ENCHANTED FOLKLORE

THE COMPLETE SERIES

Earl Gray Publishing LLC

www.bethbolden.com

beth@bethbolden.com

Publisher's Note: This is a work of fiction. Names, characters, places, and incidents are a product of the author's imagination. Locales and public names are sometimes used for atmospheric purposes. Any resemblance to actual people, living or dead, or to businesses, companies, events, institutions, or locales is completely coincidental.

Book Layout © 2024 Beth Bolden

Book Cover © 2024 Ozark Witch Cover Design

The people in the images are models and should not be connected to the characters in the book. Any resemblance is incidental.

Ordering Information:

Quantity sales. Special discounts are available on quantity purchases by corporations, associations, and others. For details, contact Beth Bolden at the address above.

Enchanted Folklore: the Complete Series/ Beth Bolden. -- 1st ed.

YOURS
FOREVER AFTER

PART I

CHAPTER ONE

She came for him in the middle of the night.

Prince Graham of the kingdom of Ardglass woke suddenly, and despite being only eleven years old, knew something was not right.

The castle fortress of Tullamore bustled with noise during the days—servants, visitors, and diplomats from the thirteen clans that comprised Ardglass talking and laughing and drinking. Led always by his father, King Gideon. But during the nights? Tullamore quieted, only the occasional creak of wood and stone as the castle shifted with the occasional servants' preparations for the next day.

But tonight, sound vibrated in the walls, the rhythmic echo of booted feet wrapped to dull the noise, pounding in harmony with the fierce beating of Graham's heart. Something was definitely not right. Had the clans laid down an ultimatum that his father hadn't told him about? Graham knew they were unhappy with his advisor and the King's own increasingly dissolute and drunken ways. Sabrina, the King's advisor, was noted throughout the kingdom as a powerful and intelligent woman. But some whispered she was a witch and a sorceress and that her magics had enslaved the King until he did not know what he did or why. But Graham believed it wasn't entirely Sabrina's fault that chaos was rising in Ardglass. His father, who was the tenth of his line, had, at the beginning of his reign, been a strong and steadfast ruler, but as time had gone on, power had corrupted him. He now spent most of his days drinking and his nights with a revolving group of girls that seemingly materialized from thin air.

Graham had asked his tutor, Rhys, about these women, and Rhys had simply affixed a bland expression on his face and told Graham that with his mother long dead, his father was lonely and desired company.

Graham had not replied that, if his father was lonely, there were many in Tullamore he could pass the time with—namely his only son, and in addition, all the many clan representatives who had begun to arrive in larger and larger numbers. But Graham did not particularly care to spend time with his father lately, so he said nothing.

Tonight everything felt different, and his apathy over his father evaporated as Graham was gripped by the real fear that something terrible had happened while he'd been sleeping.

His door opened, a wedge of dull candlelight spilling into his tower room. Graham fumbled for the little dagger his father had gifted to him on his last name-day, but even he was not naive enough to believe it would make any difference against a broadsword.

"Graham." The voice of his tutor, Rhys, was harsh. "Graham, you must wake quickly."

The one person in Tullamore, and truly in all Ardglass, that Graham trusted was Rhys. He made sure he was fed and clothed and educated—both from texts and from the members of the guard. Often it felt like the only one in all of Tullamore who gave more than a passing thought to Graham was his tutor.

Graham climbed out of bed and stared at Rhys, who was illuminated by a single candle. His face was white and drawn, as if all the blood had leaked out of it.

"Quick," Rhys repeated, his voice frantic, "put your boots on, lad. Yes, good, you have your dagger." Rhys glanced behind him, as if he expected someone to suddenly emerge from the dark shadows. "There is no time to lose."

Graham did what he was told, and even grabbed his cloak from the chair by the desk, where he had carelessly tossed it earlier in the evening.

Rhys' expression as he looked at him was frozen, and it nearly stopped Graham's heart in his chest. Something indeed was wrong, and though he wished to ask what it was, the cold look on Rhys' face trapped Graham's words in his mouth.

"There is a rope outside your window," Rhys said. "You must use it to climb down. At the bottom is a horse, with several saddlebags of supplies. You must take it and ride as far away from here as you can."

He could not help it; Graham gaped at his tutor. "I must what," he repeated, panic lancing through him.

If it was even possible, Rhys' face grew even colder, until it looked to be carved from the marble that lined the walls of the great throne room of Tullamore.

"You must go, they will be here any minute, and . . ." Rhys paused, and suddenly, there was fear in his eyes. "I promise that if they catch you, you will not survive her."

Rhys had long been the only constant companion that Graham had had. Rhys' face came more easily to him than his dead mother's. He had always been there—firm and much enamored of enforcing discipline on Graham's behavior—but always there. Did he mean that Graham should leave without him?

"What about you?" The words tumbled out of Graham, even as he tried to hold them back. He did not want to go into the forest surrounding Tullamore at night. He did not want to leave. He especially did not want to leave without Rhys. His father surely would have frowned and chastised him for his lack of bravery, but at that moment, Graham simply didn't care.

Rhys bent down, his head level with Graham's own. "I must stay, my prince. I will delay them, if I can. But you must be very brave for me now, and go."

Swallowing back tears, Graham nodded. "When may I return?"

Solemnly, Rhys just shook his head, and Graham could not hold back his choked sob. "Why?" he asked plaintively.

"It is your blood she wants," Rhys said, "and he has finally agreed to give it to her."

Graham had an idea of who "she" was, but did not ask the identity of the man who had acquiesced. He did not ask, because deep down, he knew the truth, and he did not want to see the look on Rhys' face as he told Graham that his father had agreed to sacrifice him.

He wiped his eyes. Fear still clogged his throat and held his lungs in a vise, but Rhys would not lie to him. If he needed to go, he would do as he was told, and go.

Rhys reached out and laid a reassuring hand on his shoulder. "You are brave and strong and loyal," he said to Graham. "Someday, you will need to remember that."

Graham did not ask what he meant, just nodded, and then turned towards the window.

He fumbled for the latch, and after pushing the heavy leaded glass panel, it swung open. There, just as Rhys said, was the rope, dangling right in front of the open window.

But when he glanced back, Rhys was gone, the candlelight disappearing down the darkening hallway.

Taking a breath, Graham faced the window and the rope again. It was not so much different than the exercises that the guard had set for him. Of course those exercises had been only a few feet over the dust of Tullamore's training grounds, and now there were several stories between him and the ground below.

Not that different, he told himself as he sat on the ledge and gripped the rope carefully in his hands. It was too dark to see from where it came, but it seemed solid as Graham gave it a hard tug. Still, his heart pounded as he gripped it hard, and swung his body out the window.

For eleven, he was tall and, as his father had crowed about on more than one occasion, he had inherited the hardy, muscular build of the Ardglassian line. His palms slid a little as he positioned his feet against the hard stone of the tower, and he began to carefully shimmy down the rope.

There were more windows in the tower aglow than normal at night, and each time he passed one, Graham's breath caught in his chest. His dagger was tucked in his cloak, and he could not easily draw it to defend himself if one of the windows suddenly and unexpectedly swung open.

But all the windows remained closed, though more than once, Graham saw dark-cloaked shadows pass across them.

He reached the ground, and as Rhys had promised, the horse was saddled and waiting, tied up by its reins.

"Hello, boy," Graham whispered to the horse, who dipped his head, and let Graham rub its nose. He was just about to grip the pommel of the saddle and swing up to mount when a rustling noise stopped him in his tracks.

A tall woman with long dark waving hair and a single emerald set into her gold circlet emerged from the thicket of trees surrounding the tower. Graham mounted before she could stop him, but when he dug his heels into the side of the horse, nothing happened.

"My prince." The woman's voice was dark and rich, like the honeyed wine that had so enslaved his father recently. Graham did not believe that was a coincidence.

"Lady Sabrina," Graham said, his voice calm even though he did not feel calm. He had heard much talk about how difficult she was to have as a friend, nevermind an enemy, and even though Graham did not believe he could convince her to change her mind, it was wise to proceed with caution. "Please release my horse."

"Why?" She laughed melodiously. "So you can escape?"

Graham had trusted Rhys. He had not believed Rhys would lie to him, but hearing the Lady confirm his suspicions was painful. He swallowed hard. "Gideon, the King and my father, would not stand for this," Graham insisted, because if he was not mistaken, he had few choices left and one of them was to appeal to his royal blood.

But then he remembered, with a horrifying chill, what Rhys had told him. It is your blood she wants.

She laughed again. "Here he comes." She beckoned to the trees, where a cadre of guards emerged, led by his father on his great black war destrier. "He may tell you himself."

Graham did not want to listen to his father, but even as he dug his heels into the horse's side repeatedly, the horse remained still and unbothered, like Graham was not even on its back.

Some terrible enchantment, Graham thought, but did not know how to possibly break it.

If the situation had been slightly less dire, Graham would have dismounted, come to the King's side and begged to be spared. But despite the inactivity of his horse, Graham still knew the safest place for him to be was on its back. If somehow Sabrina's enchantment could be broken, he was a good rider, and he had a chance at escaping the guard.

But before he could phrase his request, Sabrina's face shifted, like water under glass, and suddenly she was terrible and unrelenting. "My king," she said to Gideon, even as his gaze barely shifted to her. He was either heavily in his drink, or ensorcelled by Sabrina's powers.

"What is the meaning of this?" Gideon asked, words slurring together. "Graham, you have left the safety of your room."

Graham was speechless, and for a split second, he was not sure who he should trust. Had Rhys betrayed him? Had he indeed been safe in his room? It hurt to believe it, but it hurt less than believing that his father had agreed to give him to Sabrina.

"Father, I . . ." Graham stuttered. He'd meant to ask for safe passage, but the words stuck in his suddenly uncooperative mouth. He did not know whether this was another dark trick of the sorceress' or if fear and anxiety had suddenly overcome him.

"Graham," Gideon said, "you will go with the Lady Sabrina, at once."

"Where will she be taking me?" At the same moment the words tumbled out, Graham felt the horse stir beneath him for the first time since Sabrina had come into the clearing. Was her spell lifting?

"That is none of your concern," Sabrina insisted. Her dark eyes grew somehow darker in her beautiful face, and it morphed again, frustration marking it, before her features smoothed out again.

Graham's heart leapt in his chest. Something was preventing her from continuing the enchantment, and whatever it was, it wouldn't last long. He needed to make a choice, once and for all.

"Father," Graham repeated. "Where is she taking me?"

Instead of answering, the King turned his horse away, his face fading into the shadow.

Graham felt sick to his stomach, but he couldn't waste even a second, because he now knew, unequivocally, that his father had betrayed him. He dug his heels hard and fast into the horse's sides, and held tight to the reins as the horse reared and took off. Luckily, the guard had not surrounded him, probably because they hadn't wanted to frighten him, but it gave him the necessary gap between Sabrina and the guards' horses to squeeze through. Graham leaned over the horse's neck and urged it faster and faster, dodging trees and upturned roots. He knew the forest around Tullamore like the back of his hand, and he used every bit of his knowledge to wind his way through the trees, jumping over a stream as he heard the pounding echo of the guard chasing him. Sabrina's voice carrying through the dark leaves, threatening and cursing and angry. If her true colors hadn't been exposed before, they were laid bare now. Graham had no doubt that if she got her hands on him, he would be immobilized and taken someplace where he'd never see the light of day again. He did not really understand why she wanted him or his blood so fiercely, but he did know she wouldn't risk him getting away again. He'd be locked up, and not even his princely status would save him.

Graham's heart pounded in rhythm with his horse's hooves as they galloped through the forest, towards the main gate and freedom. It was the middle of the night, and Graham was counting on the fact that Sabrina, despite all her magical power, could not have raised the guard at the gate so quickly, and the way through would be open.

More shouts sounded from behind, and he heard Sabrina yell, "He's headed for the gate."

Risking a look, Graham saw that two of the guard were chasing him, but their horses weren't bred for quickness or speed, as his clearly had been. They were loaded with a lot of fancy armor, worked with gold and brass, and glinting with silver, and with those ridiculous velvet tassels that his father had once found dashing. All that extra weight meant that they might be excellent riders, but they could not overtake Graham and his light, sure-footed horse.

"Good boy, faster, faster," Graham breathed out and the horse leapt ahead, the wind streaming through Graham's hair, his cloak billowing as they gained more speed. The horses behind may not have had a chance, but he would be a fool to think that Sabrina had made no precautions at the front gate. She couldn't have raised the guard, not so quickly, but she was a woman of unusually keen intelligence, and he would be stupid to underestimate her.

They made the final turn towards the gate, hooves skittering across the cobblestones as they raced through the village. The light was better here, and he could see signs of people stirring in their beds, awoken with the noises of the chase. Please don't let her have raised the guard at the keep, Graham prayed as they approached. They were good men—loyal and obedient—and they would take him with only a word from her, and he would have no chance of evading her capture.

But it was not the keep's guard that met him at the gate.

Sabrina stood in the middle of the archway, eyes closed, murmuring a long string of words, flames spitting from her fingertips. He might have kicked his horse's heaving sides and tried to make it past without stopping, but just as he approached, her eyes shot open. Instead of their normal darkness, they glowed bright gold.

"You will not escape me," she said, her voice unearthly, and echoing with the power flowing through her veins.

He pulled up abruptly on the reins and watched in horror as her long golden cloak fell away in flaming strips, and her body began to bulge and shift into something out of a nightmare.

Graham set a reassuring hand on his horse as it bucked and skittered away from the creature Sabrina had become—head like a lion, attached to an oversized body, with a long, whip-like tail. Heart in his throat, Graham shrank as he realized the end of the tail was actually a spitting serpent.

"A chimera," he whispered out loud, remembering all of Rhys' lessons on creatures that had long ago tormented Ardglass and its neighboring kingdoms. A chimera had not been seen in many, many hundreds of years, but Graham couldn't doubt what he saw in front of him. He did not know how he could possibly evade such a creature and make it through the gate, but he would not cower in the dark and let her corral him into captivity. He would face this thing head-on, as the Prince of Ardglass, or he would die trying.

Then it occurred to him. She wanted him alive. She needed something from him, from his blood, and though he did not know what it was, it might stop her from fully attacking him if he approached.

The chimera growled and flames spit from its jaws as it paced in front of the gate, its tail whipping back and forth rhythmically.

It was expecting its very presence to cow Graham, to push him back, but he could not let that happen. Whatever occurred, Graham knew he could not stay here. His fingers trembled on the reins, but he gripped them tightly, his knuckles glowing dull white in the graying darkness.

The horse underneath him seemed to understand his purpose, and even though it shied a little under his hands, clearly terrified of the chimera, Graham knew—the way he knew he couldn't stay—that it would follow any directions he gave it. This horse had been bred for the royalty of Ardglass, and it recognized the Crown Prince on its back, and would follow Graham unto death, if that was what Graham asked of it.

But Graham hoped, fear making the edges of his vision fuzzy, that neither of them would be dying tonight.

"With me," Graham whispered to his horse, and it sprang suddenly, moving forward like a ghost in the night, weaving and dodging the chimera's flickering, hissing tail, and its spouts of flame. It screeched, the sound grating and unholy, but somehow still feminine. Graham ducked as the serpent-tail lunged for him, narrowly missing his shoulder, its teeth clacking uselessly against the heavy wool of his cloak. He reached up, blindly slashing with his dagger, disorienting the tail, and before the lion could turn and sear Graham and his horse onto the paving stones, they were gone, racing off into the darkness outside the gate.

They rode for what felt like hours, even though there had been no sound behind them and no obvious pursuers. It seemed impossible that he could have escaped so easily, even though battling a chimera could hardly be called easy. Still, he rode on, despite his horse's increasingly panting sides. They rode deeper into the forest surrounding Tullamore, and then deeper still, until between the darkness and the strange territory, Graham did not know where they had gone. They were away; that was all that mattered in the moment.

Finally, abruptly, the horse slowed, and then veered to the right, and then stopped in front of a small, bubbling stream. Light was beginning to seep through the trees, and Graham supposed dawn was only a few minutes away.

Graham dismounted on wobbly legs, still feeling like he might vomit. Between his father's betrayal and then Sabrina's enchantments, he felt unmoored and lost—and not just because he had never been to this part of the woods before. He could not easily hide, not in Ardglass. He would almost certainly be recognized instantly as the Crown Prince, and easily captured by Sabrina. Perhaps, Graham thought moodily as he watched the horse dip its head to drink in the clear water, that was why he had gotten away. Because she knew it was only a matter of time before she or the guard caught up to him. After all, he was young, and he was alone.

Not for the first time, Graham wished that Rhys had been able to come with him, to guide him, to show him what he should do. To explain what had just occurred. Why did Sabrina want his blood?

He decided that her reasons did not matter—only her purpose, and that certainly seemed terrifying enough.

"What should I do?" he asked the forest, even though he knew quite well that the forest could not answer back.

Yet, it did.

"You will come with me," a deeply resonant voice answered. Graham jumped and nearly reached for his horse's reins, but it moved away, giving him a bored, lazy look as it continued to drink from the stream.

At first, the source of the voice was not immediately apparent, and then before Graham could get his bearings or decide to wade into the stream to capture his horse's reins, a bewildering mirage appeared between the trees.

Graham shouldn't have been so astonished. After all, just tonight, he'd been betrayed by his father, then chased by a sorceress turned chimera, and now he was in the deep woods and alone for the very first time in his life. A unicorn shouldn't have felt like such a surprise, but Graham stared openmouthed and wide-eyed as it picked its way through the underbrush both elegantly and snootily. A little like all those bits of pine needle and bark were not quite good enough for it to walk across.

The unicorn shimmered—there was no other way to describe the brilliant white shine of its coat, or its single, silvery horn. Its flowing mane and tail were so ethereally pure white, they nearly gleamed blue in the muted dawn light of the forest.

Graham blinked, and then blinked again. Each time, he expected the vision in front of him to pass. Maybe he had hit his head? Maybe the chimera's serpent-tail had gotten him after all and injected him with some form of hallucinatory poison. Otherwise, what he was seeing simply did not make sense. Unicorns had not been seen in Ardglass for hundreds of thousands of years, if they had ever even existed at all. They had long since passed from history into legends whispered over the fire and a good tankard of mead. Emphasis on the mead, as most rational and reasonable men did not believe they had ever even existed.

But the unicorn remained present, as it gracefully stepped towards Graham. Then, stopping in front of him, it unexpectedly—Graham knew if he ever looked that word up in the large, leather-bound dictionary housed in the library of Tullamore, there would be a description of this night inscribed as the definition of "unexpected"—bent one knee and bowed to him, its long white mane rippling in waves to the forest floor as its head tipped towards Graham.

"My prince," the unicorn said again, in that deep, sonorous voice. "I am at your command."

Rhys had been carefully preparing him for a distant future in which he would be King, but he had never covered what one should do in the event of a talking unicorn pledging itself to Graham.

"Um," he said, because words had failed—and were still—failing him.

The unicorn raised its head and affixed Graham with a stern look. "Your Highness," it said, the two words it uttered an undeniable reprimand.

Graham flushed, embarrassed and flustered, but still not at all sure how he should proceed.

"It is very nice to meet you," he finally said. "You can call me Graham."

The unicorn huffed in surprise. "I certainly will not," it said. "But you may call me Evrard, Your Highness."

"Evrard," Graham said, testing out the name. "I have never met a unicorn before."

Evrard's face turned haughty. "I am not just any unicorn," he said, "I am King of the Unicorns." His attention flicked suddenly to Graham's horse, who had lifted its head from the stream to observe the newcomer.

"Goodness, there is no need to stare," Evrard continued, directing his comments towards Graham's horse. "How rude."

"He's not being rude. He just got ridden half to death, saving my life." Graham felt somewhat duty-bound to defend the creature who had protected him, while bravely and selflessly facing off against a sorceress-turned-chimera. For all his formality, Graham had difficulty imagining Evrard throwing himself into a fight with such reckless abandon. He'd probably want to negotiate with the chimera first, and then find a pair of seconds, and then set off at fifty paces, and make some sort of ridiculous honor-bound production out of a fight.

"Excuse me, he did not save your life," Evrard corrected him. "He prevented your untimely death. I intend to save you. That is why I have come to Ardglass."

"I'm why you're here?" Graham questioned in awe. The King of the Unicorns had come to Ardglass for him?

"I told you that you should come with me, and you will. We shall journey to the Valley of the Lost Things, and you will be safe from the sorceress who intends to take over your father's kingdom and drain you of your innocent royal blood in order to further her own filthy life."

Graham stared at the unicorn, another shock invading a system that was already over-full of them. "That's why she wanted my blood?" He shuddered, imagining her treacherous face looming over him, a silver knife flashing in her delicate, graceful hands.

Evrard dipped his head, sorrow in his voice. "Your blood is valuable for the power it contains, Your Highness," he said. "You are of the royal house of Ardglass, historically known to possess powerful magic, and you are on the cusp of adulthood, yet still innocent. It is that which the Sorceress Sabrina wishes to utilize for a spell that will extend her own life. Immortality is a powerful motivation." Evrard hesitated, the first time since he had appeared that he did not seem fully certain of everything he said and did. "That is why I believe your father agreed. Power works viciously on a weak mind."

It was one thing to have witnessed his own father's betrayal; it was entirely another to hear Evrard speak of it in that careful, sympathetic voice. Graham's throat closed and he pushed back the angry, hurt tears and wiped his eyes with hard, quick movements. He did not want anyone to see, especially Evrard. Some pain felt too great to expose to the light, and there was nothing in the world Graham had seen that was as light as Evrard. He glowed. "He was weak," Graham agreed quietly.

Evrard's eyes stared deeply into Graham's own. "He was weak because she wished him to be weak. It was not entirely of his own making. She saw the seed in him, and she exploited it. It is one of her great talents."

"How do you know all this?" Graham questioned. Evrard seemed exceptionally well-informed considering he was a unicorn. A royal and talkative unicorn, but still, a unicorn nonetheless.

"I was called here because, in the world of magic, there must be balance," Evrard said.

"Who called you here?"

"I think you know," Evrard offered. "He who was always loyal to you, and was loyal to you to the very last breath he took this night."

It was just as Graham had feared. Rhys must be dead, but his actions had also prevented Sabrina from obtaining what she wanted most—him. And even though he could not accompany him, Rhys had made sure that he was not alone. Somehow, he had summoned Evrard to help him.

Graham felt undone. Too many emotions he could not control swirled inside him like a storm cloud. Abruptly he stomped away, choosing a fallen log some distance away and sitting down upon it heavily. He had been afraid that Evrard would follow him, but he did not, and let the Prince sit there in quiet contemplation for several minutes.

The tears he'd barely held back before began to fall. He had lost his home, his loyal tutor, his safety, and his father in one single moment. Nothing would ever be the same again. Never again would he spar in the courtyard of Tullamore, or sneak honey cakes from its kitchens. Never again would his father swat at him good-naturedly when Graham made an impertinent remark. Rhys would never again tuck him into sleep or set for him too many mathematical problems or texts to be read. Life as he had known it, Graham thought dully, was over. He could not go riding back to the keep and pretend that what he had seen and heard had not occurred, even though there was nothing he wanted more.

There was nothing left to be done except move forward, one foot in front of the other.

He stood and walked back over to where Evrard and his other horse stood. "When shall we leave?" Graham asked.

Evrard gave a sharp, decisive nod. "It becomes light. We will leave immediately. Fetch the supplies and I will deign to carry them." Graham went over to his other horse, and then hesitated, his hands on the saddlebags.

"But what about this horse?" Graham asked.

"He will find his way back to the keep eventually," Evrard said dismissively.

Graham had always been a quiet boy, an observer more than an active participant, which was probably because he had grown up in a castle full of adults who usually did not wish to be bothered by a child or a child's questions. He'd long since learned to watch, and to form conclusions based on his observations. Even though he had spent less than an hour with Evrard, he could already tell that the unicorn was a snob who looked down on any creatures that could not speak as he could.

Clearly, Graham's horse had been relegated to this view by Evrard, no matter its bravery or tenacity in helping Graham ride to safety.

Rhys had always told Graham that loyalty was the most important currency he could gain as a king. And even though now, Graham had no reason to believe that he ever would be a king, those lessons still felt important.

"No," Graham said firmly. "He will come with us."

"That creature cannot speak," Evrard said, cruelty edging his voice. "Why would we need it?"

Graham shot the unicorn a chastising look not unlike the one Evrard had given him earlier. He was also a very quick learner. "We will not leave it behind because it has earned the right to come with us," he said.

"Well, I suppose we can hook his reins to your person, and he can carry the supplies. He may be useful, yet," Evrard said with resignation.

The horse gave a little whinny of agreement, and turned kind, warm eyes onto Graham, as if it knew what Graham's intervention had saved him from.

"I pay my debts," Graham murmured to the horse, and went to make sure all the saddlebags were properly secure, before looping the reins across his arm and leading the horse out of the stream and towards Evrard.

"What about the saddle and the bridle?" Graham asked, when he stopped next to Evrard. "How shall I ride without them?"

The look on Evrard's face was worth a million gold pieces. "You shall ride me like men have always ridden unicorns. Carefully and with respect," Evrard said in a haughty tone. "You may use my mane, carefully, as means to keep yourself secure."

To Graham, it seemed the utmost disrespect for him to even touch that pure white hair that cascaded from Evrard's brow, but in his hands it felt much as any regular horsehair did. He tied the reins to his cloak, and the horse trotted carefully behind as Evrard began to pick his way through the forest. There was no trail, which was a blessing, because on a trail there might be other people, and a unicorn would surely raise questions that Graham couldn't answer.

As they traveled a direction that Evrard seemed very certain of, Graham asked additional questions.

"Where are you from?"

"A place very far from here," Evrard answered patiently.

"What's it called?"

Rhys had always told Graham that one day his curiosity might get him into trouble, and Graham felt it must be true when Evrard paused in his normally very steady gait, and then continued without answering. Some questions then, Graham realized, were off-limits.

But that did not stop him from asking.

They stopped when the sun was very high in the sky by another bubbling brook. Graham chewed on a few pieces of dried meat, while Evrard and the horse drank deeply from the cool water.

"How do you know where we're going?" Graham asked before climbing back onto Evrard's back.

"I know because the valley we are headed to is one of ancient magic. Protective magic. It calls to the magic in me."

"Is it far?"

Evrard took off at a slighter faster canter than before, the horse moving behind them like it had always followed Evrard.

"It is several days' journey," Evrard said, "since we must keep to the forest, and off any known trail. For your safety, of course."

"But what if someone spots you?" Graham asked. "How am I to explain what you are?"

Evrard glanced back at his passenger. "People see what they choose to see. I do not think you will have any questions about me, Your Highness."

They slept that night in a well-hidden cave that Graham further camouflaged with several large leafy branches he had cut from neighboring trees with his dagger. There was a small ax in one of the saddlebags and a tinderbox kit, and Graham kindled a small fire with twigs to take away the chill of the night. The cave was large enough for both Evrard and the horse, though Graham knew that Evrard was not altogether pleased about sharing even a temporary domicile with the horse.

They set out bright and early the next morning, continuing to journey into the thick of the forest. By midday, there was a fine sheen of sweat on Evrard's back and Graham realized that as he'd been daydreaming, staring up at the leafy canopy of the trees, they had been steadily climbing uphill. After stopping for a rest, they continued on, and once Graham offered to help conserve Evrard's energy by walking, and leading the horse himself, but Evrard's complete silence as a response told Graham exactly what he thought of that particular idea.

By later in the evening, when the shadows were beginning to grow longer, the trees had thinned out, and the ground had gone from densely packed dirt to a much rockier, harder surface.

When they stopped, Evrard's voice finally reflected his own exhaustion. "Tomorrow, we will climb," he said, "and then we will be in the valley."

As Graham gathered branches for their fire, he asked, "What is in this valley?"

"A farm, though I do not know how inhabitable it will be. It may need repairs. It has been abandoned for many, many years." Evrard paused. "But no matter, it will be safe there."

Graham realized then that ever since Evrard had appeared in all his majestic glory, he had not felt particularly unsafe. He had been sad, mourning a life lost to him, along with Rhys and his father's loyalty and affection, but he had not once felt like they were in any particular danger. When he said so, Evrard shook his head gravely.

"We have always been in danger, Your Highness. Sabrina searches for us in many forms. Our magic has shielded us from her view, though with the taxing climb tomorrow, I may not be able to shield us for much longer." Evrard sounded reluctant to share this information, but Graham was glad he had.

"What can I do to protect us?" he asked.

The unicorn's eyes seemed to bore into his very soul. "Be brave a little while longer, my prince."

The next day was the most grueling day that Graham had ever experienced. Nothing, not even training with Tullamore's guard or the night he had escaped from Sabrina's clutches, had prepared him for the grueling climb to the top of the mountain peak. The air grew thinner, and the ground much tougher for Evrard and the horse to pick their way across. Graham descended from Evrard mid-morning, and was glad he had, because only a few hundred yards further, a hissing viper slithered out from around a rock and stood right in their way, spitting poison onto the ground, where it sizzled and bubbled.

"Graham," Evrard said sharply as Graham pulled his dagger, which he had kept much closer to hand since the unicorn's warning the night before.

He knew why Evrard had not told him of the danger previously; he still thought of Graham as a somewhat helpless child, but Graham knew he had not been a child since the night he'd escaped Tullamore. It was the same reason why Evrard warned him back now, but still Graham approached, soft footfalls on the ground as the viper eyed him with gold, flashing eyes that somehow brought to mind a woman's.

"It is her," Evrard said steadily from somewhere behind him. "She means to stop us while she still can, because once we are in the valley, you are lost to her."

Graham weighed the dagger in his right hand. If he misjudged even the tiniest bit, or worst of all, missed completely, the viper would be on them instantly, and Graham did not think their chances of survival would be very good.

"Graham," Evrard said again, and that was all the motivation that he needed to throw the dagger.

It flipped perfectly, just as Graham had practiced thousands and thousands of times, and though the dagger did not land quite as precisely as he'd hoped, it did hit the viper in its soft, meaty underbelly. It hissed loudly and angrily and then fell deathly still, its head lolling across the rocky ground.

"Is it . . ." Graham hesitated. "Is it dead?" He did not think he'd dealt the viper a mortal blow—an injurious one certainly, and one that he'd hoped would at least stop it from attacking them—but Evrard nodded slowly.

"Sabrina has many powers. One of them allows her to transport her soul into various creatures at a significant distance." Evrard looked at the dead viper with distaste. "It was once a stupendous skill, born of beautiful and good magic, but she has twisted it, like she twists all things. The viper died not just because of your blade, but because most creatures cannot survive her abrupt departure."

"What would have happened if she had been inhabiting the snake when it died?" Graham asked. If they managed to reach the valley in one piece, he had no intention of tangling with Sabrina ever again, but it wouldn't be bad information to know, just in case.

"She would also die," Evrard said. "But you are not to attempt such a stunt again. I could have dealt with the viper."

Graham walked over to where the dead snake lay, and carefully, using a corner of his cloak, retrieved his dagger, cleaning it thoroughly before returning it to the makeshift sheath he'd made. "You are struggling with the climb," he pointed out, "and I could handle this, so I did."

"My prince," Evrard said, somehow his voice becoming even more formal, "you are irreplaceable. I beg you to remember that."

"I'm also no longer a prince," Graham said bitterly. "Let's head for the peak. I don't want to risk her sending anything else."

The remainder of the climb felt strangely anticlimactic after the thrilling, heart-stopping episode with the viper. They reached the summit, and then carefully began to pick their way down. Slowly, more trees appeared, and the air grew sweet and clear. Graham leaned against a trunk as they stopped at the first stream they encountered.

"When will we reach the valley?" he asked.

Evrard lifted his head from the water. "We are nearly there," he said. "We will reach it by nightfall. But even now, I feel my magic is rejuvenated. We should be safe here."

"Should be safe," Graham muttered, and went to grab some jerky from one of the saddlebags. It wasn't that he didn't trust Evrard—after all, the unicorn had given him both imperative information about his situation and protected him from Sabrina. He had come to save Graham's life, and he was grateful, but he always felt like there was something Evrard was holding back. Important details or vital pieces of information that he kept silent on. Graham did not know what held him back. Was it that he thought Graham was too young? Too inexperienced? Too stupid? Graham wasn't sure what the reasoning was, but he didn't particularly like it.

The sun was setting across the faraway peaks on the other side when they finally climbed the rest of the way down into the meadow that carpeted much of the valley floor. From a distance, Graham could see a cluster of buildings, low and squat, and as they traveled closer, he could see that Evrard had been honest—they were not in the greatest of repair. The roof was nearly collapsed on one, and what had once been a large garden had been nearly taken over by weeds.

"So this is the Valley of the Lost Things?" Graham asked as they approached the buildings. "Why is it so empty? I'm certainly not the only lost thing in this world."

"No, but you are the most important," Evrard said, with that maddening superiority that made Graham want to gnash his teeth and demand the whole damn truth. But there was no point, because Evrard clearly did not do or share anything that he didn't want to.

When Graham wrenched open the main building's door, a whoosh of dust settled over him. The whole interior could use an intense cleaning—it was full of dust and cobwebs, but it did contain several rooms, as well as a full complement of sturdy, hand-built wooden furniture. Two fireplaces constructed of river stone stood cold and empty. The building with the mostly collapsed roof turned out to be the stable. Luckily, there were still a few bales of only slightly rotted hay. And even though Evrard turned up his nose at the meal, Graham's horse leaned down and munched away happily.

"Tomorrow, the roof will need to be repaired," Evrard said practically, clearly dictating this request towards Graham, even though he had no experience at all repairing roofs.

Graham considered saying so, but already knew his concern would be brushed aside. He would have to learn. He would have to learn to take care of all of this. This place, unceremonious and humble, was his new home, and if anything was to come of it, there was only him to do the work.

"Of course," Graham said.

"And one more thing," Evrard said, as Graham went to find a less dusty room to spend the night in, "you are lost here. Safe and lost. But perhaps a subterfuge to confuse anyone that might come upon us? As you say, you are not the only lost thing in the world."

"A subterfuge?" Graham asked tiredly.

Evrard glanced down at the heavy cloak he wore. "From now on, you shall be known as Gray."

Graham had thought he had nothing left to lose, but as Evrard walked away to the stable, he realized he'd just lost the last part of who he'd been before.

The next morning, Gray, as he was now known, tackled the stable roof, and then the dusty interior of the main house. Then, over a long, hot, arduous summer, began to clear the vegetable garden. Evrard made suggestions, but besides his own stable, he cared little of what Gray's living conditions were. As long as Evrard had sweet grass or hay to eat, cool, clean water, and a roof over his head for the occasional rainy day, he was not particular about the state of the farm. But Gray, who had been raised to rule Ardglass, felt the sting of his pointless life a little less if he kept busy. Each night he lay in his cot and thought of what he could do the next day to keep his mind and body occupied—and silent.

Being lost had its advantages. There was nobody to tell him what to do except for Evrard, and mostly Evrard left him alone, except in the evenings, when they would talk of legend and history and magic.

Gray was eventually forced out of the Valley of the Lost Things to buy supplies that could not be taken from the meadow or the woods or the valley itself. But he had grown in the two years since coming to the valley and was unrecognizable to himself in the creek as he hacked off big chunks of his dark, wavy hair with the same dagger he'd been carrying during his flight from Tullamore.

The village where Evrard directed him was exactly as he'd described, and as long as Gray kept his head down, nobody seemed to care who he was. He traded for supplies, and returned a year later, and a year after that.

Slowly, he eked out a profitable farm from the fertile ground of the valley. He built a hen house, dug a well, and began to keep sheep and cows. His garden expanded, and the next summer, he planted a whole field of hay for Evrard and his old horse.

Time both crawled and flew. Years passed, but with each successive birthday, the only marker of the passage of time were the inches Gray continued to grow. He continued to stay as busy as he could, and most nights he fell into his bed exhausted from the day's work. And that, he learned during the years, was better than lying awake and wondering what had happened to the keep of Tullamore, the kingdom of Ardglass, and his father. He heard bits and snippets on his annual trips to the village, but mostly he blocked out any talk of politics. He had no interest in the goings-on of the nobility. He was no longer a member; he was lost, and he intended to stay lost.

And so, many years passed. Occasionally, a visitor would make their way into the valley. They too would be lost, in some fashion, and they would stay for a night or a week, and then move on, but Gray stayed. He had nowhere else to go.

On the morning of his twenty-sixth year, Gray woke and did not even start at the realization that flickered across his consciousness. He would never leave this place; he would die here, lost.

Of course, the year he came to terms with the course of his life, that was when it changed irrevocably.

CHAPTER TWO

His Royal Highness, Prince Emory of Fontaine, looked up from the manuscript he was studying, and pasted on an agreeable smile.

It was much harder than it should have been—Rory knew that, but the knowing did not make it any easier to accomplish the pleasantries required when facing the Regent Queen, his aunt Sabrina. She did not bother him often, which he appreciated, as he always felt vaguely uncomfortable after her visits. Like her presence was a disagreeable reminder of everything she did that he did not.

She herself would never say anything of the kind. In fact, he was always grateful at how little pressure she put on him as the Crown Prince of the country of Fontaine. At his age, a deep, hidden voice inside told him, he should be sitting next to her at council meetings, and alongside her during the weekly audience with Fontaine's subjects. That ugly reminder that he wasn't doing enough—wasn't doing much of anything at all, except for studying his books and his languages and his ancient manuscripts—was always louder right after one of her visits.

Thankfully then, they did not occur very often.

Rory stood, and held out his hand. His aunt was still young and still stunningly beautiful, with lustrous dark hair and a pair of shining dark eyes that kindly turned down every proposal that was made to her, all under the auspices that she was far too occupied caring for her nephew's future throne and for the people of Fontaine.

She was beautiful and majestic, and therefore Rory could not fault her for being somewhat distant as well. After all, she was occupied with the business of the Crown, and he himself always seemed to be neck-deep in some important discussion or analysis or translation. Often, before he was even finished with one, another would appear, and so he passed his time as he had since he was in his early teens, in the library, situated in the tall round tower of Beaulieu.

"Your Highness," his aunt said respectfully, dipping into a graceful curtsy. After the formalities were observed, she took the chair opposite his, demurely folding her hands in her lap, even though in his personal experience, she was not exactly the demure type. She rode as well as any of their guards, and often took morning training in the yard with some of her most loyal attendants. Still, her act was excellent, and his was not—thus, another reason why neither of them had made any push to change the status quo since Rory had turned eighteen. Two years later, and there had still been zero discussion of transferring power; a situation Rory was perfectly fine with.

"What can I do for you?" Rory asked, that awkward feeling in his stomach intensifying. She never came to see him unless she needed something that only he could provide.

"You recall the terrible northern brigands who have been devastating our supply trains?" his aunt asked. Occasionally, she would provide a single parchment inscribed with some of the highlights of realm business. Rory usually read it, assuming that his aunt did not want him to be caught unawares at one of the few royal banquets he attended. The brigands looting the supply trains had been a large portion of the last installment. Rory nodded, even though he knew very little detail other than the basic facts of the case. It was not ancient, it was not in another language, and it was not a mystery to be unraveled. It needed a practical, experienced military hand to guide the problem to a solution, and therefore Rory had left it alone. He was neither particularly practical nor experienced in any military maneuvers except for archaic ones.

"We recently received intelligence that suggests they have retreated to the far north, right on the edge of our borders, to a valley lying between two mountain ranges."

Rory had no idea what this could possibly have to do with him. "Excellent," he said uselessly. This was why he never involved himself; his aunt was a paragon of efficiency.

"I would like you to travel with a squad of the guard to this valley and fetch them back to Beaulieu to see justice," the Regent Queen said primly, as if she was asking him for another translation of Gawain, and not to undertake a dangerous, active journey with the intent of capturing criminals.

Rory had very little experience concealing his feelings, even in the royal court, since he was called to participate in it so infrequently. He couldn't help his reaction; his jaw fell open. "You would like me to do what?" he asked slowly.

Occasionally, Rory wondered, since he had little occasion to witness it personally, how his aunt had achieved all that efficiency she was so famous for. He saw a little of it now, in the hardening of her jaw and the sudden ferocity flashing in her eyes. This was a woman, he realized suddenly and unexpectedly, whom you would not want to cross. He had never had any opportunity to do so, but he knew now that if he ever did, treading carefully would be of utmost importance.

The Regent Queen rose, as elegantly as she did everything, and walked to the large leaded window that overlooked the courtyard of Beaulieu, her fingertips tapping alongside the spines of the books casually piled everywhere. "I ask for so little," she said sweetly. "I assumed you would be eager to assist me with this task. Was I incorrect in my thinking?"

Rory steeled himself. "No, you were not. You know I would be honored to help you with this, but we both know I am the wrong man for the task."

She turned, and suddenly he was a bug, crawling pathetically under her gaze. Another unexpected revelation: Rory understood what it was like for those men she had rejected. Even knowing she was kind did not prevent the sting of humiliation, not when she applied it so expertly. "A man," she said. "Yes, that is what I expected to find when I ventured here. Not a boy, still enamored with his little mysteries and his picture books."

There was a very loud part of Rory that wanted to ask if she had always been this vindictive, and she had hidden it from him on purpose, but it was impossible to do so when she was staring at him like that. Rory spoke ten languages, and they all dried up under the onslaught of that hostile gaze.

"So," she continued, "you shall travel to this valley in the far north, and you will capture the criminals and brigands who live there, and you will bring them back to Beaulieu. Thus, justice shall be served."

Rory swallowed hard. He did ride well, usually when he wanted to clear his head, or examine a problem from a different angle, but he had only the most basic of defense training, and could barely use Lion's Breath, the ancestral sword of Fontaine, at all. It wasn't quite right to say that she was sending him to his death—because surely, that was impossible. But then it had been impossible to imagine her ever speaking to him with that particular tone in her voice before. Today, the impossible had become possible.

"I assume we leave at first light tomorrow," Rory said, "and I assume my guard shall accompany me."

Her face was so cold, it was etched in ice. Clearly she had not intended for him to take his guard, only the guard she had picked. Rory, who had read dozens of epic tales of bravery and disloyalty and of thrones and kingdoms changing hands, had somehow never once imagined that he would find himself in such a precarious position. After his parents had died in the carriage accident, and Sabrina had come, pale with grief but also determined to rule wisely in her five-year-old nephew's stead, he had never conceived that she would attempt to dispose of him, and keep Fontaine for herself.

And yet, it was as if a curtain had risen and Rory saw all her actions in a totally different light. Never encouraging him to learn to rule. Letting him lose himself in his studies and his books. Never once ordering him to learn to defend himself. He had no practical knowledge of which to speak, and he could not even blame that choice on her—it had been entirely his own. Her absence in his life had made it possible, but he had crafted the noose himself that would eventually be his doom.

If he let it.

"Your guard?" the Regent Queen questioned.

"I shall prefer to take my own guard," Rory said firmly. He was still the Crown Prince of Fontaine, at least until he left the walls of Beaulieu behind. He would exercise his rights—they were all that was no doubt between him and a mysterious "accident" during this dangerous journey.

"So be it," she said, smugness edging her voice. She clearly believed that his fate was in her hands, regardless of the guard.

He would just need to ensure that all was not what it seemed, at least to her eyes.

Once the Regent Queen departed, Rory hastily packed a few thin manuscripts that he believed might serve him well on this trip, and then made for the guard's quarters on the other side of the courtyard.

His guard was famously comprised of the best female warriors in the kingdom, though they saw little to no action. It occurred to Rory as he approached their barracks that Sabrina might think so little of her own sex that she had appointed his guard hoping they would be less competent, but if that was the case, then the joke was on her. Marthe, who headed the Prince's guard, was the most terrifying fighter that Rory knew, and the rest of the guard, handpicked by Marthe, had spent their lives being undervalued and underappreciated, and worked twice as hard as a result.

Rory found Marthe sharpening her longsword just inside the barracks, in the common room. He had no idea how circumspect he needed to be, because if his aunt was half as disloyal as he imagined, she would certainly have spies planted all over Beaulieu.

Marthe shot him a look over her whetstone. "Lost, are you, my prince?" she asked.

It was true, he rarely came down to the courtyard, and almost never into the barracks. A point Marthe had made many times over, but which Rory had never deigned sufficiently important to listen to. He was listening now.

"We are to leave first thing in the morning," Rory said, tempering the order with an apologetic tone. It was hardly enough time to mount a fully armed guard, which no doubt was something the Regent Queen was counting on.

Marthe raised an eyebrow questioningly. "A journey? To where?"

Certainly, she was likely expecting that Rory wanted to visit a neighboring castle with some particular tome in its library. They had done that before, on more than one occasion.

"We are tasked by the Regent Queen to travel to a valley in the far north and apprehend brigands who have set upon some of our supply trains." Rory managed to get most of it out without flinching, but his voice wavered at the end. Not enough that many might notice, but Marthe was exceedingly observant.

She sighed, a long, terrible gust. "I see," she said, and Rory suddenly had an inclination that she did. That maybe Marthe had been watching and waiting for something like this sudden journey to come to pass. Hopefully, Rory thought, she was more prepared than he was.

When she stood, Marthe was several handspans taller than Rory himself. She put a reassuring hand on his shoulder. "We will be ready," she said, confidence ringing out from every syllable. "I will gather the guard immediately and set preparations in motion." She gave him a single, knowing look, and went out the door to the courtyard.

Rory could not be entirely certain, but it did seem as though Marthe understood the potential treachery of the journey and what must be undertaken to prevent it.

At least he hoped so, because he himself was woefully and painfully unprepared to face whatever they encountered.

Dawn was a gray smudge on the horizon when Rory walked into the courtyard to meet his guard. There were five of them, led by Marthe, their heavy armor shining dully in the early morning light. Marthe's expression was grim but determined, much like Rory expected his own was.

The Regent Queen had not awoken early to see them off, but Rory was not surprised by this, as he might have been once. He had lain awake the night before and gone over in his mind so many incidents over the last fifteen years. Small, insignificant events now took on greater meaning once examined with an understanding of Sabrina's clear purpose. Rory saw just how effortlessly she had manipulated him, and in fact, much of the court of Beaulieu. Even though he was hardly alone, the thought undeniably stung. He was the Crown Prince, Fontaine was his country to rule, and he had stood aside and let her do whatever she wished to it. The land seemed to be thriving, but it was impossible to say if that was actually true, or just another of his aunt's subterfuges.

"Prince Emory," Marthe said respectfully, nodding towards a page who had appeared in the doorway from the castle proper. He carried a scroll, which was no doubt a signed declaration of their purpose, signed by his aunt. He was the Crown Prince, he should not need permission to be riding with armed guards or to apprehend criminals, but Rory realized that this act took away any agency he'd grasped when he'd requested his own guards. She was reminding him, in that cruelly subtle way of hers, that he was on her business. That he lived and breathed by her grace.

He took the scroll from the page with clenched teeth and a sharp nod. He could not thwart protocol, not so publicly, but he did not have to like it either.

They rode out in a loose triangle formation, Marthe at the front, Rory in the middle, and the rest of the guard surrounding him. Protecting him, Rory realized as they stopped for a midday break.

Deep in the forest, it was difficult to imagine there were any spies, and for the first time, he and Marthe were able to speak freely.

"I knew she would make her move eventually," Marthe said, chewing her portion of bread and cheese carefully. "I knew it would be coming, and I was still surprised when it happened. Do not feel ashamed that it surprised you, my prince."

"How far is it to the valley?" he asked. He did not want to address how stupid he had been. It was hard enough to face his own idiocy; he did not want Marthe's sympathy, as kindly as it was meant.

"Several days' ride. Perhaps a week if we take our time," Diana, one of the guards, spoke up. "And we should. No good reason to get to the valley exhausted, with tired horses."

Rowen, another guard, gave Rory a contemplative look. "A week would even be enough time to give you some rudimentary training, Your Highness." She glanced down at the sword at his belt. "Perhaps not enough to truly use Lion's Breath, but enough to make sure you can defend yourself with a dagger, if need be."

"Yes," Marthe agreed. "We will stop early every evening, and spend that time working with the Prince. He has our protection, but he must also learn to protect himself."

Rory couldn't stop himself from making a face. He knew it needed to be done; in fact, it should have been done long ago, and no doubt, would have, but his aunt had clearly wanted him to be helpless and completely indebted to his guard.

"Prince Emory," Anya laughed. "Truly, it will not be so bad. After all, don't you enjoy reading books about weapons? Skirmishes and battles? Military strategy?"

He did, but the idea of practical application made his stomach clench and then roll unpleasantly.

Marthe smiled at him. "It's quite a lot of adjustment to make at one time. You'll get used to it."

Rory had no doubt that he would eventually—he just did not particularly want to.

Later that afternoon they stopped just as the sun was just beginning to sink, and as Rowen and Acadia set up camp, Marthe, Diana and Anya worked with Rory to master using one of the small-handled sharp daggers they all carried. To Rory's surprise, Marthe even pulled a wickedly sharp version out of one of the packs, and gifted it to him, handle first.

"Is this mine?" Rory asked.

Marthe nodded. "Very useful at close range, and if you can learn to throw it, useful even at a longer range. Unfortunately, a week is not really enough time to teach the latter."

"In my country," Anya said, "we learn to throw these when we're practically in the cradle."

Rory had forgotten that Anya was not originally from Fontaine—but when you looked closer at her dark braided hair and steely gray eyes, the hint of wildness in her expression gave her away. "You come from Ardglass, right?" Rory asked.

Of all the countries bordering Fontaine, he knew the least about Ardglass. Of the Ardglass of old, he knew much, but thou-sand-year-old history could not help him much now. If by some mir-acle, he survived this journey, going back to Beaulieu might not be possible; he might need to seek asylum in another country. Ardglass was the closest, and also currently in the direction they were headed.

"I do, Your Highness," Anya said as she adjusted his grip on the dagger. "My father started teaching me to fight when I was very small, and I had hoped to wield a sword in the garrison there, but . . ." She hesitated. "After the Crown Prince disappeared, nothing was the same.

The King withdrew from court, the garrisons were mostly disbanded. The kingdom is a shadow of what it once was."

Rory knew Prince Graham of Ardglass had disappeared shortly before his own parents were killed, fifteen years earlier, but he did not know the details of the situation. Many believed he was dead and would never be found. Anya looked upset enough by divulging just that much information that he did not want to press her.

"Focus," Marthe barked at him as he practiced shoving the dagger into an old rotten log that Diana and Rowen had found and hauled upright to replace the sandbags they usually practiced on. "Put all your force behind your strike."

Next, they began to teach him defensive maneuvers with the dagger, and an hour later, he collapsed next to the fire, damp with sweat and utterly exhausted.

And the next night, Rory thought miserably, it would start all over again.

The trip to the valley took, as Diana had predicted, just over a week. The last day was a difficult climb on the horses, and on Rory himself. He was sore from a week straight of riding from dawn to late afternoon, and then hours after of swordplay and sparring. He had finally graduated, with grudging acceptance from Marthe, from the dagger to his ancestral sword, and hefting the heavy weight had left his arms weak and tired. Another man might be ashamed that he was far less proficient or seasoned than any of his guards, but then they did not speak ten languages. Rory had spent his lifetime indulging in the pursuits that he enjoyed. They might have even borne fruit, if he had truly been expected to succeed the Regent Queen and take over the throne of Fontaine. But finally, he understood that she had never had any plans to abdicate in his favor. And now that he was twenty, and of perfectly suitable age to rule, she had clearly felt the need to remove him completely.

At night when he lay in his bedroll, he should have been tired enough to sleep, but he lay awake instead, turning his aunt's actions and motives over and over and over again in his head. How could she have hated him so much? He had tried never to be much trouble, and there had always been so many servants to make sure that she was never truly bothered by his presence. She had never needed to be a mother to him; if he'd wanted one, he'd understood very quickly that that was not a position she wished to hold, and he'd lost himself in his books instead. He realized she'd undoubtedly seen the advantages of his scholarly interests and had encouraged him to cultivate them.

It was on the third night that Rory realized that it wasn't that his aunt loathed him or wished him dead. It was not about him at all. Instead, it was power that drew her and controlled her. She would do anything in search of more, and if he stood in the way, then he must be eliminated. She could not risk the chance of anyone suggesting, especially himself, that he take the throne.

Rory resolved that he would not be disposed of quite so easily.

On the eighth morning, Rory and his guard stood on the edge of the valley, their horses impatiently shifting their hooves, ready to make the descent down to the lush land below.

"If I'd known this place existed, I'd run and hide here too," Acadia said.

Rory nodded, agreeing with her assessment. Trees ringed the edges of the valley, fringed with bright green leaves and sharp sweet-smelling needles. As the ground sloped downward, the pockets of trees gave way to meadow land, plush, waving grass as soft and luxurious as velvet. Wildflowers bloomed intermittently across their view—purples and yellows and blues and reds almost blinding in their intensity. A stream meandered through the very center of the valley, far enough away to look like a lazy silver snake. And as far as the eye could see, only one set of dwellings.

"That is where the criminals must be hiding," Marthe said, extending her hand to point towards the small grouping of buildings. It was far enough into the heart of the valley it was nearly impossible to see if any people were wandering about, but even from this distance, Rory could see the farm was well-kept, with several large fields beyond its walls and a large garden on the other side, the pattern of the broken ground much different from the undisturbed land.

It did not look like a hideout populated by bandits, but Rory knew enough to understand that sometimes appearances were deceiving.

"Your Highness," Marthe said, her voice taking on the taint of deference that he rarely heard from her—and had truthfully never wanted. In this realm, away from the library and his books, he was out of his element. "Your Highness," she repeated when he did not respond, "it may be better for you to lead the way."

He shot his captain a disbelieving look. His guard may have been training him every day on this journey, but seven days of training could not possibly make up for a lifetime of skipping it. Marthe knew that as well as Rory did.

"The appearance of you leading the way, then," Marthe corrected, the corner of her lips tilting into an amused smile. "These are your lands, after all."

But Rory, who had made a considered study of his own lands, shook his head. "If they are mine, they have been on no map that I have ever seen."

"Regardless," Marthe insisted, and finally, Rory inclined his head, agreeing with her assessment.

He led the way down the incline towards the valley floor, marveling the whole way at the undisturbed and spectacular greenery surrounding them.

"It's as if someone planted a garden and then left it to grow for a very long time," Anya murmured to Rowen, her voice pitched low, as if words did not belong in such a beautiful place.

"It gives every appearance of being empty except for the farm," Marthe warned him a few minutes later, "but I would be very surprised if there were not invisible guards or booby traps, all planned to warn the inhabitants of strangers coming upon this place."

Rory couldn't help but agree with Marthe; it seemed impossible the valley could exist, and yet be so unguarded. Yet as they ventured further into the valley, they saw no evidence of any human presence. Birds chattered in the trees, their song lighthearted and free, and from a distance they caught sight of squirrels and other small animals frolicking through the tall grasses. But they were completely undisturbed.

As they grew closer to the farm itself, Rory found himself growing tenser and tenser, battling the sense of relaxation and peace the valley seemed determined to lend him. Such an unmapped, undiscovered, perfect place could not exist. It must be some kind of trap, and Sabrina was just waiting to spring it, capturing Rory and his guards in her deathly grip.

"Carefully, my prince," Marthe warned quietly as they approached the farm. It contained four well-maintained outbuildings, as well as the central farmhouse. A large garden spread out like a flawless coverlet across the front of the farm, and at the back, corn grew tall and thick as far as Rory could see. But as much as his eyes scanned the grounds, he could not see any of the people who had clearly worked very hard to make it a haven.

"It looks . . ." Diana hesitated, like she did not even want to voice the sentiment they were all thinking.

"Abandoned," Marthe finished briskly. "And yet it cannot be. This place is impeccably kept. There are clearly people about, they just do not want to be found. It is our job to find them."

Rory didn't want to dismount and leave his horse behind. He felt like he was abandoning the one advantage he had, which was his excellent horsemanship. However, Rory wasn't dumb enough to think he could properly join in the search while on horseback. So he tied up Chestnut, his fine brown stallion, and watched as the rest of his guard did the same.

"Pairs," Marthe ordered, and as the rest of the guard paired off, she walked over to Rory's side, hand on her sword pommel. "Shall we?" she asked him as they watched the rest of the pairs begin to walk cautiously around the seemingly deserted farm.

Rory nodded, and they started together towards the garden. He knew very little of such things, except in theory, but the garden looked extremely well-tended, with neat, orderly rows of vegetables, the ground around the plants entirely cleared of weeds. He reached over and plucked a small tomato from a nearby plant.

"Hey, watch yourself," a voice said, and Rory looked, and then kept looking as a very tall man, shirtless, his face and muscular chest smeared with dirt, rose from the middle of a patch of squash.

Marthe was instantly by his side, sword out of her belt, but the man simply looked at her, expression blank and bored. He spread his empty hands in front of him. "If you're hungry," he said, "take what you like. If you are lost, you may stay."

The man's hair was long and dark, nearly shaggy, but did not obscure the bright blue eyes that gazed out at him. A bead of sweat trickled down his bare and undeniably dirty pectoral muscle. Rory swallowed hard. He had never met anyone like this man before—someone rough and uncouth and utterly, completely compelling. Rory felt his blood sizzle, like a drop of water on a stove that had been stoked with firewood all day. He stared, mesmerized, by the man. Was he a bandit? He certainly did not seem like one, if his offer of food and shelter was any indication.

"Sir," Rory said, trying to find his voice under Marthe's accusing stare, "we are in search of some dangerous criminals who have been looting the supply wagons from Fontaine."

The man gave him a disbelieving look. "Does it look like we're harboring bandits here?"

Truthfully, it did not. It looked to Rory that all the man was harboring was an excellent crop of vegetables. As well as a physique that made Rory desperate to reach out and place a palm on that firm chest, even though it was smeared with dirt and sweat. Somehow, that made it even more attractive, though Rory did not think that thought could possibly be logical.

But Marthe was clearly not as distracted by such a fine chest as Rory was. Her glare was still fierce. "You will not mind if I do not take your word for it," she said. "I would like to search the grounds and buildings of your farm."

The man threw his head back and laughed. Rory did not know what was so amusing, but he discovered that he was desperate to know.

"There is nothing here but my farming implements, the animals I keep here, and the store of food to last us through the winter," he admitted. "But feel free to search all you like."

"Do you have any weapons here?" Marthe asked, her hard voice making it clear she did not believe the act. If it was even an act. Rory was strangely inclined to believe his words, but that might have been because of his beautiful eyes.

"A dagger or two," the man said, leaning against his shovel. "We have no need of weapons here."

Marthe sniffed. "We will be the judge of that." After throwing Rory another reprimanding look, she marched away, clearly intending to find the rest of the guard and do a thorough search of the farm. Rory thought she must not have thought the man was a threat, or else she never would've left him alone.

The man stared at Rory, who stared back. "Do you always travel with a full complement of lady warriors?" he asked offhandedly.

Rory blushed. It was impossible to admit to this man, who looked eminently capable of dispatching any threat, weapons or no, that Rory had to, because he could not defend himself. "It was very rude of me not to introduce myself," Rory said, extending a hand, "I am Prince Emory of the kingdom of Fontaine, but you may call me Rory."

It was as if his words changed everything. The man's eyes went blank, his face cold and hard, and he turned away, leaving Rory awkwardly standing with his hand out. "Gray," he said shortly. "Welcome to the valley."

One of the reasons Rory had always loved reading was that he felt an inescapable compulsion to know things. His curiosity was legendary, and faced with a man such as Gray, couldn't have been more engaged even if he'd tried.

"How long have you lived here?" Rory asked, as Gray returned to his squash, carefully digging around a plant. "How did you come to be here? I have never seen this valley on a map before."

Gray did not bother to meet his eyes as he responded, his tone short and hard. "I have been here many years. It's a haven for those who are lost, a magical place not found on any maps."

It did not make any sense at all for Sabrina to believe that the bandits stealing their supplies would hide in a magical valley for the lost. They might have little in the way of a moral compass, but they could hardly be lost.

"Are you lost then?" Rory asked.

Gray looked up then, eyes boring into Rory's own. He said nothing for a long moment. "Aren't we all lost?" he asked. "In our own ways?"

CHAPTER THREE

Gray knew who Prince Emory was. He'd heard them talking of him in the village, last time he was there. How the Regent Queen seemed to grip the throne of Fontaine tighter and tighter, and the Autumn Prince, as they called Prince Emory, was still seemingly unaware because his head was always in a book. Gray had turned away when the shopkeeper continued speaking of the Autumn Prince, because he'd not wanted to hear anything about any of the kingdoms surrounding his valley. But Fontaine was at least not Ardglass, and it was hardly like he could storm out without his supplies or close his ears completely.

He'd wondered why they called him the Autumn Prince, but face to face with Rory now, he understood. He looked like a particularly beautiful autumn day in the valley with his wavy auburn hair, tawny eyes, and fair skin. Delicate, Gray would have called him. He definitely had the look of someone who buried his nose in a book and couldn't see what was going on around him. Naive, that was another term Gray might have used.

Rory seemed to be a particularly terrible choice to go after a pack of criminals and apprehend them, though his guard seemed both appropriately suspicious and also eminently capable of capturing whomever they wished. Probably, Gray thought, they'd just brought him along as a particularly useless figurehead. Gray couldn't see any other possible practical use for the pretty prince.

He'd been mildly intrigued by Rory's attractive looks, but once he'd revealed who he was, any curiosity Gray had held about the younger man had died. Royalty, Gray thought with an annoyed sneer, was all the same. A complete waste of air.

Gray did not care that Prince Emory's guard was currently searching the farm; they would not find anything of value to them. He just wanted them to complete their search, confirm what he'd told them was the truth, perhaps stay the night, and then be on their way. He had no use and no time for inept princelings, even ones who stared at him like he was the most compelling thing they'd ever seen.

He knew he'd grown tall and strong, like his father had always predicted. The bloodline of Ardglass always throws true, he'd say. Gray shook his head. He did not want to think of his father, ever, but especially not today, when faced with the mirror image of what could have been. If Sabrina hadn't needed his blood, if his father hadn't been so weak, and if he hadn't been forced to run from Tullamore, he and Prince Emory would likely have met across a banquet table, or in the marble-walled throne room. They would have exchanged useless pleasantries, and maybe even eventually found their way to each other's beds for a night or two of pleasure, but they certainly never would have met in a patch of squash.

But that was what could have been, and circumstances being what they were, could never be. Prince Emory would leave in the morning, none the wiser that he had met the lost Prince of Ardglass in a mysterious valley not found on any maps.

Maybe next time Gray ventured into the village, he would hear of Rory's exile, and the Regent Queen taking over the throne of Fontaine permanently. He had never met her, but based on Rory's appearance, perhaps she would be better suited to ruling.

"Do people often come here?" Rory asked, as Gray continued to tend his squash. Rory, probably accustomed to a castle full of courtiers honor-bound to answer, didn't seem to understand that he had no interest in actually continuing their conversation.

"We're all lost, a little," Gray repeated between clenched teeth. "Or do you disagree?"

Rory smiled, the sun streaming onto his porcelain-pure features as he tipped his head back to soak in the light. "Actually, I believe you, but you also didn't answer the question."

He was intelligent then, and definitely quick, and Gray found it harder to believe that his aunt had managed to essentially usurp him without him noticing.

"After all, there is nobody here in this valley except you," Rory continued, still smiling. Gray grimaced.

"And you, and your guard," Gray added.

"But we're not lost."

Gray gave a particularly vicious shove to his spade, thought of what he'd heard in the village, but decided it wasn't worth it. If Prince Emory thought all was fine in his kingdom, then who was Gray to enlighten him? The noble game of politics and royalty and all that blasted honor that ultimately meant less than nothing was one that he had washed his hands of a long time ago. Even if Rory died at the hands of his aunt—and it wouldn't be the first time a relative bloodied their hands to gain a throne—it wasn't any of Gray's concern.

"Is this what you do here?" Rory asked, another question after a blessed moment of silence.

"What I do here?" Gray knew he should turn and walk away, find shelter and quiet in the stables or in the far-reaching hay fields. There was undoubtedly work he could do in either of those places, but then again, it had been a long time since they'd had any visitors to the valley, and even longer since he'd been to the village. Conversing with someone, even this prince, was actually kind of nice.

He could always talk to Evrard, but sometimes it was easier not to talk to Evrard.

Rory gestured towards the earth he was turning with his spade. "Work in the garden, move dirt around, that sort of thing," he said awkwardly. It was clear that the excessively clean and relatively callus-free hands of Rory's weren't a mirage; he did spend all his time with books, never working with the golden sword he carried at his hip or ever in anything resembling dirt.

"I'm mixing manure into the soil," Gray explained, and couldn't help but smile at the way Rory flinched. "But yes, this is what I do. Do you see anyone else here?" When Rory shook his head, Gray gave a short bark of laughter. "Then there is nobody else here to do what needs to be done," he said. "Only me."

"You take care of all of this?" Rory asked wonderingly, gazing around at the farm.

Gray couldn't help but be proud of what he'd built, nearly from nothing. Everything had come from sweat and blood, and was learned the hard way, which was usually doing it wrong once or twice or many times first. Others in his place might have been afraid of so much hard work, but idleness terrified Gray. Boredom brought thinking, and thinking brought a bone- and soul-deep fury that he didn't always know how to contain. Sometimes exhausting himself was all that had kept him from saddling his horse and riding back to Tullamore and demanding satisfaction for the merciless, ruinous way he'd been treated.

He did not know if Sabrina still resided in Tullamore, or if she still advised his father. It would likely be a death sentence for him to return, and ultimately, likely advantageous for her. It was the latter more than the former that usually stopped him.

After all, what use was his life? What use was his strong pair of hands? He'd created this farm, and he helped those lost souls who happened to wander by, but nobody stayed. Evrard and he kept their company, and he swam occasionally in the stream that rippled by the farmhouse. He rode his old horse through the meadows. He tended the hay and the garden and cleaned the little farmhouse. Cared for the cows and sheep and chickens. Always put away far more food than he could ever eat for their mild winters.

It was a little like being King of this valley, but Gray wasn't dumb enough to truly believe that. If he'd become a king, he'd be doing more; he'd be useful.

He wasn't even a prince anymore, and even he knew just how stupid it was to keep thinking that way.

This was his situation now, and nothing could change that. Raging against circumstances out of his control was pointless. Just as pointless as expecting Rory to do something with the position he'd been graced with—or dirty those delicate, pale fingers.

"I do care for all of this," Gray finally said, turning towards the Prince. "There is nobody else to do it, and it keeps me occupied."

"My occupation is . . ." Rory hesitated. "Not as useful as yours."

That much Gray believed completely. He had to remind himself again that when he had come to the valley, he'd been as green as Rory. Not perhaps quite as soft, or as pampered, and definitely not as naive, but then Rory was also much older than he'd been. Rory had had the opportunity that Gray never did: to grow up in the secure enclave of the court, shielded and protected. If he'd been honest with himself, part of Gray was jealous.

But the other part of him, knowledgeable and world-wise, preferred the reality of what he'd lived through. He would never again be subject to the whims of someone else. It might be a very little kingdom, but it was still his.

"What is your occupation?" Gray asked, even though he already had an idea.

"I study," Rory explained quietly, his fingers rolling up a corner of his glove again and again, until the leather creased. "I speak ten languages and can read others. I translate important manuscripts and analyze them."

Gray made sure his voice was neutral when he said, "That sounds fairly useful."

But Rory's own was scornful as he answered back. "How can you say that? You manage this entire farm. You grow the food you eat, you repair the roof over your head. You and you alone are responsible."

"And you are subject to the whims of others?" Gray observed quietly. Maybe Rory was not quite as naive as he'd believed. Maybe he understood exactly what his aunt intended. "I understand that all too well."

"So you came here from someplace else, then?" Rory asked. "Where were your parents from?"

Evrard had cautioned Gray never to give a hint to any of the people who passed through the valley what his origin was, or his real name, or anything of value. He said Sabrina's spies were everywhere, and they were still constantly hunting for even the tiniest hint that he was alive.

Prince Emory did not look much like a spy of Sabrina's, but then he had also come here on a foolish, impossible errand. There were no brigands in the valley, or in the woods, or in the village beyond. And sending someone like Rory to dispose of them was even more of a fool's errand. No, someone had sent him here, had lured him here, specifically. Gray, who had let himself get carried away with talking to someone who wasn't just here for the night or a snob, like Evrard, went still. In the years since his escape, he'd clearly grown soft and lacking the suspicious instinct that had ruled the beginning of his time in the valley. One look at the pretty prince and he'd been so distracted that he'd let Rory and his five guardswomen—capable and deadly guardswomen—essentially invade his property and his valley.

"Nowhere you need be concerned with," Gray said in a hard, resolute voice. He picked up his spade and decided that it wasn't enough that Rory's guard wouldn't find anything here. They needed to be gone. They were all armed to the teeth, and while he had not gotten the impression from any of them that they wished to harm him, Gray knew he could not take on all five at once.

He'd tried to keep up with his sword forms and practiced occasionally on a straw dummy he'd set up in the back of the stables but finding ready and willing partners to spar with was difficult. Once in awhile someone with training would pass through and Gray would challenge them to a practice bout. But otherwise, like with all things, he was on his own.

It would not be enough to handle more than one or two of Rory's clearly well-trained guards.

Definitely not all five, and absolutely not all at once.

Gray leaned down and rested his hand against the leather holder he'd fashioned for his dagger, kept strapped around his calf. He never went without it, though these days he used it more to cut stalks of wheat or to pick squash for dinner. Still, it could kill if he needed it to. He kept it clean and sharp, cautioned always by Evrard that out beyond the valley, danger still lurked.

Now it was possible that danger had actually come to the valley.

"What's the matter?" Rory asked as Gray stalked off towards the stables. He needed to check on Evrard, preferably without his annoying—and attractive—companion. Because he couldn't exactly converse with Evrard, not in front of Rory anyway.

Evrard had been correct—nobody who expected to see a horse ever saw anything other than a horse, but as soon as Evrard opened his mouth, it would be obvious he wasn't just a horse.

"You should find your guard," he told Rory as they approached the stables.

"I'm sure they're fine," Rory said, clearly unconcerned. Gray supposed it made some sort of sense; after all, the only one with very little training, except in ancient languages, was Rory himself. Everyone else on this farm could handle themselves in a fight. The guard had obviously decided that Gray wasn't a threat either, as they'd been left alone together for the last ten minutes.

"Were you really sent here to capture criminals?" Gray asked. If there was a plan to capture or kill Gray, Rory was almost certainly not aware of it.

"Yes, yes, of course we were," Rory insisted, "though it does seem like this couldn't possibly be their hideout. Unless . . ." He hesitated and his face was so open, the thoughts easily read there, Gray knew exactly what he was thinking. Unless you are lying.

"There's nobody here but me," Gray ground out. "We've established that."

"True," Rory admitted.

"So why are you really here?" Gray demanded, and took a step closer to Rory, crowding him against the side of the stables. Was he hoping to scare him a little? Certainly. Rory seemed a much easier nut to crack than some of the women on his guard. They would never tell him the truth of their journey here, but Rory? If he knew, he'd spit it right out. "Tell me what your purpose is."

"I told you already," Rory spluttered, likely flustered by the fact that Gray's bare, dirty chest was pressed right up against his own butter yellow silk doublet and fine turquoise traveling cloak. He'd probably never seen a dirty man in his entire life.

Rory felt as small and lean as he looked, but he also didn't fold the way Gray was expecting him to. Instead, he stared defiantly into Gray's eyes with his unearthly pale gaze. A thousand colors in those eyes, Gray thought, in a daze. Gold and amber and citrine. How had this backfired so spectacularly?

Occasionally he slept with men and women who passed through the valley, and once or twice on trips to the village. But they were only momentary pleasure, a moment of respite in an otherwise somewhat drab existence full to the brim with backbreaking work. But he had never wanted anyone the way he found himself wanting Prince Emory of Fontaine.

Firstly, it was terrible timing, and secondly, Rory was absolutely the last person that Gray should be wanting. But Rory's soft, pink lips were right there, and his slim body was pressed tightly against his own. It would take but a moment to tip his head down and thread his dirty fingers through the silky, fiery strands of Rory's incredible hair. Then he might know if it would be hot to the touch, flaming like its vibrant shade, or cool and soft against his fingers. Maybe he'd even end up with a knife in his back for his trouble. But before that moment, the trouble would be dizzying and rapturous.

"What's wrong?" Rory asked in a soft voice. "Why are you worried?"

Gray took a step back and tried to clear his head. It was nearly impossible to do so when Rory kept staring at him, that hopeful, somewhat quizzical expression in his eyes, like he hadn't quite understood why Gray hadn't leaned down and closed the distance between their lips.

Gray was still trying to understand it himself.

"Why am I worried?" Gray repeated, annoyed. "You've shown up here looking for something that doesn't exist. And anyone with a shred of information would have known that. Your presence here . . ."

"Could be a trap," Rory interrupted him, proving his sharp-edged intelligence yet again. How had his aunt maneuvered him into such a terrible position? Gray still did not understand it. "I . . ." Rory hesitated. "It's likely that's a correct assumption."

Gray tensed. Rory's assessment and his own were strangely similar. "Your guard," Gray said, not sure how to phrase the question.

Where was his guard? Were they lying in wait for him? Planning to kill him? Capture him? Return him to Sabrina after all these years of evading her powerful magic? He would kill himself first—simply slit his wrists with his sharp dagger. She could not be trusted with him. He did not understand entirely how she planned to use him, but it was clear that his usefulness would end with his death. And after all, Gray thought bitterly, who was even left to mourn him? Certainly not his father, who had betrayed him. Perhaps Evrard, but then, Gray had always felt like he represented more of an idea than an actual person to Evrard. A pawn, in the battle between him and Sabrina. Between good and evil.

Evrard would return to the place he had come from, and dismiss the whole time from his mind as an unpleasant experience during which he'd been forced to share a stable with Gray's stupid horse.

"What about my guard?" Rory asked, a confused wrinkle appearing between his auburn brows.

Gray took a step closer, even though there was something about Rory that was even more terrifying than the prospect of death. He leaned down, and caught the anticipation on Rory's face, even as he shifted towards his ear, not his mouth. "Can they be trusted?" he murmured.

He kept underestimating Rory. It was easy, with his soft hands and innocent eyes and stunning face. It was so easy to forget that under all that gorgeously waving hair, he had a clever, astute mind. Gray had expected an automatic affirmative, without much thought put behind it. He knew what it was like—royalty always assumed they were unassailable. Gray himself had believed that, once upon a time. But instead of what he expected, Rory furrowed his brow and gave the question serious consideration.

"Marthe is not particularly ambitious," Rory said. "She has been in my guard almost since my birth, and captain for the last ten years. Also, she was originally appointed not by my aunt, but by my father, before his death."

It was the first evidence that Rory had some inkling that his aunt was not to be trusted.

"And the rest?" Gray asked, very aware his questioning seemed relentless, but not willing to sacrifice politeness for safety.

Rory frowned. "Anya has been with me almost as long as Marthe has been captain. She's from Ardglass, but I do think she can be trusted." Gray's heart skipped a beat at Rory's admission. Would this Anya recognize him as the lost prince? It was doubtful; the last fifteen years had wrought many changes in him, but the chance still remained. "As for Acadia, Rowen, and Diana, I picked them myself after extensive interviews, and all were desperate for a chance to serve, a chance they would not have been given otherwise. I do not trust them as much as Marthe or Anya, but I would still trust them with my life."

It was enough. Still, they needed to locate the five guardswomen. Gray no longer wanted them roaming his farm unaccompanied. At least not until he could trust them as much as Rory did. His conversation with Evrard would have to wait.

Gray found them grouped together outside the farmhouse, talking in low voices as he and Rory approached.

"My prince," Marthe said, separating from the group. "Something here is . . . not right."

From the way she spoke in front of Gray, he knew the problem did not lie with him personally or with the farm, but rather the complete lack of criminal activity. They had come here expecting to find one thing and had found something entirely different. Obviously a cause for serious concern.

Rory nodded, and Marthe continued, after giving him a long, searching look. "Perhaps we should discuss this privately," she said.

Ahhhh, Gray thought, there is the strategy I would assume from a captain of the Prince's guard. She doesn't quite trust me either.

But Rory's chin stuck out stubbornly as he shook his head. "No," he said emphatically. "I believe we can trust Gray. After all, this is his farm. He has a right to know our plans."

Marthe's expression made it clear she did not agree, but she did reluctantly speak anyway. Whether that was blind obedience to her prince, or a grudging acceptance of the point he'd made, Gray wasn't sure. "I think we need to stay here," she said. "I considered seeking out the next village, and potentially evading the trap that was set for us here, but I believe we can protect you here, and we could possibly learn something useful by letting the intended action come to pass."

It was a gutsy call, but Gray didn't disagree with it.

Marthe then turned her attention to him, asking many of the same questions Rory had, except she had a different purpose. "How often do strangers come here?"

"One a month? Perhaps less?" Gray answered. Understanding where she was going with her questioning, he continued. "But it would be difficult for a soldier or a fighter to disguise themselves as one of them. They are often running away from a bad situation, wanting not to be found. An unwanted betrothal, or a father with heavy fists. They find the valley because they need it, they never expect it to be here."

"Then how were we able to find it?" Rory asked. A question that Gray had been asking himself since they had appeared outside his garden.

"I'm not sure," Gray admitted. Evrard would know, but he could not exactly excuse himself to go discuss the problem with the King of the Unicorns.

"Perhaps because we knew it was here," Anya volunteered.

"Perhaps," Gray agreed. It did seem like the most likely of explanations.

"We will set a guard," Marthe said. "Two per shift."

She did not glance in Gray's direction, so he knew she did not intend him to be part of it, but even then, he very much doubted he would rest tonight. He would lie awake, as he did many nights, and wonder who was going to come for him.

Maybe tonight the unknown threat would be coming for Prince Emory, instead. Gray had believed earlier he wouldn't care if Rory paid for his own ignorant mistakes, but to his surprise, now this thought did not bring any particular relief.

"You may rest in the bunkhouse," Gray offered. "I keep it clean for the occasional visitors. There is a separate stable, as well, stocked with hay." He had built the additional stable, even though newcomers to the valley rarely came with horses, because despite Evrard's confidence that no one could ever identify him as a unicorn, Gray still worried. Also, it alleviated the occasional awkward question, about why he would spend any amount of time in the stables, seemingly conversing with silent animals.

Marthe nodded, and one of the guards walked off with their horses, to water and feed them.

Rory did not follow them, but instead continued to stare at Gray.

"Would you give me a tour of your farm?" he asked.

Gray had hoped to slip away, to visit Evrard, and get his impression of the situation, and perhaps clean himself, maybe even find a threadbare shirt to throw on. Rory hadn't seemed offended by his lack of dress—more like the opposite, in fact—but some rules went deep. He could hear Rhys still, yelling in his mind, that meeting another prince with only a pair of loose breeches on was not done. You're from Ardglass, not a barbarian, Rhys would have insisted. And even though Rhys had been dead all these years, and his guidelines regarding attire, etiquette, and polite behavior should have died with him, Gray found himself squirming in a place he'd believed long forgotten.

"I have work to do," Gray said awkwardly, definitely not used to making polite excuses. He tried to ignore Rory's disappointed look, but it was much harder than it should have been. "Perhaps afterwards," he tacked on. He doubted Marthe would let the Prince out of her sight, but then she had done so earlier, so she must not find him too much of a threat. Gray didn't know whether to be pleased or insulted.

Gray entered the stables, his eyes adjusting to the dimmer light. He'd installed two larger windows, filling the panes with precious sheets of glass he'd bought in the village. Evrard hadn't expressed any particular gratitude, but then that was Evrard's way; expectation and then very little to follow in the way of appreciation. Still, Gray knew he enjoyed the windows, as he often found Evrard looking out them into the valley.

He found Evrard in front of one now, his expression the unicorn equivalent of discontent. "There are visitors," he said.

Evrard's great jeweled eyes swung his direction. "I saw myself," he said, "and not the usual kind."

"No," Gray said, sitting down on a stool he'd placed in Evrard's stall expressly for their chats. "A prince, and his guard."

Evrard did not seem surprised. "From Fontaine, then?" he asked.

"How did you know?" Gray did not really expect an answer; there was still much about Evrard's knowledge and his magic that he liked to keep close. Gray was never sure if it was because his methods were truly secret, or if he just enjoyed the mystery.

Evrard, unsurprisingly, ignored that particular question, and asked another. "What is your impression of Prince Emory?"

He thought for a long moment. What did he think of Rory? "He's soft, but strong," Gray finally said. "He isn't particularly experienced or skillful in the real world, but he's intelligent, and he isn't easily intimidated, even in stressful situations."

"He has potential then." Evrard sounded very pleased with himself, as if he'd predicted this result.

"Potential for what?"

Evrard just stared at him, one of those inscrutable looks on his elegant features. "Potential to be someone you could . . . trust."

Gray didn't know what Evrard had been about to say but had thought better of it at the last minute. He almost asked, but again, that was useless. If Evrard had wanted to tell him, he would have. Another mystery in a long line of infuriating mysteries.

"What does Fontaine have to do with us?" Gray asked instead.

"Much more than you realize."

"Prince Emory and his guard were likely lured here, but for what purpose, I don't know," Gray pointed out.

"They are strong and capable of protecting him," Evrard replied, "but ultimately, that job will come to you."

"So he will stay here? Is it his aunt?"

Again, instead of answering, Evrard turned his head and looked out the window. When Gray glanced in the same direction, he saw Rory practicing against a bale of hay with the sword that had sat at his waist. Anya was directing him, and Rory was just about as bad with the weapon as Gray would have guessed. Still, Evrard was right, he showed potential. Only glimpses of it occasionally, but it was there all the same. It was useless to imagine what Rory would have been like if he'd grown up like Gray, on his own, paranoid and a little desperate, but Gray imagined it anyway. He'd have been a force to be reckoned with, Gray realized. Just as strong as himself, maybe even stronger. Smarter, for sure.

"Yes, his aunt," Evrard agreed. "She is not to be trusted."

A problem Gray understood all too well.

CHAPTER FOUR

It was so peaceful on the farm, Rory could scarcely believe that danger could be imminent. After a training session with Anya, Rory sat down against the small, squat house that Gray had specified for their use. Inside it wasn't particularly fancy or luxurious. Simple wood interior, filled with basic but well-made wooden furniture. Trundle beds with mattresses filled with clean straw stood against the walls. The stable was equally simplistic, but also very clean and well cared for. Rowen, who tended their horses, hadn't had any complaints, and she could be particular about stables.

Rory watched the main house and wondered where Gray had gone. He'd been so abrupt in his refusal to give Rory a tour of the farm—then had unexpectedly softened his stance, instead claiming they could do it later. He couldn't help but wonder if later could possibly be now. Gray had been, at turns, both standoffish and clearly intrigued by Rory. And Rory, who had met plenty of men before in the castle of Beaulieu and elsewhere, had somehow never met a man quite like Gray before. He'd kissed a few boys—because now, after meeting Gray, it was undeniable that they had been boys, not men—but there had never been anyone as guarded and mysterious and exceptionally intriguing as Gray. His secrets seemed to have secrets, and Rory was just stupid enough to want him to share, even if such a possibility seemed ludicrous.

He stood, and decided that if he wanted a tour, then he would have to be the one to request one, again. Walking around the side of the main house, Rory stopped dead in his tracks.

Really, he didn't know how Gray kept stealing his breath and his words from his mouth, because he'd done it the first time they'd met, and now he'd done it again.

He was still stripped to the waist, but now he was washing, big handfuls of water cascading down his much-cleaner chest, the muscles even better defined as they shone wetly in the late afternoon sun. Reaching down, Gray groaned as he took a small wooden bowl and filled it, pouring it over his head and slicking his dark, wavy hair back. Clean, with no hair to obscure his features, his face was even more arresting, as if it had been carved by a master in one of Rory's art history texts. Rory's heart pounded and his skin felt too tight. Should he stop watching? It felt wrong to stare when Gray didn't know he was being observed, but Rory wasn't quite sure he could tear his eyes away.

He wondered if Gray was like many of Fontaine, who enjoyed the company of both women and men, and if he did, if he would ever be interested in someone like Rory. It was a wildly insane thought, as Rory was a prince, and the entire court of Beaulieu would have been aghast at the thought of Rory entertaining someone who was essentially a farmhand, but Rory simply couldn't help it. It was impossible to be faced with a man like that, with that face, and that chest, and apparently those legs, as the dripping water molded his baggy breeches to a pair of exceedingly fine legs, and not wonder. Gray was the kind of man that you saw once and thought about for a very long time afterward. And Rory, who couldn't deny he was used to getting nearly everything he wanted, wondered if he might have the opportunity to do more than just look.

"Are you done staring?" Gray asked, not even glancing in Rory's direction.

Oh, he'd been caught red-handed. Rory tried to paste on a contrite expression on his face, but he couldn't quite manage it. He did feel a bit guilty, but he didn't regret one moment of what he'd seen. Gray was too beautiful for that.

Rory had observed the behavior of some of the more romantically inclined courtiers in Beaulieu, and had long since noticed what set them apart from the other, less successful courtiers, was a brash sort of confidence. Not quite sure he could emulate that, Rory smiled and walked over, hoping a poised but purposeful saunter would do the trick.

It didn't, but that might have been the unexpected root he tripped over on his way to where Gray was wiping his face and hands with a clean, rough cloth.

"Are you alright?" Gray asked with amusement.

Rory inwardly cursed his prodigious mental abilities—because they always seemed to preclude any sort of physical grace. "Yes, of course," he said. "Is it later? I'd like my tour now."

Gray looked at him thoughtfully. "You can see all of the farm from this spot," he said. "What is it that interests you?"

You, Rory thought before he could stop the word from popping into his uncooperative brain. Always you.

But he did not quite have the confidence to say it, so he just gestured wildly to the surrounding areas. "Anywhere you like to go, particularly. Even with all the work you do to maintain the farm, you must have some time to yourself," he said. Certainly not his best effort, but not his worst either.

Gray smiled, and this time it reached his eyes, warming the blue until it reflected the sky high above. "There's a place I like that you might also enjoy," he said.

Your bed? Rory thought, but didn't say out loud, because even as a jest, he didn't know how it would be received.

He knew he was attractive, but he also remembered the way Gray's expression had shuttered when he'd introduced himself as Prince Emory. Maybe Gray didn't like members of the nobility. Maybe he'd had a bad experience, and that was why he was hiding out in this valley. Rory didn't anticipate successfully persuading Gray to tell him about his past, but he still intended to try.

"I'd love to see it," Rory said.

Gray laid the cloth he'd used to dry on a length of fence and pulled on a threadbare shirt that had been hanging from the post. Rory ordered himself not to be disappointed that Gray was covering up, and at the same time, wondered if it was because of him. Was it because Gray didn't want him to get any untoward ideas? Men didn't usually look at Rory and attempt to push him away, even if Rory rarely gazed back. They never seemed as interesting as his books did, though Gray put them all to shame.

Gray took them past the farmhouse, around the bend of the river, to a makeshift bridge, and walking over the rickety structure, he pointed out towards a meadow blanketed with flowers in a thousand different shades of purple. It gave the look of an endless, meticulously crafted coverlet, spread out across the ground, even though it was only Nature's random work. "Here," he said. "Sometimes I come here to think."

Rory knew that the man who had sat in the library tower in Beaulieu would have heard that and scoffed, imagining that a man such as Gray didn't do any thinking. At least any that was as intricate and important as the thinking Rory did. But something had shifted since he'd started this journey, and he was looking at the world and the people who inhabited it in a slightly different way now. He'd been so closed off in that tower, at first out of his own misplaced desire, and then because he suspected his aunt had never wanted him to look anywhere but at the book right in front of him. Now he was truly seeing, maybe for the first time, and he wondered at the risk she had taken to send him here, knowing that his world view might alter. Truthfully, the thought left Rory chilled to the core. Whatever was here, hidden in this valley, was important enough to be worth the risk, and he dreaded whatever consequences had followed him to Gray's farm.

"It's a beautiful place. Serene," Rory said, trying to shake his increasingly despondent thoughts from his head. He sat down, Gray following suit a few feet away. "What do you think about here?"

Gray tipped his head back and stared at the sky, an inky lock of wet hair sliding invitingly along his neck and exposed collarbone. Swallowing hard, Rory tried to follow suit and direct his attention to the sky above, but it was hard to turn away from someone so compelling.

He was silent so long that Rory was almost afraid he'd scared him away with the rather direct question. "Life," Gray finally said quietly. "Where it started, and how I ended up here."

"Was it your choice to come to the valley?"

"Choice? An interesting word and an even more interesting concept," Gray replied bitterly.

Much like some of Rory's tougher translations, he was discovering that Gray could be coaxed with space and plenty of time. Gray was suspicious and naturally cautious, and that, Rory realized, was because Gray didn't trust him.

Yet, he added to the end of the thought. Gray doesn't trust me yet.

But it was impossible to say if they would ever get a real chance to trust each other. In any other circumstances, Rory and his guard would've been on the road out of the valley first thing in the morning. The only reason they had decided to remain here was the uncertainty that awaited them. He and Gray could be separated tonight or tomorrow or any day in the near future, and an opportunity to learn and know and trust each other would never exist.

Gray plucked a deep violet flower and twirled it between his fingers. They looked thick with calluses from where Rory was sitting, but he was gentle with the flower, nearly delicate. "That is much of what I dwell on," he continued, his voice nearly as rough as his fingertips. "Choice. There is much in this life I never had the opportunity to choose, but in the end, it's not a bad life."

"I chose all of mine," Rory said, and to his own surprise, his voice was nearly as bitter as Gray's. Yes, he'd made every choice himself, and every one of them wrong.

"Doesn't sound like the choices were good ones," Gray pointed out. His hair, drying in the warm afternoon sunlight, was growing waves, and Rory itched to smooth it back, to feel those rich locks between his fingers. Unlike Gray, his fingers were still untouched and smooth, despite the week of practice, and he'd feel every single strand.

"They were selfish, and a little stupid," Rory admitted. "I'm sure you don't know what that's like. You give everything of yourself, every single day. I can see it in the way you take care of this place."

"It's a little selfish." Gray hesitated. "Working hard is a good way to avoid thinking about anything in particular."

Rory laughed, and unexpectedly, Gray smiled, his quiet happiness lighting up his blue eyes. "Don't tell Marthe that," Rory said conspiratorially, "she'd never let me forget it."

Reaching out, Gray lightly cupped his shoulder. "You look like you could use some hard work," he said, then as suddenly as he'd touched Rory, his hand dropped away. But Rory, shocked, felt the pressure radiating through his skin and muscle and bone, the heat of the single touch permeating him to his core.

It was hard to say with the sunlight and Gray's skin, tanned from working so many hours outdoors, but he might have flushed. "Sorry," he added quietly.

At first, Rory thought the apology was because you weren't supposed to touch royalty unless they invited it first. A lonely way to live, Rory had discovered. But then he realized that wasn't it at all. Gray lived here alone, with only the occasional visitor. He was likely unused to touching and being touched.

"You're not wrong," Rory said, refusing to acknowledge the apology, because Gray hadn't done anything worth apologizing for, "I could."

Gray stared at him, his eyes a penetrating and impossible shade of blue. Rory had never seen anyone with eyes like that, eyes that could bore into your very soul. He hesitated, wanting to shift closer, to be closer, but before he could, a voice interrupted them.

"There you are," Marthe said, striding into the field and ruining both the moment and the serenity. "I've been looking for you everywhere, Prince Emory."

Rory rolled his eyes.

"You should stay closer," she continued, "it's our job to protect you and we can't do that if you aren't close by."

She reached down and helped Rory to his feet, shooting Gray a look as she did so.

When they were across the bridge, Rory turned to her. "What did you do that for?" he hissed.

Marthe looked unimpressed by Rory's insistence. "Do what? Interrupt you? You should be close by. Also, that man is a stranger."

"A handsome stranger," Rory sighed.

Marthe laughed. "He may be, but he still is not to be trusted. He has yet to prove himself or his loyalty. His motives may appear pure, but anyone can hide behind an innocent mask." Her knowing gaze told Rory exactly who she was referring to: the Regent Queen.

"Fine," Rory agreed with a grumble.

"Besides," Marthe added, "Acadia is putting together a rather delightful-looking stew with vegetables from the garden, and I thought you might want to assist her."

"I don't know . . ." Rory started to say, but Marthe's single quelling look shut him right up.

"But you should learn," Marthe insisted flatly.

The sun set in a glorious wash of golds and reds and oranges. Rory stood outside the bunkhouse and watched it as it finally sank behind the trees rimming the valley, curtaining the meadow below in darkness.

"Come inside," Diana urged him, hand out, ready to corral him back into the shelter. She didn't know that what Rory most wanted was to go find Gray again and continue their conversation from earlier. He'd sat with them for the evening meal, mostly silent, and only answering questions put to him directly. He'd barely met Rory's eyes, and as soon as the food was gone, he'd ducked out, quietly murmuring that he had work to do securing the farm for the night.

"I want some air," Rory argued, and Diana shot him a fond look.

"Remember at Beaulieu, when we would have to physically drag you out of the library?" she asked. "What happened to those days?"

Rory wasn't entirely sure; only that he wasn't sure he would ever be the same after these weeks on the road. Even if, against all odds, he could return to Beaulieu and resume his life as it had been, he didn't think it would fit him as well as it had before.

"Oh," she added with a quick blush. "You want to find that farm boy, don't you?"

Diana was the nurturer of the guard, and also the romantic. She was always falling in love here and there. After a few weeks, the fairy dust would fade from her eyes, and then a month later, another girl would catch her eye. Rory knew he was not the only one who hoped that someday she might discover love a little closer to home and melt Marthe's grumpy heart.

"His name is Gray," Rory said. "And he's . . . well . . . you've seen him."

Crossing her arms across her chest, Diana's dark eyes grew bright with excitement. "But it's more than that, you like him."

"I don't even know him," Rory admitted.

"But you want to," Diana said slyly.

At Rory's nod, Diana clapped her hands happily and leaned closer. "If I distract Marthe, you could steal away for a little while," she said.

Rory raised an eyebrow and Diana blushed again, more fiercely this time. "Not like that," she insisted while Rory ducked out the front door and gave her a little wave. "If I'm not back," he said, and then thought better of his suggestion, because the last thing he wanted was, if something actually did happen, for one of his guardswomen to ruin the moment again. He shook his head briefly, and Diana gave him another grin and a happy little wave of encouragement.

First he checked the stables, but other than two horses, one occupying a stall with a large window, its face haughty and somehow familiar, the other plain and brown and steady, it was empty.

There were no lights on yet in the farmhouse Gray slept in, and even though the light was still peeping through the trees, dusk had fallen. Rory realized belatedly that he should have taken a lamp or even a candlestick if he was going to go wandering about a strange place at night. When he returned, Marthe would likely skin him. But then maybe tonight was the night that Diana and Marthe finally opened their eyes and truly saw each other for the first time. If that happened, then it wouldn't matter how late the hour it was when Rory returned to the bunkhouse.

Still, Rory remained undaunted, and headed towards the makeshift bridge and the meadow Gray had shown him earlier. It didn't make much sense to come here in the dark, but Rory was determined to leave no stone unturned. But after wandering around half-blind in a quickly darkening meadow, he finally hurried back over the bridge. Gray hadn't returned to the scene of their earlier moment. He was still nowhere to be found.

Marthe's voice whispered in his ear, maybe he has betrayed you after all. I told you not to trust him. But he shook his head, refusing to believe that someone with Gray's quiet, wry reserve, with all that kindness and determination in his eyes, could truly be bad.

He checked the stables again, heartbeat racing as he hurried from building to building, and then back to the garden, where they'd first met. But this time, the patch of squash was disappointingly empty. Where has he gone? Rory thought worriedly. Had he truly abandoned them?

It didn't seem possible, but then that was when Rory realized the pounding he was hearing wasn't just the beating of his own heart in the darkness. It was the pounding of horse hooves against the valley floor, and far more of them together than his guardswomen. There were visitors in the valley, and by the way they were riding at such a speed, they hadn't come for a friendly chat.

This was the trap that Marthe was so certain would be set for them here, and now it had been sprung, and where was Rory? Separated from his guard and hiding in a squash patch. He ducked behind a particularly tall plant and hoped he could make himself small and unobtrusive enough that he wouldn't be noticed in the dark.

He crouched down, reaching up to pull his cloak around him, hoping the bright blue which had seemed so eye-catching and flattering in Beaulieu wouldn't be the thing that gave him away to the intruders. Perhaps these were finally the brigands they had been warned of? Maybe he'd been wrong about his aunt all along, and she wasn't trying to kill him. The hope had just begun to bloom inside him—a perfectly peaceful resolution to a problem that hadn't actually been a problem at all—when he heard a female shout and then another, and he realized with lead sinking in his stomach that it was his guards, yelling at each other as they fought. He heard the first clang of metal on metal and grabbed the little dagger that Marthe had thankfully insisted he carry with him at all times, his trembling fingers closing tightly around the metal, his damp palm slippery on the handle. It was nothing, not compared to a sword or an ax or a war hammer, and he hadn't even been properly trained to wield it. A week's worth of lessons wasn't nearly enough to take on a fully grown soldier who had trained their entire life to kill silly little princes like Rory.

He could have grabbed Lion's Breath, still sitting ornamentally in its jeweled scabbard on his hip, but he was even more out of his depth with the sword than he was with the dagger, so he stuck to what he knew.

How had he come to this, hiding in a patch of dirt, trying desperately not to cry as his friends fought an unknown enemy? Rory knew one thing for certain; he was not proud of the decisions that had led him to this moment.

If I get out of this, he bargained with fate and the gods and whoever was listening, if I get out of this, and Marthe and Diana and Rowen and Anya and Acadia don't die, I will make different choices, I swear to you. I'll put others first. I'll stop being so selfish and self-centered. I'll figure out a way to take the throne and I'll rule my kingdom. Or at least figure out how to rule my kingdom. I won't hide in my books, not anymore. I'll face my aunt, and maybe I won't best her, but I won't let her win without a real fight.

He repeated it over and over again in his mind, eyes straining as he watched shadowy figures, with the occasional glint of armor, fight across the farm. If I get out of this, I will make different choices. Several of the male-shaped figures fell, and Rory prayed he had seen correctly—that it wasn't Marthe or Diana or Anya. He'd taken them for granted; their loyalty and their unyielding friendship. And then he'd selfishly made their job harder by sneaking out alone, in search of the man who had probably been the one to betray them to his friends.

Rory swallowed hard, pushing back the tears as the sound of battle echoed in his ears. If I get out of this, I will make different choices.

Hooves, walking, not riding, the sound cautious on the ground, like someone was trying to sneak towards the garden, caught his attention. Rory tensed, and tried to crouch down even lower. He wished he'd discarded the bright blue cloak; it would probably be his undoing in the end. God, what an idiot I have been. If I get out of this, I will make different choices.

More rustling, like a man was wading through the garden, but trying to be quiet about it. Rory considered giving up his hiding place and running. He also considered rising and attacking, which surely this soldier, come to kill him, wouldn't expect from useless Prince Emory.

He'd made all the wrong choices leading up to this moment, but it was surprisingly easy to choose one now. Rory didn't know if it was the right one or not, but he sprang out of the squash, brandishing his dagger, and froze at the figure in front of him.

Bright blue eyes shone even in the darkness, and even though the man wore a dark cloak, his face was unmistakable.

"Gray," Rory whispered, his heart thudding painfully. Gray had betrayed them after all. He'd been part of the conspiracy all along, probably sent here by his aunt to lie in wait for stupid, silly Prince Rory and his tiny guard, and to dispatch them to their deaths once darkness fell. And Rory, blinded by Gray's handsome face and impressive set of muscles, had pounced at the bait just as she'd intended.

It hurt, and it stung, somewhere deep inside, where he'd always been so proud of his intelligence, of how many languages he'd spoken. All pointless now, Rory thought bitterly. Anger swelled inside as they stared at each other in this dark vegetable garden, and he gripped the dagger harder and decided that if death was calling to him, then he would try his hardest to take Gray along.

A second before he sprang at Gray, fully intending to bury his dagger in his chest, Gray hissed at him. "We need to go."

"What?" Rory couldn't believe it. Was he truly going to continue this play act, like Rory hadn't seen right through it? Did he truly believe him that stupid?

"There's soldiers, assassins, I think. Your guard is holding them back but we must go," Gray begged. "They can't keep you safe. There aren't enough of them. If we can sneak out of this valley, we can find a place to be safe."

Rory stared at him. "You really think I would go with you? After you betrayed me?"

"I didn't betray you," Gray muttered. "But someone did."

There was no logical reason Rory could ascertain that he should trust Gray. It did seem extremely likely that Gray had been the instrument of his betrayal, but his heart must have been more constant than Diana's, because Rory yearned to trust him.

The sword fighting grew in intensity. He heard a heartrending yell, and his own heart turned over. One of his guards must have fallen. He did not know which, but if he was going to depend on logic, then it was clear Gray was right and they could not hold their attackers off forever. And, that quiet, annoyingly logical voice added, if Gray truly intended to kill him, he could kill him now, where they stood. He did not have to spirit him away to take his life.

Gray held out his hand. "We must go," he begged. "You must trust me."

"I suppose I must," Rory said and took his hand.

Gray took them outside of the garden, to where a horse was standing, heavy saddlebags loaded on its rump, but lacking a saddle. "We will ride," Gray said, and gave him a quick boost up to the horse, who glanced back at him, the intensity of his expression nearly matching Gray's.

You must be imagining things, Rory thought hysterically. But then Gray launched himself behind Rory, kicked at the horse's side and they were galloping away.

Unlike the soldiers, they were riding a horse who knew the land, and could also be astonishingly quick and quiet. Rory couldn't believe how little noise it made as they rode away towards the other side of the valley. Gray did not say a word to either the horse or to Rory, just clutched his back and Rory, burying his hands into the horse's mane, held on tight and fast.

The horse did not break pace until they reached the first cluster of trees on the other side of the valley, and then it began to slow.

"Nobody is following us," a voice said, almost eerie in the darkness. It was a completely different tone than Gray's voice, and yet it had to be Gray because Rory could not see anyone ahead of them, and the voice had come from very close.

"They could follow our tracks," Gray replied and his own voice was grim.

"I obscured them. It would take a very skillful tracker to follow," the other voice promised. A little smugly, if Rory had anything to say about it.

"Excuse me," Rory finally said. "Who goes there?"

Gray gave a short, unamused laugh and suddenly the horse slowed, and he dismounted. He held out his hand again for Rory to take, but Rory, suspicious and acutely aware of how alone they were in the forest, slid off the horse without his assistance.

"You said those who cannot see, do not see," Gray said, and Rory froze. His comment, unless Rory was more rattled than he'd believed, was clearly directed at the horse. "How do we open his eyes?"

"Whose eyes?" Rory demanded. "And what are they supposed to see?"

"Trust your instincts, they have yet to fail you," the voice said again, and even though the light was extremely dim, Rory swore it was the horse who was speaking. But that was completely, entirely impossible.

Gray sighed, and turned towards Rory, a wry smile on his face. "I would like to introduce you to Evrard, King of the Unicorns."

He had seen this horse twice before. Once, while searching for Gray earlier this evening, when he had walked into the stables, and again right before they took flight out of the valley. It had only ever looked like a horse to Rory, plain gray sides, normal musculature—a completely unassuming creature. But now, Rory looked closer, and suddenly, the horse's coat was not gray at all, but blinding, perfect white, like the first unadulterated snowfall. It had a horn, also white and shimmering vaguely in the moonlight.

Rory's jaw fell open as the horse—no, the unicorn—bowed to him. "Prince Emory of Fontaine," it said in its deep sonorous voice, "it is very good to meet you, though I do wish the circumstances were better."

"You always do," Gray muttered.

The unicorn—Evrard, Rory corrected, still stunned by the sudden turn of events—shifted his hooves impatiently, his long mane rippling. "Then I shall have to stop saving you and Prince Emory both from certain death," he retorted sharply.

"It's . . ." Rory found his etiquette rules falling short at being introduced to a unicorn, though Evrard was a king, so maybe that was where he should start. "It's a pleasure to meet you, Your Highness," Rory said, and bowed deeply.

"Ah, Prince Emory, the pleasure is entirely mine," Evrard claimed as Rory met his deep, jeweled eyes once more. "Your elegant manners are such a balm after spending years with this one."

This one clearly referred to Gray, who had a curious mixture of affection and annoyance on his face as he looked upon Evrard.

"Neither of us is very easy to live with," Gray offered wryly by way of explanation.

"How did such a creature come to live at your farm?" Rory wondered.

He fully expected to receive an evasive answer from Gray, and a smug one from Evrard, who clearly had not met an etiquette manual he didn't enjoy.

"I rescued him, much as I have rescued you tonight," Evrard pronounced.

"He did," Gray agreed, "and he took me to live in the Valley of the Lost Things."

"Valley of the Lost Things?" Rory puzzled. "Is that the official name of it?"

"It has always been a haven for those who have need of it," Evrard said.

"But not tonight." Gray's voice was stark and his face was full of concern. "Tonight, it was found."

Sudden guilt swamped Rory. It was his fault that Gray had temporarily lost the home he had built. Rory and his guard had led the soldiers there, which must have been his aunt's purpose in sending him in the first place.

"I'm sorry," he said, genuinely meaning it.

Evrard impatiently shook his mane. "Do not apologize for actions that were not your fault. It was inevitable the magical barriers would be breached; she has been trying for many years to find a way around them. You were a convenient pawn in her plan."

Rory straightened his cloak, brushing off some of the dirt remaining from the squash patch. "Then the soldiers were not looking for me?"

"They were," Evrard said. "But not only you."

"You should start at the beginning, you are only confusing him. Considering his reputation as one of the most intelligent in the realms, it can't be too difficult to explain," Gray said.

Evrard inclined his head. "My apologies, Prince Emory," he said.

"Rory," he insisted. "Please call me Rory."

"He won't like that," Gray inserted, "but make sure he doesn't choose to give you another name in its stead."

Rory glanced over at the other man. "Is that what he did with you? Is Gray not your given name?"

"It's his name now," Evrard said firmly, making it abundantly clear that part of the conversation was over. "We will start, but not at the beginning. There is no time for such a detailed story. Are you aware, Prince Emory, that your aunt has been making plans to usurp your throne?"

It was embarrassing that he had only just realized it, but at least he did not have to stand in front of the King of Unicorns and be surprised by that information. Rory nodded.

"Fontaine must not fall into her hands," Evrard said.

"How can I possibly prevent that? I have no army, no guard, no followers, no courtiers who would possibly be on my side." Rory had known the difficulty of his situation before, but was newly faced with it now, and the impossibility of it made his throat tight. But he'd made himself promises when he'd been hiding in the garden, and the most important had been that he would make different choices. Harder choices, Rory realized. That was what he'd really meant; that he would stop taking the easiest road, the road of least resistance.

It would not be easy to leave the throne to his aunt, most likely because she wouldn't want any loose ends, but it was certainly much harder to actually challenge her.

Add to that fact how few resources Rory actually possessed, and it took on shades of the impossible.

But Evrard did not seem much deterred. "You have more than you realize. You have me, and you have Gray," he boasted arrogantly.

Rory did not want to discount Gray—after all, he was rather in thrall to the man—but what use was a farmhand in taking back his kingdom from someone who had spent many years solidifying her position to prevent any opposition?

He was about to delicately broach this subject, when Gray entered the conversation abruptly, bluntly. "What," he declared harshly. "No."

"No?" Evrard asked.

"No," Gray said, his voice as resolutely hard as Rory had ever heard it. "No, I will not assist this silly princeling who let his aunt take over his throne." He turned and stomped off, headed into the darkest part of the woods.

Rory was left staring after him, completely lost as to his sudden change of mood. Also, silly princeling . . . that hurt more than he'd anticipated. And it hurt even more because it wasn't entirely untrue.

CHAPTER FIVE

Gray should've known it was inevitable that this whole time, Evrard had just wanted something from him—and not even to help him return to his own kingdom, but to assist some pretty little prince to pull off the impossible and defeat his shrewd, clever aunt. When it came to Evrard, there'd been a lot of things Gray had been pissed off about over the years. The unicorn's unbearable smugness was definitely one, and his high-handedness in believing he knew better than anyone or anything else was another. This was the worst of those two poor character traits combined into one singularly offensive assumption that of course Gray would be thrilled to leave the safety and peace of the valley to help another prince take back a throne that Gray wasn't sure he deserved anyway.

Initially, he'd headed towards the very edge of the valley, to the rim of trees that hid it from the world, which also happened to be the direction of the village. He could get a weapon there and come back to his farm. If the soldiers were still there, he'd kill them all and take his land back by force, if need be.

The last thing he intended to do was fall in line with Evrard's machinations and help Rory out. And there was absolutely no doubt in Gray's mind that Evrard was right in this scenario: Rory needed all the help he could get.

The closer he got to the ring of trees, the cooler Gray's temper grew. He still had no intention of leaving the safety of this valley, and he had no intention of going anywhere to help anyone, but despite Evrard's boasts to the contrary, Gray thought it was very possible their tracks could be followed. And for all Evrard's confidence, he was hardly a fighter, and Rory was even less capable. That little dagger might do a little superficial damage, and that was if—a very big if, Gray believed—Rory actually knew how to properly use it.

It was such an acute contrast to his own upbringing in Ardglass, when he'd been taught to throw a dagger with force and accuracy practically from the cradle. He could've used that dagger to stop someone in their tracks; Rory might leave a minor scratch.

"Silly princeling," Gray muttered under his breath, and turned around, doubling back on his own tracks, looping back around behind where Evrard and Rory were still speaking, making no attempts to quiet their voices or hide their location.

Typical, Gray thought as he leaned back against a conveniently placed tree. He could hear them talking as clearly as if he were still standing with them.

"What should I do?" Rory asked plaintively, and he sounded so like Gray had felt when he'd asked Evrard the same question. But Gray had been a child then, a mere eleven years old, and Rory was supposedly past the age when he normally would have taken the throne of Fontaine. He was supposed to be an adult, but he was so soft and sheltered, it was difficult to see him as a particularly competent one.

"You will need to convince him," Evrard insisted.

From his hiding place, Gray scoffed. Sure, the Prince was attractive. Sure, he'd been tempted at least twice to kiss him, but that was just a momentary pleasure. That didn't mean anything. It wasn't like Gray had ever intended to pledge his life to the other man. Evrard was a remnant of a different time, when things like nobility and honor might have meant something. And to someone like Rory, they probably still did, but then Rory was still grappling with the fact he'd been betrayed.

Gray had spent the last fifteen years living in the aftermath of betrayal, and that life had shaped his belief that honor and nobility meant very little indeed. They were just pretty words people used to control others, and Gray had no intention of ever falling into that trap ever again.

"How will I do that?" Rory asked.

"You must appeal to his greater nature," Evrard explained, and Gray made a face. He wasn't sure he had one, and surely Evrard would suspect that. "He wants to pretend it doesn't exist, but it's a part of who he is."

"Are you sure?" Rory didn't sound very sure, but then Evrard always contained enough certainty for himself and everyone else.

"Of course I am sure." Evrard's haughty voice made Gray smile, even though he wasn't looking forward to Rory's clumsy attempts to appeal to a part of him that no longer existed.

"I guess I should go find him," Rory said.

"He'll be headed towards the village, with the misguided notion that he will find weapons to help drive the soldiers out of his valley. I brought him there to save his life, and while I am pleased he's found peace there, he's grown complacent."

Gray gnashed his teeth, certain that Evrard must know he was listening in, and that was why his words were so cruelly pointed. Hadn't Evrard insisted for so many years that Gray needed to be cautious and always on alert for those who might betray him? Wanting to return to his valley wasn't complacency; it was necessity, because Evrard himself had emphasized its importance in their lives dozens of times, hundreds of times.

"There is no need to bother," Gray said, emerging from his position from behind the tree. "And," he added tightly, "I have done always as you asked. Stayed in the safety of that place, because that was the only safe place, or so you always said."

Rory looked astonished to see him; Evrard, not surprisingly, did not.

"Our circumstances have changed," Evrard pointed out, "and there is no safe place for you or for the Prince, not anymore. The valley is overrun. The Prince's guards are likely dead. We need to go to the Karloff Mountains. There is an important magical heirloom there that will be instrumental in assisting Prince Emory in gaining his throne."

"A fool's errand," Gray muttered. To reach the Karloff Mountains, they'd have to skirt Ardglass to one side, and make an arduous week-long journey. Gray believed Rory would never make it, and Evrard himself, while still in possession of his magical skill, had grown soft during their sojourn in the valley. If anyone was complacent, it was him.

"Perhaps, but it must be done," Evrard said.

"And you will do it without me, though I doubt, even if I assisted, that you would be successful."

Silence fell over the group. Gray could tell Rory was working on a plea, turning over various methods and words in his head, trying to find a serendipitous solution to Gray's adamant refusal.

Finally, he spoke, quietly and with a surprising authority. "I know you wish to return to your former life," Rory pointed out. "Before tonight, I wanted the same thing. I wanted to go back to my comfortable life that I understood, that understood me in return. I have no battle training, almost no weapons training, my guard is likely . . ." Rory paused, trying to collect himself. "They are likely dead. I am at the mercy of my aunt, who has been carefully and systematically ensuring that I am not capable of taking my own throne. I could take the easy path, and leave, and never return. I could hide. But even though victory seems uncertain, I can no longer pretend that avoiding a fight would be the right thing to do."

"You can forget about appealing to my honor," Gray said dryly. "Because I don't have any."

"I'm not trying to appeal to your honor," Rory promised. "I'm telling you that your comfortable life is gone until I can guarantee it again. And that will only happen when I have regained control of Fontaine. I can guarantee this place is erased from every map it is mentioned in. You will be left alone, entirely, if that is your wish. But I cannot achieve anything if I don't have your help."

Gray was silent for a long moment. "Logic," he finally said. "I'm surprised that's the angle you took."

"I know what you want," Rory said, "and it occurred to me that I should remind you that we actually want the same things."

"No, you want to go on some ridiculous quest to find a magical bauble in the Karloff Mountains, and I want to go back to my farm and be left alone," Gray insisted.

"Except," Rory reminded him, "that you can't go back to your farm and be left alone, not until I achieve my purpose. So you either must make do outside of the valley and leave your farm to the soldiers who are no doubt currently forming an encampment there, or you will come with Evrard and me and assist us in ejecting my aunt from Fontaine."

Evrard gave Rory an admiring, appraising glance. It annoyed Gray even more. Probably because he had never been the recipient of one of those looks, and also because no matter how much Gray wanted to deny it, Rory was actually right.

"Fine," Gray said, "but my assistance ends the moment we actually get this thing that Evrard thinks we need. And you'd better hold to your promise about the valley."

"You have my word. Shall we shake on it?" Rory asked.

"Well," Gray said sarcastically, "it's not like we have a scroll and a quill here so we can sign a proper contract." He extended his hand, and even though Rory wore a pair of those ridiculously buttery soft, pale yellow gloves, Gray felt the heat of his skin through the leather as they shook hands briefly.

"Excellent," Evrard said. "I knew you would see reason, Gray."

Gray glared at him. "Did you now?"

"And you, Prince Emory," Evrard said, simpering, "I wasn't sure whether to believe your vow, but you kept to it admirably."

"What vow?" Rory said, brows creased with confusion.

"You swore that if you got out of the valley alive, you would make different choices. Better choices. I believe that is what you truly meant, though I suppose you can be excused for being nonspecific as you were currently being hunted by several assassins sent by your aunt." Evrard paused, eyeing Rory sternly. "Or did I get it wrong after all?"

"No, no, no, that was it." Gray wasn't sure Rory was going to be able to speak at all, his eyes were so huge in his pale face, and his jaw seemed to have permanently dislodged as he gaped at the unicorn in front of him.

"Make a note," Gray murmured to him under his breath, "don't make a vow to anything unless you want Evrard to know all about it."

Rory looked like he was only a few moments from running away into the forest, despite all the inherent danger.

"How did you know that?" Rory asked Evrard. "I didn't even say it out loud."

As Gray expected, Evrard didn't answer. "Don't bother asking," Gray finally told Rory. "The best explanation I ever got out of him was, magic was intended to be mysterious, whatever that's supposed to mean."

"It was a perfectly reasonable answer," Evrard said with a sniff.

Leaning closer, Rory looked up at Gray. The only outward evidence of their sudden and rash departure and gallop across the valley was a few slightly mussed curls. This partnership would have been easier, Gray thought, if the Prince was a little less attractive. "You lived with him for years?" Rory questioned in a murmur, the edges of his lips quirking into a smile. "How?"

"Carefully," Gray retorted.

"He was a most attentive pupil, when he wasn't digging around in the dirt or fixing the stables," Evrard granted him somewhat graciously.

But Rory was still stuck on the particularly annoying vein that ran through Evrard's personality. One, that he was a king, and therefore believed himself to be infallible and two, he was a unicorn, and therefore knew himself to be unique. "I think you're right but you're also wrong. Gray didn't just dig around in some dirt or fix the stables, he created the farm out of practically nothing, and it's an accomplishment to be celebrated, not a punchline to your ego," Rory said hotly.

Gray stared at him. He knew Evrard appreciated the work he'd done over the years; perhaps he'd not always understood the drive that had kept Gray working as hard as he had, but of course it was better for Gray to be a diligent worker than a lazy ass. What he had never expected was for Rory to defend him.

"Ah," Evrard said knowingly, "you admire Gray. As well you should. You must be partners, and admiration is a good stepping-stone to trust."

Rory blushed. "He's easy to admire."

Evrard's gaze swung towards Gray but he didn't say a word. Didn't really trust himself to speak. What could he possibly say? Other than his stunning looks, Gray had yet to find something in Rory that he truly admired. Maybe in time that would change, but for right now, he liked him even though he didn't particularly want to, and he definitely did not trust him yet.

"What is this object we are seeking in the Karloffs?" Gray said, because it was better to change the subject. Better to stick to the quest that Evrard had set for Rory and get it over with as quickly as possible. Gray was already itching to go back to his valley and be left alone again.

"It is a magical heirloom of significant importance to Prince Emory, if he is to take back his throne," Evrard said and Gray rolled his eyes.

"You've already said all that. Where is it? What is it? How do we get it? All things that you clearly don't want to disclose, but all-important facts we will need to actually obtain it," Gray pointed out.

"All in due time," Evrard said smoothly, clearly much less concerned than Gray himself. Which, Gray supposed, was par for the course with Evrard. Perhaps all magical creatures contained such confident aplomb. He couldn't be sure, since Evrard was the very first he'd ever met. He wasn't counting Sabrina, because she'd been a sorceress, in thrall to dark magics, who had merely transformed temporarily into a magical creature.

The hair at the back of his neck slowly rose. "Are we going to be encountering any opposition to our quest?" Gray asked quietly. He did not want to specify Sabrina by name, but he knew from the solemn look in Evrard's eyes that he knew exactly who Gray was referring to, and to Gray's great dismay, he nodded his head.

"Many dangers on the road, and perhaps even more once we reach our destination, deep in the Karloff Mountains," Evrard confirmed.

Such a pronouncement wasn't a surprise, but Gray could grimly acknowledge it was definitely not what he'd wanted to hear.

They spent the rest of the night tucked away in the shelter of several thick trees. Gray had insisted they wait for daylight before continuing. They would need supplies to make the trek to the Karloff Mountains, and Rory was too recognizable to take into the nearby village. They'd wait for daylight, Gray pronounced, and then he would get additional supplies, while Rory and Evrard waited in the forest at the edge of the village.

Rory curled up in an empty, rotted tree trunk that had long since fallen, pulling that ridiculously bright blue cloak around his shoulders. First thing, Gray thought, we find the Prince some new clothes. He was far too recognizable with all his beautiful fabrics and arresting looks, and the last thing they needed was for Rory's aunt to discover their whereabouts.

It was too close to dawn to light a fire, so Gray hunched down into his own gray cloak, leaning against Evrard's warm body. "It feels like old times," Gray said quietly as he watched Rory doze fitfully.

Gray could feel Evrard sigh mightily. "He is not as adaptable as you," Evrard murmured, "but he will need to learn, nonetheless."

"Not an easy thing, discovering your closest relative in the world wants you dead," Gray pointed out.

"Your father never wished you dead. Sabrina had discovered a particularly powerful immortality spell that required innocent, royal blood. Not a lot of it, but enough, and the potion would need to be re-consumed occasionally, to continue its efficacy. All Sabrina told your father was she needed a little of your blood, every once in a while. Of course, she had led him to believe that he would share in the spell with her. But he was too power-hungry, and his mind too influenced by her, to understand that she could never risk you running away or growing up. She would have drained you completely," Evrard said. "You would've been dead that night."

Gray took all this information in, wishing, despite what he'd already told Rory earlier, that some of this had been given to him long ago. But then would it have made any real difference? He knew, if he hadn't escaped Tullamore, she would have killed him, one way or another. And whether his father had expressly given permission for his death or not, the end result was still the same.

"It doesn't change anything," Gray said roughly.

Evrard shifted again, and he could feel the impatience of the motion. "Semantics always matters," he insisted. "I promise you; it matters. Someday, you will see that."

"And if she wanted royal, innocent blood," Gray asked, "why is it she still apparently hunts me?"

But Evrard, who had already shared more in the last five minutes than he had shared in the previous fifteen years, went quiet, much to Gray's frustration and complete lack of surprise.

It is enough, he told himself, but he wasn't entirely sure he was telling the truth.

As dawn crept across the ground, he stood slowly, shaking off the sluggishness of his muscles, and left Rory sleeping with Evrard.

The trip to the nearby village was quick, and he made good time. The men in the village knew him well, though they also understood he often kept to himself when visiting. They did not question his purchasing of several saddlebags' worth of dried meats and crackers baked specifically not to spoil, and several good waterskins. There were some curious looks when Gray stopped by a used clothes stall in the main village market and purchased plain brown breeches and doublet, and an even darker brown cloak—none of which would fit his much taller, much bulkier build—but he stopped all questions with a single, hard glare. It was nobody's business but his own what he was buying.

The sun had barely crested over the trees when Gray returned to the grove where he'd left Evrard and Rory. The latter was now awake, sitting on another log, speaking quietly to Evrard. Their conversation largely faded as Gray approached, and he wondered, idly curious, if they had been speaking of him, and what the topic had been. Likely Rory had been asking more questions, and Evrard had been largely ignoring them.

"Here," Gray said, tossing Rory a shapeless bundle. "Put those on. You can't go fluttering around like a butterfly in a spring garden when we get on the road."

Rory opened the leather thongs to find the clothes Gray had bought. Fingering the rough cloth, he glanced up. "These are for me?"

"Like I said," Gray ground out, "you can't be prancing down the roads like a beautiful butterfly. We'll be robbed blind a thousand times over."

Gray watched as Rory retreated to a denser part of the forest to change, and just before he averted his eyes, saw Rory finger the clasp on his fancy cloak one last time before discarding it.

"I have supplies for the journey. Should be enough to last us," Gray said, directing his words to Evrard. "The saddlebags will be heavy, though."

Evrard sniffed. "I am sure I am capable of carrying a few bags," he said. "I'm only surprised you were able to circumvent your need to bring a horse on every journey we take together."

"Fifteen years in, and you still resent poor old horse," Gray said with a smile. He hoped the soldiers had left him well enough alone. Before they'd escaped out of the stable, Gray had released him and urged him to head to the opposite end of the valley, where there were streams and large fields full of clover for him to snack on. At the very least, he would not be subject to the enemy soldiers' whims. While Evrard thought the horse was quite stupid, Gray had firsthand evidence of how smart and brave he was. He'd never let himself be captured.

"Everything . . . sort of fits, I suppose."

Gray glanced up from where he was strapping the saddlebags to Evrard's back to where Rory was standing, having returned to the clearing after changing his clothes.

It was true; unlike his brilliant yellow satin doublet, the brown hung on his smaller frame, but at least he looked like so many other young men who lived in the village and outside of it.

"The idea is not to attract any attention," Gray said. "And only rich men have their clothes tailored to fit."

What he didn't say was that even though Rory was swimming in extra fabric and was lacking the brightly colored wardrobe to set off his astonishing looks, he still looked . . . incredibly beautiful. Too beautiful, if Gray was being honest.

"Perhaps, Prince Emory," Evrard suggested, "you could dirty yourself up a bit. Slump your shoulders. You still look . . ."

"Princely," Gray finished for him, afraid of what Evrard would have said, and that it would've echoed Gray's own thoughts too closely. "You look like a rich boy, slumming it in his servant's clothes."

Rory frowned. "You want me to roll around in the mud?"

"I'm sure the hard travel to the Karloff Mountains will put some necessary travel dirt on him," Gray inserted hastily. "Just keep your head down and your cloak hood up, your hair is so distinctive."

"Your reputation as the Autumn Prince precedes you, I'm afraid," Evrard agreed.

"I could cut it off . . ." Rory suggested.

Gray hated the way his heart stopped at his words. He still remembered the way he'd felt when Evrard had changed his name all those years ago. Unlike a name, hair could grow back, but without it, Rory wouldn't be . . . Rory, and that seemed like too great a crime to bear.

"We're keeping off the main roads anyway," Gray said hastily. "There's no need for such a drastic action."

Gray finished strapping the saddlebags onto Evrard, and after a quick, hushed confrontation, beckoned Rory over to where the unicorn stood. "I know the way, so I'm going to ride in front," Gray said. "You'll have to hold on to me. It won't be as easy as before." He didn't add that, without any saddle, it would take a great deal more thigh strength to stay mounted when Gray was so much larger than Rory was. Truthfully, Gray didn't want to contemplate Rory's thighs, though they looked . . . fine.

Incredibly fine, his uncooperative mind supplied, taking in the breeches he'd changed into, which were thankfully quite a bit more fitted than his new doublet.

"It won't be an issue," Rory promised. "I'm a good rider."

Gray had gotten that impression already, which was one of the reasons he was suggesting this at all. The problem was that, since the Karloffs bordered Ardglass on one side, it turned out that Gray was much more familiar with their route than even Evrard. And unlike the valley, with its magical pull, the Karloffs—other than the magical item they were after—didn't particularly exude any special feeling that Evrard could track. They would have to rely on Gray's fifteen-year-old knowledge of the maps he'd studied as a boy.

Not an ideal situation, but they had no other choice.

Without ceremony, Gray mounted the unicorn, and gracefully, Rory followed suit, tucking his cloak around him and pulling up the hood, even though the sun was bright overhead. Gray nodded in approval, and then Evrard started to pick his way through the trees, searching for the road that would take them around the village rather than through it.

After a few minutes, Evrard came upon it, and thus began their journey.

CHAPTER SIX

Evrard pulled them off the little-traveled road only when the sun began to fall behind the trees. Rory's stomach was growling; he and Gray had each chewed a little dried beef and a small piece of hard cheese during the day, but he was ravenous for real food. Something fresh and hot; he already missed Acadia's ability to make a delicious meal out of just about anything. Rory dismounted on shaky legs, stretching his muscles as he glanced around. Evrard had pulled them quite a bit off the road, deeper into the forest, where travelers on the road might not see their fire.

Of course, it wasn't likely that anyone would even be traveling this road, because they'd only seen a handful of people during the entire day. Rory had kept his eyes averted and his head tucked into his cloak, and as far as he knew, none of the few farmers they'd passed had even glanced their direction. Rory wasn't used to being quite so invisible and he wasn't sure he liked it.

On the other hand, traveling by wrapping his arms around Gray's firmly muscled midsection was definitely a positive. His legs were sore and definitely stiff, but the journey from Beaulieu to the valley had gone some distance to getting him used to long, tough days of riding.

"Shall I gather wood for the fire?" Rory asked. He wasn't much help setting up a campsite, as his guard had teasingly reminded him more than one evening on the road, but anyone could gather sticks and branches, and that was often the job he gave himself.

"What fire?" Gray asked blankly.

Rory was confused. "The fire. Aren't we stopping for the night? Having an evening meal?"

Gray dismounted, and reaching back into one of the saddlebags, rustled around for something, and then tossed it, without ceremony, in Rory's direction. He caught it, barely, and stared, more dismayed than he wanted to let on, at the piece of dried meat in his hands.

"We can't risk being seen," Gray said. "I'm sorry if your princely sensibilities can't live without a fire. Or a hot meal."

He was pathetic and spoiled. That was what Gray was truly saying, and Rory had to admit that he probably wasn't wrong.

"No," Rory stumbled, "it's fine. I was just . . ."

"Expecting something different," Gray finished, and while the words were sympathetic, his delivery was flat. "Expect it from now on. Your life is no longer as it was; it's changed." He turned and walked away, deeper into the forest, perhaps to relieve himself, or maybe just because after spending all day on Evrard with Rory, he needed some space.

Rory turned to Evrard. "Do you need anything?" he asked. After all, Evrard had been doing the lion's share of the work today. All Rory had had to do was hang on.

"Your Highness," Evrard said, "shouldn't it be I asking that question?"

"I really wish you would call me Rory," he pointed out. If Gray had been present, no doubt he would've said the request was pointless, but Evrard's constant deference was off-putting.

Perhaps because while he'd always known he was a prince; Rory had never seen himself as particularly prince-like. An impression no doubt encouraged by his perfidious aunt.

"Perhaps in time, when we get to know each other better," Evrard said. Rory had just spent the last twelve hours plastered over his backside, so he definitely felt like that statement could have been better phrased as never.

"Did you know those men who came to the valley?" Rory asked.

"Not personally, no," Evrard said, his voice careful, "but their purpose was well known to me. Her purpose has not changed since I rescued Gray fifteen years before."

"Why would someone want him?" Rory asked, resentment leaking into his voice.

Naturally, Gray would choose to re-emerge into the tiny clearing at the worst possible time. He was scowling, no doubt at Rory's words, and at the impression that he and Evrard had just been talking about him behind his back.

"There's a stream a little distance away," Gray said shortly. "You should drink some water."

"In time, yes, I will," Evrard said. Rory wished he could emulate the unicorn's abundant dignity—but perhaps without his smug condescension.

"It's a long journey to the Karloffs," Gray said, and Rory wasn't sure if the comment was directed at him or Evrard. "You should get some rest."

"Our young prince was asking important questions," Evrard said, much to Rory's surprise.

"He was?" Gray too seemed surprised, but Rory had a feeling that his astonishment had nothing to do with Evrard and everything to do with his seemingly unfavorable opinion of Rory.

"The woman you know as your aunt," Evrard said, looking at Rory, "who is currently the Regent Queen of Fontaine, is the same woman who sought to capture you many years ago, Gray."

Rory realized then that he had never seen Gray truly angry, he'd only ever been passingly annoyed. The expression on his face now was truly murderous—hard and taut, his features carved white in the setting sun. "Why didn't you tell me?" he demanded of Evrard.

Rory would have cowered if it had been him, but Evrard merely glanced up from the patch of clover he was chewing on. "It was not the right time."

"You let her take over another kingdom?" Gray challenged. "After what she did to Ardglass?"

Rory was shocked to discover that Gray was Ardglassian. Though in retrospect, he supposed he should have known. He had the big build, and the same dark hair that was so common in that country. Now that Rory was looking, he could see the similarities Gray shared with Anya, who had been a member of his guard.

Was still, he hoped, though he didn't have much faith that any of them had survived the soldiers who had descended upon the valley.

"I could not stop her," Evrard said. "It was not my responsibility and it was not the right time. But now Prince Emory, with your valuable aid, can begin to move against her."

"What did my aunt do to Ardglass?" Rory thought it safe to ask the question because Gray's face had softened, and he no longer looked like he wanted to choke the life out of Evrard.

"She was an advisor to the King," Gray said shortly. "And she conspired to control him by seducing him with power and drink."

"She is very good at getting what she wants," Rory said despondently.

"She needs to be stopped," Gray said. "I should slip into Beaulieu and gut her with my dagger."

"No," Evrard said firmly. "We will find the artifact that we seek in the Karloff Mountains and then, and only then, will we attempt to remove Sabrina from the throne of Fontaine. Things must be done a certain way. Now, I will find this stream and have a nice cool drink."

As Evrard departed into the woods, to Rory's astonishment, Gray shot him a commiserating glance. "There is no use asking why things must be done a certain way," Gray said with a sigh. "Because he will not tell you. It's infuriating."

"If you had known my aunt was behind the suffering in your country, would that have been enough to convince you to guide us?" Rory asked. It was one of the very first thoughts he'd had, when he'd realized the importance of what the unicorn had told them. Here was a perfect reason for Gray to agree—he would be able to enact his revenge on the woman who had conspired to destroy the kingdom of his birth.

But Gray shook his head slowly. "No," he finally said. "No, it wouldn't have been. In fact, I might have stayed further away. I might not have agreed at all."

Rory could not believe it. "But here was an opportunity to destroy the woman who tried to kill you!"

Gray only shrugged. "What's the point? There is always some noble who wants power and to control the people. What does it matter if it's Sabrina or some other bitch? It doesn't matter to me. All I wanted was my valley, and to be left alone in it. I don't want to be involved."

"And yet you're here," Rory said, mystified.

"I'm here because you convinced me with a logical argument," Gray said flatly. "That's all."

And Rory might have believed him before, but there was a flash of something in Gray's eyes when he talked of killing Sabrina, of marching into Beaulieu and gutting her. He might wish to be jaded and bitter and beyond thoughts of vengeance, but perhaps Evrard was right after all; there was still some unknown quantity left, hidden deep inside Gray.

"You should get some rest," Gray repeated again after a long silence.

And Rory supposed he was right; after all, even if some speck of honor remained in Gray, he could not possibly reach it tonight, and tomorrow would be another awfully long day. He sat down against a downed log and took his ugly brown cloak, wrapping it around himself. It might be hideous, but at least it was warm.

To Rory's surprise, he found his eyes growing heavy. Gray was right, their journey was long, and he would need all the sleep he could get, when he could get it. Rory closed his eyes and nodded off almost immediately.

He woke with a start, and even though the forest was quiet, the silence was eerie and wrong.

Rory's own breath was harsh in his ears, and he tried to muffle it against a fold of his cloak. He realized then that he couldn't hear even the rustling noises that Evrard generally made, or even Gray's short, compact breaths. Was he alone? Had they left him here, all by himself, in a strange, unknown forest?

A hand clamped down around his mouth before he could pant any louder, the fear and panic overtaking him. "Shhhh." Gray's voice was a harsh whisper in his ear as he struggled futilely against the much bigger, much stronger body holding him.

It was slightly less terrifying that it was Gray holding him, and Rory stilled. The night air continued to be motionless and tense, even as his heartbeat slowed back to normal.

"We're surrounded," Gray whispered so quietly that Rory bare-ly heard him. "I don't know who it is. It might be the soldiers who attacked us in the valley."

If it was the soldiers from before, Rory knew they were dead. They'd been armed and mounted, and while he and Gray were currently accompanied by a magical unicorn, they had almost no weapons, or the experience to wield them. Gray was strong, but he'd spent his entire life on the farm. And Rory had stupidly eschewed the lessons that might have saved their lives tonight.

"Do you have your sword?" Gray asked, his voice impossibly dropping even lower. "I only have my dagger, and it'll be no use against fully armed soldiers."

Exactly the problem, Rory thought hopelessly. But he did have it, it was currently strapped to his waist and he nudged Gray's left arm. Rory felt him shift the position of his fingers, searching for the hilt. One moment, he was looking, and the next he'd clearly found exactly what he'd sought, because he was thrusting Rory away from him as he drew the sword, all in one smooth, coordinat-ed movement. The sword glinted in the moonlight, silver shining along the blade. It was Marthe's job as captain of the Prince's guard to maintain the sword, with its two lion heads wrought in gold and their ruby and topaz eyes, and the blade looked impossibly sharp. Lion's Breath was the ancestral sword of Fontaine, and would no doubt announce Rory's presence to anyone who recognized it, but he knew Gray hadn't had a choice. He couldn't be expected to fight off multiple attackers with a little dagger.

Of course, it would be nearly impossible to fight off multiple attackers even with Lion's Breath, if Gray hadn't had any training in swordsmanship.

But to Rory's surprise, Gray held the blade confidently, with the assurance he knew how to use it, and called out, "Come out, and I will not kill you all."

A man, not dressed in the same unrelenting black as the soldiers from the valley, but instead in various patchwork fabrics—lush red velvet, bright green silk, and swirling orange and bright blue patterns—emerged from the trees beyond the clearing. He had long hair, even longer than Gray's, and it was almost as dark. "That sword," he said pointedly to Gray, "is not yours."

Gray swung it once, and then twice, the arcs graceful, his grip confident. Despite most of his brain occupied by frantically searching for a peaceful exit strategy, Rory had a stray thought. He cannot be just a farm boy. Not when he moves like that, not when he swings a sword like he was born to do it.

"It will kill just as easily as if it were mine," Gray said. "Tell your men to come out or I will return you to them in pieces."

It must have been an epic boast, a feint designed to possibly save their lives without having any of the skill to back up his words. Rory could come up with no other explanation. But, he supposed, he should participate as well, not just continue cowering next to a fallen log. He stood, pulling his own dagger, and wondered, not for the first time, where Evrard had disappeared to.

The man in front of Gray started to laugh. "You hold something of great value, my friend. Something we would like."

Gray took a single, menacing step closer. "The sword may not be mine, but it is not yours either."

"And the Autumn Prince? Is he yours as well?"

Panic closed off Rory's throat. They'd recognized him somehow. No doubt Lion's Breath had helped in his assessment of the situation, but somehow his hood had fallen, and his hair was embarrassingly distinctive. Maybe he should have ignored Gray and cut it off after all.

"This whore?" Gray said negligently, gesturing towards Rory with the sword. "You must not have seen the Autumn Prince up close if you think this cheap fake looks anything like the original."

Rory schooled his expression to take on the bored, indifferent look of someone who wouldn't care that he'd just been called a cheap fake. There was very little chance they could pull this off, but it was far better than any of the ideas Rory had come up with.

"You've seen the Autumn Prince?" The man took a step closer. Rory wished, belatedly, that he'd listened to Gray and rubbed some dirt on himself or something to obscure his features at least partially. There was nothing to be done about the hair, not now, but the rest? Rory knew he'd been too sure that nobody would ever recognize him.

"A real looker," Gray said. "Way more attractive than this one, for sure."

"And the sword?" A frown had appeared on the other man's face, like he was no longer quite sure. "That a fake too?"

"Real gold. Real silver. Real rubies, but," Gray swung the sword almost carelessly, "not the actual Lion's Breath. Like we'd have a priceless ancestral sword out here in the middle of nowhere." The last bit was muttered under Gray's breath, and Rory knew it was directed entirely at him.

"Still worth a pretty penny." The man crept forward half a step.

The sword stopped mid-swing, and suddenly pointed straight at the man's exposed throat. "That's close enough," Gray said, his voice growing hard.

"There's twenty of us and one of you. Two of you if you count your little prince for the night," the man said, and suddenly he was not smiling. Or laughing. Or joking. He was all seriousness, and Rory realized that they'd both been posturing, but the man had had the upper hand all along.

"This is his fake sword. He's a master," Gray tried bluffing, but the man shoved aside the words like he hadn't even said them.

"You're not unattractive," the man said, "and the 'prince' is exceedingly so, even if he's a fake. Good money there. And the sword? That can be melted down." He smiled again. "You're coming with us, either easily and quietly or with twenty arrows in your back."

The clearing grew brighter as the clouds covering the moon gradually moved away and gold glinted on the man's hands as he pushed his hair back with a clearly studied nonchalance.

Rings, Rory realized. He's wearing gold rings on every single finger.

It was a risk, but everything had felt like some form of a risk since he'd left Beaulieu. He knew if he didn't do something to diffuse the situation, they could be carted out of here with half a dozen arrows each. Rory took one careful step forward and then another, watching the lines of Gray's back tense as he heard the leaves crunch underfoot.

"Gray," Rory called out clearly, hoping he wouldn't get shot, "it's fine. We'll be fine. Put the sword down."

Gray risked a look over his shoulder, his glare washing over Rory. "Put the sword down," Rory repeated, and then remembering the story Gray had attempted to weave, affected an imperious whine. "You're creating a scene and it doesn't matter who pays me as long as I get paid."

The man leered. "You'll get paid all right," he said reassuringly, and Rory had a feeling payment wasn't all he was promising. And that was, Rory considered, not all bad. He'd need to figure out how to get the man alone, anyway. Or at least as alone as their culture generally permitted.

From the way Gray had yet to lower his sword, Rory did not think he'd guessed who the man was, or considering how he'd grown up, it was possible that Gray had never encountered this particular nomadic tribe before. Gray didn't know how to deal with them, Rory realized, and he did.

"Gray," Rory repeated insistently, "please trust me." His words didn't really fit in with their act, but without them, he didn't think Gray would ever give up his weapon.

Rory watched as he re-gripped the pommel and then, finally, lowered the edge of the sword to the ground. The man snapped his fingers, and suddenly, an arrowhead dug into the side of Rory's neck. He glanced to the side and around the clearing, men and women dressed similarly, all with rings decorating every single one of their fingers and marching up their ear lobes in graduated sizes, materialized with arrows drawn on Gray and Rory.

Of course, there were far more trained on Gray than on Rory. That wasn't much of a surprise. Rory knew he didn't look like much of a physical threat, but he could use that to their advantage.

"Rory," Gray hissed as the newcomers approached him and took away his sword and Rory's dagger, tying their hands together in front of them with rough ropes. Rory looked closer and realized they were made of woven-together scraps of colorful cloth, some with gold thread and other bits with embroidery, all rubbing uncomfortably against his wrists.

"Can you get your knot loose?" Gray hissed under his breath as they were forcibly put together and marched deeper into the forest, surrounded by so many bows there was no possible way to escape. I hope Gray realizes he'd be shot in seconds, Rory thought.

"No, and I'm not going to try," Rory hissed back.

Gray stared at him incredulously, but didn't immediately go back to wriggling, trying to loosen his bonds.

They walked for what felt like hours. They walked for so long that Rory had to wonder how the tribe had even known they'd been there—surely the clearing had been so far from their encampment, they couldn't have known. And yet, Rory knew he must be wrong, because he and Gray were currently in their hands.

"Where did Evrard go?" Rory asked under his breath, when the first rays of dawn were beginning to creep across the forest. "Was he hiding?"

Gray shot him a look that Rory didn't quite understand. "He went to get water and didn't come back," he finally admitted. "It wouldn't surprise me if he knew this was coming."

"And what," Rory asked, his voice rising despite trying to prevent it, "he wanted us to get kidnapped?"

Shrugging, Gray turned away.

Even though there were very few other options available to him, Rory—not for the first time—contemplated whether it had been the smartest choice to select a farm boy who clearly wasn't who he seemed and a snobby, elitist unicorn to help him take back his kingdom.

Unfortunately, considering his hands were currently tied, they were being marched god knew where, and Evrard was missing, there wasn't much to do about changing plans now. Rory straightened his shoulders and dove deeply into his memory, because their fates probably depended entirely on his ability to remember everything he'd ever read.

A few minutes later, they came into another clearing, this time full of tents, all constructed of the same brightly colored patchwork as their captors' clothing and the ropes that were currently binding their hands together. A few smoldering fires dotted the ground, and horses grazed off on the other side of the tents. It was exactly as Rory had expected, and he set into motion the first part of his plan.

They were taken to the largest tent, but instead of being ushered inside, the man holding Rory's hands stopped him directly in front. Rory took a breath and gathered himself for the challenge to come.

He could feel Gray right next to him, bristling with indignity, straining at his bonds, and he prayed this would work, because surely any moment now Gray would attempt to escape, and would no doubt be killed in the process.

He cast his eyes downward, and then fell to his knees, hands clasped in front of him, head bent, all adding to the subservient vibe he was attempting to communicate.

"What are you doing?" Gray demanded, as their captors murmured to themselves, no doubt astonished that a stranger would know even one of their customs.

"On your knees," Rory hissed at his companion. "Don't look and for god's sake, don't say anything."

There was a long, drawn-out moment where Rory's heart sat in his throat and Gray did not move. Rory didn't know if this would work if he followed the proper etiquette and Gray did not. Truthfully, he didn't want to find out the hard way.

Finally, Gray dropped to his knees beside him. "This better work," he muttered under his breath.

Rory couldn't speak, because everyone was watching him, and one of the books he'd read had stated very specifically that once the ceremony began, the Seeker could not utter a single word before the Giver did.

But he did think that maybe if he managed to get them out of this mess, Gray might begin to find him a little less useless.

Rustling sounds emanated from the tent, and after a few moments, an older woman with long, dark hair streaked with silver, and braided with tiny silver bells, emerged from between the flaps. She took in Rory's position, and then Gray's.

And then she too fell to her knees.

We're on, Rory thought with determination, and began to speak.

CHAPTER SEVEN

GRAY DIDN'T RECOGNIZE THE language Rory had haltingly begun to speak, but clearly everyone around him did, because they were fascinated, hanging on every single word he said.

He also had no idea who these people were, or their customs, or anything about them. And the truth was, he should have because while they weren't necessarily close to Ardglass, they were in the lands bordering Ardglass. Maybe Rhys hadn't gotten to this odd sort of tribe in his education when it had abruptly ended? But then Evrard had never mentioned them either.

Rory's head was still bent as he spoke, and when he finished, a reverent hush fell over the group.

Risking a look, Gray peeked up and to his utter astonishment, found the woman staring at Rory with tears in her eyes.

She finally spoke, but she did not use the same language as Rory. Instead she spoke in the common tongue Gray knew. "You must forgive us," she said, reaching up to wipe her eyes. "It has been many, many years since any of us have heard our language spoken out loud. For some of us, we have never heard it, only had it described. How is it you are able to speak it? I thought the teaching of it was lost to us, like many of our brothers and sisters have been lost to farms and towns and villages."

Rory looked up and settled back on his heels. He looked as shocked as she did. "I am sure I did not do it justice," he said. "I've never heard it spoken, I've only read it, and the pronunciation guide was very rudimentary."

She stared at him. "Merleen tells me that you are a prostitute, fashioned to look like the Autumn Prince. How is it you have been able to study our language?"

She did not say that whores generally didn't have access to a lot of books, especially to valuable ones containing virtually lost languages. Then a half-second before he did, Gray realized what Rory intended to do. He wanted to reach out and stop him, but then he remembered Rory's whispered words. Trust me. Gray wasn't sure he trusted him at all, not yet, but so far this entire encounter had left Gray feeling like he'd taken one look at the Prince next to him, seen a different side of him, and had come to entirely the wrong conclusions.

Yes, he was a prince. Yes, he was pretty. Yes, he did not exactly understand how to defend himself in the traditional ways, with weapons and with fists. But he was defending them now, wasn't he?

Instead of stopping Rory, Gray stayed silent and let him continue.

"I am not a prostitute, maj," Rory said. "I am indeed the Autumn Prince."

Gasps resonated from the surrounding audience, but the woman in front of them did not seem even the tiniest bit surprised by Rory's revelation. She leaned forward and took his chin in her hands. Strong, capable hands, used to hard work. Gray could see the evidence of it in the swollen knuckles and the calluses up and down her fingers. She held strong to Rory, and he didn't flinch as she stared into his eyes. Gray, on the other hand, was a total mess. Yes, Rory had caused a sensation and had made the woman sentimental and sad for times long gone, but they were still tied up and they still had no weapons. They still weren't free.

Trust me. Rory's words echoed in Gray's mind, and though he had to fight against the suspicion that had maintained such a stronghold on his mind since that desperate night fifteen years ago, he did. When the attackers had come to the valley, Rory had trusted him—even if maybe he shouldn't have. Gray took one deep breath, and then another. It was his turn to put his life into Rory's hands.

"You are very far from home," she finally said, releasing his chin. "You have come to me as a Seeker, hoping I will be a Giver. What is it that you need?"

"Freedom," Rory said, re-assuming his prior position, humbling himself before the woman. A Giver, Gray thought, this must be some ancient ritual that Rory knew because he'd read about it. Just like the language.

"You speak of something that seems of low cost to us, but in reality, is worth very much," she retorted tartly. "You are valuable prisoners. You carry expensive belongings, including a priceless ancestral sword of your country."

Gray had to force himself not to roll his eyes. Why had Rory brought Lion's Breath with him to the valley? He couldn't even truly use it, at least not the way it was meant to be used.

"Maj, I am currently a prince without a throne, without a country. I could not leave it behind to lose it to those who would use it ill."

The woman settled back on her heels. "Your aunt?" she asked, raising an eyebrow.

"A story as old as time," Rory said, and Gray was impressed at how tonelessly he could speak about the relative who had conspired to betray him.

Most of the time he attempted Rory's cool, but despite what he'd boasted about not caring, he did care. If Sabrina ever walked into his valley, he'd have killed her on the spot. Which was why, among other reasons, she'd never done it. Instead she'd sent her soft, pretty little prince, and tied them up in a nice bow for the assassins she'd sent to follow.

"If I give you this request," she said, voice thoughtful, "what would you promise me in return?"

They had nothing to give. No gold, no goods in trade, Rory had his sword—in theory only, since it was currently in the tribe's possession—but nothing much else of value. For the first time since leaving Tullamore, Gray wondered what knowledge of Prince Graham would be worth to someone like the woman in front of him.

It was his closest held secret, the one he anticipated taking to the grave, but what if he gave it up?

If you gave it up, he reminded himself, you'd lose everything. You'd lose your valley, your freedom, your independence. Probably your life.

While he wasn't against Rory taking his throne from Sabrina—as far as Gray was concerned, that bitch didn't belong anywhere near one—that seemed an especially steep price to pay. So he kept his mouth shut, and a moment later, he was very glad he did, because of course, Rory had known all about this ceremony, and had known he would be asked to give something.

And knowing this, he'd already prepared something to offer.

"Knowledge," Rory said confidently. "I would give you knowledge. Once I have deposed my aunt, and regained the throne, I would invite you to Beaulieu, and we would study your language together, and hopefully, be able to revive some of the lost parts of your culture."

"How would we know you would keep your bargain?" asked Merleen, the man who had originally captured them.

"I would give my word," Rory said. Gray almost laughed. If he was Merleen, he never would have believed Rory. But then Gray had gotten the rotten end of the whole nobility and honor thing. He could at least acknowledge that, and also acknowledge that those experiences made him never want to trust anyone of Rory's stature ever again. Others might not be nearly as suspicious.

Merleen also did not look particularly convinced, but then the woman spoke up. "Swear on your sword," she said softly.

Rory blanched, all the blood draining from his face. His reaction was so severe, Gray had a feeling that breaking a promise you'd sworn on Lion's Breath led to something extremely unpleasant.

"You know the story then," Rory said, his voice equally as soft.

"I know that your ancestor, King Francis, swore a promise to some peasants, and he swore it on Lion's Breath. And when he broke the promise, he died in an agony of fire and flame."

Rory cleared his throat. "The sword has no known magical qualities. The story of King Francis was no doubt embellished to frighten any ruler of Fontaine from lying to their subjects ever again."

The woman raised an eyebrow. "Then it has worked," she said. "You will swear on Lion's Breath, or there will be no Accord."

"And no freedom," Rory said flatly.

"And no freedom," she agreed.

For the first time since he'd opened his mouth and spoken in a language Gray had never heard before, Rory turned and looked Gray straight in the eyes. "What do you think?" he asked.

Gray stared back at him steadily. "Are you intending to lie?" he asked under his breath.

"No," Rory said, shaking his head vehemently, "but I have no guarantee that our quest will be successful. And I do not believe Lion's Breath quibbles over particular circumstances. If you break your promise, it will exact retribution in fire and blood."

"You really believe that?"

Rory looked like he did, in fact, really believe it. "I wasn't always sure," he hedged, "but then I read the original version of the story, written by a steward present at King Francis' death. The only obstacle to believing that the sword was magical was magic existing in this world." Rory glanced over to where they'd come from, where presumably Evrard was somewhere, waiting for them. "And now I believe that I was wrong, and it does exist in this world. So therefore, if I am to take the logical approach, I truly believe that if I break a promise made on Lion's Breath, I will die. Badly. Painfully."

"In a storm of fire and blood, yes," Gray said.

There was a long silence. Gray re-examined the possibilities of knocking out every guard in the vicinity before he was killed, and again came up about five guards too short. And smartly, they had kept Lion's Breath on the other side of the clearing, as far away from Gray's hands as possible.

"Is the sword particular about the person who swears the promise? Do they need to be of the Fontaine royal line?" Gray did not particularly want to swear on the sword and possibly risk his own terrible death, but somehow it seemed worse that Rory, who had so bravely tackled this, who knew ancient languages, who had studied cultures that were dying, should risk his life this way. Gray's was much less valuable. Besides, nothing had been said about regaining the throne of Ardglass, only of Fontaine. Presumably, Gray would die a farmhand, never revealing to anyone who he truly was. Rory, on the other hand, was destined for a much greater fate—if he got the chance.

Maybe Gray should give him that chance.

"It does not matter," Rory said, "because I would never permit you to do it. This is my throne, and I will make the promise." He looked up at the woman, who was watching them carefully. "Bring the sword."

But of course, they were not going to permit Gray anywhere near a weapon. Gray was a little flattered by this. Instead, they yanked Rory up by the shoulder, and marched him over to where a big, burly man was currently holding the sword. Rory rested his bound hands on the pommel, right over the lions' heads, and said, "I swear on the throne of Fontaine and all my royal ancestors that I will keep my promise to assist the Mecant tribe in regaining their original language and reviving their customs."

The woman nodded her head once, and suddenly there was a knife cutting Gray's bonds, and he was jerked upwards.

Gray met Rory's eyes across the clearing and was torn between wanting to thank him for saving their lives and berate him for risking his own so foolishly.

Didn't he see that he was impossibly precious? Irreplaceable?

Gray had not always felt that way, but the last twelve hours had forcibly opened his eyes. Without Rory, without his precious knowledge and the incredible intelligence he possessed, they would have been dead or sold into slavery. The quest would have been lost. Gray's valley would have been lost. Sabrina, through happenstance and fate, would have won without having ever been challenged.

"A horse," the woman said, in a voice that brokered no argument and one was led towards Gray. He laid a firm hand on its warm neck. It looked to be an excellent animal, and well-trained. Rory came over to where Gray stood, strapping on the sword again.

Gray's dagger was returned, and brief goodbyes were said, though they were none too friendly.

No doubt everyone had been expecting a nice big payout for capturing him and Rory, and instead, they were being let go, and being given one of their horses.

"You know the way back," Rory murmured to him, and Gray mounted, followed by Rory behind him.

With a single nudge in the right direction, the horse trotted off in the direction from whence they'd come.

Riding, the journey not only seemed much quicker, but passed by in a flash. Gray realized that in the dark, the tribe had been leading them in circles, presumably to ensure that Rory and Gray could never return to their encampment. They crossed the stream he'd directed Evrard to the night before, but Evrard was nowhere to be found.

They reached the clearing, the saddlebags still lying on the ground, and Evrard was still not present.

"What should we do?" Rory asked uncertainly after they dismounted. "What if Evrard was also captured?"

"Then we would have seen him in the camp," Gray said flatly. "And as of course, Evrard has given us almost no information on how to proceed to find this magical thing, other than it rests in the Karloff Mountains, we will stay here and wait for him to return."

Rory flopped down onto the ground, into much the same position he'd occupied the night before. "I really can't believe that worked," he said, grinning. "But as soon as I saw their rings, I knew who they were, and I knew they could be reasoned with."

"Reasoned with? Asking you to swear an oath on a sword that could bring you a fiery death?" Gray muttered.

"I had to do it," Rory said.

Except that he hadn't, and they both knew it.

"I could have done it," Gray said lowly. "You don't need my help. What you know is so much more valuable. I lived over this direction when I was a young child, and I'd never heard of that tribe before today."

Rory gaped at him. "Are you really claiming to be expendable? You?"

At Gray's refusal to answer, Rory stood up and started pacing back and forth in front of the log he'd slept against the night before. Had it only been the night before? It felt like an eternity had already passed since they'd escaped the valley, but it had been barely forty-eight hours.

"You built a farm from nothing. You're a fighter. You were going to fight those men off; I saw the way you held the sword. You know how to use it much better than I." Rory paused. "A pretty princeling. Useless. I believe that was your impression before today."

Gray couldn't deny it. He also couldn't deny that his mind had been forever altered by their encounter with the tribe.

"You're a prince," Gray said, because he couldn't quite wrap his thoughts around everything that had changed, so suddenly and so irrevocably. It was easy to condense down all his jumbled feelings into one single fact: Rory was a prince, and he was going to reclaim his throne.

Rory stared incredulously at him. "You don't think that matters."

It hadn't, but somehow, now it did.

Flushing, Gray turned away. "You barely slept before. You should get more sleep now."

"Stop changing the subject. Were you really going to swear my promise on my sword?" Rory demanded.

Rory's intelligence had already come in very handy, but now Gray wished he was a little less perceptive. Squaring his shoulders, Gray glanced over at Rory. "It was logical."

"No," Rory said with an unbearably attractive decisiveness, "it was all emotional." Closing the three steps between them, Rory reached out and put a hand on Gray's chest, right above where his heart beat faster than he'd ever admit. "Try to tell me it wasn't emotional. I can feel it. Right here."

Gray could feel it too; his heart, which had been numb and alone for so long, was waking up, the numbness receding. It felt like too much, too soon, but before he could stop Rory and say, that's plenty close enough, Rory rose up and pressed his lips to Gray's.

He wasn't just pretty; he was stunning, perfectly bringing his nickname to life, all smoldering heat with that cool thread of logic running through him. Gray reeled back, but he hadn't lied to Evrard back in the valley. Rory was strong; strong and determined. Instead of retreating, he followed, winding his arms around Gray's neck, and tugging him closer, his mouth opening under Gray's.

Almost immediately Gray lost his mind, and it sank into the warm lassitude of pleasure, growing warmer and then hotter as Rory's tongue slipped into his mouth. Gray could feel his slender frame pressed tightly against his own much larger body. He wanted to strip the ugly, ill-fitting clothes off, and glory in Rory's perfection. Because he would be perfect, Gray realized. He'd be the most beautiful creature he'd ever seen, and somehow, also the strongest.

Nothing like he'd ever imagined when Rory had first ridden into his valley.

"I leave you alone for a few hours, and you're already pawing at each other." The voice was understated and cool, and it doused the flames burning between them.

Rory froze, and removing his mouth from Gray's, glanced to where the voice had come from. Gray had to resist the urge to drag him back against him.

"Where have you been?" Rory demanded, and Gray was proud despite himself. Evrard always believed he was in charge, and sometimes you needed to remind him that nobody gave a damn who was in charge; they were supposed to be a team.

"I was down at the stream and heard the men coming," Evrard said, casually trotting into the clearing like Gray and Rory hadn't had to avoid death or slavery by sheer nerve. "I hid, naturally."

"Naturally," Gray retorted. He wasn't sure he trusted his mouth to say anything else. He wasn't sure he trusted his mouth not to simply claim Rory's sweet one again and again, and then again. He knew, without a doubt, that now that he'd had a taste, he'd always be hungry for it.

"Yes, we're fine," Rory said testily.

"I knew you would be," Evrard said, their obvious frustration seeming not to bother him much. "How did you manage to escape so quickly?"

Rory shot the unicorn a hard look. "I invoked the ancient power of the Accord."

If Gray had to guess, he'd say that Evrard looked pleased, like Rory had just eclipsed even his high expectations.

"Interesting," Evrard said, barely acknowledging Rory's quick cleverness, and already moving past it. "We must get on the road. We have lost valuable time."

Gray couldn't contain his glare. "I haven't slept," he said. He couldn't really remember the last time he slept. Exhaustion was making his boundaries blurry. Or maybe that was the kiss.

"The road is fairly straightforward for the next few days. Your Highness, you will ride in front, and Gray can rest against you," Evrard ordered.

Rory glanced over at where the horse they'd been sent back on was munching on a patch of clover. "We should take him," Rory said.

Gray was almost certain that unicorns were incapable of rolling their eyes, but he swore Evrard did. "Another useless animal you want to save," Evrard moaned. "I expected better out of you, Your Highness."

"He's a good horse," Rory insisted stubbornly. "We can even sell him later on or trade him for supplies."

Gray wasn't going to get involved in their argument. He'd never heard the end of it when he'd insisted on bringing the horse who'd saved his life all those years before.

But of course, Rory wasn't going to let him avoid it. "Gray," he begged, "tell him."

Sighing, Gray reached down and picked up their saddlebags of supplies. "You hate carrying these," he pointed out to Evrard. "We can use it as a pack horse. And Rory is right; we can trade him further down the road for additional supplies."

"Fine," Evrard sniffed, clearly annoyed that he'd been outnumbered, but all Gray felt was overwhelming gratitude that Evrard had dropped the tiny matter of finding them kissing earlier.

He didn't need Evrard to tell him that it was the height of stupidity to become involved, physically or especially emotionally, with someone like Rory. Prince Emory, Gray reminded himself. And while he himself had once been of equal stature, those days were long gone, with no hope of ever returning to them.

Gray slept on and off as they regained the old road, and each time he opened his eyes, he was pleased with the steady progress they'd made. He'd only traveled this road once or twice as a child, and the markers were faded from the elements, but they could still be deciphered.

They stopped to rest as the sun fell behind the trees, and again Gray nudged them off the main road, and they found another, even smaller clearing of trees, and there they set up a quick camp. Gray even relented, and allowed Rory a small fire. It wasn't like a lack of fire had saved them from being tracked or abducted before.

Gray sat on a downed log that he'd pulled closer to the fire, and watched the flames dance moodily. This morning, the kiss had ripped through his veins like the fiercest quicksilver, but tonight, after too many vivid, uncomfortable dreams, all the kiss made him feel was dread. He was going to grow close to Rory, and maybe even let him in further than anyone since Rhys, and he would likely lose him in this mad quest. Even if they both survived somehow, Rory's destiny was to rule his people and sit in the high tower of Beaulieu—noble and royal and far beyond Gray's grasping finger-tips.

All you want is to go back to your valley and be left alone, he reminded himself, but the thought didn't provide the same reassurance that it always had before. The kiss had changed things, as he knew it would.

Kissing Rory wasn't like kissing any of the other men and women who had passed through the valley before and whom he'd taken momentary pleasure with. Kissing Rory was willingly and eagerly sticking your hand into the fire and hoping to be consumed by it.

Gray was not quite self-destructive enough to welcome that.

To his dismay, Rory hadn't spent the last twelve hours regretting the kiss. In fact, as he picked a spot on the log right next to Gray, he shot him a very hopeful look from under those sinful lashes.

Why did he have to be so beautiful, both in and out? Gray thought with frustration.

"Did you get enough rest today?" Rory asked.

"Yes," Gray said shortly. He didn't want to have to lay out the reasons why continuing to kiss—or more—was a bad idea. But he had a feeling Rory was going to make it impossible to avoid that conversation.

"Good," Rory said, and Gray hated that his voice had slid further into uncertainty. Seeing Rory in all his brave, strong, confident glory had been life changing. He didn't want to be responsible for the disappointed look growing in Rory's eyes, but what else could he do? He was a realist. This couldn't be a passionate love affair; it was only a stepping-stone to better things for Rory.

"I'll keep the watch tonight," Gray said. "Feel free to get some sleep."

He stood and was about to go off to make sure the horse was secure for the third time, when Rory reached out and touched his leg. "Are you angry with me?" Rory asked.

At least that was easy enough to answer. "No," Gray said, "I'm angry with myself."

Of course Rory looked mystified. "I thought we both liked it . . ."

"We did. I did. Too much. You're . . . you're a prince, Rory. The Autumn Prince and the heir to Fontaine. I need to remember that, and so do you."

Rory just gaped at him as Gray shook his hand loose and walked away, ostensibly to check the horse, but really to sulk. Nothing new; he'd been spending all those years since leaving Tullamore trying to find something to do so he could avoid sulking.

But even if he'd had the farm to lose himself in, Gray knew a multitude of tasks couldn't have distracted him. Not when it was Rory.

CHAPTER EIGHT

Iᴛ ᴡᴀs ɪᴍᴘᴏssɪʙʟᴇ ᴏᴠᴇʀ the next few days for Rory to pretend that he wasn't deeply pissed. He had never imagined that his princely status might actually prevent him from kissing a man he cared about. Because that was the root of the problem: he'd begun caring about Gray. The seed had been there from the first moment, when Rory had come upon him in all his dirty, shirtless glory, and then had begun to sprout during their escape from the valley together. Getting captured and then being forced to rely on only each other had encouraged even more growth. The wide, approving looks Gray had given him over the Accord nurtured it further.

And that kiss?

If Rory had possessed any intention of steering clear of feelings for Gray, the kiss had obliterated it completely.

And yes, it was incredibly vexing that the only thing Rory could not fix was the very thing that pushed Gray away. Rory spent the past three days as they traveled towards the Karloffs stewing on the back of Evrard. There were more people on the road now, as it wound closer to the mountains, but Rory was less worried about being recognized these days. He'd definitely grown dirtier, face smudged to match his brown cloak, and the ugly patchy beard he'd always shaved had begun to grow in. Gray had chuckled under his breath when he'd first seen it one cold morning, but Rory hadn't been very amused.

How was he supposed to win Gray over when he was deliberately making himself less handsome?

The answer was, he wasn't. At least that was the gist of the cold shoulder that Gray kept giving him. Just enough clipped, shortened sentences to communicate the plans for the day, then complete and utterly annoying silence during the ride. At night, Rory might have been a tree stump for how much attention Gray paid to him.

Truthfully, after spending approximately half his time stewing over Gray's silence and the other half silent and bored, Rory would've been miserable except for Evrard's company. Evrard was certainly every bit the snob that Rory suspected, but he was also so much more. A streak of something resembling kindness unexpectedly wove its way through Evrard's conversation occasionally.

Rory had wondered how Gray could have tolerated growing up in the valley with only Evrard for company. At first Rory had been shocked that Gray was as well-adjusted as he was, considering the sole friend he'd had, and then as the hours progressed, he realized that while Gray and Evrard didn't always get along on the surface, the undercurrents between them went deep.

Midway through the second day of Gray's taciturn streak, Evrard unexpectedly brought up Rory's parents. "I met them once," he said, his voice wistful. "They were lovely, and they were kind. Too kind."

Rory, who wished he had more memories of them, asked, "How can you be too kind?"

"Sometimes an open heart can be wrenched open even further, and then something insidious worms its way in."

Rory wondered if that was his aunt, but didn't ask because he was sure that was one of those questions where Evrard would give him one of those strangely opaque looks from his beautiful eyes—and even though Rory objectively knew he was the furthest thing from stupid, Evrard would make him reconsider for a moment.

"They certainly never told me about meeting a unicorn, especially a unicorn that spoke," Rory pointed out. He'd only been five years old when they died, but he believed that a fact that extraordinary would have been one he'd have remembered.

"Naturally, I was not in this form," Evrard sniffed. Like it was unbelievably silly for Rory to have assumed that Evrard had met them in his natural form.

"You take other forms?" Rory asked, curious. Maybe when this was all over, and he was safely installed back in his library tower at Beaulieu, he would pen a manuscript on all the facts known about unicorns. Rory was mentally composing the introduction—"Unicorns are surprisingly full of themselves, even considering their elevated status as a prized, unique magical creature"—when Evrard answered.

"I was expecting more from you, Prince Emory," Evrard said. Pockets of trees flashed by as Evrard trotted along the road, but even Rory could tell the mountains were growing nearer and the air thinner. "I thought you were considered a scholar of some repute."

"Unfortunately, there is not much to be read about unicorns as a breed," Rory apologized. He could feel Gray stiffen in front of him, and not for the first time during their journey, desperately wanted to know if he was smiling as he and Evrard teased each other. His back was solid against Rory's hands, an undeniable presence, but it was hard to believe he was truly there, since he so rarely spoke these days.

On purpose, Rory reminded himself, that little pocket of frustration boiling hotter, he's not talking to you on purpose.

It was a very annoying state of affairs, and one that Rory was not at all resigned to. Occasionally—or about two or three times an hour—he had to resist the urge to beat his closed fists against that straight, rigid back, and demand to know what was so terrible about being a prince anyway.

"Of course there is nothing to be read about unicorns," Evrard said. "We are very secretive."

"And very enamored of that particular fact," Gray pointed out dryly.

Even though Rory was still annoyed—he had hardly stopped being annoyed in the last forty-eight hours—he smiled. Gray's sense of humor was dry and caustic, which was likely the result of spending far too much time with Evrard, but it existed, and he was surprisingly funny when he decided to share his thoughts.

"But how could you expect me to know more if there is very little written about unicorns?" Rory asked, the logic gap appearing very obvious after his amusement at Gray's comment settled. "That does not make any sense."

If Evrard had possessed a hand, he would have waved it airily. "Magical creatures are all very similar. Your aunt, for example, has a habit of turning into a chimera."

Thankfully, Rory did know what a chimera was. "She does?" he asked, more than a little stupefied.

"Gray faced her as one," Evrard said, and this time there was that sly edge to his voice that Rory had figured out he always used when he was hoping to manipulate Gray or Rory, or both of them at the same time. No doubt he had picked up on Gray's sudden cold shoulder just as well as Rory, and then there was the matter of the kiss he'd interrupted. Altogether, Rory felt like Evrard knew far too much about his relationship—or lack of relationship—with Gray.

"What was it like?" Rory asked, hoping that Gray would answer, but knowing better.

There was a long drawn-out moment of silence. They passed a small cottage set back from the road, smoke curling from the rough stone chimney, bright white against the gray sky. Evrard had observed earlier in the day that he was sure it would rain. Rory assumed he would likely be right, and no doubt they would not only be miserable with the wet and the mud, but with Evrard's insufferable attitude that he'd been right.

But to Rory's astonishment, it was Gray that answered. "Terrifying," he said, "but I had a very brave horse. If I'd been any older, I probably couldn't have done it. When you're a child, you always believe you can do anything."

Rory remembered so little of his childhood before his parents' death, and what had come after had never felt particularly childlike, though he'd enjoyed the many tutors and the crates of books that had continuously shown up at Beaulieu. If he concentrated very hard, he could envision a few hazy memories where his mom had held him tightly, and his father had played with him. Maybe before their deaths, his life had been a little more balanced between the books he loved and everything else, but it was impossible to say for sure.

A few hours later when they stopped for the night, Gray repeated his actions of the previous evenings and retreated further into the woods—supposedly to check the surroundings to make sure they weren't kidnapped again, but really because he was avoiding Rory. Normally Gray's behavior would have sent Rory's frustration spiking, but tonight, he had more he wanted to ask Evrard, and he thought it might be easier to do it if Gray weren't present.

Rory went over to where Evrard was munching on some nice soft grass, and sat down, drawing up his knees against his chest.

"What were they like?" he asked quietly.

Evrard was quiet for a long moment. "They loved each other, and they loved you," he finally said. "Do you remember much of them?"

"A few images. Their faces probably only because of their formal portraits in Beaulieu. I remember them encouraging me to read, but they never let me read too much." Rory hesitated. There was still a hurt, betrayed part of him that made it difficult to admit just how easily his aunt had manipulated him. How simple it had been for her to take something he loved and wield it against him. "Unlike the Regent Queen," he admitted softly. "She let me read as much as I liked. There were always new tutors, new languages, new books, new analyses that other scholars had requested. I would barely finish one project, and then another would begin."

"And you believe that your aunt arranged it that way?" Evrard asked between dainty nibbles.

Rory frowned. "If she'd asked me not to get involved in the running of the kingdom, I never would have agreed. She manipulated the situation—and me—so she never had to ask. I was so busy, so lost in my own world, that I never looked up from my work and thought, maybe I should be more involved."

Glancing up at him from underneath his rippling forelock, Evrard said, "But you're saying it now."

Rory picked at the fraying hem of his ugly brown cloak. "What if it's too late? What if I can't stop her?"

"Your Highness, I have gone to not-inconsiderate trouble to rescue you and save your life," Evrard said with a huff. "Would I do that if I believed the quest was hopeless?"

Leaning back against Evrard's legs, Rory thought for a long moment. No, he wouldn't have. The one thing Rory had learned, beyond all certainty, on this journey was that Evrard never wasted his time on anything he believed was beneath him. If he was here, and he was pushing Rory—and by extension, Gray—then he believed in what they were attempting to do. And really, Rory added, it had all been his idea, anyway.

"I am not infallible, as it turns out," Evrard continued with a sigh. "If I was, I would not have left Gray alone for so long. He's grown too used to being alone, and too intractable. Stuck in a rut of his own making, which I should have discouraged, and I did not."

"What do you mean?" Rory asked.

Evrard stared out into the darkening woods surrounding them. "I mean, Prince Emory, that he is sad, and he has been sad for a long time. I should have looked closer, and done more, but I did not. That is now on me, and unfortunately it is also now on you, because instead of pulling you closer, as his heart tells him to, he pushes you away."

Rory blushed. He wanted to ask more, but did not know which questions to ask, and there was also a part of him that wondered if they weren't better posed to Gray himself—at least when Gray was talking to him again.

Branches crackled underfoot, and Rory looked up to see Gray standing there, a load of wood in his arms. "It didn't rain," he said, "so I thought we'd celebrate with a fire."

Before he could stop himself, Rory laughed, and next to him, Evrard snorted, and pointedly did not answer.

An hour later, the fire was crackling, and Rory sat moodily watching it, lost in thought, wondering if his parents had survived the carriage accident, how much of his life might have been different. At least, he would have been a true crown prince of Fontaine, who wanted the throne and had worked for it. Who deserved it.

To Rory's shock, Gray actually did not retreat to the other side of the fire, but plopped down right next to Rory.

"I heard what you said earlier," he said, without preamble.

Rory and Evrard had said quite a lot of things today, so he could not immediately identify which of them Gray was referring to.

"The part about your aunt manipulating you," Gray said quietly, as he poked the fire with a long, sharp stick he'd whittled at the end with his dagger.

"Oh."

"It's not your fault. Not your fault that you didn't see it and not your fault that you didn't prevent it." Gray nudged his leg with his own. "She's made a career out of manipulating far more worldly and experienced men than you, Rory."

"Is that why you left Ardglass?" Rory asked before he could stop himself.

"Yes."

At first, that was all Rory believed he would get. Already Gray had said more words to him tonight than he'd said for days. But then he spoke again. "My father . . . he is intelligent and wise, or at least he was. I remember a time before Sabrina came to Tullamore, when things were different. When he was different. But after she came, everything changed, and he changed most of all. I was eleven when I escaped, with Evrard's help. By then, she had twisted his mind so thoroughly that he was willing to sacrifice me to serve her own ends."

Rory stared into the fire. He did not know what to say. Gray's father had agreed to hand him over to Sabrina? It made Sabrina's petty machinations towards Rory feel small and so insignificant. And it helped bring clarity to why Evrard had said Gray was sad, and had been sad for a long time.

"I tell you this," Gray continued, "because it's not right for you to blame yourself. You were a child, and she is both a master at this game and extraordinarily dangerous. She will no doubt try to manipulate you again, but I believe you're smarter than she is. You'll see right through it if it happens again."

Rory hoped so. "I hope you're right," he said. He did not feel quite as confident as Gray sounded, but that he thought so much of him did help to boost Rory's belief.

"I know I am."

"I'm sorry for what happened to you," Rory added softly after a long, quiet moment.

Gray cleared his throat. "And I'm sorry for what's happened to you." To Rory's complete surprise, Gray reached out and laid his hand on Rory's knee. Nothing more, but nothing less either. A peace offering, perhaps? But something, and Rory felt the anger that he'd held on to for days begin to dissipate. It was difficult to stay angry with someone who went out of their way to stop you from blaming yourself for so many terrible things.

On the fifth day of their journey, the mountains were no longer a closer promise; they were there. The road had been climbing steadily, the trees changing and thinning. They'd traded the horse in for some much-needed gold coins at the last village, as managing Evrard was difficult enough. At night there were barely any trees to take cover under, and Gray spent a lot of his time muttering under his breath about bandits on the road. Fires were a thing of the past, and it was definitely, undeniably, growing colder. Rory spent the nights huddled under his cloak, trying not to shiver and trying not to think of sharing Gray's body warmth.

They had reached a shaky truce, but there was no indication that Gray intended to touch him again, never mind kiss him. Rory, his anger gone, only had to wrestle with his own disappointment.

Today, the sun was shining more brightly, no longer covered by grayish blankets of clouds, and Rory tipped his head back, letting the sunshine and warmth fall across his face. The road curved and bent around and Rory caught a glance of something sparkling and silver out of the corner of his eye as Evrard trotted around the bend.

"What's that?" Rory asked, pointing to the flashes shining in the midday sun.

"Water? A river? Maybe a lake?" Gray answered. He had been less taciturn, but Rory also discovered that didn't mean he wanted to chat incessantly. He was still a quiet, introspective man. And Rory, who'd always believed he wanted a mate as everlastingly talkative as himself, discovered there was an unexpected peace to be found in a comfortable silence.

"We should go see," Rory said, because he was a little bored. Too many long days and quiet nights, with nothing to see or do, until he was actively fighting against the impulse to create some sort of entertaining diversion. He had a feeling that wouldn't be very well-received by either Gray or Evrard.

"Go see a river?" Gray questioned. "Why?"

"It's an excellent idea," Evrard said with an annoyed sniff. "My nose is exceptionally sensitive and you both could use an application of water everywhere."

Rory blushed. Maybe that was why Gray hadn't moved to kiss him again. But then he thought better of it, because surely Gray smelled just as bad as he did.

Gray contemplated this suggestion for a long moment. Finally, he capitulated. "It's warmer today too, which means we won't freeze to death trying to get clean for Evrard's overly touchy nose," Gray said, directing his comment towards Rory.

Without prompting from Gray, Evrard turned off the road, and after picking their way through the forest and the downed trees, emerged on the shores of a small mountain lake sparkling in the bright sunshine.

Rory dismounted, followed by Gray, and approached the water. Dipping a finger in, he found it cold, but not unbearably so. They had extra blankets they had picked up in one of the last villages, to protect against the colder nights at a higher altitude, so they'd be able to dry off properly.

To Rory's surprise, Gray didn't even bother testing the water. Just stripped off his stained shirt, yanking it out of his breeches, and then leaned over to begin unlacing his boots.

In Rory's fantasies, the first time he saw Gray completely naked hadn't been at a relatively chilly lake with Evrard as an unwelcome supervisor. The romantic streak in him protested strongly, but Rory decided that in this particular situation, practicalities outweighed silly fancies. He pulled his cloak off, setting it on a nearby rock, and then turned his attention to the rest of the clothing he was wearing. But it turned out it wasn't only romantic illusions, but an unforeseen shyness that was preventing him from simply stripping himself bare. He unlaced his boots, but after pulling them off, made no other movements to undress.

"Don't worry," Gray's deep voice rumbled out. "There's nobody else around."

But you're around, Rory thought helplessly. You're who I'm agonizing over.

"I shall go provide a lookout," Evrard said, trotting back from where they'd come. Rory couldn't help but think that Evrard, despite all his many flaws, was actually attempting to generously leave them alone for a short time.

Alone and naked.

"Right, of course. There's nobody around." Rory glanced up and wished that Gray would stop watching him. But while he wasn't staring necessarily, Gray's gaze kept straying to where Rory was toying with the ties on the oversized tunic he'd been wearing.

As for Gray himself, he'd stripped down to his smallclothes, which looked very small indeed, cupping a pair of muscular buttocks and . . . Rory blushed again. Had Gray's cock grown hard at just the thought of Rory undressing? If that was the case, then maybe there was less to be worried about than Rory had previously assumed.

Gray tucked a finger under the waistband of his smallclothes and shot Rory a hot look. "Do I need to get naked alone?" he asked.

Rory gulped, and pulled off his tunic, the cool air rushing across his suddenly heated skin.

"Better," Gray said in a teasing tone and then turned towards the lake, pulling his smallclothes down, leaving them in a puddle on the ground with the rest of his clothes, and leaving Rory with an excellent view of a very excellent butt. Rory stared, because he could not help himself. Gray was magnificent; broad-shouldered with ridges of muscles on his back leading to narrow hips and that marvelously sculpted ass. He didn't want to just look, he wanted to touch, but before he could work up the nerve to say any of that, Gray took off at a run, launching himself into the lake at nearly full speed. He came up from the water dripping, his hair sleek against his skull, and so beautiful that Rory's throat went dry.

"You coming?" Gray teased again.

God, he wanted to. More than anything.

Maybe if Gray hadn't been staring at him so intently, his gaze burning across his skin, he would have felt the chill as he stripped down the rest of the way, but Rory couldn't feel anything but heat.

"Come, jump in, it's too cold to do it gradually," Gray encouraged as Rory approached the lake, his cock bobbing with each step he took. Don't be embarrassed, he told himself firmly, Gray was hard too. You're attracted to each other. It's normal.

But it wasn't all that normal for Rory. He'd kissed a few cute boys at the court of Beaulieu, but none of them had interested him particularly. He'd definitely never been interested in going further, in touching them the way he touched himself at night.

Now, Rory wanted everything—and he wanted it so much, even though he didn't have any idea how to go about getting it. He'd read plenty of erotic texts, of course, but none of them had ever described bathing together with the man you longed for in a cold mountain lake, with the King of the Unicorns standing watch only a few feet away.

"Rory," Gray said again, and Rory didn't think he'd imagined the pleading note in his tone.

Making the choice in a split second, Rory didn't let himself hold back as he matched the speed and path that Gray had taken, the cold water hitting him in a breathless rush.

He was sure he looked far less attractive than Gray had when he came up, spluttering and cursing in every language he knew at how bitterly freezing the water truly was.

"You'll get used to it," Gray told him with a grin, as he floated onto his back and started to swim, his arms cutting powerfully through the water.

"I don't think so," Rory said, his teeth chattering.

In the water, with his hair wet and dark, Gray's eyes were an otherworldly blue, and as he swam closer, Rory was transfixed by them.

"I think so," Gray retorted softly. And somehow, he wasn't wrong, because the closer Gray came, the warmer Rory felt, like the heat between them was impossibly raising the temperature of the water.

"See?" Gray said. "It's better."

It was, but Rory was desperate to be even warmer still. He reached out and braced a hand against Gray's shoulder. His wet skin was slick and smooth under his fingertips, the muscle sliding easily under all that softness. "You're . . ." For someone who spoke so many languages, finding the words to describe how stunning Gray was like this—wet and naked and kind—was surprisingly difficult.

"Believe me," Gray said dryly, "the feeling is mutual."

Rory glanced down at his pale skin, gleaming white in the sun, and at his much scrawnier arms and chest. It seemed impossible that Gray might be as transfixed by him as Rory was by Gray. But then, Gray couldn't seem to tear his eyes away. He reached out and tucked a stray, wet curl behind Rory's ear. "They talk of your beauty for several kingdoms in every direction," Gray said softly, "and before, I never understood why, but I do now."

Even though the water was freezing, there was nothing Rory wanted more than to lean in and kiss Gray, but after how the last kiss had gone, the next one was going to have to be Gray's choice.

Digging his fingertips into Gray's shoulder, Rory floated closer, and hoped that was the last bit of encouragement Gray needed. It should be Gray's decision, yes, but that didn't mean Rory couldn't make any attempts to convince him. "Thank you," he said softly, his gaze falling again to Gray's lips.

"I keep trying to remember you're a prince," Gray finally said, the last inches closing between them, his eyes growing ridiculously bluer, "but to me, you're always just Rory."

Gray leaned in and kissed him then, gently and softly, like he wasn't quite sure Rory wouldn't turn him down after all. Rory's heart was thumping painfully, his skin prickling with heat, and now that Gray had given in, Rory could indulge in all the fantasies he'd considered from the first moment he'd seen the lake.

He pulled Gray closer, one hand reaching out to meet the other behind Gray's neck, his fingers sliding wetly across his skin. Tilting his head, Rory deepened the kiss, and as Gray's heartbeat accelerated against his chest, Rory wrapped his legs around Gray's much sturdier frame. Rory's cock, which had softened in the cool water, hardened almost instantly when it felt the brush of Gray's own.

Gray wrenched his mouth from Rory's. He was breathing hard, his pupils dilated with arousal, but he didn't push Rory away, he just stared at him. "You really want this," he said, like he couldn't quite believe it.

It was insanity because Rory had wanted Gray desperately from the very first moment he'd ever seen him—sweaty and dirty and with his hair falling in his eyes. He couldn't really understand it, but the poets had always spoken of attraction and desire and love as undefinable and illogical, and so Rory, experiencing these emotions for nearly the first time, wanted nothing more than to throw himself straight into the deep end.

"I've always wanted this, I just didn't know it," Rory confessed.

It was all the motivation Gray needed to kiss him again, and this time when Rory moved against him, hesitatingly at first, and then with growing confidence, Gray moved with him. It wasn't perfect, the slide of wet cock against wet cock, the lubrication of the lake water somewhat lacking, but it felt so good that Rory could hardly care. He'd never done this before, had never done anything more than touch himself, and he'd always believed the rapturous descriptions in the texts he'd read must be exaggerations, because nothing could ever feel that good, but this did. It felt so good, so right, so flawlessly perfect that Rory now understood why people would kill for it, would conquer kingdoms for it, would betray their own honor for it. He'd do anything right now, in this moment, for Gray to keep kissing him and touching him, and making those infuriatingly little gasps into his mouth as the pleasure began to overtake him.

Rory didn't even try to make it last, he hurtled headfirst as fast as he could, greedy and desperate, and Gray followed right behind, exploding with a deep, life-altering groan right after Rory's brain went bright and blinding with his own orgasm.

As his heartbeat slowly returned to its normal state, Rory still didn't let go of Gray. He pressed a single kiss to Gray's collarbone and opened his eyes to a world that was exactly the same, but somehow felt brand new.

"So that's what it's like," Rory said wonderingly.

Gray tensed. "You . . . you hadn't . . . with anybody?" he asked with trepidation.

"I hadn't really wanted to before," Rory confessed. "Is that okay?" He was suddenly worried, even though nothing he'd ever read stated you were supposed to make that fact explicitly clear. Maybe he had somehow made a mistake, and Gray wished he'd known. Would he have pushed Rory away? Was it unattractive to not have any experience? Inexperience was always a challenge, but he'd read the texts, hadn't he? Rory knew all the mechanics; he'd hardly consider himself ignorant.

"It's . . ." Gray hesitated again.

"I'm sorry," Rory said impulsively. "But truthfully I'm not very sorry at all."

Suddenly, a grin broke out over Gray's face, and it changed him. Made him brighter, softer, somehow. And Rory was captivated all over again.

"I'm not very sorry at all, either," Gray finally said. "I didn't mean to, and then I did. It's hard to keep looking at you, and riding with you and talking to you, and stay away. I couldn't do it."

Rory nuzzled against the damp skin at his neck. He smelled like Gray—like pine forests and warm earth and herbs.

"I didn't even try," Rory confessed, and Gray laughed again.

"We should really wash up," Gray said. "Evrard can't possibly be expected to stand guard forever."

Rory nodded, even though the last thing he wanted was to let go. But it wasn't really letting go, Rory reasoned, because he'd already decided that nothing, even Gray's own frustrating tendencies, could make him do that.

CHAPTER NINE

They dressed after a quick wash, shivering despite the warmer air and the sun shining overhead. Remembered pleasure made Gray's thoughts sticky-slow, but one stuck out further than the rest. This was the worst time to be allowing personal indulgences to matter, but fighting against Rory's indefinable charm felt more distracting than giving in. It was easier, Gray reasoned, to give in a little bit—and there was the added bonus that it brought a smile to Rory's face that warmed his eyes for the first time since Gray had met him. *Gold*, Gray thought dazedly, *his eyes are gold*. Other men wanted strongboxes full of riches and treasure, but all Gray desired was his valley, and those eyes, gazing at him like he was the only man Rory could ever want.

But, Gray shook himself as Evrard emerged over the crest of the trees, reality made that dream impossible. Rory was meant for the throne of Fontaine, and Gray was meant for something else. A smaller, humbler life. Until Rory had started batting his eyelashes in Gray's direction, that was all Gray had really wanted. But now things were complicated and complicating them even further was the secret of Gray's birth.

He can never know, Gray thought as they silently climbed onto Evrard's back again.

"Your odor is much improved," Evrard pointed out as he briskly trotted back to the road, "and your moods as well."

Gray could feel Rory's blush even though he couldn't see it. Evrard had known the events he was setting into motion when he had retreated as a lookout. Part of Gray wanted to be annoyed that Evrard was matchmaking, because he undeniably was, but his time alone with Rory had been so pleasurable it was hopeless to regret it.

"We are reaching the end of my knowledge of the area," Gray admitted a few hours later as he and Rory gnawed at the last of their dried meat stores. "But there is a village at the base of the mountains. Nargash. We should reach it by nightfall."

"A village?" Gray tried to ignore the hopeful note in Rory's voice, but it was difficult.

Ignoring anything about Rory was difficult.

And there was also that matter of the small pouch of gold coins tucked in the pocket of his breeches. They could afford a night in a proper inn, with a hot meal, before the long, arduous climb the next day. It would be good for Evrard to be sheltered in a stable, especially with the exertion of the next few days.

"If there's an inn," Gray said grudgingly, "we will inquire and see if they have any rooms available."

"Hopefully a private room," Rory said softly, leaning closer and plastering himself along Gray's back, until his voice was a whisper of a promise in Gray's ear.

His blood heating was unavoidable and his reaction undeniable. Gray must want Rory as much as Rory wanted him, and it seemed foolish not to take this chance to indulge, if they indeed had a chance.

"We'll see," Gray said, trying to make his voice gruff, but instead it came out soft and tender and anticipatory. Like he could not wait to get Rory alone and kiss him and touch him again, this time on a decent bed, behind a door that locked.

"You sound eager," Rory said slyly, and for his professed inexperience with men, he was far better at teasingly flirtatious comments than Gray would have anticipated.

Gray's fingers tightened on Evrard's mane.

"I know you are very eager," Evrard pointed out, tone annoyed, "but please do not pull out my mane in your eagerness to reach the village."

It was Gray's turn to blush. "Sorry," he mumbled.

"Before we reach the village, we have much to discuss. Our further path, and the object you must obtain," Evrard said.

It was not lost on Gray that Evrard had waited until the last moment to have this conversation. Gray did not like it because he didn't like leaving such an important quest up to chance. What if they'd gotten separated from Evrard somehow? It had nearly happened only a week prior, and only Rory's quick thinking and years of study had prevented disaster.

But if Gray had made this point, Evrard would only have replied in that infuriatingly calm tone, "What will be is what is."

"What are we looking for?" Rory asked, sounding nearly as excited to find the object that would take back his kingdom as he was to spend the evening alone with Gray. And that's the way it should be, Gray told himself, even as pain pricked him. Rory would be moving on and evolving into a leader and a man. It was right he should be excited at the prospect.

Gray resolutely ignored any feelings of envy. All you want is your valley.

"It is a ring, a ring of great mystical value and importance, and upon wearing it, gives the owner complete truth."

It sounded like complete idiocy to Gray. Who wanted complete truth? A nice gray version was always so much easier to deal with. But then Gray could see how such an object might be useful in dealing with a perennial liar and manipulator like Sabrina. For one, it would be far easier to expose her lies. And if they could get her to don the ring? The web of lies she'd woven over so many years would completely disintegrate.

"You will find this ring," Evrard continued, "called the Bearer of Truth, in a hidden cave tucked between two of the largest mountains."

"Hidden?" Gray inserted. "How do we find something that's hidden?"

"By searching for it, naturally," Evrard said.

"Not helpful," Gray grumbled.

"It can't be a huge area, between the two largest mountains," Rory reasoned. "How hidden could a hidden cave be?"

"The Bearer of Truth has remained hidden for several centuries," Evrard said, immediately ruining Rory's optimism. "It will not be easy to find it, but it is necessary to defeat the Regent Queen."

"No pressure," Gray interrupted. "Why don't you tell us something more helpful, like how to actually find the stupid cave?"

"Between two mountains of great stature lie veracity, fidelity, and certainty. Tread the peak and scale the valley. Solve the puzzle and gain the ring," Evrard intoned in a serious, ponderous voice.

"Great, a prophecy," Gray complained.

"Do you hate prophecies the same way you hate royalty?" Rory wondered.

"Prophecies, like royalty, can certainly be a waste of time," Gray said carefully, because he didn't want to give Rory the impression he hated him. He hated his title, he hated what his title represented and he sure as hell didn't want Rory's princely status to come between them—but he could never hate Rory.

"It is not a prophecy, only an ancient saying, from a time when the ring was hidden away. I thought it might add clarity to your search," Evrard corrected.

Gray rolled his eyes. Only Evrard would believe that an "ancient saying" would actually be helpful.

"Thank you," Rory said, and actually sounded like he meant it.

A few hours later, the road began to widen, and there were more men to be seen, riding carts pulled by mules or old, shabby-looking horses. The men themselves looked worse than the horses; they either ignored Rory and Gray completely, like they were too worn out from the hand life had dealt them to care, or they shot sly, avaricious looks in their direction. Their clothing was hardly rich, but more than once Gray caught a man eyeing them up and down, seemingly mentally pricing out every visible item of clothing and the saddlebags. Evrard was exempt from these thorough examinations every time, their eyes sliding right over his figure. Just as Gray expected.

Still, this part of the road was much rougher than Gray remembered, and he began to worry what Nargash would be like when they finally reached it. Would they feel comfortable stopping there and renting a room? And if they did not, would they be any safer camping out a distance from the town? Even off the road? Gray did not particularly think so, not if the road continued to be full of such unsavory characters. He transferred his dagger from his calf to his belt, and when they stopped to rest for a minute at a stream, Gray approached Rory.

"We have almost no weapons," Gray began, uncomfortably aware of how inappropriate his request was. Maybe if he'd truly been Gray the Farmhand, and never raised to be a prince, the question would have felt different, but Prince Graham of Ardglass knew what he was about to ask was completely wrong and in many areas would have been considered both a betrayal of trust and a fighting offense.

"I know," Rory said, and his gaze was anxious as it met Gray's. "You have your dagger, and I have the dagger and the sword."

Gray cleared his throat. "About the sword."

Sometimes Gray still forgot how very different their upbringings were, and so was shocked when Rory unceremoniously unbuckled his sword belt and thrust Lion's Breath, still in its protective sheath, at Gray. "You carry it," he said. "It doesn't make sense for me to have it, I can't even use it."

It was what he'd wanted, specifically what he'd approached Rory for, and still Gray hesitated to take it. "You can use it," Rory added impatiently, pushing it closer. "You used it before."

But that had not been premeditated. They'd been surrounded, and Gray hadn't thought through the action before he'd done it. He'd simply taken the sword because, if he hadn't, he'd believed they would either be captured or killed.

"It's . . ." Gray looked down at Lion's Breath. Another reason why Rory could never learn about his past or his true parentage. A nameless farm boy taking a royal sword because they needed it was one thing; a prince of a neighboring kingdom appropriating a royal sword was entirely another. In some circles they might even consider this an act of aggression or Gray declaring his intention to usurp Rory's throne.

The problem was that Rory's throne wasn't currently Rory's, and it might never be Rory's again if Gray didn't wield this sword.

"I know it's not usually done," Rory said. Of course he knew. He knew all the ancient traditions, and what carrying a sword of Fontaine would mean. "But if you don't take it, I'm not sure we're going to survive the night."

Gray reached out and clasped a hand around the decorative scabbard, encrusted with rubies and topaz. "Thank you," he said, "you're likely not wrong. Nargash will be much rougher than I anticipated when we began this journey."

Rory's eyes glowed as they gazed up at him, and the honesty in them was humbling and terrifying. "I trust you," he murmured. "Maybe I shouldn't, but I do. I know you won't betray me, and I know you'll do everything in your power to help me regain my throne. You won't take Lion's Breath and use it for your own gain."

Gray was speechless. Rory's words meant even more because he wasn't quite the silly, naive princeling that Gray had assumed the first time they'd met. He had strength—albeit a different kind than Gray had always recognized—and intelligence. He'd been manipulated by Sabrina, but then Sabrina was a master manipulator. And now? Gray thought it would be extremely difficult, maybe even impossible, for anyone to manipulate the man in front of him.

"You know a lot of things," Gray said softly.

"I know you," Rory said with earnestness, "even though I don't know as much about you as I'd like."

It was the wrong time and the wrong place to kiss him, even though that was nearly all Gray could think about. Tonight, he thought, if we can survive the journey to an inn and after we bar the door . . .

Still, Gray raised his fingers and brushed them, even as dirty as they likely were, against Rory's cheek. The reddish-blond stubble there was patchy and he'd caught Rory grumbling about it more than once, but Gray loved it for the sole purpose that it helped keep Rory invisible and protected.

Rory smiled as Gray's hand fell to his side. "Maybe someday you'll tell me," Rory said, and while there was nothing more that Gray wanted than to be honest, the truth about who he was had to remain hidden.

"Are you going to stand there and stare raptly into each other's eyes all afternoon?" Evrard interrupted.

Gray turned towards the grumbling unicorn. "You did this, you know," he murmured to Evrard as he mounted him.

"All you needed was the slightest of prompts," Evrard countered back primly. "Barely even a push at all."

As Evrard continued to canter down the road to Nargash, their surroundings edged closer and closer to disreputable. The outskirts of the village were particularly unpleasant, consisting only of broken-down buildings, some with collapsed roofs, some with their windows and doors hanging crookedly open, like teeth knocked out of an ugly man's face. And even worse, as they passed some, there were clear signs that people were still living in what Gray could barely term shacks: small fires in the front yards, clotheslines hanging between two straggly trees, and in one particularly unsightly home, children running around the ramshackle walls of the structure.

"Why is it like this?" Rory wondered aloud after they passed that particular dwelling. "Why does each village we pass look worse?"

Gray did not answer, because he didn't trust himself. They were on the edge of Ardglass now, and the village of Nargash was considered one of the very western borders of the furthest western clan. This responsibility was his father's, and eventually would have fallen to him. As it was, it seemed to be that Gideon had let his kingdom continue to slide into ruin even after Graham's departure. As insidious and evil as Sabrina was, at least Fontaine was not overtly falling to pieces, shabby and ill-used, its inhabitants forced to live in squalor.

Evrard answered instead. "Taxes," he said. "This technically falls under the purview of the kingdom of Ardglass, and its king has let unscrupulous advisors pick his treasury clean. As a result, has raised taxes throughout his kingdom to compensate."

Gray felt the burn of shame rush through him, but what could he do? Raising his head out of obscurity would only likely end in it being chopped off.

"Something must be done," Rory said quietly but with purpose.

Turning his head from the children in their threadbare clothes and dirty faces, Gray said nothing. Maybe, with his own throne recovered, Rory would eventually turn his attention to Ardglass. The thought might have been a comforting one, but the injustice for himself and for every other creature living in Ardglass raged too strongly inside him for Gray to listen to reason.

"Something will be done," Evrard promised. "You will see, Your Highness."

Gray gripped Evrard's mane tighter and nearly lashed out in anger and frustration. How did he know? What did he know? Why did he never share with Gray? Why were they going to all this effort to restore Rory to his throne when it was Ardglass that needed help? Gray had long since learned that Evrard only answered questions he chose, and they were almost never of any importance. Still, it was only by biting his lip until blood welled that he managed to stay silent.

Finally, they came upon the village proper. The marketplace was a sad sight, with wilted vegetables and rotten grain. Gray turned away and wondered how long he could bear to look, only to look away again. "There is an inn," Gray said, pointing to a faded sign. "The Chimera," he read, the irony definitely not lost on him. "I will inquire for lodging and a stable berth."

Rory stayed with Evrard and Gray approached the inn, opened the door and went inside. The inside was somehow worse than the outside—the smell of years of burned meat embedded in the exposed wood of the great room. The beams were dark with smoke and grease, and even though a little dirt never bothered Gray, he flinched when he walked across the floorboards. The innkeeper was wearing a dirty white shirt with an open neck, and a stained leather apron torn in one corner, wiping his hands on a filthy cloth as Gray approached.

"I would like a room for the night," Gray said, "and a meal, as well as lodging and feed for my horse."

The innkeeper looked Gray up and down, and though Gray knew his clothes were poor, they did nothing to conceal his tall, strong frame or his straight back. Greed flashed in the man's eyes and if they'd had any other choice, Gray would have turned back and taken them all far away from this place. But there was a particularly masochistic part of him that stayed put and let the innkeeper look his fill. None of this was Gray's fault, but it had been irrevocably set into motion when he'd left Ardglass all those years ago.

"Two gold pieces, and another if you want hot water," the man said.

It was high above the going rate for shelter, but Gray handed over the gold without arguing. He took a deep breath of semi-clean air when he walked outside, but one glance in Rory and Evrard's direction told him that, even though he'd hurried, he might have tarried too long. Several rough-looking men were eyeing Rory with interest, despite his patchy beard. The problem with Rory was, that even in ugly ill-fitting clothes with that awful facial hair, he was still beautiful, and in the middle of this muddy yard, he shone like the brightest diamond.

As Gray hurried over to them, his face must have reflected his worries, because Rory glanced at him and flinched. He's seen the men looking, Gray thought, and didn't know what to say. Rory had promised him trust, and Gray couldn't fail him, even in this depressingly bleak place. He pushed back his cloak, hoping the sight of his sword would warn away anyone who was considering an attack. He did wish the scabbard of Lion's Breath was slightly less ornate and contained far fewer gemstones. Some idiot might decide the threat wasn't nearly as great as the prize, and would come for it anyway, and the last thing Gray wanted was to fight off robbers.

"You'll be fine in the stables," Gray said to Evrard under his breath. "The hay will no doubt be moldy, but you will have to suffer through it."

"And us?" Rory asked, clearly concerned.

"The door will have a latch," Gray promised. "And if not, I will fashion something that will keep them out." He looked straight into Rory's eyes and, as best he could, told him without words, you put your trust in me, let me prove it to you that it wasn't unfounded.

"It's barely early evening," Rory pointed out. "And we must eat, too."

"It's a crowded public room, and I will not leave your side," Gray promised.

"We will all be careful," Evrard said, "for the coming days will be a test of our strength."

This night will be a test of my strength, Gray thought as he delivered Evrard to the stables.

When they walked into the common room, Rory could not quite contain the disgust in his expression as he took in the stained walls and floors, and the plates of corn mush and burned, fatty meat.

"This is not . . . not quite what I was hoping for," Rory whispered under his breath as they passed down the row of occupied tables to an empty space by the great hearth. Putting the fire at their backs was not ideal, but at least it would be difficult for anyone to approach from that direction.

"We must make the best of it," Gray said, though he was equally disappointed. He'd wanted a respite from the stress of their journey, but instead, what they'd gotten in Nargash was a rude awakening and an increasingly dangerous situation.

They sat and the innkeeper motioned to a sullen serving boy, who brought them warm mugs of ale and two plates of the unappetizing-looking food.

"I cannot believe I am complaining about a hot meal," Rory said, but he shuddered as he pushed the corn slop around his plate with a spoon that was likely none too clean, "but I would rather have some of the dried meat from the saddlebags."

"It's not so bad," Gray said, shoveling a spoonful into his mouth. "It's hot, at least."

"I guess," Rory said, clearly not convinced.

His voice must have carried, because a moment later, a man with a wicked facial scar bisecting his bushy gray eyebrow and then meandering down from cheek to chin, sat down opposite Rory. "This one seems a lot of work," he said to Gray, motioning towards Rory. "Seems haughty. Rich, even. A pain in the ass."

Gray might have felt that way at first, and still occasionally, but he was hardly going to agree with the newcomer, at least not in front of Rory. In Rory's defense, the food was bad and the atmosphere even worse.

"I am not," Rory answered hotly, obviously offended.

Jabbing Rory's side with his elbow under the shadow of the rough-hewn tabletop, Gray gave the scarred man a ferocious smile, baring his teeth. "He's not for sale," he said.

Rory made an affronted noise as Gray's words revealed the man's real purpose in visiting their table.

"I meant it," he said, "he looks damn expensive."

"Too expensive for you," Gray said steadily. He pushed back from the table, and risking it again, exposed the scabbard of Lion's Breath to the man's gaze.

"As are you, my friend, though you take pains to hide it," the scarred man pointed out.

"We are just traveling through and have no interest in deals or discussions," Gray said in a flat voice.

"As you wish," the man said and stood. "But you may find your mind changed."

After he left, Rory turned to Gray and the expression in his eyes was definitely anxious. "Was he really trying to buy me? And what did he mean, you might find your mind changed?"

"He assumed you were my property," Gray said, not wanting to address Rory's second question. He was edgy enough and might lose whatever nerve he had left if Rory knew they'd just been threatened.

"But slavery isn't allowed in Ardglass. Or Fontaine, for that matter," Rory argued.

Gray gave a short, unamused laugh. "Do you really believe that stops anyone with enough money?"

Glancing down at his plate, Rory shook his head. "He threatened you," he stated.

"Us," Gray sighed. "He threatened us. Finish your meal, because I intend to go to our room and bar the door and not leave it until morning."

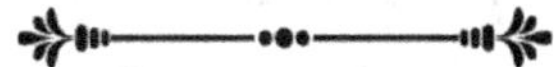

Rory ate slowly, but he did eat. Gray had long since finished his meal and was savoring the last few drops of the warm ale when Rory finally finished cleaning his plate. Glancing around, Gray realized that the hour had grown late, and the main room had emptied out somewhat. They weren't alone, but as Gray observed each of the groups left, each one looked more villainous than the last. And even worse, they were watching Rory—and to a lesser extent, Gray—intently.

"Do you have your dagger?" Gray asked, leaning closer to Rory so they wouldn't be overheard.

Rory nodded.

"Keep it close," Gray said. "I hope you won't have to use it, but I don't want you undefended while I have to fight off the rest of this crowd."

Rory's eyes grew wide. "Is that really going to be necessary?"

Gray watched as Rory's gaze followed his own, taking stock of each man that was left in the room.

"They think we're rich," Gray said softly. "Rich and easy pickings. Especially you."

Swallowing hard, Rory looked over at Gray. "We can't be. Not tonight."

"Not tonight," Gray agreed, and slowly stood. Rory followed him as he skirted around the tables against the hearth, always keeping it at his back.

Every step they took was observed, and Gray swallowed hard against the nerves that had settled low in his stomach. He'd promised to protect Rory, but he could not hope to take on a dozen men with only a small, sharp dagger and Rory's ancestral sword, no matter how fancy the title. Anyone who approached would need to be dispatched quickly, before the rest decided to join in.

Gray's destination was the staircase at the other end of the room. The key the innkeeper had given them dug into his palm and he slid it further, exposing the rough iron edge. It too could be a weapon if they were pressed. None of the men in the room moved, but there were shadows at the base of the stairs.

A perfect place for several men to lie in wait for their prey.

Gray edged closer, Rory not far behind him, and finally they made it to the corner of the room, right where the concentric circles of candle and firelight ended.

A man stepped out of the gloom. The scarred man, which did not surprise Gray at all, though worry billowed in his chest. He'd warned them, after all. No doubt anyone else who came here with any coin to speak of did so with a whole troop of armed guards.

Gray put his other hand on the hilt of Lion's Breath. "Let us pass," he said in the sternest voice he could muster. He felt Rory tense behind him and pull his own dagger.

He might not have much knowledge of how to defend himself, but he was brave—Gray would give him that much. And unfortunately, unlike with the nomadic tribe, there was no way to talk their way out of this one. It would have to be done with fists and blades.

"I don't think so," the scarred man said, a devilish smile lighting up his face. "Boys, why don't we relieve our good man here of his valuables, including that sweet, pretty boy?"

There was no time to think. Gray lashed out, punching the scarred man in the face, taking a blow back, blinding his vision for a split second. Another two men materialized out of the shadows, and he saw Rory lash out with his dagger out of the corner of his eye as one of the men attempted to grab his arm. Blood spurted, and Gray was too busy fighting off the man with the scar to check if it was Rory's.

He hadn't pulled Lion's Breath yet because he didn't want to give the men any more financial motivation to win, and it was a very small, closed-in space. Perfect, Gray thought grudgingly, for a good fist fight. But not exactly ideal for a swordfight.

Gray's training hadn't been very formal after leaving Tullamore, but he'd picked up what he could, where he could, and he'd never forgotten those first eleven years of lessons and advice. He gripped the key and slashed out at the man's eyes. He defended the blow, landing another in the vicinity of Gray's ribs, the pain and breathlessness winning for a split second, before he countered with his other free hand, a satisfying crack of bone echoing through the room.

Blood started to pour and the man gazed at him incredulously for a second. "You're a tough one, you are," he said with disgust as he snorted blood and then, with a quick, sickening motion, wrenched his nose back into place.

Shit.

These men were tougher than Gray had anticipated, living for years on the rough, lawless edges of Ardglass. You're their rightful prince, a voice inside Gray reminded him, you were born to subdue them, to remind them who sets the rules.

He was bigger, Gray realized, and started putting more of the brute force of his larger body into his blows, landing a few on the ribs and stomach, and then finally cracking one on the man's shin. He took some back, sweat dripping into his eyes, and he just prayed that Rory hadn't been dragged away in the length of time it had taken to subdue the scarred man.

Gray landed one last forceful blow and the man's head lolled back and eventually he fell back against one of the rough-hewn walls, and he finally had a moment to glance behind. There was blood on the floor, and one of the men who'd gone after Rory was holding his arm, from which red flowed freely, and Rory held a dagger at the throat of the other.

"You good?" Rory asked breathlessly. He had a dark bruise forming on his cheek. There were drops of blood on his hands. But he seemed otherwise uninjured.

"I'm good," Gray said. "Let's go before anyone decides to steal you."

They retreated up the stairs, and thankfully, the men didn't follow. Too much effort, Gray thought, we made it too tough for them to follow through. No doubt they'd look and likely find easier men to prey upon, and perhaps Gray should have felt guilty about that, but he was all too aware that they'd barely escaped with their lives. For now, that had to be enough.

Their room was three doors down from the top of the staircase, and Gray shoved the key in the lock, turned it, and they stumbled into the doorway. A single candle flickered in the corner, lighting the corners of the room well enough that Gray was reassured nobody was waiting to ambush them. He slammed the door shut and threw the heavy metal bar across it.

"There," he said, relief pouring through him, "that should hold them until morning, and by then, attacking won't be prudent."

"Do you truly believe that?" Rory asked as he crossed the room and examined the rest of the contents. A simple trunk bed with a mattress of certainly dubious cleanliness and a few blankets folded at the base. A basin of water sitting on a simple wooden stand. Dipping a finger in, Rory turned to Gray. "It's actually warm," he said with surprise.

Gray's knuckles felt sticky with blood. "We should wash," he said, gesturing to the droplets that had fallen on Rory's cheek.

He lifted a rag from next to the basin, but Rory reached over and stopped his hand. "Let me," he said quietly.

Gray watched as Rory took his hand and examined it—the split knuckles, the smears of blood, the bruising already beginning to appear. They didn't look good, but then Gray looked up at the red splotches on Rory's flawlessly pale skin and wished he could scrub them away until they'd never existed.

"You saved me," Rory said, dipping the cloth into the water and wringing it out. Gently he began to clean Gray's hands, carefully dabbing off the blood and cleaning out every wound.

Gray closed his eyes, suddenly exhausted. "You helped," he pointed out.

"It was more accidental than purposeful," Rory admitted. "I swung with the dagger and it was only happenstance it hit somewhere important."

"And the other man?" Gray asked.

"I grabbed the dagger, and I think he was so surprised by all the blood, he didn't move. I held the dagger to his throat before he could take me."

"I think he was so surprised you came out swinging," Gray said dryly. "You don't look like the type."

"They weren't very quick, and I don't think they were very smart either," Rory confided as he continued to clean Gray's hands with soft, careful strokes.

"They're robbing men at the local inn," Gray pointed out.

"Still, things could have turned out far worse." Rory took a deep breath. "This wasn't quite what I'd hoped for when you said we might get a room. Alone."

"Nor me either." Gray's voice was wry.

One hand finished, Rory rinsed the cloth and picked up Gray's other hand. Glancing down, Gray saw how huge and rough his single hand looked in two of Rory's. While he might have once been royalty too, it felt like all that polish had long since been scrubbed away. Still, he remembered how much Gideon had boasted that the men of Ardglass had always been brave and determined fighters. "Ardglass never loses," he had always been fond of saying. And Ardglass, Gray realized, hadn't lost today.

Now that he had a clean hand, Gray reached up and his fingertips gently probed Rory's bruised cheekbone. "I didn't realize someone got a blow in," he said, anger mounting despite his attempts to dismiss it. How could men see someone who looked like Rory and put their rough hands on him? It was a crime to take something so beautiful and attempt to ruin it. Even if they hadn't succeeded, Gray still wanted to go seek them out and break all their noses.

"I ducked at the last minute, I thought it had mostly glanced off me," Rory said, bending over Gray's hand. "But I suppose it didn't. It doesn't hurt so much now."

"It will in the morning," Gray pointed out. "I wish I could find some ice, take some of the swelling down."

"I'm fine. You've done plenty. I'm alive, and not in the clutches of those men, about to be sold, aren't I?" Rory observed.

"If I'd been quicker . . ." Gray said softly.

Those glorious golden eyes glanced up at him, skewering him with a single, pointed look. "If I thanked you more eloquently for saving my life would you stop lamenting at how poorly you did it?" Rory asked sharply.

The heat of the violence had just about finished leaking out of Gray, but Rory's words brought it roaring back, with teeth and claws and a very specific hunger that Gray didn't quite understand. He'd been with men before—and women too—and none of them had ever made him feel the way that Rory did, a helpless, desperate mess of terror and desire.

Gray didn't answer, but Rory must have seen the look that passed across his face—all that starving desperation—and he let go of Gray's hand. "Take your clothes off," he said, casually, like it was of no great importance. Meanwhile, Gray's insides were trembling and his fingers wouldn't cooperate, pawing helplessly at the strings of his tunic.

Finally, Rory took pity on him, and after prepping another cleaner cloth, reached out and began to untie the laces. His nimble fingers moved efficiently and soon Gray was pulling his tunic off, followed by his boots, and then his breeches. He stood in front of a kneeling Rory in only his smallclothes, his cock pulsing awkwardly between them.

He knew what he wanted, but Rory had so little experience. Almost none, by his own admission. What if he didn't even understand Gray's desires?

You may not be a scholar, worthy of delivering a lecture on sexual satisfaction, Gray told himself, but you can always show him. You're better with actions than with words.

"Let me," Rory said, and Gray was hardly going to stop him as Rory reached up and pulled down the cloth hiding his cock. It bobbed free, hard and red and wet at the tip. Gray took a deep breath.

But Rory didn't take him in his hand or even, as Gray had so wished, into his mouth. Instead, he took the clean, damp cloth and ran it down his chest, to the dark hairs that began at his pubic bone. He cleaned him thoroughly and efficiently, but gently, with careful touches that shouldn't have set Gray on fire but did anyway.

He was beginning to realize that anything Rory did had that effect. Him contradicting Evrard? Definitely arousing. Him shoving a knife into a brigand's shoulder? Unexpectedly arousing. Him giving Gray a bath? The most arousing thing in the whole universe.

Finally, just as Gray thought he was not quite above begging, Rory put down the cloth and looked up at him, his gaze steady as he leaned closer. "Let me," Rory said again, and this time it was his tongue on Gray's cock, Gray's head tipping back against the wall as he gasped in pleasure.

"Do you like that?" Rory asked and Gray's only answer was a moan, much louder than he'd intended. "I guess you do," Rory said, and Gray realized as he glanced down, that yes, that was absolutely a smirk on his face.

While Rory might not have had much practical experience, Gray could guess that he'd likely read about this particular act before because he seemed determined to wring every ounce of bone-melting pleasure out of Gray, and did it shockingly well. After only a few moments, Gray already felt alarmingly close to the edge of orgasm, the pressure building inside of him, even as he wanted to make it last. The problem was that Rory was a vixen, teasing and coaxing and impossibly beautiful as his eyes fluttered closed and he slid Gray's cock inside his mouth. I will remember how this feels forever, Gray thought, and his control splintered as Rory twisted his hand and sucked on the head.

It took a long moment for Gray to recover his bearings. The violence followed by the intense bliss he'd just experienced had left him feeling hollow and suddenly exhausted. Finally he glanced down and his heartbeat accelerated again.

Rory was sitting there, his breeches untied, his cock in his hand, his head thrown back and his teeth biting down on that perfectly plump lower lip as he stroked himself.

"Let me," Gray begged this time and when Rory nodded soundlessly, he reached down, his own much larger, much rougher hand joining Rory's, and that was all it took to push him right over the edge into ecstasy.

They cleaned up, and this time Gray refused to let Rory take the cloth. He cleaned Rory, and their hands, and then after fetching a new cloth, carefully wiped the blood spatters off his cheek and neck.

"I guess we should get some sleep," Rory finally said quietly, rising up and walking over to the bed.

It was not a large bed, and for a second, Gray nearly offered to sleep on the floor. But after what they had just done, sleeping close together felt right. So he followed Rory's lead and climbed in next to him, pulling the blankets over them.

"Sweet dreams," Gray said, the tenderness in his voice surprising him as he brushed away a strand of bright auburn hair from Rory's bruised cheek. "May they be better than this place."

CHAPTER TEN

WHEN RORY WOKE UP the next morning, the inn was blessedly quiet.

Gray was still sleeping next to him, stretched out on his back, one hand carelessly thrown across Rory, and the other partially covering his face, no doubt to shield his eyes from the bright morning sunshine spilling from the dingy window. He looked more peaceful and more relaxed than Rory had seen him before, even under the bruises scattered over his face and torso. Rory didn't want to wake him, but in the next moment, one brilliant blue eye opened.

"We're still alive," Gray croaked groggily.

Not quite the romantic words that Rory had hoped he'd hear this morning upon waking; especially after the night before. What did you expect? he thought A confession of love? And maybe he hadn't expected it necessarily, but he'd wanted it. Nobody had ever loved him in spite of being a prince, and Rory discovered that was something he dearly desired. He wanted to be loved not because he was royal, not because he was beautiful, not because he was rich, and not because he spoke so many languages and was famous throughout the kingdoms for his translations and analyses.

After all that, what's left? that annoying voice inside Rory's head asked.

Rory didn't know, and he knew enough to realize that if he himself was in the dark, he couldn't possibly expect another to discover it. Even someone as clever as Gray.

"We're still alive," Rory finally murmured.

Gray groaned and stretched. "You look like you're thinking too hard for this early in the morning."

Rory might be inexperienced, but he knew he couldn't say, *I want you to love me, but I don't know what I want you to love me for.*

"I was thinking of the riddle Evrard told us yesterday, about the cave, and what it could mean," Rory lied.

Gray groaned again. "It's definitely too early to think about anything Evrard says."

Rory secretly agreed but admitting so would also mean admitting he'd lied. "We need to find the ring, the Bearer of Truth," he offered instead. "We should get up and get ready to go. Didn't you say the road up to the mountain is rather difficult?" He didn't want to get out of bed. He wanted to stay here and stay naked with Gray, but he remembered the promises he'd made that night in the valley.

If I get out of this, I will make different choices.

The Rory of old would have self-indulgently let the quest for the ring slide, trading the unpleasant realities of their journey for the much more pleasant pastimes to be found in bed. But he'd already acknowledged that he needed to leave that Rory behind, so instead of reaching for Gray, he climbed out of bed, searching for his clothes.

"You really mean it, don't you?" Gray asked, watching him with eyes suddenly and intently awake.

"Find the ring and take back my throne?" Rory pulled on his tunic. It pulled slightly against his bruised cheekbone as it slipped over his head, and he grimaced. "I do mean it."

Gray was quiet for a long moment. "You are not what I thought you were when we first met."

Glancing back at him, Rory smiled. "I believe the feeling is mutual. I didn't know you were familiar with so much territory outside of the valley, and I didn't know you could wield a sword as well as some of my guardswomen."

"That's one thing I'm good at," Gray grumbled, sliding out of bed and also reaching for his clothes. "Fighting for my life."

When they were dressed, Gray slipped the bar off the door and opened it only a fraction, checking both directions to make sure that nobody had lingered overnight, waiting for them to emerge. But the hallway was empty, and as they descended the staircase, the main common room was quiet.

"Any food?" the innkeeper asked as they paused by the door to the outside yard. "It's included with your room."

Gray looked him up and then back down. Rory was startled to see his gaze suddenly blazing with righteous anger. "I wouldn't take another scrap from your table, sir," Gray said, the edge of his voice hard and uncompromising.

He turned and walked out the door, leaving Rory to scramble to follow.

"Do you think he gave those men information about us?" Rory asked as they walked towards the stables to fetch Evrard. "Why didn't you say so last night?"

"Of course he did," Gray said, his voice still hard. "How else would they know? It's not an uncommon practice."

"Oh," Rory said.

"And I didn't say so last night because I was too . . . distracted to think clearly," Gray admitted, and this time this tone was softer. "A good distraction."

They entered the stables and stopping in front of Evrard's stall, received a snooty look from him. There were people milling about, including a stableboy cleaning out a stall, so he could not speak, but words were often unnecessary for Evrard to express his feelings.

Gray led Evrard out to the water trough, let him drink his fill, and then they both mounted, and rode out of town. The outskirts on the other side of Nargash were equally as poor, but Rory still had a smile on his face that he couldn't quite dismiss.

"I see you two had an interesting evening," Evrard said. "Bruises, Gray?"

"Robbers," Gray said between clenched teeth. "Unsuccessful robbers."

"Did you draw Lion's Breath to fight them?" Evrard asked, his deceptively casual tone cluing Rory in that this was actually a rather important question, though he could not figure out why. Evrard knew that Gray was currently wearing Rory's sword on his belt. Why would it matter if he used it?

"I didn't want to and I didn't have to," Gray said dryly. "I had no intention of motivating them any further." He turned his head to glance back at Rory. "Did your ancestors have to be quite so generous with the gold and jewels on the scabbard? It's like you wanted to announce to everyone you're carrying a priceless weapon."

"I think . . ." Rory hesitated. "I actually think they did want to announce that particular fact."

Gray shook his head in disgust and muttered something under his breath that Rory couldn't quite make out.

"Not everyone is hiding," Evrard pointed out primly.

"No," Gray said, his annoyance clearly spiking. "Just me."

Rory thought that he was also in hiding, and that Evrard spent every moment hiding his true existence from anyone who couldn't understand it, but despite waking up in a seemingly good mood, Gray's mood had worsened with every step Evrard took toward the Karloffs. Rory didn't understand it, but he wasn't stupid enough to ask why.

The road grew rougher and steeper the further they rode, and the further from Nargash they got, the less people they saw on the road. By midday, they had not passed a single traveler in some time, and even though Evrard seemed to be in good spirits, Gray insisted they stop to give him a chance to rest.

"The rest of the way is difficult," was all Gray would say, and even though Evrard grumbled at Gray's lack of belief in his strength, eventually he stopped by a small shallow pond, and drank his fill.

While Evrard was refreshing himself, Rory wandered over to where Gray stood, silently staring at the tall, craggy peaks over-shadowing the road.

"I've been thinking of the riddle Evrard gave us," Rory began. This time it wasn't even a lie.

Gray glanced over at him. "Have you really? Why?"

They'd been riding for several hours from Nargash, and Rory had had lots of time to consider the riddle, how they should approach the search, and how he should approach Gray about his thoughts. He'd remembered how he had managed to convince Gray to accompany them at all; it had been all logic. Emotional entreaties weren't going to work on Gray. Rory was going to have to stick to basic, solid, irrefutable fact.

"Because it's early fall," Rory said, "and those mountains are large. The area between them won't be small, either, and if we want to have a hope of finding this cave before the snows start and we have to give up or freeze to death, we need to use the riddle to figure out where to look."

Gray was silent for a long moment. Rory decided that in this particular case, silence was acceptance, and continued. "Between two mountains of great stature lie veracity, fidelity, and certainty. Tread the peak and scale the valley. Solve the puzzle and gain the ring."

"And that means?"

"I'm not sure yet," Rory admitted.

Gray crossed his arms over his broad chest. "So, when you figure it out, get back to me."

The last thing anyone would ever have accused Rory of being was stupid, and it seemed to him, with several events as evidence, that each time he and Gray grew closer, he always retreated back behind his walls of cold, icy disdain afterwards. It was undoubtedly annoying, but now that he had more than one incident to analyze, it was easy enough to separate out the emotion and compare the differences and the similarities. No doubt Gray would've been upset if Rory told him his reactions were predictable, but it turned out there were very few differences and many similarities. Once he'd realized it, Rory could set aside his own emotional reaction, firmly telling himself getting mad served no real purpose. It wouldn't change Gray's behavior; the only thing that would do that was continuing to chip away at those formidable walls.

That realization reached, it made perfect sense to find a topic of mutual interest. Finding the ring was easily the best choice.

"I do have a few thoughts, though," Rory added hurriedly, not ready to be dismissed quite yet. Not at least until he'd made some progress on demolishing Gray's boundaries.

Raising an eyebrow, Gray motioned for him to continue.

"We begin by breaking down the riddle into its parts. Three synonyms for truth, when the composer could have simply used truth."

"Maybe it was for annoying embellishment," Gray said, his voice warming just enough that Rory was encouraged to continue.

"Or maybe for a purpose," Rory insisted. "So there may be three of something. On top of that, the riddle asks the recipient to tread the peak and scale the valley."

Gray frowned. "Those are . . . switched? Are you sure you remember it correctly?"

Shooting him a look, Rory shook his head. "I'm not wrong. It's tread the peak and scale the valley."

"And that means?"

Though Rory was considered one of the brilliant modern minds, Gray was certainly no slouch either. He cut through all the extraneous information and always managed to single out the most important fact.

"Again, I'm not sure, but I do have an idea."

Gray snorted. "Do I need to pry it out of you?"

"It's . . . it's a stretch. You probably won't like it."

"You're assuming I like any part of this," Gray said dryly.

It shouldn't have hurt. Rory had come to the conclusion that Gray always pushed him away once Rory grew too close for comfort. It wasn't personal. It didn't mean that Gray didn't like Rory as much as Rory liked Gray. In fact, all evidence pointed to the opposite. But despite all that application of logic, he couldn't quite deny the emotional sting of Gray's words.

"Right, of course." Rory hated how flustered he sounded. How emotional. He remembered when he could approach problems rationally for days—for months—on end. But since meeting Gray, he'd never felt as controlled by his emotions as he did now. They fluctuated all over the place—good and bad and every shade in between—and still, despite the annoyance of it, Rory wouldn't trade this experience for a coldly clinical one. Gray made him feel alive in a way he never had before.

He cleared his throat and continued. "My theory is that the riddle is telling us to look in the opposite location than it's actually telling us to. Specifically, since the riddle states we need to search between the two mountains, in the valley located in the middle, I think we need to go higher."

"To the top of the mountains," Gray added flatly. "No, I don't particularly like it. It'll be a lot of extra time and effort and energy misspent if you're wrong."

"And then, there's the question of which mountain."

"Do you have any idea which one it might be?" Gray asked with a frown.

Rory internally cringed. There was so much of this he was piecing together with the theory that the author of this riddle had meant their inconsistencies of verbiage to be secret messages to the listener. But maybe Gray was right after all, and they were simply extraneous authorial flourishes. "It's possible that the number three, based on the number of adjectives used for the word, truth, is somehow related to which mountain we would need to climb. You know the geography of the Karloffs, do you remember any-thing that might help us?"

"Really?" Gray scoffed. "That's what you were hoping for? That I might remember something from a book I read fifteen years ago about a faraway mountain range?"

This time Rory externally cringed. "Yes?"

Gray sighed. "You really are desperate, aren't you?"

"You've met Sabrina," Rory said, raising his chin and trying to remember all the promises he'd made. If I get out of this, I will make different choices. "I can't let her continue to rule in my stead. I must find a way to stop her, and this ring is my best chance. So yes, I am desperate."

The incredulity on Gray's face softened. "I do know her, and I wish the best way to stop her were to march to Beaulieu and put Lion's Breath through her heart, but it seems like it isn't, so I guess I need to trust you."

On this? Rory wondered. Or on everything? But he wasn't naive enough to ask the question out loud, because he knew Gray was burying himself with denial, and Rory probably wouldn't like his answer.

"You do," Rory said. "The number three. Anything to do with that number or what it might represent, when it comes to a mountain."

Evrard had finished drinking, and while he had slowly trotted over, he had surprisingly elected not to involve himself in the conversation he and Gray were having. Evrard refusing to add his opinion wasn't completely unheard of, but it certainly felt unusual, and Rory tucked the thought away to unpack later, when he was working less intently on the problem at hand.

"What do mountains have?" Gray asked rhetorically. "Rocks? Trees? Cliffs?"

"What about water?" Rory asked. "Mountains have streams and rivers, and they usually feed into larger bodies of water."

Suddenly, Gray flashed Rory a bright grin. "Waterfalls! The Larger Karloff, it has three waterfalls! And the biggest one? It's right at the top."

Rory grinned back. "Tread the peak and scale the valley."

"Exactly what I was thinking."

Gray was still smiling and looking at him like he was a miracle as Evrard cleared his throat. "Are we ready to journey to the Larger Karloff then?"

It was hard to tear his eyes away from Gray's handsome, beaming face, but Rory managed it, barely. "We were right, then?"

Evrard glanced down his nose at Rory. "If I knew, wouldn't I tell you?"

"Not likely," Gray muttered, the edges of his lips still curling into that irresistible smile. Rory wanted to tell him how much he liked it when he smiled, but he was afraid his confession might cause Gray's walls to go back up—and that was the very last thing Rory wanted.

"Of course you'd tell us," Rory soothed, but he shot Gray a commiserating look. The list of things Evrard would share did seem to be considerably shorter than the list of things he wouldn't. But maybe that's why he'd repeated the riddle—he'd hoped Rory would be able to solve it, and he had, with Gray's help.

It wasn't the first time Gray had been essential to this quest, and Rory had a feeling that it definitely wouldn't be the last.

I don't ever want to do this alone, he thought, but pushed it aside, because no matter what they were sharing together now, it was impossible for Rory to imagine Gray giving up a future in his valley. It was why he'd agreed to come on this journey at all.

"The Larger Karloff it is," Gray said and mounted, holding a hand out to help Rory mount Evrard—something he'd never done before. It wasn't like Rory wasn't eminently capable of doing it himself, but it meant something for Gray to keep helping him. It made them feel less like two random people coming together to accomplish something and more like a team committed to each other.

"Of course it had to be the Larger Karloff," Gray grumbled as they continued climbing. They'd been heading higher and higher for hours. A little while ago, Gray had suggested that they dismount and walk alongside Evrard, since the incline of the path had made it impossible for Evrard to even trot.

Rory shaded his eyes from the sun and stared up at the looming peak. "Do you think we'll reach the top by nightfall?" he asked.

He almost regretted the question, because Gray frowned, the lines settling deeply into his face. "We need to. I don't want to be exposed out here on the side of the mountain after it gets dark."

Wordlessly, Evrard increased his pace, and Rory scrambled to keep up. "Do you think it's possible the cave is hidden behind the waterfall?" he asked Gray.

Gray shrugged. "I think it'll be a miracle if we find the cave at all. We've figured out one interpretation of Evrard's riddle, but who knows if it's the right one?"

"It needs to be the right one," Rory vowed. He knew they didn't have the supplies to spend weeks, or even days, on the mountain. And there was so little time to lose. He needed to get back to Fontaine, before Sabrina could plan more unpleasant surprises. He also wanted to travel back to the valley, with the hope that maybe some of his guard had survived.

"What are you going to do after you get this ring?" Gray asked. "Waltz right into Beaulieu and shove the ring onto her finger and demand she answer questions?"

Rory frowned. "I don't know."

He'd hoped that Evrard would be able to shed some light on the plan after finding the Bearer of Truth, but despite the subject of their conversation, Evrard stayed frustratingly silent.

"I could put it on," Rory offered. "I could put it on and be interrogated in front of the court."

"She has not truly exposed herself to you, which was no doubt part of her calculated plan," Evrard inserted. Of course, now that he chose to speak up, it was to prove how Rory's suggestion wouldn't work after all.

"Then what is the point of this ring?" Gray demanded. "We're nearly killing ourselves climbing this mountain to get it, and we don't even know who's going to wear it?"

"The plan will be clear in time," Evrard answered serenely.

Rory definitely did not feel as calm as the unicorn, and Gray seemed especially agitated, even for him.

I swore I'd make different choices, Rory thought. My new choices can't be any worse than the old ones.

But the problem was there wasn't any certainty that was true. They didn't know what they'd be forced to face at the top of the Larger Karloff, they didn't know if they'd find the ring, and even if they did, they had no idea how to use it to its best advantage. It seemed to Rory that everything hinged on a series of unknowns, and the realization dimmed even his natural optimism.

Gray was not naturally optimistic, and it showed as their journey continued up the mountain.

They passed the first, lowest waterfall, a small, steady trickle. "The Wash," Gray called it as they walked past.

"It's impressive that you even remember their names," Rory said. He thought he'd known much about the geography of the area, but Gray kept proving that belief to be false. He was incredibly, intimately familiar with the geography of the roads and paths around here, even though technically none of this territory was part of Ardglass.

"My old tutor, Rhys, he loved geography and was always assigning me maps to study," Gray said, in a rough, low voice.

His tutor? Rory wondered what position his father had occupied in Ardglass that Gray would have had a tutor. And then there was the confident certain way he held a sword, which spoke of extensive—and expensive—training that was not usually available to boys who grew up to work on farms.

Who had Gray been before he'd run away? As much as he disparaged Evrard's closemouthed attitude, Gray had plenty of secrets of his own. Secrets Rory didn't expect him to share even if he asked about them.

"Well, that was lucky," Rory said.

"Something like that," Gray retorted darkly.

The sun was falling lower in the sky when they heard the roar of the second waterfall. Much larger than the Wash, it fell in crashing sheets of white-tipped waves to the rocky pond below. "What is this one called?" Rory asked, as they walked by. He kept his voice low, despite the noise. The path had essentially fallen away, and now Evrard was just picking his way through the forest, always heading up, further and further until Rory felt his lungs burn with the thinner air. A ring of trees surrounded the pool, and it seemed that no human had ever been here before. But it was named, and it had been on maps, and Gray had seen them.

"The Thunder," Gray said, turning away. The frown was now ever-present on his face, and Rory knew he was concerned about the coming darkness and the final climb, which was taxing all their energies. They would reach the final waterfall at the top of the mountain, and despite their exhaustion, would need to conquer whatever stood between them and the ring.

But even though Rory felt the echo of fear in himself, he'd also discovered a deep-seated, intense desire to not only survive this test, but to win.

They pressed on, passing by the Thunder without any further comments.

The third and final waterfall—the waterfall all their hopes rested upon—was silent in comparison to the Thunder. They were nearly on top of it before they actually heard it. The sun was setting, but the water was a shining, rainbow-hued wonder of fog and mist, cascading over the smooth cliff into a peaceful, ethereal turquoise pool below. "The tallest waterfall in the Karloffs," Gray said softly.

Rory didn't speak, but peered closer, hoping to see through the thick cloud of mist to what might lie in the darkness behind it.

"We will rest here," Evrard announced, not even consulting Gray, "and you will swim through the pool to the cave behind in the morning. It's not safe to try it in this growing dusk."

"How do you even know there's a cave behind there?" Gray demanded.

Naturally, Evrard ignored this question.

"I suppose a fire would be too much to ask for," Rory said.

The look Gray shot him was what Rory had expected. There was no point in asking for a fire, because he couldn't have one.

"In the morning," Evrard answered instead. "The water will be very cold. You'll need the warmth a fire provides."

If you make it back, was unspoken between them.

Rory arranged a bed of pine boughs and needles, which felt slightly more comfortable than simply curling up on the forest floor. Evrard tucked in between two trees and nibbled at a bit of ivy poking out. Gray did not bother prepping the ground at all, just tucked his cloak around him and sat, cross-legged against a fallen log.

"I'll keep watch," Gray said when Rory gave him a questioning look.

"No," Evrard interrupted shortly. "I will keep watch. You will need your energy, Gray."

Rory was surprised when Gray didn't argue, but maybe he was more tired than he'd let on, because soon his soft snores were resonating throughout the little campsite.

I made different choices was the last thought Rory had before joining him in a deep, dreamless sleep.

"It's called the Veil," Gray said, as he and Rory gazed at the waterfall, which was even more spectacularly eerie in the morning light.

"Do you know who named these?" Rory asked, but Gray shook his head.

"The maps were old," he said. "Very old."

"As old as Evrard?" Rory asked, teasing. It was so much easier to joke with Gray than to face the intimidatingly deep pond and the hidden cave beyond.

"I did hear that," Evrard said stately, coming up next to them. "You should take your daggers, but leave Lion's Breath here," he added.

"For a unicorn that does next to no fighting, you certainly have a lot of opinions on weapons and arming for battle," Gray retorted.

"The unicorn is merely my chosen form," Evrard said. "I could defend myself if required."

"Hopefully it never comes to that," Rory said. The higher they'd climbed yesterday, the pricklier Gray had become, and the more he poked at Evrard. Rory found himself occupying the mediator position in their group, even though he wasn't sure he was very good at it.

But you'll need to be, if you have any hope of being a fair, honest, trustworthy king, he thought.

Gray leaned down and began to unlace his boots. "We'll leave our boots here," he told Rory, "but stay in breeches and tunic. They'll slow us down, but I don't want to fight whatever is back there naked."

If their situation had been less dire, Rory might have impudently responded that he would love to see Gray fight naked. But the concept that they might not win this fight was sobering enough for Rory to keep the thought to himself.

Rory followed Gray's suggestion and left his boots sitting next to Evrard and watched as Gray reluctantly unbuckled the scabbard of Lion's Breath, the gold scabbard shining brilliantly in the sunshine.

Evrard bent his head over the sword as Gray carefully placed the sword next to his boots. It seemed that Gray was far more reluctant to leave the weapon behind than Rory, but then surely that was only because Gray was uncertain which kind of foe they would be facing, and no doubt he wanted every advantage they could find.

This time Rory did not wait for Gray to resurface for him to dive into the pool after him. If the mountain lake had been chilly, but warmed by the sun, the Veil's water was bitterly cold, and it stole Rory's breath.

Still, he forced his legs to churn and his head broke the surface right after Gray's. The frigid water turned Gray's skin pale, and his eyes shone starkly out of his carved white features. "After you," Gray said bitterly, "before we freeze to death."

Swimming helped keep some of the worst of the cold at bay, and luckily the pool itself was not very big. They crossed it in a few minutes, Rory's shorter strokes leaving him slightly behind Gray's longer, stronger ones. When Rory reached the mist, he held his breath, not because of the water, but because of the icy fear clogging his lungs. But as he passed underneath it, nothing happened except air even colder and much darker. A smooth ridge of stone greeted them, and Gray climbed up out of the pool with no difficulty. Rory's hands, shaking with nerves and the temperature, scrabbled helplessly against the smooth stone. He felt his panic rising, making it hard to think—logically or emotionally, or in any way at all. I'm going to die here, freezing and alone, his mind screamed.

But then a hand shot out of the gloom, strong and sure, and Rory would have recognized it anywhere. He grasped it and it hauled him out of the water.

"Thank you," Rory gasped as he shivered in the cool air of the cave.

"It's what I'm here for," Gray said shortly, and then turned away to peer through the gloom.

You're here because I want you to be, because I need you to be, Rory argued inside his own head. But he pushed the stupid thought away because right now it didn't matter why Gray was here, only that he was, and Rory knew he couldn't face any of this alone.

The cave was dark, shielded by the Veil's mist, but even as they crept deeper in, nothing interrupted the smooth stone walls except for a few pebbles Rory stumbled over. "Careful," Gray warned after he'd accidentally sent a few skittering across the floor.

It was all Rory could do to prevent whole-body shivering tremors from overcoming him completely. Putting one foot in front of the other was all he felt capable of.

They'd gone several dozen feet when a voice behind him made everything in Rory freeze.

"I knew I would find you here," a melodious voice exulted. Light shone behind them, and Rory knew what he'd see the moment he turned to face her. Had Evrard known she would appear? If he had, why hadn't he warned them? But of course, what could you possibly bring to fight a cold-hearted, manipulative sorceress?

Rory hesitated, but Gray turned immediately.

"And I you," Gray responded tartly. "You've gotten predictable in your old age."

Rory turned to see the shimmering form of his aunt, golden and perfect, toss her dark hair and smile mysteriously. "Old age? I think not. But you will not live to see it. Or you, my sweet, naive nephew."

"Sweet, but not as naive as you might think," Rory insisted, forcing his teeth not to chatter as he answered her.

She held out her hand. "I assume you are here to fetch this." A shining silver ring shone on her palm. "Truth is so overrated."

"You're wrong," Rory insisted.

Gray fell back into a fighting stance, pulling his dagger from its sheath at his calf. "We will be taking that with us," he answered, his voice cold and deadly.

She laughed, as beautifully as she always had, but now Rory heard a darker, uglier edge to it. Like she was laughing at them, but never with them.

I will make different choices. I have made different choices. I'm not the naive boy you watched ride out of Beaulieu.

Gray was partly responsible for that, but so was the world he'd encountered outside of his tower library's walls.

"I always think the old standards work as well as the flashy tricks," Sabrina said, and to Rory's horror, she closed her fingers tight on the ring, and then began to morph, her human form falling away to reveal the thing that Gray had once admitted to fighting before.

A chimera, that's what she was. Snarling lion head and big bulky body, with the tail of a serpent hissing and spitting as it flicked around her mane.

"A good thing I've had many years to consider how I would have killed you," Gray said roughly and re-gripped his dagger.

Rory knew it had to be bravado talking, because evading a chimera once was luck; they could not hope to defeat it with two small daggers and no other weapons.

She must have known it too, because she roared, crowing her triumph before she'd even achieved it, and it echoed through the cave and must have leaked through the wall of mist. Evrard would have heard it, Rory thought despondently, and he would know they were about to be defeated, if they were not defeated already.

But Gray did not flinch even for a moment, and then, suddenly, the dagger was flying through the air, light flashing along the deadly sharp edge, and landing right in the meat of the creature's broad chest.

Rory's breath caught and he hoped that Gray's impeccably true aim would be enough to defeat her, but the chimera only laughed, the human sound from its lion's jaws eerie and terrible.

The dagger fell from its chest, like it had never even hit her, and Gray gasped, disbelieving.

Rory froze, unsure of what he should do. He could never throw his dagger, not nearly as well as Gray could, and even that, with such perfect aim, had not managed to harm her.

Still, as the chimera began to prowl closer, and Gray still seemed stuck in place, disbelieving that such a flawlessly aimed blow hadn't killed the chimera.

Pulling out his own dagger, Rory stepped in front of Gray and pointed directly at the creature's growling snout. He might be terrified, nearly shaking inside with fear, but he wasn't going to let her touch Gray, not when he'd sacrificed everything he held dear to make sure they made it this far. It wasn't Gray's responsibility to kill his aunt, it was Rory's. She was his flesh and blood, and she had betrayed not only their family, she had betrayed their kingdom.

In the dim light of the cave, Rory's dagger shone less silver, and more bronze. He'd never noticed the particular hue of the blade before, and he wondered, as he tried to hold his ground, what material it was made of, and where Marthe had found it.

"You already know that will not stop me," she announced, her voice rising with exultation. "Finally I will have your blood, and even time will bow to me."

"You will never have his blood," Rory insisted. It was one thing for her to claim dominion over him, but to kill Gray? To hunt him so mercilessly he was forced to escape at a young age and remain in hiding all these years? Anger rose in Rory. How dare she? He swung out and the blow was not particularly skilled or even well-placed, as it only swiped across a single heavily furred leg. It was the kind of blow that likely wouldn't have stopped a human man, never mind a magical creature hell-bent on destroying both of them.

But for some reason the blow didn't glance off the skin, but sank in, bright red blood welling at the cut. She stumbled, clearly surprised, and then glanced down at the blade in Rory's hand.

Her shriek was deafening, and Rory realized very quickly that there was something special about this blade. Something that could actually reach her and could actually cut her. He lunged again and sliced her again, her shrieking tripling in volume.

"Keep going," Gray urged him, "it's hurting her."

But Rory had no intention of stopping now. The serpent kept dodging in and out of the space between them, threatening with its wide, needle-fanged jaws, but then Rory got a particularly lucky blow in and it screeched along with the lion's head as Rory partially cut through its long, sinuous neck.

When Rory had landed five strikes against it, blood gleaming on its fur, on its scales, the chimera took a step back, and then another. And then Gray shouldered him to the side, grabbed Rory's dagger, and right before he stepped up to land a killing blow, the creature disappeared completely, a singed scent to the air as the sound of metal against stone rang through the air.

Rory fell to his knees and with shaking fingers reached for the shining silver ring. He finally closed his hand over it and stood, holding it out to Gray with wonder in his eyes.

"We got it," he said, voice trembling. "We got it."

CHAPTER ELEVEN

When they finally climbed back onto the bank on the other side of the pool, dripping wet, Rory couldn't stop shivering. Evrard had made use of their time in the cave and had rolled together a handful of logs and other small sticks, gathering everything together into something resembling a pile. With trembling fingers, Gray pulled matches out of one of the saddlebags. It took three unsuccessful attempts to get a handful of the pine needles lit, and then another few minutes for the fire to spread to the larger pieces of wood.

Rory was still standing on the wet bank of the pool, staring across the water to the cave where they'd just battled and then defeated Sabrina. One of his shaking hands was clasped tightly around the dagger and the other was clenched in a fist around what Gray presumed was the ring they'd gone in search of. He hadn't spoken, and he'd ignored two of Evrard's kinder entreaties to come over and try to get himself warm.

It was freezing; that was undeniable. But Gray wasn't even sure it was the temperature causing Rory to shake. The letdown after violence and confrontation could be a harsh one, and Rory was undoubtedly not used to the feeling. Gray, who'd spent most of his life poised and ready for the sort of encounter they'd just experienced, felt shaken. He could only imagine the physical and emotional exhaustion Rory was dealing with.

It was one thing to know your aunt wanted you dead; it was entirely another to watch her transform into a chimera in order to accomplish her goal.

"Rory," Gray said patiently, standing despite his cold, aching muscles, and walking over to where he stood motionless on the bank. "Come stand by the fire and get warm."

"Gray is right," Evrard said, likely breaking every rule of the universe by admitting that particular sentence out loud. "Come, before you freeze to death in those wet clothes."

But Rory didn't move and didn't speak.

"Your Highness," Evrard said after a long moment, and this time his tone was not nearly so sympathetic. "Come to the fire and tell me about the cave."

Rory did glance over, but he still didn't move. "Did you know she would be there?" he asked in a small, hard voice.

"I thought she would find a way, yes," Evrard answered gravely.

"Did you know my dagger would wound her where Gray's would not?"

Finally, Rory took one step and then another, stopping right before Evrard, and extending the dagger until it was right under Evrard's aristocratic nose.

"Yes," Evrard admitted. "Bronze is not something magical creatures enjoy. Myself included." He gave a delicate shudder and turned away from the warm glow of Rory's blade.

"We got back here alive, and we have the ring, that's all that matters," Gray pointed out. "We got what we wanted, and we didn't let her stop us."

"She tried to kill me, but we still got the ring," Rory said moodily, and now instead of the misty wall of the Veil, he was staring into the now-crackling fire. It wasn't much of an improvement, but at least he was growing warmer now. Gray understood how he was feeling all too well. He'd felt much the same way after he'd escaped Tullamore, but then he'd had months and years to dwell on it. Which, Gray could admit now, perhaps had not been truly all that advantageous.

"The ring?" Evrard questioned.

Rory's eyes snapped to his, suddenly blazing and alive in a way they hadn't been only a moment before. "The ring! The Bearer of Truth. The thing you sent us in there to find, so we could return to Beaulieu and defeat her once and for all. The thing we needed to take back my throne and rescue Fontaine from her evil grasp."

"May I see it?" Evrard asked, and Rory reluctantly opened his palm. He'd been gripping the unadorned silver ring so tightly it had left a circular indentation in his palm.

"Is it what you expected?" Gray asked, because not only was he curious about the ring's significance and ultimate role in achieving their goals, he also intended to distract Rory from agonizing over his aunt.

"I did not know what to expect." And that, at least, felt like an honest answer.

Rory stared at the ring in his hand. "How will we use it to defeat her? Perhaps we should discuss the plan going forward."

"Your Highness, you should put your cloak on, and sit by the fire, continue to warm yourself," Evrard said, and again, his words felt very honest to Gray. A little too honest.

"I think it's time to divulge this great plan," Gray inserted. "How will we use this ring to defeat Sabrina?"

Before he had met Evrard, Gray never would have believed he'd witness an animal blanch, all the blood rushing from its face. But Evrard defied human understanding, and even though Gray had never personally seen him blanch before, he was not as shocked as he could have been when he did it now.

"It's difficult to explain," Evrard hedged.

Rory's hands curled into fists, and Gray had to work to keep the frustration out of his voice. Evrard didn't tend to respond well to threats. "Explain it anyway. We risked our lives going into that cave to fetch it because you said it was important, and now I want to know why it's important."

When Evrard still did not respond, Rory said with suitably dramatic emphasis, "We almost died."

"It was dangerous, but then you knew it would be. You were armed, including with a dagger I knew could seriously injure her if she appeared."

Gray ground his teeth together. "But we did not know that. I wasted precious time and a dagger strike when if I'd used Rory's, she would have been turned away far quicker with far less danger."

"Some things you should not know, you cannot know," Evrard defended, but there was an undeniable edge of guilt in his voice.

"Does it even work? This ring? What does it even do?" Rory wondered when Evrard stayed silent. He slipped the ring on, and outwardly nothing changed.

"Do you feel any differently?" Gray asked.

"No," Rory said uncertainly. "I don't feel any different and I don't think this ring is going to force me to tell the complete truth. I just think it's . . . a ring." He turned to Gray. "Your eyes are brown," he lied, and anger coalesced into a hard ball inside Gray.

"Why," Gray repeated to Evrard, emphasizing with each crisply uttered word how furious he was, "did we go fetch this ring?"

Evrard sighed. "You went and fetched the ring because I wanted you to. Because you needed to do something before you went to Ardglass and then to Fontaine. When we escaped the valley together, you have to understand, Gray, you didn't even want to assist Rory. You didn't even like him. You distrusted him. And you, Rory, you liked Gray, but you liked him for all the wrong reasons. Because you thought he was attractive and tall and had a nice chest."

Rory made an outraged sound, but there was a swelling inside that chest that Gray couldn't identify and definitely couldn't control.

"You wouldn't work together, and therefore, you wouldn't have survived," Evrard continued. "So I gave you time by telling you that the ring was necessary. You had to work together to get it. I knew it was rumored to be located in rough country and was depending on the fact that you would have to learn to trust each other or fail in the attempt. And you did not fail, you succeeded, far beyond my wildest dreams."

"Wait," Rory said after a long, charged silence. "This isn't . . . this isn't even part of the plan?"

Gray stared at Evrard, incredulous, with fury mounting inside him like a fire roaring out of control, hungrily consuming everything in its path.

"And why do we need to go to Ardglass?" Rory didn't seem particularly angry, just confused.

But Gray? Gray was something else entirely.

"We need to go to Ardglass," Gray said, the words exploding out of him before he could stop them in, "because this . . . this . . . lying creature in front of us has been manipulating us this entire time. My entire life. You think lying about a few weeks of traveling together is bad? Try living with him for fifteen years. Try letting him make every decision, including insisting, when you are eleven years old, that you need to hide who you really are, and keep hiding, even as he insists on helping others regain what they have lost. Name-ly"—Gray paused—"your throne."

"I don't understand," Rory started to say, but Gray was done listening, he was done hiding, he was done blindly following.

"You lied to me," Gray roared, and Evrard ducked his head under his onslaught. Maybe later he would feel guilty for a lifetime of anger and frustration bursting out of him, but now all Gray felt was vindication. "You lied to him. How do we even know that we can get his throne back? You certainly never wanted me to get mine back. Maybe if you wanted me to like him you shouldn't have given him the one thing I always wanted. The freedom to choose for myself. Instead, you picked my escape. You picked my name. You picked my occupation. I've been used and abused by you since the moment you appeared to me. I couldn't help it then, but," Gray said, his voice dropping as the anger exploded out of him, "I can help it now."

Evrard said nothing.

Instead, Rory spoke up again. "I'm sorry, but I don't under-stand," he attempted again. "Your throne? Ardglass? You're not . . . you couldn't be . . ."

Gray had sworn to Evrard that he would never tell anyone who he truly was. He'd kept that promise for fifteen long years, pushing everyone away who ever could have helped him bear that burden, and then when Rory had come along, he had been so twisted up inside and angry, that he'd sworn to himself that he would never tell Rory who he was.

It wasn't like those promises didn't mean anything, they just meant less in the wake of Gray seeing Evrard for what he truly was. A manipulative monster who possibly wasn't any better or more honorable than Sabrina herself.

Gray collapsed onto the fallen log next to the fire and stared moodily into the flames. "My name isn't Gray. It's Graham."

"You're the lost prince," Rory said, awestruck.

"I told you I was lost," Gray said bitterly. "I didn't lie about that."

Rory's eyes flashed, not with anger, but with understanding. "That's why you can wield Lion's Breath, you were trained to fight with a sword. And the tutor! Of course you had a tutor, you were a . . . you're a prince."

"I'm not," Gray said flatly, but that wasn't quite true, and he knew it. He was a prince. Even if he wasn't sure he wanted to be.

But that didn't stop Rory. He kept going. "All your knowledge of the road through the edge of Ardglass. The Karloff geography. And Nargash. You knew all that stuff because you were . . . that was going to be yours, someday." Rory turned to Evrard, and this time it was his expression that was accusatory. "You told him not to tell me?"

Evrard's voice was soft. "I told him not to tell anybody. It wasn't safe. Sabrina wanted him; she still does."

"You couldn't have possibly thought . . ." Rory scoffed. "I never would have . . ."

"You liked him for all the wrong reasons, at least at first. You thought he'd help you understand why all your texts talked about sex in reverent tones," Evrard said, and this time his own voice cut deep. "You wanted something from him, but you didn't really want him. To you, he was just a simple farm boy, one you'd remember fondly when you left the valley. But you still had every intention of leaving."

"I didn't . . . I mean I wouldn't," Rory insisted, but even though Gray didn't want to, he heard the echo of the lie in Rory's voice.

"That is exactly what you thought," Evrard said, relentless. "If I must face up to my own shortcomings, then, at the very least, we must all be honest with each other."

"I . . ." Rory hesitated. "I might have thought that then," he finally admitted. "I did think that, very briefly, while we were still in the valley. But then Gray rescued me and then he kept rescuing me, and when we were taken by the tribe, and I rescued him, he looked at me like . . ."

Rory looked at Gray, and his heart was in his eyes.

"I looked at you like what?" Gray demanded. Except that he already knew what Rory was going to say, because the memory of that moment was bright and vivid in his own mind, refusing to fade away.

"Like you saw more than just Prince Emory, a pretty, useless little prince with all his books and his forgotten, dead languages," Rory said quietly. "And I knew by then that I saw more than just Gray, the man who owned a farm and shoveled manure in squash patches."

"Without this time, you never would have seen each other for who you truly are," Evrard said. "I am sorry I lied. I am not sorry that the methods resulted in you trusting one another. I am sorry that you will no longer trust me," Evrard said, and Gray would grant him this: the apology did sound genuine. It also sounded like Evrard—an apology mixed in with a reminder that he'd made the right choices and all his manipulations had worked out in the end.

"I don't think that's necessarily true," Rory said cautiously, despite the looks Gray kept shooting him. He had no intention of trusting Evrard again. He'd exposed them to the greatest possible danger and for what? To build trust? So he and Rory would like each other? In the overall scheme of things, why did that even matter? After all this was finally over, Gray knew he would return to the farm in the valley, and Rory would go on to become the ruler of Fontaine.

"I think his excuses smell worse than a load of dung," Gray muttered.

Rory came over and plopped down on the log next to Gray. "I know you feel betrayed," he murmured, "but there's something you're missing here. I know I couldn't do any of this without you, and if I'd asked you to come to Fontaine, to help me oust Sabrina, you never would have agreed. You definitely would never have agreed to go to Ardglass."

Gray didn't like it, but he had no choice but to nod. After all, how could he remain angry at Evrard's lies if he himself continued to twist the truth?

"Sometimes, we commit dishonorable actions for the greater good. Like when you told me your name was Gray, not Graham. You thought there was a chance I was an emissary of my aunt and I could betray you. That's why Evrard did this; not because he liked the idea of lying, but because without your help, there would be no chance of defeating my aunt or regaining my throne."

When Gray looked up, Evrard had also approached. Gray frowned.

"Prince Emory is partially correct," Evrard said. "I said I would be honest, going forward, and I shall be. Rory needing your help to regain what he has lost is not the only reason you are here, Gray. You are here because you are not really Gray, you are Prince Graham of the kingdom of Ardglass, and it's time you remembered that."

"You spent the last fifteen years hoping I forgot it," Gray objected.

"I never wanted you to forget who you were. Gray and Prince Graham are not two separate men," Evrard insisted. "They are two parts of one complete whole. You didn't just survive in the valley, you built yourself a miniature kingdom. You prepared for strays, and when they passed through, you took care of them. You continued to build and improve upon the foundation you were given when we first arrived. You never accepted, you always pushed for more, for better, for me and for yourself. Does that sound like an unambitious farmhand to you? Or does that sound like a man who is born to lead a kingdom of people who depend on him?"

Evrard's question was one that both required contemplation and also one that Gray thought he knew the answer to immediately. Of course, he had never thought of his life in the valley in precisely those terms before, but nothing that Evrard said was technically untrue. He had done all those things, he had planned and worked and never settled. That was how Rhys had raised him, and those lessons, instilled at a very young age by someone that Gray worshiped, respected and admired, had persevered, right alongside Gray himself.

"Do you remember," Evrard continued, his voice softening, as his head dipped closer to Gray, just as he'd done when Gray was much younger, "when I told you that you would need to be brave and strong and loyal?"

Gray froze. He remembered those words like they'd been said yesterday, but it hadn't been Evrard who'd said them. It had been Rhys, on that last fateful night, when his warning had helped Gray escape with his life.

"I will need to remember them," Gray said, a thought dawning on him that had never occurred to him before, even though Evrard had given him all the pieces through the years. "Rhys never died, did he? You only hinted that he did. Rhys was never Rhys, he was you."

Evrard's eyes were fond as they gazed at him. "I wondered if you would ever realize it."

"You came to Tullamore to be my tutor knowing what would happen," Gray said slowly, disbelieving that not only had Evrard been the stalwart, somewhat smug companion of his last fifteen years, but the dear, kindly disciplinarian of his first eleven. A man he still remembered with great fondness. "You came to protect me."

"I have only ever wanted to protect you, my prince," Evrard said, his skin beginning to glow, like a lantern, lit from within. It was the first time, Gray realized, that Evrard had called him that in fifteen years.

He did not know what to do with it. He had spent so long trying to let that part of himself go, only to discover that not only had he never been able to shake it, it was an unassailable, undeniable part of what made him who he was. "I came to Tullamore to protect you. I helped you escape to protect you. I even lied to you to protect you. I know you felt disparaged and set to the side when I asked you to help Rory. You believed that your throne was a thing of the past, but it is not. The situation in Ardglass is complex, but we must still travel there, and you must still reveal yourself to all of Tullamore. It is time."

After their ordeal, Evrard had insisted they stay another night alongside the Veil. Gray, who was unexpectedly worn out from his earlier anger and the emotional revelations, hadn't argued. Instead, he'd gone off alone with his dagger, throwing it and killing several squirrels, which he cleaned and prepped to roast over the fire.

He'd apologized to Rory, because while he might be used to eating such rough fare, surely the other prince was used to better.

"It's a hot meal," Rory argued, "I don't care."

The hunting trip had also given Gray some space, which he hadn't realized he'd needed after traveling in such close quarters with Rory and Evrard for the last week. He was far more used to being alone, with occasional visitors for company, and even though he found himself enjoying Rory so much more than he'd ever anticipated, some quiet wasn't a bad thing.

After dinner, he'd gone off to sit on the banks of the Veil, hoping the quiet mist would help to silence all the questions that kept bombarding his brain. He wasn't ready to ask them out loud yet, but they swarmed him anyway.

It didn't come as a surprise that a few minutes after he'd left, Rory left the warmth of the fire and plopped down next to him.

"How are you doing?" Rory asked.

Gray wasn't particularly keen to share in the best of circumstances, but after the day he'd had? "Maybe there's a simpler question you could ask," he told Rory wryly.

"It's quite a bit to assimilate," Rory agreed. "I keep getting stuck in the most inconsequential of facts, like you knew exactly who I was when I rode into the valley."

"I hadn't actually ever seen a picture of you," Gray admitted. "But the last time I'd been in the village, they were talking about you, and why you hadn't assumed the throne yet. I usually stayed far away from any sort of political discussion, but I needed the supplies. I do remember wondering why they kept calling you the Autumn Prince. Then you introduced yourself, and I understood instantly."

Rory flushed brightly enough that it was obvious even in the falling dusk. "It's a ridiculous nickname," he said.

"No." Gray lifted a hand and stroked a single curl resting against his cheek. "It's a perfect nickname." He cleared his throat. "It occurred to me that if things had been different, we wouldn't have met in a patch of squash, while I was shoveling dung."

"We'd have met across a banquet table or in a throne room," Rory said quietly. "I thought it too. That was actually my very next thought."

"It would've been easier maybe, but not any different," Gray said after a long silence. "Not for me anyway."

Rory reached over and placed his hand over Gray's much larger one. "Not for me either."

"I guess if I have to go back to Ardglass, I'd rather do it with you by my side."

"I would've thought that you'd be eager to do it, to take back what you lost. I feel like we can't get back to Fontaine quickly enough," Rory admitted.

"Going back to Ardglass means seeing my father again, and I would rather never have seen him again," Gray said. He knew how harsh his tone was, but it felt like it wasn't quite harsh enough.

"I guess you'd come to terms with the fact that you wouldn't be going back." Rory hesitated, but Gray moved his hand, tangling his fingers with Rory's, giving them a reassuring squeeze.

"I was just thinking," Rory finally continued, his voice dropping until Gray could barely hear it, even though they were pressed closely together, "that if I were you, I'd want to talk to someone. Then I remembered that I'd been in a similar position, and I did have people to talk to. I had my guard. Marthe and Anya and Rowen. Diana and Acadia. I miss them. I'll probably never know what happened to them."

"You could," Gray pointed out.

"No," Rory insisted. "We have far more important things to do. And I didn't come over here to complain, not when you've faced far more than I ever have. I don't have a right to whine that I've lost them, not faced with what you've lost."

"It's not a competition," Gray observed.

Rory gave a short laugh. "No, no, of course not. You're right. I just . . . I wish I knew what happened to them. If they were all dead or maybe if they survived, and I could have done something to help them. After everything they did to help me. Marthe gave me this dagger, you know, the day we left Beaulieu. She said she'd had it made especially for me.

And I couldn't help but think today that she knew and she hoped that it would be helpful when we came to fight Sabrina."

"She was a good friend to you, then, not just a captain of your guard," Gray stated. He hadn't gotten the impression that Rory had been the kind of prince to spend time training with his guard.

"She was, at the very end. And it made me realize that she was probably a good friend to me the whole time, yet I barely ever acknowledged her existence." Guilt edged Rory's voice. "I took that friendship for granted."

"You don't think I took things for granted? It was so silly, but I wished for years that Rhys hadn't died, that he'd been able to come with me, and now today, I realize he did, and I never knew it." Gray sighed. "Evrard can be hard to get to know, but I never really tried. I lost myself in the work that I was convinced needed to be done, and never reached out to him."

"He could have reached out to you, too," Rory pointed out.

"Yes, he could have. Not exactly his strong suit, reaching out." Gray gave a dry chuckle. "We can't look back. We can't live with guilt and regret, not when we have so much else to face."

"It's hard to let it go," Rory admitted.

"That's why I know it's the right thing to do. The right thing is always harder than anything else," Gray said, and to his surprise, he believed his own words. He hadn't realized that the questions didn't necessarily need to be answered, only that he needed to talk to someone, and if he could ever have a choice of someones, it would always be Rory. Another unsettling revelation.

The next morning, Gray doused the fire with a handful of water from the pool, and then stamped it out as Rory strapped the saddlebags back onto Evrard.

"One thing," Gray said casually as he placed a hand in Evrard's mane, ready to mount and continue their journey, "I think we should stop in the valley first, on our way to Tullamore."

"What? Why?" Evrard sounded genuinely astonished at Gray's request, and when he glanced over at Rory, he saw Rory's eyes had grown huge in his face. He hadn't expected it either.

"Because it wouldn't be a bad idea to fetch more supplies, and I'm nearly certain that some of the members of Rory's guard survived the attack, and it wouldn't be a bad idea at all to ride into Tullamore with some experienced fighters loyal to the Crown Prince of Fontaine at our backs."

Evrard was quiet, clearly considering the suggestion. Before, Gray knew he would have simply shut it down, because the idea hadn't been his, but Gray could tell he was making an effort to be more inclusive in his planning.

"I can see the advantages to the suggestion," he admitted, "and it's not very far out of our way."

"It's not," Gray agreed.

Evrard, because he was Evrard, drew out the suspense for another moment by appearing to still be considering the request, but Gray knew he'd already made up his mind. "Yes," he finally said, "we will stop by the valley first, and see if any of Rory's guard survived, as well as add to our supplies."

Gray gave a sharp nod of agreement, and mounted. Rory paused, placing a hand on Gray's arm. "Thank you," he said quietly, "this means so much to me."

Clearing his throat, Gray stared at the trees ahead. Initially he hadn't really done it for Rory, but now, he realized that maybe he had. And maybe that wasn't something he should be ashamed of. "You're welcome," he said.

Evrard took off at a solid canter, clearly not wanting to lose any more time. "What should I call you?" Rory asked, raising his voice to be heard over Evrard's hooves pounding against the ground. "Should I call you Graham or . . .?"

"I'm Gray," Gray replied. "I've been Gray too long to be anything else."

"Prince Gray it is then," Rory said, the edges of his tone impudent, and Gray couldn't help but smile too. "I like it."

Secretly, Gray liked it too.

CHAPTER TWELVE

On their return trip, they avoided Nargash, riding around the dilapidated village and camping far on the other side. It was much easier for Evrard to ride down the hill than up, and it took significantly less time than it had on the front end.

"I'm not taking that chance a second time," Gray said dryly as he dismounted from Evrard. "I don't have a death wish, unlike some people." He nudged Rory's shoulder, and Rory caught a glimpse of his grin before he turned away to get the fire going for the night.

It was only a day after all the revelations and their agreement to be more straightforward with each other, but Rory swore that with every hour that passed, Gray stood a little straighter and glowered far less. He hadn't hidden his lack of excitement about returning to Ardglass and facing his father, but Rory still believed that slowly dismantling his secrets was already improving his mood.

"I don't have a death wish," Rory shot back.

Gray turned, flashing that quicksilver grin again. "The number of times you've managed to place yourself directly between me and danger tells a different tale." He had his dagger out and was moving further into the woods. In search of more kindling or dinner for the night, Rory wasn't sure.

"I haven't . . ." Rory spluttered. Except that he had. First, with the tribe, and then with Sabrina. The first had been more of a calculated risk—Rory had had time to weigh the hazard and the likelihood of whether there might be another chance of escaping—but the second time, when Gray's dagger had glanced off Sabrina's magical creature? That had been pure instinct, with no time to think, only to react. He'd done it because the idea of living without Gray, without his quiet, steadfast loyalty at his side and watching his back, seemed unthinkable. And despite what Evrard had said, Rory had done it before he had any idea of Gray's royal background, and it hadn't mattered if Gray only had the valley and the farm. He'd loved him and wanted him regardless of what property and prestige he could bring to Rory.

Rory's hands froze on the saddlebags as he was unstrapping them from Evrard's back.

Evrard made an impatient noise and tossed his great silvery mane at Rory's hesitation. "Those do not feel particularly nice, you know," Evrard chastised as Rory still didn't move. "They can chafe most unpleasantly."

But how could Rory perform a task as mundane as unfastening the saddlebags when his brain and his heart were alight with the knowledge that he'd stepped without hesitation between Gray and danger, and it was all because he loved him?

Craning his head, Evrard finally got a look at Rory's face. "For goodness' sake," Evrard said, his words punctuated with an impatient shake of his tail. "Look at you, mooning. I suppose you just realized why you stupidly stepped between him and Sabrina. He's not going to like it that you didn't tell him before you knew who he really is. He's going to think it's because you discovered he's just like you."

Rory glared at the unicorn. "It's not because of that at all. And the only reason he might think that way is because of what you said to him yesterday. A nice chest? Really?" He flushed, thinking of the embarrassment he'd felt. He'd worked hard to be taken seriously, and then Evrard had tried to ruin it by confessing every humiliating thing Rory had ever imagined.

"It helped for him to think you were hiding things too. Even if they were an unnatural appreciation for his pectoral muscles."

Rory's fingers finally resumed their nimble work and he dragged the saddlebags off Evrard's back with an annoyed glare in the unicorn's direction. "It isn't an unnatural appreciation. They are very fine and absolutely worth appreciating."

"Perhaps that isn't the compliment you should be leading with, when you tell Gray how you feel." Evrard looked at him contemplatively. "The question is, which should you lead with?"

Rory dumped the saddlebags next to the area they'd cleared for the evening's camp. "That is something for me to decide. How I tell Gray how I feel is not subject to a discussion."

"But you've never done this before," Evrard pointed out. "You might not realize you were going about it the wrong way."

Wrenching off his cloak, Rory tossed it down and began picking up sticks and moss. "And you have?" he challenged.

When Evrard didn't immediately answer, Rory finally looked up from the pile he was constructing. Evrard's expression was solemn, and somehow horribly gut-wrenching. Gray had barely shared any information about his past, but Evrard had always been even more tight-lipped, to the point of always giving generic information instead of personal anecdotes. It was entirely possible that Evrard had a deeply hidden, secretive past, full of love, loss, and heartbreak.

"I'm sorry, I presumed . . ." Rory stammered.

Evrard tilted his head, accepting the apology. "I believe in the past I have spoken to you of assuming other forms. There were many periods of many years when I did not occupy the form of a unicorn, when I was a man. And yes, during those times, I experienced much."

"Including love," Rory stated softly, and Evrard did not necessarily say, but the stark look in his eyes made it clear that all those love affairs had not ended happily.

When Gray returned, Rory had cobbled together a pile of kindling and moss, waiting for the larger pieces of wood and the matches to light it. He shot Rory an approving look. "I see you've been watching me," he teased, and this new, lighter Gray who teased and whose smiles set Rory's nerves alight, was definitely different and definitely not unwelcome.

"I like watching you," Rory teased right back.

"We're all very aware of that," Evrard inserted, his dry tone nearly matching one that Gray had utilized on many occasions. It occurred suddenly to Rory that maybe that was where he'd initially come by it.

"I brought dinner," Gray added, holding up a nice fat hare that he'd already skinned. "And before you moan about me killing animals to keep our bellies full, this one was already wounded by a fox I scared off."

Rory rolled his eyes. "I never said I had a problem with you feeding us."

"I saw your eyes when I skinned the squirrels the other night," Gray retorted, even though his eyes were still a warm, reassuring blue. "There's nothing wrong with feeling bad about it, but I'm still going to do it. We need to eat."

"Prince Emory is a sweeter, gentler soul," Evrard proclaimed, even though Rory did not necessarily agree with that pronouncement. He just hadn't had a lot of opportunity to see animals being skinned before, because while he might not be sweeter or gentler, he knew he'd grown up far more sheltered than Gray had.

"No, he really isn't," Gray said, rolling his eyes. "And please don't start with that Prince Emory crap. You know his name is Rory. You've called him that plenty of times. I guess I should be grateful you haven't whipped out Prince Graham yet, though I'm sure that's coming any moment now."

"It's important you remember where you came from," Evrard argued. "I'm afraid we've been too informal on this journey."

"Not informal enough," Gray countered, lighting the fire and gently placing the smoking moss inside the pyramid of kindling that Rory had constructed. "We've been fighting for our lives half the time we've been on the road. I'm not worried about bowing or scraping."

"No, you wouldn't be," Evrard said flatly.

Gray didn't respond, just kept tending the fire until a few minutes later, it was blazing warmly. He sat down on a nearby log and began to use his knife to construct a large fork for cooking the hare over the fire. Evrard trotted closer, settling near the log, but Gray ignored him.

"It feels easier, now that you've told one person, especially since it's someone you care about." Gray didn't bat an eyelash at Evrard's terminology, but Rory figured he was also trying very hard to ignore a very persistent unicorn. "But it's going to feel differently when we ride into Tullamore and everyone is staring at you, and yes, everyone will be bowing and scraping. How will you feel then?"

The dagger in Gray's hand stilled. Rory watched as he breathed in and then out again. "Like a fraud," he finally admitted.

"Then you should get used to it now, Your Highness," Evrard insisted.

Gray resumed his whittling, his dagger making short, angry strokes against the soft wood he was shaping. "I don't have to like it," he finally said, his words sharp. "I just have to live with it."

Tentatively, Rory sat down next to Gray—close, but not close enough that he'd be in danger of the sharp edge of the dagger—and reached out and put a reassuring hand on Gray's suddenly tense shoulder. He wasn't thrilled that Evrard had forced the issue now, not when Gray had been so much happier and so much lighter today. Rory shot Evrard a disgruntled look. It was clear Evrard could read some thoughts though he had never explained the extent of his ability. So Rory thought very hard in his direction, Couldn't you have saved that for another day? Didn't you see how happy he was to tell someone? To tell me?

Evrard tilted his head sideways and the clear expression on his beautiful face made it clear he'd understood every word and wasn't particularly pleased at Rory's thoughts. Too bad, Rory thought again.

"You may be both men—Gray and Prince Graham—but we know which has taken precedence in the intervening years since you were last in Tullamore. Perhaps Prince Emory and I should give you a refresher course on courtly etiquette."

Gray's expression went from slightly frustrated to downright disgruntled.

"Not happening." He grunted as punctuation to the denial, proving, at least in Rory's mind, that maybe a few etiquette lessons might not go amiss.

"In Tullamore, perhaps, rude and crude behavior might not be remarked upon," Evrard retorted, "but in Beaulieu? The crown jewel of Fontaine, where the Autumn Prince studies in his castle tower with all his intelligence and grace?"

His pronged fork complete, Gray shoved his dagger into the ground blade-side down and grabbed the hare, unceremoniously mounting it and holding it over the fire. "Feel free to tell him off," Gray said, directing his comment towards Rory, but not bothering to look his way. The wall, which Rory had so painstakingly been tearing down, piece by piece, brick by brick, was back up, and it felt pricklier and sturdier than ever. Rory shot Evrard another glare.

"Beaulieu is a gracious place," Rory allowed, "he isn't wrong about that. But he's wrong about me. I've never fit in there. I wasn't intelligence and grace. I was awkward and uncomfortable and much preferred the company of my books."

Gray didn't say anything.

"We are really not that much different. I'm hardly a prince, no matter what pretty names they call me," Rory continued, all too aware of how desperate he sounded. "If I were a true prince of Fontaine, I wouldn't have hidden away from my duties and let Sabrina take my throne in the first place."

"That we can agree on," Evrard murmured.

It seemed like the kind of comment that Gray never would have let go unanswered, but now he merely sat, turning the hare to brown it evenly on all sides. His silence was more infuriating than any of his bitter retorts. See what you've done, Rory thought in Evrard's direction, now he won't talk to either of us.

"When you have finished sulking," Evrard added, "we will be ready to discuss the plan moving forward."

But Gray, who had been all eagerness to hear Evrard's plan after they'd fetched the useless Bearer of Truth, said nothing.

Rory threw up his hands and went to search for a stream to fill their water flasks. The quiet of the forest helped Rory feel less like he'd like to leave Gray and Evrard to seemingly annoy each other to death, and after a few minutes of walking, he began to smell moisture on the air. It was one of the tricks Gray had taught him to figure out if water was near. When Rory bent down to check the earth, it was damp with moisture. When after a few hundred yards, he came upon a bubbling brook, he smiled even though nobody was there to see his success. Still, Gray would enjoy his triumph later when he was thirsty, Rory thought as he filled up the skins with cool, refreshing water.

When he came back to camp, the hare was done roasting, and Gray silently divided up the portions as Evrard stood at the edge of the camp, chewing happily on some tender clover.

Gray poked at the fire as he ate, clearly grumpy and wanting to be left alone. Rory decided he had no intention of disturbing him, and instead curled up in his cloak on the other side of the fire, staring into the flames and picturing each of the texts he was going to study when he finally returned to Beaulieu.

Evrard announced he was going to find the stream, and went flouncing off, mane and tail rippling with what Rory could only identify as annoyance.

"One day and we're already at odds again," Rory said morosely, mostly to himself since he had no expectations of Gray actually answering him.

To his surprise, Gray looked up, his eyes dark in the firelight. "That's all I wanted," he muttered, "a little respite. A day or two not to think about anything, to be happy that I was actually able to tell someone—you—who I was. And instead the stupid unicorn starts in on etiquette and Your Highness." Gray shoved the dirt at his feet with his boot. "Sometimes I don't know how we survived each other."

Rory had also wondered occasionally how that had worked—but then the valley had been fairly good-sized, and he assumed that most days there hadn't been any obligation for Gray or Evrard to actually converse about anything at all. He didn't think it would help Gray's mood to point out that it was likely they'd survived their life together before by never talking about anything of actual importance.

"And then, sometimes," Gray continued, his voice growing softer and less frustrated, "I don't know how I would have survived without him."

"He saved your life," Rory pointed out dumbly, and then flushed. Of course Gray knew that. Gray knew that better than anybody else. Without Evrard's help, he would have died in Sabrina's dungeon, likely drained of his blood, and she would have become invincible. Rory's life too, probably would have been forfeit, along with his parents, because one kingdom wouldn't have sufficed if two were available for the taking.

"He knows me better than anyone else, and that's not always a comfortable thing," Gray admitted. His voice dropped. "I'm not ready to face anyone bowing to me. I'm not ready to be Prince Graham again. Maybe not ever again. I don't know. And a few days isn't going to change anything, but he's annoyingly right. I suppose I should start thinking if I can face it."

"We're going to Ardglass," Rory said, still feeling stupid, which wasn't something he normally faced, but there was something about Gray that brought out the worst—and yet, the best—in him. "How could you possibly avoid it?"

"The whole court believes Prince Graham to be lost or dead. I don't have to be him. I could just be Gray. I'm lost, remember? Nobody's looking for me." Gray chuckled darkly.

Rory tried to reel in his shock and didn't succeed very well. "What about your father? You'd come face to face with him and not acknowledge that you are his son? Surely he knows you live? And surely he would recognize you?"

Gray shrugged, seemingly unconcerned about his father, which Rory couldn't quite believe. If he'd had any opportunity at all to know his parents, he would have taken every chance, suffered any price. Gray's attitude was baffling to him.

But then Rory's parents hadn't forced him to run away as a child.

"I'm not sure he thinks of anything anymore besides his women and his drink," Gray said. "I doubt he even remembers that he once had a son."

Rory thought even if King Gideon was as far gone in his vices as Gray insisted he was, he could not possibly forgotten his son. Even though Evrard's methods could sometimes be a trifle overbearing and absolutely underhanded, Rory could understand some of his frustration with Gray. There was a well of bitterness and anger deep inside him, and Rory had a feeling that it fueled many of his beliefs.

It definitely fueled the wall that kept Rory out.

"I don't think you should return to Tullamore as anyone but yourself," Rory said, a trifle recklessly. Gray would likely not agree with him, and it might push him away even further, but one thing Rory had learned from his years hiding in the great library tower of Beaulieu was that hiding never altered a situation for the better. "Whether you want to be or not, you are a prince, and you are your father's heir. Don't make him hide that part of you away. If anyone should feel shame for what transpired, it is him—not you."

Gray was quiet for so long that Rory worried that he might have done irreparable damage. Maybe Gray would never talk to him again, he thought morosely, but at least Gray might finally decide being lost was overrated. Some good might come of this journey, even if it never resulted in the love Rory felt being returned.

"That's why I want to hide," Gray admitted very quietly, still staring into the fire. "I'm afraid he won't feel any shame."

Rory couldn't imagine what that might feel like; his parents had loved him very much and had never wanted to leave him alone. It was inconceivable that a father would cast a son away, willingly.

"I'm sorry," he said, knowing the words were not enough. His heart was breaking for Gray; even as he'd lived with his father's rejection and betrayal, he'd grown into a fine man and a fine leader. Perhaps Rory could not exactly fault him for the bitterness and anger that overflowed out of him occasionally.

"Why are you sitting over there?" Gray changed the subject and then shot Rory a diminished grin, an echo of what he'd done earlier in the evening. But he'd still tried, despite all the fears and worries weighing heavily on his mind.

Rory raised an eyebrow. "Because I was afraid I might get my head bitten off?"

Hanging his head, Gray laughed, the sound rusty. "I guess I can't fault you for that. I'm sorry for my rotten moods."

"I'm only sorry for the cause of them," Rory pointed out earnestly, picking up his cloak and moving around the fire to where Gray was sitting. "Is this seat taken?"

"No, Your Highness, it's been waiting all night for you," Gray said, and the smile on his face was deep and genuine.

Maybe Gray was not in as much need of an etiquette refresher as Evrard had believed.

Rory sat down, and Gray put a hand on his knee, squeezing it gently. "I really am sorry," he said, and sounded earnest. "And I'm sorry for not telling you, before. I can't even say I wanted to, because I didn't. I was afraid it would change things. I was afraid that it would give everything between us weight."

It was impossible not to feel the sting of his words. Rory had wanted whatever they shared to have weight, but Gray had been hoping the whole time that it wouldn't.

Gray must have seen the hurt flash across Rory's face, because he flushed, and stammered out an explanation. "No, that's not what . . . I mean it was, but not for the reason you think. I remember thinking that you could never know, because you'd think I could leave the valley, maybe even come to Fontaine with you—and at that point, I didn't even consider it a possibility. I was lost and couldn't see beyond staying lost. I'm still not sure I can, even though there's a voice inside telling me that it's time to rejoin the land of the living. It could be Evrard, but I don't think it is. I think that voice is the part of me who wants more, who wants you."

Taking a deep breath, Rory was really proud of how steady his voice stayed. "If you still want to stay lost, you can. I . . . I really care about you." He couldn't quite manage the word love, just yet, but he was trying. "I want you with me, but I won't . . . I can't ask you to abandon the life I promised to help you reclaim. That would be selfish."

Gray smiled, soft and sweet, and reached up to cup Rory's cheek. "God forbid you get selfish," he murmured.

They'd never kissed before when there wasn't violence or undeniable need pounding in their blood. Rory hadn't known that when their lips met tonight, their secrets laid bare, it would make such a difference. It didn't feel anything like that first, charged kiss they'd shared in the forest after Rory had saved them from the nomadic tribe, or in the lake, cold and wet, or even after escaping the bandits who'd hoped to rob them. It felt both new and old, and Rory knew he'd never felt closer to Gray than he did at this moment. As Gray angled his head, kissing him sweetly and then deeply, the fire of desire rising in their blood, Rory realized while Gray might be rebuilding some of his walls, he was doing it with Rory inside. As hard as it was, Gray was opening himself up to him, one confession and one hard-won truth at a time. Evrard might have been with Gray the longest, but Rory was no longer sure that he truly knew him the best, after all.

Their kiss was beginning to turn heated, Rory panting lightly into Gray's mouth as Gray's hands skated across his chest and then lower, briefly stopping at his waist before reaching in and rubbing at the front of his breeches, where Rory was hard and aching.

"I may take to wearing bells," Evrard said wryly, making Rory jump as Gray pulled his hand away from his hard cock.

"Yes," Gray said, and Rory felt inordinately pleased at the rough edge to his tone. All this annoyance was because they'd just been interrupted—not because Evrard kept pushing him. "Some bells or another sort of auditory signal might come in handy, especially if you keep sneaking up on us."

Evrard sniffed. "I had not realized that you two had progressed to the point of nightly romantic rituals," he said.

Gray rolled his eyes. "You're a meddling fool, so I'm going to let that one slide."

"Next time, I will announce my appearance more obviously," Evrard conceded.

"You do that," Gray retorted, but his tone was amused rather than annoyed. Maybe their "romantic ritual" hadn't solved all—or any—of Gray's problems with his past or his future, but it had seemed to lift his dark mood.

Rory started to move a little further away, when Gray leaned down, and caught him by the shoulder with one firm hand. "Evrard always sleeps soundly after clover and a drink. After he falls asleep, we'll head into the woods towards the stream. There's a cluster of trees, in the middle of a clearing."

That much was something Rory had also observed, but he didn't know why they needed to sneak off to indulge in more "romantic rituals." Couldn't they do it here, a respectable distance from Evrard?

"He hears everything," Gray said, and the look in his eyes made it very clear he had no intention of letting Evrard observe any more of their relationship. Since Gray had grown up with Evrard, that did make quite a lot of sense. "Come with me, please," Gray added, and Rory would have to be deaf not to hear the pleading note in his voice—desperation that Rory felt right along with him.

"Yes," Rory said. "After he starts that snoring noise he likes to claim he doesn't make."

It took Evrard an unconscionably long time to make the noise that signaled he was well and truly asleep. Rory, who had restlessly been pretending to sleep, but in actuality waiting for the sound that meant they were in the clear, stood almost immediately after it began. Gray appeared the next moment, reaching out in the darkness and clasping his hand. "Come," Gray said, and even though it was pitch black, began to lead them through the forest, to the clearing he'd described earlier.

Rory's heart was beating quickly, both in anticipation of what might occur once they made it to the clearing, and also at how eagerly Gray kept pulling him along, like he too couldn't wait until they were finally alone.

They reached the clearing and Gray tugged his arm, drawing Rory against him, as his own back settled against one of the trees. "I couldn't wait to do this," Gray said, and he sounded equally as breathless as his mouth descended upon Rory's, passion flaring between them like it had never been extinguished by Evrard's untimely interruption.

Gray's kiss was ravenous, and after only a few blissful moments, he switched their places, pressing Rory gently but inexorably against the trunk of the tree as they continued to kiss. His lips skated down Rory's neck, finding a whole chain of sensitive spots to kiss, until Rory was moaning and squirming under the onslaught. He wanted Gray to return his hand to the front of his breeches and give him the relief he'd so tantalizingly promised earlier. But instead, Gray sank to his knees, and Rory, who could barely make out his face in the dark, gaped.

He'd done this, yes, and he'd thought about it plenty of times, but somehow he had never imagined that powerful, controlled Gray would ever give himself up to it like Rory secretly wanted him to. But he showed no hesitation as he untangled the knot of Rory's breeches and then stroked his hard cock after Gray had pulled it out from the restraining fabric. "Do you want this?" Gray asked.

Rory worried his swollen bottom lip, afraid to say yes, and terrified to say no. "I want you," he said instead. Gray shook his head, his dark hair shining in the even darker night. "Tell me," he insisted. "I want you to say it."

"I want you to," he practically whispered. "Please."

The single word was all the encouragement Gray needed, because he bent down and Rory's head tipped back against the trunk as Gray's lips enveloped his cock.

He'd read about this so many times, imagining being the giver, and being the recipient, but he'd never dreamed that it would feel as good as this. His hands settled uncertainly on Gray's shoulders, and to Rory's surprise, he pushed against them, encouraging him to do more. Rory wasn't exactly certain what it was that Gray wanted, and as he sucked on the head, pleasure blurred out every logical thought process he'd ever claimed to possess. He wanted more of this, and then he would want it again, and then he would want it always.

Finally, Gray decided to help, as he plucked one of Rory's hands off his shoulder and deposited it on his head. Oh, Rory realized, that's what he wants. And he'd seen this done, in a handful of very tasteful erotic etchings, but nothing came close to the visceral joy of it, being able to sink his fingers into the silk of Gray's hair and pull, giving himself exactly what he wanted. Gray made a happy, encouraging noise in the back of his throat, and Rory felt the last of his reservations evaporate as he carefully thrust, pleasure exploding through him.

There was so much they hadn't done, so much time they hadn't been able to steal, and even taking a little now made Rory feel wild and greedy and desperate for so much more. All those etchings raced through his head, and his orgasm, barely held at bay by the tiniest shred of self-control, roared through him at the thought there might not be a finite end to this after all. They could have more, if everything fell their way. They could be, Rory thought dazedly, everlasting.

He sank against the tree, spent and worn out from the day's journey and from his spectacular orgasm. His cock slipped from between Gray's lips and Rory reached down to help him to his feet and to hopefully, return the favor. Except he found Gray's own breeches undone and his cock softening. "I couldn't help it," Gray said, and Rory could see the glimmer of a grin in the darkness. His voice was a little rough, and between that and the evidence that doing that to Rory had been as arousing to Gray as it was to Rory himself—it nearly sent another rush of desire flowing through him.

"I know," Gray added, "but we'll have more time. We'll make more time, if we have to. But for now, we should get some rest. Else Evrard will be insufferable in the morning."

"Alright," Rory said, gazing up at him. "As soon as my muscles can move again."

Gray laughed and leaned down to kiss him again. Rory tasted himself on his tongue, and thought to himself, we can be everlasting.

CHAPTER THIRTEEN

THE REST OF THE journey back to the valley was, thankfully, uneventful, and they made excellent time, stopping only to rest when they were so exhausted they could not keep moving. Gray should have been worn out by the speed of their travel, but he felt buoyant, even as they began to draw closer to their end, and his eventual return to Ardglass. Gray told himself, whenever he could not force the thought from his mind, that if he had Rory beside him, then he could face anything—even the betrayal of his father. If he felt no regret over what he'd done, then at least Gray wouldn't have to figure out how to forgive him.

Because of all the scenarios that Gray envisioned, him being able to stand in front of Gideon, the man who had so callously given him to Sabrina, and offer forgiveness seemed to be the most difficult for him to fathom. Still, he would go, if only because Evrard was right, though Gray was loath to ever mention that out loud. He'd lived his life trying to hide from that giant pit of bitterness that rose up at the most inopportune moments, waiting and hoping for a day when he could be found again. To rid himself of it, he'd come to the conclusion he would not only need to be found, he would need to make whatever peace with his father was possible. If no way forward existed, then at least he could tell himself that he had made the effort. Then, he would help Rory obtain his throne and decide, once and for all, where he belonged. Was it with Rory? Was it in the valley? Or was it where he'd always dreamt during the nights when he was too tired to deny the thought: ruling from the Ardglassian throne?

On the fifth morning, they descended into the valley, the bright purple flowers dotting the waving green grasses a balm to Gray's soul. Had he really only been gone from this place for a few weeks? It felt like so much longer, like he'd been a different man who had lived here, overflowing with resentment, even as he'd tried to pretend that this place fit him. And it had, maybe, before this journey, but now he'd been back in the world and one less soul thought he was lost.

"Does it feel good to be back?" Rory asked.

It did, and it also felt like a slightly uncomfortable reminder that nothing ever stayed the same.

"You were content here," Evrard observed, "but not happy."

It would never feel comfortable for Evrard to know him better than he knew himself, but it helped, understanding that Rory knew him, too. From behind, Rory's hand reached up and grasped his shoulder, squeezing reassuringly. "You will not be the first or the last," he said softly. To settle, Gray thought, that's what Rory meant. And he knew then that while he might return occasionally to this beautiful, peaceful place, he would never again live here. Because that's exactly what it would be—experiencing a glimpse of what a true life, filled with companionship and love and purpose would feel like, and then rejecting it in favor of a smaller, less fulfilling echo.

"It was a good place to grow up," Gray finally said, hoping that his words told Rory what he wanted to say later, in more privacy—that this was no longer his home.

As they rode toward the farm, Gray was surprised to see that no evidence of the battle remained. There was only a lazy, sunshine-filled silence as they approached the first outbuilding.

"Someone has cleared the bodies," Rory said, dismounting from Evrard, a perplexed frown on his face. "Did they take away their comrades?"

Gray sniffed the air. "They certainly did not burn them. You'd still smell it."

"There is another possibility," Evrard spoke up. "Your guard overcame them and then buried them."

Just as his words faded in the air, a figure emerged from the stables, a sword drawn. Rory gave a shout and ran, falling to the ground in front of one of his guardswomen. She wasn't in her armor, Gray could tell as he approached, but was only dressed in a simple pair of breeches and tunic. Her hair was unbound, rippling in the wind, even as she kept a fierce grip on her sword.

"Rowen," Rory breathed out unsteadily. "You survived."

She still did not lower the sword, and Gray took a step closer, and then another, his own hand braced on the pommel of Lion's Breath. It only occurred to him once he was nearly between them that Rory's guard might not look fondly on a man who was not Rory bearing his ancestral sword. But it was too late to hide the distinctive lion heads, the rubies and topaz sparkling in the sunlight.

Rowen pointed her sword directly at Gray. "How am I to know you did not capture and spirit away our prince?" she demanded. "He disappeared, with no trace to be found of him, right in the middle of the enemy's attack."

Rory had stood and was staring at her incredulously. "He saved me, Rowen. I was about to be set upon in the garden, and he rode up and saved me. We could not be sure you could turn the soldiers away, and so we left."

"And did not return?" Rowen questioned, her expression hard and unrelenting. "And left us here to wonder what had become of you?"

Guilt swamped Rory's features. "I assumed you had all perished in the fighting," he murmured, eyes cast down low. "I wanted to return, to check on you and the others, but there were more pressing matters."

"What pressing matters?'" Rowen demanded, and Gray flinched. Rory could not say that the pressing matter had ended up being some sort of pseudo-bonding mission and the one magical artifact they'd managed to get their hands on was actually completely useless and not magical at all. Damn Evrard and his meddling, Gray thought.

Of course, that was the moment Evrard chose to involve himself. He walked up, head erect, mane waving in the breeze, and Gray knew immediately that he had not cloaked himself as he usually did. Rowen, jaw dropped, saw him in all his majestic and true glory.

She fell to one knee, her sword forgotten, and breathed out, "Marthe was right."

"Not entirely a rare occurrence," Rory said with amusement, reaching out with a hand to help her to her feet. "But I can understand your surprise."

"That's a unicorn," Rowen said, "I thought they did not exist."

"We most certainly do, kind lady," Evrard said and to Gray's surprise, he ducked his own head. "You are the lovely creature who cares for the guard's horses."

Rowen's surprise morphed into wide-eyed astonishment. "It speaks?"

"I am Evrard, King of the Unicorns," he said, "at your service. Of course I speak."

Rowen's eyes flitted to Rory and took in his amused expression. "You are not surprised! You knew he was a unicorn? A talking unicorn?"

"Not when we first escaped," Rory admitted, "but he revealed himself very shortly after. Evrard is helping us defeat my aunt."

"And you?" Rowen directed towards Gray. "You knew too?"

Gray took a deep breath and stepped into the unknown. I am found. "Evrard rescued me from Rory's aunt when I was just a boy. He raised me here, in this valley. You might know me under a different name, Graham of Ardglass."

Rowen shook her head, even as the truth dawned across her face. "But Prince Graham is dead."

"I am very much alive," Gray confessed. "I've been in hiding, in this valley."

Rory reached out and took Gray's hand. "We have a very dangerous and important task ahead of us," he said, "we must take back my throne and see if we may restore Gray to his own. Will you help us?"

Falling to her knee again, Rowen said solemnly, "I vowed to protect you with my life, Prince Emory, and that vow remains steadfast. I vow additionally to protect Prince Graham, now that he has finally been found."

Found. It felt to Graham like the word resounded through the valley—a rumble of joyous sound that could not be diminished or hidden again.

"Please rise," Rory said, and shyly glanced in Gray's direction. "Prince Graham and I are very appreciative of your service."

While Gray didn't necessarily like it, he understood the point Rory was making. Maybe he'd always be Gray to Rory—just as Rory was Rory—but he'd need to be Prince Graham to the world. Especially if they were headed into Tullamore, and then Beaulieu. Gray was a lost boy, who'd desperately wanted to stay lost; Graham was a man looking for a place to belong.

"Did any of the others survive?" Rory questioned.

A wide, deep smile bloomed across Rowen's gentle face. "Indeed, my prince. All five of us survived. Acadia sustained a small injury, but she is recovered now." Rowen turned to Gray. "Your stores here are impressive, Your Highness."

Gray held up a hand. "I'm glad to know they were able to serve you well," he said, "and please, call me Gray, or if not Gray, then Graham. I may have been born a prince, but I grew up as a simple farm boy."

Still smiling, Rowen nodded. "I shall go fetch my sisters-at-arms. They will be thrilled to see you back with us, Prince Emory."

She set off towards the fields behind the farmhouse, with Evrard beside her, and when she was out of earshot, Gray turned to Rory. "You have never asked them to call you by your chosen name?"

Rory shrugged.

"But you asked me almost immediately," Gray objected. "I believe in our first conversation, you told me to call you Rory, and you could not have known . . ."

"Known that you were also of royal blood? Of course not. But . . ." Rory hesitated. "I know what Evrard said, about how I thought of you back then. A handsome, pleasant diversion. But he was not being entirely truthful. I knew you were important the first moment I met you. I knew your appearance in my life would change it."

Gray had figured out as much; Evrard's machinations were not as opaque as he usually hoped they were. "Your face revealed as much," he admitted, squeezing Rory's fingers. "I knew you never believed me to be a simple farmhand you could enjoy and then dismiss."

"I did think you were quite rude," Rory said, laughing. "But never simple."

"Tonight," Gray said, lowering his voice even though there was nobody to overhear, "tonight, come to me."

Rory's eyes shone as he looked up at him, the sight more precious than any gold or riches accompanying his resurrected title. "I would like that very much."

"There are some things I would like to show you, and some things I would like to say. And . . ." Gray leaned down and brushed a kiss across Rory's sweet mouth. "Much I would endeavor to enjoy with you."

Rory nodded, but before he could reply, movement out of the corner of his eye must have caught his attention, as it caught Gray's. He turned and saw Evrard cantering towards them, and on his back was Marthe, the leader of Rory's guard, followed by the other four women, running behind the unicorn and his rider.

Evrard stopped in front of them, mane rippling, and face as smug as ever. Marthe dismounted, her face glowing with happiness. "My prince!" she exclaimed and belying her words, reached out to embrace him. Rory did not hesitate for a single moment before embracing her back, tightly. And Gray remembered the bronze dagger had been a present from Marthe, who had so clearly hoped that even if she could not save him, then her gift could.

Here was someone who cared as much about Rory as he did.

Gray dropped to one knee and bent his head. Marthe gazed at him in confusion. "Captain," Gray said, "thank you for all your foresight and care of the Prince. I am most grateful for it."

It was the sort of speech that Gray would have made if he were Rory's betrothed—a formal acknowledgment of the captain's services, before the task could be turned over to his husband. Of course they were not engaged; Gray did not know what he was doing the next day and the day after, or where he would belong, as much as he wanted desperately to belong with Rory. Still, he hoped his words would show Rory a little of how much he'd come to care for him.

Marthe reached down and offered a hand, helping Gray to his feet again. "And you have my gratitude for saving Prince Emory's life outside of this valley. It seems he has been on an important journey, and still has another remaining, before we may return to Fontaine and banish his aunt from the throne."

"It is true," Gray acknowledged.

Acadia, bearing a bandage on her arm, Diana, and Anya arrived, breathless. "Your Highness!" they exclaimed, all exceedingly glad to see him.

Anya, whom Rory had mentioned was originally from Ardglass, quickly switched her gaze from Rory to him. Gray tried not to flinch. Telling Rowen was one thing, confessing his lineage to another of Ardglass? That felt much harder.

"You," she said, directing her words towards Gray, "you are very familiar, sir. Are you from Ardglass?"

Gray bowed his head briefly. "I am, good lady."

"You have the look," Anya said speculatively. "I have not met many of our country outside the borders, though that surprises me still, as difficult as the situation is within Ardglass itself."

"Anya," Rowen hissed, and Gray assumed she wanted to tell her friend that such speculation was entirely unnecessary.

But it wasn't Rowen's place to confess who he truly was.

"I have been living here in this valley for many years," Gray said slowly. The words were still difficult, and he was not entirely comfortable with the truth they contained, but it was time. Evrard had not been wrong about that. "Before I came to live here, I indeed lived in Ardglass, in fact in Tullamore itself. I was also known by another name. Graham."

Anya breathed out in shock and awe. "You cannot be," she said, "but you have his look, very much like King Gideon, and I saw the young prince once, when he was touring the clans with his father. He had your eyes. You must be the lost prince." She knelt, and Gray's heartbeat thudded uncertainly in his chest. Duty, Rhys had told him more times than he could possibly remember, duty is tempered with honesty and loyalty and kindness.

"While I might have been Graham a long time ago," he said, setting a hand on Anya's shoulder, "you must still call me Gray. It has been many years since I was a prince, and I must accustom myself to the title again."

"I pledge my sword to yours," Anya said, "as I am pledged to Prince Emory."

Gray looked over at Rory. It was technically not correct, as Anya had not asked Rory for his permission to resign from his guard, but since Gray had no intention of leaving Rory's side now or at any time in the near future, there could be no harm in it. In fact, it would be meaningful to him to have a countrywoman at his side as he rode back into Tullamore.

"I am very pleased you have found each other," Rory said softly, the happiness in his gaze making it clear he was not worried at all about precedence.

"As am I," Gray said, discovering that his words were astonishingly accurate.

"We will convene after the evening meal to discuss many important plans," Evrard announced, "but until then I would very much like to retire to my stable."

Gray thought of his large tub and could not help but nod enthusiastically at Evrard's simple request. A bath and a bed. Rory. "I think we could all use some rest," he said.

Steam rose from the surface of the tub, and Gray eyed it appreciatively. On their journey, there'd been cool streams and the even colder lake, but the one time he'd hoped to find a hot bath—in Nargash—the thieves had inconveniently gotten in the way. He'd missed his big tub with its clever pulley system he'd designed, more than he'd even realized. Another bucket dumped into the tub, water sloshing over the side, and Gray's hands hesitated on the ropes.

If he stopped filling the tub now, the water would be a little shallow for just him, but if he added another to the warm water? Like someone . . . Rory-sized? He'd initially intended to spend a quiet hour alone in the tub, trying not to think of what faced him in Ardglass, but what he really wanted wasn't silence. It was that particular wrenching sound of pleasure Rory made when he was close to exploding.

Gray tied the ropes off and was about to reach for his shirt so he could go find what he truly wanted—who he truly wanted—when a knock on his door surprised him.

He was in the middle of slipping his shirt on when he opened it and smiled when he saw who it was standing in front of him.

"You said . . ." Rory said, flushing, and fidgeting with the hem of his tunic. "I wasn't sure when you meant, but I thought if the planning goes late tonight then right now might be . . ."

Gray didn't let him finish his sentence, which was surely that it would be far more advantageous to indulge now. Instead, he reached for Rory and pulled him inside, nudging the door shut with his foot. He bent down and kissed Rory thoroughly, who melted against him like he'd been afraid at how he'd be greeted but wasn't anymore. And the very last thing Gray wanted was for Rory to ever be afraid of him or think that he wouldn't want to see him.

The truth was Gray always wanted to see him, with an all-consuming focus that probably should have scared him more than it did.

Instead it just felt . . . good. Like he wasn't alone, for the first time in a very long time.

"I guess you agree," Rory said as Gray lifted his mouth, his voice breathless and edged with anticipation. "Oh!" he exclaimed suddenly, and Gray realized he must have just spotted the full bathtub. "I've interrupted your bath."

"No," Gray said softly, and reached for the hem of his own shirt, pulling it back over his head. "It's our bath."

"Oh," Rory said again, and that breathlessness had tripled, leaving him starry-eyed and flushed. He plucked at the edge of his tunic. "I guess I should . . ."

"Yes," Gray confirmed, smirking impudently "You definitely should."

He was already picking at the laces to his breeches, his socks and boots already sitting next to his bed. Glancing up at Rory, he grinned. "Why does this feel like the lake? Me nearly naked and you hesitating?"

"I'm not hesitating," Rory claimed, though Gray had seen him undress much more quickly than he was doing now. "I'm . . ." His words died as Gray shucked his breeches, and bare as the day he was born, stepped over to the tub. "I'm just appreciating the view," he said in an impressed voice.

"You can look any time you want," Gray said, pleased. "But let me look too, please."

Gray's pleading must have worked because suddenly Rory's fingers were flying, untying his breeches and pulling them off, and suddenly, he was just as naked as Gray.

Their gazes met, and maybe it was the steam or the heat of the water, but Gray's palms grew damp. He wanted to touch, his fingers itching with the need to feel the expanse of Rory's cool, smooth, pale skin. But it wasn't just his skin Gray wanted; he wanted to crawl inside Rory and understand his thoughts and his logical analyses. He wanted to understand how his heart beat, and how he could remain so kind when the world kept conspiring to destroy his life. He wanted so much more than just the fleeting physical pleasure, and that might have scared him, but all his fear was reserved for the possibility that he'd never get the chance to have it.

"Come here," Gray said softly, and Rory fell into him like he'd been waiting for exactly those words. Rory's leg was a long, cool brand against his own, his cock a wet, hot reminder of just how much they both wanted from each other.

Rory kissed him, soft and sweet and trusting at first, but with their bare skin pressed together, his kisses quickly grew hotter and deeper and dirtier, until Gray was drowning in them. There was so much he wanted to show Rory—how good it could be between two people, even though Gray had an inkling that he'd barely touched the real possibilities, at least where Rory was concerned. He'd kissed men and women and taken momentary solace in them before, but he'd never felt like this—a driving, undeniable need to possess this man and let him possess him in return.

"Tub," Gray said, pulling away from Rory's mouth with a desperate gasp. "We should really . . . it's here."

Rory shot him a demure look from under auburn lashes. "Whatever you want."

Chuckling, Gray offered a hand to help Rory into the tub. "If you knew what I've imagined, you wouldn't be so cavalier about it," he teased, and Rory smiled serenely as he settled into the water, his back against one curved side.

"Maybe, maybe not." Rory watched intently as Gray climbed into the tub, facing him. "I seem to like most of your ideas so far."

"And what about you?" Gray murmured, reaching for soap and cloth and Rory's leg, starting at the foot and beginning to cleanse it. "Do you have any suggestions we've neglected?"

The cloth traveled higher, and then higher still, and Gray's hand paused at the top of Rory's thigh. His head had fallen back, his reddish curls shining in the candlelight, his mouth falling open in pleasure.

It was an image that Gray knew he would remember forever—Rory lost to the world, only from Gray washing his leg. "You're killing me," Gray ground out, and let the cloth fall into the water.

This time it was his hands coasting along that sweet, wet skin, until they nudged up against Rory's erection. Rory moaned, his eyelids fluttering in supplication. "Please," he begged, and Gray had never heard anything sweeter in his whole life. Carefully he began to pump him with one hand as the other fished for the cloth and made quick work of Rory's other leg, until he reached the apex of his thighs and the hard cock he was stroking.

Then he shifted lower, fingers brushing up against his balls, and then lower still, until they found Rory's hole, tightly furled against his inquisitive fingertip.

"Oh, oh," Rory moaned, and Gray, fire burning through his veins at even the thought of breaching Rory there, took that as enough encouragement to continue.

"You like that?" Gray asked, hearing the desperation in his own voice.

"I've . . . I've . . ." Rory gasped and his words were lost as Gray slipped just the tip of his finger in and Rory's erection pulsed to completion in his hand.

Rory opened his eyes slowly, the deep amber of them hypnotizing in the low light of the room. He took a deep breath. Slow, Gray reminded himself, he's never done this before, he's never felt this way before—and neither have you—but don't you dare scare him away.

"I've read about that," Rory finally said softly. "I . . . I wondered what it would feel like."

"It feels even better than that," Gray said.

"You've done it?" Rory's voice wasn't judgmental, but inquisitive. Curious.

"There isn't much I haven't done," Gray admitted. Then hesitated. It was a bit like earlier today, when he'd come clean with Anya about his lineage. Being honest wasn't always easy, but there were some watershed moments where if you pushed truth away, you simply couldn't live with yourself after. And this, Gray realized, was another one of them. "But it's different with you. It's . . . I care about you, Rory."

Not entirely what he'd meant to say, but close enough.

Rory stood, water sluicing down his slender, perfect body. "I want to be the one you do it with, I want you to make me feel even better," he said. "Can you do that with me?" He'd taken a very brave stance, but Gray could tell he was slightly nervous, because his voice wavered just the tiniest bit at the end of his question.

"Yes, but . . ." Gray hesitated. It was a big step. He'd be the first, and if he listened to the rumblings of his heart, he'd want to be the last. Would Rory allow that? Would Rory even want that?

"No buts," Rory said and held out a hand. "Take me to bed, Gray."

A stupid man would continue to hesitate, once their greatest desire made their own wishes known, but Gray was definitely not a stupid man. He stood and pulled Rory fiercely against him, his own cock heavy and hard between them. "It would be my honor," he said, picking Rory up and cradling him against his chest as they made their way to the bed. He deposited Rory gently on the bed. Their skin was wet against the rough sheets, but Gray didn't notice as he knelt between

Rory's legs and with one hand gently opened them, while the other rummaged in the chest by his bed for the little vial he used when nothing else would satisfy him except being filled.

"This," Gray murmured as he finally pulled it from the depths and began to slick up his fingers, "will make it easier."

"Is it hard?" Rory asked with a giggle, his innuendo seeming to relax him as Gray began to massage the oil into the skin around his hole. Every few rotations he would dip his fingers in, and after the third or fourth movement, Rory was moaning again, his chest flushed against the pale sheets.

"It's very hard," Gray teased back. He wasn't even lying. He didn't think he'd been so engorged in his life, so tightly drawn that it felt like he could pleasure his man all night.

"More, please," Rory finally begged. "You don't have to be so gentle."

But Gray absolutely did. He wasn't small, and the last thing he wanted was to hurt Rory. Not when this was a moment primed to be full of ecstasy. Still, he could do a little more, he reasoned, and slid one of his thinner fingers in, rotating it as Rory grew used to the sensation.

One finger grew to two, and then to three, which had Rory restlessly pushing against Gray's hand, desperate and hard again, leaking profusely at the tip of his cock.

"I'm ready, I'm ready," he insisted. "Please, please."

How could he resist when Rory was begging him, his forehead dotted with sweat, his eyes wild? It was impossible.

Gray slicked himself up with the oil and then carefully positioned himself at Rory's entrance, pushing in as slowly as he dared, even as his blood boiled at the need to go faster, to claim him, once and for all.

His thoughts were a cacophony of nonsense, but the one that stood out the most clearly and the loudest was, you're mine now, as Gray finally slid home.

Rory thrashed in his grip, overwhelmed, and it was only a control born of so many years' waiting that Gray was able to hold back. "Is it okay?" Gray whispered. He didn't want to hurt him; he wanted only the opposite.

Golden eyes locked onto his, unbelievably determined and hazy with pleasure. "Move," Rory insisted through bared teeth.

So Gray did as directed and moved, short little strokes at first, stoking the fire higher in both of them, leaving Gray panting and sweat-slicked as he began to let go and go harder, deeper. Rory keened, reaching down to touch himself, only the barest touch of his sending him spiraling into bliss. Rory's body—hot and tight and unbelievable—before this moment, tightened even further, rippling around him, and Gray lost it, thrusting hard and spurting deep inside Rory.

For a breathless moment, neither of them moved, they simply stared at each other.

Gray didn't think he had words for what had just happened. There'd been heat between them before, an inescapable, driving need, but what had just possessed them? It was bigger than that, and not only did it have claws, demanding more, if not now, then very soon, it was somehow also soft and kind and unbearably sweet.

How could a feeling be all those things at the same time? Gray didn't know, and he thought from the wonder in Rory's eyes that he didn't know either. It was something, maybe, that they were both lost in this together.

Slowly, he climbed off the bed and fetched another cloth, cleaning first Rory and then himself.

"They were right," Rory said quietly as Gray climbed into the bed next to him, pulling him against his chest. Rory went pliantly, his face settling against Gray's pectoral muscle like he'd done it a thousand times before—and intended to do it a thousand times after.

"Who was right?"

"The books," Rory said, with an amused giggle that made Gray smile. "They always said it was earth-shattering and all-consuming and I didn't really believe them. But they were right, after all."

"It's . . ." He'd said as much before, but that had been in the heat of the moment, and now it was quieter. Softer. The words, which always held meaning, held more now. "It's not usually like that."

"I assumed as much," Rory said thoughtfully, surprising him. "If it was, nobody would ever leave their beds."

Gray grinned, this time the smile nearly splitting his face. "Unfortunately, I wouldn't be surprised if Evrard has us up at first light tomorrow."

"I know." Rory seemed quite disappointed at this. It warmed Gray's heart. He not only wanted to do it again, he was upset that they couldn't immediately. "And I don't suppose we could on the road."

"With Evrard and your entire guard present? I don't think so," Gray said. He didn't want anyone else to hear Rory's gasps of pleasure. They were his, and his alone.

"I suppose we will just have to defeat my aunt, and then we can do it whenever we like, wherever we like," Rory said, his voice growing sleepy. "One of the perks of being a prince, you know."

It was funny, because Gray had spent the last fifteen years thinking of all the negatives of being royal. Holding on to the reasons why he never wanted to reclaim his lineage. But here was one: Rory.

Rory, everlasting.

It wasn't a particularly honorable reason, and Evrard would have been appalled, but Gray, who had wondered if his doubts over returning to Ardglass would ever cease to trouble him, decided there was at least one reason he didn't need to dread it. And with that thought, curled around the man he loved, Gray fell asleep.

CHAPTER FOURTEEN

Later that night, Gray, Rory, Evrard and the five members of Rory's guard gathered around a bonfire outside the farmhouse. Evrard began the planning session by insisting that timeliness was one of the most pressing factors. "We need to rally who we can before Sabrina gets the chance. It is exponentially more difficult for her. You"—Evrard swung his head in Rory's direction—"are the Crown Prince of Fontaine. She cannot outright accuse you of treason, because any treason you would be committing wouldn't be treason at all."

Rory nodded thoughtfully. "Because the throne is already rightfully mine," he said.

"Likely she has already spread the word that you aren't a particularly sound choice to rule, but that won't be enough to turn everyone against you." Evrard hesitated. "There has been talk for the last two years of why she has not encouraged you to take the place that is rightfully yours. That works in our favor."

"Then why do we not ride for Beaulieu?" Gray asked, and he hadn't even tried to hide his eagerness at the possibility they could indefinitely postpone his return to Ardglass. He'd really been hoping they could put off their journey to Tullamore as long as possible.

"We have no army," Evrard said. "How do you propose we find one?"

"You don't mean . . ." Gray faltered. "You don't mean for me to muster the Ardglassian army."

"Unless you have another army at hand that you are willing and able to call to arms," Evrard said pointedly.

This was not at all how Gray had hoped the meeting would go. He'd been hoping that Evrard's plan for returning to Ardglass, back to the castle fortress of Tullamore, would be both slow and steady. Emphasis on the slow. It would have been silly to believe that he'd get more used to the idea with additional time, but Gray had hoped he could put off the inevitable at least a few more days. Give them more time to rest and gather supplies.

But clearly that was not in Evrard's plans.

Instead of continuing to participate, he sat and stewed in his own pointless, annoying thoughts as the meeting continued around him. He barely listened as the rest discussed provisions, weapons, the route, even the formation they would ride into Tullamore in, but it was only at the very end of their summit that Gray chose to open his mouth again.

"What about Gideon?" Gray finally asked flatly. "I very much doubt he will just let me waltz in and confiscate his army."

He met Anya's eyes from across the fire, flashing in the dancing lights. "Your father is in no position to deny a returning prince, wielding his consort's magical sword, the army of his birthright," she said fervently.

Consort? Gray had to force himself not to glance over at Rory to see his reaction. That kind of permanence had never been discussed between them, though Gray had a feeling Rory would not exactly mind it. Still, a commitment of that kind was serious, and should be approached seriously, and not decided by others. Still, Gray didn't address her terminology, because that was a whole other issue, and a voice in his head pointed out, with much of Evrard's inflection that right now is not the right time for that discussion.

"What is the matter with Gideon?" he asked instead, refusing to identify him as Anya had. Gideon might be his sire, but he had not been his father for a very long time.

"I think," Evrard interrupted, "that is a matter you will need to see for yourself, Gray." His voice made it abundantly clear that nobody was to discuss Gideon's state of mind any further.

But, hearing Anya's opinion of Gideon's state had certainly not made him any more eager to return to Tullamore.

Gray slept poorly, tossing and turning in his bed, despite Rory snoring delicately next to him, his dreams full of fire and blood and beautiful women melting into fearsome beasts.

As he'd suspected the evening before, they were on their horses at first light.

The only surprise was that Evrard refused to be ridden. Gray's old horse had returned to the stables, mostly intact, and so he mounted him, and Rory his own horse. Gray did not want to admit it in front of Evrard or any of Rory's guard, but he immediately missed the feeling of Rory's slender frame pressed to his back, reassuring and grounding him.

The truth was, he needed the comfort and encouragement of his touch more than ever, because it had become increasingly clear that Evrard did not only mean for him to reveal himself as the lost prince, but to take his rightful place next to his father like nothing had ever forced him to abandon it. That was a whole other thorny problem that Gray had not even begun to wrestle with—and yet he already felt bruised and battered and stung by its sharp points.

Returning to the place which had once been his home was one thing; returning to command the Ardglassian army was entirely another.

"Are you alright?" Rory asked when they stopped for a meal at midday. "You've been very quiet."

Marthe and Evrard had chatted on and off most of the morning, about various topics such as magical weapons, geographical points of interest, and history. Rory had inserted his opinion several times. Gray had not, and not only because he was not nearly as widely read as the others, but because he'd been sulking.

It was not something Gray was proud of, but the closer they grew to Tullamore, the more out-of-sorts he felt. He knew that he was in no real danger, not with Rory's guard and Lion's Breath at his hip, but the feeling of dread grew in him anyway.

"I'm tired," Gray told Rory shortly, which was not an inaccurate statement. He had slept terribly.

Rory pushed that excuse to the side like it was entirely inconsequential. "Is it because we're growing nearer to Tullamore?"

"Of course not," Gray lied.

Rory shot him a reprimanding look and reached out to take Gray's hand. "It's perfectly understandable if you are nervous or apprehensive."

Nervous? Apprehensive?

Gray was something else entirely. Frightened, perhaps? Fearful? Anxious? He seemed to feel all of the above at the exact same time, the emotions roiling around in his stomach until even the thought of food made him want to lose what little was left in his stomach.

"It's a big step you are taking." Rory tried again, and made a face, scrunching his nose, which normally Gray would have found endearing, but he was not finding much endearing at the moment. "I'm saying all the wrong things, aren't I?"

Gray sighed. "I don't know what the right ones are. If I did, I would tell you so you could say them."

"How about this?" Rory asked and reached for him, pulling Gray into a fiercely protective hug. After a long moment, he leaned back and looked Gray right in the eyes, his golden gaze as fierce as Gray had ever seen it. "I vow to stay by your side, no matter what. You will not have to do this alone."

There was a part of Gray that shrieked loudly that the only way he could do this was alone, but he didn't want to listen to that voice anymore, so he merely nodded his agreement. "I would like that very much," he said. He leaned down and brushed a quick kiss across Rory's lips. "You're a good friend."

Friendship was not entirely all they felt for each other—Gray could hardly deny that his romantic feelings were very strong indeed—but he did not want to unpack another problem by bringing up the particular term Anya had used earlier. Consort.

Rory didn't seem to be upset by Gray's word choice, though, he merely smiled and let him go, drifting over to his horse. "We'll get through this. The worst is always the anticipation."

Gray wasn't sure he quite agreed, but it was undoubtedly not helping. He remounted his horse and tried to clear his mind as they set off again on the road to Tullamore.

During the afternoon's ride, Evrard switched positions from trotting near Marthe and her mount to moving back to where Gray brought up the rear of the procession. Anya had objected to this orientation, claiming that he would not be as well-protected, but Gray had merely laid a hand on the pommel of Lion's Breath and she had stopped arguing.

Gray had also expected to receive some form of protest that he was wielding, at least for now, Rory's ancestral sword, but his guard had accepted it silently. Even Marthe had not argued, which was surprising, considering how many strongly held opinions she seemed to have. He wondered if it was because they'd all accepted him as Rory's consort, and as such, it was his right to hold any weapon he needed to protect the Crown Prince.

"I see you did not correct Anya's use of the word, consort," Evrard said, as if he was reading Gray's mind, which, knowing what he did about Evrard's magic, might be entirely possible.

"Neither of us is eager to place such a label on our friendship," Gray said placidly, refusing to give the unicorn the reaction he was clearly in search of.

"You've only known each other for a few weeks," Evrard pointed with a serious nod of understanding. "But they have been fraught weeks. You are growing very close."

Gray ground his teeth together. "You are clearly aware of what you wish to know, why don't you just pluck it out of my head? You're capable of doing it."

"It would not be nearly so satisfying if you did not admit it freely and out loud," Evrard observed placidly.

"You should just go back to discussing the weather every fifth year with Marthe. You'll get much further in your quest."

Evrard was silent for several minutes as their company made its way down the road, thick forest rising up on either side of the well-kept trail. Whatever state Gideon was in, at least he had not let his kingdom entirely go to rot.

"Yes," he finally said, "that is why they have said nothing about you wielding Lion's Breath. You will be Rory's consort."

Gray stared straight ahead. "Which am I to be?" he questioned darkly, "Rory's consort or the leader of Ardglassian armies? Because I cannot do both. I cannot be both."

"Graham," Evrard said softly, "you are capable of anything you set your mind to. I know you understand that, as I raised you to believe it.

And as yet, I do think there may be a different solution to the problem of Ardglass that we have yet to see."

"I was hoping such an enormous problem would solve itself," Gray grunted. Any comfort he'd had from Rory's embrace had evaporated under Evrard's pointed questions, and though he knew he'd regret it, all he wanted was to turn around and ride at breakneck speed back to his valley and never, ever leave. Maybe it would mean losing Rory, which would be difficult, but at least this relentless pressure on his chest might finally lessen.

"I think when we arrive, I will see things differently, and there may be a solution I have not considered," Evrard said, clearly unconcerned. "I do know your love affair with Rory was foretold, and therefore there must be a satisfactory answer to whether you should become Rory's consort and help him rule Fontaine or continue to lead Ardglass and its armies."

Gray rolled his eyes. "The kingdoms could always be united," he pointed out, and then regretted his words instantly. That had likely been Evrard's goal all along in drawing him into this particular conversation. He'd wanted to know if Gray had spent any time considering the problems at hand and had devised any possible solutions.

He would have liked to deny it, but Evrard was right—he'd been raised to be a leader and to face obstacles without flinching. He would have to be an entirely different person than he was to not consider what could be done about his lineage and Rory's birthright.

"Possibly," Evrard said, "though that seems like an inordinate amount of work and statecraft for one royal marriage. Easier, I think, to leave them separate."

"Maybe easier to leave us separate," Gray said morosely.

But Evrard only whinnied in disapproval. "We both know you're lying when you say that would be a simpler solution," he observed.

"As I said, your mutual love was written long before either of you were born. You are fooling yourself if you believe your feelings are so weak that you could easily turn away from him and the future he offers."

That was always the problem with Evrard; sometimes he knew Gray's mind better than Gray knew it himself. Because it was not just Rory himself, it was the promise of a future with companionship and love, nothing like the last fifteen years, where he'd been forced to rely entirely on himself. What he had always wanted, much as he tried to deny it, was someone by his side, and now that he had met Rory, there was no other possible person he could ever envision in that place.

"Ah, I thought so," Evrard continued, his knowing tone doing nothing to lessen Gray's annoyance.

They reached the edges of Tullamore midday on the third day of their journey.

The spires of Tullamore stood like solemn gray figures, reaching toward the bright sky. Gray had not seen their unusual spiky shapes in so many years, yet they were so familiar to him it felt like yesterday that he had looked upon them for the last time.

As they rode through the village, Gray noticed many changes from when he had last been here. The houses and huts seemed much worse for the wear, repairs done poorly or not done at all, and a malaise of spirit lay over property and person alike. Everybody they passed gave them a cursory, dead-eyed stare, but nobody inquired who they were or seemed to have any interest past observing they existed. Gray felt himself grow gradually more and more uncomfortable as they rode closer to the gated entry to the keep.

He knew upon the deaths of Rory's parents, Sabrina had returned to Fontaine, and left Ardglass behind. Why then, once Gideon had shaken off the influence of her magic and rotten advice, had Ardglass not returned to its normally thriving state?

The only comfort Gray took was at least the village was not in worse shape than Nargash had been. But with a few more years of neglect, he was not certain anyone would be able to tell the difference.

They approached the gate, the very same one Gray had faced Sabrina's chimera over, but there were no magical creatures present, only a few bored soldiers who barely glanced up at their party before moving for them to pass.

The night before, they had originally planned to approach Tullamore in a diamond formation, surrounding Rory, who would change back into his fine clothes that befit a crown prince, and Gray would take up the rear, next to Evrard—who was, at least for now, remaining in his disguise as a regular horse.

But now, Gray felt his gorge rise at the lack of discipline, and at the appalling lack of security. These men were simply going to let a troop of heavily armed guards ride directly into the heart of Ardglass, and do whatever they wished. Additionally, they were accompanying a man of clearly noble or royal blood. Gray could bear it no longer.

"Halt," Gray called out abruptly and pulled up on the reins of his horse. The rest of the group hesitated, but did not stop immediately, as he had. "I said, halt."

A man with greasy hair and a sullen attitude separated himself from the group of soldiers and approached Gray. Marthe and the others had finally turned around and were trotting back to where Gray had suddenly come to a stop.

"What's the problem?" the man slurred.

Drinking? Gray wondered, a fierce and devastating anger taking hold of him as he observed the rest of the soldiers behind him, one unashamedly taking a long swig from a flask he carried at his hip.

"Are you not on duty?" Gray asked between clenched teeth.

"Aye, yes, we are on duty. Protectin' this gate," he said, expansively waving to the large stone structure on either side of the tall archway.

"Then you are doing a criminally terrible job," Gray said. "Poor enough that I would have you arrested for treason against Ardglass, right here, right now. You are not guarding the gate, you are merely observing the people who move in and out of it, not caring a single bit what their business is or who it is with. An army could come charging through this gate, and I doubt you would even bring yourselves to care."

The man gaped at Gray. "Who are you?" he asked, a little less bored now, but no more concerned about the massive gap in training than he had been before.

Gray heard a horse trot up next to him, and wondered if it would be Rory, there to push home the fact that the guards had just allowed in the Crown Prince of a neighboring kingdom without a single inquiry. When he glanced to the side, he saw it was not Rory at all, but Anya, green eyes flashing, her expression the fiercest he had ever seen it.

"On your knees, soldier," Anya said, drawing her sword, the steel scraping against the scabbard, a sound that nobody in this keep would ever mistake for anything else.

Glaring, the man took a step closer to Anya, which Gray normally wouldn't have recommended. It seemed an especially precarious choice considering Anya's skill with the sword she'd already drawn. All he would have to do was take one look at her, and the quiet, confident way she held it, grip firm but loose, and coupled with her flawless stance, to know he wouldn't want to cross her. But the whole problem was that the guard had clearly stopped thinking.

"I don't know who you think you are. . ."

"Anya, of the Sheahish clan," she retorted calmly. "And you, sir, are too close to His Highness."

The man looked from Gray to Anya and then back to Gray again. He seemed baffled. "His Highness? Who is he?" he finally asked.

It had likely been inevitable from the moment Gray exited this very gate, fifteen years ago. No doubt his return had been foretold in the stars, just as his love for Rory had been. Inevitably, someday he would ride back to Ardglass, back to Tullamore, and reveal himself not to be just Gray, the simple farmhand, but Prince Graham, who had been lost until this moment.

I am not lost. Not anymore.

Gray dismounted and rested his hand on the pommel of Lion's Breath. Rory was behind him, but with his sword in his hand, it felt like he was much nearer. And Gray knew he needed that extra bit of courage for what he was about to say.

"On your knees," he repeated, "I am Prince Graham, come home at last to regain my place in the marble-lined halls of Tullamore."

Incredulous, the man stared at him for a long, drawn-out second. Would he recognize him? Had he ever met Prince Graham before this day? Would it matter? Surely, Gray would be required to provide some proof of his claim, but he could hardly do so now, not in front of this humble soldier.

Then, without a word, the guard fell to his knees. "Your Highness," he mumbled, face practically in the dirt. "Your Highness has finally returned. We are blessed and we are mighty."

The words echoed through him like they'd never been missing from his life for so many long, interminable years. "We are Ardglass," Gray finished.

A hard wind whipped through the courtyard as his words echoed through it.

Evrard stepped up, and as he walked towards the guard, his disguise as a regular horse melted away, revealing his shimmering white body and the single, arresting horn, touched with shades of blue, on his forehead. "We are Ardglass, indeed," he said. "The winds of change come, and nothing shall be the same after."

The man glanced up to see who had spoken and fell back to the ground. "A unicorn," he exhaled in hushed, reverent tones. "Come to Tullamore with our prince."

The other men began to walk over, and seeing the vision of Evrard, also took to their knees.

Gray didn't know whether to be relieved or annoyed that the Ardglassian guard seemed to be much more interested in Evrard than in him. But then, that was exactly the sort of thing Evrard lived for, Gray thought darkly.

But just as the thought crossed his mind, Evrard drew himself up to his full intimidating height and said, "This display is embarrassing. Get to your feet and take us to King Gideon at once."

They scrambled upwards, and that was when Rory and his guard, surrounding him, approached. "All is well?" Rory asked, his concern clearly more for Gray and his chaotic emotions than for their safe passage.

"All is as it should be," Evrard said beatifically.

Gray didn't speak, because he wasn't sure he trusted himself to answer.

As they rode towards the keep itself, the guard walked ahead and cried every minute, "He is returned, your prince has returned."

This time they were not ignored by anyone in the courtyard; every eye was on them—watching their party intently, whispering amongst themselves and pointing, quite obviously, at Gray himself.

Gray found himself wishing that he had heeded Evrard and Rory's advice and had worn something a little less threadbare than his usual shirt and breeches, with his dark, serviceable cloak tossed over his shoulders. No doubt he did not look much like a prince.

But then, he told himself firmly, that was entirely the point. He had not been a prince for the last fifteen years.

Finally, they reached the inner gate, and the steward standing there. Gray did not recognize him, but then that was not so surprising; he had been gone a very long time.

On the other hand, the steward certainly seemed to recognize him. He stared with no shame, so intently and at such length that any other time, he'd no doubt be dismissed for his rude, uncouth behavior. For all they were considered "barbaric," in comparison to the elegant, refined people of Fontaine, Ardglassians were prickly about the impression they gave others. None more so than Gideon himself.

Or at least he had been, before the lady of Fontaine had come to his court and sucked out every other care he had, except for drink and the pleasures of the flesh.

"Your Highness," the steward said after his long examination. He dropped to a single knee his arm crossed over his chest in a gesture of deep respect. "Your father will be so pleased that you are returned to us."

Gray did not really think so, but he was not going to confess that to the steward. "Please tell His Majesty that I, and Prince Emory of Fontaine, wish for an audience." He paused. "Immediately."

"Will Your Highnesses wish to clean up first?" he asked, rising to his feet.

"No," Gray said at the very same time Rory said, "Yes."

The steward looked between them in confusion.

"Yes," Gray corrected, rolling his eyes. Wiping a damp cloth over his face wasn't going to change his very un-prince-like appearance, or his un-prince-like manners, but he was willing to defer to Rory, because Rory had a much better idea of proper etiquette these days.

The guard dismounted, and their horses were led to the stables to be watered and fed. The guards had hesitated, awed expressions on their faces, as they had stared at Evrard. He was of horse-like stature, but he spoke and was gleaming, flawless white. He did not seem the type of creature to take being banished to a stable very well.

"I will wait here," Evrard said, enunciating his words with dignity. "Then we shall go into King Gideon's throne room together."

Rory and Gray were led to a medium-sized chamber near the main gate, shown warmed, scented clean water, and additional clothing items in a large carved wooden wardrobe. Gray was glad they had not separated them, because he desperately wanted to talk to Rory privately at least once before he was forced to confront Gideon.

"This must seem very strange to you," Rory said, untying his bright blue cloak and carefully pushing up the sleeves on his yellow doublet, so he could dip his hands into the shallow basin of water.

"It is very something," Gray admitted. He supposed, after three days on the road, he could do with a wash. He took his own cloak off, and after a moment of hesitation, also pulled his shirt off. Dipping one of the cloths into the water, he washed quickly and efficiently.

Rory eyed him as he was finishing. "Perhaps you should see the different options available," he pointed out. "Not that your current sartorial choices are not . . . diverting."

Gray sighed. "I'm not a pretty prince. I'll never be like you. It seems foolish to even try."

"You would feel better if you walked into your father's throne room and you weren't wearing the same tunic you wore to shovel manure," Rory pointed out.

He wasn't sure when Rory had started to sound so much like Evrard, but Gray didn't know if he liked it. Still, he walked over to the wardrobe and pulled the large, carved doors open. Rows upon rows of tunics, in a rainbow of colors and sizes, lay before him. Deep drawers with different breeches, and even decorative metal belts greeted him when he gazed down from the racks.

"Here," Rory said, elbowing him out of the way, and plucking a forest green tunic of fairly simple design, but luxuriously soft fabric out of the wardrobe. "You need no belt as you will wear Lion's Breath at your hip."

Gray took the tunic and pulled it over his head. The size was spot-on, and the color flattering. He even felt like he stood a little taller as he gazed in the mirror. Carefully re-buckling his belt with the sword, Gray glanced up at Rory. "Are you certain you wish me to carry it?" he asked. He did not want to necessarily remind Rory that walking into the throne room of Tullamore wielding Rory's sword would give a certain impression, but the last thing he wanted was to fool Rory into doing so without him understanding the full ramifications.

If Gideon saw him bearing Fontaine's sword—and he would certainly recognize its distinctive design—he would assume Gray had pledged not only his defense, but his future, to Rory. That was not entirely a bad thing, but it would be if it wasn't what Rory wanted.

But Rory put his hand out, covering Gray's own as it loosely held the pommel. "The sword is yours," Rory said softly. "And all that it entails."

So he did know, Gray thought, and his world realigned with the idea that Rory not only wanted him by his side, but he wanted him there for the rest of their lives. "I know," Rory added, "how big a decision it is, and I am not asking you to make it now, not when so much is uncertain with Ardglass, but it would be my honor for you to bear Lion's Breath today."

Gray swallowed hard. There were words of love on the tip of his tongue, and surely those would need to be spoken before they made any promises to each other, but for right now, Rory was right. This was enough. "And I am honored beyond measure to wield it," he answered, leaning down and brushing a kiss against Rory's mouth. "Nothing would give me greater happiness, in fact."

"Then it is decided," he said, his smile bright and unwavering. So certain that Gray felt his breath catch with all that he could mean.

When Gray and Rory rejoined Evrard, he gave a quick, supportive nod. "I see you have worked your good influence over him," Evrard said towards Rory. "I am impressed."

Gray glared. "I am not so bad as that," he argued.

"No, but very stubborn," Evrard sniffed.

It was hardly like he was the only stubborn creature present. It would be easier to focus on this silly, circular argument with Evrard, but there were far more important matters at hand that required Gray's attention and his concentration, so he kept his mouth shut, and watched as Rory's guard approached. They'd not shed any of their armor, and it shone in the shafts of sunlight that fell into the large entry hall from the enormous skylights above.

"Are you ready, my prince?" Marthe asked, directing the question towards Rory, who nodded. Then, to Gray's surprise, she switched her attention to him. "And you, Prince Graham?" she asked.

Gray did not particularly like that suddenly everything felt so formal between them and that she'd addressed him by his title, but to do anything else, he realized, would undermine his position. And frankly, his position already felt precarious.

"I am, Captain," Gray said.

"Then," Marthe said, gesturing to the steward, "let us proceed."

This hall that led to the main reception and throne room was one Gray remembered all too well. He'd trodden it numerous times over his eleven years residing in Tullamore. Sometimes it was because his father had asked him to meet nobles who had traveled from the clans, and sometimes it was because he'd done something particularly naughty and Rhys had insisted he confess the misdeed directly to his father.

It was very odd to be back here after so much time, and to be walking in the same hall, next to Evrard, who was and also was not, the tutor who had enforced his discipline all those years back.

Finally, they came to a halt at a pair of enormous double doors, worked in silver and studded in iron. "Your Highnesses," the steward said, "I will announce you now."

He pulled the doors open, and Gray dug his fingernails into his palm at the sight. The throne room, with its walls of green marble and intricate silk hangings, was still spotless—every bit as awe-inducing and spectacular as Gray had remembered it being—but the man sitting on the silver throne mounted on the dais was a stranger.

Gideon had always been a broad-shouldered, largely built man, famous for swinging his enormous war hammer from his destrier. But the man sitting on the throne now was bent and weak, his body shrunk and his hair thin and graying. He looked nothing like the man Gray remembered.

"Your Majesty," the steward said, his voice growing louder as he approached the throne. Was he also now hard of hearing? Gray flinched at the thought of his powerful, majestic father brought to this humiliating end, and vowed to do whatever it took to eliminate breath from Sabrina's lungs.

"Who is it?" Gray could barely hear the King's tremulous voice.

"Your son, Your Majesty," the steward said, excitement leaking into his voice. "Your son has returned."

It might have been Gray's desperate imagination, but he thought Gideon sat a bit straighter at the news.

"It cannot be," he said slowly. "Graham is dead. Lost. This must be an impostor, come to torment an old man."

It was no more than Gray had expected, but it still hurt.

"Who else is there?" the King asked, and Rory stepped forward, his guard flanking him.

"I am Prince Emory, Your Majesty," Rory said, bending slightly, as befitted his stature and the man in front of him. For all his bookishness, Rory clearly knew exactly the etiquette required for a prince to meet a king. Gray had known the same rules once, but he'd banished them from his mind, and now found that they did not return as easily as he'd hoped. Well, he thought, I have no intention of bowing to Gideon anyhow.

"Prince Emory, of Fontaine," Gideon said, rising slightly from the throne, his hands braced on the sides. Upright, the sight of him was even more awful. Gideon looked as if every ounce of health and vitality had been sucked out of him, leaving a decrepit, waning shell.

Gray pushed the despair away because the last thing he wanted was to feel for the man in front of him. He'd brought all this downfall on himself. He'd allowed Sabrina to become an advisor. He'd allowed her to take control. He'd ultimately allowed her to take his only son.

"Your appearance in my kingdom is a surprise," Gideon continued. "What is it you need?"

"I come to present your son to you, returned after many years of absence," Rory said.

Gray flinched again at the denial shadowing the King's features. "You are certainly led astray easily," Gideon said. "My son is dead."

Evrard, who was standing next to Gray still, chose that moment to walk forward towards the dais, and shock replaced the denial on Gideon's face. "Your Majesty, nobody has been led astray. The man before you now is indeed your son, as I am the one who rescued him from your creature. And, I am forced to add, yourself."

Guilt flushed Gideon's features. He said nothing.

Evrard glanced backwards at Gray, whose feet still seemed to be rooted in place, unmoving. He did not want to walk any closer, he did not want to see any more that could not be unseen, and yet this was another thing that he must do. He took one step and then another and then ten more, until he was standing directly next to Rory. Gray reached for his hand and took it, squeezing it tightly.

"I am indeed Graham, and I am no lie," he said, and while he'd hoped to keep his voice neutral, fury leaked into it.

The King took a hesitant step forward and then another, and Gray had to hold himself steady as he came closer and closer, until he was right in front of him. He could see the remnants of who Gideon had been, but they were slight and they were buried under trembling fingers, hazy eyes, and a waning strength that would never again dream of picking up a war hammer and brandishing it.

"Perhaps not," Gideon said slowly, reaching up to tremulously touch the side of Gray's face. "You do look much like him. Much as I'd imagined . . ." His voice trailed off, and Gray had not been mistaken. The guilt and shame in his eyes were unmistakable.

The King knew exactly who he was and he was only attempting to pretend because he did not want to face the enormity of what he had done.

"I am Graham," Gray repeated firmly. "You may either choose to accept me or continue to waste away in your disgrace. That is your choice. But I will not keep Prince Emory and his representatives here, subject to your uncertainty. Nor will I stay. If you have a question you wish to ask of me, then you should ask it. Otherwise"—he paused, remembering finally, some of the rules that Rhys had taught him about oration—"we will be gone from your borders by nightfall."

He started to turn, intending to leave, and a single desperate wail broke the silence. "Wait!" the King shouted. "Wait!"

Gray turned back, and knew his face was hard and unrelenting. This had been the hardest thing he had ever done, and instead of welcoming him home, the King had claimed he was a fraud.

"I was mistaken," the King said in a quiet, despairing voice. "I was wrong to call you a liar. You could be a pretender, but we both know you are not. But mostly I was entirely wrong to give you to her, all those years ago. If you are here, and willing to hear my apology, I would hope to hear your forgiveness." The King looked pitiful and pathetic, tears rolling down his cheeks, and Gray might have been more moved by the sight, but all he felt was righteous and indignant anger.

"You were wrong, yet I have no intention of offering any balm to your conscience," Gray stated. "I was given no quarter and had no choice but to abandon my home and my friends and my father, for fifteen years. There is no forgiveness left in me."

"I understand," Gideon said, his head bowed. "I would expect no less from the Crown Prince of Ardglass."

"Your Majesty," Evrard cut into the uncomfortable silence that followed. "We are also here to discuss the woman who convinced you to condemn your son to death. Certainly you are aware she is attempting to usurp Prince Emory's throne."

Clearly miserable, Gideon nodded. "I had heard of this," he finally acknowledged.

"We are here to formulate a plan to defeat her," Evrard said. "And for that we will need your assistance."

Gideon said nothing for a long, drawn-out moment. As if he almost did not trust himself. "I am willing to give whatever help you need," he said. "But my kingdom has, unfortunately like myself, grown weak. I am not sure we can offer much."

"Ardglass will offer whatever assistance is requested by my party," Gray said. "It is the very least you can do."

Gray collapsed onto the bed in the suite of rooms he'd just been shown to by the steward.

The rooms were not his own, or even the rooms of the Crown Prince, something he knew he was entitled to, but Gray was so exhausted, he couldn't find it in himself to care at the moment. From the moment he'd spotted the spires of Tullamore, he'd been braced for . . . something. Rejection? Acceptance? Apathy? He couldn't have predicted how Gideon would react to his arrival, but what he'd ended up facing had been truly worse than anything his imagination could have conjured.

There'd been a time when all he'd wanted was for his father to regret his actions. Gray had never guessed that regret could be so much more dangerous, so much more upsetting than dismissal. Regret carried claws with it and struck at his most tender, vulnerable spots. Regret brought visions of what could have been, and those hurt so much more fiercely than any memory of what had actually been.

He sighed, lying back and staring at the tapestry hung above the bed. Detailed and finely wrought, it told the story of the first Ard-glassian king, the one who had originally united all the clans, and who had become their leader, at the people's insistence. Without him, Gray would never have existed. This castle would never have existed. And yet, he found himself not being particularly grateful this evening.

A knock sounded on the door, and Gray groaned softly, not wishing to rise from the bed. Only the thought that it could be Rory, come to find him, got him up and moving. Except when he opened the door, it was not Rory's slender figure and auburn curls he saw, but a stooped, wizened figure with thinning gray hair.

Gray stared at his father. "What do you want?" he asked. They'd parted—not on good terms, precisely, but at least under the assumption that Gray and Rory could summon the clans and request they lend their swords to defeat Sabrina.

Kill, Gray had corrected firmly, because after all the devastation and destruction she had wrought, he had no intention of letting her breathe past their inevitable confrontation. After all, she would have killed both him and Rory to serve her own purposes, and while his own life did not feel particularly valuable anymore, Rory's was priceless, and that could never be forgiven.

"I wish a word with you," Gideon said stiffly. One of his guards was a good distance away, watching the interaction between father and son intently, but made no move to follow when Gray eventually waved him in. He supposed they were not particularly worried that Gray would decide to perform patricide in retribution for Gideon's betrayal all those years ago.

"What is it?" Gray demanded, awkwardness at finally being alone with him overwhelming any manners he might once have had. He hadn't known that being alone together would make him alternately want to cry and shake his father so hard his teeth vibrated.

"You stated your ultimate purpose is to defeat Sabrina and place Prince Emory on the throne of Fontaine," Gideon said, and Gray would have to be a lot stupider to miss how careful his words were. "And you also stated your intention is not to leave her alive."

"I will kill her if she can be killed," Gray said grimly.

"You may . . ." Gideon cleared his throat. "You may hesitate when you hear what I am about to say. Or maybe you will not. I cannot say. I wrestled with my conscience if I should tell you the legacy Sabrina left me with, but I decided that it is only fair that the decision lie with you."

"What decision?" Gray did not like where this was going. Sabrina's legacy?

"Her magical hold on me was exceedingly strong. Otherwise"—Gideon glanced at the floor, and Gray was astonished and embarrassed to see his eyes were suddenly full of tears—"she never could have controlled me to the extent she did. I wished for many years I was stronger, not only because her hold over me devastated this kingdom, but because it cost me you."

"That is water under the bridge." Gray knew his tone was unrelenting, but only because if he did not stay strong, he too would break down. He'd been eleven when he had been forced to flee this place. A home and a father were supposed to be a bastion of safety and comfort, and it was a cold, hard realization when they were not.

"It is, but it is not," Gideon said regretfully. "Because when she removed herself, she let me know unequivocally that I would return to making my own decisions, but that I was also forever weakened by the void left by her power. The remnants are what keep me alive. Without the weak spark of her magic remaining inside me, I would . . ."

Gray swallowed hard. "You would die. Her death means your death."

Gideon spread his hands. In supplication? In apology? Gray was not sure, and truthfully was not sure he wanted to know. "She has known from the beginning that you could be her doom."

"And this is supposed to be a barrier forcing me to stay my hand?"

"I do not know, though I suspect yes, that is a convenient complication for her." Gideon leaned against the edge of the huge bed. "I know you are very angry with me, and you have every right to be. I simply . . . I did not want you to be ignorant of it when the moment came, even as I urge you with all haste that you must be her undoing."

The anger inside him surged dangerously. Gray's hand clenched into a tight fist. "So it is to be patricide, after all," he said bitterly.

"I do not tell you this to stay your hand against her," Gideon said. "I tell you this because if this is the last time we meet, I would like us to do so at least under honest terms."

CHAPTER FIFTEEN

It was not very surprising that when he was shown to his chambers for the night, Rory felt unsettled. It had been an eventful day, and even though eventually King Gideon had technically welcomed both him and Gray, Rory knew the King's refusal to believe who Gray truly was had been upsetting for both of them.

Why had he so fiercely insisted it had to be a lie? Rory wasn't sure, but with every second of the King's rejection, his heart had broken for Gray.

Up until those fateful minutes in the throne room, Rory had believed he'd understood Gray's reluctance to return to Ardglass. But the King's reaction had been even more complicated and difficult than Rory could ever have foretold.

He walked over to the window of the tower room he'd been shown to and sighed deeply, wishing they hadn't been forced to come here. Maybe Gray would eventually have wanted to come of his own accord, to settle things with his father. But then, considering how poorly King Gideon looked, Rory thought that time was certainly not on Gray's side.

Rory, lost in his own thoughts, gave a sudden, terrified yelp as a shadowy figure emerged on the other side of the darkened window. Was it another magical creature, come to claim his soul? Rory pulled out his dagger, and though he did not know if he could defeat this monster as he had defeated Sabrina's chimera in the cave, he had to try.

But then the window swung open, and it was only Gray, dangling in front of the window, his hands and feet tangled in a thick rope.

"Gray?" Rory exclaimed. "Why are you here? And like that? Couldn't you have come in through the door?"

Gray simply shrugged, easily climbing over the stone threshold of the wall, and lightly landing on his feet. He pushed the window closed, and after he turned to look at Rory, he finally got a good look at Gray's face.

It was . . . ravaged, nearly.

Rory reached out for him before he even registered what he was doing, taking his arm and leading him to the bed, where he sat him at the edge.

"My father just came to see me," Gray said.

Rory had carefully noted all the names that Gray had used to refer to King Gideon, and most conspicuously, father had been entirely missing from the list. But now, now, he was using it, though it hardly felt like a conscious choice either. Instead it felt to Rory as if Gray had momentarily forgotten why he'd been refusing to call King Gideon his father.

If Gideon had come to see him, alone and apart from everyone else, it must have been serious, and nothing was as convincing an argument as the currently stunned look on Gray's face.

"What did he have to say?" Rory asked.

"Sabrina . . . her magic weakened him, and yet is the only thing keeping him alive." Gray looked up at Rory, who had knelt in front of his lover. "If I kill her, he will also die."

Rory did not know what to say in response to this. One of the things they agreed upon the most—and that was saying something, as they were usually in complete agreement—was that Sabrina could not be allowed to live. But now, how could Rory continue to hold to that line if doing so meant the death of Gray's father?

Pushing suddenly to his feet, Gray began to pace back and forth in the room. "Do you know," he asked, his voice surprisingly conversational, "that this used to be my room? That these are the Crown Prince's chambers?"

"I . . ." Rory was having difficulty keeping up, yet he knew he was considered one of the brightest minds of their age. "I didn't know that."

"I escaped from this room," Gray said, his voice hardening. He turned around in a circle. "The bed was there. I woke up a moment before Rhys warned me, because the noise in the castle was suddenly too loud. I knew something was wrong."

Rory walked up to him and placed a hand on his chest, right over his heart. Felt it beating true and strong. "You are the bravest man I know."

"For escaping when I was a child?" Gray laughed, the sound ringing with bitterness. "I was not brave at all. I was petrified. If not for Rhys and then Evrard, I would have died that day or someday very soon after."

"Not just for that day," Rory corrected softly. "For that day and for all the days after. For this day."

Abruptly, Gray went back to the bed. "I wish he hadn't told me," he finally said, in a devastated murmur.

Rory wished he hadn't told him either. "Was he attempting to sway your opinion?"

"No." Gray was silent for a very long time. "No, he still wants me to kill her."

Frankly, Rory could have wrung Gideon's neck himself, at this point. How dare he place that sort of responsibility on his son's shoulders? After leaving him to the wolves—or one very ruthless chimera?

"It is the right thing to do," Gray added, with grave finality. "I know it is. I know. And yet . . ."

Rory, who had never been lucky enough to know his own father, felt horribly torn. On one hand, he agreed that Gray was right—Sabrina deserved to die and should die, not only for the crimes she had committed, but also to prevent her from committing any in the future. Anyone with her magical power and particular ruthlessness could never be trusted, and prison or exile would mean they were never truly safe from her machinations. But then this was also Gray's father, who had betrayed him, yes, but there was still love between them. Without love, guilt couldn't exist, and Gideon's conscience had seemed very guilty indeed. Added to that fact was the additional wrinkle of Gray's anger—the furthest thing possible from apathy. He would not be so angry if he did not care.

"There is time to consider the choice, and to weigh our options," Rory said.

Gray stared at him starkly. "I usually find very little to argue with when it comes to your logic," he said, "but I'm afraid you are wrong this time. In fact, I believe we have very little time and very little choice."

Wrapping his arms around Gray, Rory held him tightly. He was afraid Gray was all too right.

"She's your aunt," Gray murmured roughly, and Rory squeezed his eyes shut. He had been trying, very hard in fact, not to consider Sabrina in those terms. And he realized, Gray had been doing the exact same thing with his father. Trying to separate himself, trying to pretend he wasn't the only family he had left.

"And he's your father," Rory responded softly. "We will find a way out of this, I promise. And . . ." He hesitated. "If the worst comes to pass, and we have no choice, I will stand beside you, no matter what. You'll not be alone."

The dampness on his shoulder told Rory that at last, he had said the right thing.

After a long, dreamless sleep and a subdued breakfast, Rory and Gray went to meet with Evrard in the stables.

Gideon's stewards had been at a loss as to where to house the noble unicorn, but finally, Evrard had put them out of their uncertainty. "Anywhere that is clean with good, clean hay and water will be perfect-ly sufficient," he'd snapped at them, annoyed at their own indecision.

"I trust you both slept well, at least better than I," Evrard said after they greeted him. "The horses in this stable are most restless."

Gray said nothing, and Rory hadn't wanted to be the one to speak of King Gideon's confession, so he'd merely nodded. "I was thinking," Evrard continued, "it might be nice to get some fresh air. A ride, perhaps?" He leaned down, nose brushing against Rory's shoulder. "Perhaps someplace with less open ears."

"I know just the place," Gray said shortly, and in no time they were both back on Evrard's back, galloping out of the keep itself to the town beyond, and then further than that.

The place Gray brought them to was awe-inducing. Rory had known the keep of Tullamore was built at the peak of a tall hill but had not realized the keep overlooked a large canyon, with a river below, and at the head of the gorge, a spectacular waterfall. Gray had navigated them around the keep, to a spot further down the canyon, and the thundering water would likely drown out their voices to anyone who had attempted to follow.

"Now," Evrard said, when they both dismounted. "Your father said the messengers would leave early this morning for the clans, to ask them to gather. Do you know if they left?"

Gray nodded. "I asked three separate stewards. They indeed rode out first thing this morning."

"Good, they will be back on the morrow," Evrard said with a satisfied nod. "Prince Emory, you will need to work on composing your plea, as none of the army of Ardglass are required by anything other than honor to come to your aid. Even Prince Graham cannot force them. They must come willingly."

"If they don't?" Rory asked, suddenly apprehensive. He was not a great orator and had never before given a speech designed to lead troops. He'd read plenty of them, but that had hardly prepared him to give one himself.

"They must," Evrard said, and the pressure settled on Rory's shoulders like a heavy cloak.

"If they don't, that is not our only problem," Gray said. Rory found himself holding his breath. Surely after Gray confessed about his conversation with his father, Evrard would come up with a creative, inventive solution. Surely, he must. Gray could not be asked to kill his own father, as he killed Rory's aunt. Every man had his limit, and Rory was terrified that asking Gray to do this would be straining his.

"You spoke to your father, then," Evrard said gravely, and Rory's heart squeezed. Did Evrard know? How had he never said? Gray should have been warned.

"You suspected then," Gray said with a heavy sigh.

"You yourself remember the conversation we had after our first fight against her," Evrard said quietly, all smugness leaking from his voice. As if he knew how hard this would be for Gray, and wished he could be spared it, but knew he couldn't. "She leaves creatures in much worse shape after she departs their forms. Most die, but your father is—was—strong, and he resisted her for so long that a spark of his own power remained behind to keep him functioning after she left Tullamore. Unfortunately, it will not be enough to keep him alive after she dies."

"Then he was right." Gray stared at the waterfall, expressionless.

"I wish very much that he had not been, but I'm afraid his intuition is correct here."

Gray turned back to stare at Rory and Evrard, his eyes like two unbearably hot fires. "She cannot be left alive."

Evrard nodded again. "I do not believe there is a safe way to hold her that she would not eventually subvert to her own purpose. She is dangerous, but then you know that already. You've experienced it firsthand."

"There is one problem then," Gray continued, his voice relentless. "One you partially foresaw. Without my father alive, there is no ruler in Ardglass. I will have to return and take up the throne."

"Will you?" Evrard questioned softly.

Gray's eyes burned. "There is hardly any other choice. I cannot simply shirk my duties." He swallowed hard, his Adam's apple bobbing with emotion. "At least not because I wish to be somewhere else. With someone else."

That was when Rory, breathlessly, realized the inherent problem. Gray wanted to stay with him, actually wanted to accept the mantle that had been offered to him with Lion's Breath. He was saying he wished to stay with Rory and be his consort and help Rory rule

Fontaine. But he could not, at least not when Ardglass was in desperate need of a ruler, and the only one who could take the throne was Gray himself.

"What if there was an alternative?" Evrard asked.

"There isn't one," Gray scoffed. "We already talked about this. The options available to us aren't good."

"What about combining the kingdoms?" Rory offered.

He didn't think it was a horrible thought; it was one he'd considered before, at least peripherally. But Gray made a face.

"I don't think it's fair to ask two kingdoms with very little in common, despite a geographical border, to merge together simply because we want to be together," Gray said. Rory frowned, because he was precisely, completely right. It wouldn't be fair. "And," Gray added, "how would we possibly convince the clans? There'd be a rebellion."

"And maybe there should be a rebellion," Evrard said with great satisfaction.

"Excuse me?" Gray said.

"Maybe there should be a rebellion. Why does Ardglass need to be ruled by a king anyhow? Ardglass began as a loose collection of clans, who fought together occasionally, and held summits once a year," Evrard pointed out. "Your father has grown weak. The clans are already ruling themselves. Let them."

"I . . ." Gray hesitated. "Would that even be a good idea?"

"Thirteen generations ago your ancestor conquered the clans and styled himself King. Back then, there were more inter-clan wars. But the acrimony has faded over time, and I no longer believe that a central figurehead is needed to mediate. Maintain your relationships with the clan chiefs and let them rule themselves."

Gray was silent for a long while, digesting Evrard's point of view.

Rory was afraid to offer his own opinion and accidentally sway the other man unfairly. But he did, desperately, want Gray with him, now and in the future. He wanted to grow old with him, to watch him bear Lion's Breath until they were as gray and withered as King Gideon.

"I suppose we could discuss this with the clan representatives after . . ." Gray hesitated. "After our victory." Because until that was achieved, there was no point in discussing this plan with anyone. Gray could die, Rory could die, they could both die and then there would be no need to change anything about the governance of Ardglass. Though if they were defeated, Rory was sure it would only be a matter of time before Sabrina overcame Ardglass' defenses and took that kingdom for her own, along with Fontaine.

Maybe, in the end, the two kingdoms would end up merging regardless of anything Gray or Rory or Evrard did.

"After the victory," Evrard agreed. "Now, about your speech, Rory."

Rory grimaced. "I suppose there is no point in arguing that a speech won't be necessary."

"It will very much be necessary." This unexpectedly came from Gray, not Evrard.

Rory's expression must have reflected surprise because Gray gave a short, humorless laugh. "I was raised to be the Crown Prince of Ardglass, and the future leader of its armies, until I was eleven years old. Rhys taught me well." Gray's voice took on an ironic tone, because essentially he was praising Evrard at that moment, and not really Rhys at all. "I know the clans. They respond to strength and honor. You may not possess much physically of the first, but you have an abundance of the second. And the throne is yours, not hers, which will sway them further."

"It will not be easy, but there are several key facts on our side that will win at least a few clans to our defense, which is all we need," Evrard added. "Still, we will hear your speech."

Rory had certainly not expected to make the speech now and was unprepared. His first version was halting, and painfully awkward.

The second was a slight improvement.

The third time he went through it, he'd grown more comfortable with the most effective phrases, and delivered it, he thought at least, with more than a little aplomb.

Evrard's and Gray's eyes met. "It will do," Gray said. "I'll stand next to him, Lion's Breath prominently displayed. They'll know what it means. Rory might not have the physical strength, but I can project it for both of us."

"It will have to do," Evrard said. "For we have no other choice."

The sun was high in the sky over Tullamore as representatives of the thirteen clans gathered in the main courtyard. Gray and the stewards had overseen the quick erection of a wooden platform, since Rory was on the shorter side. "And," Gray had added, wiping the sweat from his brow as he'd pounded in nails with the rest of the workers, "it has an added bonus of giving you a slightly more physically imposing appearance, since you'll be up higher."

Rory had glanced at him questioningly. "I'm not sure there's much that can truly improve that," he'd admitted.

"Just trust me," Gray had responded. "I can make this work. All you have to do is give the best speech, the most persuasive, speech you're capable of."

Rory had practiced for several more hours with Evrard the evening before and the morning of, as clan members started to pour through the main gate. The only advantage of practicing with Evrard was he refused to lie and claim Rory was doing better than he truly was. The opposite was true actually. Even when Rory felt like he was improving, his dictation and the soaring rise of his voice capturing all the fervor and excitement of helping him reclaim his throne, Evrard would gaze at him with a bored expression and ask, "But are you really trying, Your Highness?"

He was trying, very hard in fact, and so Evrard's words were galling. But they also helped to push Rory to improve much quicker than he would have otherwise.

"Again," Evrard said, and then, "again."

Finally, just when Rory was about to reach over and see if a unicorn could be strangled, Evrard gave him a thoughtful—and extremely rewarding—nod of approval. "You are not as hopeless as I thought you might be," he said.

Not entirely a compliment, but then Evrard was hardly the complimenting type.

As Rory climbed the platform, Gray behind him, sweat dotted his forehead. Nerves, or the heat of the day, Rory wasn't quite sure. But something he did know was that he'd never felt so determined in his life. Not even when they'd left Beaulieu an age ago, or when he'd escaped from the mercenaries come to kill him in Gray's valley, or when he'd faced down the chimera in the cave behind the Veil. It felt as if all those moments were building to this last, great one. He was going to give his speech, and the clans of Ardglass would listen.

He situated himself on the platform, and felt Gray stop next to him, and out of the corner of his eye, watched as he pushed his cloak back, revealing the distinctive pommel of Lion's Breath. A murmur went through the assembled men, as they recognized the sword.

"Clans of Ardglass," Rory exclaimed after a long, drawn-out moment of silent anticipation, "you have been called here today by your king, because your assistance is needed to right a wrong."

Initially Rory had been determined to lead with the fact that their prince had returned to Tullamore, but both Gray and Evrard had immediately dismissed that idea. "This is about you, not Gray," Evrard had cautioned.

"It's a little about Gray," Rory had argued, fiercely. And had then lost, because Gray had spoken up and refused to be mentioned in the speech. From the glint in his eye, Rory knew he wouldn't be easily forgiven if he broke his promise not to do so.

"You know the woman who has taken my throne in Fontaine," Rory continued, voice growing in strength. He tossed his cloak behind him, the bright blue reflected in the sky high above, and strode confidently over the floor of the platform, even though it squeaked and groaned dubiously. Would it stay intact for long enough for Rory to finish his speech? Rory really wasn't certain, but he couldn't let the doubt show either on his face or in his voice. He needed to look the part, like a true leader, and he couldn't do that while worrying the entire structure would collapse under his weight.

"She is dangerous and conniving. In fact, she manipulated and seduced your own king with foul, dark magic. Without her spells, King Gideon would be healthy and strong and your kingdom would mirror his own well-being. Instead, your kingdom is growing weaker, and is prey to others, including a Fontaine led by my aunt. If we do not defeat her now, the chances of doing so later are slim."

Rumblings grew in the crowd. Rory took that as an encouraging sign and continued speaking, his tone growing increasingly impassioned. "That is why you have been called here today. There is an evil lurking in our lands, and it is our responsibility to root it out, destroy it and salt the earth underneath it so no more can ever grow here again. Tomorrow I march on Beaulieu, with my guard and my sworn shield beside me, determined that she will no longer control us with her malevolence. Who is with me?"

His voice died slowly across the echoing courtyard, and he panted a little. Giving speeches was far more difficult and far more exhausting than he'd ever imagined, but he'd done it, at least as well as he ever had, the moment grabbing him and propelling him along.

The only problem was that dead silence had met his fervent plea for assistance.

Not exactly the conclusion he or Evrard had had in mind.

Rory met the stubborn gazes of the clan representatives and quailed. They did not seem at all interested in participating in a war over the throne of Fontaine. Their clans were weakened by what Sabrina had wrought in Ardglass, and in their own king, and that was obviously less pressing than Rory's immediate problem. And that, as Evrard had worried, was exactly the problem with trying to rally soldiers of another country. They were always more interested in fixing their own problems, than meddling in anybody else's problems.

He knew he needed to do something, but what he knew he needed to do was dangerous—as in Gray might not ever forgive him for it. But without saying it, Rory did not know if they would have any men to march with them to Beaulieu. Without an army, they would have no chance of making it anywhere near Sabrina. Definitely not close enough to kill her.

In the end, Rory's decision was surprisingly easy. He was stuck between one stubborn near-consort, and the rest of the even more stubborn men of Ardglass.

I'm so sorry, he thought fervently in Gray's direction. I know this is not how you wanted to do it, and I did not want it this way either.

"I stand here today, not only as a prince of Fontaine, a neighboring country to your own, but also as a man who has found what has been missing from Ardglass for all these many years." Rory heard Gray's intake of breath behind him, sharp and tight, and Rory figured that since he didn't grab him or physically stop his mouth, then that was as good of permission as he was ever going to get. "I present to you," he continued, "the lost prince returned, Prince Graham of Ardglass, here bearing my sword, the Lion's Breath, and sworn to protect me til death."

That got their attention immediately. Murmurs swelled in the audience to shocked gasps and confused exchanges among the different clans.

One of the clansmen stood. "How can we be sure?" he demanded. "Aye, he looks much like Graham did, but His Highness was small when he was killed."

Come help me answer these men, Rory thought, glancing backwards, where Gray was staring at him with a mixture of anger and resignation. Nobody else is going to convince them who you are except for you.

Rory held out his hand and urged him with his eyes. Come, please. And finally, he did, albeit very reluctantly. Gray stepped forward, and even though he'd clearly accepted the position that Rory had placed him in, he did not look thrilled about it.

"I am indeed Prince Graham, and yes, I was quite small when I was lost. Because that is what I was. Lost, not dead."

A louder rumble echoed through the gathered crowd.

"Prince Emory found me and restored me to you," Gray said, his voice rising perfectly with the rising excitement of the crowd. He didn't even practice, Rory thought glumly. "And with me at your side, it is our duty, our responsibility, to make sure that the woman who forced me to abandon my home does no other harm. To Prince Emory or to any of the clans of Ardglass."

A great yell reverberated through the men—first one and then another and then a hundred resounding confirmations, followed by foot stamps and clapping.

He had won them over when Rory had failed. At least they had been successful, Rory thought, because if this gamble had failed and he'd been left with no army and no Gray, he'd have had no chance of ever retaking his kingdom. He'd probably, Rory contemplated moodily, have died unhappy and alone, with Sabrina's unearthly eyes the last thing he saw. It was not a pleasant vision.

The exclamations coming from the crowd were excessive enough, but then one by one, the men fell to one knee, arms crossed over their breasts, to honor the man who stood on the dais. Not Rory, but Gray.

Rory could see he wasn't outwardly frowning, but the edges of his lips had drawn together so tightly they'd turned white. Gray was clearly displeased, and it was not a stretch to believe that it was Rory he was the most displeased with.

Finally, the painful exercise ended, but the moment he and Gray descended from the platform, they were overtaken by maniacally happy, rejoicing soldiers, who believed that their savior had finally come, all in the guise of a lost prince returned to them. Rory, watching Gray borne away on a tide of goodwill, eventually turned away from the crowd in the courtyard and made his way back into the keep, listlessly meandering through the hallways. He hadn't seen where Evrard had gone to, because he'd tucked himself away, not wanting to overwhelm and distract the clans with his magnificence.

That, Rory thought despondently, was a real irony. Because in the end, all he'd done was to overwhelm and distract with his reveal of Gray's true self.

After a few minutes, he found himself at the huge carved double doors leading to the throne room. He'd overheard one of the stewards mention the King rarely used it, and since all the guests were outside, falling to their knees in front of Gray, surely it would be empty now. At least, this would be a great place for Rory to hide, since he wasn't quite mentally ready to come face to face with Gray just yet.

He pulled open one of the doors and slipped inside.

The candles were not lit, but the skylights still brought impressive light to the enormous space. The throne on the dais was empty, and Rory skirted it, instead choosing to walk near the silk banners lining each side of the hall. Heavily embroidered with gold thread, the overall number must mean they depicted the sigils of each of the Ardglassian clans.

"Hiding? How unprincely of you."

A voice started Rory and he turned to see the King lurking in one of the shadowed alcoves between two of the fluttering emerald green banners. He stepped out, and slowly hobbled over to where Rory stood.

"I'm sorry," Rory stammered, slightly ashamed at being caught in another country's throne room, clearly hiding from the chaos he'd just created outside. Then he realized that the King had been in here too, by himself. Hiding as well? Rory wondered.

"How unkingly of you," Rory added, giving him a sheepish smile. "But it's alright. I won't tell anyone."

"Even my son?" Gideon asked with a heavy sigh.

Rory thought this over for a moment. "I'm not sure he's truly interested in anything I have to say, now," Rory said slowly.

"He is very proud," Gideon pointed out. "But then it's likely you already knew that."

Rory nodded.

"He must have been very surprised that you chose that moment to reveal who he was," Gideon said.

Surprised? Rory wasn't sure that was exactly the right term. He couldn't have been all that surprised. Perhaps disappointed, instead. "He asked me not to and I did it anyway," Rory confessed. "I suppose I'm not a very convincing orator." Of all the shame he felt, this was the strongest. If he'd given a better speech, perhaps it never would have come to revealing Gray.

A glimmer of a smile emerged on King Gideon's face. "You're not as bad as you think. The Ardglassians are bitter, indignant, and excessively stubborn. Graham knows that, even if he's tried to forget it. He'll forgive you."

Rory was not quite so sure. After all, Gray had explicitly asked him not to, he'd agreed, and then he'd done it despite his promise.

"I do know," Gideon continued, "how much my son cares about you, because I do not think he ever would have returned here otherwise." It was impossible to guess how difficult an admission that was for both a king and a father, and the pain in Gideon's voice echoed that fact. "He'll come around."

"Perhaps," Rory said, not feeling particularly optimistic despite the King's words.

That was when Gideon's prediction was put to the test, as that was the moment the doors swung open, and then Gray came stalking through them, a dark glower on his handsome face.

"There you are," he said, only to Rory, ignoring his father completely. "I've been looking for you everywhere. You're missing the summit to plan our attack on Beaulieu."

"I didn't know we were having one," Rory said hesitantly.

Gray frowned. "Of course we are. And you have important information we need." He turned to go, assuming, Rory supposed, that he would simply follow when summoned. For someone who didn't think he was a born leader, he certainly seemed to take naturally to it. Behind Gray's back, Rory glanced over at the King, who was staring sadly at the floor. Rory gave him a shrug and went to follow Gray's long strides out of the throne room.

CHAPTER SIXTEEN

Though he'd hoped to feel differently, Gray wasn't any less furious at Rory the next day. His anger had been building from the moment on the platform when Rory had glanced back at him, shot him an apologetic look, and had proceeded to blow his life apart.

He'd hoped after a few pints of ale with the clansmen and a dreamless night of sleep, he might feel differently about Rory's betrayal, but the self-recriminating look on his face had haunted Gray and he'd not slept a single wink. Rory had known how much revealing Gray's parentage, as publicly as possible, in order to convince the clansmen, would hurt him. And yet, he'd done it anyway.

Gray wasn't stupid; he'd known that enough of Tullamore knew the truth, including the stewards—the biggest gossips in the whole keep—so it would be impossible to hide it forever. But Gray had been counting on being able to slowly reveal who he was. Certainly not blurt it out without any finesse and without any preparation, and all because Rory wanted men to march with them to Beaulieu?

He knew just how much Rory wanted his throne back, because at one point, he'd felt the exact same way. There hadn't only been seeds of uncertainty and doubt that anyone else could do as credible a job as himself but going from prince to farmhand had been a blow to his pride. For the first eleven years of his life, he'd been raised to be one thing. Being the Crown Prince had defined who Gray was. That was no longer true, but he still felt the painful echo of loss. Strangely, he'd felt it less since returning to Tullamore. Seeing his father, incalculably diminished, and the clans hampered rather than helped by his rule over them, had sweetened much of his bitterness. He'd listened to Evrard's suggestion, and then spent the last few days considering the possibilities. If they survived—a very big if—then Gray knew he would do his part to help untangle the monarchy of Ardglass, suggesting to the thirteen clans that they might rule themselves.

Gray also wanted Sabrina dead just as much as Rory. Perhaps more, if he was willing to sacrifice his already-failing father over it, but the point remained. Rory had taken precipitous action yesterday, and he hadn't apologized for it, which Gray could only assume meant he wasn't actually sorry.

Considering how many men were saddling in the courtyard, fires extinguished in the early morning dew, smoke rising from their ashes, Gray thought maybe it might have been worth it. But surely, surely there had been another way.

Evrard trotted over to him, ignoring all the awed expressions in his wake. Gray knew a little how he felt now. Everywhere he went, Gray was treated like a savior, the man who could rescue all of them from ruin.

I rescued myself, Gray thought as Evrard stopped in front of him. You should do the same.

"You aren't riding with Prince Emory," Evrard said, his tone chastising. "You cannot be angry with him for doing what needed to be done."

Evrard had yet to discover that telling Gray he could not do something ever actually prevented him from doing it.

"I can and I am," Gray retorted, swinging his leg over his saddle and placing a calming hand on the twitchy neck of his horse. Like Gray, he was used to solitude, and there were so many people in this courtyard.

All willing, Gray thought, to help them kill Sabrina. It was a heady thought, and for a second, he hesitated. Rory's words had given them this chance.

Gray's eyes snapped to Evrard. "Get out of my head," he insisted coldly. "You are not welcome there, and certainly not to change my mind about Rory."

Evrard did not look the slightest bit apologetic. "I hardly had to insert any thoughts at all. There's a part of you that doesn't just want to forgive him, it needs to forgive him." He shook his mane out, his voice growing just as strident at Gray's. "You should think on that during the journey to Beaulieu."

Gray did not think Evrard had much power over his mind. Not enough power anyway to force him to do anything he did not want to do, and certainly not enough power to force him to think on something he did not wish to think on. Yet, for the whole morning of the first day of their journey, it was difficult to think of anything else. It was true, he wanted to forgive Rory, but as Evrard had said it was definitely more than that.

Was this the power of fate driving him towards Rory? Or was it his own feelings? It was so difficult to separate one from the other anymore, and though Gray believed his feelings were true, he couldn't help but wonder if they'd been impacted by his and Rory's intertwined destiny.

Ten of the clans had sent troops, and Gray thought their number was at least five hundred. Easily enough to march upon Beaulieu, especially if they were not expecting an invading force. Beaulieu did not hold a particularly large garrison, Marthe had explained, there were only a few dozen guards stationed there at any given time.

This would hopefully be an easy march, followed by a quick defeat.

Gray tightened his fingers on the reins and refused to let himself contemplate the terrible possibility that he would not be staying on at Beaulieu at all, but that he would end up returning, alone, to the valley.

Only a month ago that was all he'd wanted out of this quest, but now, coming to the end of it, it was impossible to deny how much more he wanted.

A life. A future. Companionship. Love.

Gray shook his head, wishing the physical motion could dislodge the frustrating thoughts from his uncooperative mind, but as they continued to ride down the road, they stuck persistently. And this time, he couldn't even blame Evrard.

When the sun was high in the sky, Marthe, whom he had elected to lead this combined company because of her experience and her knowledge of the Fontaine fortifications and armies, held up a hand to signal they were to stop in this clearing for a midday break.

Supplies of dried meat and bread and cheese were distributed, along with flasks of cooled, refreshing water fetched from a nearby stream.

Gray must have had a thundercloud on his face, because to his surprise, he was left alone, an empty circle around where he sat under a shady evergreen tree.

The abrupt delineation between him and the rest of the soldiers made it very obvious when Rory finally approached him.

Who are you kidding? Gray sneered at himself. You would have spotted him in a crowd of a thousand men. And not just because of that ridiculously bright blue cloak.

He refused to let himself touch the pommel of Lion's Breath as Rory approached, contrite expression on his face. His fingers had wanted to stray to it so many times during the morning, and he'd forced them to remain at his side. He did not need to touch a sword to remind himself of his obligations or his feelings.

"Gray," Rory said, the single word punctuated with a heavy sigh.

It was difficult, but Gray did not look up. Instead, he fixed his eyes on a small pile of evergreen needles to the right of Rory's boot.

"Gray," he sighed again. "At least look at me."

Rory clearly did not understand that avoiding his gaze was the only thing keeping Gray from immediately getting to his feet and wrapping his arms around him. It was self-preservation, only.

"I understand how upset you are with me," Rory continued, as Gray's fingers dug into his thigh. "I really am very sorry that I said what I did, but you have to understand how little choice I felt like I had in the matter. Something needed to be done. Evrard made it very clear that it was my responsibility to convince the clans, but truthfully, they didn't care about me. What they care about is you."

Worst of all, Rory's apology made plain and indisputable sense. Of course the clans of Ardglass wouldn't care about Rory's plight. They were struggling, after the departure of Sabrina had made Gideon so weak, and it was all they could do to keep their own borders and lands intact. Marching out to defeat an enemy currently entirely occupied with another country? It didn't make sense and it provided them with no tactical advantage whatsoever.

But bringing the lost Crown Prince of Ardglass into the situation? Using him to convince the clans that fighting was necessary? Logic was no longer a part of the discussion; they had volunteered based on emotion alone. He was their savior and even if he was marching them off to free another land, he would return and free their own.

In a manner of speaking, anyway.

Rory had known this, maybe not before his speech began, because he'd wanted to believe he could deliver a rousing enough argument that would convince them anyway. But Evrard? He surely had known Rory's oratorical skills wouldn't be enough.

"That meddling unicorn," Gray spat out under his breath. "Someday . . ."

Rory looked at him in confusion. "What does this have to do with Evrard?"

"Everything has to do with Evrard," Gray said, rolling his eyes. "I'm sure you've realized that by now. You're a very smart man, Rory."

Slowly, Rory nodded. "I do see that . . . but . . . how does Evrard have anything to do with this?"

Gray sighed.

"He wanted to show me that we were much stronger together than we are apart. I knew it already, but . . . I let my bitterness overwhelm me. I'd believed it was fading, over time, that I didn't care anymore, but I guess I do."

Rory, encouraged by this confession, sat down next to Gray, unceremoniously plopping himself on the ground, regardless of his buff-colored breeches. He put a hand on Gray's shoulder, an earnest expression on his face. "Honestly, Gray, how can I blame you for being bitter? We are stronger together than we are apart, though I don't find I understand how Evrard telling me explicitly not to mention your lineage and then me being forced to do so is supposed to convince us of anything." Rory stopped, a suddenly blinding, lopsided smile freezing Gray's heart. He could sit here and watch Rory smile forever. "Unless he was trying to convince us he's a meddling, foolish creature. Because that I understand completely."

"It's a common military technique," Gray said slowly. "Pretend battle. A minor skirmish to prepare your troops for the larger, much more real fight. He wanted us to understand our strengths now, before we approach Beaulieu, where Sabrina will do everything she can to sow doubt between us."

Rory was quiet for a long moment. "I still should have asked you first," he said quietly.

But Gray knew he'd been wrong. Evrard hadn't come out and said it. Rory hadn't even done so, though he'd obliquely referred to it in his apology. But the truth of it was currently blinding him. He reached out and clasped Rory's hands in his own. "You see these men around us? Five hundred of the clans of Ardglass marching with us to a battle that isn't even theirs. We wouldn't have them if you hadn't announced to them who I was. This army wouldn't even exist, and without it, our future wouldn't exist."

Rory's eyes warmed, amber turning to gold. "You truly mean that," he whispered.

"After this is over, and we survive, and you have taken your proper place on the throne of Fontaine," Gray said, more certain of this than anything he'd ever been in his whole life, "I will take my place, which will always be by your side."

After lunch, Gray retook that place, by Rory's side, as they rode towards Beaulieu.

Rowen had shot him an amused glance. "I see that you have returned to us," she said.

"Like he could possibly hope to keep away," Anya said with an affectionate smile for Gray.

"If you're theorizing that I'm irresistible, I won't object," Rory had inserted, with a delighted laugh.

They rode in loose formation for the rest of the day, Gray refusing to leave Rory's side. He wore Lion's Breath proudly, never keeping his fingers from touching the hilt if they wanted to. He might have been born in Ardglass, and raised to be the Crown Prince of that country, but the years in the valley had changed him and now he no longer felt taking over the throne from his father was the right path for either him or for his country. He was meant to protect Rory, to shield him from harm, and help him become the fairest, kindest ruler that Fontaine had ever known. The sword, which wasn't supposed to be his ancestral bequest, had begun to feel like it anyway. As for Ardglass, Evrard's words kept echoing in his head: it had originally been thirteen clans.

Two days passed, much the same, and then on the last night, Marthe announced over the fires that on the morrow, they would be in Beaulieu. The reckoning had arrived.

Rory's tent was bright blue with dangling golden ribbons. Gray glanced at it, fondness in his gaze, and even though he'd set up his own, much plainer tent, he had no intention of letting Rory sleep alone tonight.

He'd kept to his own tent the previous two nights, because Marthe's pace, directed by Evrard, had been intense and exhausting. They needed to reach Beaulieu before Sabrina managed to call up any additional armies to her cause and before she spread any more poisonous lies about Rory's preparedness for the throne. They'd been worn out each night, but tonight, they'd stopped early in preparation for the battle tomorrow. Marthe, who many of the clansmen had initially muttered about following under their breath, had proven to be an adept leader of their forces and Gray felt justified in her appointment with every thoughtful, wise choice she made.

But tonight, he'd not keep to his own tent. Gray could not imagine spending possibly his last night on earth with anyone other than Rory.

Acadia had cornered him before the evening meal was served, and offered the tidbit of information, under her breath, that she had deliberately pitched the guards' tents further away tonight. "Privacy is important," she'd told him quietly. "We understand that."

Gray joined Rory's fire as he had the other nights, the rest of the guard sitting around it, except for Marthe, who was very busy with preparations for tomorrow's final march.

"Are you ready for tomorrow?" Diana asked Rory softly. "You may have to do things you would not normally choose to do. Battle is like that."

It was clear from the shadows in Rory's eyes that he had considered this possibility already, and had come to terms with it, even if he did not necessarily like it. Gray himself had been forced to do so, with his own father's confession. He did not know if his father would die the moment Sabrina perished, but he did not expect to ever see him again.

Their goodbye, brief but fraught, had been additionally on his mind the last few days.

"May your sword swing true," his father had said, offering him a handclasp. Gray had hesitated for a long moment but had finally taken it.

"May my shield guard you," Gray finished, the words an ancient Ardglassian adage for those headed to war.

And that was all they had said to one another. Somehow, it was going to have to be enough, Gray thought as he stared at Rory.

It would have to be, because Gray had no intention of returning to Ardglass without Sabrina's blood on his hands.

"We may all have to do things we would not normally choose," Rory said carefully, and he glanced over at Gray.

"Some things are bigger than us," Anya offered. "I would give my life to ensure the safety of both your kingdoms. And I do not offer it lightly, because in all honesty it's a good one and I wish to keep it, but this quest is more important than a single life."

Gray could not help but think of his father, sitting in Tullamore and waiting to die. Wanting to die, if it meant the woman who had destroyed him preceded him.

"Tomorrow will bring many changes," Rowen said, and her quiet, decisive words left a thoughtful silence.

She did not need to say that some of the people sitting around the fire in a loose semicircle might not be there the next evening.

"Enough," Rory said suddenly, and stood. His eyes glowed in the firelight, intent and purposeful, his gaze settling directly onto Gray. "Yes, we might all die tomorrow. Yes, we might all do terrible things so we can survive, but tonight we're alive still and I'm not going to waste this moment by worrying about what the morning might bring." He held out a hand to Gray.

Gray stared at him, surprised and more than a little aroused. If Rory wanted to spend this night—the last night they might possibly have—proving he was alive with Gray, he certainly was not going to turn him down. Reaching out, he took Rory's hand and rose to his feet.

"Goodnight," he said, and it was hard, following Rory, who was very clearly leading him to his tent, not to flush. There was something about Rory being so overt about his intentions that unmanned Gray. Rory never flaunted his affections, but there was a bluntness to his behavior tonight that Gray discovered he really enjoyed. Everyone who was watching—which was basically everyone in the whole camp, since Gray was their long-lost prince, and Rory was the famous Autumn Prince—knew exactly how it was between them.

The tent was much smaller inside than Gray had anticipated, even though his own was barely any bigger. He tried stooping, but the height of the bright blue fabric eventually defeated him and he sank to his knees, gazing over at Rory, who'd sat down at the edge of the low-slung cot.

"I see you're properly kitted out," Gray teased him. "I don't think I even got one of those."

Rory smiled. "If they'd tried to give you one, you'd have given it back."

That was definitely true, and it made Gray's hands feel warm and clammy to hear Rory knew that about him. Knew it and not only didn't mind but enjoyed it enough to bring that amused little half smile to his beautiful face.

"I won't deny," Gray said, rising up to move over to the cot where he gently sat down next to Rory, "that I'm pleased we won't have to make love on the ground tonight." He picked up one of Rory's hands. They were still smooth-ish, but Gray could feel the beginnings of callouses from the reins, from sword practice, and from the much harder living he'd been doing. He raised it to his mouth and dropped kisses on the tips of each of his fingers.

"Is that what it would be?" Rory asked quietly. "Making love?" His eyes met Gray's, questioning. Unsure, still, which was something Gray couldn't abide any longer.

"I'm ready to dedicate my life to your service. Not only as your guard or your sworn shield, but as the man who stands by your side every single day, through the good and the bad and the worst you can imagine and loves you through all of it." Gray had imagined it would be harder to say those words, since he'd always longed to say them, but had never actually imagined he would meet someone he'd feel comfortable saying them to. But to say them to Rory felt natural, like breathing. Like he was confessing something he'd known was true for a very long time, and his brain was only just now catching up to his heart and soul.

"You truly mean that," Rory exhaled slowly. "You love me."

Gray grinned, and maybe he should've been more nervous that Rory wouldn't return his feelings, but he knew Rory as well as Rory knew him, and it was indisputable, like the sun rising in the east, that Rory loved him too.

"I do. I do love you." He hesitated. "I know you want to celebrate being alive tonight, but I couldn't let you go into Beaulieu tomorrow without you knowing. It would be the biggest regret of my life."

Rory's eyes were luminous as they locked onto his. "Do you have any right now? Regrets?"

"Only that I'm not kissing you right now," Gray said, and Rory laughed.

"I do think I will like having you by my side," Rory said, laugh lines still creasing his face. "I would be honored if you would be with me."

"The honor would be all mine," Gray said, and leaning down, covered his mouth with his own. They kissed and kissed, Gray drawing the kisses out forever. Soft and slow and gentle giving rise to fast and hot and damp, his mouth slanting over Rory's as he memorized every single part of what it meant and what it felt to kiss him this deeply.

He couldn't think that this could be the last time, but the words lay between them anyway, unspoken but very much present in the air.

Gray undressed him slowly, carefully, dotting kisses over every bit of pale skin he exposed, until he finally sank down, bending over Rory's boots to unlace them.

Glowing, Rory reached for him once the rest of his clothes had been disposed of. "I do love you too," he said, the tender look in his eyes something that Gray knew he would take to the grave. Whether that was tomorrow, or in fifty years.

"Lie back, my darling," Gray murmured, and Rory, who usually tried to push or argue in bed, went quietly, like he understood how important this was for Gray to do this.

As he slicked his tongue up Rory's hard length, he remembered the first moment he'd ever seen this prince. He'd been dressed like a peacock, all shining satin and gold thread, and his very presence had been a confusing revelation to Gray—a bright intrusion of a world that he'd long since come to terms with losing. But it had hurt that day, not just because he'd been jealous of Rory's peaceful childhood or his title, but because he'd believed then that there would be no chance to get to know the beautiful boy with the auburn curls any better. They were meant for two different worlds, and Gray knew he shouldn't even bother hoping for better.

But now he had better, he had the very best, and he'd earned it, not because he was Prince Graham, but because he was Gray. He knew it wouldn't have mattered to Rory if he'd claimed his lineage or not. Or if he'd never had any lineage to begin with. Rory bucked and groaned, Gray's tongue wrapping around the head of his cock. It was easy because what lay between transcended the right and wrong of the world.

Fated, Evrard liked to say, and Gray, who'd never particularly believed in fate one way or another, believed in it now.

"Gray," Rory gasped, reaching down to tangle his fingers into Gray's hair as he rolled his hips, searching for the bright hot heat of Gray's mouth. He knew Rory was growing closer, the tension tightening between them, and he slipped a spit-slick finger down between Rory's thighs, teasing his entrance, circling it. That, and a single fierce suck, was all it took for Rory to give a fierce shout, his orgasm pumping into Gray's mouth as he swallowed.

"You are perfect," Rory said drowsily as he recovered, eyes golden and languorous, the most beautiful thing Gray had ever seen. "Let me," he added as Gray loosened his own breeches.

How could Rory say he was perfect, when Rory's small delicate hand moving over his own rampant erection felt like the most spectacular thing in the world? He'd never understood before why men and women killed and died for this fleeting physical pleasure, but when it was with someone you adored, who adored you back, the truth of it undeniable and undiminished? It was only enough to feel that pressure and feel the love spreading through him, and Gray was groaning too, exploding all over that small, surprisingly adept hand.

Rory dug for a handkerchief and wiped Gray's come off his hand. He was unhinged enough, the magic of this night wrapping around them so tightly Gray wasn't sure it would ever let go, that he was almost sad to see it disappear.

"Come," Rory said, and held out his hand again. He'd reclined in the cot, pulling the blankets back to make a spot for Gray. He didn't need any further encouragement, he quickly unlaced his boots and shed the rest of his clothes, lying down next to Rory.

Placing a hand over his heart, Rory cuddled close. "Tomorrow," he said softly, "I'm afraid everything will be different."

It would be. Tomorrow, if they were both very skillful and very lucky, Sabrina would be dead. "This won't be different," Gray promised. "That will have to be enough."

And it was.

CHAPTER SEVENTEEN

Very early the next morning, they marched for Beaulieu. Rory hadn't felt much like eating—anxiety and nerves coalesced in a tight, unpleasant ball at the base of his stomach—and even Gray hadn't pushed him.

They'd camped half a day from the tower gates of the castle, and by the time they'd been on the road for a few hours, the advance scouts Marthe had bidden to ride ahead were already beginning to return.

After the third had arrived in a cloud of dust and echoing hoof beats, Marthe ordered a halt.

Gray, Rory, and Evrard rode up to where she stood, with the rest of Rory's guard and several of the clansmen. She glanced up as they approached, a frown on her face. "Somehow, I believe Sabrina has been alerted to our presence," she said. "I suppose it cannot be too surprising. We are a company of nearly five hundred men. She could have had spies alongside the road from Tullamore." They had taken a lesser-known route, trying to avoid any of Sabrina's informants, but clearly she was better prepared than they'd anticipated.

"I would have," Gray volunteered. "And she is far more conniving than I am." Evrard nodded, his own face grim.

"Regardless, she has managed to put a force together, and they are currently encamped in front of the first gate." She shot Rory an apologetic look. "I'm afraid, Your Highness, that our original plan of using the men as an arrow to drive you into the castle proper is not going to work."

"How many men?" Gray asked. It occurred to Rory, after hearing Gray's question, that he had been raised much differently for those first eleven years. He'd truly been educated and trained to be a king, as well as a leader of the Ardglassian armies. And while they might not have been the reasons Rory loved him and wanted him by his side, those were skills that were undeniably helpful now and would continue to be in the years to come.

"Approximately as many as we have mustered, Your Highness," one of the advance scouts said, pushing his hair back, as he addressed this answer to Gray, not to Rory. Who definitely did not feel a tiny twinge of guilt, despite Gray's forgiveness. He'd done this—revealed Gray's lineage to the clans and brought this force together. It was entirely his fault that Gray made a face at the way the soldier addressed him. Maybe it had been a necessary evil, but Rory couldn't pretend he wasn't responsible for it.

"Theoretically, then," Marthe said, "we could engage this force, and perhaps be a distraction to help a much smaller force sneak into the castle proper, in order to confront the Regent Queen. Her men will not continue to fight for her if she is dead. Rory is the heir. Once she is gone, then their loyalty should be easily won."

Rory did not particularly like the idea of anyone fighting and potentially dying for him, but since he'd called this army for exactly that purpose, he could hardly express this thought.

"This plan is . . . risky," Evrard offered. Nothing else. In Rory's experience, Evrard had an opinion about everything. Right now might be the first time Rory had ever heard him demure. But then it occurred to Rory why he was doing it; he was letting Gray, who had been born to be a leader, lead.

"Sabrina is dangerous, but I agree it's best to engage her with a very small force. The distraction will help." Gray shifted in his saddle. "I will take Rory and a handful of his guards. Rory—do you know a different way into the castle?"

"I do," Rory said slowly. "Through the sewer would probably be the best for what you have in mind."

"An excellent choice of route," Anya added. "I will come with you."

"As will I," Diana said.

"I would also be honored to accompany you and Prince Emory," said the scout who had given them the earlier information.

"Thank you . . ." Gray said.

"Kristian," the man said, bowing his head.

"Thank you, Kristian," Gray repeated, with a smile. "Then we are decided. Marthe and the main force will distract and delay with their attack on the army at the gate, while we go through the sewers to reach Sabrina."

Marthe nodded. "Do you have a plan on how to kill her?" she asked.

Gray had a troubled but unsurprisingly resolute look in his eyes. "I intend to kill the bitch any way she can be killed," he said.

The rest of the force's progress crawled nearly to a halt as they crept closer to the army waiting for them at the gate of Beaulieu.

Before separating, Gray and Rory consulted with Evrard, who, to Rory's astonishment, demurred from participating in their small group. "I will stay with the army," Evrard said. "They are vulnerable. You are strong. I must continue with whoever needs my help the most."

If Gray was surprised at Evrard's identification of their five-person group as "strong," and the five hundred soldier force as "vulnerable," he did not look it. Instead, he asked Rory where the best place was to enter the sewers.

"Not at the front of the castle, by the gate," Rory said. "Instead, we should go around the side, where an extension of the drainage system runs down to a creek that's a few thousand feet away from the castle. That's the best place to go in." Admittedly, Rory had never actually seen this part of the sewer system, but he knew it existed because he could picture very clearly in his mind the layout of the castle and the detailed drawing of the sewer system laid over it.

"Then we will head toward this stream. It's also advantageous as Marthe's force will move slower, forestalling a confrontation as long as possible, whereas we will need to move quickly and urgently. It also takes us away from the main force in case there's a trap that Sabrina's laid for them."

"If she's breathing, there will be a trap of some kind," Evrard warned.

And that fact, Rory assumed, was why the main force was so vulnerable. He prayed that Evrard was able to identify the trap and unravel it before it caused any terrible damage.

"If you're right and there is a trap," Gray said grimly as they tightened their saddles, disposed of any superfluous baggage, and armed themselves for the skirmish to come, "we will be their only remaining hope."

Five of them, Rory included, did not feel like a particularly hopeful number, but Gray sounded grimly determined that this plan would work.

It had to work, Rory reminded himself. If they were defeated today, then it would give Sabrina more time to muster additional soldiers, and their own small force could not possibly hope to overcome those odds. They might not be catching her entirely unawares, but they would have to find and kill her nonetheless. Rory gripped the hilt of the bronze dagger he'd hung at his belt, remembering their confrontation in the cave behind the Veil. He'd injured her then, but none of the blows had been mortal. Despite Gray's grim confidence, they did not really know how to kill her.

"Evrard," Rory hissed as Gray gave directions to the rest of their group, "Evrard," he repeated again, when Evrard seemed disinclined to answer him right away. "How can we possibly kill her? Do you know any weaknesses that she might possess?"

The unicorn swung his great head towards Rory. "Between you and Gray, you are capable," Evrard said. "Did he not tell you he asked me?"

Rory frowned. "No, he did not."

"I told him the identical thing. What I know is you are capable of it, but that is all I can share."

That was all Evrard, being exceptionally helpful to the end. But Rory also couldn't be angry with him, not when he was staying behind, and attempting to protect the five hundred men Rory himself had convinced to come on this quest.

"Good luck," Rory said, heart suddenly in his throat. He realized that if anything went wrong, this might be the last time he ever saw Evrard. Impulsively, he dismounted and reached out for the unicorn, wrapping him in a quick, tight hug. "Thank you for saving my life, and for bringing Gray into it."

"I did very little," Evrard insisted, but Rory didn't think he'd imagined the pleased note in his voice.

"Farewell," Rory said, remounting his horse, and turning to join Gray and the rest of the group.

As Gray had planned, they rode hard towards the creek. Rory, who was not used to riding at the point position, was directed there by Gray because he was the only one who knew the way.

Even though he was terrified down to the marrow of his bones at what the rest of the afternoon would bring, Rory discovered that it was easier to be expending energy on a solid plan, working towards a concrete goal. As they continued to ride, Rory discovered that both his hands and his confidence felt steadier.

He did not know how Gray had felt, seeing the spires of Tullamore for the first time in fifteen years, but when the generously round towers of Beaulieu appeared for the first time, Rory abruptly drew up on his reins, slowing his horse, and as a result, the rest of their group.

"What is it?" Gray asked, concern leaking into his voice. Surely, he was afraid that Rory had spotted something untoward that might not bode well for their party, but instead it had just been the towers of his home that had given Rory pause.

It's only been a few weeks for me, even though those days have irrevocably changed my life, Rory reminded himself. It was fifteen long years for Gray. Stop being silly, it's not the same.

But it felt something like what Gray must have experienced; a lesser echo of that same feeling. The joy of seeing home again, crossed with dread at what entering it again might hold. The realization that after this day, he might be solely responsible for its sturdy brick walls and thousands of people living not only within its walls, but scattered throughout the countryside.

"It will be all right," Gray finally said, when Rory said nothing. "I will be right here, by your side."

Rory would never deny that this promise helped him enormously, but he knew now it could not be all his strength.

The rest of it he needed to find inside himself.

He took one deep breath, and then another. A voice inside him said, you were born for this. And he had been, hadn't he? He'd not been raised to it, like Gray had, but the same blood ran in his veins that had run in the veins of his father, whom Evrard had said was a fair and benevolent ruler. He would never get the chance to see what sort of king he would be, if he didn't forcibly eject the woman who had taken his throne.

Purpose coalesced inside Rory, and he looked up at the towers of Beaulieu with a firm, steady gaze. "Yes, you will," he said to Gray. He didn't need to tell him that he'd found a similar well of strength inside himself, because Gray's approving glance told him that he looked it.

Strong. Kind. Honorable. Determined.

He had read so many texts about the great kings of old, and he knew what separated them from the rulers that history didn't remember. Rory vowed that, if given the chance, he would live up to his father's example.

Anya gave a shout, and Rory looked over where she stood, and realized she'd found the creek the sewer system dumped into.

Unfortunately, the diagrams Rory remembered hadn't detailed exactly the state of entrance of the system, and when they approached it, he realized it was covered by a very sturdy-looking grate. The holes between the iron bars were small—far too small for even Rory to fit through.

Gray sighed, and dismounted, walking over to the opening of the sewer. "We must take this off," he said. "Did anyone bring an ax?"

Kristian brought one over from one of his packs. "You never know what you might need in a battle," he said, handing it over to Gray. "D'you need any help?"

Dubiously, Rory eyed the grate. It seemed immensely strong. Impenetrable, in fact. Yet, Gray took the ax and headed towards it anyway.

His first strike was slightly higher than the foundation of the iron bars, set into the wide stone entrance of the sewer, but the next were perfectly aimed, and he swung again and again.

Still, when he took a step back to shrug his cloak from his shoulders, it appeared that he hadn't made any progress in even denting the bars.

"Wait," Anya said, approaching. She was carrying a pickaxe. "Let's chip away at the stone, instead. It's got to be softer than those metal bars."

It was a difficult and exhausting process, if everyone's expression was any indication. There were not enough real tools to go around, and Gray had forbidden Rory to use his bronze dagger—truly, that did make sense as the dagger was the only thing they knew of that could cause Sabrina any harm—but the other four spent the next hour taking turns to gradually demolishing the stone around the grate.

When it finally fell away, Rory cheered loudly, but the other four looked too tired to celebrate.

Gray collapsed against a tree and wiped his face with a sleeve of his tunic. "A few minutes of rest," he suggested, "and then we will proceed into the sewers."

Rory sat down next to him, offered him first his waterskin, and then his handkerchief. It had been laundered in Tullamore, but after being on the road for several days, it had grown dusty again. Still, Gray didn't seem to notice as he took it and wiped his face, exhaling slowly.

"Somehow," Gray said, "it doesn't feel right that Evrard isn't with us."

"I think. . ." Rory hesitated. "I do think he stayed to protect the rest of the army, but I also think he wanted us to know we could do this on our own."

"That sounds very much like Evrard," Gray pointed out dryly.

Rory shrugged. "Once you get to know him, he's quite predictable."

"What about you? Do you think we can do this on our own?" Gray, who had sounded so determined and sure only a few hours before, now had an edge of uncertainty in his voice. Maybe it was exhaustion from pulling out the grate, or maybe it was doubts, beginning to creep in. They didn't know how to kill Sabrina. They didn't know how effective the sewer routes would be in finding her. So much in this very important quest was being left up to chance, and if Rory dwelled on their chances for success, he knew he'd be overwhelmed by terror at the incredibly slim possibility they'd actually succeed.

"I think we can't do anything else," Rory said softly. "We were always meant to be here, right here, right now, and I think that has to count for something."

"You're right." Gray shot him a lopsided, incredibly charming smile. "Why do you always have to be right?"

Rory grinned back. "You love it."

"I do, I do. I love you." Gray said it softly, earnestly.

"I love you, too." Rory stood and held out a hand for Gray to take. "Let's go reclaim my throne."

Their journey through the sewers was just about as unpleasant as Rory had been expecting it to be. It was dark, smelly, and extremely tight. At moments, Rory felt like the walls were going to close in and simply swallow him up, but he kept breathing, despite the horrible stench, and continued to plow ahead, following the makeshift torch that Kristian had constructed and then given to Anya.

Anya had insisted on going first through the sewer. When Gray had questioned why, she'd merely fixed him with a single-minded glare. "Because I can," she'd said.

That was enough reason for Rory. He didn't want to ask anyone to put themselves in danger for them, but he also wasn't going to stand in the way and stop anyone either, because as much as he hated it, he and Gray needed Anya and Diana and Kristian. With them the chance of succeeding was incredibly slim; without them, it was nonexistent.

Occasionally, a rat would skitter through the puddles lining the tunnels, and Rory would jerk and then force himself to calm down. He wasn't happy about it, but eventually he stopped being surprised by the random creatures that showed up alongside them in the sewer tunnel. They'd been in the dark, creeping forward, for what felt like an eternity, when finally the light bobbing ahead of them came to a halt.

"Rory," Anya called out. "This tunnel splits ahead."

Luckily, when he thought back to the diagrams he'd seen, he remembered the split. "Left is towards the throne room," he said decisively. "I'm assuming that's where we want to go. That's where she spends most of her time."

Gray's expression in the dull light was thoughtful. "Will she be there? Could she possibly be with the rest of the forces at the gate, instead?"

"She'd never do that," Diana spoke up. "She doesn't believe women should involve themselves publicly in the matter of war."

"Publicly?" Kristian asked, a frown creasing his face. "But she'll do it behind the scenes?"

"There's a general she likes, well," Diana hesitated, "a little too much if you get my meaning. In any case, he's essentially her puppet. She'll have him out with the forces at the front of the gate, while she directs the action from the throne room."

"So the throne room it is," Anya said.

Initially, Rory was surprised by Diana's matter-of-fact answer. He'd never heard his aunt make any comments like that, but ultimately, her words made sense. Sabrina had been enamored of her public visage of beauty and grace. She could fight as dirty as anyone, with skills she gained privately. But her training was always done in secret, like it would somehow diminish her authority if anyone knew how ruthless she truly was.

But somehow, Rory had always known. Perhaps, she'd made sure he knew, in anticipation for this day.

Course decided upon, Anya continued moving, with the four of them behind her. At some point, Rory recognized a particular configuration of turns, and observed that they had moved from below the courtyard into the castle proper. Another two turns, and with Rory's heartbeat pounding in his ears, he announced they should be very close to the throne room.

"I think we're here," Rory whispered. They'd all dropped their voices since entering the main section of the castle, as nobody was sure if the sound would carry.

"I see a grate," Anya said. "It's in the ceiling."

Everyone peered up into the gloom as Anya held up the torch closer to the ceiling. "I hope it's not set into the stone," Gray muttered.

Kristian boosted himself up briefly, using the sewer walls. "It's not set in," he confirmed. "Diana—let's use your spear to pry up a corner of the grate and then push it over."

"It's going to be heavy," Diana warned. "It might take more than one of us." She hefted up her spear and Anya helped her position it in the corner of the grate.

Kristian put his hands on the spear, alongside Diana's, and at the count of three, they pushed upwards with all their combined might.

The grate did not move. Rory exhaled slowly, trying not to panic that they might be stuck in these claustrophobic tunnels quite a bit longer.

"We need more force," Diana said reluctantly. "Gray, can you help?"

Gray moved to one wall, and feeling up it carefully, found a good handhold in a stone that had not been placed with the same care as the others. He gripped it and leveraged himself up, gripping the spear at a much higher point than Diana and Kristian. "Now," he barked. Rory couldn't imagine the coordination and balance it took to hover there, nearly suspended in mid-air and then add his strength to the others as they thrust upwards.

This time the grate moved, and with a great screeching groan, it shifted to one side, just far enough for a person to fit through.

"Quickly," Anya said. The grate moving had indeed not been very quiet and if this opened into the throne room itself, the sound would draw any soldiers left to guard the Regent Queen.

She braced her hand on the ground, and Gray, after lightly jumping down from his perch, used her boost to pull himself through the opening.

After a moment, Gray's face reappeared, framed in the opening. "It's all clear," he said. "I'm in a hallway outside the throne room itself. It's empty, at least for now."

Anya then assisted Kristian and Diana, and finally Rory. "What about you?" he asked her. "How will you get up?

Anya just smiled. "Ardglassians are adaptive," she said. "I'll manage."

Then she set her hands out for Rory, who embarrassingly struggled for a moment to get a good handhold on the smooth edges of the stone. Luckily, Gray was there to give him a hand, and pulled him up as Rory pushed.

Once Rory's eyes adjusted from the gloom, he saw they were indeed outside the throne room, just as he'd hoped they would be. This was a lesser-used passageway, and it was indeed empty.

Anya joined them, barely breathing hard at all, and Rory wondered if she'd actually managed to climb the walls like a spider.

"Cautiously," Gray mouthed and this time, he took the lead.

Pulling Lion's Breath from its scabbard, Gray gestured towards a side door. Rory nodded, afraid to speak, lest the sound travel too much and alert Sabrina to their presence. Gray was right; it was a side door into the throne room.

He opened the door a crack, and then at his signal, weapons raised, they ducked through the opening to enter into the throne room of Fontaine.

Sabrina, despite all their attempts at secrecy, sat on the throne, the wrought gold lions' figures on either side of her head shining with the reflected light of the dozen chandeliers above. She might have been expecting them, but at least, Rory thought as they approached, cautiously, she was alone.

Perhaps this meant that she was so certain of her own magical power that she had relegated every member of her army to the front gate, where they would hope to repel Ardglassian force.

"Nephew," Sabrina said in a particularly silky tone, "how pleased I am to discover that you have returned." Her gaze fell upon the rest of the party. "And you," she sneered, voice changing from sickly sweet to dangerously angry, "you are here."

Rory knew Gray wanted to protect and shield him. His positioning made that clear enough, but Rory couldn't let him take the brunt of whatever attack she flung at them first, and instead stepped around him.

"You," Rory said calmly but certainly, "are trespassing."

She erupted in peals of honeyed laugher, tossing her long dark hair, completely unconcerned at his words. "You really think you can remove me?"

Rory was not certain at all, but they had come all this way, and everything was resting on the idea that Rory believed he could.

It was so easy to let that belief show now, to let it radiate out of his expression and hit her, perhaps not where it hurt, because Rory doubted she had anything as primitive as feelings anymore—but right at the heart of all her conviction.

"I do," Rory said, his words echoing his expression. "I intend to remove you, if you will not remove yourself."

Then she stood, her brilliant cerise gown falling around her in graceful folds, and she gestured, absently, like she was swatting a fly. "Then, come and try."

An iron grip took hold of his upper arm, and Rory glanced up to see Gray frowning at him. "No," was all he said.

Rory considered arguing, but instead, decided that what Gray needed the most right now was certainty that he was safe, before he took on this age's greatest sorceress. And, Rory thought, he'll also need a bronze dagger.

He held out the weapon towards Gray who considered it for a long moment, then glanced back at Diana, and it was clear he was ordering her to stay with Rory—no matter what. Rory was fine with that; he truly didn't know anything other than how to perform basic maneuvers to defend himself.

Gray took the dagger, and then began to advance on the throne, with Kristian and Anya flanking him, one hand carrying Lion's Breath and the other Rory's dagger.

It was obvious the moment Sabrina realized that he was bearing her country's ancestral sword into battle against her. Her face grew dark and furious, and suddenly she was no longer the most beautiful woman, she was the most horrifying.

"How dare you bear that sword with your filthy hands and filthy blood," she spat in Gray's direction, her voice rising enough to echo off the great carved wooden beams holding the roof in place.

"They're a hell of a lot cleaner than yours," Gray said calmly. Rory's own blood was roaring at this point, in fear for Gray and in anger at how callously she'd dismissed his importance.

"Go shovel manure," she hissed, and then, as Rory had expected all along, she muttered a sharp phrase and began to shift into a chimera.

Her dress and then her skin fell away in long, tattered, flaming shreds, like it wasn't the woman changing into the chimera, but the chimera emerging from the woman.

Rory didn't want to know what sort of evil spirits Sabrina had promised her soul to in order to wield this sort of power.

But Gray was prepared for this form, as he had been for her other, and taking a step forward, threw Rory's bronze dagger, the metal flipping gracefully end over end until it ended . . . embedded in a giant silver plate that Sabrina had suddenly flung up in front of herself.

She cackled with delight at their confused expressions. "As if I would let you try that again," the chimera roared.

Anya yelled and charged, tossing her spear, tipped with bronze, at the chimera's head, but at the last second, the creature ducked and her snicker was triumphant.

"You cannot hope to defeat me," she announced, reckless and over-confident.

Use it, Rory prayed, use all that certainty against her.

The trio regrouped, and after a quick, whispered consultation, Rory watched as they split, approaching the chimera on three sides. Kristian bore a heavy ax, its blade dully shining, and even though Anya had yet to retrieve her spear, she had pulled out a short but deadly-looking sword from a sheath at her hip. They stepped closer even as the chimera roared, fire beginning to ferment in its mouth, spittle becoming specks of ash and red-hot burning coal.

Rory's heart stuttered. Any moment, as they pushed Sabrina towards the throne, the chimera would lash out and turn someone into ash. He wasn't ready to witness anyone's death—certainly not any of the three in front of him.

But then, shocking Rory and no doubt Gray, she suddenly sprang up, wings extending from either side of her golden-hued body, and she flew over Gray's head.

Gray frantically turned and met Rory's eyes. He looked wild and unhinged, terror leaking out of him as they could only watch as the chimera easily flew over their heads and then settled behind Rory and Diana, its feet landing with a resounding thud.

Gray was strong and fast, but he was not quick enough to forestall a magical creature, and Rory realized, the thought racing through his mind like quicksilver, that it was just him and the chimera now.

Anya tried to step around him, but the viper-tail whipped out and snapped her in the chest, sending her flying back, skidding across the marble floor until she was an impossible distance away. Rory could hear the others yelling and running to his rescue, but there was no time. They couldn't reach him before she turned him into dust.

"Nephew," the chimera said, Sabrina's voice deepening and lengthening. "The time of reckoning comes."

It would be easier if he'd had his dagger—Rory missed the feel of it in his hand—but he knew it wouldn't have done him any good. Gray had already made the best effort they could with the bronze weapon, and they'd gotten nowhere. Still, to face her with no weapon? Rory's heart beat faster in his chest, and it took everything, but he still straightened and looked her dead in the eyes.

"Good," it said. "You face me as a man, not a sniveling boy. As your father did."

Realization sank deep into Rory's bones, with teeth and claws and pain. "You killed my parents," he said tonelessly. "That's why they died. You killed them."

"Just," the chimera echoed gleefully, "as I will kill you now." It took a step and then another and then, with no weapon, Rory could only brace himself for the inevitable impact of the chimera's jaws around his neck.

He had just a single moment to think, as hard as he could in Gray's direction, I'm sorry, and I love you.

Just as it seemed preordained that Rory would die as his parents did—at his aunt's hand—suddenly Gray was there, panting with the effort it had taken to cross the length of the entire throne room. He'd skidded in front of Rory and he was wielding Lion's Breath as if he had been born to it.

"Don't you dare touch him, you traitorous bitch," Gray shouted, and thrust the sword just as the chimera opened its massive, deadly jaws.

If we die, Rory thought hopelessly, at least we will die together.

But instead of death, there was fire.

Sudden, hot flames flung from the tip of Lion's Breath and the chimera reared back, trying to dodge the fire burst, but it was too close, and it was too late.

Gray looked just as astonished as Rory felt, but he held the sword steady, the flames continuing to envelop the chimera, its skin blackening and curling up at the edges.

The chimera shrieked, an unearthly female sound, and then abruptly, it went still. Unmoving. A flaming mess of fur and skin and cerise silk.

The fire finally drew to a close, and after it extinguished, he took one hesitant step forward and then another. When he was close enough, Rory held his breath as Gray poked the shapeless, still smoking heap with the sword. It did not move.

"I think. . ." Gray said, his voice wobbling. "I think she is dead."

Rory flung his arms around his neck and tried very hard not to sob with incredible relief into Gray's shoulder. He failed.

CHAPTER EIGHTEEN

More than once after Sabrina's defeat, Gray felt the urge to duck away, behind a convenient gold-fringed curtain or into a shadowy alcove, and when he was certain nobody could see, pinch himself. In the month since Sabrina died and her forces had been defeated, there were so many moments when he could scarcely believe that this was truly his life. Before he'd met Rory, he'd come to terms with his jaded loneliness, with seeing only those who needed help as they passed through the valley, and with the final, inescapable thought that there would never be anyone special to wake up next to in the morning.

But now every single morning, he woke up to Rory's auburn curls in his mouth and his slender body pressed insistently against Gray's own.

He'd never again be alone, unless he chose to be.

It was hard to trust his sudden, blinding happiness, but at the same time, impossible not to.

Gray could still remember what the sword felt like, flaming in his hands, and he'd understood then why he'd been the one who needed to wield it. He was Rory's sworn protector, his consort, and even though they'd said no true vows to each other, every moment together since they'd first met had felt like a vow. The sword must have agreed, and as Evrard had said, adopted him as an honorary member of the Fontaine royal house, as it had responded to Gray's extreme need when it had truly meant death for both of them otherwise.

"It was not a revered artifact of many generations of Fontaine royalty for nothing," Evrard had told him dryly after he and Rory had emerged from Beaulieu to find Marthe and the unicorn holding their own with Sabrina's small army. After seeing her charred body, the general had lain down his own sword and surrendered.

It had, as Rory put it afterwards, been surprisingly easy.

The nobles of Fontaine had welcomed the Crown Prince back as if he'd never left, and even accepted his taller, darker shadow as his consort. Of course, knowing that Gray was, in actuality, Prince Graham likely had something to do with their effortless acceptance of him.

Of course, who would have the nerve to deny Gray his place when he'd demonstrated Lion's Breath's rather astonishing hidden talent?

Nobody dared, and as Rory had said, it went easily.

Anya had ridden the fastest horse they could find and had reported back three days later with the news that the King was surprisingly still alive.

"He feels no different," Anya reported, to everyone's shock. Gray hadn't understood and had confronted Evrard about how this could possibly be, when everyone had been in agreement that killing Sabrina would also mean the death of Gideon.

"Magic works in mysterious ways," Evrard simply said, but that didn't mean that Gray ever trusted it. Something so slippery, with so many rules and yet so many exceptions, wasn't something you could ever depend on.

This particular opinion was a source of very minor strife between Rory and Gray. The former wanted to believe in the power of magic in changing the world. The latter wasn't sure they could trust in something they could never see or touch. And Gray's opinion was actually proven correct a month after Sabrina's defeat.

Rory's coronation was planned for the very next day. The rooms of Beaulieu had all been aired out, invitations to all the neighboring kingdoms had been sent. Messengers had been sent to the Mecant tribe, and a handful of representatives had arrived, and would, per Rory's agreement with the tribe leader, begin re-learning their lost language. Even King Gideon had sent back an acceptance, dependent on his ability to travel. The Fontaine crown, with its roaring lions and giant rubies and topazes, had been polished over and over again until it shone like a star in the deepest darkness, all in readiness to be placed upon Rory's head. Gray had been pressed into too many clothing fittings to count, to his excessive complaints, and had finally come to a compromise with the tailor. Less gold braid on his tunic, and he would agree to wear the fancy, bejeweled sword belt that had originally been designed to be worn with Lion's Breath.

Gray was having one last security check with Marthe, when Rory rushed up to him, breathless, with a distraught look on his face.

"What is it?" Gray asked, fear curdling in his stomach. Things had been too good. Too pat. Too easy. Life and love weren't supposed to be simple. The other shoe would inevitably drop. And it seemed, from Rory's expression, that it finally had.

"It's from Tullamore," Rory said grimly, drawing him off to the side of the courtyard. "It's news from your father."

Gray still didn't know how comfortable he felt calling Gideon his father, but he certainly wasn't going to correct Rory right now, especially with that look on his face.

Rory extended a sealed letter toward him. "Anya came ahead from the royal party, with this."

He wasn't proud, but his fingers shook as he took it. It had been too easy, and Evrard's explanation for his father's continued survival too deliberately vague. He'd known this would happen, and Gray didn't know whether to be angry with him that he'd let Gray enjoy this respite of happiness and rest, or grateful.

The one thing Gray had learned in his life was that you always paid the cost of your deeds; even if it was much later, after you'd imagined your slate already cleared.

"Do you . . ." Rory hesitated. "I can stay with you while you read it, if you want."

Gray looked down at the letter, recognizing his father's spidery handwriting, even finer and wobblier in his decline. Did he want Rory to sit with him? Wasn't that why he was so grateful for Rory's existence? Because his presence made it easier to bear the terrible burden life brought sometimes?

But then he glanced up into Rory's troubled amber eyes, and knew he didn't want to share this particular burden.

He'd killed Sabrina knowing it would, in all likelihood, kill his father too. He'd done it, understanding how difficult that particular cost was, and he'd followed through with his intent, because the benefits still had outweighed it. It wasn't a decision that he'd let Rory help him make, and so Rory shouldn't have to take that weight onto his shoulders. It was Gray's to bear.

"No," he said. Rory frowned more deeply. "I'll read it and find you later."

There was an enormous banquet tonight, in celebration of Rory's coronation, and he and Gray were intended to be the guests of honor. Gray had a feeling that after reading this letter, he wouldn't feel much like celebrating.

"If you're certain . . ." Rory said, clearly not agreeing with Gray's decision.

"I'm sure," Gray retorted, more brusquely than he'd intended.

"All right," Rory agreed finally. "As long as you promise to find me later."

"I promise," Gray said—more to himself than to Rory. He'd need the balm of Rory's love and care in the wake of this, even if he didn't want to believe it now.

He took the letter and headed out the main castle gates, passing by the guards with a single, friendly wave of his hand. They knew he liked to wander alone sometimes, when he craved privacy. After so many lonely years in the valley, he wasn't quite used to spending so much time around so many people, but he was trying.

At first Gray wasn't sure where his feet were leading him, but then after a few long minutes of walking, he looked up and realized he'd headed towards the creek where he, Anya, Diana, Kristian, and Rory had first snuck into the castle. There was the grate, still with bits of stone attached, sitting on the ground next to the entrance. He would have to remind Marthe that breach would need to be re-sealed.

But for now, it was as good a place as any to sit and read what were certainly his father's last words to him.

With trembling fingers, Gray fumbled the letter open, breaking the wax seal, bearing the imprint of his father's ring.

It had been shakily embedded into the bloodred wax, and Gray inhaled sharply as the ring tumbled out of the envelope. He gripped it hard, the edges cutting into his palm as he opened the letter and began to read.

DEAR GRAHAM, it said.

I WAS SO HAPPY THAT I WAS ABLE TO TRAVEL TO BEAULIEU TO CELEBRATE YOUR PRINCE'S CORONATION AND YOUR COMMITMENT TO HIM AS HIS CONSORT. I THINK YOU TWO WILL BE VERY HAPPY TOGETHER. IT IS TO MY IMMENSE REGRET THAT AFTER WE CROSSED OVER THE BORDER FROM ARDGLASS TO FONTAINE, I

BELIEVE MY BODY BEGAN TO FAIL ME. MY HEART IS ACHING FOR THE TERRIBLE NEWS THAT WILL BE DELIVERED AT THE EVE OF RORY'S CORONATION, BUT THE SILVER LINING IS THAT I HAVE JUST ENOUGH STRENGTH TO PEN THIS LETTER AND TELL YOU THINGS THAT I WISH I HAD SAID THE LAST TIME WE SPOKE.

SEEING YOU AGAIN WAS SOMETHING I WISHED FOR AND DREADED IN EQUAL MEASURES. WHEN YOU ARRIVED AT TUL-LAMORE, I KNEW WITHOUT A DOUBT THAT THE FORMER FAR OUTWEIGHED THE LATTER. I HAVE NOT BEEN THE FATHER TO YOU THAT YOU NEEDED, OR THAT YOU DESERVED, BUT IT SEEMS THAT DESPITE MY GRAVE MISTAKES, YOU GREW INTO A STRONG, HONORABLE MAN THAT ANY FATHER WOULD BE PROUD TO CALL SON. I DO NOT EXPECT YOU TO FORGIVE ME FOR THE EVIL THAT I LET INTO MY MIND AND INTO MY HEART, BECAUSE I DO NOT FORGIVE MYSELF. EVEN NOW. ESPECIALLY NOW. BUT I DO HOPE THAT YOU WILL BE ABLE TO MOVE FOR-WARD, INTO YOUR NEW LIFE WITH RORY, AND AT LEAST BE ABLE TO LET GO OF YOUR BITTERNESS AND ANGER, BECAUSE THE LAST THING YOU DESERVE IS TO CARRY THAT PARTICU-LAR BURDEN WITH YOU FOREVER. ALL I CAN SAY NOW, EVEN THOUGH I KNOW IT WILL NEVER TRULY BE ENOUGH, IS I AM TRULY, EVERLASTINGLY SORRY.

YOUR FATHER,

GIDEON.

Directly after his father's wobbly signature was an impersonal notation, inscribed in another hand. Gideon, rest his soul, died this day, and has been borne home to Tullamore.

Gray looked up into the canopy of trees, the sun shining so brightly overhead, and the birds chirping happily, as if they had no cares in the world, but he did not see the green of the trees or the blue of the sky or the red of the robins. The colors blurred together with the sheen of tears he could no longer hold back.

Perhaps his hand had not been the one responsible for his father's death, but at least he had avenged Gideon by slaying the one who was. Still, revenge was less reassuring than Gray had always believed it would be, and far colder. He shivered and wiped his eyes, only to have them fill again with tears.

There was perhaps nothing Gideon could ever say that would erase those fifteen years, and all the pain and uncertainty of them, but he had come close in his final letter. If Gray was painfully honest with himself, there was a part of him that did forgive his father, because he'd apologized sincerely, he'd done it with love, and he'd done it not expecting to ever be forgiven. And that, Gray realized, counted for more than he ever would have thought possible.

"I'm sorry," a voice called out, and Gray was so startled to find himself not entirely alone that he nearly dropped the letter and his father's ring into the stream. He looked up and saw it was Rory standing on the other side of the bank, with an ashamed look on his face.

"I'm sorry," he said again. "I meant to leave you alone, I really, truly did, but I saw the way you looked, and I knew how hard it would be to read the letter, and I just . . . I love you and I didn't want you to be alone."

Gray hesitated. He'd truly believed he did want to be alone, but after reading his father's words, especially about his future with Rory, suddenly that seemed not only unimportant, but categorically stupid.

He'd already been alone for so long. It was an ugly habit that he couldn't seem to break, even though he could acknowledge all the benefits of having a consort and friends and thirteen clans who had agreed to come to his aid if he ever had need of them again.

"I'm the one who's sorry," Gray said, extending an arm to help Rory across the creek. "I shouldn't have pushed you away."

Rory settled down next to him and gazed at the ring in Gray's palm. "Your father's ring," he said softly. "Anya told me what happened."

"It seems . . ." Gray's voice choked in his throat, stuck on absolutely nothing at all. "It seems crossing over from Ardglass to Fontaine was the key to his demise."

"Your father was living on borrowed time, and he was so happy he could come see us," Rory said softly. "To see you."

Gray nodded. "He said as much." And because he didn't have the words to express what his father had, he handed the letter to Rory. It was his future too, and he deserved to read it.

Rory did so, carefully holding the parchment in both hands as Gray turned over and over the ring in his own. Finally, Rory lifted his head, and his own eyes were also full of tears.

"I wish . . ." Rory said, his own voice clogging. "I wish he had been able to say this to you in person."

Gray wished that too, but he couldn't be sad or upset or angry, because in the end, his father had still expressed what he'd felt. And while the speaking of the words might have been transformative, the writing of them had been equally as important—maybe even more so, because this was his father's dying wish. His last thought, before he departed this world, had been saved for Gray.

"I think it will be okay," Gray said, and to his own surprise, it was.

It wasn't a sudden transformation; the hurt he'd carried around forever was too big and too broad and too ingrained to just instantaneously disappear, but maybe, just maybe, each day it would fade a little.

Rory reached over and grasped Gray's hand tightly in his own. "It's more than okay," he said. "It's going to be magical."

Gray knew tonight, he'd take Rory's arm and lead him into the banquet thrown in his honor. There'd be tables groaning with every delicacy from Fontaine, and even from Ardglass, and the best of the wine and ale from the Beaulieu cellar house. Tomorrow, Rory would take his throne, and Gray would be standing right next to him, uncomplaining in his new tunic and the splendid jeweled sword belt designed to showcase Lion's Breath, and he'd be the first one to congratulate and greet the new King of Fontaine. That night, there'd be a private, much more personal celebration between just the two of them. And, Gray realized, Rory, who was usually right, was right once again.

Their happily ever after was indeed going to be magical.

PART II

CHAPTER NINETEEN

Six months later

Gray woke very slowly, his brain rousing in tiny increments. First he was aware only of a warm figure pressed against his back, and then breath tickling his neck, lifting the hairs and causing him to twitch. Then a brightness against his closed eyelids, and the sounds of rustling and hushed whispers.

He'd been waking up next to Rory for months now, and it never felt less miraculous. Each and every morning felt like the first time. Without opening his eyes, Gray turned and drew the soft, sleeping bundle closer to his own body, and his sleepy brain reveled in how perfectly Rory fit next to him. Like they'd been made for each other. Maybe they had—Evrard dropped hints aplenty, because that was Evrard: always hinting and forever evading any direct inquiry—but Gray had decided that whatever the truth was, it didn't matter, because he knew what it felt like when he was at Rory's side. And something so extraordinary, that gave him this much strength of purpose, had to be born of the strongest, brightest kind of magic.

The rustling departed, and for a single moment, Gray thought another kind miracle had just occurred: Rory sleeping through the servants who prepared the fires every morning.

For the last six months, Rory, with an increasing sense of kingly devotion, had risen with the dawn, and worked long past sundown. There was indeed much to learn and much to do, and even more to administer, now that Rory was the ruler of Fontaine, but even though Gray knew how much his responsibilities encompassed, he still selfishly wished, every once in awhile, that he could keep Rory all to himself.

This morning . . . maybe. Gray held his breath, and carefully tightened his grip around Rory's waist. He sighed, still asleep, and snuggled closer. But then, just when Gray was trying to decide if it was better to let Rory continue to sleep, or to wake him for much more pleasurable activities, Rory jerked awake.

"What time is it?' he asked groggily, and Gray, who had long since learned that beginning their morning with an argument was a counterproductive waste of time, moved his arm, releasing Rory. Gray finally opened his eyes and took in Rory's sleep-mussed curly hair as he stretched his arms upwards, his limbs milky white in the dawn sunlight.

It wouldn't have mattered if he'd been unattractive or even ugly, Gray still would have thought him the most beautiful man in the world. So much of his beauty radiated from within: kindness and cleverness and an indomitable strength that nothing could ever dim.

Gray chuckled tiredly, and rolled over onto his back.

"The fire's already going," Rory said, and Gray heard his feet hit the floor. "I'm going to miss my lesson with the Mecant elders." He paused, turning back to Gray. "What's so funny?" he asked, and Gray would have to be a lot sleepier to miss the aching tone in Rory's voice. He didn't want to leave their bed, even though he knew he needed to. Maybe it should have helped, but even that particular fact didn't really make Gray feel any better.

"I was remembering the first time I met you, and how naive and silly I thought you were," Gray confessed.

"And that was amusing because?" Rory arched an eyebrow as he reached for a shirt, pulling it over his head.

Their gazes caught and held. "Because it's very far from how I feel about you now."

Rory smiled, the sight nearly as bright as the sun shining through the windows of their shared bedroom. "Well," he said, bending over and giving Gray a tantalizing little glimpse of his pale, peach-shaped arse, glorious and muscled from all the riding he did, "it's very far from how I feel about you, too."

Laughing in spite of himself, Gray found his grumpy mood dispelled by just how much he loved the man in front of him—all the parts of him, including the annoyingly responsible part who wanted desperately to care for his kingdom and make sure it was ushered into a new age of enlightenment and prosperity. "You are going to be late now," Gray said. "But first, before you leave, come give me a kiss."

Rory did, leaning down over the bed, his mouth moving confidently and passionately against Gray's own. It was a good kiss, because all their kisses were. This one, however, felt anticipatory, like a dry pile of kindling, desperately waiting for a spark. It didn't take more than a second to light, and Gray's fingers were tightening on Rory's hips, and even as he tried to ignore his hardening cock, it seemed to demand a much different response.

"Sorry, sorry," Rory said, hastily breaking away, mouth wet and red, panting a little. He wanted it too—Gray could see the hard line of his own cock in his breeches. Maybe it should have helped Gray feel better that Rory was suffering just as much as he was with how little alone time they had together anymore, but it didn't. Not even a little. "Tonight," Rory promised.

Gray made a face. "Tonight is that banquet that Evrard has been rattling on about for weeks." *And that I've spent the last month of my life planning.*

"After the banquet?" Rory said hopefully, and Gray didn't have the heart to remind him that after the protracted formality of a banquet and a few glasses of wine, he'd absolutely come back to their room and fall asleep the moment his head hit the pillow. His schedule was so brutal and exhausting that Gray couldn't even be angry about it.

Gray wanted to help ease his burden—desperately, in fact—but whenever Gray brought it up, Rory changed the subject or brushed his concerns away. Gray had been trying a more subtle method up until now, but with his frustration and worry mounting, maybe he needed to be more direct.

While I'm planning banquets and deciding on seating arrangements, you're running a country.

"Sure, after the banquet," Gray said with a reassuring smile. Maybe if by some miracle, Rory wasn't completely exhausted, they could even have a conversation about it. But before that, it would almost certainly be worth his while to consult Evrard on how he could demand to help without being too forceful or accidentally offending Rory, because that was the very last thing he wanted.

Gray knew he'd been meant for more than tending the farm in the Valley of Lost Things, and he knew he could absolutely do more than physically protect Rory's back. And not only that, he wanted to do more, if only because that might mean the enormous burden currently resting on Rory's slim shoulders was lessened.

"I love you," Rory said, and while the gaze in his eyes was dimmed from exhaustion, the bright happiness in them hit Gray square in the chest, leaving him breathless for a moment.

He'd never expected to have this, not for the rest of his life, and even though it wasn't perfect right now, it was still so much more than anything Gray could have dreamt, when he'd been so alone in the Valley.

We're going to figure this out, Gray swore to himself as he smiled at his lover. "I love you too," he said.

It was not quite as easy to be that optimistic a few hours later, when Gray, who'd been looking for Evrard, had ended up being cornered by a handful of courtiers instead.

Evrard, in the form of Rhys, had spent the first eleven years of Gray's life attempting to burn courtly manners and formal etiquette into his brain. Evrard had been resigned, but not surprised to discover that they hadn't imprinted quite as well as he'd imagined, as the informal years in the Valley had eradicated most of this knowledge and every single bit of the diplomacy Gray had once learned. Since then, Gray had been trying to regain the lost language, but truthfully, he still found it difficult to bother. If it had been anybody else's kingdom, even his own, he wouldn't have even made an effort, but for Rory he knew he needed to make peace with the nobles. They were understandably rather perturbed by the Autumn Prince's new consort, whose manners seemed more suited to a stable than a throne room.

"It is imperative that you deliver this message to His Majesty," Count Aplin said stiffly. "The rooms assigned to my party for the banquet are hardly acceptable."

Gray, who was having difficulty refraining from rolling his eyes, counted to five—a technique Evrard had suggested to help deal with frustrating situations—and then counted to five again. He desperately wanted to remind Count Aplin, who knew this particular fact, that it had not been Rory who'd assigned the rooms, but Gray himself. And, as there were only so many rooms available in Beaulieu and apparently a multitude of nobles who wanted them, facts were not on Count Aplin's side.

He turned to Anya, who had pledged her sword to him, even as Gray had pledged his to Rory. He did not have much need for a personal guard, a job which Anya was greatly overqualified for anyway, and so she had appointed herself as both a reminder to Gray that he couldn't tell off the nobles, and also the person he turned to when he wanted to work off his frustration in the practice ring.

"Anya," Gray said, his calm voice deceptive, "as the King's consort, do I not have the task of assigning various rooms in Beaulieu?"

Her gray eyes were glimmering with amusement. "You do, my prince."

At first, he had wanted her to stop referring to his lineage—especially since after the death of his father, the kingship of Ardglass had been disbanded entirely—but then Evrard had intervened and claimed that it was good for the Fontaine nobles to remember that while Gray might have very little patience with niceties, he did in fact outrank them.

"Ah," Gray said, still calm, but his gaze now pinning Count Aplin to the floor. He squirmed, visibly. "I thought so."

"But, Prince Graham, the rooms are truly unacceptable. Only four! And so small! And terribly located, very far away from the throne room and the great hall. I served the King's aunt loyally, and that loyalty should not be repaid with such poor lodgings." Count Aplin was clearly not going to give up without a fight.

"The King's aunt?" Gray prowled a step closer to Count Aplin. "The sorceress who sold her soul for dark magic? Who threatened the King's life? Who threatened my life? Three times?"

Count Aplin stared at Gray. "Three times?"

Gray stared back, hard. Maybe later, much later, he would feel guilty about how harsh he was being with Aplin. It would almost definitely happen when Evrard inevitably cornered and lectured him about diplomacy and using honey instead of vinegar. But right now, playing nice with one of Sabrina's ex-supporters felt impossible.

"Three times," Gray confirmed.

Aplin flushed. "I . . . Just please pass on my complaint to the King."

Nodding sharply, Gray didn't say he would—because he wasn't going to and he definitely wasn't going to lie and pretend like he was going to bother Rory with such a silly request.

Finally, the Count seemed to understand and turned away. Gray let out the unsteady breath he hadn't known he was holding. Anger and frustration were still coursing through him, the indignity making his blood boil. Maybe if Rory finally let him do something important, he wouldn't have the time to listen to the sort of petty complaints Count Aplin and many others had.

Gray was just about to go find Evrard so he could ask for advice on how to convince Rory to help share some of his burden, when a sound stopped him short.

Slow, arrogant clapping.

Turning, Gray saw one of Sabrina's other supporters, the Duke of Rinald, approaching. While Count Aplin was annoying, he was ultimately harmless—like the complaint he'd just made about a bad suite of rooms. But the Duke was an entirely different problem; he was clearly disgruntled and intelligent enough to actually do something dangerous about it. Out of all of Sabrina's old supporters who still lurked in the Fontaine aristocracy, the Duke of Rinald was by far the most worrisome.

Gray felt his anger congeal into ice. He'd stupidly lost his temper with Aplin, and the Duke of Rinald had witnessed the entire exchange—and likely would find a way to use it against him.

"You certainly have no love for Count Aplin," the Duke drawled. He had dark hair, and even darker eyes. Beady, unforgiving eyes that brought to mind dark deeds and even darker purpose. Gray could very well imagine him standing next to Sabrina as she cast her spells, dooming Gray's father, and then Rory's parents. Aplin might have enjoyed Sabrina's influence in the court at Beaulieu, but the Duke of Rinald had run it with her. Had been so influential, in fact, that Evrard initially had been concerned about leaving him free to continue plotting. But Rory had insisted that without any actual proof of his misdeeds, the Duke and any other of Sabrina's supporters, would remain free. It had been a calculated risk, and Gray still wasn't sure it had been the right path to take.

"Sir," Gray said, acknowledging his presence without actually saying anything of substance. Because what else could he say? He certainly had no love lost for the Count and his whining, and he certainly felt even less kindly inclined towards the Duke.

"Highness," the Duke said icily, inclining his head. "You certainly have made your influence felt here at court."

Maybe without that clutch of fear for Rory and his somewhat precarious position, Gray would have been proud of the Duke's statement. He'd tried to do what he could to keep an eye on the men who could hurt the man he loved and the future they'd so miraculously created here. Sometimes all he could do was exercise the little influence he had to inconvenience them, like Count Aplin. Until Rory let him become more involved in the day-to-day running of Fontaine, he'd take every path available to him—even the ones that felt insignificant.

"Thank you," Gray said. "I'm so pleased you've noticed."

"Count Aplin might be satisfied with complaining about accommodations, but others will not be," the Duke said. "I will warn you, not everyone is so pleased that King Emory has taken his aunt's throne or brought a prince of Ardglass to Beaulieu as his consort. We must be vigilant against those who would threaten the King."

The Duke would never be stupid enough to say it was him who was unhappy about these two events, but the message was clear enough. Watch your back. Watch Rory's back.

"I appreciate your concern," Gray offered stiffly.

"Of course you do," the Duke said, his voice oily and ingratiating. "Shall I see you and the King tonight at the banquet?"

"Naturally," Gray said. "Until tonight."

"Tonight," the Duke agreed.

When Gray finally found Evrard, tucked away in one of the brighter corners of the royal stable, his hands had finally stopped trembling.

"What is the matter?" Evrard asked, his tone annoyingly complacent. Gray knew when he heard what had just transpired, he would not be nearly so calm.

"The Duke of Rinald," Gray groaned, leaning against the rough-hewn wood of the stable wall. "I think he just threatened me and Rory." Gray paused. "Mainly Rory."

To Gray's surprise, Evrard's expression remained unconcerned. "We knew that he was going to be unhappy about Rory ascending to the throne," he said.

"Also, Aplin is complaining again," Gray said with a resigned sigh. "This time about the bad rooms I gave him."

"Perhaps if his focus remains on those indignities, he will not be interested in additional conspiracies," Evrard pointed out.

Gray was secretly afraid this wasn't true at all, and that both Evrard and Rory were frighteningly certain of their own invincibility. But Gray, who was the one somehow relegated to actually addressing their complaints, was increasingly concerned. All it took was one or two nobles grumbling, and discontent could spread like wildfire. He remembered when Sabrina had first come to Tullamore, and when her influence on King Gideon had grown by leaps and bounds very quickly, how angry the Ardglassian clan chiefs had been. An interloper, and a beautiful woman at that, suddenly had their King's ear. Gray remembered when he had first awoken that fateful night, how certain that the threat came not from Sabrina, but from the clans themselves. Perhaps that was why she had chosen that night to finally exercise her control over the King, forcing him to relinquish Gray—she'd known she could not continue to hold the clan chiefs off for very much longer. Of course, he would never be able to ask her, because he and Lion's Breath had turned her into a harmless pile of ash.

But now Gray was the interloper at a foreign court, and he had strange, inexplicable magic. The people of Fontaine loved Rory, and would willingly follow him—but it was unspoken that they were not quite as thrilled that along the way, he had discovered the lost prince of Ardglass and insisted on bringing him home.

"I need to be doing something else than listening to Aplin's petty complaints and the Duke's veiled, ambiguous threats," Gray said, squeezing his fists together. He'd felt this way once before, when he'd first come to the Valley, and the only thing that had kept him sane was as much useful work as he could possibly accomplish in a day. Assigning rooms and listening to the nobles' squabbles and being available for whenever Rory had a spare moment for him—that could never be classified as useful and absolutely was not enough to keep him occupied.

Evrard cocked his head, considering. "You have, I would assume, discussed this with the King."

Gray rolled his eyes. "Yes, of course I have."

Evrard's silence prompted him to continue. "And he keeps saying he will find more for me to do, but deep down, I don't think he intends to find me an occupation. He wants to do it all, even if the attempt leaves him bedraggled and exhausted."

"He feels guilty," Evrard supplied, and then hesitated. "Perhaps that is an expected emotion. Rory let his aunt control him and his kingdom for many years, without complaint or interruption."

"But that doesn't mean he needs to take care of every single thing in the kingdom now," Gray argued. "He's made it right by taking responsibility. In fact, he's taken on much more than he could possibly handle. We both know I could help with the burden."

"You pointed this out, and he still refuses?" Evrard asked—even though he already knew the answer. Of course Gray had asked. Rory had never even turned him down. But then he'd never actually made an effort to include Gray either.

"He never outright refuses," Gray explained. "But it's become clear that he's not going to assign me more important tasks until he believes that it's a good idea."

"Perhaps . . ." Evrard paused for dramatic effect, something he'd always enjoyed and now used far more than was necessary, now that he was back at court. "Perhaps your position needs to be more official. Then it would not be a matter of Rory choosing to include you, but a matter of royal protocol."

It took Gray a long moment to realize what Evrard was saying. "You think we should be married?" It was hard to keep that edge of disbelief out of his tone. He and Rory were already committed, already in this together through both the successes and the failures. Their union was even official enough that Lion's Breath had decided he deserved to wield the power it held.

"Did you not intend to be married?" Evrard inquired mildly.

That was an even stupider question. "Of course. Someday," Gray said. Except that, truthfully, there had been much unspoken assumption and no actual conversation about it—except when Rory had asked him if he wanted to continue carrying Lion's Breath. They'd both known what that meant implicitly, and what it meant when Gray said he did. But somehow, in all their time together, they had never discussed having an actual wedding.

"It didn't seem important right now," Gray added ruefully. "Rory being crowned officially seemed much more pressing."

"It was much more pressing, but I do believe having a wedding, in which you both commit yourselves to each other and to the kingdom of Fontaine, will solve both your problems admirably."

"So humble," Gray grumbled.

If Evrard had been in human form, Gray could imagine his insouciant shrug. Both elegant and infuriating, a special skill of Evrard's. "You have come to me for a solution to your problem with Count Aplin and the Duke of Rinard's displeasure and a way to convince Rory to transfer some of his burden of kingship to you. This does in fact solve both problems admirably. It solidifies your position and gives the kingdom a chance to celebrate, thus muffling any discontent and also requiring Rory to share his duties with you as his official consort. A neat, tidy solution, and one, I might add, that you already had planned on performing, someday."

Per usual, Evrard was not wrong. His overconfidence was then not misplaced, and his ego continued unchecked.

Annoyingly unchecked. Gray sighed.

"I do not doubt the solution, only the timing," Gray said.

"Ah, then this hesitation is borne of romance. You wish to get married because of love, not because of matters of state." Evrard sniffed. "You are a prince, and Rory is a king. Your love affair might have been foretold for many years, but that does not mean you are not incredibly blessed to have your soulmate be your chosen mate. Many others are not so lucky."

Gray knew the marriage between his parents—which had eventually become a happy one—had been arranged. It wasn't that he didn't want to marry Rory; indeed, the opposite was true. But he could not, with a clear conscience, suggest marriage now to Rory, without further explaining why the timing was ideal.

"Rory isn't going to agree," Gray finally said. He wasn't lying, but he wasn't being entirely honest either.

"You should still ask." It was framed as a suggestion, but Gray knew better because Evrard's tone had become particularly stern.

I will try one more time to convince him, before this step is necessary, Gray thought to himself as he took leave of Evrard to return to the royal suite and dress for the banquet. Surely I can convince him.

CHAPTER TWENTY

The banquet was as crowded as Gray had worried it might be. He'd gone over the invitation list himself, and then helped undertake the onerous task of assigning seating based on rank. But it was one thing to see hundreds of names in tiny print on a long scroll of parchment, and quite another to see the faces all those names represented, crowded together, even though the reception rooms at Beaulieu were enormous and dwarfed even the throne room in Tullamore.

It was no surprise that since he had spent so much time in the Valley, with only his own thoughts for company, Gray still found such crowds daunting. He put on a good face for Rory, because this couldn't have been easy for him either, as he understood Rory had rarely participated in such gatherings prior to his coronation, but like all things, they were in this together.

"I feel like I cannot even catch my breath," Rory muttered as he and Gray stood at the very end of the receiving line, bowing to every noble and aristocrat that had deigned to attend—which, it seemed to Gray, was all of them.

So far, they had yet to see either Count Aplin or the Duke of Rinard, and for that Gray was extremely grateful. Still, there had been a distinct coolness in the air as they'd greeted some other members of the court—nobles that prior to this evening, Gray might have counted as at least impartial.

Rinard had warned him, Gray thought morosely. They needed to combat this growing discontent quickly and without drawing any additional attention. Maybe Evrard was right, and the best way to fix all their problems would be to make what was currently unofficial, very official.

"I think we are almost at the end," Gray reassured Rory, tightening his fingers on the back of the gold embroidered white silk tunic he wore. "It will be over soon."

Rory glanced up at Gray, his amber eyes wide and filled with exhaustion. "Sometimes it feels like it will never be over."

Straightening, Gray greeted the next guest, and then the next, before he had a chance to respond. "You should let me help," he repeated. It was the kind of entreaty he'd made many times before, and always Rory had kindly but firmly brushed him off. But now, Rory hesitated.

But before he could answer, the Duke and the Count, arm in arm, stopped directly in front of them.

"Highness, Your Majesty," the Duke of Rinard said. He bowed, as befitted both Gray's and Rory's positions, but Gray remembered enough of his own etiquette training to know it was not quite low enough to greet a king. Perhaps not an overt slight that anyone else might notice, but enough that it made Gray uncomfortable. Rory shifted next to him, Gray's hand falling away from his back.

"Duke," Rory greeted Rinard coolly. "And Count Aplin is with you as well. How appropriate."

The Duke leaned over, brushing a quick, possessive kiss over the Count's cheek. "I did not realize you were aware of my consort," he said. His voice slithered across Gray's consciousness, and his anxiety, already heightened, ratcheted higher. Maybe Rory had been aware the Duke and the Count were committed consorts, but Gray hadn't known. Not for the first time, he thought what good he could do by creating a network of informants, even within Beaulieu itself. It would prevent anyone from developing unsavory ideas, and keep Gray informed when they did.

Not only was Rinard developing them, but Aplin clearly was as well. The hair on Gray's neck prickled as Aplin's eyes, usually a mild gray, flashed an odd glowing green.

But as soon as Gray had seen the change, it was gone, leaving him wondering if he had really seen anything at all. Surely, if another member of the court possessed magic, the same kind of magic as Sabrina, someone would know. And since nobody ever kept their mouth shut here, someone knowing typically meant everyone knowing. But he had heard nothing of this phenomenon and it filled Gray with an anxious dread.

"Of course I am aware of Count Aplin," Rory responded smoothly, "I made sure that my own consort supplied him with rooms appropriate to his station for this very banquet."

Aplin frowned, and then his expression smoothed. "Of course, Your Majesty," he said, bowing at precisely the same height as Rinard had.

Watching their backs as they departed, their figures melting into the thousand invited nobles, Gray realized that if Aplin was Rinard's consort, he could not be nearly as harmless and easily dismissed as he'd hoped. There was a conspiracy afoot, and Gray was going to have to untangle it before it suffocated Rory.

"How did you know about the rooms?" Gray asked. Aplin had passed along the message to Gray, but Gray had declined to ever give it to Rory. Had Aplin found another method to deliver it?

Rory shot him a long-suffering glance. Gray looked down the line and saw there were easily another twenty-five aristocrats in the receiving line. Under any other circumstance, he'd have cried off, suggesting that the King was exhausted and would hopefully find time to greet the rest at a later time. But if Rinard and Aplin were conspiring to depose Rory from the throne, then he couldn't afford to alienate any other possible supporters.

"We're almost done," Gray reassured him—unfortunately all too aware of how much of a lie that was. They weren't almost done. In fact, it felt like every day they were only beginning.

"Aplin sent along about twenty messages to my personal steward," Rory explained under his breath. "He said he spoke to you."

Gray ground his teeth together and gave the next noble, Countess What's-Her-Name, an entirely faux smile. "I did speak to him. I declined to pass on his complaints because I believed they were silly."

The look in Rory's eyes was stark. "Silly, yes, but unwise to ignore."

Gray didn't like the feeling he'd been chastised, but then whose fault was it that he was currently on "placate nobles" duty? Especially when he was terrible at it?

They made it through the remaining twenty introductions, and then had at least a few minutes where they could retreat to a small adjoining room before the banquet began in earnest.

Rory looked slightly surprised that Gray led him out of the receiving room, but also seemed resigned as Gray pulled him into the antechamber, and then closed the door firmly behind them.

"I need a minute," he said.

Rory leaned against the wall, still impossibly beautiful in his white and gold silken finery, but when his eyelids drooped, the dark circles underneath them stood out starkly on his pale skin. "We have a minute," he said, and then paused. "Aplin and Rinard aren't harmless, you know."

It was difficult, but Gray restrained his eye roll. "Yes, I'm aware," he said. "They're incredibly dangerous, especially Rinard." Gray took a deep breath, trying to calm his suddenly racing heart. Why had he ever believed that once Sabrina was dead, they would be safe? Safety, after all, was something he could never take for granted.

"Aplin is far more dangerous than Rinard. Rinard postures, and talks a lot, but I believe Aplin's naivety and pettiness hides a deeply calculating mind."

It was a possibility that had never occurred to Gray before this moment. And once he thought about it, his conclusion chilled him. He'd wanted to wait, but waiting wasn't possible. Not now.

"I spoke to Evrard today," Gray said. "There is a possible solution he suggested to help balance out your duties as well as dismiss any insidious talk amongst the court."

Rory's eyes opened and he gazed into Gray's own. "What was his suggestion?"

This was entirely the wrong time to suggest it, and Gray was hardly prepared, but he was not going to ask Rory to marry him without some semblance of romance. He had no ring, but he could at least get down on one knee.

He did so, and Rory blinked in shock once, and then twice. "What are you doing?" he asked, his voice a surprised squeak. Lately, especially, Rory acted older and wiser than his years, but occasionally, his playfulness would return, and Gray would be reminded that he was really a young man, taking on too many burdens at too young an age.

"King Emory," Gray said, praying his voice would remain steady, "Rory, it would give me the greatest happiness and honor to take your hand in marriage, if you would be so willing."

Deafening silence filled the air between them. Rory was still gaping at him, clearly shocked that Gray had chosen this moment to propose—frankly Gray was shocked he had selected this moment too, so he could hardly fault Rory for that—but the automatic agreement that Gray had expected was nowhere to be heard.

Finally, Rory took a step towards him, and then another, reaching out to grasp Gray's hands in his own and lift him to his feet. Rory's expression was full of regret and Gray experienced a sudden burst of anxiety that maybe he had made assumptions all along that could not possibly be justified. "This was Evrard's idea," Rory stated, but didn't ask. He clearly already knew why Gray was proposing. And even though Gray had not gone out of his way to prevent it, he'd hoped that happiness over being together forever would help make the origin of his proposal more palatable.

Unfortunately, that did not seem to be the case.

"It was Evrard's idea," Gray agreed, but tightened his grip on Rory's hands, pulling the man closer to him, pressing him against his own body. "But I love you. I want to spend the rest of my life with you. The idea to get married now might be Evrard's but it was always my intention to be with you, for as long as you would have me, you know that."

Rory did not look quite as convinced as Gray had hoped.

"I do know that." Rory's voice was regretful, and Gray felt the immediate loss of contact as he pulled away. "But I do not want to get married because it would silence my critics. Especially Aplin and Rinard. This is my life, not theirs, and they do not get to control it simply by existing."

"Then marry me because you want to," Gray begged, uncomfortably aware of his own pleading tone, but also painfully aware that he had just been turned down. For fair and just reasons, but they didn't prevent the rejection from stinging.

But Rory didn't say anything, just continued to look pained, like somehow his own heart was cracking, right along with Gray's. "We should go back to the party," he said gently, and this time he did reach for Gray, tucking his hand into Gray's much larger one. "We will be missed."

Gray wanted to tell him that for once, Rory's royal duties shouldn't come before his personal ones, that they should stay here and decide how to move forward, how to eliminate the threats against them while staying committed to one another, but the distance in Rory's eyes—the first Gray had ever seen—kept his mouth shut.

Gray didn't stop the servant from filling his wine glass again with the ruby red liquid in the glass pitcher. Rory shot him a look.

"What?" Gray asked, "I'm enjoying this party."

"You don't usually enjoy parties," Rory pointed out. "And banquets, those you especially dislike."

It was impossible to keep his hurt inside. It felt like it showed on every inch of his body, radiating out of him like the sun and its warm rays. Except that Gray felt like the exact opposite. "This is my first banquet," he pointed out slowly.

"And you seem to be having a much worse time," Rory retorted. At least they were seated at the very head of the gigantic table, separated by enough sparkling glassware, delicate porcelain, and shining silver that nobody could hear them bickering. Or notice that perhaps Gray had imbibed much more than he usually did.

"Perhaps that has nothing to do with the event, and everything to do with the proposal you just rejected," Gray said.

Rory's gaze shuttered close. "I didn't reject you."

"You didn't say yes," Gray pointed out, gesturing with his glass. "I think I would have noticed if you had."

"Can we not do this now?" Rory hissed. "At least save it until we're alone. Please."

It was not fair, but then life felt particularly unfair right now. Maybe it was that he was seeing everything through the haze of the wine, but to Gray, it felt like all he had done since arriving at Beaulieu was to be everything he thought Rory wanted, to be available whenever Rory had a free moment, to take care of every pressing matter that he could, so Rory could be free to rule his country. And in payment, Gray received very little if any personal time, possibly treasonous nobles, and a rejection of his marriage proposal.

If Evrard was here, at this stupid, blasted banquet, then Gray could at least complain to him, but he was in his stable, snug and undisturbed, and likely completely unaware of the chaos he'd created with his simple suggestion.

Gray had resented the unicorn many times in his life, but his resentment had never burned as acutely as it did right now.

He leaned back in his chair and glared at the liquid in his glass. "I think I should go back to the Valley." The words came out without him even thinking about them, and definitely without him considering the effect they could have. For when he'd lived in the Valley of the Lost Things, it was not as if he had felt life was any more fair. In fact, he remembered all those painfully lonely nights, wishing to meet someone he could share his exile with, and never, ever glimpsing even a possibility on the horizon.

Then Rory had arrived, changing everything, but now, somehow, life as Rory's consort was nowhere near like he'd imagined it during those lonely nights. But then, Gray thought, watching as Rory's expression went pale, he had never imagined that his consort might be a prince or a king. He'd only ever wanted some poor shepherd boy or a sweet milkmaid. He'd never dreamt that he would find himself back in a place similar to where he had been born.

Maybe . . . just maybe . . . he had had the right idea all along.

"Do you mean," Rory hesitated, "do you mean to leave? To go back?"

Gray didn't know what he meant. He knew, objectively, that he was still in love with Rory, and that he never wanted to leave him, but there was something about Beaulieu that was driving him slowly insane and was making him say things he'd never have considered under normal circumstances. But then, becoming the consort to a king and wielding a magical weapon was hardly normal, even for someone who'd grown up with a unicorn as a father figure.

Maybe what he needed was a little break. Some space, for both of them. Maybe Rory would miss him more when he was gone, and realize they were meant to be together, regardless of circumstance. "Not forever," he admitted softly, setting down his glass and catching up Rory's hand in his and raising it to his lips. He brushed a kiss, agonizingly slow, over Rory's skin. "Just . . . for a little bit. I could use some time away."

It was impossible to miss the hurt in Rory's eyes. Truthfully if anyone needed a break it was him, but he was the King now, and he felt the obligation so keenly that Gray knew he didn't believe a break was something he deserved.

Another problem, heaped upon the million others on Gray's plate, and he couldn't hope to solve any of them.

"I will put together a small company to escort you in the morning," Rory said, and this time his voice wavered and Gray would have to be blind to miss the sudden sheen in his amber eyes. "But I will miss you."

This time, Gray's kiss landed on Rory's lips, and it crossed the line from polite to something else entirely. He didn't care. "I will miss you too, you know that. I don't want . . . I don't want to end up like this, me drinking too much wine, you working all the time, and us bickering at banquets."

Rory wiped a tear away. "We won't. I swear it."

"I'll forego the company," Gray added. "I'll take Evrard. I have Lion's Breath. I shall be fine."

"You'd best promise you will be," Rory said, a smile threatening to break through the thundercloud on his face. "I will not tolerate anything less, and I hear the King of Fontaine is completely unable to compromise."

Gray smiled back. He felt better already, like he could already feel the hard dirt of the road beneath Evrard's hooves, and the wide-open grasslands of the Valley. "He's still learning," he said, brushing another kiss across Rory's perfectly flawless nose, "but I believe he will get there. Someday."

"Someday," Rory agreed with a sniff.

As predicted, Rory fell asleep nearly the moment his head hit the pillow when they finally returned to their quarters from the banquet. Gray stayed up later, packing a bag, but mostly watching Rory sleep, his auburn curls spilled across the ivory sheets, his face so peaceful.

Even though Gray knew in his gut that going back to the Valley was the right thing to do, his stomach clenched at the inevitable sorrow they'd both feel at being separated. Even a few weeks was far more than they'd been apart since the first time they'd met.

Still, in the end, he wouldn't be leaving if he didn't believe this wouldn't lead to a breakthrough. At the very least he had to try because they couldn't keep going as they were.

When the first rays of early morning sun crept over the castle, Gray gently rolled Rory over and watched as his eyes fluttered open. For a split second, only joy and love were reflected in their depths, and then after a moment passed, and Rory woke further, he remembered why his lover might wake him, and a shadow crept in.

"You're leaving," Rory said, and there was an edge of hurt to his tone.

"I wanted to get on the road early," Gray said softly.

Maybe leaving Rory right now wasn't particularly kind, but at least to Gray's mind, it was necessary. "Of course you did," Rory said. Bitterness joined the hurt. "When should I expect to see you again?"

"I won't be gone very long. Maybe a few weeks. Just to make sure the Valley is secure. Give you time with the Mecant elders."

Rory could hardly argue that while the elders were at Beaulieu, and he was fulfilling his promise, there was very little time for Gray. Still, he'd just begun to frown, before Gray leaned down and kissed the disgruntled expression right off his face. Gray poured everything he felt into that kiss: the hope and happiness he felt whenever he thought of their long, glorious future, the pride in Rory's accomplishments, the deep pervading heat that filled him at just the thought of Rory, panting and aroused, perched above him. They were both breathless when Gray finally lifted his head.

The shadows had disappeared from Rory's eyes completely.

"I love you," he said, and it wasn't that Rory didn't say it often, but this time it sounded fervent—like a vow. And Gray took it as such, holding the words close to his heart and letting the balm of them soothe the wounded hurt he'd felt when Rory had chosen to answer his proposal with silence.

"I love you too," Gray responded, leaning in to brush one more kiss against Rory's glorious curls. "I'll be back home before you know it."

"I thought we had solved this particular set of problems," Evrard said, sounding incredibly put out, "and then I discover, to my utmost shock and horror, that we are going back to the Valley. The Valley! You hated the Valley."

"I didn't hate the Valley." Gray made sure to keep the amusement out of his tone. Evrard wouldn't appreciate Gray finding his outpouring of melodrama funny. "I was lonely there."

"Yet, here we are, going back, and for what reason I am still endeavoring to discover."

"We needed some space. I . . ." Gray took a deep breath. "I did as you suggested, and it was a disaster. Rory hated the idea."

Evrard stopped trotting down the road so abruptly Gray nearly lost his seat. "He what," he exclaimed.

Gray was even more relieved he'd decided Evrard needed to accompany him back to the Valley, because if he'd discovered the truth with Rory within lecturing distance, he probably would have put Rory so firmly off marriage, a wedding never would have occurred.

"I told you that he wasn't going to want to be married because of Aplin and Rinard's gossiping," Gray said, despite the fact that he was truly afraid what Aplin and Rinard were doing was far worse than a little loose talk.

"Well," Evrard sniffed, "I never suggested you inform him of that particular benefit. That was all on you."

"I wasn't going to lie to him." That was something Gray had vowed never to do.

"Still," Evrard hedged. "There is a method of communication called diplomacy."

"And I'm exercising it by putting some distance between us," Gray insisted.

"You are so sure this will work?" Evrard did not sound particularly convinced.

"It's better than continuing the same thing and continuing to let it separate us further." Gray took a deep breath. "By the time we get back, the Mecant tribe will have departed for the season, and perhaps Rory will have had some time to reflect on what he really wants his rule to be like."

"And some time to miss you?" Evrard chortled. "Perhaps you are more conniving than I had given you credit for."

"It's not . . ."

"Yes it is, and I applaud it," Evrard said, sounding very final about his decision. "After all, you are doing it with every intention of it helping Rory, not hurting him. You mustn't worry. You're not Sabrina. You could never be her."

Gray let out the breath he hadn't known he was holding. It was annoying that occasionally Evrard knew him better than he knew his own mind, but then it could be illuminating too. He'd never have thought what bothered him about being labeled "conniving" was that he never, ever wanted to resemble the sorceress he had slain.

"A half day and a hard ride and we will be at the Valley," Evrard continued. "That is plenty of time to not only review your plan for Aplin and for Rinard, but to continue your etiquette lessons."

Gray groaned, hard.

Maybe he shouldn't have left Beaulieu after all.

CHAPTER TWENTY-ONE

Rory wished fervently that Gray hadn't left. He missed him already, more than he had ever imagined he would—and his imagination, from all the many years of burying his head in books, was extremely well-developed—and it was all quite a bit worse because Rory placed the entirety of the blame for Gray's departure on his own shoulders.

"Your Majesty," Anya asked, breaking her silent position near the doorway to his office, and coming to stand near his desk, "are you alright?"

"No," Rory said miserably. "I'm not."

"I did wonder, because you were making a quite pitiful groaning noise just then," Anya offered, a glimmer of a smile breaking through her solemn expression.

Rory didn't know whether it was better or worse that Gray had left Anya behind, ostensibly to guard him. If he'd wanted Rory to think of him every minute of every day, and never be able to escape his memory, he'd have accomplished that even without Anya. But with his countrywoman right there as an additional constant reminder, Rory's suffering felt particularly acute.

"I miss Gray," Rory said, not that this revelation was particularly new to anyone, especially not to Anya, who had been present for the last two days and had witnessed every ounce of Rory's regret.

"If you miss him so much," Anya said, resting a hip against the edge of Rory's enormous, intricately carved desk, "why did you let him leave in the first place?"

It must have been Rory's somewhat shocked expression—in the six months since he'd ascended the throne of Fontaine, it was rare that anyone, barring Gray and Evrard, actually told him the blunt, unadorned truth. Anya must have realized a moment too late that she was addressing Rory, who was the King, and not Gray, with whom he knew she had a much more informal relationship.

"I . . . uh . . ." It was unusual to witness the Ardglassian warrior feeling anything other than supremely self-possessed and confident. "My apologies, Your Majesty," she added, with an apologetic frown. "I appear to have overstepped my boundaries."

Rory was not jealous, precisely, of Gray's easy way with people, even those who did not like him, but he was beginning to see that his own stiff formality was doing him no favors. Another blame to lay at the gravestone of his aunt, who by allowing him to hide away, had neglected to teach him some vital lessons about social interaction.

"No, no," Rory said, "it is I who should be apologizing. You said nothing wrong. In fact, I . . . I find I need more people who tell me the truth." There was Gray, of course, but it was not the same. "And you are right, absolutely right. If I did not want him to go, I should have asked him to stay."

"Your Majesty," Anya said, absently reaching down to pet one of the enormous carved lions holding up each corner of the massive desk, "you have recently taken your throne. Gray is still coming to terms with his own legacy and his own power in your kingdom. Some . . . growing pains are to be expected, I think."

Rory, who had spent the last two days, and in many ways, the last few months, beating himself up mentally for the problems he and Gray were experiencing, gaped at her.

"You really believe that?" he asked slowly. In all likelihood, it was entirely inappropriate for Rory to be having this conversation with Anya, but he knew she was good friends with Gray, and if he couldn't talk to someone, there was a strong chance he would simply explode.

"Both your lives completely changed when you became King," Anya said simply.

Rory knew Anya was right, and that even as they had both struggled to adjust to their new reality, their feelings for each other had remained steadfast and true. He still loved Gray, he still wanted and needed him in equal parts, and he hoped—no, he believed—that Gray's feelings were similarly unchanged.

"Has Gray ever told you about how he came to terms with his exile in the Valley of Lost Things?" Anya asked.

Gray did not typically like talking about his feelings, especially feelings surrounding him leaving Ardglass. He had mentioned it offhandedly once or twice, but never in any depth, and Rory found himself more disconsolate at the fact Gray was talking to Anya, but not to him. But then, Rory reminded himself, when would you have time to have these deep conversations? You barely have any time to ask each other how your day was.

Rory was forced to shake his head, at least a little embarrassed that they were supposed to be soulmates, but Gray was talking to his countrywoman instead.

"I explain this because I have the impression that your upbringing, at least after the death of your parents, was quite different," Anya said seriously. "But Gray was raised to be a king. He was trained from a very young age to not only be a statesman, but to be a general. Nearly everything he did was in service of helping him become a better, more just ruler to his people. And then, at age eleven, everything changed for him. Every bit of foundation that he had was ripped away, and instead of being a king, he was essentially told that he would be a farmhand the rest of his life."

Of course Rory knew the facts of the situation; that at eleven Gray had fled Ardglass, and then had settled in the Valley of Lost Things. He also knew, from offhand comments Gray had made from almost the very beginning, that such an abrupt change weighed heavily on him then, and now.

"He dealt with this," Anya pointed out, her voice gentling, "by staying so busy he couldn't dwell on the sudden changes that had overtaken his life."

Rory was renowned for being one of the most intelligent men of his age. With Anya's words, he realized just how stupid and blind he had been. Instead of giving Gray something to do to help him adjust to the new circumstances in which he'd found himself, Rory had rebuffed every single attempt Gray had made to find an occupation.

He was silent for a long moment as so many of their conversations were re-framed in his head, taking into account this new angle. And all of them suddenly felt quite different. Gray, not dissatisfied with Rory, or thinking that Rory was not good enough or Rory was not working hard enough, but desperate for something to do because he was struggling and because he was bored. Here Gray was, with half of the education normally given to a king, and no way to use it, because Rory was too stubborn to let anyone else help.

"I'm an idiot," Rory finally pronounced, disgusted with himself. He'd become so self-absorbed, juggling all the new duties he'd taken on, that he'd failed to notice the man he loved was struggling. It wasn't like Gray hadn't said anything; he'd asked more than once if he could help. But Rory, feeling his own heap of guilt from letting his aunt rule unchecked for years, had never made an effort to make a place for his lover.

A smile glimmered at the edges of Anya's mouth. "Not an idiot," she said, "merely a king trying to do right by his people and a man in love, trying to navigate a new relationship."

A new relationship.

Was that why Gray's proposal had bothered him so much? Rory, too, had taken it for granted that they would be married someday, and had been unpleasantly surprised that Gray would decide now, when they barely saw each other, was the perfect time.

Maybe it was the perfect time to use a wedding to silence any treasonous gossip, but it certainly wasn't anything close to the most ideal time for Rory and Gray personally. He'd known they were struggling a little bit, had inevitably seen it, but had been un-sure how to solve their problems. Had hoped, somewhat naively, that with time for them both to adjust to their new roles, every-thing would revert back to how it had been at the very beginning.

But that wasn't right either, Rory realized. That wasn't even something he should want. Their relationship shouldn't march backwards, back to the beginning, but progress and move forward.

"I can see why Gray keeps you around," Rory said to Anya, who only shrugged.

"I think he likes having me around because I'm from Ardglass and I make sure his head stays the same size," she said.

"Maybe we can share your service, and you can assist me simi-larly," Rory proposed.

Anya regarded him speculatively. "I don't think a huge ego is your problem, Your Majesty," she said.

"Perhaps not, but an application of brutal honesty never goes amiss," Rory said firmly. Too many advisers were treating him like particularly delicate glass, afraid to see how much he could bear. The Rory of six months ago might have been equally concerned about his strength of purpose, but the Rory of today had dug deep and discovered he was much tougher than he'd ever imagined.

Somehow, miraculously, the Valley looked unchanged as Gray and Evrard rode down the slope towards the farm.

"It never changes because I wish it that way," Evrard pointed out, answering Gray's unspoken question.

"Magic," Gray muttered under his breath, even though he was perfectly aware that Evrard would hear it.

"You hardly disparaged magic when you summoned it with Lion's Breath and saved Rory's life as well as your own," Evrard pointed out.

"There's a place for it. That I won't argue with. But to keep this valley green and bright and perfect?" Gray shook his head. "It feels like a waste."

"It's not my magic that keeps this place pristine," Evrard observed. "But a much deeper, much more archaic magic set in place long before I even existed. I could hardly change it, even if I wished to."

The crops Gray had planted in the spring before Rory's arrival with his guard to the Valley were still sitting in the fields, seemingly frozen in time. He'd fully expected to ride in and immediately have to rip rotten crops from the fields, but everything was preserved, like the last six months hadn't passed at all.

"You could have told me that we didn't need to check in on the Valley," Gray grumbled as he dismounted, running his fingers along the tall corn stalks Rory had once hid in.

"And deprive you of an excuse to run off when you and Rory were having problems?" Evrard said, clearly much amused by himself. "I wouldn't dare."

Gray glared at the unicorn next to him. "That isn't why we came. We came . . ."

"Because Rory wouldn't listen to you? Because he won't let you help him? Because he turned down your proposal of marriage?"

Gray stalked over to the farmhouse and yanked the door open. He was already missing Rory and regretting leaving in such a huff, but Evrard was not making this any easier. A common problem with Evrard; he tended to rub your nose in it before you finally admitted he'd been right all along. Gray's hands tightened into fists as he took in the main room of the farmhouse. It was just as he'd left it, like he'd merely stepped outside for a moment. "It wasn't like I thought it would be," he finally admitted in a low, despondent voice. "I thought . . . I don't know what I thought."

Evrard paused in the doorway. "You thought even though Ardglass was lost to you, you could pick up where you left off with Fontaine." He tilted his great head, his bright white mane falling to the side. "You thought you'd found a purpose again."

"I did," Gray said savagely. It annoyed the ever-living hell out of him that Evrard knew him so damn well, but it turned out there was some benefit to discussing his problems with someone who could read Gray's mind. He wasn't used to Evrard being so entirely wrong. "I found a purpose, I did, I had adopted Fontaine as my own, and Rory as my future and . . ." Gray broke off with a muffled oath and stomped over to a chair and slumped down into it.

When he glanced up, Evrard was carefully picking his way across the threshold, despite Gray's longstanding order that animals, even animals who talked, didn't come in the house, they stayed outside or in the stables. "You thought being Rory's consort and protecting him would be enough," Evrard said softly. "But it's not."

"I'm angry with myself for believing that was the case. For thinking that loving Rory would be enough." Gray's head fell into his hands. "I want it to be."

"How could it be? You," Evrard said, his voice growing, and taking on that magical quality of excessive confidence, "you were born to be a king."

How was that supposed to make him feel any better? "And now, thanks to Gideon, I'm not," Gray observed wryly.

Evrard's mane shimmered in the dim light of the farmhouse. "You are not listening," he said, clearly frustrated. "What do you think you would be if you and Rory were married? An assistant? A mere consort? You would be a king, same as him. He is able to bestow the title and powers onto you, same as his own. And you should share the throne. You possess some of the knowledge and the skills needed for ruling Fontaine, and while Rory's learning was different, it's complementary. Together, you are the balance."

"That means asking him to share his birthright," Gray said. He wanted to believe Rory would be willing, but then very few men who obtained power were ever able to give it up. Rory definitely was not most men, but he was still a man, with the same weaknesses, no matter how fiercely his intelligence shone.

"He would do it and more, for you, and for Fontaine," Evrard pointed out softly. "And regardless, he cannot, if you do not ask."

"But I have asked," Gray burst out.

Evrard's gaze seared into him. "Did you truly ask? Or did you hedge, afraid that he'd turn you down?"

Gray stared moodily at the floor. "I did ask him to marry me, and while he didn't outright reject me, he certainly didn't agree either."

"It sounds to me like you both need to talk through your problems." Evrard's voice was unbearably wise. And Gray was fairly certain he was also trying to point out that the last thing he should have done was run away instead of talking through everything they were struggling with. Because that was what he'd done, wasn't it? At the first overt sign of trouble, he'd packed up and left.

"I needed to know this was still here, in case . . ." Gray hesitated; he didn't even want to say it out loud.

"Rory has taken on a huge responsibility, but you've given up your life twice now, without hesitation." Evrard paused. "Looking back to make sure that what you left still exists isn't the worst thing you could have done. And as you can see, the Valley is still here. If you wanted to come back here and live, you could."

Even though Gray didn't respond to Evrard, he already knew what his answer was. He wouldn't be coming back here, not permanently. He belonged in Beaulieu, with Rory. They just needed to figure out his place there, and how to rearrange things so he fit a little better.

After settling Evrard into his stable with fresh straw, Gray collapsed into his old bed, and to his surprise, slept well, and then rose with the dawn, feeling his mind settle on a decision.

He'd cared for this farm for too long to see it stand stagnant, even with the strange preservation magic that had settled over it.

"We made the effort to come," was all Gray said when Evrard questioned their schedule, "and so I'll harvest this crop. We'll leave at the end of the week." His heart was already yearning to return to Rory, but another part of him—the part that had worked so long and so hard to make this farm his home—knew he couldn't leave it like this.

"We talked about this . . ." Evrard began to say, but Gray held up a hand, stopping him.

"I don't care if it stays frozen like this for a hundred years. I'm not leaving these vegetables behind when the people of Fontaine could eat them."

He'd have to be a lot blinder to see Evrard's satisfied expression as he turned away.

The days passed more quickly than Gray anticipated. He worked hard from sunup to sundown, harvesting the crops in the fields, and then packing them away in crates he'd put together during many past winters. Evrard could not be expected to carry such a heavy load, as well as Gray, so he traveled to the village, and with his coin purse full of Fontaine gold, bought a solid work horse and a brand-new cart. It was the first time he appreciated not having to bargain for every piece of dried meat or stick of wood. He'd had the results of his hard labor to barter with before, but never before had he been able to outright purchase anything. He hadn't even wanted to take the gold, but Rory had insisted. Now Gray was glad he had, because, when he returned to Beaulieu, he'd have something to show for his absence. Without the gold, and the transportation it had purchased, the crops never could have left the Valley.

The day before they were planning to leave, Gray was out in the corn field, sweat dripping down his forehead even though it was very late autumn—nearly winter—and the weather had definitely turned cooler. This was the last field he had to harvest and pack onto the already full cart, and he wanted to get done earlier so he might have time to relax in the bath, in anticipation of the journey home.

The noise of hooves pounding the ground startled him out of his rhythm, his knife falling to his side as he glanced up.

Since they'd arrived almost a week ago, he'd seen not a soul except for the quick trip he'd taken to the neighboring village. He was certainly not expecting to see anyone, though he supposed that the rules of the Valley still applied. If someone was lost and needed shelter, the Valley was accessible to them.

At first, Gray couldn't see anything, even as he shaded his eyes from the weak wintery sunshine.

Then, like a vision from his fantasies—or perhaps from his memories—he made out a group of riders, horses in formation, with a slight, but erect figure crowned with bright auburn hair riding at the forefront.

Gray's first thought was sweet, blessed relief. He'd known he was missing Rory terribly, but he'd pushed the feelings away because they'd hurt, and keeping busy helped numb him, at least a little. His second thought, as Rory and his guard rode closer, was that something terrible had happened to make them flee Beaulieu again. *You never should have left him. You weren't there to protect him when he needed it the most.*

Gray wiped his face with an already dirty sleeve, and stepped out of the corn patch, waiting for the riders to come closer. When they were finally near enough to make out which of Rory's guard had come with, joy swept through him in a dizzying rush. Marthe was not with him, which hopefully meant that all was well, and Rory had left her behind to maintain Beaulieu's defenses.

Which meant only one thing—Rory had come for him.

Finally, they stopped. Gray met Anya's gaze, and she smiled brightly at him.

Then Rory swung his leg over his horse and Gray couldn't look at anything except his lover as he walked towards him.

Rory was smiling too, so sweetly that Gray could barely stop himself from rushing and throwing himself into his arms, no matter how dirty and sweaty he'd gotten.

"I hear this is an excellent refuge for the lost," Rory said, his hot, possessive gaze making it clear that he didn't care how dirty or sweaty Gray was either.

Rory might be one of the most brilliant minds of this age, but Gray could still keep up. "Are you lost, then?"

Rory didn't say a word, but walked closer, closing the last few feet behind them. He reached up, cupping Gray's cheek, rough with the beginnings of a beard because Gray hadn't been bothered to shave while he was alone in the Valley. "I was lost without you," he admitted softly. "I'm so sorry, more than I can even say."

Gray let out the breath he'd been holding—maybe from the moment the crown had been placed upon Rory's brow, or maybe even earlier than that, from the first moment they'd entered Beaulieu.

"I'm sorry too," he said. "I was coming home. I swear." He gestured towards the loaded cart. "But I couldn't let all this go to waste when our subjects could use it."

The corner of Rory's mouth quirked up. "Our subjects?"

Gray steeled himself—reminding himself that they both wanted the same things, that they were still wildly, madly in love, and that most important fact hadn't changed, even though nearly everything else had. "I hope to call them my subjects too, whether or not you consider my proposal," Gray said quietly. "I want to help you. I want to help them. Please let me."

Rory's expression didn't waver. "I think we can work something out. But first, there is something you should know." He paused, and his gaze grew darker, more determined. "I'm afraid that Sabrina isn't quite as dead as we hoped."

CHAPTER
TWENTY-TWO

A WEEK BEFORE

Missing Gray, while slightly more manageable with every passing day, was a feeling that didn't abate merely because Rory had realized how many mistakes he'd made with the man he loved. Still, he couldn't stay in bed, feeling sorry for himself, or stare moodily out the window and not attend to the mountain of paperwork heaped upon his desk. Still, he made time—time he realized he should have been making all along—to summon Marthe to his office.

"Your Majesty," Marthe said dipping into a quick, economical bow.

"I told you that you needn't bother," Rory said, but Marthe's lips compressed into a stubborn line.

"You are my king, and I am your general," Marthe said. "Anything else would be unseemly."

And even though she would continue to resist, Rory knew he would continue to ask, and maybe someday, she might relent. Probably not though, Rory thought with an internal grin.

"You've summoned me?" Marthe asked.

"Please sit," Rory said, indicating a chair opposite his own. "I wish to discuss tradition with someone I trust. Someone who knows the nobility, but isn't a member of the court."

Marthe's gaze sharpened as she sat down. "You are thinking of changing things," she said, and Rory was pleasantly surprised to see that she looked delighted at the possibility.

"I am," Rory admitted. "I . . . perhaps for other men, or other women, ruling a kingdom isn't overwhelming, but I am still learning, and still want to make many of the decisions myself. So I find myself with more work than I know what to do with."

"I know Your Majesty wishes to stay involved," Marthe suggested, "but there are some that would be willing to assist."

"Some?" They both knew exactly who she was referring to, but just like Marthe refused to concede to informality, Rory wasn't going to make this easier on her.

"I know Prince Graham was raised and educated to be the King of Ardglass, and you trust him completely. Perhaps you could share some of the burden with him."

Rory smiled. "I could, unofficially. But what if I wished to make such a division of labor more formal?"

She didn't reply immediately, and Rory knew that now he'd surprised her. "You mean," she asked slowly, "to give him some of the power traditionally held by the throne?"

"I mean to marry him," Rory said simply, "and upon our marriage, elevate him to kingship, alongside myself. Some decisions, those impacting the whole of the kingdom, would be ones we would need to make together, but others . . . I was thinking of splitting the traditional duties in half."

"I . . . I was not expecting this, Your Majesty," Marthe finally admitted.

Rory stood and wandered over to the window overlooking the courtyard. "I haven't found many references to such action in the past. But even more than myself, I know you to be a scholar of history, especially of Fontaine. Is there any precedent?"

"I . . ." Marthe hesitated. "Whether there is precedent or not, this will not be popular with the nobles and with the court."

Rory turned. He knew he was still too pretty, still too young, to have a truly kingly bearing, but he was working on it. He drew up to his full height—wished he had a few more inches—and leveled his most royal look at Marthe. "This throne is my responsibility and my birthright and those who oppose me should take care to remember that."

Marthe had known him since he was a young child, bookish and quiet, and he was pleasantly surprised to see how astonished she looked. "Of course, Your Majesty," she said. "I do not know of any precedent, though if I remember correctly, there were some ancient documents, from the beginning of this kingdom, giving you the permission to do so."

"I have read them too," Rory said, returning to his seat and leaning forward, capturing her gaze. "I was hoping you would say so, and that we could agree on this particular interpretation."

"Your Majesty." Marthe took a deep breath. "Rory. You are the King. You are free to do whatever you wish. Your aunt saw fit to do the same, but while she was clearly corrupt and sold her soul for the use of dark magic, she did so without the kingdom knowing. Plainly speaking, to the majority of your subjects and your court, she was a decent regent. There is no saying once she held full control that she would have maintained fair and just rule. The common people, they do not care who holds the throne as long as they are treated well, and as your aunt treated them well, there is belief that you will do the same. For the nobles, however, it is different. She cultivated many of them, elevated them, spoiled them with power and riches. They are not so easily persuaded to support you, especially when they never knew she was an evil sorceress."

"She was power-mad," Rory said. "It would have shown eventually, but you are right. It was not evident to the country when she was killed, and that hurts my own position."

"The kingdom does not trust Prince Graham yet. Ardglass is not, and has never traditionally been, an enemy of Fontaine, but the court sees him as a prince from another country—one you are very close to, one whose bed you share."

Rory drummed his fingers on the table. "I'm not trusted."

"Perhaps an exaggeration, but there is a current of distrust, and I am sure you know of whom I speak, but there are those who curry that distrust, to their own benefit."

"Count Aplin, and the Duke of Rinard," Rory said bluntly.

Marthe nodded.

"It would be a great benefit to me and also to Gray if I could somehow expose my aunt's treachery and dark magic to the court," Rory thought out loud, "but it cannot be as simple as merely saying so."

"There needs to be evidence," Marthe agreed. "Evidence they can see with their own eyes."

"They must make the decision that she would have been a poor ruler themselves. But . . ." Rory smiled. "Perhaps we can lead them there."

"I have yet to do much investigation of the catacombs underneath some of Beaulieu. You knew there was an existing structure, when your great-great-great-grandfather began the construction of the existing castle?"

"I was aware," Rory said, "though I was under the impression those areas had been sealed off."

"They were, but I have long held the belief that Sabrina opened some of the rooms and used them as a secret lair to experiment with her dark magic."

"Why would you think so?"

Marthe held out her hands. "Have you found any evidence of dark magic in the castle proper? I have not, and I have searched. Yet we know unequivocally that she had it. I was hoping to leave the place where it was kept buried, deep in the ground, but perhaps we should expose it—and her, along with it."

"I too would rather leave it buried but . . ." Rory could not help but think of Gray's soft expression on the early morning of his departure, and the desolation in his eyes when Rory had turned down his proposal. He could not lose him, no matter what the cost. And this plan of his, where they married and shared the ruling of the kingdom, was instrumental to their future. "We must find it and we must show it to the court."

To Rory's surprise, Diana came to fetch him, short of breath and with panic in her eyes, the very next morning. "Marthe needs you," she said, giving Rory a quick, perfunctory bow that made Rory's heartbeat accelerate with uncertainty in his chest. The only one of his guard who was more of a stickler for protocol than Marthe was Diana. So the fact that she essentially eschewed it this time in favor of speed did not bode well at all.

"Is everything alright?" Rory asked as he and Diana, with an accompanying Anya, hurried in the direction of the throne room.

Diana's expression was grim. She led them past the throne room and they stopped in the hallway, where they had entered Beaulieu six months ago, trying to surprise Sabrina and defeat her before any of the armies could engage. The grate had been pulled open, and Rory could see the flickering of torches in the dark tunnel below.

"You must see what we discovered," she said, and refused to say anything further as she held out an arm to assist Rory in descending down to the tunnel below. Within moments, Anya and Diana had followed him, and his eyes slowly growing accustomed to the dim light from several torches, posted a few dozen feet apart down the length of the dank sewer.

"Follow me," Diana said, and picking up one of the torches from the makeshift holder, led them in a direction that Rory was fairly sure was opposite of the one they'd taken that fateful day.

"How did you find it?" Anya asked.

"We started here, in the sewer, as that seemed the most obvious method of entry from the castle itself," Diana said as they picked their way down the waterlogged stone. "It did not take us very long to find it." She shuddered, and Rory was sure, with a growing sense of dread, that it wasn't because she was cold, even though there was a distinct chill in the air down below.

Finally, they emerged into a central meeting of several of the large pipes, and there, at the very end of the most forward tunnel, stood Marthe, a bleak look on her face.

"Your Majesty," she said, inclining her head. "I have found what you requested." She gestured, indicating the large metal door that had blocked Sabrina's lair off from the rest of the tunnels.

"Should we not go inside?" Rory asked.

Marthe hesitated. "Your Majesty, we can collapse this tunnel and everything in it, and ensure that the likelihood of it being found and anything inside it ever being used again would be extremely slim."

"But you said earlier, just yesterday in fact, that you thought we should use it to expose Sabrina as the dark witch that she was," Rory objected. He'd been hoping that with the execution of her plan, he could enact his own, and ensure that his and Gray's future was as happy and joyful as he'd always hoped it would be. But now instead Marthe wished to close all the evidence away? Hide it?

"Before you make the decision, you should see inside," Marthe said, her voice as hard as the stone walls surrounding them. "And we should hurry."

Anya placed a hand on the sword hilt on her belt and Rory began to comprehend why Marthe might have changed her mind.

He followed Marthe, pulse thudding dully, into the darkened chamber, secretly (or perhaps not so secretly) terrified of what he would find.

The room itself was fairly basic and non-threatening, with no corpses lying around or blood splashed along the walls. Merely a few old, battered wooden tables, covered in glass jars filled with a creepy assortment of animal parts and some rather more innocuous-looking herbs, and parchments scattered every which way. An enormous deep black cauldron stood in the middle of the room, its interior crusted with burned-on bits that had Rory shuddering.

"This, Your Majesty," Marthe said, pointing to one of the tables, "was what concerned me the most."

Rory stepped over to the table. On it was a vial of some substance, and it was open and clearly fresh, as it had not yet dried out in the container. Next to it was a large stone mortar with a matching stone pestle. Rory put a single fingertip inside, and felt the wetness of whatever mixture had been in process. "You interrupted someone," Rory said softly. "Someone knows about this place and has been using it since Sabrina's demise."

"Or it could be Sabrina, back from the dead," Diana piped in fearfully.

"She's dead, Gray burned her to ash," Anya answered flatly. "But this is clearly one of her sycophants, trying to continue her evil work."

"Unfortunately," Marthe added, "the person fled before we could get a good look, and it was so dark and the terrain so uneven, it was impossible to follow them. However"—she pointed to a scrap of parchment next to the mortar—"they were using one of her recipes. You know it's not her, because look, see the handwriting?" Rory peered closer, and made out his aunt's distinctive handwriting, though he did not recognize the language, and then the very different notations that had been made next to some of the lines.

"Someone is trying to take her place," Rory said in a hard voice. "No, we cannot expose this. We must destroy it. Everything in it. And I must go get Gray, now."

Marthe frowned. "Is it such a good idea to leave the castle at this time of unrest? Surely we could send a messenger to bring Prince Graham back to Beaulieu."

Rory had known she would suggest that; after discovering this lair, she wouldn't want him to leave the relative safety of the castle. But was it truly safe when someone within the walls was attempting to practice Sabrina's particularly warped version of magic?

"We will be quick. I will travel light, with only a small guard. After all, the person who opened this chamber will be here, and not in the Valley." Rory could see Marthe was unsure, but she finally nodded her approval. He hadn't necessarily needed it, because he was the King, after all, but it was certainly easier if she agreed.

"Hopefully we caught whoever was here mid-spell, and they will be unable to complete it," Anya said ominously.

"Hopefully," Rory repeated, but he did not feel particularly hopeful. He felt afraid, and until Gray was back, safely within these walls, and they were again united, he wouldn't sleep easy.

CHAPTER TWENTY-THREE

Telling Gray about Marthe and Diana's discovery hadn't been the first thing he'd wanted to lead with—there were definitely other subjects he was dying to discuss with Gray—but after Rory's confession, that was all Gray wanted to hear.

"Tell me everything," he said, pulling Rory towards the farmhouse, as Anya directed the guard towards the stables. "What do you mean, she isn't dead? I fried her."

"You did," Rory agreed. "We all saw it. But, Marthe found a room, deep in the catacombs, near where we snuck in using the old sewer tunnels, where Sabrina performed her magic spells. And it seems that someone else is using it."

Gray stared at him, as Rory sank into one of the chairs near the fireplace. Gray's old home might be very simple, but it was comfortable. "Someone else? Who?"

"Unfortunately, they seemed to have run off just before they were discovered. But," Rory sighed, "I do have my guesses."

"Aplin or Rinard," Gray said in a hard voice. "Of course it would be them. It surely has to be Rinard."

"Perhaps not. I have my concerns about both of them."

Gray sighed, and began to pace back and forth. "I won't disagree with you. But why were Marthe and Diana searching in the catacombs in the first place?"

This was less easy for Rory to admit, because so much of the explanation why touched on the other reason he'd been desperate to talk to Gray.

He held out his hands towards Gray, who came nearer and took them in his own, clasping tightly. Rory's heart beat a little faster, and even though he knew this was the right thing to do, he still felt a frisson of nerves. "It was actually Marthe's suggestion. She said many of the nobles didn't fully understand what Sabrina was capable of, and perhaps I should show them what she was truly like. It was good timing, since I was looking to curry favor with the court, because I'm planning to announce a new proposal that might not be popular."

Gray frowned. "Is that really the best idea right now? Even if you can convince them Sabrina was evil, the risk might not be worth the reward."

He couldn't have known it, but his words gave Rory the strength—the certainty—he so desperately needed. "The risk," he told Gray seriously, "would be worth every bit of the reward. At least I hope so."

"What could possibly be worth it?"

Rory stood, and tugged their still connected hands in the direction of Gray's room, where he knew the bath was set up. "Let's take a bath and talk about it, more privately," he said. "I've been thinking about your bathtub since we left Beaulieu."

Gray laughed, his expression was baffled. "You have marble tubs the size of whole rooms in Beaulieu; why on earth would my tub be worth dreaming about?"

"Because you're in it," Rory said, closing the door behind them and wrapping his arms tightly around Gray's neck. He rose on his tiptoes and kissed Gray square on the mouth. From the moment their lips touched, Rory realized that they hadn't been kissing nearly enough.

Touching, either. Or really talking, when it came down to it, but tonight, at the very least, other than one important question, he didn't intend to do much talking. Touching and kissing? That was another matter entirely.

Rory's fingers made quick work of the buttons on Gray's stained shirt, and he quickly shoved it aside, resting his palms against Gray's heart, beating hard in his chest. He pulled away, momentarily entranced by Gray's damp red-tinged lips. He didn't believe it, but he was so handsome. Gray was always telling him that he was the beautiful one; the most stunning man he had ever seen. But Rory had been looking at Gray that way from the very first moment they met, and he had no intention of ever stopping.

"Bath," Gray said breathlessly. "I thought you wanted a bath. I know I need a bath. Harvesting corn is no minor job." He hesitated. "I wanted to finish this afternoon so we could leave tomorrow."

"Tomorrow," Rory said firmly. "Bath now. Talk now."

Gray started working the pulley system, bringing water from the cistern to the bathtub. "What is this new plan of yours? You should've talked to Evrard about it."

"I don't think I need to. I think . . . I know now, at least I think I know, what you were trying to do the other night, when you . . ." Rory hesitated.

"When I proposed," Gray said flatly.

"Yes, when you proposed," Rory responded softly. "I didn't know then. I was too overwhelmed and drowning in my own problems to see it, but now I see what you were trying to do. And it would be a good start, but I think we can improve upon it."

Gray shot him a quick, pointed look. "Improve upon it?"

This is it, Rory's subconscious unhelpfully supplied. Now you find out if you waited too long. If you refusing to answer the other night was the nail in the coffin of your relationship. Carefully, he dropped to one knee. His riding breeches were stained and dirty, his tunic had not fared much better, and his hair was mussed from the ride and from Gray's own fingers. But hopefully what his attire lacked, he could make up for with his words. After all, words were his thing.

"I love you," Rory said. "I do want to marry you. It would give me the greatest happiness in the world if you would do me the honor of becoming my husband. But something that would make me even happier—and you too, I hope—would be if you would take the throne of Fontaine with me. Share it. Rule with me, Gray. I don't just want you to be my consort, I want you to be my partner. My equal. My king."

There was no other word for Gray's reaction than complete shock.

"You . . . this is what you want?" he asked, and Rory could only nod in agreement.

"But, every time I asked you, you . . . you put me off!" Gray answered. He sounded frustrated and Rory couldn't say he blamed him. Rory had been blind, and had a lot to apologize for.

"I've not been treating you right, not for awhile now. I wasn't thinking of you, and all the adjustments you've had to make since you came with me to Beaulieu. And when I did, it became so obvious to me that the solution to so many of our problems was to stop trying to handle them alone and share them."

Gray crossed his arms over his bare chest, but didn't say anything. The water continued to fill in the tub, and Rory, feeling awkward that he was still kneeling with no answer in sight, finally stood and walked over to the vessel, dipping his fingers in to test the temperature of the water. Rory supposed he couldn't really blame Gray for being angry, for wanting to make sure Rory wasn't merely trying to placate him with empty promises. And perhaps Rory did deserve a little payback for his own non-answer to Gray's proposal.

Finally, he spoke up. "This will not be a popular choice for you, as King," he said softly. "You are taking an enormous risk here. We could do this more slowly. First, an engagement. Then marriage. Then gradually involving me more in sharing your duties until you finally appoint me as your equal. We don't have to do this . . . I'm not going to leave you just because I'm frustrated."

Rory couldn't deny he'd considered a plan very similar to Gray's suggestion. It was slightly terrifying, trusting to chance and his very newly won ability to govern his people, that they wouldn't become frustrated and find a new ruler to take his place. "Gray," he said, reaching out to him again, and pulling him close, pressing their bodies together. "You were born to be a king, and more importantly, you were trained to be a king. What kind of husband would I be if I chose to diminish that part of you? Not a very good one. I would not have the first choices of our committed life together be half-hearted compromises."

"You do mean to do this, then, fully. No turning back."

It might have felt more difficult than it was, except that Rory knew how much they could accomplish if only they worked together, if only they married Rory's knowledge with Gray's strength. "I am as fully committed to this as I am committed to you," Rory vowed.

Gray stared at him for a long, measured moment. "I love you," he finally said, and leaning down, kissed him soundly, passionately. Lifted his mouth briefly and smiled. "And yes, of course I will marry you."

Relief and happiness cascaded through Rory. He reached up and cupped Gray's bristled cheeks, kissing him again, and then again. "You won't regret this," he vowed. "I swear that you won't."

Gray was smiling now, as widely and as brightly as Rory had ever seen. "I haven't yet," he confessed. "Even all those times we ended up fighting because men lose their heads around you."

"They do not," Rory scoffed. But Gray's gentle teasing, after a week apart, and what felt like months where they barely saw each other, was a balm.

"They absolutely do," Gray said, and he was definitely grinning now. "But then so did I, so I can hardly blame them."

"You did?" Gray had always seemed so sure, so confident, so purposeful, that it felt strange for Rory to consider that it was him, and not circumstances out of Gray's control, that had been enough to change his path.

Gray bent down, his dark blue eyes growing serious, as he swept a hand through Rory's hair, pushing it back gently. "I thought you were everything I hated, condensed into one person, but then I discovered who you really were, the man underneath the Autumn Prince, and it wouldn't have mattered if you were an emperor or a beggar, I was yours. Heart, soul, and body."

Rory couldn't help the glimmer of a smile that escaped him. "Body?" he inquired hopefully.

Laughing, Gray scooped him up and, depositing him on the edge of the tub, made quick work of his clothes and boots. Rory slid into the tub and watched expectantly, with his blood racing and heat building in his stomach, as Gray shed his own pants and boots.

He was every inch the warrior that Rory always fantasized about: all that smooth golden skin covering muscle that bunched and flexed as he leaned over to untie a stubborn lace. When Gray raised his head again, his gaze had darkened. "I like you watching me," he said softly, but with clear erotic purpose. His cock was growing harder, and Rory watched with rapt attention as Gray's hand gripped it, stroking from root to tip and back again. "But I think I like you touching me even more," he admitted.

"Then come here," Rory pleaded, and Gray did as requested, stepping into the tub and positioning himself opposite Rory.

Reaching out, Rory was surprised when the other man batted his hands away. "But . . ." Rory pouted. Hadn't Gray just said he liked Rory touching him?

"Wash first," Gray insisted, and he was already scooping out the soap, suds trailing across his broad chest. Rory shut his mouth and followed suit, washing up quickly and efficiently. The moment the soap returned to the dish, Rory was pushing off from one side of the tub, floating over to where Gray sat, waiting, his eyes gleaming with so many possibilities that Rory felt breathless.

When Rory finally settled on his lap, knees on either side of Gray's thighs, they both let out a sigh. "Better," Gray said, and that was the last word he said for awhile, as Rory leaned down and kissed him thoroughly, tongue slipping inside his mouth and exploring every inch that he'd missed over the last few weeks. His fingers, trying to grip Gray's damp shoulders, slipped, and their heads nearly knocked together. Gray gasped and then suddenly, without warning, picked Rory up, his powerful muscles straining as Rory wrapped his legs, water streaming off them, around Gray's waist.

"Bed," Rory agreed, answering Gray's unspoken question.

It had always been hot and perfect between them, even when they'd been in a half-frozen lake, and it was just as perfect now, but now, as Gray lay down on the bed and Rory crawled up his chest to continue kissing him, it wasn't just unrestrained lust. There was tenderness and care between them. Every time Gray touched him, fingers sure on his skin, Rory experienced an echo of every bit of love Gray felt. And hovering behind every kiss, every touch, every gasp and every moan was the knowledge that they would be doing this for a long time, and every moment of that forever, they would be together.

"Please," Rory begged as Gray's touch fleetingly brushed against his own hard, leaking cock. "Please touch me."

"As my king commands," Gray teased, but this time his fingertips didn't just graze his skin, but settled with purpose against the cradle of his hips. "How did you want me to touch you?"

Rory, panting and half-crazed with want, opened his legs, spreading them wide in an open invitation.

Invitation received, Gray slicked his fingers up from the bottle by the bed, and when he slid the first finger inside Rory, he threw his head back and moaned. No matter how much they did this, it always felt so good, somehow even better than it had the first heart-stopping time they'd indulged.

"You feel so goddamned perfect," Gray ground out, his voice growing low and intense, gritty around the edges. Another finger joined the first one, and as they delved deep, touching that electric part inside him, Rory gasped.

Typically this was the extent of the preparation Rory needed, usually both of them were so incredibly eager to have Gray inside him, but this time, Gray kept fingering him, alternating his deep thrusts with shallower teasing brushes, until Rory was panting, sweat beading on his brow, his cock painfully hard as it tapped his stomach wetly.

"Please, please, please," Rory pleaded, feeling at the very edge of his self-control, driven there by Gray's own. He was clearly as ready as Rory was, but still he held off, apparently content to drive Rory mad with pleasure.

He only relented after Rory felt like he might explode from the tension wracking his body, and at the very least, orgasm before Gray could even slide his cock inside him. Gray carefully withdrew his fingers and slicking his cock up, positioned himself between Rory's legs.

"I love you," he said, his intense gaze boring straight into Rory's own as he finally slid home.

Rory trembled with the effort it took not to give himself over to the overwhelming bliss. When Gray's cock slipped in those last few inches, Rory's head fell back against the pillow, and he groaned, "So good, so full."

"I'm gonna make you feel even better," Gray promised, and began to thrust, his rhythm overwhelming Rory almost immediately. "See, I promised you," he grunted, as Rory found himself hurtling right over the edge without even a single touch on his own cock, spurting all over his own stomach and Gray's too.

Gray followed him only a moment later, letting out a loud, incredibly sexy groan that might have made Rory hard again if he hadn't just finished coming as hard as he ever had in his life.

"That was," Gray said, pulling out and then collapsing next to a completely worn-out Rory. "That was something else."

"You're a closet sadist, as well as the sexiest man in the world," Rory said, pulling together the energy to roll over and gaze at the man he loved. The man he was going to marry.

"It's part of my charm," Gray said with a rough chuckle.

"You're perfect," Rory said as his eyes began to droop. "You're perfect, and I love you."

It was clear; Rory did not think Gray was perfect the next morning. "Come on," he said, half-dragging Rory out of the warm cocoon of the blankets. During the last six months, it was always Rory pushing to get up earlier and earlier, and somehow get more done in a day than was physically, humanly possible, but maybe that was finally catching up with him, because he was resisting Gray's efforts to coax him out of bed so they could finish the harvest.

"Your guard is already out, they're in the fields right now," Gray grumbled, pulling Rory's leg out, only to have him retract it rather forcibly.

"Then they should keep it up," Rory mumbled into the pillow. "I'm tired. So tired."

"You've been pushing yourself too hard," Gray said, sitting down with a hard thump on the side of the bed. "I told you that you were, and you wouldn't listen."

"No need to say 'I told you so,'" Rory complained. "I already figured out how to fix it, didn't I?"

"But we can't really fix it if we don't harvest this corn and travel back to Beaulieu."

Rory's head tilted to the side, as if he was considering this. "And we can't plan our wedding either," he pointed thoughtfully.

"Exactly," Gray said. Six months ago, he might have asked why a wedding would take a lot of planning—but then he'd entered the rank-fixated and event-obsessed court at Beaulieu, and he'd discovered that everything he knew about events was wrong. At Tullamore, they'd prided themselves on keeping state occasions simple. As long as there were plenty of roaring fires, enormous roasts over them and plenty of ale and whiskey to go around, the clansmen had not been particularly hard to please.

At Beaulieu, a court event was an event. And a royal wedding was likely a whole other level of obsessive planning that Gray wasn't sure he was prepared for. Yes, he desperately wanted to marry Rory, but he also didn't want to worry about who was going to sit sixteen seats down from the royal table.

"Why don't we just . . . get married," Gray said.

Rory stared at him blankly. "I thought that was what we were going to do."

"I mean, without all the pomp and circumstance." Gray sighed. "The banquet to honor the Mecant tribe took a whole month of planning! I don't want to wait that long."

Reaching out and stroking his arm, Rory smiled up at him sweetly. "I want to get married now too, but unfortunately, part of what will help distract the court from stewing about your future kingship is plenty of pomp and circumstance."

Gray sighed. "So we can't avoid it?"

"I'm afraid avoiding it will likely be impossible."

"Then," Gray said, suddenly rising to his feet and wrapping his arms around a squirming bundle of blanket-swaddled Rory, and lifting him up, "we'd better get started." Rory grumbled, but finally he discarded his blankets and began to get dressed.

It took the rest of the day to get the corn harvested and packed into the cart. When Gray went to visit Evrard and prepare him for the next day's journey, the unicorn merely stared at him.

"Go with you? Why would I go with you?" Evrard asked, clearly uncomprehending what Gray was asking.

"We're going back to Beaulieu," Gray said slowly, enunciating every word, knowing it would likely annoy Evrard, but doing it anyway. "Rory and I are getting married. He came here with nearly the same plan you had."

"Imagine that," Evrard said smugly.

"Don't you want to be at the wedding?" Gray asked, trying to prepare himself if Evrard claimed that he didn't. Or if he maintained this charade that he wouldn't be coming back to Beaulieu at all.

"The wedding is merely a formality, and mark my words, it will indeed be a formality. I will miss seeing you stuffed and glittered and wrapped in enough gold-embroidered thread to decorate a regiment."

Gray couldn't understand. "Why will you not be there?"

Evrard's gaze finally turned towards him, and to Gray's shock, it was soft and empathetic. "I know you wish me to be there for you, but the last thing the royal court will need at your wedding is a reminder of Rory taking the throne. I am associated most strongly with that event. You need to present a front of unassailable strength."

"Wouldn't us standing with a royal unicorn help present that strength?" Gray asked slyly.

But Evrard's expression never wavered. "I wish I could return with you, I do. But it cannot be helped. Your life is situated. Rory's life is situated."

Gray had told himself that he would not let his feelings be hurt if Evrard refused to come. But it was inevitable. Evrard, while hardly the most appropriate father figure for a child, had been the only one he had known. And now that his own, real father was dead, Evrard was all that he had remaining.

"You have your family," Evrard said, reading his mind yet again, even though he knew it annoyed Gray, "and they will be there, and on that day, I will be thinking of you and Rory and sending you all my good wishes and happiness for the future. But as you well know, I have served my purpose here. I saved you. I saved Prince Emory, and saw him to his kingship, and now I have seen you to yours, and also to marriage with your soulmate. There is little to keep me here. I am like the Valley; I come as needed, and now that we have both outlived our usefulness, we will fade into the ether."

"I'm sorry to hear that but I understand," Gray said, but truthfully, he couldn't feel anything but hurt and bewildered. Part of him desperately wanted to say that Evrard should stay for him, and for all the good, measured advice that he would surely need in the future. But he also had his pride, and his pride stopped his tongue. "Then this is goodbye." He placed a hand on Evrard's neck, and Evrard bowed, his mane flowing to the straw below their feet.

When Gray came out of Evrard's stable, Rory immediately knew something was wrong, and came up to him, a concerned expression on his face. "What has happened?" he asked.

"Evrard will not be returning with us. Not for the wedding. Not ever again, possibly." Gray took a deep breath. "If you wish to say goodbye to him, now would be the best time."

"I shall say something, certainly," Rory said, and marched off to the stable. No doubt to inform Evrard that he was being an idiot and that he would be coming back to Beaulieu with them in the morning.

But Rory returned from the stables with a defeated look in his eyes and they did not speak of it again.

In the early morning light of their departure, Evrard did come out of the stables one last time, white coat shining and glimmering in the dawn, and if Gray had to turn his head away to prevent anyone from seeing a tear fall, then it was between him and his horse.

When they departed the Valley of Lost Things, Gray took everything of value to him, as he knew, instinctively, that it would not remain any longer. This was the last of its magic, and with Evrard gone, it too would dissipate after their departure.

CHAPTER TWENTY-FOUR

RORY HAD BEEN CERTAIN that they could not possibly organize a royal wedding in under a month, but three weeks and six days later, he was standing in the enormous throne room at Beaulieu, watching as Gray went toe-to-toe with Rowen, who had appointed herself as the wedding planner. Normally, the steward would have done the job, but after Rory had announced his intention to crown Gray to conclude the ceremony, the grumbles had increased exponentially, leaving some, like the curmudgeonly steward who had spent nearly his entire career in service to Sabrina, to either accept the changes or leave. At first, Rory hadn't been certain they could even pull off such an intricate and complex event without someone who had any experience, but Rowen had scoffed at Rory's concerns.

"I've spent my whole life at court," Rowen said. "I know how to plan an event."

And it turned out she did, at least when Gray allowed her to do her job properly.

"I've discovered the problem here," Anya told Rory under her breath. "You didn't give the Prince enough to do, thus he had enough time and energy to interfere with Rowen."

Rory shot her a look. "I gave him plenty to do."

"The Prince used to run an entire farm with practically no help. I don't think either of us is good at estimating what he's capable of handling."

It was difficult to argue with that, or with the fact that Gray was here, and despite ten council meetings this week, and shadowing Marthe in her role as General of Fontaine's armies and Rory keeping him occupied for hours each evening in bed, he apparently had plenty of energy to argue over floral arrangement placement with Rowen.

"If only the Prince had been able to apply himself so successfully to finding the person who used Sabrina's lair," Anya said, and Rory had to nod his agreement. No matter how they'd searched, it was hard to find someone who clearly did not want to be found. The room, buried deep in the catacombs, had been guarded night and day, and nobody had even attempted to approach. They were no closer to finding the culprit and they were about to lose their best tool—the day after the wedding and Gray's coronation, the room was to be demolished entirely.

"The biggest one should go in the front, right over the dais," Gray argued. Rowen didn't say a word, only nodded. Rory already knew that she was going to put the floral arrangements wherever she wanted, no matter what Gray said. Rory had agreed with putting her in charge for a reason; she knew what was needed and how to accomplish it.

Which was why this was an enormous waste of time when they could actually be going over the complicated ceremony—the entire reason why they were in the throne room today.

"Darling," Rory said, approaching the pair, "why don't we leave these minor arrangements to Rowen, and go over the ceremony itself. The etiquette is rather complex, and well . . ." Rory gave him a look that was both fond and exasperated. "Well, we know formal etiquette is not your strongest skill."

Gray glanced over at him, eyes warm—quite possibly just as warm as Rory's own. "No? I'm hurt, sweetcheeks."

Rory blushed. It was one thing for Gray to try this new nickname out in private, in their bed, but to do so in front of Rowen, Anya, and the handful of nobles who had chosen to witness the rehearsal? Entirely another.

"Darling," Rory repeated between clenched teeth, still amused and still fond, despite the nickname and despite a hundred other things that should drive him crazy but somehow, never did, "we are wasting time."

Gray smiled broadly, like wasting time was his favorite thing and not at all the opposite. "Well, then, lead the way, Your Majesty."

A slight improvement over sweetcheeks.

Truthfully, in less than twenty-four hours, Gray wouldn't be required to use that particular honorific for Rory any longer. Not that he had ever been particularly diligent about its use. But after his own coronation, there would be no need, because he and Rory would be equals, both Kings in their own right.

It hadn't quite caused any outright riots just yet, but it wouldn't matter if it had. Rory was adamant and completely sure that this was both the best choice for him personally, and for the kingdom he ruled over. He'd given a speech to the court, which was something he was finally getting the hang of doing, detailing why it was a necessary step. It must have been fairly convincing because afterwards, the grumblings had mostly died down. Along with the steward, the Duke of Rinard had left Beaulieu, followed very shortly after by Count Aplin, and Rory knew he wasn't alone in hoping that was the last they'd seen of those two—and that the reason they'd been unable to catch the magical practitioner was because they'd already departed and would hopefully never return.

Rowen led them through the lengthy ceremony, and thankfully, Gray had only a few questions and remarks for her until they reached nearly the end of the marriage rite. "And now," Rowen said, pulling a length of cloth from behind the podium they stood in front of, "Prince Graham will bestow upon King Emory a length of valuable tapestry from his kingdom of Ardglass, as a symbol of his commitment to this union."

Gray blanched and stared at the cloth like it was a coiled serpent, poised to strike. "What is this?" he demanded.

Rory barely held back a resigned sigh. It had been his idea to add this particular flourish to the ceremony, and he'd known that Gray wouldn't like it—at least on the surface. Gray still held a lot of complicated feelings towards the country of his birth. "This is a part of the Ardglassian commitment ceremony," Rory began to explain, hoping that the bored, informative tone he adopted would calm Gray down and not inflame him further.

"I know what it is," Gray said, gesturing to the cloth. "I meant, why is it being included as part of our ceremony? We are being married in Fontaine, and approximately ten minutes after this, I will be crowned a king of Fontaine. Do you think we should further remind everyone that I was born to be a king of a neighboring country?"

Rory had struggled with whether they should include it for exactly those reasons—but then he'd realized that those concerns could be reframed, and therefore seen in an entirely different way. Gray's lineage should be seen not as a detriment, but as an advantage. The court was concerned that Rory had no experience, and had never been trained to be a king. Well, here was someone who had been trained to be a king. It was one of many reasons why Rory had become convinced that Gray needed to share his throne.

"I think we should, yes. We can hardly make everyone forget it, and why should you not celebrate your country on the day of your wedding?" Rory said, but the glower on Gray's face only grew.

"I need to talk to you," Gray said, and the edge to his voice made it abundantly clear that it was not optional. "Privately."

"One moment," Rory said, and followed Gray over to the edge of the throne room. The massive room, with its enormous vaulted ceilings, was a feat of engineering and virtually guaranteed that even a hushed whisper could be heard, but Rory wasn't going to remind his betrothed of that particular fact.

"Are you insane?" Gray demanded.

"The last time I checked, no," Rory responded quietly.

"Then why do you insist on possibly jeopardizing your throne with these stunts? We've just barely got the court calmed down over me sharing your throne. And now, you're going to stir up all this talk all over again by adding this to the ceremony." Gray crossed his arms over his chest and Rory was reminded of how Rowen must have felt, feeling absolutely sure the flower arrangements were in the right place, but having Gray argue with her anyway—for no real purpose except to argue.

"Are we doing this or not?" Rory finally asked. "Because when I suggested this plan to you and then I proposed, I meant to commit to it, without flinching, no matter how difficult the path got. You are from Ardglass, that's something you could not possibly change, even if you wanted to, and you shouldn't want to—even if the reminders can be painful. You are who you are because of what happened, and I love you for that strength. It brought us together and it should be celebrated, especially on our wedding day."

Gray stared at him, expression inscrutable. "You really believe that."

"I do. I believe in it," Rory said firmly, "and I believe in you."

"I don't want to bring you to ruin," Gray admitted softly, brokenly, his eyes haunted. "I love you too much to do that."

Rory reached out and took his hands, squeezing them tightly in his own. "You could not possibly. And I prefer to see that we bring each other strength, not ruin. I could not do this without you, and I like to believe you could not do this without me. So let us do this without flinching, without hiding away those parts of ourselves that might make others talk."

Gray did not say anything for a long, drawn-out moment. His expression went from sad to resigned to finally one that Rory at least wanted to believe was hopeful. "And," Rory added, "Anya has spent many evenings embroidering this cloth that came from Ardglass. It has great significance to her, and I believe she hopes it will hold the same for you. It is a gift, from the remnants of a kingdom that you gave the best chance to succeed, and they wish to thank you for it."

Tears glimmered at the edges of Gray's eyes then. "It's from the clans?"

Rory reached up and pressed a firm, loving kiss on his cheek. "In another life, you would have been their king. In this one, you're mine."

Gray couldn't say exactly why he had been arguing with Rowen over floral arrangement placement. He could say why he'd argued with Rory over including the Ardglassian custom in their marriage ceremony. Evrard would have told him that both definitely boiled down to one thing, and one thing alone: fear. Fear that he wouldn't be a good husband or a good king. Fear that taking this step would hurt Rory more than it would help him. He wished he could be as confident as Rory was, but the truth was, Fontaine felt balanced on a knife-edge these days, and the smallest thing could send it toppling over into chaos.

Evrard would also have told him he was being overdramatic; something he enjoyed accusing Gray of on a regular basis.

Gray stared moodily at the pile of documents on his desk, in his brand-new office opposite Rory's own, and tried to ignore the pulse of pain at every thought of Evrard. Of course Evrard could not hang around forever, just in case Gray or Rory got into trouble, but still the thought of never hearing another of his sarcastic and smug retorts filled him with a strange kind of anguish. He'd never thought he would miss those things; in fact, he'd hoped many times to never hear them ever again. But that particular wish coming true had ended up being far thornier than Gray ever could have imagined.

A knock on the door shook him out of his reverie. The night before his wedding, and he was pouting. Gray walked to the door and opened it with a smile. It was Anya, and she smiled back. "And here I thought I would find you worried about all the ways this could go wrong," she said, slipping inside Gray's office.

"I was," Gray confessed. Anya shot him a reproachful look.

"You thought I could be Rory," she finally deduced. "And you didn't want him to know that you were pouting."

"I was not pouting. I was merely . . ."

"Contemplating every which way this could go wrong?" Anya finished helpfully.

"Essentially," Gray admitted.

Anya sighed. "Well, regardless of how fatalistic you're being, I thought you might want this." She held out the package in her hands, wrapped in plain brown cloth, and tied with string.

Gray took it and turned it over in his hands. "Is this the fabric you embroidered for the ceremony?"

Nodding, Anya gestured for him to open it, and carefully, Gray did so. To his surprise, the embroidery was pristine and intricate. "I had no idea you could do work like this," he said, his eyes meeting Anya's with surprise.

"Why? Just because I can wield a sword better than you?"

"Well . . ." Gray had to admit that had been part of his assumption.

"You're not entirely wrong," Anya continued, shrugging in a slightly embarrassed fashion. "I'm not usually interested in needlework, but this was important, and I wanted it to be right."

Gently, Gray unwound the cloth and was shocked to see an abbreviated version of both his escape of Tullamore at age eleven, and then his and Rory's triumphant return to Fontaine fifteen years later. And then, finally, on the last panel of the tapestry, the last council meeting of the clans that he had presided over himself, after the death of Gideon. The meeting where the clans had, with Gray's support, voted to officially disband the monarchy of Ardglass.

"It might have been the most convenient choice," Anya said, still self-consciously refusing to meet Gray's gaze, "but it was a noble one, too. And we of Ardglass appreciate it more than you can know."

"Anya," Gray said slowly, "thank you. Thank you for all the time and care you put into this, and for wanting me to have something of Ardglass when I marry Rory."

Her eyes were bright and fierce as they finally met his. "Even though you will be Fontaine's king now, you were ours first. And you shouldn't forget that."

"I won't, I swear I won't," Gray said, and to his own complete surprise—and definitely Anya's—he pulled her into a tight hug. "Thank you, again. For everything."

Her gaze was slightly damp when he finally released her, and his own was definitely not any dryer. "I said someday that I would serve the

King. It's not as I imagined it, not exactly, but I'm honored to be in your service, Your Majesty."

Gray cracked a smile. "Not quite yet."

"But soon. You need to get used to it."

Gray didn't think he ever quite would, and maybe that was what would make him a good king. Never entirely believing he deserved a part of the throne, or the entirety of Rory's heart. It would keep him working hard and giving his all, even when the road felt smooth and easy.

If that ever happened. With the way things were going now, that future seemed both very far off and also right around the corner—if only he could reach out and grasp it.

"I'll do my best," Gray promised.

Rory had promised himself that when some of the kingly responsibilities shifted to Gray—tomorrow, it's actually tomorrow, he thought, triumph mixing with a little bit of panic—that he would do so with a mostly clean desk.

Which explained why, the night before his wedding, he was working late in his office, sorting through the last of the parchments he'd been asked to read.

A quiet knock interrupted his concentration and he glanced up, sure it was Gray, insisting he not work quite so late tonight, but then, Gray would not bother knocking.

"Come in," he said, and to his surprise, Shaheen, the leader of the Mecant tribe, entered his office.

"Your Majesty," she said, bowing low, nearly as low as she had long ago, when Rory had begged for their lives in the middle of the Mecant camp. "I wondered if I might have a word with you."

Rory stood, and gestured to one of the comfortable chairs opposite his desk. "Of course you may," he said. "You know you never need ask. My office is always open to you."

Shaheen's glance was swift and cut him to the quick. "You are the King of Fontaine," she said, her tone remaining kind, "and I am the leader of a dying tribe. Of course I must ask. We continue to survive only due to your graciousness."

Rory sat, somewhat humbled. Whenever he met with Shaheen, which had been frequently since their arrival at Beaulieu two months earlier, he often felt the breath punched from his lungs with painful realizations.

"My apologies," he said. "I did not think."

"You are young, very young," Shaheen said, settling in the chair, her multicolored robes flaring around her, "I was much more foolish when I became the leader. You must give yourself room to breathe, to grow. And also a little credit, as you are not nearly as poor as you think you are."

Rory was touched. Being a leader was much tougher than he'd ever anticipated, his decisions having far-reaching effects he did not always foresee. As much as Shaheen's tribe was learning from him at their daily lessons, he enjoyed talking with their leader and gleaning as much knowledge of leadership from her as he could.

"Thank you," Rory said. "What is it I can help you with today?"

"It is Merleen," Shaheen said with a heavy sigh. "I think . . . I think I would like for him to stay behind, when we leave next week."

Rory liked Merleen very much—he was blunt and amusing and very good with a weapon, from the sparring he'd seen out his office window—but also had the impression Merleen was anxious to return to the forest and to the rest of his tribe. It was understandable, considering the ultra-civilization of Beaulieu and its many high walls might certainly be stifling to someone who had grown up in the forest, living in a tent, always on the move, never being settled.

"Have you spoken to him about this?" Rory asked.

Shaheen nodded. "He is willing to remain behind. I intend him to be a bridge, between Fontaine and the Mecant, if that is acceptable to you."

"Of course it is acceptable, and an excellent idea." Rory mentally kicked himself for not thinking of it first. The Mecant, their ways slowly being lost, would need to adapt or die out. And Shaheen, like every good ruler, was doing her utmost to assist in that transformation.

"Then it is settled," Shaheen said, a small, mysterious smile blooming on her face. "I think he will discover that his place here will do him much good."

Rory was not quite as certain, but envied Shaheen's confidence.

"How do you know?" he asked, leaning forward and setting his elbows on the desk. "How do you know what is the right thing and what is the wrong path to take? I find myself constantly questioning whether I am making the best choices for Fontaine, and in a lesser sense, for myself."

Shaheen was quiet for a long moment, contemplating his question. "I believe that your very doubt is what will make you a good leader, Your Majesty," she finally said. "You worry about your people. You place them above your own happiness and comfort, much of the time. You may not always know the right path immediately, but you search for it, and it is that quest that will bring peace and prosperity to Fontaine."

"Sometimes I am not always selfless," Rory admitted.

"You are a man, not a figurehead. You matter, too." Shaheen's voice was firm, and brokered no arguments.

"A man," Rory thought out loud, pondering her words.

"And tomorrow, you will also be a husband." Shaheen smiled.

The morning of the wedding and coronation dawned clear and cold, the bells in the very highest tower of Beaulieu ringing so brightly and so loudly that Gray thought, as he lay in his bath, that if Evrard was still in the Valley, he might have heard them.

To his surprise, it felt like the day passed very quickly. First, his bath, then being dressed—as of course, a future king of Fontaine could not possibly dress himself, even though he'd told everyone who would listen more than once that if he couldn't dress himself, he certainly wouldn't make a very competent king. But nobody wanted to listen to him, and they sent the valet in anyway. Gray, who had finally decided that it was worthless to argue when it felt like the entire court, including Rory, was against him, let the man dress him.

"You look very handsome, Your Majesty," the valet said, voice worshipful as they both took in Gray's very fine reflection in the floor-to-ceiling mirror dragged into their bedchamber just for this occasion.

Gray's first inclination was to make a face at all the glittering silver and gold embroidery on his forest green tunic, but he could hear Evrard's voice in his head, asking, is that what a king would do? Gray knew the answer to that particular question—and this time, decided that he should be embracing this new change, instead of constantly fighting it. He'd have to send Rowen one of the biggest floral arrangements as an apology for being difficult.

It was different; thinking of others first, instead of himself, but he'd already had some practice, because from nearly the first moment he'd met Rory, he'd been putting him first.

He straightened and without any silly or gross expressions, looked at himself seriously.

He'd turned out as tall and broad as Gideon had always hoped. As he looked, Gray realized the evergreen of the tunic, trimmed with all that silver and gold thread, as well as the broad red epaulets—distinguishing him as royalty and not merely a high-born noble—actually suited him. His breeches were supple and butter-smooth leather, fitting to his legs like they had been tailored just for him, and to Gray's embarrassment, they actually had been. His dark hair shone under the candlelight of the chandelier overhead, and though his head was bare now, a brand-new crown that Rory had commissioned especially for him was waiting in the throne room, for the moment of his crowning. It combined the fiercely sparkling amber of the traditional crowns of Fontaine with the deep green emeralds of Ardglass. A special piece that Gray knew Rory hoped would help establish his blending of both heritages.

He reached for the final touch; his leather and gold sword belt, from which always hung Lion's Breath.

"Wait," the valet said, reaching out to stop him, "the King left especial instructions that you should wear this instead." He indicated an even more ornate belt made of gold links and more amber and emeralds.

"But I can't wear a sword with that," Gray objected.

The valet frowned. "A sword would completely ruin the line of your ceremonial tunic," he said.

It felt wrong leaving Lion's Breath behind, like he was only half-dressed. For the last eight months, the sword had been always at his side or in his hand. But then, Gray reasoned with himself, practically all of Marthe's army would be guarding the outside of Beaulieu, as well as inside the castle and even the throne room itself, for the ceremony. Of all days, he shouldn't need to carry Lion's Breath. He was being crowned a king, not a general. Certainly anyone of importance or with any influence already knew he bore Lion's Breath. It was hardly a secret. He did not need to have the extra reminder today, of all days. Not when Rory was about to place a crown on his head.

Gray reached for the jeweled belt, and told himself the weird voice in his head, begging him to reconsider, wasn't the remnant of Evrard's influence, but merely what remained of his nerves.

"Excellent, sir," the valet said and helped to position the jeweled belt around his middle. "I believe you are ready, Your Majesty."

"I'm something," Gray said under his breath, looking one last time in the mirror. The next time he saw himself, he would be a king, and perhaps even more life-changing, Rory's husband.

"Shall we meet the King's party?" the valet inquired and Gray nodded.

A few minutes found them outside the hallway of the throne room. Ironically right where it felt like his entire journey to the throne began; when they'd sneaked into Beaulieu in an attempt to remove Sabrina from both life and power. Anya was already there, her armor shining and her eyes sparkling. She was carrying his length of embroidered cloth that she had labored over. Gray had decided that she needed to be the one to present it to him at the appropriate moment, so he could bestow it upon Rory.

Rory approached with several of his guard surrounding him. He was dressed in finery typical of the Autumn Prince—golds and burnt oranges with a bright turquoise silk cape falling from one shoulder. A delicately wrought gold crown with carnelians, amber, and topaz adorned his head. He looked stunning, a fairy tale brought to life, and somehow all Gray's own.

"We would like a minute," Rory finally said, staring at his betrothed. The guards around them moved away, but Gray noticed that they did not leave entirely. Smart, considering he was not wearing Lion's Breath and the trespasser had yet to be caught.

"You look . . ." Gray reached out and took Rory's hands, laughing self-consciously. "I'm afraid words fail me."

Rory's eyes shone just as brightly as the jewels crowning his brow. "From the first moment, I have never looked away from you. Whether you are as beautiful as you are this day, or are stooped and worn and aged, I will love you all the same," Rory vowed. "One kiss before all the dull ceremonial processes?" he asked hopefully.

"Just one?" Gray teased.

"I'm not sure we have time for much else," Rory said earnestly, "and if we are off-schedule, Rowen may cry and that would be a catastrophe."

"Marthe wouldn't be very happy with us," Gray agreed. "One kiss, then."

"And make it a good one," Rory suggested, with a twinkle in his eye that promised that he knew Gray would apply himself properly whether he reminded him to or not.

Gray did as asked, his hand sliding to the small of Rory's back as he bent them both back, and captured Rory's perfect mouth with his own. He kissed him deeply, feeling Rory's fingers come to clutch at his shoulders, and then smooth back his hair as he pulled back just enough to see the shine of his beloved's eyes.

"Promise me something," Rory said softly.

"Anything," Gray vowed.

"Kiss me like that at least once each day, for the rest of our lives?"

Gray chuckled. "Like what?"

"Like you love me more than you imagined you could, and you're surprised by it every single moment."

"I think that can be arranged," Gray said, and reaching down, tucked Rory's hand into his own. "Are you ready to get married?"

"I've never been more ready," Rory said, his smile luminous and happier than Gray had ever seen it.

They walked down the central aisle hand in hand, their progress slow but stately, and even though Gray knew he was supposed to be staring ahead, expression solemn, he couldn't help sneaking a look every foot or so, smile breaking through his serious demeanor. He'd been so afraid that at the last moment, he'd be nervous and terrified and sure they had made all the wrong decisions, but instead, all he felt was the unimpeachable rightness of this moment.

Marthe, in her golden armor with a stern countenance, was to hear their vows between themselves, and then Gray's vows to Fontaine.

"I'm but a general of an army," she had protested, because she never wanted to make more of her position than she should, but Rory had held up a hand, quieting her argument.

"You are the most right person I know for us to make our vows to," he'd insisted. "You saved my life, you made it possible for us to regain the throne of Fontaine. You hold the armies, while we hold the support of the people of Fontaine. Who else should we make such vows to?"

Finally, Marthe had conceded the point, and as they stood in front of her, Gray could think of only one additional person—or one additional unicorn—who would have been more appropriate for Rory and him to swear their fealty in front of. But Evrard wasn't here, and he wasn't going to be here. Gray needed to let that go, no matter how much it stung. He refocused on Marthe, who was giving the short welcome.

"Ladies and gentlemen of Fontaine, of this royal court, we are here today to see our king pledge his faith and his hand to Prince Graham, his consort and his protector, and for Prince Graham to return his own promises, both to our king and to the kingdom. Will you hear their pledges?"

A rush of sound met Gray's ears. He'd been most concerned about this section of the ceremony, as there was a definite possibility that the court would not want to hear their pledges. But it seemed that was hardly a problem at all. All Gray saw was smiles and encouragement reflected back at them from the crowd.

Everyone loves a wedding, Evrard echoed in his head. Gray supposed he'd been right the whole time. It was only too bad he wasn't here so Gray could tell him so and Evrard could gloat properly.

"I, King Emory of Fontaine, take you, Prince Graham of Ardglass, to be no other than yourself. Loving what I know of you, trusting what I do not yet know, I will respect your integrity and have faith in your abiding love for me, through all our years, and in all that life may bring us." Rory's fingers tightened on Gray's own, like he was trying to calm their trembling, and Gray understood. His own heart was thumping irregularly, excited and a tiny bit terrified.

"I, Prince Graham of Ardglass, take you, King Emory of Fontaine, to be no other than yourself. I take your faults and your strengths, as I offer myself to you with my own failings and successes. I will do everything in my power to help you when you need help, and vow to turn to you when I need assistance. I choose you as the person with whom I wish to spend the rest of my life." Gray took a deep breath as Anya took a step forward and extended the embroidered cloth, which he took. He ignored the rustle that went through the crowd; they were surprised, but it remained to see if it was a good or bad surprise. "And now I will pledge my past, and my present, and my future to you, and your kingdom. My promise is represented by this tapestry, illustrated with the story of my birth, and of the most important journey of my life—my journey to finding you."

Rory reached up and wiped a single, crystalline tear from his cheek. "Nothing would honor me more," he said, letting Gray wind the cloth around his neck and cinch it down by his turquoise sash. The golden threads echoed his eyes and as Gray caught a glimpse of Evrard, immortalized in silver thread, he realized that Anya had made sure that he was present for this most important day.

"Now that you have made your pledges to one another . . ."

A snarl rose from the crowd, and Marthe hesitated, Gray's gaze immediately dropping from Rory, to scanning the crowd.

It parted, and stalking towards the dais where he and Rory stood was Count Aplin, looking worse for the wear. Mud smeared up one side of his silvery tunic, his hair looked as if he had just ridden for hours, and his eyes were wild and unfocused.

Panic lanced through Gray in a sickening rush as the guards stepped in front of the Count, who with a single wave of his hand, sent them toppling backwards in a frightening rush of power.

"Guards," Marthe called out, and Anya stepped in front of Gray and Rory, pulling her sword from its sheath.

But Gray knew it wouldn't do anything, not when the Count was clearly the magic user who had utilized Sabrina's lair in the catacombs, and who had tried to enact a dangerous spell, before he'd been inter-rupted.

Or had he been interrupted? Gray wasn't sure if he had or not, but his deepest fear was that the only one who could stop Aplin was him and the magic of Lion's Breath. Gray reached for the sword, and only realized, after his fingers closed around dead air, that he had stupidly allowed himself to be dressed without it today. Today, of all days, he was unprotected, and Aplin was possibly going to murder both him and his almost-husband before Marthe could even complete the wedding vows.

"Ah," Aplin cackled, "missing something, Your Majesty?" His snide tone made it horrifically clear that he had interfered with the valet, and made sure that when Gray dressed this morning, he would be without the one weapon that could possibly defeat the kind of magic that the Count wielded now.

"You will not get away with this!" Rory shouted, his tone deadly angry.

"Oh really?" Aplin questioned, brushing aside more fully armed guards like they were children's toys as he made his way even closer to the dais. Gray's heart constricted. "It seems as if I am. And very easily, too."

Gray clenched his fists. How could he have been so stupid? Maybe he was a king, but he was also protector of this kingdom, and of its ping, and he was failing utterly.

Marthe let out an appalled gasp as pieces of Aplin's face began peeling away to reveal an enormous silver serpent in his place.

"This is . . . really not good," Rory muttered between clenched teeth as Marthe drew her own sword and joined Anya in front of them. But Gray knew the two women, despite their experience and skill, would be no match for Aplin's magic. The only way he could be defeated would be with the purifying and cleansing fire of Lion's Breath, and without the sword, Gray could not hope to summon it.

He reached out and gripped Rory's hand. At least if they fell, they would fall together, and at least it would be in front of the entire court. Unlike Sabrina, who had carefully worked behind the scenes and concealed all evidence of her dark magic, Aplin was doing it front and center, stroking his ego with every slithering movement he made towards the group huddled at the back of the dais.

"I want you to run. You and Rory both," Marthe ordered under her breath. "Perhaps you can escape him, lose him in the halls of the castle."

"And expose more people to his dark treachery?" Rory shook his head. "This will end now. What he wants is me."

"You and that usurper," the serpent rasped out. "That foul-mouthed Ardglassian that you permitted to touch you, to protect you, to marry you. And then you were going to allow him to destroy the throne? I could not let him or you take that step."

The crowd gasped as the snake approached the group. Anya's grip tightened on her spear and she threw it with deadly accuracy—perhaps one of the best throws of her life. The serpent ducked at the last moment, its huge head wavering on its neck, sharp teeth shiny with venom in its great mouth. The spear glanced off its neck, but green blood flowed from the injury.

"He's not as strong as Sabrina was," Rory hissed. "He can be hurt."

"If one could get close enough," Marthe retorted testily.

It was a split-second decision that later, Gray wasn't sure he'd truly thought through at all. But the truth was, after the age of eleven, he'd never expected to be anything at all. He'd believed, without a single doubt, that a great life, a meaningful life had passed him by, and that any opportunity to truly change the world was gone. Rory's love had given him a glimpse of a different future, and it evolved even further with his new plan of crowning Gray King. But what else could give the most meaning to a life? Sacrificing his own for a greater purpose.

Gray reached out and grabbed the dagger from Anya's belt, and darting forward, moved past the protection of the two best warriors in Fontaine, so he could face the deadly serpent alone.

"Gray!" Rory cried out, but Gray blocked out the voice, because it already hurt that the beautiful future that he'd hoped for with Rory was going up in flames. But he could do this.

He ducked as the great head swung, its jaw snapping shut and just missing his arm. Rolling closer, he eyed the exposed underbelly of the snake, hoping that it was as vulnerable as its real-world counterparts. He poised, hoping to strike with the dagger, praying it would be deadly enough to stop the Count from continuing his attack, but before he could swing with it, flames suddenly erupted out of the pointed end.

The serpent reared back, screeching as flames engulfed him. Gray, as surprised as the first time Lion's Breath had summoned its deadly magic, couldn't believe that this little dagger, of no ancestry whatsoever, was summoning the same flames the ancient sword had.

Abruptly, it was over, the remains of Aplin smoking on the marble floor, a horrified hush spreading through the enormous chamber.

"Gray!" Rory yelled, running towards him, after finally loosening Marthe's grip. He fell to his knees next to Gray, who dropped the dagger like it had scorched him, even though the metal was as cool as the first moment he'd held it. "Oh god, what happened?"

Gray stared at his almost-husband. "I don't know . . . I didn't have the sword. I just thought I could hurt it, hurt him. Enough to maybe stall him, maybe give Anya another shot, enough to save you."

Rory was crying, tears dripping down his cheeks as he clutched at Gray's shoulders. "You insane idiot, you saved me, you saved us all." He put his head in the crook of Gray's shoulder and hugged him fiercely.

"I think . . ." Marthe approached now, her voice as uncertain as Gray had ever heard it. He supposed that it wasn't every day a gigantic serpent was burned to ash in front of her. "I think it is my utmost honor to pronounce you committed partners and Kings of this realm." She extended her hand and Gray realized that she carried in it his new crown. Rory glanced back, and smiled, taking it in his own two hands. Gray, who had knelt down to be closer to Rory, found he did not have to move at all. So it came to be that in front of the smoldering ruins of their second-worst foe, Prince Graham of Ardglass became King Graham of Fontaine, and to his own shock and his husband's, the entire court erupted into wild applause.

CHAPTER TWENTY-FIVE

A WEEK LATER, IT was as if a magical fight had never happened in the throne room. The ash from Aplin's body had been cleared away, and the floor cleaned. A second throne had been moved to join the first, and today, in their first audience as Kings, Gray and Rory sat side by side, holding hands across the space between their respective seats.

"Your Majesties," Anya said, approaching the platform they were sitting on, "one last report, this is a message from the unit you sent to track Rinard. He has not been found, and no trace of him exists."

Gray sighed. He had not expected Rinard to be found, not after what had happened to his consort in this very room, but the effort had been the very least Gray could do, now that he was nominally in charge of the defense of Fontaine. Still, it did appear from Anya's reports, mostly given in her guise as the head of the new informant network, that the nobles had mostly, if not entirely, pledged their support to the new Kings.

"And," Anya continued, "I believe that is everyone who has submitted a proposal to be heard before you."

Gray let out a breath he hadn't known he was holding. He knew he'd been trained, at least until age eleven, to be a king, but he'd discovered that king-ing was not as simple as he'd believed it was when he'd been a child. It was complicated and difficult and mostly involved making a lot of compromises and then couching those in such attractive terms that everyone believed they'd gotten their own way, when in fact nobody had. And it turned out, he did have a surprising affinity for it. Or maybe that was the man at his side, who had believed in him, and who he believed in, to the very last breath in his body.

"See?" Rory said with a bright grin. "It was not so bad, was it?"

"Well," Gray grumbled, because it had still been slightly stressful. He hadn't been entirely sure he was going to convince John the farrier to accept only three cows for his daughter's hand in marriage, and not five. But love had prevailed, as love had only a week ago, and now the farrier's daughter was going to marry the farmer.

Gray decided it had a pleasant symmetry.

"You did great," Rory said, leaning in to give him a quick kiss.

"You were . . . tolerable," Gray teased, and then turned to get up to lead Rory away from the throne room and hopefully to more pleasurable pursuits, but then out of the corner of his eye, he saw a sight he had never expected to see again.

Gray dropped Rory's hand and stood up slowly with shock racing through every vein in his body.

"You . . ." Gray whispered as a man approached the dais. His face was as familiar to Gray as his own face, his own body, his own mind. He'd been sure a month ago, when they had left the Valley, that he would never again hear that voice, or that smug, certain tone ever again.

And like so many other countless times, Evrard had made sure that Gray was wrong.

"Your Majesty," the man said, bowing, "I would like to offer my stewardship services to the throne of Fontaine."

"You would?" Gray knew his own voice was strangled, but he wasn't as young as he once had been, when he'd been equally as shocked.

"I have heard," the man continued, as if Gray hadn't spoken, "that you had a bit of excitement at your wedding, only last week."

Gray would have rolled his eyes but that was almost certainly not kingly, and likely he would never get away with anything un-kingly ever again. Especially not with the man currently standing in front of them around. "We did," Rory said, a puzzled expression on his face, as he approached where Gray and the man stood.

"I like to think that if I were on the job, nothing of that sort would ever happen again," the man said confidently.

"You would be able to prevent . . . a disgruntled member of the court from unearthing his predecessor's magical lair and turning into an enormous poisonous serpent, hell-bent on interrupting a royal wedding?" Rory asked archly. "That is quite a promise, indeed."

"Indeed," Gray echoed.

"I have much experience in negotiations, and on councils of various kingdoms. And . . ." The man flashed a knowing smile at Gray. "And much experience in educating future princes to be kings. I assume you do not have a child as of yet, but there is still time . . ."

"I would say so," Gray muttered. "We were just married."

"Regardless," the man said, "I offer you my services, such as they are."

"I think . . ." Rory hesitated. "I think we could find a place for you, good sir. And your name?"

The man flashed Gray's husband an incorrigible smile. "My name is Rhys, Your Majesty. And it is excellent to finally meet you."

YOURS EVERLASTING

PROLOGUE

A THOUSAND YEARS AGO . . . or so

Evander was incensed. Vexed. Entirely exasperated.

"Are you telling me that you do not want me to address the situation that has developed on the surface?"

Deimos did not blink.

But then, Deimos never blinked. His was the coiled, dead-eyed, hypnotized gaze of a poisonous serpent.

Evander had known Deimos for a thousand years, and would know him for thousands more, but even with all his power to uncover secrets, he'd never exposed a single one of Deimos'.

Death held no secrets, and Deimos was the Guardian of Death.

"I do not wish you to address it," he said.

"It is important. We do not allow humans to possess the powers the sorcerer is gathering." Evander knew it was a risk to continue to argue. After all, Death brokered no arguments, either. But Deimos would occasionally be convinced to listen to reason.

Speaking of reason . . . why was Vanya not speaking up, either?

Evander had discussed the situation at length with him, before the meeting of the Conclave, and while Vanya was the Guardian of Belief, both knowledge *and* reason fell under his purview.

He knew how important this was. Evander had stressed it, both *before* he'd tumbled into bed with the other Guardian, and *after* as well.

"Why does this concern us?" Deimos asked. His voice was calm. Deadly calm. Evander had never heard him raise it once, but then, there was no place in death for anger.

"If we are Guardians, then we are the Guardians of the humans' safety, and their sanity, and their continued existence," Evander argued. "We are meant to protect them. It is our sacred charge. Our duty. What we were tasked with, why we were created. The sorcerer might not be causing problems today, but if they grow in power, as they intend, they will."

Deimos held up a hand. The other eleven stayed silent.

They knew better than to interfere when Evander's stubborn streak collided with Deimos' intractability. Vanya, Evander realized, a chill sliding down his neck, must have foretold the impossibility of this conversation. He did sometimes.

He had not told Evander to leave it alone, either.

But would you have?

"I ask what concern it is of *yours*, Guardian," Deimos said. "You are the Guardian of Secrets. You are not meant to defend the surface." His gaze slid to Marcos, whose job it *was* to defend the surface.

Marcos blinked.

How could he not? He was so many things that were human: fear and courage and a blood-curdling, berserker rage. He was all instinct and no thought.

Evander had been dismissing him forever, and it seemed on this point, he and Deimos actually agreed.

Marcos was useless. Good in a battle, perhaps, but utterly hopeless here, in this chamber where the Conclave met, each word a move in the chess match that constructed fate.

"I would defend them, if others will not," Evander said. "I know the sorcerer's secrets. He craves power. So much power. Forever life, as we have been given. If he is able to obtain these things . . ." He trailed off, because the Guardians would all know what this could mean.

They would be threatened.

"Guardian Marcos, you are our Guardian of War," Deimos asked, "have you been consulted by our brother on this apparently grave situation below?"

Marcos shook his head, his eyes flashing. He was clearly offended, and unable to hide it.

Evander was not surprised.

"Then you must not be so very concerned," Deimos said dismissively to Evander. "There is no problem. It will resolve itself. No human has ever amassed enough power to threaten *us*. We are everlasting."

The other eleven recited back with Deimos.

We are everlasting.

It was a habit, after a thousand years, to repeat the words back. They came easily.

"We are everlasting."

Vanya had warned him, a hundred years before, the time slipping by so smoothly, like beads on a necklace, that Deimos was increasingly uninterested in what happened below them.

We will eventually fade from memory and concern, he'd said. *We will become legend; we will be everlasting.*

Evander hadn't been convinced. After all, he knew countless secrets. So many still believed, would never be swayed from their beliefs. Vanya should have known that, too.

But while he hadn't taken Vanya's warnings seriously, he'd not entirely dismissed them either. He'd been preparing for a day when the Conclave retreated. When the Conclave no longer concerned themselves with petty human matters. The day had come much sooner than Evander had anticipated.

"But . . ." Evander began to argue again.

It was a risk.

It was always a risk to argue with Deimos.

"The decision is made," Deimos said, his steely tone growing harsher.

This time the risk had not paid off.

"I do not ask for assistance, *especially* the Guardian of War's assistance," Evander said, "merely permission to deal with the situation myself."

Deimos' stare contained millennia of dread.

Even for one such as Evander, powerful and knowing, it humbled.

"Guardian of Secrets, your audience is finished," Deimos said with finality.

"You are taking far too many chances."

Evander was not surprised to see Vanya lounging on his bed when he entered his chambers. The oil lamps in the corner flickered with flame, and touched on Vanya's bare chest, his olive-toned skin glowing in the light.

He was beautiful, but then they were all beautiful, even Deimos in an unnerving way.

"That was not taking too many chances," Evander retorted as he crossed the room, examining the tray of meats and cheeses that had been left on his desk. Vanya had likely ordered it in. Their assignations were not regular, but happened often enough that nobody would have blinked at him asking for food to be sent to Evander's rooms.

"You also insulted and angered Marcos," Vanya pointed out silkily.

"That hothead?" Evander muttered.

"He is not stupid, no matter how much you wish him to be. And Deimos is certainly not stupid."

"No, but he is wrong," Evander said steadily.

"And yet you will do nothing about it."

Vanya was rarely as forceful as Deimos. He had no need to be. Love bred belief more strongly than power ever did.

Evander popped a piece of meat into his mouth. "I have not yet decided," he said.

"Come here," Vanya said, patting the soft ivory coverlet next to him. "Come here, and we will forget all about this."

"I cannot," Evander said wryly. "You know that I can discover every secret and every lie and, more importantly, every single truth people hold close. The sorcerer will be a problem. He must be dealt with."

Vanya looked irritated. "Then let Marcos deal with him. Or Hyperion. Maybe mauled by a wild animal, he will be less power-hungry and more bent on basic survival."

"You would really give him over to Hyperion?"

"Oh, you know I am joking," Vanya said, smiling now. The persuasive smile that won more belief than any orders in the universe. "I mean that we should forget about it tonight. Forget about it tonight, and tomorrow, and for the next thousand years, if you know what is good for you."

"How could I?" Evander was good at hiding his own bitterness. But there was no reason to hide in front of Vanya.

He was his best friend. His lover. The only one on the Conclave that he felt like he could truly trust.

"Not this again," Vanya said, and stretched out further, his nude body on full display. "Come, let me help you forget. About this sorcerer, and about this silly resentment you have for your Guardianship."

"It's not silly," Evander said. "You would not know what it's like to have everyone distrust you, because you are the opposite."

"There are plenty of discordant beliefs," Vanya reminded him.

"But secrets?"

"I am not trying to dissuade you from your feelings," Vanya said. "I am merely pointing out that you can do nothing about them. You were the Guardian of Secrets from the moment you were created, and you will be the Guardian of Secrets for many, many years to come. Embrace it."

He had. For a long time.

For what felt like an eternity, he'd put one foot in front of the other, gathering secrets, and for much of that time, he'd found at least some satisfaction in being the receptacle for things that people both desperately wanted and had no more use for. Nobody trusted him, not completely, because he always knew too much, but he did have Vanya, and occasionally one of the others. Hektor was not so bad. Kadir, either. He even got along with Gael.

Evander wasn't sure when he'd gotten so dissatisfied. Was it when he'd started hearing the whisperings and the rumblings of this sorcerer and he'd realized he could do more, *be* more? Other Guardians had more defined powers. Jae and Hektor tended the earth. Marcos dealt with violence and anger. Kadir was the master of time. But Evander? He could discern secrets, but not always. There had to be purpose to his scrying for them, or else they needed to be attached to a strong emotion for him to sense them. Many believed that he could read minds, but he had never been able to. He could hide, he could skulk around in dark corners, he could change shape at will, far better than any of the other Guardians could, and he often knew people better than they knew themselves. He'd even discovered a nifty trick of transporting his spirit away from his corporeal body, unbeknownst to those around him. But as for an actual task? He'd never felt he had one, not like the others. Not like Gael, who controlled the wind, or Lyric, who gave the gift of song.

He didn't know when exactly his discontent had begun, but he *did* know that he could not lose himself—not again—in the feel and pleasure of Vanya's body.

Not when he finally felt like he could finally set his powers to good use.

"What is it you always say? *We choose our own destiny?*" Evander did not mean to say it so mockingly, but he heard the derision in his words. None of this was Vanya's fault. None of it was anybody's fault, that was the biggest problem.

There was nobody for Evander to blame.

Nobody he could exact slow, painful revenge on.

Just himself.

Vanya shot him a reproving look. "I don't actually say that," he reminded him. "It's only attributed to me. A fact you are perfectly aware of."

"If you're here to tell me things I already know or to try to make me forget what happened in the Conclave, you might as well leave," Evander said bluntly.

Vanya knew his bad moods better than anyone, knew them well enough he shouldn't be hurt by them, but Evander saw the flash of it in his eyes before he could hide it away.

"You're going to do something very stupid and ill-advised," Vanya said as he rose from the bed, smoothly and gracefully. He draped his linen shift over his head, then fastened a bejeweled golden belt low on his hips. "Let it be known that I tried to change your mind, and that I did try to distract you from whatever insane course you're plotting."

"You did," Evander acknowledged. "But you had to know I wouldn't change my mind."

Vanya nodded, and as he passed by him, as gracefully as he did everything else, pressed a kiss to Evander's forehead. "I knew," he said simply. "But I had to try anyway."

The door closed behind Vanya with a soft click.

Evander turned to the plate of food on the desk.

He noticed then that there was only enough food for one.

Vanya had known that he wasn't going to be sharing the meal after they fucked. He'd gotten it just for Evander.

He slumped down into the chair, and picked at the meats and cheeses, shredding some of the honey flatbread that was his favorite as he considered the plan he was forming.

Vanya was right; it was inevitable that Evander was going to do something about the sorcerer.

The thirteen of them were evidence that too much power corrupted, and for a human it would be even more dangerous.

Something had to be done, but the question was . . . *what*?

Whatever he ended up deciding, there was no way around making more exploratory trips to the surface. Three or four hundred years ago, that would not have been so unusual, but as time had passed and Guardians involved themselves less and less in human affairs, they'd naturally spent less time with humans.

But to gather the information Evander needed, there was no way around it—he needed to go to the surface, and that was a risk because Deimos, like Death, was all-seeing.

He'd occasionally used Vanya to distract Deimos' attention from what he was doing, but he could not rely on Vanya to help out with this. He'd made his feelings plenty clear.

There were other Guardians he could ask.

They would know why, even if he lied, and he couldn't be sure of any of them, not like he was sure of Vanya.

Vanya's suggestion of using Hyperion resurfaced in Evander's thoughts, and he was in the midst of considering involving the Guardian of the Wild when there was a knock on the door.

He wasn't in the mood to talk to anyone, but he stood anyway and walked over, pulling it open with more force than was strictly necessary.

A figure filled the doorway—the *entire* doorway.

Of course it was Marcos.

Evander should have expected that he'd show after the discussion in the Conclave.

"I saw that Vanya left . . ." Marcos said, his voice trailing off.

Evander stared at the man, daring him to say more.

But he didn't. Because that was Marcos.

Why use words when his fists, and his sword, and his many, many knives worked so well?

"What do you want?" Evander finally asked.

"The sorcerer," Marcos stated succinctly.

Evander pulled the door open further. "Come in," he said, "we don't need to discuss this in the hallway."

The door shut behind Marcos, who'd barely crossed over the threshold.

"Is he truly a threat?" Marcos asked.

Evander studied the man in front of him. He was beautiful, like they were all beautiful, but instead of elegant perfection, like so many of them, Marcos was the beautiful fierceness of a hawk, with the intensity and steel-sharp focus of his dark eyes. His hair was shorn short, much shorter than anyone else's, but all the no-nonsense cut did was leave in stark relief the wild magnetism of his features.

Gael had once said—or maybe it had been Hektor—that Marcos was the most attractive of any of them.

Of course Vanya had taken that to heart, and Taavi had sulked about it for ages with him.

But looking at him now, Evander could see it.

Everything about Marcos, even after a thousand years of knowing him, was alien to him, but Evander couldn't deny he *was* attractive.

Not that he'd ever do anything about the realization; Marcos had the single-minded focus of one of the human monks, the ones who worshipped them and eschewed every single comfort and indulgence.

Marcos would never dream of entertaining a pleasurable dalliance.

He was just not built for it.

"The sorcerer is a threat," Evander finally said.

Something about Marcos, always on alert, relaxed. "What will you do about it?" he asked.

"Who says," Evander asked, as he walked back to his desk, digging around on the demolished platter for a hunk of cheese, "that I will do anything about it? After all, I have been forbidden to interfere by Deimos himself."

Marcos did not roll his eyes. That would be just as foreign to him as indulging in a quick, pleasurable fuck. But Evander felt the look he gave him just as viscerally. "I am not stupid," Marcos said, enunciating each word slowly and carefully. "You will not leave this alone."

"Why do you think so?"

"Because you know the very worst of all of us, and of every human. You know what lives in this sorcerer's heart. What eats away at his brain. If he is a problem, then you know it, better than anybody else."

"Yes," Evander said shortly.

Vanya's words echoed in his head. *You were the Guardian of Secrets from the moment you were created, and you will be the Guardian of Secrets for many, many years to come. Embrace it.*

How could he embrace something that was considered so vile and abhorrent without becoming vile and abhorrent himself?

Evander had yet to discover *that* particular secret.

"Then you know he is a threat. A real, true threat. And you will not rest until the threat is extinguished."

"Now," Evander teased, even though Marcos was hardly one for flirtatious banter, "you make me sound just like you."

"Maybe we are not so different, you and I," Marcos suggested softly.

Except Evander knew there was nothing soft about the man. Nothing.

Just like sometimes it felt like there was nothing true about himself.

"Are you suggesting we work together?"

In all the many hundreds of years the Conclave had existed, he and Marcos had worked together only a handful of times, usually with a group of other Guardians—but never just the two of them.

"You know the mind of the sorcerer, and the heart of him, and I can stop him with whatever weakness you can discover," Marcos said.

"If it was so easy as to simply slip a dagger between his ribs, I could have already done that," Evander pointed out, standing and beginning to pace back and forth.

"As you don't merely collect and keep secrets, I do not merely kill," Marcos pointed out dryly.

Maybe the man had a sense of humor, after all.

Evander was not surprised that it had taken almost a thousand years to come to fruition.

"He *and* what he knows must be destroyed," Evander said. "He must be erased. Eradicated. As if he never existed."

"We do not need his power passing on to the next," Marcos agreed. "We must burn it from the earth. Are there others, yet?"

Evander did not know. Something he very rarely liked to admit to. "There is more to discover about this sorcerer still," he said. "There must be reconnaissance, before a final plan is formulated."

"You mean to make repeated trips to the surface?" Marcos sounded surprised.

No doubt he also realized the inherent difficulty of preventing Deimos from seeing them.

"Just two—one journey for information, and then a second journey, to unfold the plan," Evander said. "Two may go unnoticed by Deimos."

"Except it is unlikely," Marcos said, his dark brows drawing together. "I think it best we deal with this in one trip. I will go with you. We will burn out everything we can, everything we can find. That is the best solution. Deimos might be unhappy we defied him, but if we have already accomplished our goal . . ."

"You would risk angering Deimos?" Evander did not mean to sound so surprised, but he was.

He was further shocked when Marcos stilled for a second, then his spine straightened, and he seemed to grow inches, or perhaps even feet, and his magic filled the room in a dizzying rush.

He makes himself small. He makes himself forgettable because he is so dangerous.

The realization alone was perilous, because now Evander knew *this* secret.

A secret that Evander guessed Marcos had never wanted him to know. But he'd revealed it anyway, likely to build some kind of trust between them.

"Deimos," Marcos said in that deep, dark voice of his, "does not scare me."

Death would not scare a Guardian as strong as Marcos.

It was then that Evander realized just how much he'd been hiding.

"Deimos does not scare me either."

Evander had always *wanted* to be scared of Death, but even though he found the Guardian unnerving, he'd never been afraid. But perhaps he should have been. Vanya was right, he'd taken too many risks over the years. Done a hundred tiny, petty things that annoyed Deimos, and every one of them had pushed Death closer to the edge.

"I know," Marcos said, and that was the third surprise. Three surprises, and one was usually extraordinary for Evander.

"We shall meet and travel together," Evander suggested, deciding that he needed to get Marcos out of his rooms before he discovered anything else astonishing, like that Marcos actually *felt* things. "We will meet at the main portal in four hours. It will still be late enough, after a Conclave meeting, that nobody should miss us."

Evander saw Marcos hesitate.

"No," he finally said. "I have an alternate route I have been cultivating. I will meet you on the surface, near the Well."

"You have created another method to reach the surface?" There it was—the fourth surprise.

Marcos shrugged. "You should understand. The enemy needs to not see you coming. Everyone knows the portal exists."

Evander almost asked who the enemy was, but then decided that perhaps, in this one circumstance, it was better not to know *every* secret of Marcos'.

"I will meet you in four hours," Evander said with a quick nod. "Do not be late."

Marcos astonished one last time before he opened the door and left—he flashed Evander a quick smile, full of white teeth, fierce and unexpectedly charming, and said, "I am the Guardian of War. I cannot be late, and I cannot be early. The skirmish cannot begin until I arrive."

The Castle at the Top of the World, where the Guardians lived and where the Conclave met, was silent and dark as Evander crept down the hallway.

Being the Guardian of Secrets, he was exceptionally good at moving undetected—the one vulnerable location would be the portal, set into the floor in the main Conclave chamber, that combined with a Guardian's magic, could send them to the surface.

He passed Vanya's room without hesitation, because he knew if his friend and lover had another opportunity, he'd try to forestall or stop him again. And now that Evander had found an unexpected ally, he had no intention of letting Vanya attempt to change his mind again.

He'd promised Marcos he would meet him in four hours, at the Well. Then they would do a short reconnaissance of the sorcerer's dwelling, and commit every bit of magic and knowledge they had to eradicating his power from the surface.

It was a simple enough plan—and foolproof—if he could get to the Conclave and its portal undetected.

The Castle was full of artifacts from their history. A thousand years of battles and victories and advancements of the human world below.

Evander sidestepped around the shadowed outline of a plow, the first to be constructed, that Hektor, Guardian of the Earth, had brought to the Castle and had preserved in gold.

A sundial, courtesy of Kadir, the Guardian of Time, stood on a tall column at the end of the hall.

Lyric, the Guardian of Music, had an entire room of instruments that he fussed with.

To say nothing of the massive armory that Marcos had spent the centuries filling with every conceivable weapon.

And then there were the gardens, property of Jae, Guardian of Plenty, that Hyperion, Guardian of the Wild, had filled with statues and marbles of every known creature that existed below them.

Perhaps that was why he and Vanya had always gravitated towards each other: they had no artifacts, no concrete reminders of the power they held. Secrets, like belief, could not be seen or held or touched.

The antechamber was empty and still dark, only a few candles set into the wall recesses lighting Evander's way, but he wouldn't have needed them anyway. He functioned better in the dark, another point that he continued to feel bitter about.

An enormous tapestry filled one entire stone wall, a joint effort between Taavi, the Guardian of Love, and Abram, Guardian of Healing, that depicted the first marriage, the first family and the blossoming of the humans' relationships.

Evander had always hated it.

Sure, it was ugly, and it was unnecessarily flashy, but it wasn't the colors of the embroidery or the composition that truly bothered him.

Vanya's words from earlier came back to him: *You were the Guardian of Secrets from the moment you were created, and you will be the Guardian of Secrets for many, many years to come.*

Below, Vanya's followers preached that anyone could set their own destiny.

It was an irony that Evander had never had the chance.

He turned away from the tapestry, and had just entered the main chamber, his goal the portal set in the middle of the mosaic floor, when a movement just out of vision caught his attention.

He pulled up, still half a dozen steps away. "Who's there?" he said sharply.

A tendril of dark smoke weaved through the air, and then another, and Evander's stomach sank.

"After all this time," Deimos said, gliding out of the shadows, his black hair gleaming in the dim candlelight, his smile oily and wretched, "you still believe yourself the only Guardian who thrives in the night."

Evander considered making a break for the portal. He could make it through, and Deimos could not stop him. But what if Deimos had laid a trap for him on the other side? He would be unprepared and vulnerable, coming through the portal. And when he returned? *If* he returned? Deimos would still exact a punishment for Evander's disobedience. A punishment likely to be more severe if he attempted to dodge it the first time.

"We are not alike," Evander said. "I resent the implication."

"As do I," Deimos retorted. "I ordered you to not interfere with the sorcerer. And yet here you are, ready to commit disobedience."

"Is it disobedience? I thought your orders were merely suggestions."

The frown lines on Deimos' handsome face deepened. "You know very well they are orders. I lead the Conclave. My word is final. I ordered you to leave the sorcerer be. And now you must pay the consequences."

Evander fully expected some sort of tame slap on his wrist. He'd received them before.

But this time, Deimos drew himself up to his full height, and Evander was suddenly reminded of Marcos.

Marcos, who had been the only one who had known he was going tonight.

Marcos, who knew when.

Marcos, who knew *where*.

Marcos, who he had been right never to trust.

A surge of anger and resentment crested through him. "You," he spat out at Deimos, "have only the word of a traitor, and it is the word of that traitor against mine. I could be going to do anything on the surface."

"But you are not. I know you are not. The so-called traitor knew you were not." Evander felt his fury growing at Deimos' confirmation that he had been betrayed. "Thus, you will face your fate." Deimos was inexorable. As far as Evander was concerned, it was one of his worst traits.

"As you wish," Evander said, giving an insolent little half bow towards Deimos, who had always wanted to be a king.

But he had only ever been a Guardian.

"You are growing in insolence and also in power," Deimos said, his voice booming, and suddenly, the chamber was lit. And it was full.

Every chair was full, with a Guardian. Except Evander's, which was empty.

Out of the corner of his eye, he saw Vanya, disappointment in his eyes.

He saw Marcos, too.

His face, however, was completely blank.

Later, Evander would think back to this moment, and that empty chair.

The herald of his doom.

And the one who had brought it.

"You have defied me. You have searched for allies to array against me," Deimos continued. "You resent your place, and your Guardianship. To my other Guardians, I propose that a Guardian who does not wish to be a Guardian, who does not *act* as other Guardians act, *not be a Guardian.*"

Deimos' words fell into the utter silence of the room.

This, Evander realized much too late, was not going to be a petty punishment.

Vanya had tried to warn him. This time, and so many other times.

Panic swept through him as Deimos continued intoning his judgement of Evander's many crimes against the Conclave.

". . . disrespectful, dismissive, rude, and unbecoming nature," Deimos concluded. "He does not belong with us. He never belonged with us. I propose that Evander, Guardian of Secrets, be forevermore banished from this Conclave, with his vote going empty in absentia. I propose that his powers be stripped down, and as he cares so much for the humans, that he be sent to the surface until such time as he learns humility and his place in this Conclave. Who agrees with this proposal?"

Slowly, Evander watched as hands went up.

Gael, the Guardian of the Winds, perhaps even more inexorable than Deimos ever was. He had never seen anything in shades of gray, only ever in black and white. Of course he would vote with Deimos.

Hektor and Kadir.

Jae. Hyperion. Osias, the Guardian of the Oceans. Lyric, Taavi, and Abram were the last to raise theirs.

No, that was not true.

There was still Vanya.

And Marcos.

Marcos, who had betrayed him.

Why was he hesitating now?

Then finally, Vanya's gaze met Evander's. There was a thousand years of love and friendship and laughter and pleasure in that gaze. But layered over it all was disappointment. Disappointment and hurt.

Vanya raised his hand.

That left only Marcos.

Evander knew the condemnation had to be unanimous, or Deimos could not cast him out.

Why, then, did Marcos not complete his betrayal and raise his hand?

Deimos looked to his Guardian of War.

"Why the hesitation, Marcos?" he asked.

"There is supposed to be a proper trial." Marcos' chin tilted in a stubborn angle. "You know this."

Deimos waved a hand. "That is merely a formality. We are all in agreement. Evander has expressed that he does not *wish* to be a Guardian. A trial would be an unnecessary waste of the Conclave's time."

But he hadn't. He'd only wished to not be the Guardian of *Secrets*.

Marcos looked straight at Evander. For a second he was burning with righteous indignation, with the flame of unquenchable courage and strength. But then, like it had never existed, it was gone.

Marcos raised his hand, and it was over.

"I, Deimos, Guardian of Death and leader of the Conclave, thereby do banish and cast out you, Evander, Guardian of Secrets, until such time as you have learned to be humble and obedient."

Through the burn of humiliation and fear, Evander heard the chuckles around him at Deimos' words.

Nobody believed that he would ever be either.

And he *wouldn't* be.

They could banish him, but they could never take his pride. He straightened, and stared straight at Deimos as he muttered the incantation.

Then he was falling, falling, falling, not through the portal, but through a funnel of fire and wind and rain, hot and impossibly cold at the same time, the sensations dancing across every nerve ending.

He only knew a second before he was going to land, had only a breath to brace himself for the jarring pain.

For a very long time, it might have been minutes or it might have been hours, Evander lay there, on the hard ground.

He felt . . . *different.*

Deimos could not strip him of all his powers. He would still, always, be immortal. He could feel pain, but he could not die.

Otherwise, surely the impact from falling all the way from the Castle would have killed him.

Finally, Evander leveraged himself off the ground.

It was as good a time as any to take stock of his powers—or what remained of them.

One by one, he tested them.

He could no longer turn invisible.

He could no longer project his form in another place.

Without another being in front of him, he could not determine whether his power to tell if someone was lying or not was intact.

But what did remain angered him.

One of his fundamental powers, the one he'd always resented the most, the ability to shape-shift into something else, was the one he still possessed.

All the Guardians had that ability, to some extent, but his had always been the strongest, the most potent. He could become an exact copy of anything or anyone, just by thinking it.

But Evander usually resisted using that power, because he had only ever wanted to be *himself*.

Deimos, Evander decided with anger surging through him, was even sicker than he'd imagined, to leave him with the only power he'd never wanted.

He flopped down on the ground. He considered, briefly, changing form, but what was the use? What was the purpose?

He had no purpose any longer.

It took days.

Maybe even weeks.

But eventually Evander began to explore the land around him.

It was uninhabited. He'd seen no evidence of any humans in the length of time Evander had been in this valley.

Because it was a valley. It was ringed on one side by mountains, and shaded by trees, but the valley floor was a meadow.

Hektor and Jae would have loved it here, Evander thought as he walked through the wildflowers, blooming riotously.

But Hektor was not here, and neither was Jae, and Evander realized, as he did every single time he thought of one of his friends and companions, that he would probably never see either of them again.

It was easier to think of Guardians he would not miss, like Hyperion.

Like Lyric.

Like Taavi.

He could not think about Vanya. The wound was too fresh, and far too painful.

He *did* think about Marcos, and what he would say—what he would *do*—to him, if he ever laid eyes on the Guardian of War ever again.

Marcos was deadly, but Evander was *angry*.

He'd betrayed him, as easily as breathing, and then pretended to argue with Deimos, a faux sham of insisting on a trial, and then in the end, he'd voted to condemn him anyway.

There was not much else to think about in the valley.

Evander subsisted on berries and edible plants, and lay there in the grass, thinking of Marcos' betrayal and how he would exact his revenge.

But revenge, with no end in sight to his banishment, grew to feel pointless.

One season turned to the next.

It grew colder.

And Evander realized that time passing so easily, so quickly, had been far more comfortable in his tower room, with its soft, comfortable bed, and Vanya for warm companionship.

Here, on the surface, time seemed to crawl.

There came a point in which Evander no longer had a choice, and he was finally forced to leave the valley. He had no tools with which to build a shelter, and he would need food, with the autumn turning to winter.

He found a village, and for the first time since he'd fallen, shape-shifted. Not significantly. Just enough, making himself taller, uglier, rougher, so that he would not seem particularly noticeable.

When the first man he met asked his name, he could not give his Guardian name, so instead he said he was named Rhys.

Nobody looked twice at him.

Evander had often gone unnoticed in the world of humans before, but always by *his* choice. It was an entirely new experience to do so because there was nothing particularly memorable about him.

Trading a few days of labor for some old tools, he returned to the valley.

He could have stayed in the village. They had not welcomed him with open arms, but his presence had been tolerated. But Evander could not forget that he was different. There was no longer a place he fit in.

He was not human, and he was no longer a Guardian.

He was something in between, a cast-out, a reject, an outsider.

So he retreated back to his valley, casting what remnants of magic he had around it so he would not be bothered.

He built a crude shelter. He planted crops. He returned to the village now and again, always in the rough disguise of Rhys, to obtain a cow, chickens, and occasionally a lamb that he would raise.

It was a boring existence. Crude. Unimaginative.

Evander nearly forgot what it was like to be anything other than a recluse—except he could not quite forget.

Late at night when he lay in his bed—not as comfortable, nor as warm as his in the Castle had been—he remembered, and he burned with indignation.

And so life went on, full of hard work and a hand-to-mouth existence, until one day when a vaguely familiar power pushed, almost haphazardly, at the edges of the valley, at the edges of his mind.

While Evander had never forgotten the circumstances of his banishment, he'd focused entirely on the ones to blame: Deimos and Marcos. He'd ruminated on Vanya and how much he missed his friend.

He'd even learned to miss some of the others. Hektor and Jae. Hyperion. Kadir. Even Taavi.

But he *had* forgotten about the sorcerer. In his rage, he'd forgotten entirely about the sorcerer who he'd been so determined to quash, the power he'd insisted did not belong on the surface, with the humans.

Now it was back, and it was pushing at the magical barrier he'd raised around the valley so he could sulk properly—alone, with nobody to bother him.

Someone was bothering him now.

It had been many, many years since the sorcerer had lived. It was possible, but as Evander froze in the fields, his fingers tight around an iron trowel, he realized that the taint of the magic felt different from that of the other sorcerer. This was a new power.

So the magic had not died out with the sorcerer. And unsurprisingly, Deimos and Marcos had deigned it unimportant and insignificant, and had not dealt with it either.

It was still here, that power.

The trowel dropped from his fingers.

It took two days, but after Evander closed up his farm tightly, he rolled everything he owned into a tight bundle, slung it over his shoulder, walked through the magical barrier of the valley, and went to find the power, power that never should have existed here to begin with.

He had a new purpose.

CHAPTER ONE

Rhys—in this iteration of his life, he was going by Rhys, which he found particularly ironic, because that was the first name that he had ever gone by besides his own—had no purpose.

That was not entirely true.

He had *had* a purpose.

It had been a purpose he'd devoted hundreds of years to—solidifying the kingdoms of Fontaine and Ardglass, and in the process wiping out the lineage of sorcerers and sorceresses who would use the people of those countries for ill.

Sabrina, the final sorcerer in her line, was dead, killed by a magical relic that Rhys had used the last of his waning power to imbue with fire.

Lion's Breath, the Fontaine king he'd gifted it to long ago had called it.

And it had hung, somewhat innocuously, on the sword belt of many kings of Fontaine, until it was needed, and the right man, the crown prince of Ardglass who also happened to be the lover of the crown prince of Fontaine, had picked it up and had used the power within it to kill the last sorceress.

Always, before Rhys could manufacture a scenario in which the wielders of too much power were eliminated or killed, they had trained others.

It had been a blight on this land and on the others around it, for hundreds of years.

But finally, the blight was gone.

Sabrina had been power-hungry and had declined to ever share what she'd gathered. She'd had followers, but Rhys had done his due diligence. They'd never had true access to the power.

Her selfishness had been her doom, and finally, Rhys' success.

And now he was back at the kingdom of Fontaine, playing an advisor, and playing at being Rhys again.

He had been many people in his thousands of years.

He had been Evander, the Guardian of Secrets, the longest, but it was still painful to think on everything he'd lost, so he'd rejected that name.

For a time, the guise of the King of the Unicorns had been both useful and a pleasant boost to his ego. Evrard, he'd styled himself then. Nobody knew that Evrard was not his original form.

Nobody except the remaining twelve Guardians, and since in the hundreds of years since he'd been banished, he'd never seen any of them again, he believed they'd forgotten all about him.

The main problem with being Rhys again was that he did not *want* to be Rhys. Rhys was boring. Rhys had always been a means to an end. First to protect his original identity. Then to gain access to power and influence, both in Ardglass and Fontaine.

He'd intended to retire as Rhys, once he'd accomplished what he'd set out to do, but he had not anticipated that without any purpose driving him, being Rhys again—possibly being Rhys forever—would feel so uncomfortable and foreign.

He had not thought of himself as Evander in hundreds of years, but he was beginning to wonder if maybe *that* was the form that had fit him the best.

"Rhys, I asked you a question."

He raised his head, realizing that he had actually *drifted off* during a council meeting, and Emory, King of Fontaine, was looking at him like he'd just grown a second head.

He checked, very briefly, to make sure that he *hadn't*. Because with his shape-shifting powers, he could, in fact, grow a second head.

"Ah, yes, you did, Your Highness, and I was currently contemplating the answer."

Rory shot him a look that made it clear he did not believe this for a second. Gray, his husband and partner-king, was sitting next to him, smirking.

He knew better.

Of anyone, it was likely Gray knew him the best. Gray had known both Rhys, when he'd been Gray's tutor during his childhood in Ardglass, and Evrard, the unicorn.

He'd never known Evander.

But then nobody did anymore.

Evander was better left dead and buried, banished and vanished, but for some reason, *now*, he could not stop thinking about that life.

It's because you are so very bored.

"Then, what is the answer?" Rory asked.

The problem was that Rhys had not been paying attention. He'd been thinking—not the sane, routine kind of thinking that led to productivity and intelligent analysis, but the dangerous kind. The kind where he could not help but wonder . . . *what if*?

He already knew *what if* was pointless.

He was never going to be Evander again.

But he could not stop thinking about it anyway.

Rhys gritted his teeth. Gray was openly grinning now, and there was nothing more he'd have liked than to wipe that smug look off his former student's face, but that would mean being able to move backwards through time and actually *listen* to the question Rory had asked. That was a talent he had never possessed. Kadir could. But Kadir was not here. He was likely still at the Castle at the Top of the World. Maybe he was even staring down at Rhys now, laughing at him.

"Could you please repeat the question, Your Highness?"

"I asked, did you have an opinion on the amount of grain allowances for the North Mountain villages?"

Rory did not gloat, he merely repeated the question. Rory was growing as a leader and a ruler, gaining a reputation over the last year of being strong, but just. Gray had helped with the strong part, but he could often be hotheaded. Rory, on the other hand, approached things with a more analytical mind, with an eye to fairness. It was what made theirs such an excellent partnership.

Rhys comforted himself by remembering that he had arranged this partnership, and it had worked out—with only a few hiccups—just as he'd planned it would. Rory and Gray had always been meant for each other, but even Rhys had not foretold how well they would suit each other. How deeply they'd fall in love.

"I do, in fact," Rhys said, summoning his most dignified tone. "We have the extra grain, yes?"

Gray checked the parchment in front of him. "Yes, in fact, we do," he said. "The summer was mild, with plenty of rain, and the lowlands produced a record surplus."

"Then instead of letting it rot in the storehouses, we should give everyone an additional amount," Rhys said.

Rhys could have sworn Rory was hiding a smile. "That is an excellent suggestion," he said.

"And it's exactly what I said," Gray muttered under his breath.

Not for the first time, Rhys wondered what he was doing here. Gray and Rory might have needed his help at first, but they'd been ruling for a year now, and married for six months. They were happy and settled and the kingdom was growing and healthy again.

But where else could he go?

The valley again?

He'd always retreated to the valley whenever he was lost or frustrated—but the idea of being alone was . . . for the very first time, unpleasant.

Gray had clearly gotten under his skin, a situation Rhys was still trying to be annoyed about.

"Next on the agenda . . ." Rory began, before Rhys interrupted.

"Next on the agenda should be the succession of Fontaine," he said.

Gray rolled his eyes. "Not this again," he said. "We've only been married *six months*."

"And Rory has been king for a year, with no succession plan in place," Rhys reminded them.

"Rory is *fine* with that," Rory inserted with an easy smile on his face. He shared a glance with Gray. "Someday, we'll figure something out."

"Figure something out?" Rhys asked archly. "Is one of you miraculously going to be able to birth a child? No? Then you can't just *figure something out*. You're more intelligent than that, Emory."

"That's King Emory to you," Rory said, voice pleasant, but his eyes blazing with indignation.

"Maybe we should ask what *you're* intending to figure out," Gray said.

Yes, Graham of Ardglass had known him far too long, and knew him far too well. It was a problem, and a problem without a solution, which was Rhys' least favorite kind of problem.

"I don't know what you are referring to," Rhys said stiffly.

"Yes, you do," Gray said, leaning forward. "Your help has been invaluable, but surely there is something more that you'd like to do. Go establish your own kingdom? Where *are* the other unicorns?"

There'd been a time when Gray had spent very little time or effort thinking. There'd been a good ten years when Gray had been a purely physical being—between when Rhys had helped Prince Graham escape from the fortress at Tullamore, and Evrard had shepherded the hidden prince, now named Gray, through adolescence into adulthood in the Valley of the Lost Things. He'd put one foot in front of the other, rarely thinking or analyzing or considering. Then Rory had come along, *all* thought, and they'd changed each other.

Now Gray was just as dangerous with his brain as he was with a sword.

"Gone." Rhys licked his lips. "They're gone. They've been gone for a thousand years." Technically, they'd never really existed at all, but he'd enjoyed styling himself as Evrard, King of the Unicorns, because it had felt so different from Evander.

Evander would never be king of something so pure and innocent.

"Right," Gray said. "So, what are *you* going to do? Because we've got this all figured out."

"If you're looking for suggestions, I am sure Merleen might have a few," Rory said slyly, referring to the Mecant tribe member that their leader, Shaheen, had left at the court of Beaulieu. The Mecant had arrived after Rory had ascended to the throne, after he had sworn to help them gain their language back. Shaheen had studied with Rory, with a few of her family members, and then left Merleen to act as an ambassador when they'd returned to their nomadic ways.

Rhys had never met anyone *less* suited to being a diplomat than Merleen, except perhaps Gray, but what bothered him the most about Merleen was the unfortunate crush he'd developed on Rhys.

It was awkward, to have such a devoted follower, and then it had become worse when Gray and Rory had discovered Merleen's feelings.

"Merleen is going to birth your child?" Rhys asked with faux wide-eyed surprise. "I didn't realize he was capable of that."

"He's not. Though if it was going to be *your* child, I'm sure he'd find a way," Rory teased.

"This is hardly conversation fit for a council meeting," Rhys said stiffly.

"Yet you continually interfered in *our* personal life, and still do," Gray retorted. "Maybe we just want to be together for now. We don't need to create a family just yet."

"If you weren't rulers of Fontaine, I would agree," Rhys said. "But your situation is less stable than you imagine it is."

"No," Rory said resolutely, "it's plenty stable. Fontaine is peaceful, and its people are going to be well-fed this year. Ardglass is holding its first invocation of the clans in three hundred years. Things are . . ." Rory took a deep breath, like he was a little unsure of it himself. "Things are good. Which you're aware of. You're just bored, trying to find problems where they don't exist."

Rory's immense intellect could be astounding, and it could also skewer like a rapier.

"I'm not *bored*. Bored is for . . ."

Except that Rhys knew that Rory was right. He *was* bored.

"Go take Merleen and visit the valley," Gray said with a smile. "He'd like that."

Rhys had tried very hard not to encourage Merleen. His affection was determined, and he'd been stubborn about it. He'd never actually propositioned Rhys, but the implications of his feelings were clear enough.

And it was not that Rhys could not possibly return them . . . it was just not something he *did*. Not anymore.

Not for a very long time.

Not since Vanya.

But Merleen wanted more than just a quick fuck, and he seemed to realize, despite his persistence, that Rhys had no intention of giving in to his desires.

But still, he persisted.

It made Rhys uneasy, and so did Rory and Gray's teasing—even though they clearly meant well.

"Yes," Rory said decisively, "you should take Merleen and go on a trip to the valley. Take an extended leave."

"What about the council?" Not the official council of Fontaine, though Rhys did sit in on those meetings too, but the more unofficial council meetings that Rhys, Rory, and Gray held several times a week.

"I think we can manage very well without you," Gray said with amusement.

Rhys had no intention of going anywhere with Merleen, and he definitely did not intend to *ever* take the man to his valley.

Merleen was quiet and at first Rhys had found him all silent muscle and no brain, but then he'd realized, sometime in the last six months, that while he rarely spoke, he *watched*.

He watched Rory and Gray; and had watched Count Aplin and the Duke of Rinald, had even warned Shaheen about them, when Rhys had still been convinced they were annoying but ultimately harmless; he watched Marthe, who had been the leader of Rory's guard, but now served as the general of his armies; and he certainly watched Anya and Diana and Rowen and Acadia, who now made up Rory *and* Gray's guard; but most of all, he watched Rhys.

Sometimes Rhys wondered if Merleen had uncovered all his secrets merely by watching, but that was impossible.

He had too many, so many he had never even said out loud.

"Thank you, but I feel I must decline your generous offer," Rhys said stiffly. "My place is here, not chasing after some ephemeral dream."

"Right," Gray said, grinning. "Because that's what you would have told *us*, a year ago."

"You were a very different scenario," Rhys said. "You were fated to find each other."

"And you have no fate for yourself?" Rory's tone was kinder, softer, but it didn't hurt any less.

"None," Rhys said with finality, and stood. "Now I must consult with Marthe about a . . . about a situation."

He didn't need to consult with Marthe about anything, but he had to get out of this chamber, with its walls closing in, before he lashed out.

He'd learned the hard way to not be angry, to not make decisions and act before he'd thought through every possibility first. He thought he'd long since trained away Evander's impetuousness—hoping to avoid paying that steep cost ever again—but now it seemed it was back in spades.

All it took was a little aimlessness.

Rory and Gray let him walk out, even with his painfully bad excuse, and didn't try to stop him from leaving; for that, at least, Rhys was grateful.

On days he needed to escape, there was nothing better than shedding the skin of Rhys, and donning a new one.

This afternoon, he took on the form of the fastest thoroughbred in Rory and Gray's stable, galloping over the countryside for hours, letting the wind stream through his mane.

He used to do this as Evrard, but Evrard was a mystical form that had never really existed, except in men's imaginations, and so it was harder, more of a drain on his internal magic, to maintain it.

Besides, he'd created an entire persona as Evrard. And that persona would never have gone running, without a destination in mind, across muddy fields and up grassy knolls, and would absolutely have given a shit if his mane got tangled or he got spots on his glossy white coat.

This way he could . . . be a little more anonymous.

Nobody else knew he could shape-shift, except Rory and Gray. They only knew that it *could* happen, not that he did it regularly—though he'd promised himself that he *wouldn't*, now that there was no purpose—so it was a surprise after running for hours, until night had long since fallen across the castle of Beaulieu, to see Merleen melt out of the shadows as he emerged, newly changed into Rhys, through the castle gate.

"Where have you been?" Merleen asked, voice low. There was something about it, something about his demeanor, unassuming yet tinged with an undeniable physical power and prowess, that reminded him of someone.

Rhys had yet to put his finger on exactly who it was, but he assumed that if he hadn't remembered, it wasn't important. Surely it must be one of the inconsequential soldiers he'd met over the years—and there had been thousands of them. So many that Rhys could not possibly remember all their names or why they'd been important.

"Out," Rhys said shortly. He was not in the mood for Merleen's games tonight. The way that Merleen would push right up to Rhys' boundaries and then hold there, unwavering, making it clear that he had no intention of giving up.

He continued to stride into the courtyard, pockets of light dotting the cobblestones. But even though he avoided them, and he did not look back, he could sense Merleen following in his footsteps.

"Out where?" Merleen finally asked, after the guards had opened the main doors, letting them into the castle proper.

Rhys glanced behind him, even though he'd told himself that he wouldn't.

It was that weird taste of the familiar, that was why he hadn't dismissed Merleen completely. Or at least that was what he kept telling himself.

Merleen took a step forward, shadows creasing his face.

"Out," Rhys repeated again, making his tone inexorable, his point inarguable. "I was not aware my movements were the business of the Mecant ambassador."

Merleen chuckled. "You are the counselor to kings. How could you be anything else but of interest?"

He wasn't handsome, not in a traditional sense. His features were too harsh for that, like they'd been carved not from marble, but from plain stone and then worn down from too many years exposed to the elements. His nose was too big, and his eyes were sunken, a dark, dark brown that seemed to look at Rhys and really *see* him.

Not just Rhys.

Not Evrard.

Not any of the fleeting forms he'd taken over the years.

But . . . someone he hadn't been in a very long time.

He was big, too—built like a mountain. Even in the muted fabrics, unlike what the rest of his tribe enjoyed, a cacophony of color and pattern, he was formidable.

"I am nobody and, as such, am of no real importance, no matter who I counsel," Rhys said. Such humility was not his typical style, but the way Merleen kept looking at him made the back of his neck itch and his blood burn.

Rhys supposed if they ever fought, he *could* win, but it would take every bit of his ingenuity and magic to defeat Merleen's pure physical force.

He knew this, because when he was supposed to be pretending that Merleen didn't exist, he would occasionally watch the training that Merleen shared with the other members of Rory and Gray's guard.

Gray himself had even praised Merleen's sword work on many occasions, and it took serious skill to impress him. But Rhys hadn't needed Gray's word to believe that Merleen was both talented and powerful. He'd seen the evidence with his own two eyes, even as he'd tried to pretend that he hadn't.

Then again, it would be seriously easy to disarm him now.

All it would take would be Rhys drawing closer, slipping right under Merleen's guard, and reaching up, pressing their lips together.

One night in Rhys' bed, and Merleen would be his to command.

Except that Rhys wasn't interested in commanding *anyone*. Not anymore.

Not even Merleen.

Merleen chuckled again. "No real importance? Then why did Shaheen task me to keep an *especial* eye on you?"

"I do not think you needed an assignment to keep an eye on me," Rhys said, deciding he was done playing around. Or maybe it was merely the boredom talking again.

Merleen did not so much as flinch. Rhys had to give him at least a little credit; the man had nerves of steel, surprising for a human of relatively young age. "You've been paying attention."

Rhys rolled his eyes. It was undignified but what did it matter? Merleen was like him—*nobody*. "I'm not blind."

"No." Merleen's voice was entirely steady, and Rhys did not see him flush. Then he took a step closer, and suddenly he was as close as he'd ever been.

Rhys would have denied it til the end of time, but his mouth went a little dry, and he had to crane his head back. Rhys was short and unassuming, which was the way he'd been designed, and well, Merleen was *not*.

Suddenly, it occurred to him who Merleen reminded him of.

Marcos.

A name he had not thought of in hundreds of years.

He'd been too busy trying to right the wrongs the Guardians had let fester to worry about something as petty and small as revenge, but the anger surged through him again, as fresh as it had been a thousand years ago.

Before he could tell him off, once and for all, Merleen ducked his head. "You see everything and everyone," he said in a hushed tone, as if people could overhear them.

But nobody would, the corridor was empty, as the residents of the castle were currently packed into the Great Hall for the evening meal.

Rhys realized, suddenly, the knowledge unsettling him, that Merleen had picked precisely this time for their conversation so they wouldn't be interrupted.

"You are certainly difficult to miss," Rhys said bluntly. "Even if I was not quite so observant, your presence wouldn't go unnoticed."

Merleen's smile was unexpected. "I know," he said, without any self-consciousness whatsoever.

It occurred to Rhys that maybe he'd underestimated him, the same way he'd underestimated Marcos.

Marcos had fooled him, hadn't he?

That took skill and audacity.

Merleen apparently had the same traits in spades.

Rhys pushed away thoughts of Marcos. After all these years, he had no intention of letting the Guardian of War unsettle him again.

This isn't going to hurt anything, he reasoned with himself as he let his body sway closer to Merleen still, *and it might even alleviate your boredom for five minutes. Or so.*

But before Rhys could close the distance between them, the corner of Merleen's lips quirked up to the side. "You never said," he pointed out, his voice hushed, "where you were this afternoon. If you think a kiss is enough to distract me, then you are sorely mistaken."

Rhys jerked back. Annoyed. More at himself, even, than at the smug look on Merleen's face.

He's not even handsome. You're just bored. So utterly bored.

"Where I was is none of your business," Rhys said in a harsh voice. Hating how fast his heart was beating.

Merleen knew now that his attraction was not completely one-sided.

Rhys had given that secret away—for *free*.

He straightened and turned away.

"Where are you going?" Merleen asked. Still completely unbothered. Like he hadn't been *this* close to kissing Rhys, something he must have been wanting for some time.

Anger flared through Rhys. Anger and humiliation.

"Wherever it is," Rhys said in a biting tone, "it is *also* none of your business." And he turned and walked off.

Rhys wished that he had somewhere he could go that would be infinitely more interesting than his chambers—some place that Merleen would have *really* liked to know about and wouldn't—but his life here was surprisingly simple.

He could have gone to the Great Hall, and eaten with Rory and Gray. He was always invited. But after running into Merleen, and having him not only school him, but realizing his similarities to Marcos . . . well, Rhys was not in the mood.

He stalked back to his chambers, and on the way, stopped a servant in the hall, asking for a tray of food to be brought to his room.

He would just have a nice quiet meal in front of the fire. Then he'd go to sleep, and everything would be normal again in the morning.

He didn't really believe it, but telling himself the lie was easier than dealing with the possibility that he was so dissatisfied with his life here that he'd nearly been tempted into kissing *Merleen.*

Vanya would have laughed at him for a hundred years, and never bothered to hide it.

Rhys slumped into the chair by the fire and sipped the wine that the servant had brought with the food.

As advisor to the kings, he'd been given a gold goblet, worked with a few carvings and even a subpar ruby set into the expanse just under the rim.

There'd been a thousand pieces better than this, in the storerooms at the Castle at the Top of the World.

He and the other Guardians had lived in luxury there, never wanting for a thing, merely needing to envision their desires in order for them to be made real.

Even a hundred years ago, he'd have said that he was missing the ease of that life. But he'd never minded living simply, without gold and silks and a dozen servants bowing and scraping.

He had no need of that. His growing relationship with Rory and Gray had shown him that. He'd been perfectly satisfied living in the valley with Gray for all those years, never wanting for anything.

Gray had become the son he'd never wanted, and then Rory had come along, and he'd somehow taken *him* under his wing, as well.

He supposed that if he was going to be honest, Rhys thought morosely, staring into the fire, he'd discovered that he *could* love, after all.

Not romantic love, though, that had died with Vanya, even though he'd never really been *in love* with him, not the way he knew love could be. Not the way he saw the love blossom and grow between Rory and Gray.

It was the affection and care he felt for them that kept him from leaving now.

That, and the fact that if he did leave, he had no earthly idea where he would go.

He finished the wine, his head swimming with it.

He would take his own advice to heart, and go to bed. Everything would seem better after a good night's sleep.

Except, after he settled in, under the velvet coverlet, he was still unsettled.

Rhys told himself that it was just his sudden realization that Merleen reminded him of Marcos—and that he'd almost kissed him anyway.

When he finally fell asleep, it was a light and fitful sleep.

He tossed and turned for hours, and woke, in the dead of night, at least an hour or so before dawn, with a voice—*the* voice—echoing in his head.

Rhys recognized it instantly.

Hundreds of years could go by, and he'd remember it all the same.

Vanya.

"Evander," the voice echoed. "*Evander.*"

Rhys shot up in bed, his eyes wide open. He fumbled for the candle on the little table beside the bed, and it took four tries to get it lit.

When he did, finally, he waved it around, the flame flickering, the light dancing on the stone walls and the tapestries that covered them, but there was no Vanya.

Then he heard it again. "Evander," he called, "*Evander.*"

He nearly answered him, out of habit, but then he snapped his mouth shut, biting down so hard on his lip that he tasted blood.

It was a dream.

A hallucination.

A vision.

Vanya was *not* calling for him. He was not here. It was just . . . a remnant of memory, from back when he'd known him almost as well as he'd known himself, and they'd been partners and friends and Guardians together.

Realizing that Merleen reminded him of Marcos, that thought had merely shaken loose some of his very old memories. The ones he'd tried very hard to forget.

He stayed in bed, upright and alert, for what must have been an hour, and then another, the candle finally sputtering in its own melted wax, until the first tendrils of dawn began to creep across the walls in his chamber.

"It was just a dream," Rhys told himself.

But he was not so certain.

CHAPTER TWO

It happened again.

This time, Rhys was walking down one of the many corridors of Beaulieu, headed to the library to meet Rory to discuss a new trade agreement with Ardglass.

The voice echoed off the stone walls, and Rhys nearly dropped all the papers he was carrying.

"Evander," Vanya called, faraway and yet so familiar that Rhys' knees felt weak. "*Evander.*"

He'd just passed Anya, and when he heard the voice, he turned back and nearly ran to her, almost knocking her over in his enthusiasm.

"Did you hear that?" he demanded of the dark-haired guard. "Did you hear that voice?"

She frowned in confusion, her brows crinkling together. "No?" she said. "What voice?"

"Evander, Evander, *Evander,*" Vanya called again.

"*That* voice," Rhys said, resolute. "That voice just then. The one that said . . ." He hesitated. It had been so very long since he'd said that name. But then Anya would have no earthly idea that Evander was him. She did not even know that once upon a time, he had been Evrard. "Evander. The voice called for Evander."

"I didn't hear a thing," she said gently. "Not Evander, and not anything else."

"Oh. *Oh.*" Rhys didn't know what to say. He'd wanted so much for it to be real and hadn't even realized how strong the desire was, until it had turned out to be all in his own head.

An invention of a brain occupied with nothing more important than council meetings and avoiding Rory and Gray's haphazard matchmaking attempts.

You are so very bored, you must find something to do that isn't trade agreements and pretending not to spy on Merleen when he fights Rowen in the courtyard.

"Are you alright?" Anya's smile was kind and she put a hand on his arm, gripping him tightly. Rhys realized that he had been swaying.

Exhaustion? Perhaps. He had slept terribly last night, when he'd slept at all.

He was just so very unsettled by the voice.

"I'm fine, thank you," Rhys said, and it felt good to use his most certain tone of voice. "It must have been a dream."

Anya smiled, softly. "Must have been. I will let you know if I hear it myself, or I hear of someone named Evander."

"Thank you," Rhys said, knowing that she would not.

Because Evander was *him*, and he had no intention of answering to that name ever again.

That evening, instead of retreating to the silence of his room, where he'd have no choice but to hear the voice, loud and clear, he took his evening meal in the Great Hall.

"We missed you last night," Gray said, as Rhys took his regular spot next to Their Highnesses.

"I noticed that Merleen was *also* missing," Rory added, with an impudent smile. "You two didn't happen to be together . . ."

Rhys was very old, and had been lying for every single one of his years, but he was still surprised at how easily the falsehood rolled off his tongue. "No, of course not," he said, shooting Rory a look that was intended to discourage any further speculation in that direction.

But Rory, who had not always been so, was now both fearless *and* confident in that fearlessness, and he merely stared back, blandly.

It had been so much easier when he'd been afraid of his own shadow.

"I think Rhys and I did work out the new Ardglass trade agreements," Rory said.

Gray finished chewing and swallowed. "Good." He lowered his voice. "I debated all day whether it was right for me to excuse myself, but I think now that it was right."

"You'd never have done the wrong thing, and given too much, just because it's Ardglass," Rory objected.

"It wasn't that I would, but the relationship between our two countries is still so new," Gray pointed out, "and even if I was the most objective negotiator in the world, I don't want to give anyone any ideas."

Rhys nodded in approval. There'd been a time, not so very long ago, when he'd despaired of forming Gray into the prince he'd once been. Rory was a good influence, of course, but what had made the most difference was that now Gray actually *cared* about making good decisions.

In that vein, he'd learned, not only to be the protector that Fontaine desperately needed, but to give his own reasoned opinion.

They don't need you, a voice in the back of his head whispered again.

Not Vanya's voice. At least that hadn't shown up yet, though Rhys wasn't sure how this one was any improvement.

It still skewered him right where it hurt, in the place deep down, where he wanted to be *needed*.

Rhys watched as Rory struggled. He wanted to say that nobody would believe that Gray would give the Ardglassians a more favorable trade agreement because he'd been Ardglassian, but he couldn't.

Because it was true.

There was still work to be done here, progress to be made in closing the gap between public opinion and the truth, but not for the first time, Rhys wondered if it was actually *his* work.

He'd told himself that it was, but how could it be, when Rory and Gray understood it so completely and were the only ones who could truly sway the kingdom's old prejudices?

"Perhaps the next step," Rhys suggested as he speared a roasted squash chunk with a silver fork, "is to adopt a child, and make sure the child is of Ardglassian ancestry. Even better, find one that combines both Fontaine and Ardglass in its bloodline."

Rory frowned, but it was Gray who spoke.

"Not this again," he said. His tone was joking, but his gaze was serious.

"You need an heir, and let me remind you *again* that you won't spontaneously birth one."

"We know that," Rory said, then hesitated. "We don't want to pick a child like . . . like we're at the horse fair and selecting a new mount. That doesn't seem right to either of us."

"Even if we were ready," Gray pointed out.

Rory nodded his agreement.

"It's only a matter of time before another Duke of Rinald decides that it's sacrilege for an Ardglassian to hold the throne of Fontaine, and bed its king," Rhys reminded them.

"Is there going to be another Duke of Rinald?" Rory asked archly. "I thought that threat was eliminated. And you said the count was harmless."

"He is," Rhys said, lowering his voice. "I took care of him, myself."

He'd ultimately been a mere pawn, as had the duke, but even pawns could be dangerous. He'd lured the count into a trap, waiting and watching to see what he'd do to extricate himself, which power he'd reveal he possessed, but when he hadn't, Rhys had let him go.

He wasn't worth killing.

"I think, my love, what Rhys is trying to say is that rumors can be almost as dangerous as shape-shifting sorcerers," Gray said, amused.

"True," Rory said. He grinned. "It's too bad you can't demonstrate your particular talents in front of the whole court again. That would keep them in line."

"What would keep the court in line?"

Rhys looked up and realized it was Merleen and he was sitting down at their table.

He was usually invited to dine at the kings' high table, but he rarely chose to do it. Instead, he liked to sit a few tables away, and stare, like Rhys was a tall, foaming tankard of mead, and Merleen was dying of thirst.

Rhys did not know whether it was better or worse to have him sitting next to him.

Worse, definitely worse, especially after he humiliated you last night.

"Remember when Gray leveled a man with only the fire from his mind?" Rory teased. "That would keep *anyone* in line."

"It would indeed," Merleen said.

Rhys forgot that he had been there, at the wedding.

Rhys had been there too, but he hadn't been in any of his regular forms. He hadn't been Rhys, or Evrard, or anybody that either Rory or Gray might recognize.

He'd nearly revealed himself and intervened, when the battle with the duke and the count had grown dire, but in the end, Gray had proven just how powerful his connection to Fontaine was, by calling up the fire of Lion's Breath without even wielding the magical sword.

Rhys had been so pleased that day, and a week later, after he'd verified that Count Aplin was harmless, he'd returned to Beaulieu, ready to finally lay down hundreds of years of responsibility.

He hadn't realized then that settling into such a quiet, uneventful life would be so boring or that he would fit so poorly into it.

The thought had barely crossed his mind, when it began again.

"Evander," the voice called, "*Evander*. I know you hear me. I know you are listening."

No, Rhys thought desperately, *not here and not like this.*

But his mind—because that was what it *had* to be, it could not be Vanya calling for him, that was impossible—wouldn't see reason.

It was not exactly impossible, but it *was* improbable. Because surely if Vanya had been able to speak to him during any of the last few hundred years, he'd have done it already.

"Are you okay?" Gray asked, turning to Rhys, concern shading his voice. "You went white."

"I didn't think anything scared you," Rory said, leaning in. "What happened?"

"It's nothing," Rhys said, wishing that he could brush away the voice in his mind as easily. But he couldn't. Especially not when now the voice was just not merely calling his name, but *speaking* to him.

"Evander, *Evander*," it called again, "why are you ignoring me?"

Because you're just me finally losing my mind, Rhys thought pointedly.

"Of course he can be scared," Merleen said, between bites of roasted meat. He said it matter-of-factly, as if he had personally witnessed it.

He's not talking about last night.

Because last night, he had not been afraid. He'd been . . . tempted, and unsettled, by the realization that Merleen reminded him of Marcos, and then he'd been embarrassed.

See? Rhys felt like telling him, *none of those are fear. I was not afraid of you. I will never be afraid of you.*

"You certainly claim to know me very well," Rhys said stiffly.

He did not want to engage with the man, but he kept making it impossible *not* to. Of all the ways Merleen infuriated and annoyed him, this was the most frustrating.

He made it impossible to be ignored.

"He'd like to know you even better," Rory said under his breath, chuckling.

Rhys watched as Gray tried to subtly elbow his husband beneath the table.

Rory had grown up at court. He was used to its politics, even its sexual politics. While Gray had been raised on a farm, with only Evrard for company, he'd always been less earthly than Rhys had imagined he'd be.

Gray had always liked private business to stay *private* business. Rory was far less particular about that, probably because he'd grown up with a whole court watching him. Waiting for him to mature and to grow into the beauty he now possessed.

"I like to observe," Merleen said. "It was why my aunt believed that I'd be suited to this position."

"Have you heard from Shaheen?" Rory asked, clearly attempting to change the subject.

"Evander, *Evander, Evander, Evander,*" the voice called again.

Rhys stood, abruptly.

He'd believed that by coming to dinner in the Great Hall, he'd be too distracted for the voice to bother him.

Except he was now more bothered than ever.

"Excuse me," he said as an afterthought as Rory, Gray, and Merleen regarded him. "I . . . I must have forgotten about an appointment."

"What appointment?" Rory asked, bewildered, but Rhys did not stick around to answer. He turned and left the Great Hall as quickly as his legs would carry him.

As soon as he reached an empty hallway, verifying that Merleen had not followed him, he took a deep breath and leaned back against the stone.

"What do you want?" he asked, out loud.

"I knew you could hear me," the voice responded.

Could it be? Could it really be Vanya? After all this time?

Rhys could barely believe it.

"I can hear you," he said quietly. "But I do not *want* to hear you."

The voice laughed, so like the Vanya that Rhys remembered that the knowledge made him *ache*. "Surely you believed you were going insane."

"The thought occurred to me," Rhys said dryly. "I have not answered to that name for many, many years."

An understatement. He'd not answered to that name since the day he'd been stripped of his title and most of his powers, and cast out of the Castle at the Top of the World.

"Do you remember the Well?" Vanya asked—because even though the voice could be the devious work of others, others that meant to do him ill, Rhys found himself wishing that it *was* truly Vanya.

"I do," Rhys said.

"Meet me there, at the Well." Vanya's voice rang with finality, brokered no argument.

"What?" Rhys asked, shocked. "Meet you?"

But there were no more voices, no more questions, no more proclamations.

Meet me there, at the Well.

Vanya had delivered the message he'd set out to convey. There was clearly no need to communicate further.

Rhys thought of Vanya's request for the next week.

Truthfully, he thought of little else.

That was the blessing and the curse of adopting such a simple life. He had plenty of attention to give.

Almost immediately, he concluded that it could be a trap.

It could also be the beginning of a new life—in fact, the return of an old life. Perhaps Vanya was extending a hand, ready to welcome him back to the Thirteen.

But if he was, wouldn't Deimos have been the one to contact him? After all, he was the leader, and he was the one who had made the decision to banish him all those years ago.

It still made sense, Rhys reasoned, because he had completed his task, had accomplished what he had set out to do.

Perhaps all his hard work was being rewarded and he was being given his place back.

Or, that other voice cautioned, *it's a trap.*

Rhys knew what he wanted it to be, and he also knew what was more likely.

But because he could not decide which it was, which outcome made the most logical sense, he did nothing.

Just brooded about it.

He rambled around the countryside and avoided the Great Hall at night, waiting for the voice to return, but it did not.

Just when he had come to the conclusion that the voice had gone silent, that it didn't matter if he left for the Well or not, it came to him again.

Rhys was standing in the hallway above the center courtyard of Beaulieu, looking out the window at the training happening below, as Merleen took on both Anya and Rowen, but barely seeing the movements as he was lost in thought.

He had barely seen Merleen this last week, though that had been entirely purposeful, but then when he'd passed by the window and realized it was him fighting, he'd stopped.

Stared.

For the first time not pretending that he'd been distracted by someone else.

Maybe it was the voice, maybe it was that it had been *Vanya's* voice, a voice from another time and another place, but he'd looked down at Merleen, and he'd seen Marcos instead.

The efficient, brutal movements, the confident surety of his decision-making, the unusual forms he'd no doubt picked up from his childhood with the Mecant.

It all reminded him of Marcos.

"Evander," the voice called out, shocking him out of his reverie.

Rhys' head snapped up.

"Evander, Evander, *Evander.*" Vanya's voice caressed as it commanded. Just as it always had. "You were not always so disobedient."

"Perhaps I cannot leave, cannot go on a fool's errand to the Well."

"And yet you are so bored, here you stand, admiring this *human.*"

I am not admiring him.

Yet, it was difficult to disagree, because it turned out there was so much to admire.

"I am needed here," Rhys said firmly. "I cannot go."

"Lies," Vanya hissed. "You were always a good liar, Evander, but not so good that I could not see through you. You must come to the Well."

"Must?"

"I did not ask." Vanya's voice echoed in his head. "I said come to the Well. And you must."

"In case you need a reminder, I am no longer the Guardians' to command."

"Perhaps not," Vanya said. "But the Guardians still have power. What if . . ." He trailed off, and there was a strength and a heft in whatever he did not say.

Merleen was right; Rhys *could* be afraid.

"What if?" he demanded.

"What if something were to happen to upset this delicate balance you have spent so many years perfecting?"

"Guardians, hundreds of years ago, did not deign to interfere," Rhys pointed out. After all, he'd been banished for making an attempt.

Rhys could feel Vanya's resigned sigh through their connection. "Are you truly willing to take that risk?"

He was not.

And Vanya knew it.

Rhys ground his teeth together. "No."

"Then," Vanya repeated, "you will come to the Well."

Rhys considered continuing to argue, but the faint connection he'd felt, it was gone, and he knew that Vanya wouldn't be returning.

Trap or not, Vanya or not, he was going to have to journey to the Well. He had no choice, not if he wanted to protect Rory and Gray and the beginnings of what they were building here.

He turned away from the window, and headed towards the library. He had some research to do, and then he would need to pack for the journey.

For a fleeting moment, he considered traveling as Evrard, but then decided against it.

He would go as Rhys.

Because Rhys, whether the skin felt better or worse than others to him, was who he was now.

Rhys considered saying goodbye to Rory and Gray and telling them where he was going. He'd miss them, and he hoped they would miss *him*.

But considering the possibility that Vanya's demand was a trap and he was not Vanya at all, Rhys did not want to drag anyone else into the situation, and Gray and Rory would never let him travel alone.

They'd insist he take some of their guard members, perhaps even Marthe or Anya, and Rhys was not willing to leave Beaulieu and Their Highnesses unprotected, especially not with Vanya's last threat.

No, he would travel alone.

He still had the remnants of his magic.

He could still change shape.

He could still sense when evil was approaching.

Therefore, it would be better for him to simply slip out in the middle of the night, with nobody the wiser.

Rhys penned a quick note, setting it on the desk in his chamber, informing Rory and Gray that something had come up, and he'd been forced to depart suddenly—but that he *would* be back.

Because he had every intention of returning, from whatever this was, even as he could feel his heart beat a little faster at the possibility that while on the road, he might find excitement again.

You don't need excitement, Rhys reminded himself, except that there was undeniably a part of him that hadn't stopped craving it.

He shut the door to his chamber and pulling his pack up higher on his shoulder, turned to walk down the dark corridor.

"Trying to run off again?"

Rhys froze.

Merleen melted out of the shadows.

How did he keep doing that?

When he'd been Evander, nobody had ever successfully snuck up on him—except Deimos, the one time it had truly mattered—but Merleen seemed to do it easily.

Not for the first time, Rhys wondered if he had some kind of buried power.

"Running off, now that you've made yourself indispensable?" Merleen questioned again.

Rhys took a steadying breath. "No," he said, "and I am hardly indispensable. Not that it is any of your concern, but there's a situation I must take care of."

"By yourself?" Merleen paused. "And don't try to argue, because you're clearly trying to sneak off in the middle of the night so nobody will stop you—or nobody will go with you."

"It's not worth bothering the guard," Rhys lied.

Merleen's gaze narrowed. "Somehow I doubt that."

"Whether you doubt it or not, I'm going alone because nobody else needs to be drawn into it."

Rhys turned to leave, but before he could take another step, Merleen's voice stopped him again.

"Take me with you."

Turning back slowly, Rhys eyed him up and down. Having someone of Merleen's skill would undoubtedly be useful, but there was much that he did not know about Rhys. Namely, that he wasn't even Rhys.

Allowing Merleen to accompany him on this journey would complicate everything.

"No," Rhys said firmly.

"Why? Because it'll be dangerous?" Merleen smirked. "I would think that would be an issue for you, since I wasn't aware you could even protect yourself."

Rhys told himself not to rise to Merleen's bait, but even in thousands of years, he hadn't been able to train himself out of every gut reaction. "Perhaps I don't look it, but I can protect myself better than you could ever imagine," he snarled.

It was Merleen's turn to eye him, from the top of his head, to the bottoms of his worn traveling boots. The look on his face made it clear just how much he didn't believe him.

And Rhys could give him that, at least. Rhys was slight and somewhat unassuming. He didn't wield a sword. He had a knife in his boot, but that was for appearances and emergencies, and because Gray never would have let him leave the castle walls without it.

For a brief second, Rhys considered changing into something else. He could take Gray's form, or even Merleen's. He could prove, without a single question, just how powerful he was.

But then Merleen would never look at him the same way again.

"You're not going alone. That's not up for debate," Merleen said.

"Oh? And how are you going to stop me?" Rhys challenged. Stupidly. Because in this form, Merleen could *absolutely* stop him.

Merleen shot him a look. "All I have to do is wake King Graham, because he would certainly never let you go off alone."

"Fine," Rhys said through clenched teeth. "You can come with me to the border."

"Where are you going that's beyond the border?"

"Again," Rhys said, not very patiently, "it's absolutely none of your business."

"It's my business now, because I'm coming with you," Merleen said, and before Rhys could argue *again*, Merleen was taking his arm, and he was completely, utterly unprepared for the power that shot through him at the contact.

Rhys stared at him.

None of the sorcerers he'd ever come in contact with had ever held power that strong. This wasn't routine, human-held power. It was so much more electric, with a feel and a taste to it that Rhys had once known as well as his own.

"What . . ." He gasped.

Merleen had the nerve to look sheepish. "Shit," he said. "I forgot you'd feel it since you aren't . . . well, you aren't *you* anymore."

Rhys could still feel the remnants of the power coursing through him. Wild and heady, it thrummed through his body.

Only one Guardian had a power signature like that.

"Marcos?" Rhys questioned.

Questioning his own sanity. Just a few weeks back, he'd realized that Merleen reminded him, in some small way, of Marcos, but he'd never imagined that Merleen *was* Marcos.

Merleen sighed, and like a snake shedding its skin, he slowly morphed into the form that Rhys still recognized.

The power was still there, but it was the difference between a glancing blow, and a strike that hit home.

Marcos electrified, just by affixing his dark, intense gaze to Rhys'.

He remembered, a second too late, that Marcos had been the root cause of his downfall and he wasn't supposed to be pleased to see him. Even if it was wonderful to feel all that power again, to be back in the presence of another Guardian.

"How dare you follow me," Rhys lashed out. "Not when you . . . when you betrayed me."

Marcos sighed. "That wasn't me."

Rhys rolled his eyes. "Of course you'd say it wasn't."

"It wasn't. And I'm not following you, well, not for the reason you believe."

"Oh?" Rhys asked archly. "And what reason do I believe?"

"That I've been tasked by Deimos to watch you, to make sure you don't betray the Guardians." Marcos said it matter-of-factly. "But I came for myself. I was . . . I was concerned about you."

"Well, you can see for yourself, I'm doing just fine." Rhys said it bitterly. "Now, if you'll move out of my way, I'll be going."

"What?" Marcos demanded. "Now that I know you're not a weak human, but have power, and this . . . this . . . *form* you've assumed is out of choice, not necessity, you think I'll let you go alone?"

Rhys stared at him. "I don't trust you."

"You don't have to trust me," Marcos said. "That's not required to protect you."

"We just established I can protect myself," Rhys said in a clipped voice, "so your presence is hardly required."

"But I can still wake Graham and Emory and make sure they know that you're leaving." Marcos hesitated. "They don't know what you *really* are, do they?"

Rhys ground his teeth together. Hundreds of years had not helped make Marcos any more likable. "They do not."

"Just a regular old shape-shifter?" Marcos chuckled under his breath. "Like those even exist."

"It doesn't matter if they do or not, that's what they believe and that's what they'll continue to believe."

Marcos had the nerve to look regretful. Like he didn't really want to force Rhys' hand this way. "Only if you let me go with you." He paused. "It's a trap, you know."

"What's a trap?" Rhys pretended ignorance, but Marcos just smiled.

"The voice. It's a trap."

"You heard it?" Rhys was so surprised he asked before he could continue pretending he didn't know what Marcos was talking about.

"Yes," Marcos said heavily, "and I do not believe it's what you think it is."

"I don't know what it is, but I can't ignore it," Rhys said.

"I know. I knew you'd leave. You'd never leave the people of Fontaine, or Graham or Emory unprotected and exposed."

"Which is why you've been spying on me," Rhys said bitterly.

Marcos nodded.

"Fine, you may accompany me, but do not talk to me, do not intervene, and do not think for one second that you are in command of this expedition. You are not."

"Naturally you would be in command," Marcos said. Rhys swore he caught a glimpse of a smirk before it disappeared swiftly.

Perhaps it was a bit ridiculous considering that of the two of them, Marcos was undeniably more powerful. But power didn't equal trust, and despite his protestation that he hadn't been the one to inform Deimos all those years before, Rhys did not trust him.

He was the most likely culprit, and if he'd betrayed him once, it was likely he'd try to betray him again.

"Let's go, then, before someone sees us, and I have to explain why I'm with . . ." Rhys glanced over at him as they began moving down the corridor. "Why I'm with a human the size of a small mountain."

Marcos grinned. "Merleen wasn't exactly small, either."

"No, but everyone knew Merleen. As far as they're concerned, you're a stranger."

Marcos did not respond to that. In fact, it was a blessing that he stopped talking entirely as they wound their way through the castle. He did not even point out that Rhys was taking the best possible route out of the castle—the one that would ensure that the guards did not see them leave.

They emerged into the courtyard, but stuck to the dark shadows that clung to the outside walls.

"No horses?" When Marcos finally spoke in a hushed voice as they passed by the castle stables, it was apparently to criticize Rhys' planning.

"Too noisy, too messy, and far too much work," Rhys said.

"You're not planning on becoming a horse for me to ride, are you?"

Rhys shot him a venomous look. "Hardly," he said. "We will travel on foot."

"It'll take longer, too," Marcos pointed out.

"Are you in a hurry to arrive at the trap?" Rhys questioned.

When Marcos just shrugged, Rhys skewered him with another deadly look. "I didn't think so," Rhys said.

It was easy enough for Rhys to slide through the little door set into the stone wall, next to the massive iron grate door that protected the castle itself.

It was a little tougher for someone the size of Marcos, but he managed it too, shrinking himself slightly with barely a blink.

Rhys told himself as he watched Marcos slide through the doorway that he was not jealous of how easily the Guardian wielded his power still.

An ease that Rhys had not been able to enjoy for a thousand years now. He'd missed the endless wellspring of power, desperately, at first, but then he'd gotten used to conserving his magic, only using it when he absolutely needed it.

It still did not come quite naturally, and now, watching Marcos, he realized that it never would.

He'd never been a creature created for conservative purpose. But now he had no choice in the matter.

Deimos—and *Marcos*—had stolen it from him.

"The Well is to the north," Marcos said as they took themselves off the path, away from questioning eyes, and turned towards the mountain ranges that ringed the north side of Fontaine. On the tip of the tallest mountain lay the Well.

"I have not forgotten the location of the Well," Rhys retorted. "It has been many years, but I remember that much."

"Then I will let you lead," Marcos said gracefully, and they turned towards the north.

CHAPTER THREE

Marcos knew he would not tire easily, but Rhys—*Evander*, that was Evander under that unassuming exterior, a marvel that would never fail to astonish him—undoubtedly would.

After watching him for hundreds of years, both keeping near to him, and also keeping his distance, Marcos was still not sure how reduced his power was.

Marcos knew he'd retained some of the magic he'd possessed before, but unlike when he'd been the Guardian of Secrets, now, he was clearly more particular about how and when he used it.

"We should stop for a rest," Marcos said, after they'd been walking all night and partway into the day, almost without pause.

They'd stopped once, to fill their waterskins at a cold, bubbling stream. They'd long since left Beaulieu behind, and they had not even passed through a single village. Out of choice, Marcos had assumed, but it still surprised him that Evander kept to the disguise of Rhys.

Surely now that Marcos had revealed himself, Evander would let the shape of unassuming, gruff Rhys melt away until he finally was himself again.

Except not once, as far as Marcos knew, had Evander taken his normal shape since he'd been banished.

But now, now that he was with Marcos again, surely the subterfuge was unnecessary.

Rhys glared at him. Even after all these hundreds of years, watching Evander be someone else, he was not used to seeing Evander stare out at him through someone else's face. "Do you need to stop?" he asked.

"No, of course I do not," Marcos said. "I am a Guardian, I could walk all the way up the North Mountain without stopping. But . . ."

"But I am no longer a Guardian," Rhys interrupted him. "Your point is clear."

But even if it was clear, Rhys was obviously annoyed that Marcos had brought it up.

He doesn't trust you, he thinks you're to blame, which isn't all that surprising, and now he thinks you're patronizing him.

It was not the most auspicious beginning, but Marcos still held out hope that maybe they could forge a partnership, even after all this time had passed.

He just had to stop himself from saying the wrong thing and angering Evander—*he is Rhys*, Marcos reminded himself—even more.

So far, he had not managed even that.

Rhys stopped when the sun reached its zenith in the sky, finding a shady grouping of trees, with a large fallen log they could rest next to.

"Is this sufficient?" There was still a bite to Rhys' words.

"Perfectly sufficient," Marcos said, taking care to make sure there was no additional inflection to his words that would anger Rhys further. He certainly was not going to be stupid enough to remind the ex-Guardian that he did not need to rest at all.

Rhys settled down against the log. He looked tired. Perhaps if he changed forms, back to Evander, he might find additional strength. Maintaining a different form could be a strain on his power reserves.

Marcos would have suggested it but the silence that had fallen between them, and Rhys' defensiveness every time he made even the simplest suggestion, kept him quiet.

He waited until Rhys closed his eyes, and then shut his own, sure that Rhys, who was obviously exhausted, would fall asleep quickly.

But a moment later, Rhys spoke up. "You did not mean to reveal yourself to me."

Marcos had never been as accomplished a liar as Evander had been. He'd never needed to be. Fighting was often straightforward, with little need for deception, and he'd never gotten into the practice of telling falsehoods well.

He *could* lie, but it was unlikely Rhys would believe him, and the chances of Rhys being even angrier at the lie were considerable.

"No," he said carefully. "No, I did not mean to reveal myself."

Rhys looked like Rhys, and not anything like Evander, not like . . . not like the Guardian he'd known for so many years . . . but Marcos' heart beat faster anyway when he opened his eyes and Rhys was staring at him—like he was trying to figure Marcos out, still.

It was disconcerting, seeing Evander's stare come out of another man's face, and his personality and his unique intonation come out of another man's mouth using another man's voice. Marcos wasn't used to it yet, not even after a few hundred years, and he wasn't sure he'd ever truly adjust.

"If you were sent by the Guardians, why bother keeping it a secret?"

"I told you before, I was not sent by Deimos *or* the other Guardians."

"You just *chose* to leave the Castle at the Top of the World, *chose* to leave the Enclave of Guardians?" Rhys asked archly. "I find it very difficult to believe that Deimos would just let you go."

"Perhaps Deimos banished me as well." It was not a very good lie even for him, but he told it anyway.

Marcos could *feel* the scorching look Rhys shot him. "You forget, I was the Guardian of Secrets," he said. "I can tell when you're lying. Even now, because you're not very good at it."

"Never have been." Marcos rolled onto his back and stared at the slivers of blue sky he could see through the overarching branches of the trees.

"The more you persist in lying, and lying *poorly*, the more suspicious you are," Rhys said. "And the less I trust you."

"You said you didn't trust me to begin with," Marcos said.

"And yet, somehow I trust you even less now," Rhys said sarcastically. "At least tell me who sent you? Was it Deimos? Was it . . ." Marcos heard Rhys' voice catch and he willed away the bitter resentment that flared at the hesitation. "Was it Vanya?"

"I told you before and that was *not* a lie; I sent myself."

Rhys made a scoffing noise at that particular revelation, which made Marcos very glad that he had told *some* of the truth, but not the entire truth. Maybe he couldn't lie, at least not effectively, but he didn't have to tell Rhys everything.

"Out of guilt?" Rhys demanded.

"No, not out of guilt." Marcos hesitated. "Though I did feel some shame, but not because I betrayed you to Deimos, because I did not. It felt dishonorable that you paid for both of our mistakes."

"And so you left the comfortable, luxurious environs of the Castle, and came here, to . . . what? Watch me? Assist me?"

"You know very well you never needed any assistance," Marcos responded gravely.

"And how do I know that?" Rhys' voice was harsh. "Maybe you're the one who was responsible, in the end."

"You know that is not true," Marcos retorted. "I was part of the Mecant tribe during much of your final struggle against the last sorceress. What could I have possibly done to assist?"

Rhys didn't say anything for a long time, and Marcos had hoped that he'd actually fallen asleep, but then he spoke up again.

"Why the Mecant? And how long were you with them? A considerable time, I'd suspect."

Marcos risked a look over at him. "How do you know that?"

"You were comfortable. At least a generation or two, I'd guess. Maybe more."

"Three," Marcos said. "They suited me."

"I did wonder how we were discovered by them, as deep in the woods as we were."

"As if that has ever mattered to the Mecant," Marcos said. "Which is why I liked them. The quiet. As for why, the Mecant traveled considerably, and I heard much of what was happening in both Ardglass and Fontaine."

"But you want me to believe you didn't interfere," Rhys scoffed.

"Did I interfere when Rory and Gray were captured by the Mecant?" Marcos asked archly.

"According to them, they saved themselves."

"Am I supposed to believe you weren't watching the entire time?"

Rhys sighed. "I was, and they did save themselves. But you certainly did not assist, though you should have, because you couldn't have possibly known that Rory would know the key to the old kind of negotiation. Almost nobody does anymore. The Mecant are a very old tribe, nearly as ancient as we are, and even they have lost some of their traditions."

"I had faith that Prince Emory was intelligent, and Prince Graham was resourceful."

"Faith," Rhys scoffed.

"You know there is a very thin line between faith and the rhythm of the universe, how events occur as they're supposed to. You used to be able to feel it."

It was why he didn't regret touching Rhys, even if it had revealed his true identity before he'd intended to. He'd known the moment that it happened that it was *right*, because the universe had sung to him that it was.

Rhys stared at him, naked frustration and annoyance plain in his expression.

Shit. He had fucked up again, reminding Rhys of another power that he no longer possessed.

"I . . . I'm sorry." The words weren't much. Marcos had never been particularly good with them. He'd always been better with his fists—or with a blade.

Rhys sighed, and rolled over. "Go to sleep, Marcos."

But Marcos didn't, even as Rhys' soft snores finally echoed through the little valley they'd settled in.

He didn't need the rest the way that Rhys did. He could go much further, on much less sleep, with little food or water and still barely deplete his magical reservoir. But traveling with Rhys was going to be more difficult. He'd need regular sleep and food as well as clean drinking water. And the weather as they headed north? That was going to be an even bigger issue. Rhys was going to need warmer clothes, much warmer than what he was wearing, which was a light cloak, over plain shirt and pants, and a worn pair of boots.

Unassuming clothes for the advisor to the Kings of Fontaine, but especially unassuming for a Guardian.

Of course, Rhys had developed this particular character when he'd been in Ardglass, at the fortress of Tullamore, when he'd been Graham's tutor for most of his childhood.

Unassuming attire was the Ardglassian way, but surely he could have . . . spruced himself up a bit when he'd come to Beaulieu? But he hadn't, and Marcos, coming face-to-face with him for the first time as Merleen, had been shocked into near speechlessness.

It hadn't just been Rhys' thick, gruff brogue of a voice. It had been everything else, too. Rhys had been the antithesis of Evander, who'd been shorter and slender, and a graceful work of art with his loose blond waves and sea glass eyes.

Eyes that cut through everyone and everything—except that he'd miraculously never figured out Marcos' most closely held secret.

Marcos had known, even a thousand years ago, that Evander's attractions were far more than his appearance, but this proved it.

He was just as inexplicably attracted to Rhys as he had been to Evander.

But that wasn't important. What was important now was finding a decent village, where Marcos could earn some coin so they'd be properly stocked and outfitted for this journey.

Rhys might want to travel light, but Marcos wasn't willing to risk his health or his safety.

He hadn't been looking after it for hundreds of years to fail now.

Rhys woke up a few hours later, and from the disgruntled expression on his face as soon as he spotted Marcos, it was obvious he was still upset that he wasn't making this journey alone.

They didn't speak as Rhys drank more water and he pulled some dried meat out of his traveling sack as they stood back up.

Marcos stretched, strapped his sword onto his back, and headed to the stream to splash some water on his face.

He hadn't slept, but just the cool water hitting his skin refreshed him enough. He would make sure they stopped at the next village.

"Ready to go?" Rhys asked in clipped tones, nothing like the semi-hushed questions of the night before. Marcos wasn't disappointed or really all that surprised. He'd known it would take a long time to win Rhys over, once he discovered who Merleen really was.

Perhaps he'd never feel the same way about him that Marcos had always felt about Evander, but what he hoped for most was that they could be partners.

"Yes," Marcos said briefly.

They set off towards the north, following the main road, but keeping a good ways off it.

They walked in silence as they had the day before, for many hours, but as dusk was beginning to fall, Marcos began to see more people on the road, and when Rhys stopped abruptly, with a crossroads in sight, he was not surprised.

Rhys had been very clear that he was in charge of this journey, but Marcos also had no intention of letting him make stupid decisions.

"There's a village up ahead," Rhys said.

"Yes," Marcos agreed. "A larger one." That was an even better situation, as many people would be coming and going, and they could easily vanish into the crowd. With a smaller village, they would stand out, even in their humble attire.

He watched as Rhys considered the situation and all the potential benefits as well as the potential pitfalls.

"We should go around it," he finally said. "I have a little more dried meat, and as established, all you probably need for another few days is fresh water."

"What we *should* do is spend a few days, and gather the supplies we will need for the journey. Furs and proper coats and boots. The right kind of food and water for an undertaking like this. And horses to carry it."

Rhys shot him a bland look. "I see you don't enjoy walking. I'm not particularly surprised by this revelation."

"It's not enjoyment, it's *logic*," Marcos said with exasperation. "We will need supplies to make it all the way up the North Mountain, and horses can carry a lot more than we can. I didn't suggest we buy horses to ride, though I admit some confusion about your disdain for them."

"Why?" Rhys challenged. "Because on occasion I will take the form of one?"

Marcos barely held back an eye roll. "Yes, exactly."

"I knew you had caught me a week or so back," Rhys grumbled. "You were not particularly subtle about it, and I wondered if you had power, because you were so clearly drawn to mine."

Marcos wondered how, for a Guardian so fiercely intelligent, he could also be so utterly blind.

You want him to be utterly blind, Marcos reminded himself. *You've always wanted him to be blind to you.*

"If you're asking if I could sense you changing forms, the answer is *yes*, and also *yes*, you're changing the subject."

"I don't like them," Rhys finally confessed. "Horses. I was in the form of a unicorn for many hundreds of years, and I often disguised myself as a horse."

"Well, we don't need you to be a unicorn, so no need to further confuse your appearance," Marcos retorted.

That had never made sense to him, during all the hundreds of years he'd kept an eye on Evander-turned-Evrard. Why choose a form that required additional camouflage and an additional power drain?

If Rhys was not already so prickly, Marcos might have asked him why he'd done it.

But he wanted him to give in, gracefully or not, about the supplies, so he wasn't going to push Rhys on any other subject.

"I'm only surprised that you didn't decide that I needed to be a horse to carry all the supplies," Rhys grumbled.

It had never occurred to Marcos, likely because he would never have suggested a Guardian be used to merely *haul* something.

They were ancient magical beings, created to protect. Not to haul waterskins and dried meat and extra blankets.

Rhys sighed, no doubt at the shock on Marcos' face. "I have done far worse," he said. "The end justifies the means, but I would rather not do it again."

"I believe we can find the coin for a horse or two," Marcos said slowly. "My skills are usually in high demand in villages like this."

Rhys eyed him suspiciously. "High demand for *what* exactly?"

Marcos supposed he should be embarrassed by this. "There is always someone or something who needs to be . . . evicted, shall we say, or controlled, or dealt with," he said, "and as it happens, I am well-suited to those particular tasks."

"Evicted? You're hired to remove people from their homes?" Rhys sounded shocked.

"Bad men, sometimes. Thieves or robbers or murderers. Or men who would hit their partners or their children. And occasionally, they will have me hunt for a wild animal in the forest who continually preys on the village."

Rhys shot him a look. "You're a regular hero, Marcos. How much coin do you take for such work?"

"As much as they can give me. It's . . . well, it's not *honest* work, but do you see many generals who are needed? Much battle strategy? Any gladiator battles to be fought? No? Then I take what I can find."

"How do you find it?"

Marcos grinned. "That is the easy part."

"Why do I think I will not like this very much?" Rhys asked with a resigned sigh.

There were two local pubs, both with accommodations on the second floor, but one looked quite a bit rougher than the other, and Marcos could *feel* Rhys' annoyance emanating from him as he selected the worse of the two.

"Really?" Rhys hissed under his breath as Marcos pushed open the door.

Above it hung a worn sign that read, *The Ass & Bee.*

"Always better to take the rougher place," Marcos said under his breath. "There's more money here."

Rhys looked around at the plain, shabby interior of the big common room. There was a large fireplace at one end, with a few logs in it, flickering lazily, and roughhewn tables, filled with what looked to be crude and dirty men, all drinking out of ugly carved wooden tankards.

"Somehow, that does not seem to be true," Rhys said disdainfully. "Money . . . *here*?"

"Trust me," Marcos said, and then remembered too late that Rhys did not.

Rhys clearly remembered though, because he shot him a look that spoke volumes about just how much he didn't trust Marcos, and that this scenario was certainly not helping the situation improve any.

But Marcos couldn't help that. He'd done this enough times to know that at the nicer establishments, nobody was ever willing to open their purses. The way he looked almost always scared them off.

Here? All these men would rather face his sharpest blade than admit he intimidated them.

"Just . . . sit, and keep your head down," Marcos suggested, waving to a table close to the fire.

"What are you going to do?" Rhys sounded skeptical. "Whip your knives out, and start polishing them?"

Marcos laughed, before he could help himself. He noticed at least half a dozen heads swivel his direction. No, he would have to do no knife polishing tonight.

"Something like that," he said. "Go sit down." He gave Rhys an encouraging push on the back, and then when he finally saw him sit, he turned towards the bar.

It ran the length of the room, and it was just as roughly carved as the tables and benches, stained with grease and mead and what could've even been blood.

Rhys might be disgusted by a place like this, but truthfully, it felt like home to Marcos. He didn't need to pretend or smile or even talk. He just needed to grunt and, when the opportunity presented itself, demonstrate his skill.

A man, in a dirty white flowing shirt topped with a grungy brown vest, patched in two places, gave Marcos a look as he approached the bar.

"Two meads, cheapest kind you got," Marcos muttered, "and a plate of whatever you have to eat."

The man eyed Marcos suspiciously. "You got coin?"

He had the miniscule amount he'd owned as Merleen, but it would be enough to feed and lodge them for at least a few days, at least until he got more.

Digging into the pocket of his tunic, Marcos set the worn cloth bag on the bar. "Yep," he said laconically.

The suspicion in the man's eyes did not dim.

Marcos supposed if you owned a place like this, you kept it by being continually paranoid of everything and everyone.

"Who you with?" the man asked as he turned towards the keg set back, behind the bar. "That mousy-looking man over by the fire?" He gestured towards where Rhys sat, disdain written plainly across his features.

Marcos wouldn't have called him mousy. Unassuming, yes. But as soon as that big brain and big mouth ended up on the same page, the *real* man underneath the trappings roared to life, and Marcos had spent too many years trying to resist the irresistible pull of *that* man.

"He's an associate of mine," Marcos said.

"Associate in what?" the owner of the pub wondered.

See, Marcos thought, *no knife polishing necessary.*

"A little bit of this, a little bit of that. Whatever people need, in exchange for coin."

The man set the two tankards down, mead slopping over the side of one of them and wetting the bar. "You look like you'd be handy," he said, his dark, shuttered eyes taking in every inch of Marcos' size and musculature.

"If you hear of anyone needing a hand, we'll be staying a few days."

The man gave Marcos a sharp nod as he counted out a few silver coins from his purse. "Need a room?"

"Yes."

"I'll send the girl over with the food and your room will be top of the stairs, second from the left," he said tersely.

Marcos picked up the tankards, and left the bar with only a brief nod.

He'd done his work for the night.

Rhys was frowning as Marcos sat down and pushed one tankard in front of him.

"We have a room," Marcos said, "and we should have plenty of coin in a few days."

Rhys shot him an unimpressed look. It shouldn't have fired his blood, but it did.

"And how," he asked, delicately picking up the roughhewn tankard and taking an experimental sip, "did you manage that so quickly?" He made a face at the taste of the mead.

It was watered down, Marcos discovered as he drank his own, but it wasn't a *terrible* flavor. Of course, Rhys was used to living at court, both at Beaulieu and before that at Tullamore. Even though the Ardglassians were less particular than the Fontainians, Tullamore had still been a ruling seat of power with all its inherent luxuries.

Of course, the valley and its farm buildings, where he'd stayed with Gray, had not been particularly well-appointed, but as far as Marcos knew, Rhys had always been Evrard then, and even a unicorn couldn't be *that* particular, when all he'd needed was a warm stable and some sweet hay to chew.

"It was not difficult," Marcos said ruefully. "A few of the right kind of grunts, and he understood my meaning."

Rhys did not look convinced. "It would have been just as easy to meet some rich merchant on the road and take what we wanted."

"You have become unscrupulous during your time here," Marcos teased. "Robbing merchants on the road!"

"Like you aren't going to do much of the same thing now," Rhys grumbled. "I doubt anyone is going to hire you for particularly scrupulous reasons."

"No, but they are going to pay me for a service, which I intend to render," Marcos said.

"Apparently so long has passed that I forgot entirely about your obsession with honor," Rhys said wryly.

Marcos finished his tankard of mead. It was not particularly good, but it was wet and he was thirsty, and he'd long since learned during his time here to take what he was given and not complain.

"War should be honorable," Marcos said quietly. "Anything less, and it is merely cruel chaos."

"Yes, well, there is no honor in secrets," Rhys retorted evenly. "So you understand my complete lack of familiarity with the topic."

Marcos wanted to argue with him. He'd seen the toll that Evander's Guardianship had taken on him, during all the time they'd sat on the Conclave together, and he'd also known, for a thousand years and more, that Evander was wrong.

A Guardian without honor would never have risked everything to protect the people here. And even after the worst possible scenario had come to pass, he'd still devoted his entire life to making it right. To doing the honorable thing.

Even with his diminished power, he could have easily usurped any kingdom, or created his own. But he hadn't.

However, that was the thing about Evander—about Rhys, about Evrard—he never liked listening to another opinion besides his own.

So Marcos stayed quiet on the subject, and did not argue.

Instead, he asked, "During your years, was that how you earned your keep? Stealing from rich merchants on the roads?"

Rhys' look was chiding. "You were following me for many of those years, weren't you? Keeping an eye on me? You should know the answer to that question."

"I was not *keeping an eye* on you," Marcos said, even though that was not very far from the truth. "There were many years when I kept to myself, with the Mecant, or in other places, and I did not know where you were or what you were doing."

He was never going to be good at lying, but this was close enough to the truth that Marcos hoped it would pass muster.

"No," Rhys said decisively. "No, I was not *stealing*. I did not need to."

"Of course not. You created yourself an influential and important personage, who wouldn't need to whack rich merchants over the head to steal their purses."

Rhys glared at him.

"Just an observation," Marcos said lightly. "In any case, we do not need to resort to it now, as I believe that tonight we will see a development that will make going to such lengths unnecessary."

"What is it?"

But instead of answering, Marcos stood. "I will fetch more mead. Would you like another?"

Rhys stared sulkily at his half-full tankard. He was clearly unhappy that Marcos would not divulge all his secrets so easily. "No."

When he returned, the food had arrived, and Rhys was picking at it with a frown on his face.

"How long will we be here?" Rhys asked. "The food is . . . distasteful at best."

"Not up to your regular standards?" Marcos asked. "And to answer your question, we will be here as long as it takes."

CHAPTER FOUR

RHYS WAS IN AN exceedingly bad temper.

First, Marcos had been incredibly high-handed, demanding that they postpone their journey for at least a few days, in order to be "properly" outfitted with supplies.

Rhys had brought a handful of coins with him, enough for some periodic lodging and food along the journey, but based on the standards Marcos was insisting on, it wouldn't be nearly enough.

And now, they had come to this dirty, ugly tavern, with its watered-down mead and slop for food. As for the lodgings, they were hardly an improvement. The bed was small and narrow, the mattress filled with lumpy straw that Rhys did not want to question the origin of. And to make things worse, there was only *one* of these uncomfortable beds.

Marcos insisted that he take it. "I will be keeping watch," Marcos said, sliding a rough piece of wood across the door. "You can take the bed."

And *now*, the very worst part of this entire situation was that Rhys was required to be grateful that Marcos had been so generous.

Rhys did not want to be grateful.

He wanted to be angry—but it was difficult to be angry with someone who offered you the only bed in the room, no matter how poor it was.

Rhys shifted to the other side of the mattress, trying to find an area without lumps, but was unsuccessful. He sighed, not even bothering to temper his frustration.

"Trouble sleeping?" Marcos asked kindly.

Even in the dark gloom, Rhys could see where he had settled—opposite the doorway, back against the rugged plank walls of the room, booted feet drawn up to his chest. Rhys could even see the wry expression on his face.

He'd always enjoyed his ability to see in the dark, always considered it one of his favorite gifts, but now he wished he could do it a little less well.

"The bed is lumpy," he said, aware of how ungrateful he sounded. He could very easily be on the floor. Marcos was still, as far as Rhys knew, a full-fledged Guardian. He could have overpowered Rhys in an instant, with merely a crook of his fingers, never mind all those very impressive muscles.

But he hadn't.

Rhys still had not figured out what ulterior motive Marcos had for accompanying him, and that annoyed him most of all.

"You could always transform. The hay might suit you better if you were of an equine descent," Marcos teased.

Up until now, Rhys was unaware that Marcos *teased*. This was new. But then, even though they had served on the Conclave together for hundreds and hundreds of years, he had never really *known* Marcos. He'd kept to himself, more at home on a battlefield or in the armory than he was the Castle at the Top of the World.

"I certainly will not," Rhys said firmly. "I will . . . adjust."

He'd slept in far worse. Admittedly, not in some time. He'd gotten spoiled and lax. But at the very beginning, when he'd first been banished to the surface, there had been some lean, cruel years.

"Then I suggest you do," Marcos said. "We have a long journey ahead, and there will be little time for resting after we leave here."

Rhys turned over, plumping the straw underneath him, and attempted to banish the questions that kept swirling through him. Particularly all the questions he had about Marcos.

He'd just managed to lull himself into a relaxed state that at least approximated sleep when he heard a rustling outside the front door.

Not a rustling. A *scratching*.

"Is that . . . is that a mouse? A rat?" Rhys hated how wobbly his voice sounded. He'd *been* both a mouse and a rat. Of course, not very frequently, and only out of extreme necessity.

But that didn't mean he wanted to share his bed with either.

"No," Marcos said shortly. "Be quiet. Stay in the bed."

Rhys took that to mean that whatever happened, he was being told not to interfere.

The scratching intensified.

And then suddenly it was not just scratching, but a screeching sawing, the dissonance of the sound breaking through the silence of the inn, and in the dark, Rhys watched as Marcos sprang to his feet so quickly that one moment he was still seated, muscles poised to act, and then he was standing, and bracing himself as several men busted through the door.

They were all of the same big build and wore the same home-spun, dirty attire as the men downstairs, except these men held various weapons clutched in their hands. There was a knife, long and definitely sharp, glinting in the dim light pooling from the hallway, and a pickaxe, a fist clenched around a rough wooden handle, and finally, the tool that Rhys recognized that had made that horrible screeching noise.

It was a saw blade, sharp as anything, and notched, each tooth dangerous, and Rhys realized the man must have stuck it through the gap between the door and the doorframe, and used it to partially cut through Marcos' makeshift lock, until they'd been able to break it entirely with their strength and bust through the door.

He had only a second to take this in, take in *them*, before Marcos was moving towards them in a whirlwind of action. He dodged the pickaxe's blow, with a quick duck of the head, and then jabbed a sharp elbow into the knife wielder's stomach, forcing him to lose grip on the weapon.

Rhys nearly yelled, because the other man, the third, with the saw blade, as sharp and deadly as anything Rhys had ever seen, was on Marcos an instant later.

But Marcos must have anticipated his attack, because instead of disengaging, he charged, pummeling the man's midsection with a series of hard blows, then smashing his jaw with his fist, sending him flying.

The third dismissed, Marcos began to turn back, but even a fighter as skilled and talented and *gifted* as Marcos could not handle three adept fighters at once without a single weapon, and Rhys saw, through the darkness, what was about to happen.

The pickaxe hovered, for a single spit second, behind Marcos' back, where the man was about to drive the pointed end into his back, incapacitating him.

The man didn't know that Marcos was immortal and therefore impossible to kill, but Rhys knew he could be hurt. And while they might have time to stop here to gather supplies, they did not have time to wait around for Marcos to recover from his injuries.

Rhys had but a split second to decide.

Even though it was never a question of which action he would take.

He rose from the bed, hand outstretched, and called the power, feeling it as it surged through him, from the ends of his toes, through his midsection in a thrilling rush, to the tips of his fingers, and then, finally, at the last possible second the flame shot out of his palm.

It was nothing compared to what he'd wielded as a Guardian. When he'd been at full strength, he'd shot fireballs from his pinky finger. But this shot of magical flame, while not quite intense enough to touch the man attacking Marcos, was still enough to make him duck with a sudden yelp of surprise. Marcos' head swiveled and he turned, bringing the weight of his full strength down on the crown of the man's head, sending him crumpling to the floor.

Rhys had been in battles before. He'd fought, though not frequently because he far preferred addressing an enemy by subterfuge and not direct confrontation. But the blood rush after a battle was not new to him.

Still, it *felt* new, when Marcos turned his dark, intense stare onto him.

"What," Marcos asked, his breath short and the tiniest bit labored, "happened to staying on the bed?"

Rhys looked down at his palm, still smoking, and fought a sudden, inexplicable urge to burst into hysterical laughter. "I did not leave the bed?"

Marcos grinned then, and he couldn't help himself any longer. He threw back his head and laughed. "I even stayed quiet," Rhys crowed.

"Yes, but you nearly roasted someone who came to hire me," Marcos said, still clearly amused by the turn of events.

"What?" Rhys exclaimed. "Those men . . . they were here to rob us!"

"No, they weren't," Marcos said, crossing to the bed, and kicking one of them, who rolled over, groaning in the process. "That was the only reason why the fight even lasted as long as it did. I did not want to kill them all outright. If that was the outcome I'd desired, they'd have been dead a minute ago, without any interference from you."

"They were testing you," Rhys said slowly. He might not be as powerful as he'd once been, and he'd never been a brilliant fighter, not like Marcos, but he still possessed considerable intelligence. "They broke in to see if you were skilled enough to hire."

"It was a test," Marcos agreed, inclining his head in Rhys' direction. "I did not realize you still possessed that much magic."

"It's not much, and it is not particularly useful, as it drains me for days after, but you said that we will be resting here at least that long . . ."

Marcos grinned again, bright as the sun in the dark. "You exerted that much power, because you believed you could save me?"

"I knew he could not kill you, because the chance of them taking your head was zero, I was just trying to avoid nursing you," Rhys muttered, trying to make the action sound far more logical than it had actually been. In truth, it had been rash and foolish. A child's move.

He'd believed himself long since cured of the notion of being a hero.

The man underneath Marcos' feet groaned again, and Marcos bent down. "You feeling good enough to take us to your boss?"

"Us?" the man questioned. "He didn't say anything about *us*, only you."

"Where my friend goes, I go," Marcos said, his tone brokering no arguments. Rhys nearly made an argument for him, that he had no intention of endangering himself more than he needed to. But he knew better than to question Marcos' authority in front of these brigands.

If they were smart and they realized he and Marcos were not truly aligned, they'd do whatever they could to drive a wedge between them, to create even more problems. Not that Rhys truly believed that they *were* smart enough, since that was a move *he* would've made. But still, it was smart to be cautious.

"We weren't supposed to bring the other one," one of the other men argued. "He won't like it."

"I am sure *he* refers to your superior," Rhys inserted smoothly. "Let me promise you, while my associate here might be the brawn of the operation, I am the brains. Your leader will not be disappointed."

Marcos shot him a glare, but the man underneath him nodded slowly. Reluctantly.

"Fine," he said, "we will take you both."

If Rhys had realized that accompanying Marcos would mean having a dirty bag made of rags thrown over his head, and then literally being *tossed* into the back of a rank-smelling wagon that had clearly not been cleaned in some time, then Rhys would not have been so eager to present a united front.

"You owe me," Rhys hissed under his breath at what he believed was the Marcos-sized lump next to him as the wagon jolted and jarred them, moving across what seemed to be a very poor road.

"*I* owe *you?*" the lump responded incredulously.

"You owe me," Rhys said firmly.

"The only reason I am going to all this trouble," the lump retorted, "is to keep you from being malnourished and your toes and fingers from freezing off. I certainly would not go to any of this trouble for *me*."

It was unbelievably annoying, how superior Marcos could be, when he was supposed to be—when Rhys had *declared* him to be—merely the muscle of the operation. Rhys had permitted his inclusion because he'd had no real choice in the matter, but also because surely having a Guardian of untold power and skill along could only assist whatever difficulties Rhys discovered while heading north.

Marcos was *not* here to take care of Rhys.

The very idea was insulting.

Rhys harrumphed, loudly, to ensure that Marcos heard his displeasure. Not that he had any reason to suspect otherwise.

Next to him, he felt the Marcos-shaped lump tense, and Rhys braced himself for another annoying lecture, when the wagon stopped abruptly, throwing them against the wood barrier separating the front from the back.

"*Oomph,*" Rhys grumbled.

"Are you alright?" Marcos asked after a second had passed.

Apparently he could not help himself.

"I'm perfectly alright," Rhys said, grinding his teeth. "It was just a very sudden stop."

"No, it wasn't," Marcos said, and Rhys could nearly hear the amusement in his tone again. "I could tell it was coming. And you would have been able to tell too, if you'd been paying attention to the movement of the wagon, and not arguing with me."

Rhys decided that did not deserve a response, so he merely lay there and let the men with the questionable sanitary history unload him from the back of the wagon. First him, and then Marcos. He noticed it took only two men to dispatch him, but they used all four for Marcos.

They were cautious, then. Perhaps not brilliantly intelligent, but with some idea, at least, that Marcos was powerful and worth keeping an eye on.

They led them through what had to be a clearing—Rhys could feel the tall grass brush against his trousers—and then into the mouth of a cave. It was dank smelling, and cold, and he barely held himself back from shivering as they walked deeper and then deeper still into the cave.

Finally, they came to a stop, and their hoods were removed.

Rhys blinked slowly. There was a man sitting on a dais in front of them, made crudely out of what looked to be old broken-up shipping crates. His eyes were dark blue, and he would have been handsome, except for the dirt all over his face, and the even dirtier hair, hanging in lank waves across his features. The clothing he wore was just as rough as his men's. But the thing that most surprised Rhys was that he was big, perhaps even as big as Marcos, though it was hard to tell while he was still sitting.

The sitting was the most extraordinary part, because the chair was no ordinary chair, scavenged or even *bought.* It had clearly been made, or much more likely, stolen.

It was of dark, smooth carved wood, with engraved symbols and decorative flourishes picked out in gold leaf. The back was especially impressive—the spire of each side of the chair back was topped with a gold finial.

Rhys was fairly certain that what he was staring at was a throne, lifted from perhaps one of the old kingdoms to the north.

Or perhaps, he thought, wishing he could get a closer look at some of the engravings, one of the old chairs from Ardglass, that had once sat in the council chamber of the thirteen clans.

His memory was not as clear as it should have been, but if he could get nearer . . .

He found himself pulled abruptly back by his collar.

"What do you think you're doing?" one of the men snarled.

Sorry, Rhys nearly said, *I just thought I might have remembered your leader's chair, from back three hundred years ago, when the clans of Ardglass used to meet.*

But he couldn't, because this group was already suspicious enough.

"I was just looking at your leader's magnificent . . ." Rhys hesitated. He wanted to say *throne,* because that's what it was. Even if this man only ruled the local gang, he certainly aspired to more. But he settled for . . . "Chair. His chair."

"It's very fine, is it not?" The man rose from it, and yes, as Rhys had wondered, he was nearly as tall as Marcos.

Maybe once he'd been as muscular as Marcos, but he clearly spent too much time in the chair—the *throne*—now, and also too much time drinking terrible mead at the pub, because he'd started to grow fat.

There was still an imposing charisma to him, and Rhys mentally warned himself to be careful.

"Very fine," Rhys agreed. "Is it from Ardglass?"

The man's gaze narrowed. Marcos coughed under his breath next to him, clearly not pleased that Rhys had derailed the conversation.

"Are *you* from Ardglass?" the leader asked in a hard voice.

"Oh, no, *no,*" Rhys said. Even though he could still hear some of the remnants of the accent he had picked up during all those years at Tullamore.

"I told you," one of the underlings argued, "he's not from anywhere 'round here, at all. He made *fire* with just his hand."

The leader's eyes widened.

Oh, *damn.*

Marcos muttered under his breath again.

"A . . . momentary lapse," Rhys said, shooting the leader his most charming smile.

"You can't do it again?"

"Not right away," Rhys answered honestly, hoping that would be the end of the conversation—but knowing that it wouldn't be.

The leader turned to Marcos. "You know he could do that?"

Marcos gave a short, succinct nod. And then added, "I can do far more than that."

All true, Rhys thought ruefully.

"What?" The leader was smiling belligerently now as he stalked back and forth in front of them. "You can shoot fire out of your cock?"

Rhys barely held in his chortle of laughter.

"No," Marcos said, in a tone that Rhys remembered all too well from before, when he was barely holding in his temper. "I can fight anyone you need. In any number."

The leader rested back on his heels. "Have a high and mighty opinion of yourself, don't you?"

"Yes," Marcos said unapologetically.

"Barely bested my three men," the leader said. "You needed your friend to shoot some fire at one of them."

"No, I didn't." Marcos hesitated. "He just likes to show off."

Rhys didn't know whether he should be pissed off at how obnoxious that accusation was, or how obnoxious it was that Marcos had figured him out so easily.

The leader was silent a moment, thinking to himself. Finally he said, "We need a man to attack a convoy traveling through the village in a day's time."

"I can do it," Marcos said confidently, even though he did not know *any* of the particulars.

Egotistical maniac, Rhys complained to himself. *Even if it's likely true, he could at least pretend that it might be difficult.*

"You are very sure."

"I am very good," Marcos retorted.

When the leader finished reciting the particulars, Rhys nearly laughed out loud again.

They were . . . robbing a merchant. On the road.

And only getting a miniscule percentage of the final take.

If they'd been alone, he'd have reminded Marcos that *all* the final take could have been theirs.

Instead they were giving most of it to this huge pompous ass, who felt like he needed to sit on a *throne* to bolster his ego.

Rhys was not impressed.

When they were *finally* alone, grabbed again and taken to a deeper cave fitted with a makeshift set of bars Rhys supposed were intended to stop them from escaping and warning the intended target, he said as much to Marcos.

"Quiet," Marcos said, "this is a cave, our voices carry."

"I know that," Rhys retorted. "What I am trying to say is that we could have performed this theft ourselves, with *no* help from the locals, and none of it would be going to these people."

"We don't need all of it," Marcos reasoned. "We only need some of it."

Rhys rolled his eyes. "You are painful, sometimes."

"I hardly think you are one to talk. I am not the one who was banished from the Conclave."

That was a sore point, Rhys could admit it. It had been sore for a long time, and it was sore still. It was not exactly fair that Marcos had brought up his lowest point, but he supposed he could not really blame him. After all, Rhys had been needling him.

Justifiably, but then most people did not respond particularly well to Rhys' needling.

"So you are going to perform this theft for these men," Rhys said instead, changing the subject.

"Yes. It should be easy enough."

"The merchant is traveling with fifteen armed men," Rhys pointed out. He knew Marcos could do it, because no human could fight the way Marcos could. He was faster and stronger, and impossibly skilled.

Rhys had seen him turn the tide in battles just by being on one army's side.

"And they will be traveling through a culvert, and vulnerable to an attack from the sky," Marcos said, sounding like it was perfectly reasonable that he fly down and attack from up above.

"And no," Marcos added, a twist to his mouth almost giving Rhys a smile, "I will not be *flying*. I will be falling towards them. Or I suppose you could say *jumping*."

"A much further distance than most men could manage," Rhys sniffed.

"We have established that I am no man." Marcos walked over to the grate that penned them in, and tested it, jiggling one side and then the other, proving that just as Rhys had suspected, they were staying locked in because Marcos did not want to be free, not because these iron bars could actually keep him incapacitated.

"And what will they say when you perform as admirably as I know you can?" Rhys questioned.

"You saw the throne," Marcos said, shooting him a knowing look. "The leader has a mystical streak. Or he *wishes* he had a mystical streak. That chair came from Ardglass, it was one of the original thirteen."

"You think so too? I could not get close enough to verify."

Marcos smiled. "I was one of the original thirteen. It was the chair across from mine, in the council chamber. I would have recognized it anywhere."

"Of course you were," Rhys said. He was not surprised. The line of sorcerers had moved between Ardglass and Fontaine frequently over the years, and he'd always been near at hand. And to hear Marcos tell it, so had he.

For what reason, Rhys had yet to discover.

But he would. There was no doubt in his mind that he would eventually uncover Marcos' secret, because he'd never failed to do so before.

"Like I said, this man is mystical, or fascinated by the mystical. He will not detain us, even after I display my abilities. Instead, he will let the legend of his gang grow, after we are gone." Marcos sounded very sure.

Rhys was less sure, but what he *was* confident about was this crew's complete inability to hold them if they wished to go.

"Get some sleep, if you can," Marcos continued, gesturing to the straw-covered floor. "It's much worse than the mattress at the tavern, I'm sure, but it's better than nothing."

Rhys settled down, annoyed that he'd been abducted without even his big heavy cloak, because the ground was wet and cold. But Marcos was right about one thing, it was better than nothing.

"I suppose you want me to say I'm grateful," Rhys said a few moments after Marcos' eyes closed.

One of them opened again. "I do?"

"If you were taking advantage of the poor conditions to remind me that it will be an improvement to be better outfitted in our journey north, you are right. It *will* be an improvement."

Marcos smiled, but did not say anything.

The morning might have dawned clear and cool, or cloudy and humid.

It was impossible to say, since they were still locked up underground.

Rhys could smell the day dawning though, and he paced in their cell, waiting for the leader to come release them so Marcos could lay waste to this merchant's traveling caravan.

They had already wasted enough time on this ridiculous attempt to earn enough money to buy supplies.

"Where are they?" he demanded testily.

"Give them time, they'll be here." Marcos was still lying on the cold, hard ground, seemingly unbothered by either.

"I don't know how you can be so calm about this," Rhys complained testily. "We are *stuck* in here." Except they weren't. Not really. They were only still here because they wanted to be here.

Not *wanted* necessarily, Rhys conceded, but *needed* to be here.

"They need us," Marcos reminded him. "Or rather, *me*, though I think the leader is allowing you to accompany us, if only because he's hoping to see your fiery party trick."

"It's not a party trick," Rhys objected.

Except that was essentially what it amounted to now.

Marcos shot him a look. "Promise me you won't use it," he said. "You don't need to waste the energy, not when I intend to create some distance between this village and us by tonight."

"You *are* concerned, then," Rhys said.

"Not because of this gang," Marcos countered. "But we could be slowed down due to complications or interference, and I am ready to get on the road after this. We'll steal a horse and then buy the rest at the next village."

"You seem to have it all planned out." Rhys hated how sulky he sounded. What happened to *him* being in charge of this journey?

"Promise me," Marcos insisted.

Rhys nearly didn't. It was none of Marcos' business if he wanted to use what little power remained to him. But Marcos had also made a very strong, very logical point. They would need to exit the scene of the upcoming crime quickly. It would be best to be out of here before any additional suspicion fell.

He could still feel the drain on his body, on his energy, after the last use, and after the mostly sleepless night he'd just passed.

"I promise," Rhys said, finally relenting.

He'd just finished saying the words when a man approached the gate. "It's time," he said in a gruff tone.

Marcos was on his feet in a moment. If the man was surprised at how quickly he moved, he did not show it.

This time they were not covered in dirty hoods, but they followed the man out of the tunnels, through the room with the throne, and then out of the mouth of the cave. Rhys realized he had missed the fresh air as he took a long gulp of it.

They were directed back to the wagon, and seeing it wasn't an improvement over merely smelling it. Sharing it did not help, but Rhys kept his thoughts on the gang's hygiene to himself. Marcos did not need to fight all of them, *plus* the merchant's men.

The wagon traveled for ten minutes and then twenty, then Rhys lost count. It climbed up a hill, on a steep, rocky path, and then finally pulled off. The men jumped out, and Rhys followed, watching as they came to a stop right in front of a precipitous drop-off.

"This is the culvert the merchant's caravan will pass through," Marcos said pointing below. "I will jump down, assaulting them from above, and the rest will swarm in when I have established control of the situation."

"*After*?" Rhys questioned. "You don't want them to help you? Against fifteen armed men?"

Marcos merely shrugged with one shoulder, as he checked the straps of his hard leather armor.

"They will only be in the way," Marcos explained.

The armor he wore now was nothing like the armor he'd worn as a Guardian—perfectly fitted plates of silver and gold, gleaming and covered with symbols of power, intertwining and interlocking. Rhys had seen him arrive on a battlefield and men shield their eyes from the shimmering, shining vision of Marcos, a literal beacon of hope.

He was wearing the Mecant armor now, and like his original armor, it was embossed, but the leather was dark and worn, and many of the embellishments that had once been gold and copper and bronze, had faded away.

He pulled out his knife and, after checking the edge of the blade, shoved it back into the holster in his boot. Only then did he remove his sword to check it, unsheathing it with a screech of metal on metal, and Rhys was shocked to see that it was not a Mecant sword—but *his* sword. The Guardian of War's sword.

Rhys had only seen Marcos pull his sword a handful of times. He usually relied on his fists, and on the few knives he had secreted away on his person. One of them that he'd carried had been three hand spans long, and wickedly curved.

But the sword was a sight to behold.

Rhys heard several men around them gasp and utter oaths under their breath as Marcos pulled it from its sheath. Nearly five feet long, with a curved guard, and a simple silver grip, crossed with dark leather, it was the golden etching on the blade that was so mesmerizing, and how it seemed to magically morph, swirling and rippling down the long expanse of sharp steel.

"That's some sword," one of the men said, coming up to stand next to Marcos.

"A family heirloom," Marcos said shortly.

If Marcos was smaller or slightly less capable, Rhys imagined that one or more of them might try to appropriate it, no matter how long it had been in Marcos' family. But one look at the fierce expression on Marcos' face, and Rhys guessed none of them would be stupid enough to try.

The man asked a handful of other questions, but the look on Marcos' face made it clear that he wasn't interested in answering any of them.

Finally, he seemingly gave up, and returned to the other group, gathering a hundred feet away.

"Why the sword, but not the armor?" Rhys asked as Marcos slid the sword back into its sheath, strapped across his back.

"Do you remember that armor? It was not only ridiculous, it was like a beacon, way too bright, way too shiny, and also completely unmistakable."

"And the sword isn't any of those things? Not shiny? Not unmistakable?"

"It was also uncomfortable and heavy," Marcos added. "I didn't like fighting in it. No range of movement. Besides . . ." He hesitated. "A sword is personal. I've fought with this sword for thousands of years."

"Yet you never draw it."

"But I can. It's right here," Marcos said, patting the sheath, "where I can use it if I need it."

"You just never need it?" Rhys already knew the answer to that question, though. He'd seen Marcos fight enough times. He likely *didn't* need it.

Marcos just grinned. "Your memory must be shorter than I anticipated, Evander."

"That's not my name," Rhys answered automatically.

Marcos' gaze grew somber. Contemplative. A descriptor that Rhys had never imagined that he would use while describing the Guardian of War. He gave a short nod, and turned away.

It's not my name, not anymore, Rhys yelled to himself—but really to the Guardian who wouldn't talk to him.

You don't know who or what you are anymore, another voice, buried much deeper, reminded him.

CHAPTER FIVE

Men through the ages had called it many things.

Bloodlust.

Berserker rage.

Bloodthirstiness.

Marcos had experienced all of them, the siren's call through his body, through his blood, to fight and to destroy.

He felt it now, rising in him, an irresistible pull.

Marcos let it spiral higher, let it move through him, strip out all the distractions, all the other variables. His mind focused, narrowing in with a pinpoint accuracy, on the first two riders in the merchant's caravan, just about to enter the beginning of the open culvert.

He was gifted in many things, but his ability to time things perfectly was one he enjoyed the most. Withdrawing his favorite dagger—the long, curved one with the hilt that fit perfectly in his hand, the leather binding molded to his palm—he took one breath and then another. It was a balance: the blood coursing through him in a dizzying rush and the deadly calm that allowed his mind to make calculated decisions.

Waiting until just the right moment, he braced himself and then dropped down, right behind the first set of riders. Less than a second later, he had them on their backs, using the hilt of his dagger to knock them out.

Death was easy; it was a challenge for him to offer defeat without destruction, and after so many thousands of years of battle, it was that challenge he sought more than any other.

Marcos turned, clubbing the next rider in the throat with his arm, sending him falling, hitting his head on the hard, rocky turf.

A shout went up through the ranks of the caravan.

There were two more, now, on their feet and not on horseback, and as Marcos charged, they withdrew their own swords. Marcos' stayed in its sheath. He liked the challenge of only drawing his sword when absolutely necessary.

War was not a game, but over time, he'd learned to set these special trials for himself. It kept his skills sharp, but more importantly, it kept him in check.

Lashing out with a quick, well-positioned slash, he sliced one with his knife, right above the upper thigh, blood spurting, and without hesitating, turned to the other as the first dropped to his knees.

The second had had an extra moment to prepare for his attack, and he met Marcos' blow with one of equal force, his sword and Marcos' knife clashing together once and then twice.

The man's swordsmanship was skillful, and it took an extra parry for Marcos to find a way under his guard, slamming him with a shoulder into the ground.

It was that extra second that he paid for, because now the rest of the guards were massing.

Marcos had taken on this many men before, but they were also well-paid, and clearly had some skill, and as he advanced towards the next three guards, he realized he might have slightly miscalculated.

He had just enough time to pull the second knife, shorter but no less deadly, from his boot, before they were on him.

His movements were faster, quicker, more efficient, and he could think further ahead, even dueling three opponents, but defeating them still took more time than he'd envisioned.

He blocked a blow, and then another, flicking his knifes in and out in patterns so well-practiced and well-remembered they felt like part of his body. A jab with a sword made it through his defenses, and he lunged out of the way in the nick of time.

Whacking a man out of the way with a solid punch, he disarmed the second with a parry he'd invented for that purpose.

Leaving only the third, and a growing mass of men behind him.

He fully expected to hear the gang's cries behind him, as they charged into the battle, but he heard nothing, only his breathing and the thundering of his heart as he struck the back of the man who tried to pivot away from him.

Leaving only eight men remaining.

Four of them were arrayed around the coach that must be carrying the merchant and his gold, but the rest began to approach, moving carefully, deliberately.

They'd clearly marked him as a serious threat—even if there were far more of them.

It was time.

Even Marcos could not hope to defeat four men—and then another four—with two knives. He slid the shorter one into his boot and unsheathed his sword.

It sang as it rose from its sheath, as metal scraped metal, and he watched as the men in front of him hesitated just long enough.

He sidestepped the first, spinning around and whacking the second in the back, leaving him on his knees, and then began to drive the other three back with heavy blows, blows they could barely deflect.

The second fell to a jab that would need to be seen by a doctor. Hopefully the merchant would part with some of his remaining gold to take care of his men.

Marcos was not usually so sloppy, but the rest of the gang had still not materialized, and he was beginning to think that he had misjudged and they would not.

He was on his own.

The thought had just teased at his mind, as he attacked the third and fourth man, switching back between them with slashes and piercing blows, when he heard a noise behind him.

A heavy thud.

Someone had just landed on top of the coach from up above.

Finally, Marcos thought, as he dispatched the third, and then turned to the fourth, who was by far the biggest and most skilled of the group that he'd faced thus far.

They came together in a flurry of blows, swords clanging as they hit and then fell away.

Another man might have given up, after seeing Marcos defeat the rest of his comrades, but this one didn't shirk or blink, until all of a sudden, he took a step back, his jaw falling open.

Marcos risked a look behind him and nearly yelled.

Rhys—no *Evander*, was up on the roof, a flame shooting from his outstretched palm, and he was breathing hard, but he was holding it and he was clearly mustering his energy to firebomb the rest of the guards around the coach.

Marcos was so shocked to see the Evander of old that he nearly missed the penetrating thrust of the other man's sword, but he parried it just in time, pushing him away and down, and giving him a rap on the back of his head that he wouldn't soon forget.

He realized a second too late that he'd been hoping, deep down, to defeat the rest of the guards, before Evander marshaled the rest of his power, but he was too late.

A fireball flung out of his hand, and Marcos could sense just how strongly Evander had wrenched it out of himself, pushing it away with all his force. It flattened three of the remaining four guards, and with the shock written on the fourth's features, it was not that difficult for Marcos to stab him solidly through the shoulder.

His sword lowered, and he tore open the door, coming face-to-face with a whey-faced man, dressed in rich scarlet robes, hovering over a solid-looking lockbox.

"That," he said in clipped tones, "is mine."

When he emerged with it, setting it at his feet, he found that Evander had jumped down from the roof.

"What were you thinking?" he demanded as Evander walked towards him. "Where are the rest of the men?"

"They wouldn't join in, not when they saw you fight. They said you didn't need any help, not with how you moved." Evander's blue eyes—bright as cornflowers—followed his. "They didn't want to risk their lives, only yours."

He'd seen Evander in Rhys—it had been impossible not to. But coming face-to-face with the *real* Evander again, for the first time in so very long, was making him short of breath. At least Marcos was fairly certain it was the familiar specter of the Guardian in front of him, and not the battle.

Marcos raised an eyebrow. He was flattered and furious. Angry and awestruck. It had not been unusual for Evander to evoke such strong and parallel emotions in him, but he was unused to it, after so long without. He felt the rush of them now, right alongside the burn of the battle, and his fist clenched tighter around the pommel of his sword.

"And so you decided to come assist even though I had the situation well in hand?"

"You pulled your sword," Evander argued, the flawless curve of his jaw jutting out stubbornly.

"You *promised*," Marcos said, and suddenly, he found himself pushing Evander back against the side of the coach. Evander's hair glowed gold against the dark olive paint. The sight of it made him insane. It made him lightheaded. He wanted to make the men behind bleed, he wanted to make them all suffer, and he wanted to stroke Evander's hair, and find out finally if it was as soft as he'd always imagined.

He couldn't touch him, his hands were full, of his favorite knife, and his sword, but he could *look*, and Evander was looking back, that particular heat in his eyes that had always pulled Marcos towards him, inexorably.

He'd never *wanted* it. But he'd dreamed of it, anyway.

"I had to do it," Evander said quietly. "You know I had to do it."

"And this?" he said, his eyes raking up and down Evander's form. His dark coat, with its high collar, emphasizing the flawless pearl sheen of his pale skin. "You revealed yourself?"

Evander licked his lips. *That is not an invitation*, Marcos reminded himself. "You said the leader, that gang, was obsessed with mysticism. When they saw me change, when I became . . . *me*," he added bitterly, "they ran, terrified out of their wits by my magic. We will be but legends in a few months' time."

He had just said, before the battle, that he was no longer Evander.

He'd been *angry* that Marcos had referred to him by that name, even though that was who he was. Who he would always be, no matter how he ran, no matter how many forms he took.

He *was* Evander.

Seeing him like this only convinced Marcos more.

It was like seeing home, for the first time in a very long time.

"I had to, anyway," Evander said, sounding self-conscious. Like he too had just remembered that the last words he'd spoken to Marcos before the battle had been a denial of who he was. "I'm more powerful like this. Well, not as powerful as I was. But I will recover faster and I knew . . ." He trailed off.

"You knew I would be angry, because you promised."

Marcos knew it was the latest in a long line of bad decisions. At least questionable ones. But he leaned in, pressing his much larger body more firmly against Evander's much slighter one. Evander's head tilted up. In stubbornness, perhaps. Or so he would not lose the connection of their gaze?

Marcos did not know.

But he knew the question would haunt him.

"I had to," Evander said again.

"You said it yourself. I am immortal. These men could not kill me if they tried."

"I know," Evander retorted. "I *know*."

"You just did not want to play nurse, I'm aware," Marcos said dryly. What he should do was move away. Check the lockbox. Take two horses. Escape before the gang who hired them decided that a shapeshifter who could throw firebombs and a man who could defeat fifteen men were too valuable to lose.

Instead he was pinned down by Evander's eyes.

It was not the first time that had ever happened, and it would certainly not be the last, but unlike all those other occurrences, Evander was gazing up at him with surprise and wonder.

Like it was the first time he was truly *seeing* Marcos.

There'd been a moment, a mere echo of what he was feeling now, when Marcos had stood in Evander's chambers before he'd been cast out, and even though the bed had likely been still warm from Vanya's body, he'd *wanted* more than he'd ever thought possible.

And yet that moment paled in comparison to this one.

Evander's head tilted up another fraction, and Marcos' grip on his sword tightened. He knew better than to drop it, especially on a fresh field of battle, when threats could still lurk in the shadows, but the temptation was strong.

He'd been waiting for thousands of years to touch Evander, and now, finally, Marcos thought that possibly Evander *wanted* to be touched.

Evander opened his mouth, and he found himself anticipating and dreading what he was going to say.

But he was left wanting, because instead of actually speaking, Evander made a distressed noise, and eyes fluttering shut, he collapsed at Marcos' feet.

He was running through the gardens.

They were lush, almost overgrown, because Jae could never leave well enough alone, and was always trying some new arrangement, some new planting, flowers blossoming so plentifully and so strongly that the entire air smelled of perfume. He could never bear to cut anything back, so the gardens kept proliferating.

There was a canopy of the bluest wisteria above his head, blossoms dropping like rain on his head, and he laughed, brushing them away, feeling them tickle his face as they fell. Shaking his golden waves of hair, he left a shower of blossoms behind.

He turned a corner, feeling the man behind him closing in, and he faded into the shadow of the maze that Jae had constructed over seventy years earlier, creeping along the edges, waiting to catch the man who believed he could catch him.

After all, he was the Guardian of Secrets, and he was the only one of the Thirteen who had managed to find his way through the maze the very first time.

That dent in the dense brush to his left was where Marcos became frustrated and used his big curved knife to hack his way out.

And the red roses there, climbing up that wall, that must have been where Taavi and Hektor liked to steal away from everyone else, one bloom for every kiss they'd ever shared.

He'd stopped hearing the footsteps, and he crept out, carefully, not wanting to reveal himself too soon and ruin the game.

"Found you," a voice behind him exclaimed triumphantly.

Before he could turn around and face him, he was overwhelmed by the other Guardian, arms wrapping around his chest, firm lips kissing down the lean column of his neck.

The scent surrounding them was intoxicating, but it was the feel of his hands and his mouth on Evander that made his head swim.

He leaned back, and let the other Guardian take his fill, cock hardening in his loose linen trousers.

And then he reached back, and instead of Vanya's smooth cheek, he touched the rough bristles of another.

Marcos.

Evander woke with an abrupt start.

You were just dreaming.

It was only a dream.

And yet it had felt so much more real than a dream. An imagined fantasy?

The dream—because that was what it had been, he told himself firmly, a *dream*—began to fade away, and he began to take inventory.

He'd been enough different men and creatures through the years that he'd learned to carefully categorize who or what he was before he ever opened his eyes.

But in all these hundreds of years on the surface, he'd never woken and been *himself*.

He'd been Evrard or Rhys or one of another dozen fleeting disguises that he'd used as needed.

He'd never permitted himself *this* disguise, because it had never been a disguise.

It had been *him*, before Deimos had stripped what made Evander who he really, truly was, away.

Squeezing his eyes shut, Evander wished himself back into the dream.

It had been simpler to be that carefree, easy Guardian.

Which was why he'd never permitted himself to occupy this shape again.

Down here on the surface, nothing was easy, and he needed to remember that before he remembered anything else.

Evander took stock of his surroundings. He was upright, and he was also moving, in a slow rolling gait that was unmistakably equine.

He was on a horse.

There was a warm, hard body behind him.

Marcos.

"I can feel that you are awake." Marcos' voice was deep and rumbling. "I felt you startle."

"It would be easier if you were slightly less aware," Evander grumbled.

He finally opened his eyes.

It was nearly dusk, and they must have made good time since . . . Evander realized he did not remember *how* he'd gotten on the horse.

He certainly would not have chosen to share with Marcos. He'd have demanded his own mount.

That was the moment he realized that he had no memory of what had happened after the battle.

Clear as day in his memory was standing above the battle, watching Marcos as he took on fifteen of the merchant's armed men. He remembered waiting for the gang leader who'd hired them to give the signal for the rest of his men to attack.

But he hadn't. He'd merely watched, an amused grin on his face as Marcos had torn into the defenses of the caravan as if they were wet parchment.

But then he'd taken a second longer with one of the men, and it had thrown off his timing. Evander had seen it immediately, understood the consequences of it, and he'd felt a swell of panic rise inside him that he hadn't quite understood.

He'd reminded the leader politely at first. Then he'd yelled. Then he'd screamed.

But the man had merely laughed at his distress.

The anger that surged through him had been a shock.

He'd promised Marcos that he wouldn't interfere or intervene, but even though he'd reminded himself very firmly that Marcos did not need his help, did not *want* his help, he'd reached for the power before he could reconsider or think about what he was doing.

Not the fire magic. Not at first.

He'd known he didn't have the energy for it, not when he was maintaining a different form, the cloak of Rhys.

No, to access that kind of magic, the kind of magic that could really help Marcos, he'd need to be someone else.

He'd need to be Evander.

The change had swept over him as easy as breathing, and it had felt like a veil had lifted over his features and his magic had surged through him as he'd returned to himself.

He'd grasped for the power and hadn't hesitated, dropping down to the roof of the traveling carriage, letting it flow through him in a sickening wave.

"I thought you taking your real form would make it easier for you to access your magic. I guess I was right."

Marcos' casual observation interrupted his disordered, panicked thoughts before Evander could get to the moment when everything had gone black.

But then it was back, the memory flashing through him in a nauseating wave.

He'd felt the rise of the battle in his blood. Marcos' eyes had been wild with it, with recognizing him, stripped of all his normal artifice.

And then they'd come together, bodies pressed close, and Evander wanted to feel a wave of embarrassment at how he'd acted, how he'd wanted, so desperately, for Marcos to lean down and press his lips against Evander's, but he felt no humiliation whatsoever.

He'd wanted it.

He . . . wanted it still?

Evander shook his head, trying to clear it.

"I didn't know," Evander retorted. "I . . . I suspected, I suppose. But I have not taken this form since . . ."

"I know," Marcos said, and naturally, it was not the almost-kiss or the embrace, or the burn of want still coursing through him that made him blush. It was that Marcos had known he'd never re-taken this form, and that he'd done it today, for *him*.

"You have been out for almost a whole day," Marcos said. "You collapsed . . . do you remember that?"

He wished he didn't, but he did.

"Yes," he said shortly.

"I took the strongbox and several horses and got out of there," Marcos said, reciting the order of events tightly, succinctly, leaving out anything about what had *nearly* happened, right after the fight.

That is better for everyone, Evander told himself firmly. *You don't need to discuss it because it is irrelevant.*

Evander stroked at the horse's mane, and felt its pleasure at his touch.

"I might have overdone it," he admitted. "My power . . . well, you know it is not what it once was."

"Which is why I asked you, in fact made you *promise,* that you would not intervene."

"If I told you that you were right, would you cease this endless lecturing?" Evander asked crossly.

There was silence behind him for a long moment.

Finally, Marcos spoke, and his words were quiet. Soft. So much softer than Evander could've imagined. "I am appreciative. Your help, while ill-advised, *was* invaluable."

Always when Evander believed he had understood Marcos and relegated him to the right kind of box, with the right purpose that he could serve, he surprised him.

And Evander was not much surprised by anyone.

"You're welcome," Evander said.

"How are you feeling?"

"Better. Much better. Less drained." He'd recovered faster than he had since coming to the surface.

"We will stop at dark, and then you can eat something, which should help you regain more strength."

"Did you get the supplies?" Evander wondered. He realized, there was another set of reins, tangled loosely in one of Marcos' big fists. Turning back, he glimpsed first, Marcos' stern face, and ignored how the sight of it sent a tremor through him, then spied the second horse behind them, loaded with saddlebags.

"Yes, as you can see," Marcos said, amused.

Maybe he'd felt the tremor.

Evander hoped he didn't understand what it meant, though if Marcos did, that would make at least one of them.

"It was not exactly simple," Marcos continued, "because you were out cold, and I had to make sure you weren't unprotected. So I slung you over my shoulder, and told everyone that we were just married, and you'd over-indulged during the celebration."

"You . . . you . . . *what.*" Evander had not been mentally present for this humiliation, but he felt the sting of it spike inside of him nevertheless.

"It was the easiest explanation. The merchants I approached at first were worried that I'd kidnapped you, and I had to invent an explanation that made sense. And I couldn't leave you, not when you were insensible." Marcos' tone was matter of fact, but the truth was, he hadn't looked unaffected at all, right after the battle.

He'd been shaken.

And not just because, Evander thought, he had returned to his original form, which was not exactly unpleasing to the eye.

"So you have married us now," Evander said dryly.

"Like I said, the simplest explanation." Marcos' voice was still so easy, like there was nothing else he wanted.

And perhaps there wasn't.

"Is that why I smell like . . ." Evander sniffed at his tunic. "Mead? Terrible mead?"

"I sprinkled a little over you," Marcos admitted with a chuckle. "Had to sell it, right?"

Evander rolled his eyes. "I can hardly blame you for paying attention to detail, when there is nothing I enjoy more than the details. I suppose, then, if you were that detailed in your approach, I should find nothing missing in the supplies you purchased."

"There is food, several waterskins, a bedroll for the hard, cold ground that we'll be likely to find, and one last thing that I found, just for you."

"Just for me?" Evander asked skeptically.

He could *feel* Marcos' grin, even though he could not see it. "Call it a wedding gift, courtesy of the merchant and the gang leader, who abandoned the battle before he could take most of the gold."

"I also hope you obtained me a new change of clothes, since you doused these in mead," Evander said.

"That too," Marcos said. "I remember just how fastidious you've always been.

"But then," he added in a teasing voice, "it never made much sense to me. Because how could you possibly be fastidious when you're something else? Like a horse? Or a mouse? Or Evrard?"

"I will have you know that Evrard was perhaps even more fastidious than I am," Evander said.

"But mice? Horses? They . . ."

"Don't," Evander warned him. "Just . . . don't. Leave it at I *am* fastidious now, in this form, and you would be smart to remember that."

Marcos laughed. "With you wearing that face, it will be difficult to forget." He hesitated, likely because he'd felt Evander stiffening in front of him. "Are you considering staying Evander?"

Even though he could *feel* Evander, in every inch of skin and every bone in his body, it still felt dangerous to remain as him.

He'd almost been sure that when they stopped, he would dismount and become Rhys again—but the truth of it was he did not *want* to be Rhys.

He wanted to be himself, even though he'd told himself that he couldn't be Evander again, because Evander was missing and gone forever.

But there he was. He'd reached for his oldest form, and even though he might only be a shadow of what Evander had been as a Guardian, while he could be anything in the world, what he wanted most in his heart, deep down where he never wanted to look, was still Evander.

"It seems the most convenient solution to the problem. It takes effort, magical and otherwise, to change forms and to maintain other forms," Evander admitted. "I have more power at my fingertips if I stay Evander. Not much more, but enough."

Evander told himself that he was imagining the satisfaction rolling off Marcos in waves. He could not possibly know anything about how Marcos felt. But he *did*. It was impossible to mistake.

"That," Marcos said slowly, with consideration, like Evander couldn't *feel* how pleased he was, "is a wise decision."

Evander's stomach grumbled. "Are we stopping soon? I find that I am, in fact, starving."

"Really?" Marcos' voice was a rumble behind him. "I couldn't tell."

Evander only remembered how sharp a weapon his elbows had always been when he struck Marcos in the chest and heard his *oomph*.

"We will be stopping shortly; I believe there will be a nice creek coming up. I have scented the water on the air." Marcos' voice had grown formal, and Evander found himself craving the teasing.

"My apologies," he said. "I'm still . . . I'm still adjusting to this body again. Rhys' elbows were not nearly so weaponized."

"What is that like?" Marcos wanted to know. "Being in a new body? Or an old, familiar one? Is there always an adjustment?"

"Sometimes, it's a rush of feeling, especially if I become human again, after so long as an animal. I was Evrard for a very long time," he admitted. "When I became Rhys, it was exhilarating. Even if Rhys was not a particularly exhilarating form."

"I liked Rhys just fine."

"Really?" Evander was skeptical. Rhys had been created because he was easy to forget, a kind of form he'd perfected over the years.

"Truly," Marcos said. He pulled the reins, moving the horse off the road and down a small incline, dotted with trees and brush underfoot, until they did, indeed, come to a nicely bubbling stream.

"And now," he added as Evander dismounted without waiting for his assistance, "you can even bathe."

Evander turned, and it was a jolt to see Marcos again, even though he'd been hearing him speak since he'd woken up.

But this was the first time he'd truly seen him, since the moment before he fainted.

Evander ignored the shivering of his insides, and tromped right over to where the other horse had ducked his head, beginning to chew on a clump of grass next to a fallen log.

The horse was loaded down with more supplies than Evander was expecting. He started pulling off the saddlebags one by one, inspecting each one. There were four waterskins, a whole saddlebag full of dried meat and the hard kind of bread that rarely went bad.

"Looking for your gift?"

Evander glanced up and saw Marcos standing there, a glimmer of a smile on his face.

"No," he said, "I'm looking for the clothes. It's warm now, but when dusk falls, it'll grow chillier, and I want a bath." He shot Marcos a look. "You could use one as well."

Underneath the blankets, he finally found the clothes.

They were simple enough, and good for traveling, in shades of olive green and brown.

"I did not know whether you'd be staying Evander or not, but Rhys is about the same size," Marcos said casually, like there was nothing unusual about sizing his body up.

There isn't, Evander reminded himself. *This is a simple arrangement. He is helping you—only because he refused to be left behind—and once it's over, once I have uncovered the source of the voice, I will return to Beaulieu and Rhys, and this chapter will be closed.*

"Thank you," Evander said stiffly.

But no matter how many times Evander recited that admonition as he marched down to the creek, he did not quite believe it.

He just hoped that Marcos would take a hint and not follow him as he took the new clothes and set out for the stream.

Ducking behind a tree, he braced himself as he yanked off his boots, pulled off his tunic, and then loosened his breeches, dropping them in a pile. Naked and beginning to shiver, Evander regarded the water in front of him.

The stream was not too swift, though there was no doubt in his mind that it would be cold.

Selecting a shallower spot, where Evander could see the smooth gravel of the bottom, and the water eddied and swirled, he took a cautious step in. Muttering an oath under his breath, he took another handful of steps in, until the water was nearly to his waist. The temperature took his breath away, but it also felt good to be able to clean off the sweat and dirt of the road, and the night spent in that makeshift cell.

It was one of the things that had always annoyed Evander about his transformative abilities—surely he should have been able to shift away from blood and gore and dirt and sweat, but he never could. Evander was just as filthy as Rhys had been, and he set out to scrub it all away with the cool, clean water.

It was far too cold to wash his hair, so after a minute or so of rinsing, his teeth chattering the whole time, he turned to step out of the creek when out of the corner of his eye he saw the worst possible scenario.

Not a bear.

Or a cougar.

Or the gang, come to find them and exact revenge for taking all the gold.

Not even the merchant, angry that they'd stolen from him.

No, it was Marcos, standing near the creek bed, and he was in the middle of unbuckling his chest plate, loosening it enough to remove.

"What do you think you are doing?" Evander asked, hating the panic that had leaked into his voice.

Marcos shot him an incredulous look. "I am bathing. You yourself said I needed it." He pulled off the armor, and then knelt down to remove his studded leather greaves from his legs. "Don't tell me," he added, "that you've become prudish over the years."

"No," Evander said. "Hardly. I only meant . . . is it safe to bathe at the same time? What about the horses and the supplies? The gold?"

Marcos did not look particularly convinced by this argument, which made plenty of sense, because it was a terrible argument.

"We haven't met a single person on the road. We left a great distance between us and both the merchant's men and the other thieves. I think I can take a little dip in the stream without compromising our safety."

"Right."

Evander had just been about to get out of the water, because it *was* cold. He would have done it, without flinching, but then there had been that moment between them after the battle.

When Marcos had pressed that big, powerful body against his, and he'd felt weak in the knees with the force of it.

Vanya would have told him it was just sex, and he could even have it with Marcos, if that was the direction his tastes were headed these days.

But even though many of the Guardians treated sex as just another way they could enjoy themselves and the immortal life they'd been gifted, Evander had never been able to be cavalier about it.

He'd only been physically intimate with Vanya, even though he knew Vanya shared his favors with many. That had never particularly bothered him, because he trusted the connection they'd always shared. But he'd never been tempted to explore or experiment, and then after his fall to the surface, he'd been too busy to contemplate trusting anyone that much.

Occasionally he'd considered taking a different form to find release, but he'd never actually been able to do it.

Maybe he *had* gotten prudish.

Evander took a deep breath. "I was just finishing," he said.

Marcos glanced up from where he was untying his boots.

"Then *you* can protect our supplies," Marcos teased.

"Yes," Evander said, and realized too late that it was a mistake to get out of the stream when he did, because that was the very moment

Marcos stood, pulling his loose linen tunic over his head and dropped his breeches.

Vanya had always claimed that Marcos was like a weapon—*so unimaginative, so stolid, so plain*—but as Evander took in Marcos' body, he realized that Vanya was right, but he was also wrong.

Marcos was big and he was strong, unbelievably so, but he was also beautiful.

That was smooth skin, over all that muscle, and they weren't bulky or too big. He was formed in an impossibly elegant way, the slopes of his shoulders leading to the bulge of his biceps, and the ridges of his abdomen leading to . . .

Evander gulped. He'd told himself over the many years alone that he hadn't missed sex or physical release, but clearly he had, because his lack of it was suddenly the most pressing problem that he could imagine.

In a moment, Marcos was going to understand it too, because even with the cold water, and the way his bare skin had chilled in the growing dusk, he felt hot, and he found himself growing hard.

Marcos' dark eyes were amused as he came to a stop right in front of where Evander stood, near the bank of the stream.

"Are you alright?" he asked.

"I must be tired still," Evander said. "I feel shaken."

Marcos reached out and took his wrist in his hand.

Evander could feel his pulse leap at the skin-on-skin contact. His thumb, rough and calloused, rubbed across where his blood beat the hardest.

"Your heart," he murmured, glancing down at where he'd left a streak of dirt on Evander's pale skin, "is beating just fine."

"You are hardly Abram," Evander retorted, referring to the Guardian of Healing.

"No, but he taught me many things. A good skill to have on a battlefield. The ability to take people apart, and then to put them back together," Marcos pointed out.

His voice was as soft and gentle as his touch, even as the roughness of his fingers sent a thrill up Evander's spine.

"I didn't . . . I didn't know that," Evander stammered.

At any moment now, he was going to flush red, and this pale skin of his would do nothing to hide it.

"You do not know everything about me," Marcos said, sounding surprisingly delighted.

"But you know much about *me*," Evander said.

Another puzzle he had yet to untangle.

"Yes," Marcos admitted. He reached down, and trickled cool water down over the dirt he'd left on Evander's skin, and then released his grip.

Evander caught back the plea of *don't* before he could embarrass himself any further.

"Go get dressed," Marcos added. "It's freezing."

When Evander reached his clothes, his fingers were trembling. Not from the chill, no, it was not that simple at all.

CHAPTER SIX

Marcos spent longer in the water than he probably should have.

It was cold, *very* cold, and yet the icy water seemed to do little to calm the raging fire in his blood.

He'd wanted so badly to reach out and just *take* what he wanted. What he'd wanted for so long that the unfulfilled ache felt like an old familiar friend. But there was so much Evander didn't know, and Marcos would have to be blind not to realize that he had yet to fully trust him.

It was why the attraction between them made him so uneasy.

He didn't like it, even as he craved it.

Marcos was going to have to exert every bit of his self-control to not give in until Evander understood everything, and unfortunately it was nowhere near as simple as just sitting him down and reciting it.

Evander was going to have to *believe it*, and that was so much more difficult.

Finally, when he felt his fingers turning blue around the edges, he hefted himself out of the water and threw back on his tunic and trousers, picking up his armor.

He could not avoid Evander forever, even though seeing him in this form sent a tremor through him still that he could not quite control.

With Rhys, he'd seen little bits of Evander. His gaze, his tone, his brilliant brain. But it was blinding when it was all those things coming out of Evander himself.

And Marcos was stupid enough that he'd always dreamt of being overwhelmed by the light of him.

When he approached where he'd tied up the horses, he discovered that while he'd been washing up, Evander had made himself useful.

He'd gathered sticks and even a few logs, sawing away at them with his knife, and with the tinder he'd picked up in the last village, Evander had even started a tiny fire.

"You've been busy," Marcos said, dragging one of the bigger log pieces towards the fire and setting it opposite where Evander sat, cross-legged, teeth ripping into a piece of dried meat.

"Yes," Evander said. "And I was hungry."

I was too, but not for food. Marcos shut the thought down quickly.

He was always going to crave Evander, but he could control himself. He *had* to control himself.

"I could eat something myself," Marcos said, hoping that filling his empty belly would take his mind away from other hungers.

Evander reached into the bag at his feet, and tossed a large chunk of dried beef his way. Marcos caught it and took a big bite.

"It's not a roast or a haunch of pork, but it will do," Evander said.

Making a small bow, Marcos responded with, "I am gratified at your appreciation."

Evander made a scrunched-up face. "You are so much sillier than I remember."

"You barely ever glanced my way, when we were at the Castle at the Top of the World," Marcos pointed out. He wasn't bitter about that; he *wasn't*. He'd even managed, over a few hundred years, to banish the ruefulness from his tone.

"I suppose not," Evander conceded. "But I think you will be gratified to know I no longer believe you're to blame for my banishment."

"I told you that I wasn't."

"And yet," Evander pointed out lightly, "your word is not all it took to convince me. I had to see for myself. You had every opportunity to do me harm. To hit me over the head and take me back or take me away, but as far as I am aware, we are on the road to the north, as I intended."

Marcos nodded. "We are."

"Then, I do not believe you were sent by Deimos. And," he added with a heavy sigh, "I do not truly believe that you betrayed me either. It is not in your nature."

"I told you that I did not, and also as I said before, I sent myself," Marcos said.

"But *why*?" Evander demanded. "Why come to the surface if you did not need to?"

"Like you, I always spent more time here than the others. How could we be Guardians otherwise?"

"And what, now I fall under your protection because I am no longer a Guardian?" Evander's glare and his voice challenged from across the fire, the light of it dancing in the waves of his hair.

"We planned to eradicate the sorcerer's line *together*," Marcos pointed out. "I came to your chambers and suggested the plan that we undertook. It was not fair that only you were punished."

"Only I was caught," Evander said wryly. "And yet I find it difficult to believe that Deimos did not suspect you."

"Deimos is afraid of me."

Marcos had never said the words out loud before, and he hadn't expected them to fall, with a painful hush, into the falling dark.

Evander stared at him.

"What do you mean?" he demanded to know after a long second of silence.

"After you fell, I waited some time, maybe a dozen years or so? And then when you decided to emerge from your valley, I came down to the surface, too. Just to make sure you were fine."

"I *was* fine," Evander said, enunciating each word carefully and clearly.

"Yes, you were. You had a purpose. I figured that out quickly. You were going to continue the plan that we had begun together. I did not think you wanted my help, so I watched. I waited, in case you did. And during that time, during the first hundred years or so, Deimos sent the other Guardians to bring me back to the Castle at the Top of the World."

"They came to take you back?" Evander sounded shocked. They had all spent time on the surface. Of course, none as much as Marcos, but still.

"They *tried* to take me back," Marcos corrected, with solemn satisfaction. "I am fairly powerful, a fact that I have tried over the years to undermine."

"You didn't want them to know, so they wouldn't feel threatened," Evander guessed.

Marcos nodded. "It was not always easy. But they came, and they left without me. And then a hundred years after that, Deimos himself came."

"Deimos was here?"

Marcos could feel the tremor moving through Evander even from across the fire.

"Deimos came. Deimos tried to employ persuasive tactics, at first. He promised me power. Love. Many riches. Storerooms full of gold. Anything he could think of. But I had a purpose, and I was not easily swayed from it."

"But he is *Deimos*. He is the most powerful of us all. How did he not overpower you?"

"I did not let him get that far," Marcos admitted. "I knew . . . rather, I *suspected*, that some events had come to pass. I did not have evidence, but I knew enough about what he had done. Enough to make sure that I would not be bothered."

"You threatened *Deimos*?" Evander sounded incredulous. And it *was* astounding. Marcos could barely believe now that he'd done it. It had been an incredible risk.

But he was the Guardian of War. He could smell fear, and Deimos had been afraid.

"He left me alone, after that," Marcos finished.

Evander was shaking his head still, disbelieving that he had invited so many hazards.

"And you have not seen any other Guardians in your time here?"

"Oh, I see Gael occasionally," Marcos said. "And Jae. Hyperion. Though not for a few hundred years. I sailed once, upon the ocean, and Osias greeted me. But none of them have forced me to return. They know better now."

Marcos knew what Evander wanted to know. Perhaps it was silly and petty to make him ask for it. "And Vanya?"

"You know there is little belief here anymore," was all Marcos was willing to say. "You have walked among the people. You know."

"I know." Evander's gaze as he stared into the flames was moody. Disappointed. "That is why you think it is a trap."

"I think it is *something*," Marcos offered. "I do not know what it is yet, and the unknown worries me. That is why I insisted on coming with you."

Evander shot him a look. "Yes, you are an exceptional protector. Leading us right into a band of thieves."

Marcos considered defending himself; he'd made solid decisions—maybe they had not turned out like he'd envisioned—but he hadn't been reckless. It was difficult to be reckless when he knew what he was capable of. But Evander was going to believe whatever he wanted to believe.

And he'd always wanted to believe that Marcos was stupid and thoughtless.

Even though they'd shared a handful of moments where he thought that Evander's opinion of him might be changing. They'd felt intimate and charged, like for the first time, Evander might truly be seeing *him*, but now he realized that it had only been blind hope.

He'd always had a weak spot where Evander was concerned, and nothing had changed.

"We should get some rest," Marcos said gruffly. "I can take watch, if you'd like."

"I slept most of the day. I should take the first watch. Honestly, I should take the *whole* watch," Evander said, standing and stretching. Marcos pointedly avoided looking at his body, all lean, perfect lines. Before, he'd have always looked his fill, but what was the point now?

Marcos had believed himself to be resigned to looking and never touching, but he'd started to dream, to wish, to *hope*. And reality was a colder, harsher blow than he'd anticipated.

"You are still recovering, and I am . . ." Marcos hesitated. "I do not need any sleep right now."

Guardians could go days without sleep. During a particularly difficult campaign when he'd been the leader of one of Ardglass' thirteen tribes, he'd gone a week without sleep.

But Evander was no longer a Guardian, and surely he needed the rest. After all, he'd overexerted himself.

"Fine," Evander grumbled, and wandered off, presumably to fetch the blankets.

Marcos stayed on his log, pretending that he was not staring moodily into the fire the same way that Evander had earlier, when they'd discussed Vanya.

He heard Evander rustling around, talking under his breath to the horses, and then abruptly, an exclamation. And then another.

He must have found the gift that Marcos had gotten him.

Evander emerged back into the circle of firelight, the fur coat wrapped around his body, pulled up close to his chin. He was carrying a pile of worn blankets in front of him. He dropped them next to the fire and shot Marcos an unimpressed look.

"You bought me a fur coat?"

"They were selling it for a very reasonable price, and it'll keep you warm in the north," Marcos said.

He'd also imagined that the light brown fur would look glorious on him—and he was not wrong, though looking at Evander now, the collar pulled tight around his neck, his blond hair tousled around his face, a spike of painful longing shot through him.

"It looks like some rich merchant's wife's coat," Evander complained, spreading out one of the blankets, and flopping down onto it. "I look ridiculous."

"You also look warm," Marcos pointed out dryly.

"It is *quite* warm, I will give you that." Evander stretched out his legs. "Maybe even too warm for this night."

"But not for the next, when we are a day's travel closer to the north."

"We should be there in less than a week, if we are traveling on horseback," Evander said. "I suppose I will be grateful then that you found this."

"That was the idea," Marcos said. He pulled one of his knives out of its sheaths and began to sharpen it on a whetstone. He did not anticipate finding much action on this road. It was well traveled, and relatively safe. It was why he had selected it, instead of a shorter route. Still, he could not help but be prepared for anything.

"Maybe I will thank you, then," Evander said, his voice growing sleepy, his eyes beginning to flutter shut.

But Marcos wasn't laboring under any kind of false impression any-more—Evander wasn't going to thank him, not the way he'd always hoped he would, and he would have to be satisfied with making sure he didn't freeze to death on the way to the Well, and making sure he didn't spring whatever trap awaited them there.

They did not see anyone on the road the next day, and Evander, sensing Marcos' poor mood, kept quiet. Marcos pulled them off the road as dusk grew, and this time there was no suggestion of a bath. Even a single day's ride north had made it far too cold to consider.

Evander had built the fire again, and they huddled around it. Marcos had even grabbed the thick cloak from his pack and wrapped it around his shoulders, even though he was usually impervious to cold.

"Will there be snow tomorrow, do you think?" Evander asked, speaking for what felt like the first time all day, since Marcos had refused to be pulled into polite small talk.

"Possibly," Marcos said. "But the ground will freeze tonight."

"Of all the things I dislike about the surface," Evander said morose-ly, "the worst is the cold."

"It's not my favorite either," Marcos said.

"It was one thing to look out the windows of the castle, and see the snow falling on the surface, it is entirely another to sleep on the cold, hard ground, with only a puny fire for warmth."

Marcos was surprised. He had not expected Evander to talk about the past, when he'd lived at the Castle at the Top of the World. When he'd had all the power in the world at his fingertips.

"I may not talk about it, but that does not mean I don't *think* about it," he said, shooting Marcos a rueful look. "Surely there are things you miss, too. You've been on the surface nearly as long as I have."

And out of choice, not necessity. Evander didn't say the words, but Marcos heard them anyway, echoing in the silence between them.

"The food," Marcos admitted. "Some of it is so poor." He held up a piece of the dried meat he was currently chewing on. "And all of it terribly seasoned."

"You mean, *most* of it is so poor," Evander said with a commiserating glance. "The food at Beaulieu was excellent."

"King Emory and King Graham do set an excellent table. Is that why you stayed?" Marcos had not intended to ask the question, even though he had been curious from the moment he'd arrived at Beaulieu, as Merleen. Beaulieu was no Castle at the Top of the World, but Marcos had assumed it was an improvement over many lesser places.

"At Beaulieu?"

"You could have gone anywhere, done nearly anything. You could have created your own kingdom. Had your own legions of followers. You did not need to be the unassuming advisor to Rory and Gray."

"Maybe I have seen the ruin that so many kingdoms come to," Evander said lightly, and Marcos knew he was avoiding the real answer.

Would he ever hear the real answer? Deep down, Marcos wasn't sure.

Evander had always held his secrets close.

"We should get some rest," Marcos said.

"You mean *I* should get some rest," Evander said. "I know what you are doing, and it's ridiculous. I am fully rested and recovered from using my magic."

"Are you?"

Evander glared. "I am," he said haughtily. "And you have not slept for at least four days, which I remember very well is about the point at which you will get very tired."

"I haven't slept for a week before." Marcos didn't know why he'd said it. Maybe he didn't like the idea of Evander taking care of *him* very much.

It felt too close to what he truly wanted, deep down in his heart.

"That was stupid," Evander said archly. "Do I want to know why you were so foolish?"

"It was a war," Marcos said, wrapping his cloak closer around himself. He would find a blanket and let Evander take the first watch—because if he did not, Evander wouldn't stop arguing about it. "War is the exception to everything."

"Which war?" Evander asked, sounding genuinely curious.

"One of the Ardglassian tribal wars. The last one, I believe."

"*I* was there," Evander said, clearly surprised.

"Yes," Marcos replied steadily, while admonishing himself to stay calm, "I know."

"I was there . . ." Evander trailed off, making a face. "You were there to watch me."

"To *help* you. I knew you wanted a united Ardglass. I didn't know why, but I could see that it would help the people to be less fractured and warring with each other constantly."

"You were part of Dougal's contingent, then," Evander said thoughtfully.

Marcos cleared his throat. He had known if he mentioned the sleep deprivation, they would end up down this road, and here they were.

He should have just kept his stupid mouth shut.

"I *was* Dougal," Marcos said.

Evander's mouth dropped open. "You were . . ." Marcos could see the thoughts flying quick and fast in his eyes. "You disguised yourself."

"You know I can, though not as well as you," Marcos pointed out. "You did not suspect I was Merleen until you touched me and felt my power."

"There was something about you, something I recognized," Evander argued. "And Dougal too, though I could never put my finger on it."

"And now, you know," Marcos said, and stood. He unpacked a blanket from his pack, made sure the horses were settled for the night, took a piss, and when he returned to the fire, Evander was thankfully quiet.

Marcos had already shared more than he wanted to.

He unfolded the blanket on the ground, banked the fire, and settled down next to it. Evander had been right about one thing; four days was when a Guardian *did* start to get tired, and it took almost no time for his eyes to close.

The ground *was* frozen the next morning.

Other than making several disgruntled noises and shivering inside his fur coat, Evander continued to be silent.

Marcos pulled a piece of meat out of the pack and, as he mounted his horse, took a bite, chewing it.

As they rode through the forest, the trees were growing scarcer, and each evergreen branch was covered in a thick encasement of ice, weighing the branches down until they looked like they were bowing to them as they passed.

Evander was quiet for nearly three quarters of the day.

High noon came and went, and he merely nodded his thanks at Marcos when he tossed him a piece of meat and bread. As they had the last few days, they did not stop. Marcos was carefully monitoring the horses, and had assessed that if they did not ride them too hard or fast, there was no need to stop in the middle of the day to rest them.

And the colder it got, the less inclined he was to take extra time for breaks.

The sun was just beginning to creep down in the sky when Evander finally broke his silence.

"You were following me. Closely."

Marcos sighed. It had clearly been too much to ask for Evander to let it alone. That enormous brain of his could not stop churning, even for a moment.

"And not just as Dougal. Or Merleen. I can think of half a dozen men that were probably you. Familiar, in some way, that I could not identify. But they were always you."

There was nothing Marcos wanted more than to lie and say he did not know what Evander was talking about.

But there wasn't just a half dozen. It was more like a solid dozen, or more. Even Marcos had lost track over the years.

"Some of them, probably," he finally admitted. "Why does it matter?"

Evander stopped suddenly, pulling the reins up on his horse, and turning it around, exasperation on his face. "Why does it matter? You were following me *that closely* for hundreds of years, and you ask why it matters?"

"I already told you that I kept an eye on you, that was why I was here, on the surface," Marcos said reasonably, hoping that would be the end of the conversation, but knowing better.

Evander had found the thread of *something*, and because he was Evander, he was bound and determined to follow it to the end.

Even if the end was a conclusion that he wouldn't want to hear, and that Marcos never wanted him to realize.

"You did not say you were so close so many times." Evander rode closer, gaze narrowing. "Why did you not tell me who you really were?"

There were many answers to that question.

But only one simple one—and it was not *quite* a lie, which meant that maybe Evander might believe it. "It seemed easier not to," he admitted.

Evander glared. "You did not have the right to make that choice, to take that choice away from me. If you were helping me, if you were *there*, I'd have wanted to know."

"Perhaps if I was Vanya." It was harder than Marcos had anticipated to make his tone come out so light and unconcerned. When really, the truth had haunted him for years.

"You couldn't have known that I blamed you for the betrayal." Evander's forehead creased in confusion. "Even you are not that all-knowing."

"It was an easy enough assumption to make," Marcos said.

"I would have wanted to know it was you," Evander insisted stubbornly. "And *why* do it at all? That is what I still don't understand."

And you never will, as long as I am drawing breath to keep it secret.

"I told you, I felt responsible for your situation, even if I was not directly to blame. Also, your goal was laudable. The sorcerers did not need to control the people of the surface. They owned too much power."

"For that, you sacrificed your existence as a Guardian and your life at the Castle at the Top of the World?" Evander sounded incredulous. To him, it must sound like an utter waste. But for Marcos, it had felt like a fair and just trade.

And to be close to Evander . . . even if he was not Evander, and Marcos was not really Marcos . . . that alone had been worth it.

Every miserable campaign, every war, every fight he'd endured. Every terrible meal. Every sleepless night. The snowstorms, the rainstorms, every single bit of bad weather.

But Evander couldn't possibly understand.

"Come, let's continue our journey," Marcos said with finality, nudging his horse closer to Evander's, but Evander still did not budge.

He continued to stare at him.

Incredulous.

Upset.

Uncertain.

Wary.

Then Marcos watched, the weak cold sunlight illuminating the beauty of Evander's face, every plane and curve of it, his blue eyes narrowing, as he realized the truth.

"Vanya teased me about it sometimes, but it was a *joke*," Evander said, so quietly that it might have been to himself, and not to Marcos at all.

"Come," Marcos said brusquely, and this time, he led his horse off the path and around Evander's blockade. He was not going to discuss this. Especially not when Vanya and Evander had treated it as something to laugh about, late at night when they shared a bed.

He could hear Evander's horse following behind him, but he resolutely did not look back. No matter what Evander said, he was not going to look back.

Humiliation and frustration warred within him.

Why couldn't Evander have just left it alone? Why did he feel the need to push everything to its inevitable conclusion?

Because he's Evander, and you love him, you've always loved him, every single part of him, even this part. Even when he uncovers your deepest, darkest, most painful secret.

Marcos shoved the thought away. It hurt more, just thinking it.

He focused on their surroundings. The trees were growing sparser, bigger boulders, the color of slate gray dotting the landscape. The ground was packed hard, with little in the way of extraneous weeds and plants. He would need to be careful and perhaps stockpile some for the horses, for when snow and ice eventually blanketed the way.

Everyone always assumed that the Guardian of War would only concern himself with fighting—but the best generals always sent their troops into battle well-fed and well-supplied.

Thankfully, after a few minutes, Evander ceased his babbling. Marcos had stopped listening to it, anyway, purposefully blocking his ears so he wouldn't have to hear any more stunned realizations.

Or how Vanya used to tease Evander about it.

For being alive so long, he was always so surprised at how absolutely terrible Evander was with people. Anyone with a modicum of sense or empathy wouldn't have brought up Vanya and his tendency to make Marcos' feelings a joke, and yet that had been Evander's first reaction.

Marcos, half his attention on the landscape as they trotted past, and half on his outrage and annoyance, remembered how once at Beaulieu, Gray had told a whole sequence of stories about how Evrard had raised him in the valley.

"Not exactly a warm and cozy father figure," Merleen had commented at the time—and Rhys had glared at him. Of course, Rhys hadn't known that Merleen had known just who he was.

Or that Merleen was actually Marcos.

But the point remained.

Evander might be good with secrets and hiding in shadows and transforming into a flawless copy of something else, but he was utter crap at anything resembling emotion.

Not that Marcos himself was any better, though at least he'd had the sense to refrain from confessing everything to Evander when he'd realized why his gaze always returned to the other Guardian. Why he always strained to hear everything he said. Why he couldn't get him out of his mind, even though they rarely spoke.

Why he'd gone out of his way to defend him on more than one occasion.

Perhaps he had not been as circumspect as he should've been, but he hadn't marched up to Evander and revealed his undying love, either.

His horse maneuvered around a rock, and Marcos glanced up, attention suddenly sharp. He swore that the horse had made a similar movement only a few minutes earlier. He'd been in the middle of burning with embarrassment and frustration when it had occurred, so he'd been understandably distracted, but it felt so familiar, he shifted his weight automatically, expecting the next adjustment as the horse maneuvered past a larger boulder, set half into the packed dirt of the road.

That boulder . . . it was memorable.

There was no question in Marcos' mind as he stared at it, head turning as they passed by it.

They had been by it before.

At least once.

Marcos picked through his memory, and found it again. No wonder feeling his horse shift that way had pricked at his consciousness.

They'd been by this exact same spot at least *twice*.

"Evander," Marcos called out sharply, "does any of this road look familiar?"

At first, there was only silence behind him, and for a single heart-stopping moment, Marcos wondered if something had happened to the other Guardian while he hadn't been paying attention.

But then Evander spoke up, and his voice was sulky, in a way that Marcos recognized from his time as a Guardian whenever he hadn't gotten his way. Trust Evander to be pissed off that Marcos wouldn't talk to him, after the way he'd reacted. "Familiar?" he asked. "What are you talking about?"

Marcos would be way more annoyed by Evander's sulk, except every nerve and sense was alight and buzzing with his sudden realization.

"I think we're trapped in some kind of repeating spell. Or the road is charmed, or something."

"Or something," Evander grumped.

"I'm not the magical expert here," Marcos reasoned. He knew enough. He had some power of his own, but he'd never made a particular study of it. What need did he have, when he could defeat his enemies with his fists and his knives and his sword?

"Tell me exactly," Evander finally said, "I haven't been paying close attention to our surroundings."

"I wasn't, either," Marcos confessed. "But I felt the horse sidestep around a smaller stone, and I thought the movement felt familiar, and then, like I remembered it from before, I shifted my weight, expect-ing the next, bigger boulder."

"That one that's set into the road," Evander said.

Marcos pulled up the reins, slowing down and Evander pulled even with him. It was hard—but not impossible, not now—to look over at his profile, concern written all over his beautiful face.

It was easier to face him, now that he knew, because the situation had at least forced them both to focus on this new problem and on finding a solution.

"I think we've passed by that boulder at least three times," Marcos said.

He watched as Evander cast his mind back, trying to remember every minute of the last hour. "More than that," he said, shaking his head. "I can't believe I didn't realize it. I was . . ." He hesitated. "I suppose I was thinking of other things."

"Me as well," Marcos admitted. "How many times, do you think?"

"At least five, perhaps more. I think it must be at least a ten-minute loop, or else we would have noticed sooner."

With how distressed he'd been, Marcos wanted to say that *yes, he'd have noticed* but he was not entirely sure.

"At least," Marcos said, because he was not prepared to admit that maybe it could have been shorter.

"We should time it," Evander said. "Figure out the edges of the loop."

"Really? We should continue to walk through it? Not try to get out of it?"

Evander shot him a look. "You asked for my opinion, I'm giving it. The loop hasn't hurt us so far. It's only trapped us. I think as long as we stay trapped, we're not threatening whoever or *whatever* created it."

"We should use the big boulder as a marker," Marcos suggested, pointing to the boulder behind them.

"Yes," Evander agreed.

They set out cautiously, Marcos counting his horse's tentative steps, as he held tight to the reins, eyes scanning through the trees and the brush on both sides of the road. It was understandable, he realized, that he'd missed that they'd been through here so many times before, because the foliage was so repetitive. If you were going to set a trap for someone—and Marcos, while less knowledgeable about magic, knew *all* about the mechanics of setting a good trap—it was the perfect location.

Finally, they reached the boulder again.

Marcos quickly calculated the ratio of steps to estimated time, something he'd done many times on the road, as early on, there were so few maps of the surface. "Approximately seven minutes," he said.

Evander sighed. "That is not an inconsiderable trap," he said.

"A loop of this length would take power," Marcos agreed. "I thought you eliminated all the power that wasn't ours."

"As did I," Evander said dryly. "I am as surprised as you."

"I did not spot any other inconsistences in the landscape," Marcos added.

"Actually, there was a bit of a shimmering around the far edges," Evander disagreed. "I recognized it, though I am not surprised you missed it. It's Guardian magic. Or it *was* Guardian magic. It has that same taste. The same flavor. The same look to it. I would recognize it anywhere."

"You could set this trap," Marcos said, not liking the way this was going at all.

Evander might be a Guardian no longer, but he was still powerful, and Marcos, though he'd tried to hide the extent of his own power, knew just how much of a prize he was.

"Yes," Evander said.

"You've done this before." Marcos knew before Evander even answered what his reply was going to be.

"Many times," Evander said. Paused. "This was one of my favorite traps, when I was a Guardian."

"Someone knows who you are."

"We are not precisely hiding," Evander retorted. "I'm in my original form. I threw a fireball at a merchant's private army only a few days ago. You unsheathed your sword. Your *highly recognizable* sword."

"Yes, I could have disguised it, but I didn't, because it is *my* sword," Marcos said, annoyed that somehow Evander was laying the blame for this at his feet. He hadn't been the one to demonstrate his magic *twice*.

He'd merely fought like a demon.

There were men out there who could do *almost* the same.

Almost.

Evander held up a hand. "There is no point in arguing about this. We have to face the facts: someone knows who I am, and who you are. How they found out is irrelevant."

"I don't think so," Marcos added under his breath.

Evander glared at him. It was so much better than the galling sympathy he'd been directing his way only an hour before that Marcos almost welcomed the return of the normally prickly Evander—because that was an Evander he recognized.

"It *is* irrelevant," Evander argued. "So, whoever did this knows who we both are, and knows what we are capable of. And, even more importantly, knows my history, knows the kind of magic I liked to employ."

"It has to be a Guardian," Marcos said.

He resolutely ignored how Evander's eyes lit.

No matter what Marcos had said the other night around the fire about men on the surface and belief, Evander still believed it was Vanya. It didn't even matter that if it *was* Vanya, it meant that he'd trapped and deceived them. It just mattered that it was Vanya, after all these years.

That shouldn't have angered Marcos, but it did, all the same.

"Who could it be?" Marcos continued. "Jae could do this magic. Gael, perhaps, though I do not feel anything more than a slight breeze, so it is unlikely to be him."

"Kadir," Evander said. Then paused. Marcos watched him shift uncomfortably. "It could also be Deimos."

"It is not Deimos," Marcos said resolutely. He felt sure of that fact.

Deimos would not come at him directly—not after their last confrontation.

He would use one of the other Guardians.

Evander did not look particularly convinced by Marcos' certainty.

"We need to continue in the trap, until I can find a hole in it."

"How long will that take?" Marcos asked.

Evander shrugged. "However long it takes."

CHAPTER SEVEN

Evander knew this whole process would have been *much* simpler and easier if he still had the full extent of his powers.

Even with the inherent power of this form, Evander had trouble grasping at the edges of the magic as he reached out with his mind, and tried to touch it. It kept sliding and slipping and squirming away from him, avoiding any attempts he made to hold on to it.

Whoever had made it was powerful. Extremely powerful.

Perhaps even more powerful than Evander had been at the height of his skill as a Guardian.

Marcos had said, unequivocally, that whoever had trapped them could not be Deimos, but he had not encountered such pure, unadulterated magic for a thousand years—not since he'd brushed right up against Deimos' power as Deimos had stripped him of his own.

Evander shook his head in frustration as they passed by the large boulder again.

"Nothing?" Marcos' voice was clear of inflection. There was no judgment in his voice whatsoever. But Evander found he was judging himself.

"Nothing," Evander said. They'd been traveling this strip of road, aware now of their problem, for several hours. This was the twenty-fourth pass they'd made past the boulder, and Evander was no closer to figuring out who had sprung this trap, and how he was going to release them from it, than he had been on the first.

The urgency meant he was trying very hard to focus on the problem at hand—considering they were currently entirely at someone's mercy, and had been for a good portion of the day—but his brain kept wandering off.

Wandering off in the direction of Marcos.

The answer to all his questions had ended up being simple enough.

Evander *knew* people felt love. He'd felt it himself, in various forms, over the years. But not romantic love. Not romantic love in such a capacity that would motivate him to follow someone for a thousand years.

To watch over them.

To protect them.

To never reveal themselves.

He'd never even felt that way about Vanya.

It made sense now why Marcos had never announced his presence, merely revolved around Evander as one of half a dozen characters. Evander knew he shouldn't be annoyed about that, considering how many characters *he* had played over the years, how much wool he had pulled over people's eyes. Rory and Gray knew he was both Rhys and Evrard—but they were the only ones who knew.

Besides Marcos.

Who knew everything.

Who knows everything and who is still here, caring about you. Protecting you. Revealing himself to you.

Except he wasn't sure that was entirely true, Evander considered as he reached out again for the magic that shimmered right around the edges of the illusion, because Marcos had most definitely *not* wanted him to know.

He'd only discovered the truth because of Marcos' confession about Ardglass and his participation in their history. And he'd only realized then because the thoughts kept swirling inside of his head, refusing to be denied, but also refusing to coalesce into a conclusion that made sense. Coincidences never felt truly coincidental to Evander. Then he'd cast his mind back, considering all the many men he'd met over the last thousand years.

He'd realized, suddenly, like a lightning bolt hitting him, that Merleen had not been the first man to remind him of Marcos.

It had happened before.

Perhaps not as clearly as it had with Merleen. But it had happened a long time ago. And then it had happened again, and again, and again.

Evander couldn't believe that he'd missed it, all those times.

Or that of all the men that had felt vaguely familiar, tickling the back of his brain, he'd never realized that those particular men had gone out of their way never to touch him.

Because as soon as Merleen had touched him, Evander had *known*. Had felt Marcos' power and its particular scent and intensity and he'd been instantly recognizable, even before he'd stripped away his disguise.

"That's it," Evander said suddenly. "I don't recognize the way this power smells."

"What? The way it *smells*?" Marcos said, pulling his reins in and stopping his horse, right before they approached the boulder yet again.

"I don't recognize it. I'd recognize another Guardian."

"Are you sure you don't recognize it? You could have just . . . forgotten the way one of them smelled?"

Evander pushed the insult in that suggestion away. Normally he'd be pissed off at the assumption that he could forget the way the other Guardians' magic felt and smelled and *was*, but his brain was brimming full. Too full of the problem at hand, and also with Marcos' inadvertent revelation, to truly get angry.

"I didn't forget. I wouldn't ever forget," Evander said. "Have you ever forgotten how to wield a sword?"

Marcos gave him a sheepish grin. "Point taken," he said.

"The *point* is that I do not recognize the way this magic feels or smells or behaves. I would, if it was another Guardian."

"But it's powerful, so powerful, I thought it could only be another Guardian."

"Yes," Evander agreed uncertainly.

Nothing about this made sense, and now joining his frustration at the inability to solve the problem, and the perplexing matter of Marcos' feelings, was a frisson of fear, running right up his spine.

He was not afraid often.

But whoever had done this could hold them in the palm of their hand, for as long as they wished, and Evander didn't think there was much he could do or say about it.

"What if we went off the path?" Marcos suggested.

"Into the forest?"

"Yes, where the magic shimmers, or whatever you said it does." Marcos' voice was impatient, and Evander realized he was afraid too.

And if *Marcos* was afraid . . .

"We're safe, *I think*, as long as we stick to the expected role," Evander said. "That would not be sticking to the expected role."

"If we stick to the expected role, we're going to be trapped in this forest for the next thousand years," Marco pointed out dryly. "Is that what you want?"

"Obviously not," Evander retorted. "But trying to breach the edges of the magic physically . . . whoever did this *will* know."

"Good," Marcos said with satisfaction, pulling his knife from his boot.

Evander watched as Marcos nudged his horse, guiding it off the path, and he sighed. Of the two of them, he was the most naturally cautious, but then he'd also paid the steepest price for his reckless behavior.

But Marcos had always said there was nothing to be gained if there was nothing to be lost, and it seemed that he still believed that.

Evander hesitated for a moment longer, then clicked his tongue, sending his horse after Marcos'.

The closer they got to the edges, the stronger the power felt. Evander could feel it, almost luminous the more he concentrated on it, the taste of it thick and foreign on his tongue. It did not *feel* dangerous or particularly like dark magic, but he knew that power of any kind could easily disguise itself.

Marcos' horse whinnied uneasily, and he soothed it, pressing a hand to its neck.

They continued on, but then Marcos spoke into the silence. "I can feel it too," he said.

Evander nodded grimly. "It's very strong."

"I know what you mean," Marcos said. "I don't recognize it, but at the same time, it feels so familiar."

He could feel the power pushing back at them now, a nearly visceral force, and if he closed his eyes, he knew he'd *see* the golden motes of it sparkling in the air.

"We should stop here," Evander said.

Marcos didn't question, but did exactly as he suggested.

Evander came to a stop next to him, and dismounted.

"What are you doing?" Marcos questioned. "You shouldn't . . ."

But he trailed off when he saw what Evander was doing and didn't finish his sentence. Just waited. Like he respected what Evander was about to try.

As he walked closer, he felt like he was pushing through the magic. The closer he thought the barrier was, the tougher it was to take a step. Then when he couldn't move one more foot, he closed his eyes, gathered his own force, and pressed his palm outward.

The flame that flowed through him and out his body was not nearly as violent as the one during the attack on the merchant's traveling party had been. This, Evander reminded himself as he controlled the rush of the power, was just an experiment.

The moment the flame touched the edge, a flash of bright white light blinded him, and when he opened his eyes again, he froze.

They were back on the road.

Right next to the boulder.

From behind him, Evander could hear Marcos draw his sword.

A very bad sign.

"That is entirely unnecessary."

But that voice, that was not Marcos'.

Evander turned, and saw a woman standing in the middle of the road, a few yards off.

She was old, and yet young. A lined, creased face, but the eyes that shone out of it were ageless, eternal, the dark purple blue of Evander's favorite wildflowers that had once dotted his valley.

Her hair was long and tangled, as bright as the sun, bright yellow mixed with a glowing perfect white. She wore a long brown cloak, torn and dirty, but when she took a step towards them, she walked like she was a queen, wearing the finest garments.

"That's close enough," Marcos warned, taking a step closer to Evander.

Evander knew his first inclination was to shove Evander behind him, but he gave Marcos points for not doing it.

For only *wanting* to do it.

For only getting close enough to do it if he *had* to.

"Who are you?" Evander asked.

She laughed then, the most beautiful, clear, bell-like sound he'd ever heard.

"I am surprised you do not know me, Evander, Guardian of Secrets," she said coyly.

He'd been so sure that he'd eliminated both Sabrina and all her sycophants. But then, nothing about this woman reminded him of the evil sorceress Rory and Gray had defeated. Her magic had been miniscule and grasping, always desperate for an infusion of power.

This woman *breathed* power. It multiplied and grew just because she wished it to.

Evander, who had possessed plenty of his own, and knew others who possessed just as much, had never witnessed anything like it.

"Why have you trapped us here?" Marcos demanded. "You must release us at once."

"And you, Marcos, Guardian of War," she said, "you fear me, but yet I fear what you can do. Does anybody know what you are capable of? Do *you* know what you are capable of?"

"Yes," Marcos said shortly.

"Is that why you trapped us, you're afraid of what Marcos is capable of?"

"Marcos," she said, eyes suddenly so grave that Evander felt the burst of her power like a wave of sadness cresting over him, "has been many men, and all of them have been impressive." Her voice turned sly. "Don't you agree, Evander?"

"What I think is not the question," Evander said ruthlessly. "Why are we here, in your trap? Why will you not let us go?"

"A trap that would not have worked so well if you were not both so distracted," she pointed out. "You," she said, waving her hand gracefully at Marcos, "were embarrassed and angry that he discovered your deep, secret yearning. And *you*"—her gaze turning to Evander—"are conflicted. You do not know if you can love anyone. Though," she added thoughtfully, "you are not averse to discovering what Marcos is like in bed." Her smile turned wicked around the edges.

Evander blushed.

"We are not . . . we are not your . . . *playthings*," Marcos said in a harsh voice.

"Are you not?" She paused. "I am your Mother after all."

Then she snapped her fingers and everything went black.

Evander's eyes fluttered open slowly, his heart beating wildly. He didn't remember anything, not after the woman calling herself the Mother had snapped her fingers.

She'd clearly teleported them somewhere—a form of power he *knew* none of the Guardians possessed, not even Kadir.

Trying to force his eyes open, he didn't feel pain exactly, but they were slow to respond, almost as if they'd been magically glued shut.

Finally, he got them open, and to his shock, discovered that he was lying on a massive pile of furs, in a cabin, snug and cozy, with a roaring fire in a stone grate at one end, and shelves upon shelves of herbs. There was a gigantic iron pot suspended over the fire and something in it smelled delightful.

It could be poison, Evander warned himself, but it smelled so good, like rich broth and roasted vegetables and meat, that he nearly climbed to his feet and found out.

He heard a sound, and when he glanced over, he saw it was Marcos, his own eyes fluttering open.

Marcos was on his feet, immediately, knife in his hand.

"There is no need for that here," the Mother's voice said, and she snapped her fingers again and the knife was *gone*, disappeared completely from Marcos' grasp.

Marcos growled. "That is mine," he said.

"I will give it back," she said simply, "but I had to take it because you persist in believing that I intend to harm you, and I have no interest in being cut to smithereens by your suspicions or by your knife."

"Who *are* you?" Evander asked again.

She stared at him with that inscrutable expression. "And who are you, Evander, Guardian of Secrets? Are you Evander? Are you Evrard? Are you Rhys?"

"I am all of them, and more," he retorted.

"And I," she said mysteriously, "am all of you."

"You are not. If you were, you would not be unknown to us," Marcos argued. He shifted his weight again, and Evander found himself half behind Marcos' bulging bicep.

The thing was, this Mother could take all of Marcos' knives and his weapons, and even his sword, but she could not take the thing that made him most powerful of all.

Marcos himself was the effective component of Marcos' power.

"I have been greatly wronged," she said simply. "And you will right that wrong. I have selected you, because I believe you are the most capable of defeating Deimos."

"Deimos?" Marcos arched an eyebrow. "I do not intend to *defeat* Deimos."

"It would be a suicide mission," Evander said, annoyed he even had to say it. "Deimos is the Guardian of Death."

She turned, and somehow her profile was beautiful and terrifying and ancient, all at the same time, the fire sparking light in her hair. "I know what Deimos is, and what he is capable of," she said quietly. "I created him, after all."

"*You* created him? Then why can you not defeat him?"

"Because I am the *Mother*," she said, turning towards them, and suddenly she was more than terrifying, she was fierce. Resplendent. Her power sparking off her in waves that nearly overwhelmed Evander. "I do not destroy, I only create."

"You're saying you . . . you . . . you *can't*?" Evander couldn't believe it. Someone this powerful, they could do anything. And yet the frustration in her eyes, nearly boiling over, made Evander believe that she was actually telling the truth.

"I think," Marcos said, and for the first time since they'd both awoken, he was seemingly relaxed, sitting back down on the furs, "you should tell us the whole story."

"You will help?"

Evander glanced over at Marcos, because surely he would not be stupid enough to attempt to fight and defeat *Deimos*. He'd already challenged him once, and that had been a wild and potentially dangerous choice. *He did that, he took that risk for you*, Evander reminded himself, and suddenly felt both warm and cold all over. But Marcos did not have that look about him, when he was about to do something reckless, and Evander realized that he wasn't agreeing at all. He was biding his time.

"We will listen," Marcos said firmly.

Evander settled down next to him, and before he knew it, he was leaning into Marcos' firm shoulder. It felt reassuring in a way he could not explain, and he didn't move, not even when Marcos glanced at him, confusion in his eyes.

He loves you, why would he be surprised that you choose to touch him?

But that was a question for another time, and another place.

The Mother wrung her hands. "There is nobody else."

"I said we would listen," Marcos reminded her. "Tell us the story."

A wooden spoon bloomed from between her fingers and she turned towards the pot, still bubbling away on the fire. She was quiet for so long that Evander almost spoke, almost begged himself, because he *was* curious now. After all, he was the Guardian of Secrets, and the one secret he'd never come close to discovering was where they had all come from. They'd all appeared one day, fully formed and grown, with purposes and powers at the Castle at the Top of the World. If Deimos had known, he'd never said. He'd merely taken control of the group, as he seemed to be the most powerful and nobody had ever wanted to go against his word.

But try as he might, Evander had never been able to discover *who* created them or *why*.

He was beginning to think the Mother might be telling the truth.

She *might* truly be their Mother.

Finally, she spoke.

"I was alone for a very long time," she said, her tone quiet and contemplative, as if she was thinking of those years. "Nobody but myself and my thoughts to keep me company. For a while, for thousands of years, that was enough. And then, I realized, I could create anything I wanted. I could create . . . *more*. Someone to keep me company. I created a girl, and she became my companion. For a lifetime, we were happy, and then . . ." The Mother's voice broke then. "And then she died. I was alone again."

Evander could *feel* her sadness, her loss, her grief, floating in the air. It was a grief he recognized, from when Deimos had banished him from everything he'd known. He reached out, and before he could even *think* about it, he tucked his fingers into Marcos' hand, big and calloused, and squeezed.

Marcos squeezed back.

But he hadn't been alone, had he? He'd had Marcos, he just hadn't *known* he was there. Now he knew, and he also knew, deep down, without a single uncertainty, that he wouldn't ever have to be alone again. Not unless he chose to be.

"For a long while, I grieved her. I did not want to do anything else, because nothing could replace her. But then, slowly, I realized that she had awoken something in me that needed to be satisfied. A question that needed an answer. I knew the people I created would not last. They would grow old and they would die, so this time I did not just create a companion for myself, I created an entire people.

"The people, they begat more people, and then more, growing so much that while I still walked among them sometimes, I did not feel connected. I felt overwhelmed. But I could not let them be on their own, so with the help of another god, I created another kind of being."

"You created us," Marcos said.

She nodded. "I created Deimos. With his power and with his assistance, I created the immortal Guardians, and as Guardians, your task was to watch over them, to protect them. To usher in their life, and to make sure the life they lived was full of plenty, of joy, of love and music and belief, and then they were to be ushered into their death."

Her voice grew mournful again.

"I retreated. It was overwhelming, to think of all that I had done, and then lost. I needed the quiet again. And I enjoyed that quiet for thousands of years, again. Until . . ." She lifted her eyes, and they burned, right into Evander like a brand. Marcos made a sound, under his breath, and he knew he'd felt the power, too. "Until I woke up and realized that the Guardians no longer cared for protecting my people. They only cared for their own ability, their own immortality, their own consequence. Deimos, whom I had charged with leading the Conclave, had instead led the Conclave of Guardians astray. He had even banished one of *my* Guardians. But," she added wryly, "he could not strip you, Evander, of everything, because he did not create you. *I* created your power, and only I could uncreate it."

Evander had always wondered when he fell, when he was banished, why Deimos had left him with *some* of his magic. In some cases, it felt like only a remnant. A useful remnant, but only a fraction nonetheless. He'd finally come to the conclusion that Deimos had done so out of clemency, but now he realized that had been an easy lie he'd told himself.

If he could have, Deimos would have taken it all, stripped him and left him with nothing.

"See," the Mother said, "you see now why he needs to suffer, why he needs to be removed. He has grown too powerful."

"We cannot remove him," Marcos said with finality. "No matter what he has done. He is too strong. He is *Death*."

"And you are War," she said inexorably. "Do you not defeat Death with every battle you fight?"

"That is not the same," Marcos argued.

"But it is," the Mother said.

Marcos glanced over at him, intensity in his gaze. "Evander, you've been very quiet."

He'd been thinking. In actuality, analyzing the situation. He did not necessarily disagree with Marcos, but if there *could* be a loophole, a way they could remove Deimos and return the Conclave to its original purpose?

It might take a bit of convincing, but the other Guardians would eventually fall into line. They'd gone along with the corruption

Deimos had spread throughout the Conclave, but at least before Evander had been dismissed, he did not think Deimos had truly infected any of the others.

But there was one thing the Mother had said that made him wonder if it *was* possible, after all.

"If only you can uncreate my power, then why can you not uncreate Deimos'?" Evander asked.

She looked regretful. "Even my powers have limits," she said regretfully. "You do not believe that I would have done anything for my first companion to have lived with me forever? I would have. But that is a power I do not have. I can create, I am very good at it, but making it everlasting? That is Deimos' contribution. I cannot unmake him nor fully take his powers."

"And yet you want us to do it," Marcos said dryly.

She turned back to the fire and was quiet for a long time. Finally, she spoke. "Together, you are very powerful. You are drawn together. And together, you could defeat any obstacle."

Evander was not sure he believed as strongly that he and Marcos were as powerful as the Mother claimed, but he could feel the truth of her words resonating through him. He *was* drawn to Marcos. It was difficult to understand the why of it, though he was sure if Taavi was here, he could tell him all he needed to know.

But you don't need to know the why, you only need to know that it is true.

He also knew another truth: he felt a fierce and strong desire to destroy or at least defeat Deimos. He had been in power too long. He had grown corrupt. He had hurt Evander only because he could. If any of the other Guardians refused to follow his rules, he would do the same to them.

If Deimos had been fair and just, as he had been, in the very beginning, then perhaps he would have told the Mother that there was nothing to be done.

But deep down, he did not *know* that. He suspected it was possible, but Marcos was extraordinarily powerful, and he had already proven equal to Deimos in mettle.

The possibility existed that they *could* do something about Deimos.

"I think you could be right," Evander said.

Marcos looked shocked, his mouth falling open a little. He dropped Evander's hand, and he shouldn't have felt the loss of it, but he did.

"You are not thinking straight," he said.

"No, I am thinking straight enough," Evander retorted. "I know that he has grown too powerful."

Marcos said nothing. But the look in his dark eyes was plain enough.

"You must figure this out together," the Mother said, "and for the night, I will leave you here, alone, so you may discuss it."

"Thank you, kind Mother," Evander said, bowing a little.

She inclined her head. "It has been a long journey for you, and it will be longer still. Take the night and rest. Eat a hot meal. You have earned this." She snapped her fingers again, and suddenly, through the doorway on the other side of the room, they could see a huge wooden tub, steam curling around the edges.

And then, as suddenly as she'd appeared, she was gone.

"Have we though?" Marcos asked into the silence she left behind.

"Have we what?" Evander asked, standing and moving over to where the pot bubbled over the fire. The meat smelled delectable, large chunks of it floating in a spiced, dark brown gravy. His stomach grumbled. It had been too long since he'd eaten a hot meal, and this one was going to more than make up for it.

There was bread, tucked away in a basket, hearty and full of berries and seeds. And a large pitcher of golden mead, so much better than what he and Marcos had shared a few nights back, at the ugly, run-down inn.

"I hardly think we've earned a respite," Marcos grumbled as he walked over, his boots making punctuated thumps on the floor. "We've only been traveling for a handful of days, and it was hardly the most grueling campaign I've been a part of."

"Yes, we know, you are big and tough and built of stronger stuff than the rest of us," Evander retorted. "But the Mother isn't wrong. If we don't need to suffer, we shouldn't. Yes, I know this journey has only been a few days, but there were *years* I spent on the road. I have not been settled into Beaulieu that long."

He picked up several bowls and began to ladle out the stew. "Come sit, and stop pouting," he added. "Nobody says you must suffer to prove your worth."

"I didn't . . . I don't . . ." Marcos made a face, but sat down at the table anyway. "I hesitate to indulge in the Mother's hospitality when we must say no to her request."

Evander set the bowl on the table with a thump. "I disagree."

"That we should say no, or that taking her hospitality means we are obligated to consider the proposal?"

Marcos glared at him. "You want to say yes."

"I think it's our duty to say yes. To at least do what we can."

"When we could stay here, on the surface, forever, and never risk our comfort by indulging in Conclave politics? We have both done it for a number of years," Marcos pointed out. "We could do it for thousands more. There is nobody to stop us. We can live whatever life we choose."

"You could, perhaps," Evander said bitterly, spooning up his own bowl of stew, and setting it on the table, but he did not come sit down.

Instead he paced back and forth in front of the fire, feeling the warmth seep through him. Warm him in a place where it felt like he had not been warm for so long.

"I was *banished*," he finally said between clenched teeth. "I was not given a choice. I am here because I cannot be anyplace else."

"You want to punish Deimos for that," Marcos said.

Evander could see that he was trying to be understanding, but how could he possibly comprehend what it had been like?

Deimos had destroyed a fundamental part of what made him *him*. He'd mourned for it for hundreds of years.

Evander wasn't sure he'd ever stopped mourning it.

He'd felt a pang of it even now, only a few days ago, when he'd transformed into Evander again. When he'd looked into the reflective water of the stream and seen *him* again. But not him, all at the same time. He'd never truly be Evander, Guardian of Secrets, ever again.

"He should be punished for it," Evander said, hearing the alien harshness in his own voice. "He should have his own life, his own comfort, his own selfish superiority ripped away from him, until he knows how it feels."

"Would he though? Would we actually be able to do it? *Should* we do it?"

Evander whipped around, and the first thing he saw was the hard, firm line of Marcos' mouth.

"What?"

"We shouldn't do it. It's not prudent, and it's a risk we shouldn't take." Marcos sounded so sure, Evander felt a spike of temper.

"I don't know what risk *you* could possibly be talking about," Evander said, the fury already simmering away inside of him beginning to heat up to a much hotter temperature.

"If you could go back, to when Deimos told you to ignore the cult of sorcerers on the surface, you *would* ignore them. If you knew what it would cost you . . ."

"It wouldn't have mattered!" Evander was vaguely aware that he was yelling now. He didn't know where the Mother's house lay, but he hoped that it was far from anyone.

"How can *you* say that, when you know how much it cost you?" Marcos answered back, that inexorable, unflappable tone driving Evander wild, because how would Marcos know what it had cost him?

He'd not been the one to suffer through it.

He'd only watched from the sideline, thinking he knew all about it, but in reality, knowing nothing.

He had chosen; Evander had never chosen.

And Marcos sitting there, smug in his belief that they were exactly the same, that he'd taken the fall right with Evander, even though he'd barely even lost anything—in fact when he had in all honesty, *gained* from the transaction—made Evander's temper flare so much hotter.

Vanya had once told him that he could be evil if he chose. That he always had a choice between doing the right thing and the wrong thing.

Evander had retorted, the memory bright but faded in his mind, that only one thing ever muddied the waters for him: his temper.

Whenever he got angry, he lost perspective and control.

He'd lost it during the Conclave meeting when Deimos had ordered him to stay off the surface.

He lost it now.

Evander turned and, locking eyes with Marcos, saw the emotions flash across his face, the ones he'd always been successful at hiding before. The awe and the attraction and the inevitable, inexorable *pull*.

But Marcos couldn't hide them anymore; not when Evander knew his secret.

He didn't think it through. He didn't think at all. He emptied his mind entirely, and strode over, and Marcos went very still as he dug his palms into the table on either side of his body, and leaned in.

He'd only wanted to shut Marcos up. Needed that split second when Marcos *understood* that he wasn't in charge, that it didn't matter if he thought he presumed what Evander felt, that Evander held him and his balls in his fingertips.

Marcos didn't move. Didn't flinch. Just sat there and let Evander kiss him.

It had been a very long time since he'd done this, but he didn't remember how it had felt, not at all.

The heat, the moisture, the way it felt natural to lean in and let his tongue sweep across the closed seam of Marcos' lips. He was so much warmer, so much softer, than he'd ever imagined—and he swore that he *hadn't* thought about this, but the truth was uncomfortably different—and deep down, he felt a flare of something that wasn't temper at all.

Then Marcos let out a deep, shaky breath, and then he moved, reaching up and cradling Evander's cheek in his rough palm. For a single moment—that stupid single moment Evander dreamt that he would *own* Marcos, body and soul—that flare became a fire and then became a conflagration, raging in his belly as Marcos angled his head, and finally kissed him back.

It was scorching, yes, but it was sweet too, and Evander felt himself begin to sway on the edge, right before tumbling into something impossibly even hotter.

Before he could fall, he wrenched himself away. Heard his own breathing.

Wrong, Vanya would have said, chuckling in amusement, *you did something very wrong.*

"I shouldn't . . ." Evander licked his lips. Tasted Marcos on them. Salt like steel, but sweet too, so insanely sweet. Maybe it was those feelings, the ones he'd pretended for that split second that Marcos didn't have. "I shouldn't have done that."

Because it was the best kiss you've ever had in your life, and you've been kissed enough times to know it shouldn't have been like that.

But it had been.

CHAPTER EIGHT

MARCOS' FINGERS WERE TREMBLING so hard that he could barely pick up the rough-hewn spoon that Evander had set in front of him.

They were supposed to be eating. This was the first hot meal they'd had since leaving Beaulieu—since he barely counted what they'd eaten at the run-down tavern—but Marcos was stuck in a moment five minutes earlier.

How long had he dreamed about kissing Evander? Ravishing him until his knees grew weak and Marcos followed him to the floor?

But then he'd never imagined it under these circumstances either.

That Evander would kiss *him*, and that he'd do it because he was angry, and wanting to prove a point. That he would regret it afterwards.

Or that Marcos would discover that he simply did not care.

That he'd want to throw his spoon down, splattering stew every which way, and pin Evander's body to the table, and kiss him the way he'd *really* been dreaming of doing for all these years.

But doing any of that would be a mistake. Just as much of a mistake as Evander had claimed he'd already made.

"How is the stew?"

Tasteless. Bland. Probably would've been delicious, if I hadn't just had my mouth on yours.

Marcos knew that Evander was trying his best to be polite after the argument and then the cataclysmic finale to the argument, but being polite took more than he had to give right now.

In response, he grunted.

They sat in uncomfortable silence for another handful of minutes, and then because Evander couldn't give up—it was simply not in his nature—he spoke again. "Would you like some bread?" he asked, still with that innocuous, overly diplomatic tone, like he was back at Beaulieu, in charge of one of his interminable council meetings.

Marcos chanced a glance up. There was something still wild in Evander's eyes, even if he sounded so calm, so collected. He'd felt something. He was *still* feeling it.

"No," he said, and then returned his gaze back to his bowl, mechanically eating without really tasting anything he was putting in his mouth.

"I suppose," Evander said, like Marcos hadn't just made it plenty clear that he wasn't interested in polite dinner conversation, "that the Mother would be an excellent cook. I should not be so surprised that the fare at her table is excellent."

Marcos rolled his eyes. Annoyed, in spite of how he kept trying to clamp his temper down.

Temper meant something cataclysmic almost certainly happening again.

He was trying very hard *not* to let Evander seduce him into a temper.

Or seduce him into anything at all.

"Maybe," Marcos said sarcastically, "you should suggest to King Emory that he hire her for the kitchens at Beaulieu."

He felt the heat of Evander's look.

Not so bland now, he thought with satisfaction. But the heat, that was definitely the problem. Not the solution.

Evander sighed. "Are you never going to look at me? Or talk to me again?"

"Both seem like very possible outcomes," Marcos said.

"I apologized, twice if I recall. And you didn't acknowledge either of them."

How could he? Acknowledging Evander's apologies would mean acknowledging that the kiss *was* a mistake.

It hadn't felt like a mistake. Not a single heart-stopping breath of it.

He grunted again.

Marcos knew he was leaning into the worst kind of cliches about who he was. Only mindless fools avoided conversation by grunting, but maybe he *was* more of that mindless fool than he'd imagined.

Evander had certainly turned him into one with that kiss.

"Don't do that," Evander said. "I suppose you aren't going to look at me again, either."

Oh, but he *wanted* to. The desire had always been strong and fierce. But now it had grown claws. One taste and the grasping beast inside of him wanted a thousand more.

But instead of looking up, meeting Evander's eyes, he kept his gaze glued to the bowl.

"You are the most infuriating man," Evander continued. "You'd think . . . well, *I'd* think you were disappointed."

Marcos rolled his eyes.

"Why," he said, in clipped tones, daring a glance up at where Evander sat, leaning back in his chair, arms crossed over his chest, "are you trying to provoke me? Why can't you just leave me alone? Haven't you done enough today?"

"You *are* disappointed," Evander said, and now *he* sounded disappointed.

"You're talking even crazier than usual."

Marcos didn't understand why but this finally, *finally* silenced the other Guardian.

They ate the rest of their dinner in silence.

It didn't taste any better than it had before, but Marcos kept scooping up bites and then chewing, and swallowing. He didn't know what they'd face at the Well, but chances were it wasn't going to be good. He'd need his strength.

Marcos heard Evander stand. "I'm going to take a bath," he said. "I'm disgusting, and I'm not sure you're much of an improvement."

He wasn't.

And still, Evander had practically crawled into his lap.

He shook his head, trying to clear it.

"I will get in after you," he said.

"What?" Evander said, in a pseudo-shocked voice, "you don't want to share?"

He *was* trying to provoke him, and for the life of him, Marcos could not understand why. But whatever the reason, he'd reached the end of his rope and the last bit of it was fraying with temper.

He slammed the spoon down onto the table and shoved the bench back as he stood.

"Why?" he demanded.

He had at least a foot on Evander, and generally tried not to loom, but now he didn't care. He loomed with every single bit of his extra height. "Why won't you just leave it be?"

Evander stared at him, those pansy-blue eyes as wide as he'd ever seen them.

"I don't know how you can just leave it be," he said. "Don't you . . ." He swallowed hard, and didn't finish the sentence, which frankly, Marcos thought, was better for him.

"*Yes,*" Marcos burst out. "*Yes,* I had wanted to do that for a long time, and then you did it, and you told me you wished you hadn't. So if you want me to be blunt, this is me being blunt. I'm big, I'm awkward,

I'm terrible at this, so this is the only way I know of telling you to *leave it be.*"

One of the things that Marcos had always admired about Evander was that he never shrank from a fight or a challenge, and that intimidating him was basically a useless exercise. It couldn't be done, and it was a waste to even try.

"You're not awkward," Evander said.

"Well, thank you," Marcos retorted. "I'll make sure to focus on that gracious compliment tonight when I try to fall asleep. Now if that's all, I'm going to go do a quick check outside while you take your bath."

He turned to leave, but suddenly, Evander was there, in his space. Placing a hand on his shoulder. "No," he said very clearly. "No, I didn't tell you that I wished that I hadn't. I didn't think that at all."

"But you said . . ." Marcos felt like he was a breath away from stuttering. Embarrassingly.

So many ways he'd dreamed this would play out, and none of them had been nearly this humiliating.

"No," Evander repeated again, his lips turning up into a smile. A soft, intimate smile. "I said that I *shouldn't* have done it. And I shouldn't have. It was . . . it was unfair to you, because I did it out of anger, and then it was unfair to me, because I discovered that I didn't want to kiss you only to prove a point."

Marcos wasn't sure he'd heard correctly, but the luminous way Evander kept looking at him made it difficult to misinterpret.

"You . . . I . . . *what*?" He just plain stuttered this time.

Evander patted him on the shoulder, and then removed his hand. Marcos wanted to snatch it back.

"Do your check outside, though I know the Mother will make sure we're safe," Evander said. "And then," he added, with a twinkling smile that ratcheted Marcos' heartbeat up, "I'll meet you in the bath."

"You . . . you . . . you must really trust her," he said, even though he was thinking, *you must really trust me, you must really want me, and I can't understand why, though I'm not going to argue you out of it.*

"Yes," Evander said simply. "You felt it too, I think."

He had, and he'd felt it too when Evander's lips had touched his.

Which was why it had hurt so badly when Evander had leapt away, and muttered, *I shouldn't have done that.* Except that he was finally beginning to realize that Evander hadn't regretted the kiss—only the circumstances surrounding it.

He nodded, and even though he wanted to turn back, to grab Evander back and erase the memory of the first kiss with a second, he let him go.

Evander was right; they were both filthy dirty, and though he'd had a handful of dirty post-battle fumbles with willing soldiers, he wanted more for Evander.

He wanted everything for him, and everything *with* him.

It was eerie outside, the cabin situated in a stretch of forest comprised of a handful of spindly trees with scaly gray bark, and expanses of banked white snow. Nightfall had arrived, but Marcos could see nearly as well in the dark as he could in the light, so he walked around the structure, verifying that there was nobody there, that it didn't feel like there was a single person around for leagues, and then after stamping the snow off his boots, went back inside.

Evander had disappeared, likely into the room with the tub, and he paused halfway across the room, hesitating.

Had Evander's offer been legitimate? Did he truly want to bathe with him?

You are not afraid of anything; your nerve has never failed you, not at the brink of a battle or in the middle of a fight. Are you really afraid of him?

Marcos knew he was afraid of what havoc Evander could wreak if he used him and then left him.

He'd cared for him for too long to be able to let that go.

But without risk, he knew there was never any benefit.

"Come in," Evander called out. "The water's so warm."

Steeling himself, Marcos crossed the main room, and then stood at the edge of the doorway.

The tub filled most of the room, and it did look warm, steam still curling across the surface of the water.

"I think it's a magic tub," Evander said, "charmed or something. Because the water should not still be this hot, and yet it is."

He was naked, and in the tub. If Marcos leaned closer, he could've seen the rest of Evander's body, beneath the water. But he'd seen it already, both before he'd been banished, in the huge underground cavern of baths at the Castle at the Top of the World, and then a few days back, when they'd bathed together in the freezing stream.

But just because he was familiar with the elegant grace of Evander's perfectly formed limbs didn't mean his heart stayed calm or his blood cool or his cock soft.

"The Mother has indeed been generous," Marcos said, and began the process of unbuckling and removing his light leather armor, one piece at a time.

Evander watched. Intently, if Marcos had the words to describe it.

It had been a miracle that he'd managed to hide his erection at the stream. There was no way to hide it now, and Evander, who, as far as he could tell, hadn't spent much of the last thousand years indulging in many pleasures of the flesh, didn't seem particularly perturbed by the possibility that he might get an eyeful.

Marcos leaned down, and pulled his boots off, grateful for the fur lining, and then let his last garment, his breeches, fall off him.

He looked up to see Evander regarding him steadily, gaze steady but alert, and Marcos told himself not to blush as his cock, heavy with blood, bobbed as he leveraged himself into the tub.

The heated water hit his skin and he groaned in pleasure.

"Come," Evander repeated, gesturing next to him.

It was more than he'd expected. It was probably more than he deserved, but Marcos wasn't going to be stupid enough to say no.

He floated over, resting his back against the circular wall of the tub, feet brushing Evander's.

"See?" Evander said smugly. "Isn't that better than being all the way over there?"

"I don't know, is it?" Marcos teased. Evander *knew* how he felt. He'd figured out his secret, and there was no point in denying it except the way that Evander's eyes lit at the provoking statement made Marcos smile.

Evander didn't answer his question with words. He shocked the breath right out of Marcos' chest by turning, and straddling him, wet skin brushing wet skin everywhere. Marcos' pulse skittered with anticipation. For a long moment, Evander just stared at him. It felt similar to that moment so long ago, the night of Evander's banishment, when he'd spoken to Marcos in his chambers and it was as if he'd *seen* him for the first time.

He was seeing Marcos now. There was no question of it.

Evander's fingers were slippery on his skin as he pressed them into Marcos' shoulders. "I don't usually do this," he said quietly. A confession. Something else that Marcos knew he didn't do very often.

He'd been the Guardian of Secrets for a reason.

"Only with Vanya," he added, as if Marcos hadn't already known that. "I didn't really think I wanted to, and then . . ."

It was impossible to stop his smile. "And then?"

Evander rolled his eyes, but it didn't make Marcos' cock any softer, and it didn't make *Evander's,* currently rubbing against his own every few moments, any softer either. "And then you insisted on getting naked in that stream," Evander pointed out. "You're . . . you're very nicely formed. Everywhere."

Marcos raised an eyebrow. "Everywhere?"

"Yes," Evander said lightly. "Everywhere."

"I was of the opinion it started earlier than that," Marcos said gently. "After the fight."

They'd almost kissed then. Marcos had been a heartbeat away from giving in to so many long years of denial and just pressing his lips to Evander's. It would've been reckless, but it was also nearly irresistible.

"That was just the battle. Bloodlust and all that," Evander said, biting his lower lip. Marcos' fingers trembled as he settled them on the smooth skin of Evander's waist. He had exceptional self-control, but it was only a matter of time before he gave in to everything he wanted.

Everything they both wanted.

That much Marcos could admit to now.

"I've felt that, many times," Marcos said seriously, "and it's never felt like that before."

"What does *this* feel like?" Evander wondered. Like he didn't want to just know what Marcos felt, but he wanted Marcos to give it definition, so he could understand it too.

"Everything," Marcos said roughly, and tugged Evander another inch closer, covering his mouth with his own.

There was nothing angry about this kiss. Nothing hesitant. Nothing unsure. It was all fire and heat and the slickness of their skin as Evander rubbed against him.

Marcos groaned into his mouth as he let his fingers skate down his thighs, and then up his back, reverently caressing all the places that he'd admired so many times. But only ever from afar. He'd only been able to look, but never touch.

Evander tilted his head and the kiss impossibly deepened, their tongues brushing together, delving deeper until he wasn't sure where he ended and Evander began. Marcos felt the flame of it in his blood, beating in time between his heart and his cock, and he wanted so much he felt like he might burst with it.

Then he felt the tentative reach of Evander's hand, soft and sure, as it wrapped around his cock. Pleasure surged through him and he broke the kiss, panting with it.

"You don't have to . . ." Marcos exhaled, each word punctuated with a breathy moan as Evander began to twist his palm up and down.

"I want to," Evander said, and his eyes were knowing, pupils blown dark with lust. "I really, really want to."

Marcos would have to be a much more foolish man to keep arguing. So he tilted his head back and let Evander explore. He clearly had some knowledge, but he was also a tease, giving Marcos just enough to keep him right on the edge, but never enough to send him over.

His thumb crested over the swollen head of his cock, and he gasped with the intensity of it.

"You feel so good," Evander said with wonder. Like he hadn't imagined it *could* feel like this.

It had been long enough for him, that maybe he'd forgotten.

Vanya—*no*, Marcos thought with resolution, *you are not going to think about him right now. Not when Evander . . .*

Then Evander leaned in, kissing him, deep and filthy and it was glorious, so much more than Marcos had ever let himself dream of, that he fell right over the cliff, spurting into Evander's hand.

When he opened his eyes, Evander was staring at him, impossibly smugger.

"You enjoyed that," he said.

"What gave it away?" Marcos teased again, trailing his hand up Evander's thigh. Nearly to where he strained for Marcos' touch.

"Maybe the way you moaned my name," Evander said.

Had he moaned Evander's name? He must have. He was going to count it as a win that he hadn't said anything else embarrassing.

Because the truth was, his heart had never felt fuller.

Maybe this wasn't love for Evander, but he was here, in his arms, sweet and gasping for it, and that was better than any fantasy he'd ever indulged in.

"What do you want?" Marcos asked.

"I want you to touch me," Evander said, staring at him straight in the eyes, no shame. Not a single ounce of it. "And I want you to kiss me. I really like the kissing."

It wasn't a hardship to do both, because Marcos really liked the kissing too.

It added an extra layer of thrill to an already glorious experience.

He slid his hand closer, and loved the way he felt Evander's skin tremble, and when he brushed the back of his hand against just the tip of his cock, it twitched, so eager.

"Like that?" he asked, after leaning in and nibbling right along the seam of Evander's lips.

"No," Evander said breathlessly, and he pressed his whole body closer, nudging his cock further into Marcos' palm, and then giving him the kind of kiss that would keep him warm for so many nights to come.

Marcos didn't want to tease anymore, just wanted to make him feel good, and so he worked him up and down, twisting Evander's cock with his fingers, noting how much harder he moaned into his mouth whenever the callouses on his fingertips rubbed him.

If Evander had a weakness for his sword callouses, who was he to argue with that?

With one last suck of his tongue, Evander gave a shout, and shook in Marcos' arms, falling apart in the most glorious sight he'd ever been privileged to witness.

When Evander finally stopped shuddering, they lay there, warm water still swishing around them, for a long time, not speaking.

Marcos didn't want to ruin the perfection of the moment, but he already knew Evander's brain was working, because even a really fantastic orgasm wouldn't be enough to slow it or stop it.

Finally, he *did* speak. "You don't want to try to defeat Deimos," he said.

Marcos wasn't particularly surprised by this change of subject. It didn't bother him. He shifted to the other side of the tub, and finding some soap, began to scrub the rest of the filth and sweat off him.

"No."

It had been a wild risk the first time he'd challenged Deimos, and he'd only done it because there was no other choice. Evander might not have known he was there, on the surface with him, but Marcos hadn't wanted to leave him.

He hadn't labored under the false impression that he had done much at all to help Evander, but it had been reassuring to know that he could if the need arose.

Evander joined him a second later. "And I do."

"You seem to want to tangle with him again, for reasons that I confess I don't entirely understand," Marcos admitted. "But that doesn't make your reasons any less valid."

Evander smiled. "I knew you could see sense," he said, taking the soap from him. "What do you think we should do?"

Marcos ducked his head under the water and rinsed. "You're asking me?" He was surprised. Evander rarely asked for counsel; he always thought he knew best.

"I am," Evander admitted.

"I think we should go to the Well, and determine the scope of the trap," Marcos said. "Tell the Mother that we have yet to make a final decision."

"You think she will accept that?"

"I don't think she has much of a choice," Marcos said, slowly. "She is requesting this of *us*, and has admitted herself powerless in the situation."

Evander nodded.

"Besides," Marcos added, "I would rather only fight one battle at a time."

"Do you mean, *we* should only fight one battle at a time?" The expression on Evander's face was surprisingly playful, considering the subject they were discussing.

Marcos leaned back against the side of the tub. Enjoying the hot water. Enjoying this conversation, more than he ever expected he would. "Logically," he said, "it follows that the Guardian of War would do the majority of the battling."

"I will not disagree with you there," Evander said. He rinsed and joined Marcos at the edge of the tub, their feet brushing together under the water. It felt so companionable, so much what Marcos had always wanted, that his heart ached. "But the Mother said that we needed to be *together*. To be a partnership."

"Forgive my inclination to keep you safe with my not inconsiderable skill," Marcos said dryly.

"It is appreciated but unnecessary," Evander retorted. "If you've been watching me as long as it seems, you know I can take care of myself."

"I do know," Marcos admitted.

"And," Evander added, smiling, "I might even be an asset. How many Guardians can shoot fireballs out of their hands?"

"None," Marcos said. "Which was always surprising to me. It's an oddly offensive power for a Guardian who always liked avoiding fights."

"I like to think that the Mother knew with so much sneaking around, I'd eventually need to be able to blow someone to bits," Evander said mischievously.

"You should ask her." It was not the first time Marcos had considered all of the Guardians' magical gifts. Some of them, like his extraordinary skill with weapons, made sense. Others were more obscure.

"Perhaps I will, someday." Evander hesitated. "How far do you think we are from the Well?"

"We were perhaps two days' ride when we were caught up in the Mother's trap. But I do not know how far out of the way we were taken by the Mother," Marcos said, considering the question. "It is much colder outside than it had been, less trees, more in line with the scenery I'd expect near the Well. If I had to guess, I'd say we're even closer."

"The Well being near the Mother's home . . . that makes sense. Power gravitates towards power," Evander said. "She might have even *created* the Well. That wouldn't surprise me in the least."

There was nothing Marcos wanted more than to stay floating in the hot water, enjoying the comfort of being clean, and enjoying just *talking* to Evander. It had been so long, so many hundreds of years, since he had been able to talk to someone who understood exactly what he was, the responsibility that had always lain so heavily on his shoulders.

With Evander smiling over at him, the weight of it felt less pressing.

And Evander? He'd been alone for so long.

"I wish . . ." Evander paused. Suddenly looking very serious. "I wish you'd let me know you were out there a long time ago."

He was also feeling that intoxicating weightlessness, then.

Marcos thought back to all the many times he'd come face-to-face with Evander—when he'd been in one of his many personas—and then he'd walked away.

Why hadn't he reached out?

Every one of those times, it had seemed impossible.

"You said it yourself," Marcos said finally. "You didn't need my help."

Evander rolled his eyes. "No, I did not. But the company would have been nice. This is nice." He looked at Marcos questioningly, like he was wondering if Marcos was enjoying it too.

That was frankly ridiculous, because it was everything Marcos had ever yearned for.

"Come," Evander said, rising, water streaming off his naked body. A sight that Marcos had seen before, but it had never hit him like this, like a blow to the ribs. It hurt, left him breathless with the impact, and yet, it felt so wonderful that all he craved was more.

Evander reached out a hand, and Marcos took it.

"I'm tired," he said. "And that bed was comfortable."

Marcos had been prepared to sleep on the floor. But when Evander, after drying off, settled into the nest of furs in the corner of the main room, he looked up expectantly at where Marcos stood, awkwardly, one of his knives in his hand. He never slept without it.

"Well," he said, "are you joining me or not?"

And Marcos couldn't say no.

CHAPTER NINE

Evander woke with the sound of the door opening and closing.

When he opened his eyes, he saw the broad shoulders of Marcos, as he came back into the cabin.

He cleared his throat, as he pushed the furs down, and as he reached for his clothes, Marcos' gaze turned towards him.

"You're awake," he said, looking pleased.

It was a soft look that Evander had never expected to see on the fierce Marcos' face, but it suited him.

Made it easier to not regret how close they'd become last night.

"As are you," Evander said, pulling up his breeches, shoving his feet into boots.

"I never sleep soundly in a strange place," Marcos admitted. "I was up early, trying to determine our location."

Evander decided that he would let him have the evasive answer; he could understand how waking up, tucked in close to him, might have been overwhelming.

Neither of them knew how to do this. Better to focus on the matter at hand.

The fire had banked overnight, and Evander walked over, picking up a twisty stick, charred black at the end, poking at it. "Were you successful?"

"There's plenty of snow on the ground. Large snowdrifts. I'd guess we're fairly close to the Well."

"An hour by horseback."

Marcos tensed, a knife appearing so quickly in his hand, Evander didn't know how he could've drawn it so fast.

Evander hadn't really considered how the Mother would arrive this morning, but suddenly, there she was, holding a fresh loaf of bread and giving them a look that made it clear she'd known exactly what they'd get up to if she left them alone—and that she approved.

Evander fought back his blush as Marcos slipped his knife back into its boot holster, the tense muscles of his shoulders relaxing.

"That close?" Marcos asked, raising an eyebrow.

She turned to him, tucking a strand of white-gold hair behind an ear as she pulled out a wickedly curved knife of her own, and began to cut the bread into slices. "I created it," she said offhandedly, "I would not want to make it so very far away, would I?"

"No," Evander said. "You wouldn't."

He'd been right, then. He couldn't say he was particularly surprised. If he reached back into his memory, the *feel* of the Well had the same mysterious slippery energy that the power of the trap had.

Unidentifiable, which was why he hadn't recognized it.

"Deimos always said that it was a gift, and that gifts could be rescinded, if the Well was not treated with respect."

The Mother's glance at Marcos was stern. "Deimos is wrong in many things," she said, "but right in this. I have considered removing it many times over the years. It gives Deimos power, but then"—and now her expression turned sly—"it also gives others power too."

"Who?" Evander wanted to know.

But her expression had already closed off, becoming opaque, and she did not reply. Instead she held out slices of the bread she had cut.

"Come," she said, "sit down, break your fast, and tell me what you have decided."

Evander sat, and watched as Marcos reluctantly followed.

His sense of honor was likely smarting, worried that by accepting her hospitality and not her offer, that they would offend the Mother.

"We have not decided," Evander said.

She hummed under her breath, slathering the bread with thick, golden butter from an ancient-looking pottery crock on the table. "I guessed as much," she said.

"We do not know what faces us at the Well, or why we were called there," Marcos added, more apologetic than Evander had ever heard him.

"I do not think it a coincidence," the Mother said softly. But her gaze did not accuse.

"Me either," Marcos agreed. "But we can only fight one battle, on one front. I, too, am concerned about Deimos' growing power, and the actions he took against Evander, but right now, the possibility that the voice calling us to the Well is a trap must take precedence."

The Mother's gaze swung towards Evander, and he felt pinned by the sheer age and complexity of it. "And you, Guardian?"

Evander considered correcting her use of his title. He was no longer a Guardian, not if his powers were as diminished as they were, not if Deimos had banished him from the Conclave. But she knew what had happened and must not have cared, as she still addressed him by his old title.

"I would defeat him," Evander said cautiously. "He should not get to banish any others like he did me. He should be leading the Conclave with an eye towards the surface, but he is not."

"And you are." The Mother said it with finality. Like her word was law.

"I have tried," Evander said.

"You care about my people," the Mother said. "I will hope that with the trap at the Well addressed, you will decide that Deimos is the danger and must be defeated, at any cost."

Marcos frowned, and Evander knew he was thinking about the last word she'd said.

The cost.

Evander could place himself in Marcos' shoes and see how the cost might be more than he was willing to pay. After all, they *could* make a life for themselves here on the surface, and not involve themselves in the Mother and Deimos' power struggle.

They would be happy. Evander knew that much, because it felt like the happiness and satisfaction he'd been searching for was right within his grasp.

But he also remembered how he'd felt returning to Beaulieu with no purpose.

A life without purpose, especially an everlasting life, was no life at all.

"We appreciate your hospitality and the night of rest," Marcos said stiffly.

The Mother smiled, and it was so warm it was like sunning yourself on a bright summer day. Her power was so effortless it astounded him. "It was entirely my pleasure," she said. "I have long wanted to meet you."

That possibility was even more confounding. That this woman, of tremendous power, had wanted to know *them,* even though Evander had long been stripped of what he'd thought had made him special.

"And no," she continued, her smile growing, "not because you *used* to be a Guardian, but because of what you committed to doing once that path was closed to you." She turned to Marcos. "And you did not have to follow him to the surface, at such a great personal cost, either."

"Yes, I did," Marcos said firmly, with conviction.

"Well, I am very glad you think so," the Mother said, patting him on the arm. "Is there anything else you need for your journey?"

"No," Evander said, exchanging a glance with Marcos as he finished eating his bread. "I believe we should be on our way, though."

"I wish you the best of luck," the Mother said. "Your horses are outside."

Marcos looked surprised.

"You did not think I would take them?" The Mother laughed. "I merely housed and fed and warmed them, as I did you. They are rested and should serve you well, on the final part of your journey."

Marcos bid her goodbye, and went outside to find them.

Evander turned to face her. "What if I wanted to speak to you again?" he asked.

"Then, you need only think of me, and I will be there," she said. She pressed a wrinkled, yet smooth palm to his cheek and he nodded. Turning to leave, she caught his arm. "Wait," she added. "There is one thing you should know. The Well? Is not only a portal and a magnet for everything of power, but can also restore what is lost."

"What?" Evander wasn't quite sure he understood. Was she talking about *his* power? About bringing back what Deimos had taken from him?

But instead of answering, the Mother gave him another one of those enigmatic looks, snapped her fingers, and Evander found himself outside, next to the horses that Marcos was currently checking over.

He looked over, raising an eyebrow. "Was the door not good enough for you?" he asked.

Evander stared at him. "No," he said slowly. "Not at all . . . the Mother just told me something."

"What is it?" Marcos asked. He mounted his horse.

Evander followed suit, patting his horse's neck reassuringly. "I'm not sure," he admitted honestly. "I need to think about it."

Marcos was quiet for a moment, like he wasn't sure how he should react to Evander not telling him everything. "If you want time, then take the time," he said. "I believe the road is that way," he said, pointing in a northern direction. "At least I keep *thinking* this is the way we should go, so going this way makes logical sense."

Evander nodded. "You think she planted the idea in your head," he stated.

"I don't like it much, but yes."

Evander thought again of the information she'd given him right as he was leaving.

She'd waited until Marcos was already out of earshot. It could have been accidental, but Evander had a feeling that everything she did was purposeful.

A few minutes of riding later, they found the road. Marcos gazed up it—because it was inevitably *up,* a long, winding rocky path that made its way up the mountain, to the top, where the Well lay.

"I would not have taken the horses," he said, "but she was so adamant that they were necessary to the journey."

"I doubt much she says is by chance."

Marcos shot him a look. "Including what she said to you?"

Evander chuckled under his breath. "I knew you could not leave it alone."

"Forgive me," Marcos retorted. "I do not like secrets."

"I believe many would call that an ironic statement," Evander said lightly. "But I will tell you, even though I do not believe she wanted me to."

Marcos frowned, staring ahead at the rocks that littered the path. "Because she told you after I'd left."

Evander nodded. "She said the Well was not only a portal, but could also restore what was once lost."

Marcos was silent for a long time, the only sound their horses' hooves on the path, as they carefully picked their way around the exposed stones. "You think she was talking about your power."

"I don't know what else she could have been referring to."

"It feels like a trick."

"It *feels* like an opportunity," Evander countered.

"Or an unnecessary risk," Marcos said.

"This is why the Mother waited until you had left before telling me anything about it," Evander said, annoyed. "You're too cautious. Too risk-averse."

"Should I be racing into fights and not avoiding them? That's what everyone expects from a Guardian of War, isn't it? Craving battle. Craving carnage. But I never have. I won't apologize for being careful. Or for being careful with you."

Evander glared at him. "I'm not a *thing* you need to protect."

"I am perfectly aware of that," Marcos said. Still calm. Evander realized that he *was* calm. And the one whose temper kept flaring was him.

And that hardly helped dampen his anger.

"Are you saying you just can't help it? That . . ." Evander spit out the words, until he realized what he was going to say, and he stopped abruptly.

Marcos had not even said the words yet, and it felt wrong, even as furious as he was, to spit them back at him like they were weapons in an argument.

"That I don't want you to throw your existence away on a trick? On a fool's errand?" Marcos questioned lightly. Like he didn't know what Evander had been about to say. And yet, he had to know.

"Are you saying the Mother is trying to trick us? Trick *me*? You felt her power. I know you did. Felt it better than I did, probably."

"I'm not questioning her story," Marcos said patiently. Too patiently. "I did feel her power. I believe she is exactly who she claims to be. But she also did not tell you how to use the Well to restore your powers. She did not even say it would. You concluded that, all on your own."

Evander ground his teeth together.

"This is another subject on which we will never agree," Evander said. "I do not understand how the Mother could say we make a great team when we disagree on everything."

Marcos' glance at him was sly, knowing. "Not everything," he said.

Evander huffed. Still annoyed. But *less* annoyed.

Marcos shouldn't be able to diffuse his temper like that. Nobody had ever been able to, not even Vanya.

But Marcos knew just how to take the force of his anger and twist it into something else.

"This is not over," Evander insisted, more to himself than to Marcos—who was intimately familiar with just how stubborn he was, and would likely already know that their discussion on this particular topic was just beginning.

Marcos didn't respond, merely inclined his head, and Evander caught the flash of amusement in his eyes.

They rode on for another hour.

The road became a path and then became a track.

Evander had to re-focus himself on the task of leading his horse through the increasingly icy shards of rock as they rode further.

He *had* been considering the words of the Mother, and how he could possibly use the Well to restore his power, but it was too hard to pay attention to the road and also to the conundrum that she'd raised by her statement.

Wind whipped around their heads, swirls of freezing air and icy snowflakes. The sky was an ominous dark gray, solid and unrelenting above them.

It was not a particularly welcoming place.

Power wasn't, usually.

It was difficult and prickly and dangerous.

Evander had never liked coming to the Well; he'd used the portal contained within it and always made sure to put as much distance between him and it as possible. Evrard's hooves had been particularly steady on the sheets of ice that coated the winding path down the mountain.

He had suggested, when they had stopped to unpack an additional cloak for Marcos, that he could change.

"And then what would we do with the other horse? And what kind of use will you be as a unicorn when we reach the Well?" Marcos had questioned.

"The Mother told us to bring them, thus ensuring I'd stay in this form," Evander realized, trying not to sulk. He'd been rather proud of that suggestion.

Marcos nodded. "I believe that, as well.

"I think only a little bit longer," Marcos added as they re-mounted their horses. "Be prepared for anything when we reach the top."

"I have always been prepared," Evander retorted.

Marcos didn't disagree and Evander caught a hint of pleasure on his face, before it disappeared into the swirl of his cloak's heavy hood.

The Well was a silent place.

There was the wind of course, echoing around them eerily, like it was calling to the power that massed here, and listening to its answer. But other than that, there was nothing.

Marcos' boots crunched on the ice as he dismounted, tying his horse to one of the spindly trees that circled the jutting hill. It was maybe a dozen yards to the top, where the Well sat.

Evander dismounted too, and followed suit, tying up his horse. "Will they be safe here?"

Patting the neck of his horse, Marcos contemplated this. "I don't think they will be *unsafe.*"

"You think the Mother put a charm on them."

Marcos grinned suddenly, a brightness cutting through the icy gloom. "The horse is warmer than I. I think she knew we'd need them and made sure they were prepared."

"She is the Mother, after all. She creates and she tends what she creates."

Marcos nodded.

"I would not worry about them," Marcos said. "Though if I recall, you were not a fan of anything else of equine descent before this. Why the sudden concern for them?"

Evander rolled his eyes. "The power, you can feel it around us. It has form and thought and *will.* How do you think it would react if it discovered that we were negligent of any creature?"

"You think the power comes from the Mother, and wouldn't like us leaving the horses to die."

"Put simplistically, yes," Evander said. He saw Marcos' expression darken, and hurried to add, "I do not think *you* simplistic, of course."

"Of course." Marcos' tone was wry. "You would never think that."

Except they both knew he had. For a thousand years and more.

Marcos leaned down, and pulled the knife from his boot. It shone bright silver, the curved blade wickedly sharp, even in the gray, dingy light surrounding them.

He flipped it in his hand, effortlessly, and extended it towards Evander, the leather-wrapped handle towards him.

"Here," he said.

Evander had a much smaller knife, tucked away in *his* boot. Admittedly, it was a knife that Rhys had used for cutting pieces of meat at dinner, or for slicing open messages, and not for defending himself, but there was no reason it wouldn't be perfectly sufficient in a fight.

Marcos must have seen his hesitation, because he continued. "And don't tell me you've got one, I've seen that blade. You could stick that in me and I wouldn't even hesitate; I'd keep coming. This"—he lifted the blade in his hand again—"has an enchanted blade. It'll give you a second, maybe two, against a Guardian."

"I thought we weren't going against any Guardians."

Marcos' stare was impossible to read. "I don't know what we're going against," he said. "But I like to be prepared."

Once, Gray had told him what it had felt like the first time he'd touched Lion's Breath, the flaming sword that had destroyed Sabrina. "It wasn't even *mine*, not even from Ardglass," Gray had said, "but the moment I put my hand upon the grip, I felt it, like I'd been shot with an arrow, with lightning. Scared me half to death. Later, I thought it was just that we were suddenly in the middle of a fight, but it wasn't that. The sword knew me. Knew I would use it. And then I did. The power wasn't just in the sword, then, it was in *me*."

Evander, who had helped forge Lion's Breath, hadn't been particularly surprised, since he'd been hoping from Gray's birth that he would be the one who'd finally wield the sword the way it was meant to be wielded.

But he'd never expected to feel something like that himself.

Until he reached out and took Marcos' knife, and the moment the tips of his fingers brushed the leather, he felt the jolt of it, the *shock*. Yes, it was definitely the enchantment of it, because when he reached out and tasted the power imbuing it, it was undeniably Marcos'. But it was more than that. This knife that he'd seen a handful of times before his banishment, but never made particular note of, reached out and grabbed him by the throat, the power and the magic overwhelming him. Choking him.

He dropped it.

"What is it?" Marcos was instantly by his side, concern written on his starkly handsome features. "What happened?"

Evander eyed the dagger, lying so innocuously on the ground. "I think . . . I think I am meant to wield this dagger," he said slowly.

"I gave it to you so you *could*," Marcos pointed out.

"No." Evander took a deep breath. "More than that. I think I was *always* meant to have this dagger."

Marcos hummed under his breath. "I remember when I forged this," he said. "It was a long winter. I was . . . preoccupied with other matters, but I felt myself drawn to the forge, and I poured all my worries and my fears and . . . all my other emotions, into it."

"That winter, when you started to see me . . . differently?" Evander asked carefully. Not wanting to put words into Marcos' mouth.

"Yes." He reached down and picked the dagger up. "I suppose, for as long as I've carried it, this blade has really always been yours."

This time when Evander took it, gingerly touching it with his fingers, the blade's power didn't overwhelm him. Instead, it . . . it *welcomed* him. Like it was coming home.

"I think you may be right," Evander said.

"Strange," Marcos said, and Evander, still staring at the blade, at the gold symbols engraved deep into the silver blade, heard him withdraw his sword from its sheath. "It never felt particularly powerful to me, only that I always felt like I wanted it with me, just in case."

"Just in case," Evander mused as they began to climb the last part of the path. He had to pay close attention to where he stepped because the ice was treacherous, but part of him was still singing with the way the knife felt in his hand.

How happy it was that the knife and Evander had finally come together.

"Stay behind me," Marcos ordered as they finally reached the last bit of the trail. They had only a dozen more steps, and they would emerge at the very top of the mountain.

Evander could see it in his mind's eye, the icy shards protecting the deep, turquoise-blue icy water of the Well, the power swirling around it in white clouds of vapor.

As Marcos crested the hill, Evander right behind him, he pulled the power in, centered it, focused it, ready to push it out as a flame from his outstretched hand, but as he glanced wildly around him, he realized that it was a waste, because there was nobody there to aim a fireball at.

Marcos didn't stand down yet. He crept around the Well, examining every inch of the ice and snow at their feet, every shard of it that rose in the air, protecting the Well.

Finally, he returned to where Evander stood. "Have you heard any-thing?" he asked.

Evander had wondered as they made the last climb if he would hear Vanya's voice again. After all, it was his voice that had summoned him here.

But there was nothing.

Only the eerie silence.

"No," he finally had to admit. "Nothing."

Marcos sighed. "We will wait. You were called here. Someone wanted you at the Well."

"Maybe it was the Mother," Evander suggested.

"If it was her, she would have cleared up the confusion when we were there," Marcos said. "Because the potential trap at the Well was why we had to put off doing what she wanted—defeating Deimos."

"I think she wanted us to come here, and wanted me to use this"—Evander lifted the dagger, which sang in his hand, a siren's song of belonging—"to restore the power that Deimos stripped from me."

"My dagger?" Marcos' face and voice were full of disbelief. "How would she have even known that I would give you that dagger? It was *mine* for many hundreds of years. Not yours."

"It's always been mine. You had it, yes, but you were carrying it for me."

Marcos frowned. "How do you know this?"

He'd known Marcos would ask, but the question made him flinch anyway. "You will not believe me."

"I tend to believe a lot of what you say, in fact," Marcos retorted reproachfully.

"You will not believe me, because I barely believe it myself," Evander said wryly. "I know because the dagger told me."

"It *told* you?"

"I touched it, and it was so much power, it overwhelmed me. That's why I dropped it. But . . ." Evander knew how crazy he sounded, but he continued anyway. "When I picked it up again and we walked the rest of the way to the Well? That's when I felt it."

"And you felt that it wanted you to use it to channel your power back?" Marcos sounded understandably skeptical.

Evander nodded. "I just . . . I just *know*. I can see myself, plunging the dagger into the middle of the Well. It's rough. It's . . . it's terrifying. The power engulfs me. Everything goes black. And then I wake up, and I can *feel it*. Coursing through me like it never left, like Deimos never banished me."

Everything he'd ever wanted and never believed he could have again, back in an instant.

Marcos eyed the Well, sitting, calm and undisturbed, in the middle of the protective ice shards. "I do not think it is wise to follow *this* path. It is one thing to follow a suggestion placed in my mind as to which direction to travel. It is entirely another to use a magic we don't understand."

"Why do we have to understand it?" Evander threw his hands up in frustration. He could feel something inside of him, pushing him, prodding him, *wanting* him to win this argument. Normally he'd have felt at least some of Marcos' caution and concern, felt some fear that this, just like the voice, was a trap. But all he felt was the exhilaration of hope.

After so long being hampered and hindered, he could be fully himself again. He could actually *be* Evander. Not this similar facsimile, the outward appearance the same, but the inner self diminished. He could be *all of it*, again.

"I wish I had never given you the dagger," Marcos announced, turning to him, a solemn look on his face. "I should take it back from you."

If Marcos wanted to come over and forcibly remove it from his hand, he could.

The regret written on his face told Evander just how much he didn't want to.

"You won't."

"You could destroy yourself," Marcos said.

"A risk I am willing to take."

Marcos looked away then, like the thought of losing him was too much to bear, like he did not want Evander to see the emotion in his eyes at only the idea of it.

He did not look back when he spoke, but his voice was rough and raw. "What if it is not a risk *I* am willing to take?"

"You know very well that it is not up to you," Evander said, gently. "This is a chance for me to be . . . for me to be myself again. I cannot pass it by. You know I can't."

Marcos did not say anything for a very long time.

There was only the wind, whistling around them, and the counterpoint in his head, the song of the dagger, wanting him to take back what had been forcibly ripped from him.

Finally Marcos straightened, and looked him straight in the eye. "I know," he said. "I know you have to try."

"You could stop me." Evander did not know why he was filling Marcos' head with ideas. He *could* stop him. Nothing could stop Marcos, not even Death, from taking the dagger from his hand. He was bigger, he was stronger, and his fighting skills were legendary.

"It is not my choice to make." Marcos' voice was rueful. "I wish I could reconcile myself to stopping you, but I can't. It's your decision. Your risk. Your fate."

"Yes."

Evander switched the dagger to his other hand, and began to gather his fire magic, what was left of it anyway, so he could melt away the protective shards around the Well.

"Wait," Marcos said, and suddenly, he was at Evander's side. "You should save your strength. Let me take care of the ice."

Evander shot him a look. "You have no fire," he pointed out.

"I have no *need* of fire," Marcos reminded him, gesturing towards the ice with his sword. "This will cut through the ice just as well."

Evander stepped aside, trying not to be ridiculously pleased. Marcos did not approve of any part of this plan, but he intended to help anyway.

Even though the air was frigid, and only a moment before he'd felt chilled to the bone, Evander discovered the knowledge warmed him, someplace deep inside, someplace he wasn't sure anyone else had ever touched.

"Step back," Marcos warned. "This could be dangerous."

"Of course it's dangerous," Evander called out, "but you don't see me trying to stop *you.*"

Marcos laughed, and after Evander had moved back a few yards, he swung his sword at the nearest ice shard, and it exploded into a thousand pieces, a million pieces, the icy bits falling through the air like snow, dusting his head and arms with white, sprinkling all around him.

Marcos brushed off his head, and hacked away at the base of the shard a few more times, making a clear path for Evander to walk through.

He moved the dagger back into his right hand, and stepped closer.

"Wait," Marcos said again, catching his arm right before he climbed through the gap.

Evander turned to look at him, and there it was again, that emotion cresting in his eyes, written in every line of his face.

Perhaps it was very stupid that Evander was willing to risk this—the love and devotion of someone as honorable as Marcos—but how could he accept it either, when there was a gaping hole inside of him that refused to heal? How could they ever be together as equals, as true partners, if Evander couldn't restore what he had lost?

They had both left the Castle at the Top of the World, and the Conclave, but Marcos had done it on purpose. He'd *chosen*. Evander had never chosen. He'd had all his choices made *for* him.

Now he was going to make a choice for himself.

But, still, something in the vicinity of his heart ached at the thought of letting Marcos down. Of abandoning him. Of losing him.

"Please," Marcos said, his voice low, "please be careful. If anything goes wrong, if it doesn't feel right . . ."

Evander didn't let him finish his sentence. Instead, he reached up, and wrapping a hand around Marcos' neck, tugged him down until their lips met in an unexpected and wild kiss.

He knew how Marcos felt; he did not know how *he* felt, but Evander had tried very hard over the years not to lie to himself, and right now, he knew that if he kept kissing Marcos and they kept sharing the same kind of pleasure they had the other night, and even more vitally, if he kept being steadfast and true and also an unbelievable pain in Evander's ass, that he would eventually feel the same.

That he'd abandon anything and everything he knew to follow him. Just to make sure he was safe, that he was protected. Even if Marcos was exceptional at protecting himself.

Evander had never felt that way before, not about anybody. Vanya had been a friend, and sometimes a lover, but with him, it had never felt like this wild, untamed yearning.

It hurt, to step away, to move his lips from Marcos', but he did it.

He wanted to be whole again, for himself, and also because he wanted to come to Marcos as he had been. Exactly who he'd been when Marcos had fallen in love with him, all those years ago.

"I promise," Evander said quietly, reaching up and cupping Marcos' bristly cheek with one palm. "I promise if it feels wrong, I will stop."

Marcos said nothing, but Evander knew the words weren't necessary; he could see everything he felt in his eyes, burning strong and bright and true.

Evander turned and continued climbing over the base of the destroyed ice shard, coming closer and closer to the Well.

It swirled bright blue and white, the mist above it choking him with the magic that churned in the air.

He knew it sensed him, felt him, *wanted* him.

Standing in front of the pool, he held out the dagger. It felt right in his hand, like he'd always held it, like it had been made just for him.

It was; Marcos just never realized it, not until now.

But he did now. Evander knew that if he risked a glance back, that he would see the realization in Marcos' face.

He'd set these events in motion, all those years ago, during that long winter, when he'd ached for someone he didn't think he could have.

Evander raised the dagger and plunged it into the very center of the pool.

For only a moment, there was nothing. And then, Evander felt his whole body jerk and begin to shake, overwhelmed with the magic surging through him, around him, roiling through every bit of his body, until he wasn't sure he could hold it or control it.

Don't be foolish, a voice inside his head crooned, *only a fool tries to control the wind.*

But it wasn't Gael, it was the Mother, and he forced himself to relax, to let go, let the power control him.

His vision went foggy, and then right when he was on the verge of breaking apart, everything went black.

CHAPTER TEN

MARCOS WATCHED AS THE magic of the Well swirled around Evander, as it consumed and subsumed him, until he could barely see the outline of his figure, the power seething around him until he was nearly lost.

His fingers clenched around the hilt of his sword, the leather straps digging into his skin. He'd promised himself—promised Evander, though not in as many words—that he wouldn't interfere. This was Evander's choice, and the path that he'd decided to tread.

He trusted Evander, had *always* trusted Evander, even when he hadn't been particularly trustworthy, but as Marcos watched the magic batter and battle Evander, he discovered entirely new levels of trust.

He will stop it if it's too much.

He promised.

But can anyone stop this? Can you?

Marcos didn't know the answer to that, but he knew that if it came down to it, he'd give his immortal life to save Evander if that was what it took.

He'd always known that, but as the seconds ticked by, the vow inside of him grew stronger, grew teeth and talons and dug itself as deeply into Marcos' heart as it could.

And then, nearly as suddenly as it began, it was over.

The power evaporated like it had never existed, and Marcos was already nearly to the Well when Evander fell, slumping over.

He was fast and he was nimble, and he caught Evander's head in his hands before it hit the ancient stones surrounding the Well, deeply carved runes worn from so many thousands of years.

Checking Evander's pulse with his own racing out of control, he discovered that it was strong and steady.

He was alive, then. Just knocked out.

Marcos felt a swell of relief as he lifted the other Guardian, carrying him away from the Well, and carefully setting him down. He returned a moment later with blankets and with Evander's fur cloak, wrapping him in it, and when he was sufficiently protected from the cold, he tucked himself into his own cloak, and then lifted Evander into his lap, surrounding Evander's much smaller body with his much larger one.

He sat like that for what could have been days, but Marcos knew it was only an hour, maybe two.

Every once in a while, Evander would stir in his sleep, and Marcos would soothe him as best he could, stroking the bright gold waves of his hair.

Then, finally, he woke up, bright eyes opening and fastening directly on to Marcos' face.

"It's over," Marcos said, a little stupidly.

He was thinking of the kiss they'd shared before Evander had approached the Well.

He was thinking of how it had felt, not like Evander was just exploring the option, or angry, like he had been the night in the Mother's cabin, but *more*. Like Evander was actually beginning to feel something, maybe even something similar to what had consumed Marcos for all these years.

"Yes," Evander breathed out unsteadily. "Yes. It's over."

"Did . . ."

Evander pulled a hand from inside his cloak and, for a moment, considered it, staring at it, and then he reached out and a flame, tinged violet at the edges, bloodred at the center, blossomed.

The flame coupled with the peace on Evander's face told the whole story.

It had worked.

The flame extinguished and Evander scrambled to his feet, nearly tripping over the long fur cloak in his eagerness.

And then, suddenly, he was an eagle, and he was soaring upwards through the air, buoyed by the winds swirling around the top of the mountain.

Then he landed, and abruptly, he was a lion, fierce and with a shaggy mane, roaring his satisfaction, and then he was a horse, coat the darkest pitch black of night and magnificent, and then he was Evrard.

Then Rhys.

And then, finally, he was Evander again, and he was smiling.

"Yes," he repeated again, triumph in every sound he made, "yes, yes, yes, *yes*." He laughed, and then flung himself into the air again, this time a phoenix, bursting into flame, and he came to rest in front of Marcos again, this time the fabulous feathers of a peacock flaunting behind him.

Marcos found himself laughing, happiness overflowing inside him as he watched Evander finally indulge in every wild fantasy and test the limits of his power, again. *Finally.*

Evander changed form another half a dozen times, and then it seemed that he had indulged in his fill, because in the end, he came to sit next to Marcos, leaning his head on his shoulder. "Thank you," he said quietly. "*Thank you.*"

"I did nothing. I merely *let* you risk yourself," Marcos said.

"No," Evander argued. "You made the dagger. You made it *for me*. Without it, I couldn't have touched the power in the Well. You made that possible."

"I didn't know," Marcos admitted. "I didn't know what I was doing."

"Doesn't matter," Evander dismissed.

"Where *is* the dagger?" Marcos wondered. "Is it . . . did it . . ." It shouldn't have hurt that the dagger had been lost in the transfer of power. Just seeing Evander change and then change and then change again, laughing at the freedom he felt, at the intoxicating pull of his magic, that was enough.

But it did hurt, that it had been lost. It had been a physical manifestation of what he'd felt, that long-ago winter. All the agony and the hope and the joy and the love.

"No," Evander said, and pulled it from beneath a fold in his cloak.

It was still his dagger. Still the same leather-wrapped handle, still the same curved blade, still as sharp as if Marcos had just cleaned and honed it himself. But the golden symbols of power and strength and magic that he embedded in every blade he forged, they had changed.

They were glowing bright bluish white now, and when Evander laughed, they shifted color, morphing from blinding white to violet to the deepest red.

"It's yours, truly, now," Marcos said in a hushed voice.

"Yes," Evander agreed. "It might have always been mine, but now it belongs to me."

I've always belonged to you; even before I realized it, I was yours.

Marcos wasn't sure he'd ever belong to Evander, not the same way. That was a hard reality to face, but he'd been facing it for so many years now that he'd learned to accept it.

Nothing should feel differently now, but with Evander kissing him, before he'd gone into danger, and now, with him resting his head on his shoulder, it did. Completely.

"We should rest," Marcos said, clearing his throat. "I will keep watch."

"But . . ." Evander tried to interrupt.

"This could possibly still be a trap. I haven't been convinced otherwise, no matter what you were able to take from the Well," Marcos pointed out.

Evander's expression turned grave. "You don't think Vanya called me here so I could restore my power?"

That was not what he thought at all.

"No," he said. Not elaborating any further.

"Oh. I was so sure . . ."

Marcos wanted to shake him, yell at him until the truth sank in. Vanya wasn't his friend anymore, hadn't been his friend in a thousand years. If he had truly been, he'd have been right next to Marcos, watching over him, making sure he wasn't alone.

But he knew Evander well enough to realize that he wouldn't want to hear the truth. The only path to acceptance was if Evander came to the conclusion himself.

"Regardless of what happened with you and the Well, I still think there could be a trap here, waiting to be sprung."

"Well," Evander said, voice brightening, "at least if there *is* a trap, I can help defend against it now."

"You could have done that before," Marcos countered. "You still had power. *Less* power, but you weren't defenseless. I'm going to start a fire, bring the packs up, and the horses, too." He stood, not particularly wanting to argue about this. He was thrilled that Evander had gotten his power back, because he could only imagine how painful losing it had been. But it annoyed him considerably that Evander thought he had been useless without it. Without it, he'd accomplished more than the Conclave, with their remaining eleven Guardians and all the power they had at their disposal.

He spent the next hour bringing up all the supplies, then carefully leading the horses up the rest of the steep, icy path. He settled them a good distance from the Well, giving them a nice brushing and draping cloaks over them to keep them warm, though, as he'd told Evander earlier, they were warmer than the two of them were. No doubt another gift from the Mother.

Evander had gone to collect what wood he could find, but the whole while Marcos was working, he swore he could feel his gaze on his back, watching him.

Considering him.

It made his skin tight and hot, and flashes of the kiss they'd shared earlier kept returning, and then there were the memories of what they'd shared the night before distracting him.

When he could put it off no longer, he returned to where Evander was piling up the branches and sticks he'd gathered.

"It's definitely growing colder," Evander said, as Marcos pulled his flint from a pocket and dropped down on his haunches in front of the wood, ready to start the process of starting a fire.

With the wind and the cold, it wasn't going to be easy.

But right when he was about to strike the first time on the flint, suddenly there was fire, and it was flickering bright and unwavering, the wood catching like it wasn't nearly frozen solid.

He glanced back at Evander, who was grinning unrepentantly. "That seemed like a lot of work when I knew a shortcut," he said. "A lot of effort that would be better used someplace else."

"You always were a show-off," Marcos grumbled, but he *was* pleased that he didn't have to kneel in front of the pile for ages, trying to get a flame to catch.

"If you have it, you should use it," Evander said smugly. "Besides, starting that fire was going to be a nightmare. You know that."

Grudgingly, Marcos nodded.

"Come sit by me," Evander said, gesturing towards the cocoon of blankets he'd created. He held up the leather pouch of dried meat and a waterskin. "I have excellent provisions and I'll even share with you."

Marcos didn't need to be invited twice. He tucked himself in next to Evander, already feeling a bit warmer. "I do not know if I would categorize these as excellent," he pointed out, as he took a piece of meat and began to chew it.

"What I wouldn't give for a nice roast, hot from the spit, and a nice flagon of good wine," Evander said mournfully. "And a *warm* bed."

"I can keep you warm," Marcos said, pulling him a bit closer against him.

Evander gazed up at him, and the heat in his eyes more than made up for the frigid wind blowing around them. "And I didn't even have to ask," he teased.

It occurred to Marcos then, as he lifted Evander into his lap and he nudged his cold nose against his neck, trying to warm it, that he'd wanted this too, but he hadn't wanted to ask for it.

The wall he'd been trying to keep around his heart, trying to protect it from getting in any deeper than he already was, crumbled a little bit more.

Evander hadn't thought he could fall asleep, the power still electrifying every inch of his body, and the cold seeping in bone-deep, but it turned out that tucked into Marcos, he could and *did* fall asleep.

He'd meant to stay awake, too, because Marcos didn't have to always be the one keeping watch, but then he'd gone and slipped off into sleep without being able to stop himself.

He must have been more tired than he realized, because he didn't open his eyes until the glare of the rising sun glinting off the icy ground woke him.

Shifting, he realized that during some time in the night, Marcos had moved, and while he was tucked up tightly against him, he wasn't in his arms any longer.

He shouldn't have missed touching in so many spots, but he did—even though logically of course they couldn't have stayed that way all night.

"You're awake," Marcos said quietly, but it startled him anyway.

"Didn't mean to sleep so long," Evander admitted, but the soft, contented smile on Marcos' face, like he hadn't wanted him to do anything else, brushed away his concern. "I must have been really comfortable."

"I..."

Evander would never know what Marcos was about to say next, because suddenly, the sun wasn't just bright against the flawless white of the ice and the snow, it was *blinding*, and Evander realized that it wasn't the sun at all.

It was the light of a figure, dressed in a white robe, feet bare, barely touching the ground as it walked towards them.

Evander scrambled to his feet, shocked and yet not, all at the same time. He'd known he'd come. He'd *known* that it wasn't a trap, that when Vanya had called his name, and said he wanted to meet here that he'd *meant* it.

He'd know Vanya's voice anywhere, and he'd known it, deep down in the place where he could always determine the truth from a lie, even after Deimos had stripped him of his powers.

And he knew now that this, without a doubt, was Vanya.

He heard Marcos come to his feet behind him, but he only had eyes for the man in front of him.

Vanya had come. The moment he'd become truly a Guardian again, Vanya had come for him.

"Evander, you kept your promise," he said, his voice as melodious as ever, his eyes the same warm, soft brown, his hair still shining dark curls. He couldn't change. He was everlasting.

They were everlasting.

"I said I would come, and I am here. Are we to return to the Castle at the Top of the World?" It stung, more than he thought it would, the idea of leaving the surface behind. Of leaving Rory and Gray and Anya and Marthe, and all the people he'd grown close to. But they did not need him, anymore. They would do just fine on their own, and he was *not* a human, he was a Guardian, and he felt the excitement rise in him, banishing away the hurt, just at the idea of returning to his rightful place.

The place he'd been denied.

"Return to the Castle at the Top of the World?" Vanya's voice was amused.

"You should not have come."

Evander heard Marcos' voice behind him. Heard the steel in his tone. But couldn't quite believe it. Could not understand it.

Vanya's gaze flicked to where Marcos stood. "You know nothing, Marcos."

"I *do* know I hoped it was actually a trap, and that it was not truly you who was calling Evander. He deserves better than to be finally acknowledged after all this time, *and* after what you did."

Evander was confused. "What did Vanya do?"

If he hadn't once known the Guardian in front of him so well, had not spent thousands of years at his side, sharing a bed, sharing confidences, sharing a friendship that should have endured, but hadn't, he might have missed it. But he didn't.

There was the barest flicker of unease in Vanya's eyes before he pushed it away.

Marcos walked up next to Evander. Didn't touch him, but he didn't need to. His claim was visceral, it lay in the air like a brand, or a chain.

Evander wasn't sure he liked it, probably because he didn't understand it.

"Should I tell him, or should you?" Marcos asked. He gestured. "We both know what you should do, but it remains to be seen what you *will* do."

"Tell me what," Evander demanded to know.

"Marcos is confused, he doesn't know what he speaks of," Vanya said smoothly. "He's lying."

But Marcos had never lied. He wasn't a liar. He didn't bend the truth to suit his own needs, either. He spoke the truth and he spoke it clearly and proudly, never with any prevarication. That was how he'd always been, and as they'd grown closer over the last few weeks, Evander hadn't discovered anything about him that proved differently.

"Marcos doesn't lie," Evander said.

"But he keeps secrets, doesn't he? We all do." Vanya's voice was taunting. "I bet you have even discovered one about him."

He had. But secrets weren't lies. Nobody knew that as intimately as Evander did.

"No," Evander said. "He doesn't *lie*."

Out of the corner of his eye, he saw Marcos shrug. "So be it," he said, and then turned towards Evander. "You wanted to know who betrayed you to Deimos, when he stripped you of your powers and banished you to the surface. It was not me, though I understood why you might think so. It was someone else. It was Vanya."

Evander stared at him, shock hitting him like a punch to the stomach. "What?"

"You must understand," Vanya said, "I didn't know what Deimos would do, and I *did* warn you, you remember. I came to your chambers and told you that it was best if you left the surface and the sorcerers there alone, but you wouldn't listen. You never listened. Still, I thought a reprimand from Deimos would be enough to scare you straight."

He almost sounded regretful as he tried to excuse his actions. *Almost*.

"You knew I was going to think it was Marcos." He was so angry, so completely, utterly furious that he could barely spit the words out.

Vanya waved a careless hand. "You didn't know Marcos' secret, shockingly, and so I thought, he might be a better scapegoat than I." He shot Marcos a triumphant smile. "If you'd told him when you should have about your silly crush, he'd have never believed that you'd betray him. Evander takes that kind of thing seriously."

Evander stared at the Guardian he thought he'd known.

At the *friend*.

"I should have guessed," he said, voice hard and unrelenting, because if he let himself waver, he'd do something worse, like try to burn Vanya to a crisp, or even worse, *cry*, "because you weren't here, you didn't follow me, you never tried to make sure I was protected. But Marcos always did."

"Of course Marcos did," Vanya said slyly.

And that was somehow even worse. Evander didn't even think, just raised his hand and the flame rushed through him, blossoming on his palm effortlessly.

It wouldn't really hurt Vanya, not permanently, but it would feel satisfying to throw a few fireballs in his direction.

"Wait," Marcos said, putting a hand on Evander's arm. "Wait. I want to know why he's here. There's more he needs to tell us before you try to roast him."

Vanya laughed indulgently. "Like you could. You can barely conjure a thing, these days. Though there was that silly little experiment where you shifted into a unicorn and tried to pretend to be a *king*."

The fire roared in Evander's ears and he let it rush out of him, leaving him dizzy, but still upright. That was Marcos' hand, holding him up.

He saw the shock in Vanya's eyes. And he knew then, though he'd already known, deep down, that Vanya had not brought him here so he could restore his powers. And he had not come here because Evander had figured out with the help of the Mother how to use the Well.

He'd come for another reason entirely.

The fire stopped an inch from Vanya's nose.

"I see you have each other on a leash now." Vanya sounded amused by this. "I wondered if you would ever win him over, Marcos."

Evander's temper spiked again at the way he talked down to Marcos. Like he truly was that stupid Guardian, all instinct and no brain, who was only good with a sword. Evander supposed that he too had laughed about it, a long time ago. But he knew better now. Marcos was loyal and true, and he not only had a mind, he used it well.

Vanya was wrong about him, and it turned out he'd been wrong about Evander, too.

"Tell me what you want," Evander demanded. "Why did you call us here?"

"Or what? You'll burn me?"

The fire, a wall of it, burning violet and red and white, flickered right against Vanya's nose.

"Yes," Evander said, and meant it.

He would.

Vanya would eventually shed his scorched skin like a snake, but in the meantime, he'd *hate* being ugly.

Vanya had always loved how beautiful he was. How seductive. How perfect.

Now Evander could see what he'd always been. Self-centered, and only caring about others when it suited him.

The rage inside him billowed.

"In fact, I come with a message from another," Vanya said lightly. "And he will not be pleased when I tell him you have recovered your power."

"*Deimos* sent you?" Marcos did not sound particularly surprised, only worried. Evander heard him draw his sword.

Vanya nodded. "He does not like how powerful you have grown. He did not like how close Marcos was. Even if he never revealed himself. And now it seems, he has. That," Vanya said inexorably, "is not going to do you any favors, Evander."

"Deimos banished me. He no longer has any say over what I do and how I choose to do it," Evander said between clenched teeth.

"On the contrary, he is still your leader. He punished you, and he thought, perhaps, he could bargain with you. Which is why he had me summon you. You would not come if *he* did it, but me? Your everlasting friend? I knew you would come. Deimos knew it, too."

"Bargain with Evander over *what?*" Marcos questioned.

"There's nothing you could have bargained with that would have swayed me," Evander said righteously, and wanted to believe it.

But Vanya's expression told a different story.

"I believe there might have been something we could have given you that would've convinced you to remove yourself from human politics. When King Emory took the throne, we believed you would stay in your valley."

Originally, he'd intended to. But it was so lonely, so bleak, so many years stretching out in front of him with nothing to do, nobody to talk to, that he'd ended up returning to Beaulieu only a few weeks after he'd told Gray he'd never see Evrard again.

That particular promise had not been too difficult to circumvent—he'd returned as Rhys, intending by the time he arrived to retire and stay Rhys for the rest of his days.

"Why do you care what Evander does and doesn't do on the surface? The Conclave has long since removed itself from humanity," Marcos said, giving his sword an absent-minded swing that was certainly on purpose. But then Evander's wall of flame had flickered but not moved, only a breath away from Vanya's face.

Evander thought about this for a second, his mind whirling.

They'd thought he'd stay in the valley. They would've preferred that he stay in the valley.

Evander remembered then, Sabrina's workshop that Gray had shown him when he'd come back to Beaulieu, buried in the bowels of the castle. Much of her supplies and evil magics had been cleansed from the room, but there'd been a residual smell, a *feel* about the things that remained that had reminded him of something that he hadn't quite been able to place.

And now, suddenly, he realized what it was that had been so confoundedly familiar about it.

He'd dismissed it at the time, as the impression had been so faint, he'd been sure he'd been confused.

But now he knew he hadn't been confused at all.

He'd smelled *Deimos* in Sabrina's workshop.

Suddenly, it became very clear where the first sorcerer had gotten his power to begin with, and why it felt like Evander could never quite defeat them, generation after generation.

Why Deimos had not wanted Evander to pursue the subject and had ordered him to drop it.

Why he'd banished him, instead of merely punishing him for a few decades.

It had been Deimos all along, directing those sorcerers. He'd created a cult of his own followers, and then imbued them with his own power.

Vanya smiled slowly as the realization must have dawned across Evander's face.

"You see," Vanya said, "Evander knows. Deimos hoped you would be satisfied with defeating the woman, the sorceress, and you would stop looking, stop fighting. Return to your valley and forget about it all."

"But I didn't."

"No." Vanya took a step and the fire flickered, and pushed outward. "No, you did not. I came here to try to bargain with you, Evander. But you are too clever for your own good. You always were."

"Why Deimos?" Marcos demanded. "Why would you side with him?"

"He has an entire cult of followers, and their belief is very strong." Vanya's tone turned regretful. "So much stronger than any belief has been in the Guardians for hundreds of years."

"You compromised your ideals, and the task we were charged with, *and* the very fabric of our existence, so people would *worship* you again." Evander was disgusted and could not pretend otherwise. He'd always admired Vanya so much, and to discover that he'd not been worthy of a single moment of that admiration made him sick to his stomach. But the nausea didn't stop him from pushing the fire forward again. Harder. It blazed even fiercer. For the first time, Evander saw a flicker of fear in Vanya's eyes.

"You should understand," Vanya protested. "You hated being the Guardian of Secrets. You complained about it all the time."

"Perhaps, but I never would have done this," Evander said and felt the truth of it echo in his bones.

Maybe he'd been dissatisfied with the duties he'd been charged with, but he'd never been weak, not like Vanya.

"Go back to your owner," Marcos said laconically, and suddenly his sword wasn't absently swinging but pointed, in all its deadly glory, right alongside Evander's fire. "I am sure he is missing you."

"No," Vanya protested. "No, I need you to promise me that you'll let it go."

"Now that I know this is all Deimos' doing? And that I never eradicated the sickness of the power among humans?" Evander laughed humorlessly. "I don't think so."

"We'll let you come back to the Castle," Vanya promised, clearly scrambling.

"If I forget about the sorcery cult and Deimos' involvement?" Evander let the question hang in the air.

Long enough for Vanya to hang himself.

He nodded, eagerly.

Evander laughed again and this time when he did, he pushed the fire out with a roar and Vanya scrambled backwards, running as it chased him, until he dove right back into the Well, leaving only the steam of the fire colliding with the power remaining.

For a very long moment, all Evander could hear was the roaring of the fire in his ears, the beat of his own heart as he breathed in and out.

Then he heard Marcos' boots, sure and solid on the ice, approach.

"It had to be done," Marcos said, and he sounded regretful.

Which made sense.

You should not have come.

He'd wanted the voice to not be Vanya's. He'd *wanted* it to be a trap so . . . resolution hardened in Evander's veins. So he wouldn't have to tell him the truth about Vanya's treachery. He'd known and he'd not said a word, not even when Evander had believed that it had been Marcos who betrayed him.

He whirled around, fury mounting in him again.

No, not again. *Still.*

He was so angry at Vanya, still. At his weakness, at the complete lack of honor. At how easily he'd been seduced into doing Deimos' bidding. But now he was also furious at Marcos, who owed him the truth but had refused to share it.

"You knew," Evander said, turning to confront the other Guardian. "You knew and you never told me."

"I . . ." Marcos wet his lips with the tip of his tongue. He looked uneasy. Maybe because he'd just witnessed Evander assail Vanya with an entire wall of flame. "I hoped that you wouldn't have to know. And some of it . . ." he added hurriedly, "I didn't know for sure. Deimos' involvement with the sorcerers, for example, that was not something I could prove, though I suspected."

"That's what you threatened him with," Evander said, the pieces falling into place in his head.

Did it make him any less furious now that he understood all of it? *No.*

"Yes." Marcos' answer came with a resigned sigh.

"He was afraid, because you knew, and he thought you might tell me."

"I think . . ." Marcos hesitated. "I think as long as we stayed apart, they did not care. The threat was less."

"But Vanya called to me *before* you revealed your true self. You were still Merleen when you insisted on coming with me."

"Yes, but . . ." More hesitation. Evander wanted to reach over and shake the Guardian until he spilled all his secrets.

But you don't need to do that, you've always been the best at making people talk.

The biggest problem was that he both desperately wanted to know all of Marcos' secrets, and he was terrified of them.

What they'd make him *feel*.

"Just say it," Evander spit out. Not the most persuasive tactic he'd ever used, but he'd lost his patience. Vanya had compromised it, and then Marcos had shredded it utterly.

"I was going to tell you, that night in Beaulieu, when I nearly caught you changing," Marcos confessed. "When we . . ."

When we almost kissed.

"Yes," Marcos said quietly. "I couldn't do it, not when you didn't know who I was. And honestly, I was more surprised than anything that you would. After all, you'd known Merleen for months, known about his obvious crush, and you'd never shown any interest."

"I was . . ." He could not say, *I was bored*. But it was part of the truth.

The rest of it? Evander refused to look too closely at any of the other pieces.

"It was on the tip of my tongue to say it, even though I knew you would be so angry that it wasn't Merleen, a completely uninvolved, entirely harmless man, but *me*. So I didn't. But they—Deimos, at least—must have seen, and must have realized it was only a matter of time."

"For the Guardian of Secrets, you certainly kept a lot from me." Evander didn't try to hold back the bitterness in his tone. "Even when we were with the Mother, and she made her request, you didn't give anything away."

Marcos' expression had turned pleading. Desperate. But it didn't make a dent. Evander had believed himself impervious to betrayal; that his banishment had been so utterly painful that nothing else could touch it.

He'd been wrong.

This ached, deep down, in a place that he didn't think anyone else had ever touched.

Not even Vanya.

"Were you *laughing* at me that night? I was so . . ." He'd been something. Determined. Aroused. Intrigued.

"Evander, what I said that night was the truth. No matter what I suspected, I still wanted to believe that we could leave it alone. That we could just . . .be."

"Together. You thought that we could just be, *together*."

Marcos turned away then, and the soft part of Evander, the part that ached, told him to follow. To apologize, even though *he* had nothing to apologize for.

"I know you are angry with me for not telling you my suspicions . . ."

Evander interrupted. "I am angry you didn't tell me about Vanya, *and* that you didn't tell me any of your suspicions."

"How could I tell you that the Guardian you most trusted, your friend and your *lover*, had been the one to betray you?" Marcos demanded, and suddenly there was a flare of temper in his voice.

Anger at Evander? Or anger at himself?

He wasn't sure, but it didn't matter.

Evander was only relieved that he wasn't angry alone anymore.

"By simply saying it," Evander argued, enunciating each word carefully. "Unless you thought I'd hate the messenger . . ."

The guilt Evander spotted in Marcos' eyes told the whole story. He'd thought exactly that. That telling Evander the truth about Vanya would mean that he'd never, ever see Marcos as anything else.

"I was wrong," Evander muttered darkly, "you *are* stupid."

The resignation on Marcos' face should have been satisfying. Except that ached too.

"Come," Marcos said abruptly, "we need to pack up and head down the mountain. I do not want Deimos to decide that Vanya didn't accomplish his task therefore he needs to address it himself."

"Where are we going?" Evander asked even though he already knew.

There was a very petty part of him that wanted to force Marcos to say it.

He sighed, in the middle of folding up blankets, but did not glance up.

"Beaulieu," he said. "We're going back to Beaulieu."

CHAPTER ELEVEN

It was not a mystery or a surprise that Evander was angry.

Marcos had known that if he ever had to tell Evander the truth about Vanya, he'd be upset.

But then he hadn't foretold having to tell him while Vanya was standing right there, beautiful and reproachful, or that his betrayal would be so much deeper and more pervasive than either of them could have imagined.

So, it was not particularly a surprise that he was furious or that as they'd packed up, Evander had refused to look in Marcos' direction and only spoken to him when asked a direct question.

It was not unexpected—in fact, Marcos realized this whole journey, while he and Evander had been growing closer, he'd been anticipating a moment just like this one, when it all went to hell—but that didn't mean it wasn't agonizing.

Still, despite Evander's sulking, they made good time heading down from the Well. Not for the first time, Marcos was glad they'd taken the horses, because it was so much faster than being on foot. He had to acknowledge now that the Mother had at least had some idea of what they'd been going to face, and she'd tried to prepare them as best she could.

Even her suggestion to Evander about the Well had ended up being prophetic. He'd taken the chance and gaining his powers back had proven to be the difference in the confrontation with Vanya.

Vanya hadn't been powerless. He could have fought back, but instead he'd fled. No doubt because he'd come to the Well assuming that only Marcos had any power. The very last thing he'd expected was Evander's sudden—and very fiery—determination.

Marcos could feel dusk coming as they headed down the mountain. He could taste it in the air, *and,* even worse, he could taste a coming storm in the air. *Snow,* he realized, *we're going to get snow.*

He kept a sharp lookout for the right kind of setup that he wanted to ride out the storm, and finally, half an hour or so down the road, he found it.

Large trees, with heavy evergreen boughs that would shield them from the worst of the snow, and a few additional downed logs, which he could quickly use to construct some kind of makeshift shelter.

"We're stopping here," Marcos announced, nudging his horse off the road and down into the little valley, where he hoped they could weather the storm.

"Why so soon?" Evander demanded to know as he followed suit.

"Storm's coming," Marcos said succinctly. "This is going to be the best place to ride it out, I think."

"We could try to find the Mother's cabin," Evander said.

"Why bother her? We'll be fine here," Marcos said.

"In the snow?" Evander sounded dubious.

He deliberately did not remind himself that only a day ago, Evander had trusted his judgement on matters similar to these. It hadn't taken very long to get used to how sweet it had felt for Evander to respect his opinions.

And now, it was all shattered, because he'd deliberately withheld the truth.

If it hurts, you have only yourself to blame.

"I've camped out with a thousand men in much worse," Marcos said, stopping his horse in a relatively flat, insulated area ringed with trees. "We're well supplied. And after this, it's only a few days' ride to Beaulieu if we push the horses."

"Oh, so you're *not* concerned about the horses, then?" Evander asked archly. Trying, Marcos was fairly sure, to be difficult on purpose.

"No," Marcos said, determined to be patient and give Evander no more reasons to be pissed off. "I think the Mother's enchantment is still upon them, and some hard riding won't hurt them. A week, sure, but we're not a week away from Beaulieu, not if we use the regular roads."

"Not worried about hiding either?"

"Are you? Will Gray and Rory have sent out a search party for you?" Marcos questioned, even though he already knew the answer.

Evander rolled his eyes. "No, I left a note, so they wouldn't. They know sometimes I have matters I need to tend to. They wouldn't worry."

"Then," Marcos said smoothly, "it's no problem to keep to the main roads. Deimos won't come at us yet. Come, help me get the packs out. I want to get a shelter built. These evergreens will keep out most of the snow, but in case it turns to ice, I'd like some further protection for us and our fire."

Evander didn't respond, merely dismounted and began to untie the packs off the back of his horse.

Marcos decided that maybe silence wasn't such a problem.

It was better, anyway, than having Evander argue with every single suggestion he made. With Evander quiet, he could focus on the task at hand—which was making sure they'd be reasonably comfortable for the night ahead.

He grabbed a small sharp axe from his own bundle, and spent the next hour chopping logs and rearranging them into a shelter-like formation. Evander kept silent, but he could feel his eyes on him almost continuously. Like he wanted to look away, but couldn't, and resented the hell out of that particular fact.

That's fine, Marcos told himself as he set the last log into place. He'd had long stretches, one even lasting nearly a decade, where he'd been furious with his own heart for settling on the one creature who'd barely ever acknowledged his existence.

It hadn't been fair, but then Marcos had learned the hard way that not even an immortal life, an everlasting life, was fair.

It seemed like Evander should have learned that particular lesson long ago, considering Deimos' punishment, but perhaps he had not.

While he'd been setting up the shelter, it seemed that Evander had been taking stock of their provisions, and he'd also started a fire, gathering together all the bits of wood that Marcos hadn't needed or used. He'd even constructed the facsimile of a pot, which was currently hanging on a forked branch over a magically created fire, simmering briskly away with some kind of greens and some of what remained of their dried meat.

"I thought," Evander said when Marcos examined the setup, "that perhaps a hot meal might not go amiss."

It was not an apology. Not when he still wouldn't *look* at Marcos, not really, and it was absolutely offered begrudgingly, but he'd done it anyway.

Evander could absolutely indulge in a good sulk. Marcos had seen it for himself on many occasions. But Evander wasn't stupid, and not cooperating with inclement weather on the way would be the height of stupidity.

"A hot meal on a cold day like today? With snow coming?" Marcos looked up to the sky—a dark, ominous gray that boded ill. "It will definitely not go amiss."

"Come, let's eat before we finish settling in," Evander said, gesturing towards the pot. "If you could grab it."

Marcos did, ignoring the singe of the burn on the tips of his fingers. He'd heal quickly, he always did, and there were much more pressing matters to worry about. He settled the pot between them on a nest of blankets as Evander revealed what he'd been working on. A roughly carved spoon.

"It's not perfect," Evander said apologetically, "but I think it will do." He handed it to Marcos, who was impressed.

"What about for you?" Marcos asked.

Evander shot him a surprising grin. Was he not so angry after all? Or had he forgotten how furious he was supposed to be? Marcos wasn't sure. "I made my own," he admitted, lifting up a second spoon. Still roughly carved but it would be enough to scoop up the hot broth. "I thought it might be easier."

"Than sharing when you're so angry with me?" Marcos stated. "Absolutely."

Evander shot him a glare. "I . . ."

"Are angry with me," Marcos finished for him dryly. "I know."

"It's just . . ." Evander hesitated again. "You should have told me about Vanya."

"You'd have been angry with me then, or angry with me now." He scooped up some broth and lifted it to his lips. "I don't see much of a difference."

Evander grumbled something under his breath, but didn't say anything else as they ate, methodically and quickly.

The soup wasn't much—just some dark greens and grasses that Evander had found tucked here and there between the trees, and the dried meat, reconstituted, but it was hot and filling.

"I must finish," Marcos said, getting to his feet as he watched the first snowflakes begin to fall. "We must be settled in before it starts in earnest."

Evander nodded but didn't say anything.

When Marcos finished securing the horses, and brought the fur cloak over, Evander had covered the makeshift pot with a thatch of leaves he'd woven together, and he'd half buried it to keep it warm. "The rest for breakfast," he explained, when Marcos had glanced over at what he'd done.

"I'm sure we'll be glad of it," Marcos said. He extended the fur. "The temperature is dropping, rapidly. I can feel it. Put this on, and get settled in for the night."

"What about you?" Evander questioned.

"What *about* me?"

"How will you stay warm?"

"I'll be fine," Marcos said gruffly.

"No," Evander argued. "No, you will come in here with me, and we'll bundle up together."

Marcos opened his mouth to remind him that it wasn't a good idea, considering how annoyed he was with him, but before he could, Evander snapped out, "I might be angry at you, but at the same time, I don't want you to freeze to death. Come on, be reasonable."

"Well, when you put it that way," Marcos muttered under his breath and settled down, his own cloak billowing around him as he sat down under the shelter.

He kept his distance from Evander though, because he wasn't going to be stupid enough to push himself into his space—even though with the snow coming down harder and the temperature dropping, the best tactic would have been to press their bodies together for warmth.

But Marcos would rather freeze than touch Evander when he didn't want to be touched.

They sat like that for a bit of time. It could have been ten minutes, it could have been an hour. Marcos reached down, almost instinctively, for the knife he usually kept in his boot, wanting the familiar feel of it in his hand to ground him. It could always use a cleaning and sharpening, and with his sharp eyesight, he could still see well enough in the dark to use it as a distraction.

But he couldn't.

His fingers closed around nothing and he remembered a moment too late that the knife had claimed Evander, and it was his now.

Maybe it was always his, just like you, and you're both fucked, Marcos thought bitterly.

He'd believed that nothing could possibly be worse than never having Evander, even though he'd gotten used to the idea over the last few hundreds of years. But no, he'd been utterly wrong.

Because it was so much worse to experience a taste of Evander, and never get another. He'd never even gotten to really revel in it, in *him*, and he shouldn't be disappointed, but he was.

There'd been so much he wanted to share, to experience, to savor, and now he likely never would.

Evander, more than any other Guardian or man he'd ever known, knew how to hold on to a grudge.

"I can feel you thinking over there, and it's not anything good," Evander said suddenly, surprising Marcos.

"You don't know that," Marcos mumbled.

Except that Evander probably *did*, because he knew everything, every deep, dark, ugly secret that people held close to their chests. The only reason he hadn't discovered any of Marcos' secrets before was because he hadn't *wanted* to know.

He'd been far happier not realizing how Marcos felt.

"I'm only surprised that you haven't suggested we get closer, for warmth," Evander said conversationally.

"I didn't want to impose," Marcos said roughly. Not letting himself think about what that would feel like. How much he'd enjoy it.

How Evander would likely tolerate it.

"Now you're sulking too, and it just isn't going to work. Only one of us can sulk at a time."

"I'm not aware of that particular rule." Marcos shouldn't feel bitter, but he did. Why was Evander always pushing like this? It was annoying. It also managed to be endearing, even though he didn't *want* it to be.

"Maybe we can't freeze to death, but we can be uncomfortable," Evander said breezily, like none of this was actually significant.

Marcos' fingers tightened into his cloak, and then he realized, suddenly, that Evander was doing what he always did.

Pretending that none of this mattered, in an attempt to hide just how much it did.

"Fine," he said, giving in. He scooted closer. "We can't have you being uncomfortable." Marcos' leg pressed against Evander's, and then his side, and then his shoulder. He knew none of this was going anywhere, but it felt . . .

You are not going to feel *any of this,* he instructed himself firmly, *you are just going to keep each other warm.*

But then Evander lay down, curled up, and reached over, tugging him down with him, and Marcos nearly protested but then he sighed, deciding there was no point in protesting any longer.

It was easy—far too easy—to pull Evander that last inch, and settle him right against him, his bigger body curled around his much smaller one.

Now he'd *really* need to not feel a thing, because if he did, it wouldn't matter how cold it was, he was going to want, and that was a shortcut to getting hard.

Marcos focused on keeping his breaths deep and even, when suddenly Evander wiggled against him.

That was impossible not to feel. Evander's curves rubbing against his . . .

Marcos heard his own sharp intake of breath.

"What are you doing?" he demanded.

"Just trying to get comfortable," Evander said, and the faux innocence in his tone made it clear he knew exactly what he was doing: playing with fire.

Evander might not have spent a lot of the last few hundreds of years indulging in pleasurable pursuits, but he was not naive.

"Well, get comfortable, then," Marcos muttered as Evander wiggled again.

"You feel *very* comfortable, very warm," Evander said. "I didn't know . . ."

But he wasn't stupid, he'd have to have at least guessed.

"Go to sleep," Marcos said sharply. Hoping that Evander would leave it alone. Knowing he wouldn't.

Evander's hand tucked into the front of his tunic, slipping under the edge of his leather armor. Resting against the bare skin of his stomach. He hissed, and not because Evander's fingers were icy.

"Sorry," he said, not sounding apologetic at all, "my hands are cold."

"Your hands are *freezing*," Marcos complained.

"Maybe you can warm them up," Evander suggested slyly.

Marcos' self-control was legendary, but Evander had always shredded it like it simply didn't exist. When Evander's body curled even closer to his, his questing fingers tracing cold patterns on his abdomen, lower and then lower still, until he was only a breath away from where Marcos' cock was straining for him, he snapped.

"Did you hit your head?" he demanded to know. "Are you under some kind of spell?"

Evander's fingers stopped for a second, but then they kept going, tucking themselves into his breeches. "I was annoyed with you," he admitted, "but that doesn't mean I don't want to touch you. I *like* touching you. And I thought you liked me touching you."

Marcos groaned as he finally clasped his cock. His fingers were cold, and his length was hot and straining and pleasure surged through him.

"I do," he ground out, trying desperately not to buck against Evander's hand. It felt so good, he was hanging on by a single thread.

And like Evander knew it, he gripped him harder and gave an experimental twist.

Marcos couldn't stop it anymore; it was like his body had been possessed with someone with a lot less sense and a surplus of desire.

It was easy enough to turn Evander, until he was facing him. Evander curled his fingers around him and gave another slow, deliberate jerk and fire bloomed in his belly, racing through his veins, burning away the last of his reservations.

Evander's lips were cold, too, as he leaned in and kissed him, but his body was warm as his hands searched for the gaps in his cloak, tucking into his clothing, reveling in the feel of his skin.

"Please," Evander gasped into his mouth as he tilted his head, trying to get his tongue deeper into Marcos' mouth.

And who was Marcos to deny him?

His cock was as hard as his own, slippery at the tip and Marcos' thumb slipped through the moisture, smoothing his passage downward. Oh, he wanted to get his mouth on Evander, had craved the taste of him for ages, but this would have to do. For now.

Evander redoubled his efforts, every twist of his wrist making Marcos pant a little harder. It was just a simple handjob, it shouldn't have felt so good, but knowing it was Evander's hand, and Evander's mouth he was kissing, *and* that he was so into it, desperate little pleas falling from his lips into Marcos' mouth, pulled him right to the edge.

"Shouldn't feel so good," Evander slurred as Marcos tugged him right there with him.

"Yes," Marcos said resolutely, "it *should*," and the knowledge of it wrapped around him, right along with Evander's hand, and he convulsed as his orgasm roared through him.

He felt Evander's cock twitch in his hand and then he was coming too, groaning loudly, like he couldn't hold the sounds back.

Marcos' heartbeat slowed, and he realized that they hadn't thought this through very well.

"We . . . uh . . . made a mess," Evander said sheepishly, just as Marcos realized it, too.

But while he had no intention of ever discussing this with Evander, this wasn't the first time he'd been on the road, in a campaign, and indulged in a quick jerk-off session. He knew what they could do.

"Can you reach the waterskin with your other hand?" Marcos asked.

"Yes," Evander huffed out, and Marcos could see the flush on his cheeks growing deeper. He deposited the waterskin between them, and Marcos unscrewed the lid, wetting a corner of his cloak. He made quick work of himself, and then carefully cleaned off Evander as best as he could.

"Is that alright?" Marcos asked.

"Yes," Evander said, sounding surprised. "But your cloak . . ."

"Not a problem," Marcos said, and now that both hands were cleaned, he ripped off the corner, tossing it to the side. "Just a little shorter now."

Evander stared for a long second, and then threw his head back, laughing like he couldn't stop.

"What?" Marcos asked, puzzled. He hadn't thought it was particularly funny, but Evander kept laughing.

"You're just so resourceful," Evander said between gasps of laughter.

"I didn't think that was such a bad thing. Or such an amusing thing."

"It's . . ." Evander waved a hand. "I just . . . every time I think I have you put in the right box, you find a new box, and it should annoy me, but it . . . it occurs to me that maybe I should just stop trying to find a box and accept that I simply cannot quantify you."

"And that's funny?" Marcos was confused. But he was fairly certain, at least, that this was a *good* thing.

"I was so mad at you," Evander said, not really answering his question. "But you're an impossible person to stay angry at, you know?"

"Because of the box thing?"

Evander nodded, his laughter finally quieting, his eyes growing solemn. "I never know what to make of you, and then you open your mouth or make a suggestion or just look at me a certain way, and I *know*."

Marcos thought he actually understood.

There'd been that long winter, all those years ago, when he'd spent all those months puzzled and trying to place why he couldn't seem to look away from Evander, whenever he was in the room.

His heart stuttered, as he wondered if maybe it could be the same. Could Evander be feeling the same way he'd long felt about him?

Hope was terrifying, but it blossomed inside Marcos anyway.

"So does that mean that you're not angry with me over Vanya anymore?"

"I'm . . ." Evander hesitated. "I'm very angry at him. More than angry. Every time I think of him, I could burn him to ash, all over again. But you? It's different. I *wish* you'd told me the truth, because you had it, and I didn't. But no, I'm not angry with you anymore."

Marcos tucked Evander into him, even closer. Felt his body relax in his arms. "I wish I had, too. I'm sorry."

"That's enough," Evander said with a sigh, and they were still in that position when Evander finally drifted off to sleep.

Leaving Marcos awake and contemplating how everything between them was changing, and even if he wanted to stop it, he wasn't sure he could. It was out of his hands now.

Digging their way out of the snow was the hardest part of the return to Beaulieu.

After they'd warmed up the horses, and took to the road, the next two days passed quickly. They stopped briefly, when full dark had hit, to rest their mounts, but whatever spell the Mother had enchanted them with had given them incredible stamina and energy, and Marcos had marveled at it.

Evander could see the practical applications of such a charm, but he'd also not spent so many hundreds of years planning wars and battles and campaigns, so he'd found it rather less interesting.

Or at least he would have, if Marcos hadn't kept talking about it.

As his anger at the other Guardian had faded as they'd galloped towards Beaulieu, Evander had felt his interest blooming every time Marcos opened his mouth.

Had he always been so fascinating? Or was that a symptom of how much Evander liked touching him and having him touch him in return? He wasn't sure, but it felt like he was finally casting away the last of the prejudices that Vanya had infected him with.

Marcos was loyal and kind and skillful in battle *and* he was intelligent.

Just as intelligent as Evander himself.

In some regards, perhaps more so, which was not something he would be admitting to Marcos or anyone else anytime soon.

He had appearances to maintain, after all.

And as for appearances . . .

They were only a few leagues away from the castle proper, when Marcos slowed his horse to a slow trot.

"Why are we stopping?" Evander asked, pulling his horse even with Marcos'. "Is something wrong?" The journey back to Beaulieu had been shockingly uneventful. They'd run into plenty of people on the road, of course, but none of them had seemed even remotely suspicious.

If Deimos was keeping an eye on them . . . if Vanya had reported that Evander had regained his powers . . . he was doing nothing about it.

Yet.

"Nothing is wrong," Marcos said, but the heaviness in his words proved the opposite was true.

"Yet, I don't believe you," Evander retorted, unable to help teasing him a little bit.

It was just that Marcos was so delightful to tease and flirt with—all stoic and solemn and earnest, but Evander had discovered the right joke would make him smile, and it was like watching the sun rise at the Castle at the Top of the World. It blinded him, enchanted him.

Marcos sighed. "I was wondering if it's wise to return to Beaulieu as ourselves."

"As Marcos and Evander?" Evander had been so distracted by his growing fondness for Marcos that he hadn't given it any thought.

But *Marcos* had.

That's only because he's had so long to get used to his feelings. You're just reconciling yourself to them. You don't even know what they are yet.

"Nobody at the castle will recognize you as Evander, and I have never appeared on the surface as Marcos. Before now."

"I haven't ever been Evander, either, not since the very beginning," he admitted. A fact that he was fairly certain that Marcos already suspected. "But I . . ." He didn't want to return to the form of Rhys. And Evrard, he would cause questions. Too many questions.

It would be better to change himself back to Rhys.

But as much as he'd resisted returning to his original form, to becoming Evander again, he was loath to let it go.

"Just until Rory and Gray recognize you, and don't think you're a stranger," Marcos said reassuringly. "We don't want them to think we're threats."

It was logical. It made sense.

But Evander hated doing it. A second later, he stared at Marcos through Rhys' eyes.

Marcos had never touched this body. Never shown Rhys the kind of pleasure he'd shown Evander.

Maybe he didn't care about Rhys, not the way he cared about Evander.

But then the air around Marcos shimmered and he was suddenly, inexplicably Merleen again. "A disguise more than anything else," he said. And then he was reaching out, catching Evander's cheek in his palm and he was kissing him with enough passion that there was no way that Evander could doubt how he felt.

Not about Evander. Not about Rhys.

"I guess," Evander said breathlessly, after Marcos turned away, "that you don't mind Rhys, then."

Marcos turned towards him. "You're *you*, no matter what form you take. I see you, as a unicorn or as an eagle, or as Rhys, but it's always Evander who's looking back at me."

It made sense; Evander never felt like he was truly different, no matter what form he took, but while a change could be a breath of fresh air, he'd discovered that he really *liked* being Evander.

And part of that was the way that Marcos looked at him when he was.

"That's all well and good, but don't try to deny that you prefer me as Evander," he teased.

Marcos shrugged. Evander thought he might have caught a hint of a blush high on his cheekbones. "That was how I knew you for so long," he admitted. "Do you prefer Merleen . . . or Marcos?"

That was easy enough. Merleen had unsettled him—but he wasn't sure now if that had been because Merleen had been a disguise, and with his reduced powers, he hadn't quite been able to penetrate it, or if he'd actually been attracted to the disguise, and the man underneath it, and he hadn't known how to deal with that.

"Even when you're wearing this," Evander said, waving at his Merleen form, "you're still Marcos. Always Marcos."

He wasn't sure how he'd managed to fool him in the first place.

He did it by keeping his distance.

But there isn't any more distance between you. Not anymore.

"Then," Marcos said with a grin, "I think you have your answer."

"Tonight, we'll be ourselves again," Evander said, realizing he wasn't just making Marcos a promise, but himself.

"Yes," Marcos agreed, and nudged his horse, Evander following suit.

They galloped the rest of the way to Beaulieu, to the gate, where they slowed for the guard who stood watch over the entrance.

"Is that you, Rhys?" the guard asked, looking surprised. "Their Highnesses will be so pleased that you're back."

"Hello, Godrick," Evander said, and it was like falling back into a familiar shape—and a familiar voice, tinged now with the Ardglassian accent he'd always used as Rhys.

"And you too, Merleen," Godrick said with a smile, motioning to the other guards to raise the gate.

"Why was the gate closed?" Marcos asked, and Evander could tell from the frown on his face that he was concerned.

The gate normally *wasn't* shut during the day, even though there was always a rotating guard posted at the entrance, because Marthe was thorough and incessantly concerned about the kings' safety.

"There's been . . ." Godrick paused, like he wasn't sure what he should say. "Some weird things, I suppose? And you know the general, she likes to be cautious."

"Indeed she does," Marcos said, patting Godrick on the arm as they rode past him.

They exchanged a look once they were clear of the gate.

"Weird might be a way to explain that the sorcerers have emerged again," Evander said under his breath as they stopped next to the stables, and finally dismounted.

Marcos stretched his back. And even as Merleen, Evander had discovered that it was difficult to even focus when he moved. He was so deadly and so graceful, all in the same moment, and it was mesmerizing.

He wanted to get him alone, and get all his clothes off.

But first, they needed to see Rory and Gray, tell them the truth, and find out what Godrick had meant by *weird*.

Unfortunately Evander already knew that wouldn't be quick.

"You're back."

Evander turned and Anya was standing there, with a smile on her face, but there were shadows under her eyes, and she looked . . . uneasy.

Apprehension bloomed inside Evander. While he and Marcos had been traveling back to Beaulieu, had Deimos and his sorcerers already turned their attention towards the people that Evander cared about the most?

"We rode back as quickly as we could," Evander said.

Anya nodded. "Gray and Rory will want to see you," she said.

"We have much to discuss," Evander agreed.

CHAPTER TWELVE

Anya led them into the castle proper, through the passageways, and even though he had only been gone from Beaulieu for a week, it felt alien to be wandering these halls as Rhys.

"Where did you go?" she asked as Rhys realized they were heading towards the Great Hall. Were Rory and Gray holding a public audience this afternoon?

If they were, this would have to wait.

But when Anya pushed open the doors, the dais at the end, with its two thrones, was empty. Instead, Rory and Gray were sitting around a large circular table positioned in the center of the room, and they were joined by the general, Marthe, and by Rowen, Acadia, and Diana.

Rory's eyes lit up when he saw Rhys and Merleen.

"You're back!" he exclaimed. "And none too soon."

"What has happened?" Marcos demanded, and Evander nearly laughed, because everyone at the table looked surprised to hear him make such a forceful request. Merleen had kept to himself, had mostly kept quiet; but Merleen had never really been Marcos.

He'd been afraid to step into the light, to reveal who he truly was, because it was undeniable that Evander would have recognized him instantly. Just the ringing authority in his tone would have been enough.

"There've been some odd things happening in the villages around Beaulieu," Gray explained. "Dead animals here and there, more than there should be, always drained of blood. A goat born with a sheep's head. A young man who was a shepherd disappearing and not being heard from again. Scorched ground with no explanation. Nothing particularly dangerous or suspicious on its own, but together . . . we are actually in council, trying to decide what to do about it, *if* we should do anything about it."

"You should," Evander said. "But first, before we discuss that, there is something you should know about me. And about Merleen."

Gray nodded. He looked apprehensive, and Evander supposed he couldn't blame him for that. If anyone could've guessed that there was more to Evrard's—and Rhys'—story, it would be Gray, who had met them both.

At the time, he hadn't realized they were the same person, but he did now. And the apprehension in his expression made it clear that he knew the other shoe was about to drop.

"We would be honored to hear whatever you have to tell us," Rory said, a gracious ruler from first to last.

Gray had come a long way, but he was not nearly as polished.

As a pair, the differences helped them work better together than any possible similarities.

In them, Evander could see the echoes of him and Marcos.

But he pushed that thought aside.

"My name is not Rhys," he said.

Gray snorted. "No, of course it isn't. It's Evrard."

"It's not that either," Evander admitted.

Everyone at the table looked fascinated. "My name is Evander," he said, and as he said the words, he let the transformation wash over him, until who was standing in front of them was not Rhys, but Evander. His real self.

"And this," he continued, gesturing towards Merleen, "is not Merleen, not the nephew of Shaheen, but Marcos, who is a Guardian, like me."

With Evander's gesture, Merleen's disguise melted away, revealing Marcos, and his inevitably amused expression.

"Show-off," he said under his breath.

Evander shrugged.

"What do you mean *Guardian like me*?" Gray wanted to know. He'd crossed his arms over his chest and he looked perturbed still.

Evander supposed that made sense; Evrard had been something of a father figure to him, a young boy who had been ripped from everything he knew—and now he was discovering that Evrard hadn't even been real.

That Rhys, who'd protected him in Tullamore, hadn't been real, either.

"There are thirteen Guardians," Marcos spoke up. "We each are responsible for caring for a part of the human population, for something vital to them. I am the Guardian of War. Evander is . . ."

"Evander *was* the Guardian of Secrets," Evander finished for him.

"*Was?* What does that mean?" Rory wanted to know.

"I want to know more about what a *Guardian of War* was doing hiding out in my kingdom," Gray muttered, but Rory nudged him.

"I was banished hundreds of years ago for daring to cross our leader, Deimos," Evander said. "I wanted his permission to go to the surface, to live among you, and banish the sorcerers from your midst. He would not permit it. I attempted to circumvent his judgement, and so I was banished here, and stripped of all my powers. I decided to devote my time to the task, anyway. I thought with Sabrina's death, my task was accomplished."

"Why do I feel there is a *but* coming at the end of that statement?" Gray complained.

"There is another secret group with power, and I would not be surprised if they are growing, in force, waiting for the right time to strike," Marcos said.

"Strike?" Marthe's voice grew sharp. "You think they will attack?"

"I think it is very possible, yes, because Deimos has decided that we, together, pose a threat to him." Marcos sounded grave. "This is not your fight, and we did not mean to bring it to your doorstep."

"But you did." Anya threw both of them an inexorable glare. She would always be protective of Gray—the prince who'd been lost, and who had finally been found.

"Evander has devoted hundreds of years to bringing peace and prosperity to Fontaine," Marcos said staunchly when Evander had considered intervening. "A side effect of this support and work is that now, Deimos sees this as a place he can use to hurt you. We will do what we can to steer the fight away from you, but I can make no promises that he will not forcibly drag you into it regardless of what we do."

"No," Rory said, holding up a hand. "That will be unnecessary. I know what Evander has done for me and for this country. Everyone will get a choice, but please count the two of us in. Nobody gets to banish you and then attack you, not on my watch. Or to fill my country with power-hungry sorcerers who would wreak havoc on my people."

"You said that you are the Guardian of War and . . ." Diana hesitated. "Evander is the Guardian of Secrets. What is Deimos the Guardian of?"

"Death," Evander said flatly. "Deimos is the Guardian of Death."

The words echoed through the sudden silence in the Great Hall.

Gray was the one who spoke up. He looked . . . marginally less furious. "And he is the one leading these new sorcerers?"

"We believe so," Marcos said, inclining his head.

"If you are the Guardian of Secrets," Rowen spoke up softly, "can you tell if we are lying?"

"No," Evander said firmly, then realized that *yes*, he could, again. "Actually, if I do concentrate, I can generally ferret out the truth," he admitted. "I did not have my powers for many years because of Deimos' banishment but . . . that was why we left."

Marcos glanced over at him. "That is not why we left."

"We were called to the Well, a magical portal, by another Guardian," Evander confessed. "He threatened Rory and Gray, everyone at Beaulieu, if I did not go, so I went. Marcos revealed himself and journeyed there with me. We met the other Guardian, realized his treachery, but the silver lining was that with the Well's assistance, I have recovered my magic."

"What are your powers?" Gray wanted to know. "You know how to steal our secrets, how to determine when we're lying and . . ."

"Something you might recognize," Evander said, and he couldn't help the grin as he raised his hand, flame leaping out of it.

"*You* did that," Rory exclaimed, his eyes torn between his husband and the flame dancing on Evander's palm. "At our wedding!"

"I created Lion's Breath a few generations ago, knowing you would need a weapon worthy of you. It took . . . much of my magic," Evander admitted. They did not need to know that it had stripped him for years. He'd barely been able to maintain different forms, but eventually his magic had slowly but surely built up again. "I had never merged my magic with a blade before. Unfortunately I did not have Marcos' expertise to rely on, back then, but I was unaware that wielding it would transfer some of its power to the bearer. But it seems that it did."

"And thank the Gods for that," Marthe said seriously. "We would've all died, if not for King Graham killing the count with his bare hands." She paused, and Evander could feel her gaze taking him in, *all* of him, including the flames emerging from his palm. "If you need us to fight, we are with you." Her face was grave. "You have sacrificed much to help us and to protect this realm. I would gladly give my life to assist you in this."

"I would, too," Anya said, inclining her head towards Marthe. "I understand from conversations with King Graham that you saved his life when he was just a boy, helping him to escape Tullamore and Ardglass."

Evander inclined his head. "I did my duty," he said simply.

"And we will do ours," Rowen said, adding her voice to the others.

"It will be dangerous," Marcos warned.

"Are you not the Guardian of War?" Gray's eyes lit up. "I am sure you have much to teach us."

"You should not encourage them," Evander complained as they finally, after a long council session debating the best course of action, and Evander and Marcos answering many additional questions, headed to their quarters. Or rather, Evander realized, they were heading towards *his* quarters.

Merleen's quarters in Beaulieu were the other direction.

But Marcos had followed him out of the Hall, and had yet to leave his side.

It filled Evander with a warmth he'd never felt before, and wasn't sure he could properly identify.

"I should not encourage them how?" Marcos asked, his tone teasing.

"Especially Gray," Evander said, as if Marcos hadn't responded. "He is easily swayed, easily impressed."

"I would think he is actually the opposite, because you raised him to guard himself and to question everything," Marcos said. He was still smiling.

Evander wanted to push him against the nearest wall and wipe that smug, annoyingly sly smile off with his fist.

Or with his mouth.

But Rory had already given him several knowing looks, and he had a feeling that neither of them had been particularly circumspect about how close they'd grown.

It would only confirm the king's suspicion if they were caught kissing in the hallway.

Your chambers are just down this corridor, you can wait, Evander cautioned himself. But he'd waited for days now, and his skin felt hot and itchy.

He yearned to touch Marcos, and have him touch him in return.

"If that is a compliment on how I raised Gray from boy to a man, to a king, then I will take it," Evander said formally. Trying to distance himself. Trying not to lose control completely.

Marcos made him want to throw his poise away with both hands—and Evander both loved it and hated it.

"It is," Marcos said. "And he is curious, wants to know more, then why should I not tell him more, share my knowledge of battle and war with the man? He is responsible for the security of this kingdom."

"That's the general," Evander reminded him.

"I was not disparaging the general, I am sure she is eminently capable. But Gray is a strong man, with a stronger will that I believe you helped take root, and he is also the one who bears a flaming sword that you forged. He should know what I know, or as much of it as I can teach him."

Evander rolled his eyes and finally, *finally*, they stopped in front of the doorway to his chambers. His fingertips twitched, and he nearly reached for Marcos.

Nearly.

It was a close thing.

"Evander," Marcos said quietly, turning towards him, before he could reach for the door. "I know you consider him yours, and I would never do a thing to harm him."

Evander nearly laughed. Was that what Marcos thought he was concerned about? He knew Marcos would only give Gray the information that would strengthen his defense, and he'd never place him in danger by giving him too much.

He'd only been . . . trying to distract both of them from the palpable tension and the carnal desire that had been plaguing him since the last time they'd touched.

He could still feel Marcos' mouth on his, still feel his hand, with its rough callouses and its perfect, utterly pleasurable pressure, wrapped around his cock.

And he wanted more. He knew there was more. He'd hardly been an innocent with Vanya, and they'd had hundreds of years, *thousands* of years, to explore sex.

He wanted all of that, and so much more, with Marcos.

"Of course you wouldn't," Evander said dryly.

"Then what . . ." Marcos hesitated, and then he smiled, slow and *oh*, it was so dirty, so utterly perfect, that Evander could barely contain himself anymore.

He pushed open the door and had Marcos pressed up against it in a flash, hand skating down his torso and mouth nearly in line with his.

"You wanted this," Marcos said softly. Knowingly.

He'd already talked too much. Knew too much. *Saw* too much.

Evander stopped his words with a kiss. He'd been so ravenous for Marcos that he could barely restrain himself, and he poured all of his confusion and his desire into the kiss, tongue sliding against Marcos', savoring the taste of him, the *feel* of him.

It was intoxicating, immediately, and he felt dizzy and unmoored by it.

By *him*.

Kissing Vanya had been sweet and nice, but there was an urgency, a desperation with Marcos that had Evander already pawing at his clothes.

The scrape of Marcos' scruff, dense from so many days on the road, against the sensitive skin of his neck was a sublime counterpoint to the pleasure rushing through him.

Fingers still scrabbling over Marcos' leather armor, he finally found the ties which held it in place and he pulled them loose.

Marcos chuckled against his lips. "Eager?" he questioned, teasing again.

Evander had never imagined that the Guardian of War would have such a keen sense of humor, or that he would enjoy it so much.

Nothing is how you thought it was.

But instead of drowning in the upheaval of his existence, Evander discovered that he had a firm grip on one person. One person who made it all make sense.

Marcos.

Panting, Evander sank to his knees and rocked back, just looking his fill.

Marcos' body had been designed as a weapon, and he'd honed it to the sharpest edge. But it was more than that, too. He was exquisite like this, lips red and swollen from Evander's own, his gaze soft and hot.

He lifted off his armor, and set it on the floor, his tunic underneath slipping to reveal one powerful shoulder.

Evander wet his lips and groaned as Marcos pulled off the tunic, leaving his chest and torso bare. He reached up, pressing a palm to his stomach, and felt the muscles twitch under his touch.

"As you can see," Marcos said, his voice rough, "you are not the only one desperate."

Evander could see it, the hard line of his erection in his breeches. It was easy to let his fingers slip lower and tug the last bit of his covering down.

He'd touched him twice, brought him to two orgasms, but Evander hadn't had a chance to really *look* at Marcos' cock.

And now he could sit here, and not only look his fill, but touch and . . .

Well, it seemed very obvious that he wanted even more than that.

Above him, Marcos groaned loud and unrestrained as Evander leaned in and gave his cock an experimental lick.

Marcos' palms pressed hard against the door. Like he was afraid to reach out and touch him.

His control is impeccable, and you're going to break it, anyway.

"I should . . ." Marcos took a deep breath as Evander licked again. "I should wash. We have been on the road . . ."

But he didn't smell bad, only like Marcos. Like leather and steel and something wild and dangerous, the crackle of lightning hitting the ground. As Evander leaned closer, the scent of him only grew stronger and more intoxicating, until Evander felt dizzy with it.

"You . . ." Marcos tried to speak again, to warn him? Evander wasn't sure, because he answered the unasked question by dipping his head and sliding his cock into his mouth, sucking lightly on the head, enjoying both the way it twitched against his tongue and the groan that Marcos let out.

It had been a very long time since he'd done this but Marcos didn't seem to mind, even though he was cautious. Marcos was larger than Vanya had been, a full mouthful that Evander discovered he *really* enjoyed.

Enjoyed so much that as he gave Marcos pleasure, fingertips dug into the rippling muscles of the most beautiful pair of thighs he'd ever seen—and he'd seen so many pairs over his many, many years—he found his own blood beating hot and strong, and he reached down, pressing a palm against his own erection, straining at his breeches.

Marcos' groan was rough and desperate. "Yes," he begged, "touch yourself. I want to see you."

He sounded like he'd die if he didn't see, and since Evander felt the same flavor of urgency, he pushed his breeches down, freeing his own cock, stroking it firmly as he took Marcos' length deep, tracing patterns along it with his tongue.

Precome blurted onto his tongue and he savored it, knowing that Marcos was close. And he was too, but he needed more. He slipped a finger alongside Marcos' cock in his mouth and wet it, sliding it down his body, enjoying Marcos' shocked gasp.

Raising up on his haunches, Evander trembled as he pressed his fingers lower, and then lower still, circling his hole, gasping around Marcos' cock as he pressed in.

He could imagine Marcos doing this to him, fucking him with his fingers and then his cock, big and inescapable, driving him wild with the pleasure of it.

Marcos' whine was high and needy as he sucked harder and pushed his finger in further, a second joining the first. He wanted to feel full, as full as Marcos would make him.

Then, *finally*, Marcos' hands left the door, and Evander felt them settle on his head, on his cheek, stroking his hair, soft and sweet.

And then they gripped him hard and Evander froze, for a split second, bracing for Marcos' orgasm, then as it washed over him, started to swallow.

Marcos' bellow was probably heard throughout Beaulieu, but in that moment Evander didn't care. He was frantic, sucking hard on Marcos' cock, licking up the last bit of his come, teetering on the edge of his own orgasm.

He was so close, he just needed a little bit more . . .

Marcos' softening cock slipped out of his mouth and he was panting, so aroused he felt both like he could live on this edge forever, and desperate to fall off it.

Then he was being lifted, effortlessly, like he weighed nothing, and Marcos kissed him deep, big hands cupping his backside, and then Evander felt it.

Another finger, bigger and rougher, joining his own. He pressed his cock, slippery and straining, against Marcos' stomach, rubbing it against the ridges of his muscled abdomen, and that was all it took. His orgasm was like a storm, buffeting him and shaking him, and Evander thought he might have yelled.

He came down with a shaky laugh, and as he opened his eyes, his gaze still even with Marcos', he knew he must have been *very* loud indeed, because Marcos' grin was undeniably smug.

"Don't tell me," Marcos said, his voice a deep rumble as he carried them over to the bed, "that you were thinking about that during our council with Their Highnesses."

"I won't," Evander said, chuckling under his breath. "I'll deny it until my final breath."

Marcos picked up his tunic and wiped his chest clean of Evander's come. "We should call for a bath," he said.

If they did, and they were both here, in Evander's quarters, everyone would know.

Rhys had never taken a lover.

Evander had only had one lover before—and Vanya had betrayed him.

But he already knew, deep down, in a place where truth and lies became inescapably apparent, that Marcos would never deceive or abandon him.

He had not said it, but Evander believed that he loved him.

"You do not mind if everyone knows?" Evander asked, shedding the rest of his clothes. He *could* use a bath.

He did not know if *he* minded yet, so perhaps it was best to ask Marcos first.

"Why would I?" Marcos questioned with a shrug. "Would it bother you?"

"Rhys was not . . . he did not . . ." Evander hesitated.

"But everyone knew Merleen was trying," Marcos teased.

"They do not know you are Merleen, or that I am Rhys."

Marcos shrugged again. "It is our business. If the court wishes to gossip, they will gossip. You have been at many courts, you should know this."

"I do, but it has never been *me* they were gossiping about," Evander admitted.

Marcos reached over and pressed a reassuring hand against Evander's shoulder. "If you wish to keep it between us . . ."

But even before he'd restored his powers, Evander never could have missed the hurt that flashed in Marcos' gaze. He did not want Evander to be afraid or, even worse, ashamed.

And he wasn't. Not necessarily.

He was just so very new to this. Embarrassingly.

"I have not done this," he said with as much dignity as he could muster. "Never before."

"You did it with Vanya. The whole Castle knew about you and Vanya." Marcos' tone was dry as kindling, and he looked away, like he was afraid of what Evander would see in his eyes.

"After that," Evander corrected, "I did not do this."

Marcos looked surprised.

"You were watching me, you should have known," Evander said. But clearly he hadn't.

"I believed you must have been discreet," Marcos said slowly. "Never, not once since you were banished?"

"I did not trust anyone," Evander admitted.

"And you trust me?"

It was a natural assumption to make, but it still made Evander squirm inside. He *did* trust the Guardian, but it was harder to admit it.

Especially when Marcos' gaze kept flaying him bare.

"Yes," he finally admitted. "Yes, I do."

"Then that is enough," Marcos said and rose to his feet. "I will return to my own quarters, then."

That had not been what Evander wished at all, and he found himself scrambling to fix it. "No," he said hurriedly, "no, I did not mean for you to go, for us to . . . well, for us to do *that*, and then have you leave."

He hesitated. He'd never dreamt that he'd say the next words, but he couldn't deny the authenticity of them. "I want you here. With me."

The smile that graced Marcos' features was one of his brightest, his eyes impossibly softened even further.

He loves you, Evander thought, again, because he could not help it. *And you . . . well, you are hardly averse to him. Not now.*

But he didn't know if it was love. He'd never loved that way before. Could he love Marcos?

Regardless, he could not, *would not,* mention it until he was sure. Marcos deserved that much.

"Then, perhaps I will make myself scarce while you call for the bath," Marcos said gently. "Since you do not wish to be the subject of gossip."

It felt so petty, worrying about that. Evander shook off his concern. "No," he said, "I want you here, and if people decide to discuss that particular turn of events, it's their business, not ours."

Marcos tugged up his breeches. "I will find a servant, then, and ask them to bring a hot bath, and some food," he said. But before he turned to go, he looked back. "Kadir once told me that we were everlasting, that we could never change, but I would challenge that now. You *have* changed, Evander, Guardian of Secrets."

CHAPTER THIRTEEN

The next morning, Marcos set off with Gray and Anya towards the east, with Marthe leading another contingent to the south, intending to search through several nearby villages, hoping to ascertain if any other strange occurrences had happened, and also to potentially discover where the sorcerers were hiding.

Evander found himself at a loose end, and after an hour or two in his study, unable to concentrate on other matters of state that had gathered on his desk during his absence, he got up and went to find Rory. Unsurprisingly, he found him in the first place he checked: the library.

"I thought I might find you here," he said as he entered. Rory glanced up. He had a streak of ink on his cheek, and a massive pile of ancient texts surrounded him.

This was the scholar Rory who had nearly let his aunt, the vicious sorceress Sabrina, usurp his kingdom, because he'd been too lost in books.

He'd become more involved in the running of the kingdom since taking the throne, but Evander knew that this place was still where Rory felt the most at ease.

"I thought I might dig through some of our oldest volumes, see if I can find any references to Guardians or Death as a figure," Rory explained. He paused. "It is still very odd to see you like that, like . . ."

"Like?" Evander questioned, taking a seat as Rory trailed off.

"Like Evrard, but as a person. That is what you remind me of. Is that why you took the form of a unicorn?"

"I took the form of a unicorn because it was unusual and magical and also because it reminded me of purity, of innocence," Evander said wryly. "I was quite bitter in those days about my Guardianship."

"And you are not still?" Rory questioned, though Evander had a feeling he had already discovered the answer to that question.

Evander shrugged. "With so many hundreds of years passed since my banishment, and since my powers have been lately restored, I find I'm less interested in vengeance, and more eager for justice."

"*And* since you grew closer to Merleen," Rory teased. "Or I suppose he is Marcos now. *The Guardian of War.*"

"You would not question his capabilities if you saw him in action."

"Oh?" Rory raised an eyebrow. "And I'm assuming you have?"

"We've known each other a very long time," Evander said. Hoping that Rory would leave it at that. Yet knowing that he wouldn't.

Rory could be a dog with a bone; impossibly stubborn, sometimes; even more stubborn than Gray, and that was saying something.

So many other young men would have fled to safety, and never tried to return to claim their kingdom. But not Rory. He'd acknowledged his mistakes and worked hard to fix them.

When he'd been born, to parents who'd loved him—parents Evander hadn't been able to save—Evander had cherished high hopes for the young prince.

But back then, he'd been occupied in the valley, making sure that no harm befell Gray. Sabrina would never have been emboldened enough to kill Prince Emory of Fontaine, but Gray? She'd have gone after him in a heartbeat. And Evander had known that he needed both of them to defeat her, so he'd watched and waited and hoped.

On first acquaintance, Rory had just seemed like a very pretty, slightly spoilt child.

But he'd proven himself, over and over again, and then morphed into the kind of man and the kind of king—and the kind of partner and husband—that even Evander could approve of.

Through it all, he'd always possessed such a fierce intelligence, and Evander could feel it turning on him now. Considering him. Considering Marcos.

"Gray doesn't trust him," Rory said conversationally. "Yet it seems you do."

"He said that?" Evander was surprised. Gray trusted *him*, and he'd made it abundantly clear yesterday that he trusted Marcos.

"According to you two, he's the *Guardian of War*," Rory said. "Of course Gray doesn't trust him. He doesn't want war brought to our kingdom."

"War is such a general term," Evander said, discovering he felt it entirely necessary to defend Marcos. Especially when he wasn't here to defend himself. "He's a brilliant fighter, but he also has spent thousands of years studying tactics, and supply lines, and can lead an army like he was born to do it, because he was."

"And you think that doesn't sound worrisome to Gray," Rory said wryly, setting his elbow on the table, and resting his chin in his palm.

Evander was shocked, and he was rarely shocked. "Gray thinks he wants to usurp his kingdom? *Marcos*, really?"

"We don't know him. Sometimes . . ." Rory hesitated. "Sometimes it feels like we barely know you. It's good to be cautious. After all, you raised him to be."

Rory's words echoed Marcos' from last night.

You raised him to guard himself and to question everything.

He had, because it had felt like the only way to protect a young, inquisitive boy who'd just been ripped away from everything he'd ever known. If he was annoyed at Gray's mistrust now, it was his own fault, for planting the seed.

"I did," Evander grudgingly admitted. "But I hope that today, while they are out checking on the villages, Gray will begin to learn that Marcos is who he says he is. No more and no less. He wants no kingdom for his own."

"And neither do you," Rory stated.

"All I want is . . . peace. No kingdoms. No wars. No battles. No conquering heroes. Just peace." It seemed silly to admit, when he'd had it here, at Beaulieu, before Vanya had called him, and he'd hated every minute of it. But now? The idea of it felt so very different. Or maybe *he* was different.

"Then peace we shall have," Rory said. He pushed an open book towards Evander. "I did find a handful of references," he said, pointing to a passage in a volume so old that Evander could barely make out the lettering. "It refers to Death, coming on its black steed, to conquer the people."

Evander checked the bound leather cover and its binding. It was old, cracking and crumbling, but he recognized the symbols right away. "This is from Ardglass."

"Long before Ardglass was Ardglass," Rory confirmed. "When it was just a loose grouping of tribes."

Evander considered mentioning that Marcos had once been a *leader* of one of those tribes, and had fought in one of their more important battles, but that would give Rory the wrong idea when he was already unsure if Marcos was trustworthy.

He skimmed the passage once, and then twice, and then a third time. "You are an expert on languages," he said to Rory, "are you sure the author is not merely being descriptive? Death on a dark steed?"

"You should be familiar with Ardglassian texts of this time period," Rory said. "The adversarial atmosphere, the constant fighting between the tribes, it did not lend itself to particularly florid language. They were pragmatists."

"Ardglassians have *always* been pragmatists," Evander said frankly, and Rory shot him a grin.

"No one knows it better than me," Rory said lightly. "But no, I don't think the author was being metaphorical. I believe Death, in fact, came, and Death rode a black horse."

"It could be Deimos, but the passage tells us nothing else."

"Yes, it does," Rory said, carefully flipping several pages of nearly transparent parchment. "The story continues here. Death rode a dark steed," he read, "and went to the highest reaches, seducing some women and some men away from their true path, bending them to his own merciless purpose."

"You think this describes how he assisted and created the first sect of sorcerers," Evander said thoughtfully. "The timing is . . . well, it is not quite right, there were one or two of them on the surface before this. This happened, I believe, *after* I was banished, but . . ."

"But?" Rory prompted.

The conclusion filled Evander with dread. "This is when I started taking a more active role in defeating the sorcerers. I left the valley. I refocused *my* purpose. I think he knew I could eradicate one or two easily enough. Especially if they did not work together. But as soon as I began to seek them out, there were always more, new generations cropping up, knowledge passed down. Every time I felt like I had conquered them, they sprouted in a different spot."

"You think he started adding to their numbers, and the passage refers to that."

Evander nodded gravely, and he was sure that Rory's expression matched his own.

"And you think he's done it again," Rory said, frowning.

"Sabrina was unique," Evander pointed out, tapping a finger on the text in question, "she was not like the others I faced, who *did* tend to huddle in groups because their power was greater that way. But she never wanted to share, and she was extraordinarily powerful on her own, so she wouldn't."

"But what about Aplin and Rinaldi. They were her followers, right?"

"In the roughest sense of the word, yes. But she didn't share with them. Not really. Not while she was alive. My guess is they were her lackeys. Her spies in this court. But it was only when she died and Aplin ransacked her lair that they gained some of the power. Not Rinaldi, he was useless. But Aplin, yes."

"And then Gray killed him." Rory smiled. "You should have told me that you were the one who forged Lion's Breath."

Evander laughed. "Tell you I'd been around, hundreds of years ago, and created this sword not for your ancestors but for you? For *Gray*? And a unicorn forging a sword? Would you have even believed it?"

"I suppose that would've created more questions than you could answer," Rory admitted with a smile. "And no, probably not."

"Gray wouldn't have believed me," Evander grumbled, "and he was already difficult enough by that point."

"Actually, I think he would have. I think Gray's always known there's things you didn't share, couldn't share," Rory said contemplatively.

"And he held that against me." Evander chuckled under his breath. He knew how frustrated Gray had been with him at times. How he'd retreated into his work and his everyday life in the valley, hoping for some kind of peace.

Then Rory had upended all of it by venturing into the valley, on the run, and in danger.

"Perhaps." Rory was still grinning, but then his expression grew more solemn. "But I think Gray trusts you and your judgment more than you realize."

"I suppose we'll see," Evander said.

Marcos had insisted they take him to every village in their sector where something strange had occurred.

But as they toured the villages, Marcos closely attuned for anything that felt out of place, or anything that smelled of Deimos' power, they'd come up empty.

Nothing out of place. Nothing that gave him that uneasy prickling feeling at the back of his neck.

"Maybe," Gray said as they mounted their horses after Marcos finished talking to some of the villagers at the last location, "we should have brought Evrard with us."

"Evander," Marcos corrected before he could think it through.

Gray shot him a long, contemplative look. "It's hard to remember," he said by way of explanation. "I knew him by a different name for a long time. It was hard to even remember to call him Rhys, and now he shows up and he's something different *again*."

"Perhaps his form has changed," Marcos said, "but I think if you give Evander a chance, you'll recognize Rhys *and* Evrard in him. He might look different, but in my experience, he's always been uniquely himself."

Gray swung his leg over his horse, pulling himself up effortlessly. He wore Lion's Breath in a scabbard strapped to his back.

Marcos' fingers had itched from the moment he'd seen it to hold it in his hands, to wield it, even in practice.

He'd known, of course, that Evander had, at one time, forged a sword. But he'd never gotten close enough to see it. To touch it.

But he could feel Gray's hesitation. He was holding back. Unsure of his purpose—and Marcos couldn't blame him. He was a powerful Guardian. It was why he'd never come to the surface in his own guise before. It created too much uneasiness, too much distrust.

"What should we do now?" Anya asked, as she mounted her own horse.

He'd known Ardglassian women like her before, shield maidens who could fight just as competently as their brothers, but there was a singular fierceness to her gaze that he found himself appreciating.

He would be honored to fight by her side, if it came to that.

And, he thought morosely, it likely would.

He could already feel the forces coalescing, clashing, the inevitability swirling around him that they would do battle on one of these fields, next to one of these villages.

He hadn't told Evander yet, but he would.

Soon.

"Let's see the charred spot those villagers mentioned," Marcos suggested. "I might be able to sense our enemies from the magic expended there."

"You can do that?" She sounded fascinated as they left the village at a trot. She had some of Gray's distrust, which he knew to be an Ardglassian trait—they were slow to trust, but once you'd gained their loyalty, you never lost it—but she was also interested in his skills, and what he could teach her.

She hadn't said it specifically yet, but he already knew he'd pass what he knew on to her. On to Gray, if he could reconcile himself to the possibility.

Marcos nodded. "I don't sense power as well as Evander does, but my tracking is second to none. If I can scent the sorcerers there, I can try to track them."

"That's amazing." Anya sounded impressed. "Isn't that amazing, Gray?"

Gray shrugged, clearly less impressed. "I've known many excellent trackers," he grumbled.

"But none of them could track *magic*," Anya reminded him.

Gray grumbled again, under his breath, and even with his enhanced senses, Marcos couldn't quite make him out over the sound of the horses' hooves against the packed dirt of the road.

But Marcos didn't need to hear him to understand what he'd meant.

He didn't trust him.

Didn't *want* to trust him.

Which was going to make all of this harder.

"The villagers said it was just past this field," Anya said, pointing and nudging her horse in the same direction. "They said it was hard to miss."

Indeed, when they came over the ridge of one field, and started down the slight hill to the next, the flattened, charred wheat stood out like a sore thumb.

"What a waste," Gray said as they approached it.

"Let's leave our horses here," Marcos ordered, stopping a good distance away from the mark in the field.

"Really? Why?" Gray asked. Not challenging him, not exactly, but the insinuation was there.

This is his kingdom, and he has the right to protect it however he feels is fit, Marcos reminded himself. It would have been so much easier to be here as Merleen, whom Gray had felt a kinship and a loyalty to, who'd been his friend.

Instead, Gray had discovered that Merleen had been a figment of his imagination, and had never truly existed at all.

Not the best way to begin a partnership.

"There could be much residual magic in that mark," Marcos cautioned. "I do not know how the horses will react to it."

"They can sense it?" Anya asked.

"Animals are often more sensitive than we are," Marcos said, smoothing the mane of his horse as he dismounted, tying the reins to a nearby bale of hay.

He turned towards the mark.

Behind him, he could sense Anya and Gray also dismounting. He heard Gray pull Lion's Breath from its sheath and he could smell the steel of Anya's long knife as she pulled it from one of her brown leather boots.

He held up a hand as they grew closer.

"Let me look at it first," Marcos said.

"No."

He looked back and Gray was staring at him, his blue eyes hard as stones.

"I know you don't trust me . . ." Marcos began, but Gray interrupted him.

"It is *my* mandate to protect this kingdom," Gray said, "and no, I do not trust you. You're the so-called *Guardian of War*. How do I know you have not lured us here to kill us both? You could do it easily."

"With my bare hands," Marcos said calmly. He could imagine Evander snorting, unimpressed by his tactics, but he knew Gray. Understood him. He wouldn't trust him until he had the whole truth. Deception and partial truths would only prolong his misgivings, and since Marcos did not know how much time they had before hell descended on them, it was important to settle this now.

"See?" Gray drawled. "My concern is hardly misplaced."

"Gray," Anya said, trying to reason with him, "he's *Merleen*. He isn't going to do anything."

"Yes, he came to my court and he lied about who he was, and what his purpose was." Gray's tone was still implacable.

"I'm not lying now. It would be easier if I told you a whole lot of conveniently reassuring lies. But I will not. Yes, I am powerful. I, however, am not remotely as powerful as Deimos, who will descend here in what could be days or could be months or years. I don't know. But I do know we need to be prepared, and we need to learn everything we can before he arrives."

"Somehow, I doubt that's true," Gray said wryly.

"What, that Deimos will arrive . . ."

But Gray cut him off before he could expound further on the subject.

"No," Gray said firmly. "No, that you are not as powerful as Deimos."

Marcos narrowed his gaze. He had known Gray since arriving at Beaulieu. They'd become friendly, when he'd been disguised as Merleen. Marcos rarely underestimated people he *didn't* know. And he knew Gray.

Still, he'd underestimated him.

"You are confident," Gray said. "Not the over-confidence of some-one who is over-matched and knows it and believes they will succeed in defeating their enemies, anyway. But true confidence."

"And," Anya added, shooting him a wry smile, "you said you have been away from your Conclave for years, many hundreds of years. Surely if Deimos could have made you come back, he would have." She arched an eyebrow. "You intimidate *him*."

"And yet that does not make him any less of a threat," Marcos said.

"No, it makes *you* a threat." Gray's voice was hard as steel.

Marcos gestured to where Gray held Lion's Breath.

"That sword," he said, "contains the fire magic of a Guardian. It won't kill me. But it will slow me down, and leave me in a state where I would be less of a threat to you. If I *was* a threat to you."

Gray relaxed a fraction. Marcos saw it and knew he'd said the right thing.

"You think by telling me the truth, you'll win my trust," Gray said.

"I think it's a start," Marcos admitted. "Now, I only suggest you stay back, a little ways behind me, because I don't know what kind of power lies in this field, and Evander would skin me slowly if he discovered that I'd brought any harm to you."

Amusement tweaked the side of Gray's mouth up. "You think he could? Skin you alive?"

Marcos shot Gray a frank look. "Evander could do anything to me, and if I knew I deserved it, I would let him."

"Don't you know," Anya hissed to Gray, under her breath, "they're sharing *quarters*."

That brought a full smile to Gray's face. "What's it like, being with a manipulative shapeshifter?"

Marcos hesitated. "As difficult and challenging as you'd expect."

This time Gray laughed, gesturing with Lion's Breath. "I don't necessarily *trust* you yet, but I do think I like you."

"Well, that's a start," Marcos said, and turned to head towards the scorched earth.

As he got closer, he heard Gray behind him. A proper distance back, as he'd suggested, but Marcos still heard him loud and clear as he said, "It would take a brave man to take on Evrard as a romantic partner."

"Luckily for him, and for me, I'm rather renowned for my bravery in the face of danger," Marcos said with a chuckle.

Then he turned his attention to the mark.

The wheat all around it had been flattened, like a windstorm had crushed the stalks, radiating around the charred circle in a spreading arc of destruction.

The closer he came, the heavier the residual magic in the air felt, like it was pressing into him. His fingertips tingled with it, and he could nearly taste it on his tongue.

He pulled a smaller knife from his belt, even though the field was empty except for the three of them. Just having it in his hand was reassuring. It would take a long time for this knife to replace the one he'd given to Evander as his favorite, but in a pinch, he never doubted that he could do some serious damage with it.

"What is it?" Gray asked, concern in his voice.

It took Marcos a second to realize that he'd only asked because Marcos had drawn a weapon.

He gripped the knife harder. "There was someone very strong here. Or several sorcerers of significant power. I can feel it in the air."

"I can feel it too," Gray said quietly. "Like it's a dark, greasy cloud, floating in the air, except that I can't see it."

Marcos nodded. "You might be more sensitive because of the sword. I'd guess that some of its power transferred into you. Considering what you were able to do without it."

"Makes sense," Gray acknowledged. "Do you know what they did here?"

Marcos dropped down to his haunches, leaning in closer to the charred circle. He didn't want to get too close. Dark magic, even its remnants, could be seductive, tricky, and could grab one by the throat.

Evander had murmured a warning before they'd left today, and Marcos hadn't needed it to be cautious. But it had served as a good reminder.

As he leaned in closer, he saw what could be the remains of a skeleton of a small animal. Burned. Burned to almost nothing.

He knew if he touched the bones, he'd *feel* it, but that they'd also likely crumble in his hands. Whatever fire that had done this had been very hot.

And contained.

The circle was only a few yards wide.

"I believe it was a sacrifice of some kind to bolster their power, though it could have been to practice, too."

"Practice?" Anya sounded disgusted. "They burned lambs for *practice?*"

"Most people are not good or evil, they're merely surviving, day to day. Black magic like this, dark as pitch, it takes time to take over a person. Creeps over them slowly. Sabrina didn't start the way she ended up. It's not easy to take your power and condense it into flame and then fling it at someone with the intent of roasting them to a crisp."

"So you think they can be saved?" Gray sounded hopeful.

Marcos hated to destroy that hope, but it was better to be realistic.

He shook his head. "No. Once the darkness takes a corner of their heart, they're lost." He stood and looked over at Gray. "We need to find them."

Gray gestured towards the charred circle. "Then tell us where to find them."

Marcos closed his eyes, focusing his power. Focusing on the slimy dark power of the magic, even though it made him want to retch.

There was something awful about Deimos that had always made the hair on the back of his neck stand on end, but this was so much worse, condensed the way it was. And, in addition, there was no telling how much darker Deimos had grown since the last time they'd faced each other.

The trail led away from the field. Marcos followed it on foot, and Gray and Anya followed him, without protesting or saying a word. He hoped that meant that maybe Gray was slowly beginning to trust him more, but Marcos had a feeling that he wouldn't learn if the other man could be depended on til the moment he needed to.

Evander raised him, and he did right by him. What you need is to trust him. Not Gray. Him.

He kept walking in silence, following the trail. It didn't vary or waver, and it was as easy as following a string, which made him uneasy.

Power of this magnitude wasn't usually all this steady. It fluctuated. He knew that much from witnessing Evander's own, over the years, and all the other Guardians he'd lived with.

Power could flicker. This power did not flicker. It never flinched.

They'd crossed one field, and were halfway through the next, when he abruptly stopped, holding up a fist.

"What is it?" Gray came up to him.

Marcos eyed the edge of the foothills that bordered the edge of the field they were in.

"He thinks it's a trap," Anya said, coming up on Marcos' other side and answering for him.

"How do you know?" Marcos had barely figured it out, and he was the best at what he did.

Anya shot him a knowing look. "You have this terribly suspicious look on your face, like something didn't smell right."

"Something *doesn't* smell right," Gray muttered. "It makes me want to vomit."

"That's the black magic," Marcos explained. "But Anya is right, I think it might be a trap. The trail is . . . unnatural. Not quite right. A little too easy to follow."

Gray looked out at the foothills. Marcos would imagine there could be caves in those rolling hills. Quite a few excellent places to hide.

Quite a few excellent places to stage a trap.

It was exactly what he would have done.

"What should we do?" Gray asked finally.

Marcos had been trying to decide. It was very likely a trap, but knowing about it could diffuse much of the danger, *and* it seemed a waste to not spring it, when they could learn something about whoever had set it.

It would be safest for him to spring it on his own.

No chance for harm to come to either Gray or Anya, because surely that had to be the goal. No sorcerer, no matter how powerful, could be a match for Marcos. But Gray? Taking out one of the leaders of this kingdom, the one who wielded some power *and* a magical sword?

That would be the goal.

"You know that we have to explore the trap," Marcos said steadily, staring out at where the danger no doubt awaited them, "but I also know that it was not designed for me."

"You think it was meant for me." Gray's voice was surprisingly steady. Marcos gave Evander credit for instilling in him the ability to face things, even difficult things, head-on.

I didn't do much, he was already like this. Marcos could practically hear Evander's voice in his head, reminding him of the truth.

And it seemed likely that it *was* the truth.

"I do," Marcos said, deciding that it was better to stick to blunt, brutal honesty. "On one hand, it seems prudent to leave you here. You can defend yourselves, if trouble comes up from behind. And you won't be in the line of fire for whatever trap has been set."

"But?"

Marcos chuckled dryly. "How do you know there's a but?"

"If there wasn't, you wouldn't have discussed it. You'd have ordered me to stay here, and gone off alone, already," Gray pointed out.

"I believe there is safety in numbers, and if I was laying a very smart trap, I would count on myself hoping to protect the king by leaving him behind."

"You think the trap is actually *here*," Gray mused. "That would be smart."

"Yes, occupy me while the rest converge on you," Marcos said.

"And it would have been such a good trap, too."

Marcos whirled around at the strange, strangled voice coming from behind him.

A woman stood there, several hundred feet back, and she wasn't balancing flame on her hand, the way Evander did. No, it was consuming her hand, consuming her arm, flickering almost all the way to her shoulder.

She had power, then. But she could not truly control it, because it was a Guardian's power and it was too much for her to bear.

That's more dangerous, Evander whispered in his ear. *She's volatile, because of it.*

"Gray," Anya hissed under her breath. "Get behind me."

"No," Gray said in a hard voice.

With that refusal to yield, even for his own protection, Gray rose another few notches in Marcos' estimation.

Instead of hiding behind Anya, Gray walked up right next to Marcos.

Marcos drew his sword. He doubted he could get close enough to cut her down, she was too unsteady, the flame flickering all around her in a whirlwind.

Wind.

If she had been the one to set the initial trap, that must have been how she'd kept it contained. Someone else had brought wind . . .

Gael.

Marcos pushed the thought away and raised his sword just in time. The long steel length of it glowed blue with his protective magic, deflecting the fireball the sorceress flung in their direction.

It fell to the turf, flames smoldering in the grass.

Gray glanced over at him. "That's a nifty trick," he said conversationally, like there wasn't a crazed sorceress who had just tossed fire in their direction.

Marcos raised his arm and a flickering blue light arced around them, protecting him and Gray, and Anya, too, even though she was further back.

"You know this will not succeed," he called out to the sorceress. "They would have told you why the trap was necessary."

"Because you were too powerful?" she sneered. "I don't believe it."

"You should," Marcos said steadily, and carefully, deliberately, he stepped around the fire in the grass, watching out of the corner of his eye as Gray stamped it out with his boots. One step at a time he began to advance on her, deliberately, with no sudden movements.

He could have defeated her easily. His shield would have cut through the worst of the fire, and he could have cut her down with his sword where she stood, but her volatility changed things.

She could explode in a ball of flame. Consume everything within leagues of them. Including Gray, Anya, and the village.

Fire magic was dangerous, but especially dangerous for a human, who couldn't hope to contain it.

There'd been a man once, who'd tried to hold the fire and he'd ended up destroying a whole part of the Northern Reach of Ardglass. Marcos had only survived because he was too hard to kill. But he'd walked among the smoldering ruins of too many good men that day, and he wasn't going to let it happen again.

"Don't come any closer," she yelled, the fire around her flashing red, then orange, then blue, and then violet as the heat of it overwhelmed her. "I'll melt you!"

"No, you won't," Marcos said inexorably, and he kept walking, one foot in front of the other, until he was only a few feet from her. He could see the crazed look in her eyes, the fire beginning to eat at the skin of her arm, the pain and realization blossoming in her expression.

Quickly, Evander whispered in his ear. *Do it quickly.*

She pushed out with a wall of flame, much as Evander had with Vanya, but hers was not nearly as powerful, because she was losing control.

"Watch out!" Anya called out as he braced himself and his shield for the flame to hit him. It shook around him, and the hilt of his sword grew warm, the symbols etched onto the flat blade pulsing with protective magic, but his protection held.

Adjusting his grip, Marcos stepped suddenly, with all his unnatural speed and agility, to the left, and swung the sword, trailing its bluish-white magic.

His blow hit true, and a breath later, her head rolled towards his feet, the fire extinguished as suddenly as it had come to life.

He stared down at her partially charred body, and the only thought besides pure, unadulterated rage was that Deimos had much to answer for, and he would be honored to be the one to exact it from him, one blow at a time.

"You killed her."

Marcos looked up to see Gray staring at the body, lips pressed hard together, Anya coming up behind him.

"She was lost," he said succinctly. "The fire was already consuming her. She didn't have control of it. Too powerful."

Gray glanced up at him. "Will that happen to me?" He gestured towards his sword, where he held it in his other hand. "I know this has fire magic. Evrard . . . I mean *Evander* imbued it with his own fire magic."

"He knew a human was going to be wielding it," Marcos said. "He wouldn't have ever given it too much, given you too much." He heard his own voice turn hard, unrelenting. Unyielding. "Someone gave this woman too much power. Knew it was too much power. But did not care."

"They should pay for this," Anya said, her teeth clenched as she stared down at the remains of the woman. "They used her, didn't they?"

Marcos nodded, watching as Anya's fist clenched tighter on her knife, knuckles turning white, face etched with fury.

"Tell me that we can make them pay, for taking one of my countrywomen and turning her into *this*," Gray said.

"Yes," Marco said. "We will make them pay."

CHAPTER FOURTEEN

"Are you sure you're not mistaken?"

Concern was etched on every line of Evander's face, as he frowned down at Marcos, sitting in the bath in his own quarters.

He'd smelled of sickening dark magic and smoke, and he'd insisted on taking a bath before meeting with the council to discuss what he and Gray and Anya had found—and what their next steps should be.

"I know what I saw. A sorceress attempting to wield fire magic far more powerful than she could contain, but it *was* contained. By wind."

"Are you sure she didn't just burn up all her control with the sacrifice?" Evander trailed fingers in the water. "Maybe the sacrifice helped her steady it so she could lay the trap."

"No," Marcos said. "She set the fire, made the sacrifice, and then someone with wind power, they contained it. Contained *her*."

Evander's frown deepened. "I can't see Gael joining Deimos. He was always above the petty concerns of the surface."

"You didn't think Vanya would either," Marcos reminded him.

Anger flashed in Evander's stormy blue eyes. Anger at him, or anger at his old friend? Marcos didn't know which, but he wouldn't take back his words.

They had to speak frankly and bluntly about this situation, because if they were not honest with each other about the realities and the very real consequences of this fight, then they might not survive it.

And then there would be nobody to stop Deimos obtaining what he wanted most, which was apparently an entire legion of followers.

"I should be angry with you," Evander said.

"But you're not," Marcos interrupted. "You understand."

"I understand what we're fighting against," Evander said, standing and beginning to pace through the room. "I understand it because I've been facing it for a thousand years."

Reassured that he no longer smelled of death or fire, Marcos lifted himself from the bath, reaching for a length of linen to dry himself.

"Then you understand how serious this is," Marcos said gently. "We can't let more Guardians join Deimos, or else we have no hope of defeating him."

"The Mother . . ." Evander trailed off.

"The Mother isn't here," Marcos said.

"You want to go attack them now."

"I don't want to attack them at all, but I think the longer we wait, the longer we hold, the more difficult it will be." He reached for his clothing, pulling on breeches, a tunic. He left off his armor, because this was only a council meeting—but then he reconsidered.

He wasn't a general, he wasn't even the general of this country—that was Marthe, and she *was* capable, he'd seen that for himself—but maybe to be at his most persuasive, he should come to them as a Guardian, fully armored.

But before he could pull the leather chest plate on, Evander appeared in front of him, and pressed his palm to where Marcos' heart beat. "She could've hurt you," he said softly, his voice low.

Marcos didn't think he'd ever seen fear in Evander's face. He'd always been so brilliantly gutsy and daring. Never flinching. Invariably unruffled. But he was afraid now.

"She could have, but only because she didn't have any control," Marcos said as reassuringly as he could.

"And Gray . . ." Evander said. "I'm grateful you were there, it would have been . . ." He clamped his lips tightly together, like he couldn't even speak of what would have happened if Marcos hadn't been there, if the sorceress had trapped Gray and Anya the way she'd planned.

"They thought they knew me, thought they could predict how I would behave. That I would protect, above all else, and the thing is, I did. I didn't let them out of my sight. That was the best way I could protect them."

"With yourself." Evander's voice was rough.

"I might be the Guardian of War but I've always wanted to be meant for more than just battles and blood," Marcos said softly.

I'm meant to love you and protect you, and protect everyone that you love.

Evander let his head fall to Marcos' damp chest, and he wrapped his arms around him, tugging him closer.

He knew he was seeing a side of him that nobody except perhaps Vanya had witnessed. Evander trusted him that much, believed in him that much.

And Marcos would never let himself fail.

Ten minutes later, Marcos stood in the Great Hall, facing the rest of the council as they sat again at the circular table.

He repeated in a steady voice what had happened with the sorceress, watching the faces of the council members morph from surprise to concern to fear, even though he'd gone out of his way to not try to overdramatize the incident.

Evander glanced his way, and he heard his voice again. *It's okay that they're afraid, they should be afraid.*

"Is that the way it happened, Gray?" Rory asked.

"That is exactly how it happened," he said with a grave nod. "Though, I am still uncertain as to how Marcos was able to ascertain that it was a trap."

"It was the way the magic felt . . . too steady, too clear a path to follow," Marcos explained. "Magic often wavers. Especially magic contained in someone who isn't a Guardian. You saw how it was too much for her to bear."

"I did," Gray admitted. "But your first inclination was to leave me and Anya, and go ahead, to flush out the trap."

"It was, but the first inclination is not always the wisest path. It's good to not be predictable. Besides," he added, hoping that his argument didn't sound impossibly smug, "I knew the best way I could protect you and Anya would be to be with you myself. To protect you personally."

"He's not wrong," Anya said wryly. "His sword glows blue and can deflect fireballs. That doesn't even count the magic shield."

"Magic shield?" Marthe questioned.

"I wish it could protect more than just me and a handful of others," Marcos said ruefully. "It's useless for an army. I've tried."

"Hmmm," Marthe considered.

"I am most concerned," Evander said, speaking up for the first time in the meeting, "about the origin of the trap. That charred circle in the wheat field. The sorceress wouldn't have had the control to burn just a small circle, for a sacrifice. It would have grown unwieldy for her almost immediately."

"What do you think it means?" Rory asked.

"I think it indicates there's other powers at play," Evander said heavily. "Potentially other Guardians."

Rory's face turned white, and Evander's pronouncement seemed to suck most of the air out of the room.

Marcos could taste the doom that descended over the table.

"How many did you say there were again?" Rowen asked quietly. "Thirteen?"

"So, ten, without Evander and Marcos and Deimos," Rory said, scribbling on a piece of parchment in front of him. "Who else would be likely to join him?"

"Marcos believes that wind is what contained the sorceress' fire," Evander said. "That would be Gael, the Guardian of the Winds."

"Is it likely that he would partner with Deimos?"

Marcos glanced over at Evander. "I think it's honestly more likely that Deimos somehow usurped some of his power, rather than he joined him himself. Though I suppose it is a possibility."

"It's a possibility," Evander said firmly. There was a haunted look in his eyes that spoke one word and one word plainly: *Vanya*.

Marcos regretted making a point of it in his chambers earlier.

"Gael was never much for surface politics," Marcos argued. "He'd never have involved himself without a good reason."

"Deimos is conniving. You don't believe he could have invented an excellent excuse for Gael?"

Marcos had to concede that point, inclining his head.

For a long moment, everyone at the table was silent.

"Who *would* be likely to join him?" Rory asked.

He knew how hard it would be for Evander to voice the truth out loud, so he did. "We know that Vanya, Guardian of Belief, has joined forces with Deimos. For better or worse, he has less . . . *offensive* powers. Though he is exceptional at joining conviction to will. Every single man and woman that Deimos has seduced to the dark side, and infected with that magic, will believe, unequivocally, that they are doing the right thing, the *just* thing."

Rory continued to write on the parchment, barely glancing up.

"Can this Vanya fight?" Gray wanted to know.

"As much as any of us can," Marcos said. "But not particularly well, if I remember."

"No," Evander said, his voice a dark rasp.

"Who else?" Rory asked.

"I think it would be easier to identify who wouldn't," Evander said. "Abram, Lyric, Hektor, Kadir, Taavi. Osias, he is much like Gael. He would not involve himself, unless Deimos did something particularly devious."

"Jae might. And Hyperion," Marcos said.

Evander frowned. "Yes, perhaps."

"So *perhaps* Deimos has three other Guardians on his side. One who will cause the men and women who fight for him to believe unwaveringly in his cause. What could Jae and Hyperion do?"

"Jae will make sure they are well provisioned. I believe they are holed up in the caves dotting those foothills," Marcos said. "Normally I would suggest we wait them out, wait until they're starving and weak. But Jae's power will make sure they won't want for anything."

"And Hyperion?" Rory asked archly.

He and Hyperion had never been as close as Evander and Vanya, but nonetheless, he had been a friend. The closest thing to a friend, anyway, that Marcos had had at the Castle.

Marcos pushed the pain of his betrayal away. If Evander could face Vanya, then he could confront the possibility that Hyperion had joined Deimos.

"He's the Guardian of the Wild," Evander explained. "He's always been . . . well, *wild*. Angry. Uncontained. The chaos that Hyperion thrives on means he might see the benefits of Deimos' appeal."

Marcos nodded. "If Deimos succeeds, that would create an atmosphere here that he would . . . enjoy."

But Hyperion had always been so much more than that.

He'd been fierce and free and throbbing with life in every inch of his being.

Marcos pushed the throb of pain away.

"What can he do?"

"What *can't* he do?" Evander said dryly. "He can command animals. He can conjure animal visions with enough power to create physical damage. He's powerful. A worthy opponent for Marcos."

"I thought *Deimos* was an opponent for Marcos," Gray objected.

"We will not be evenly matched." Marcos laid the statement out with the bluntest honesty he could have. "Which is why we need to act *now*, before Deimos seduces any more sorcerers or Guardians to his purpose."

"You don't want to wait for them to attack, you want to go on the offensive," Marthe said flatly. "That could be death, for all of us. We do not have *power* or magic or anywhere near this kind of strength."

"No," Evander said steadily. "No, you don't. But you do have strength and will, and Marcos and I are not only powerful individually, we're powerful together."

Rory raised an eyebrow at Evander's choice of words and Marcos found himself, despite the seriousness of the topic, momentarily amused.

"And," Evander added, "we have the blessing of the Mother. I think that will count for something."

"The Mother?"

"She created this world, she created us, and she created you," Evander said simply.

"I suppose she wouldn't like the havoc that Deimos wants to wreak on her creation," Gray said, voice wry.

"She asked us to defeat Deimos, but we were . . . distracted by another quest," Marcos explained. "I do not know how she can help, only that if she gets the opportunity, she will."

"So we have the hope that a goddess figure of untold power *might* assist," Marthe said. "What else do we have?"

Marcos appreciated the general's practicality.

"Evander has his full powers back, and he has control over them. I am . . ."

Evander rolled his eyes. "Marcos is the most powerful Guardian of the Conclave. I believe he is even more powerful than Deimos, a fact that he's carefully hidden from him for thousands of years. I would wish for nobody else by my side."

"Then, if time is truly a concern, we should plan an attack," Marthe said simply.

"None of you are obligated to join us," Evander said, and Marcos would have to be blind to not see his gaze fall to Rory and Gray.

He'd spent a thousand years planning for their peace, for the peace of this kingdom.

And now it was going to be destroyed in the space of a single council meeting.

"You sent for me?"

Evander stood in the doorway of the library and watched Rory look up from his stacks of parchment and much higher stacks of books.

"I found more references to Death on a dark steed," Rory said, "as well as mentions of a man in early Ardglassian history who could defeat any fighter, who could circumvent any trap, who invented battle plans that never failed to lead to victory. This is your Marcos, isn't it? He was in Ardglass."

Evander should have known that Rory was too sharp to miss it.

"He's not *mine*," Evander said carefully.

Rory shot him a look. "Yes, he is," he said simply. "The same way that Gray and I have always been each other's."

"It is not the same at all," Evander said. He hadn't wanted to discuss this, especially not with *Rory*, but perhaps he was a better option than discussing it with nobody at all.

"Whatever is between you," Rory said carefully, because if anyone knew the power of words, it was him, "that *is* him, is it not?" He pushed forward a large, leather-bound text, and unlike most Ardglassian texts from that particular period, this one had a single, stark illustration. Bold lines, sketched in black ink, took up almost half a page. The face wasn't Marcos', but the eyes? The expression? That was all him.

"Yes," Evander finally said. "That's him."

Rory looked at him more carefully. He'd spent so long analyzing his precious texts, he'd become equally good at analyzing people. It was the same set of skills, Evander supposed, just applied differently. "You didn't know he was here, on the . . . what did you call it? The *surface*."

"No," Evander said shortly.

Pulling the book back, Rory carefully slid a piece of parchment in to mark the page and then shut it. "Watching you, was he?"

"Not exactly like that," Evander said. He was remembering, fondly, the beginning of their association, when he'd thought Rory pretty and spoiled and not stupid, but too esoteric to glean much from everyday life.

He'd grown sharp.

Or maybe he'd always been sharp, and now he was allowing Evander to see it.

"Hmmm," he said, leaning back in his chair. "It's not the same as Gray and I, and he wasn't *exactly* watching you. What was he doing, then?"

How was Evander supposed to answer Rory's questions, when he couldn't answer them for himself?

Rory burst out laughing. "You should see your face," he said, very amused. "You must really, really hate not knowing everything, not understanding in minute detail something that's happening—and not just happening in your general vicinity, but *to you*."

Evander didn't bother to hold back his scowl as he collapsed into the chair opposite Rory's. "You are not helpful," he muttered.

Rory's expression softened. "How *can* I be helpful, then?"

"You asked me to come *here*, to *you*," Evander reminded him. He hadn't wanted to have this conversation. He hadn't wanted to have it at all.

Except he'd known that he would be having it with Marcos, because the minute he stepped back into his chambers, he would be there.

The night before they attacked the sorcerers and Deimos?

Possibly the night before nothing was ever the same again?

Potentially the last night of thousands and thousands of nights?

While Evander knew the generalities of how Marcos felt, he had been scrupulously careful to never say a word himself. He had yet to actually confess feelings of any kind.

But he would tonight.

Evander knew it. He longed for it and dreaded it in equal measure.

I know you don't feel the same, you couldn't possibly feel the same, he could imagine Marcos saying, *so please don't say anything at all.*

Except Evander didn't want to stay silent. But he didn't *know*, not for sure.

Maybe it would be worse to say something, if it was the wrong thing, if it turned out to be untrue, than it would be to stay silent.

"I did ask you to come, because I wanted to ask you if this was Marcos. I thought so, but I wanted to be sure."

"Why?"

Rory's smile was secretive. "Several reasons. Starting with I like to know who is residing in my castle, and directing my troops, and planning battle strategies with my general."

"Gray is growing to trust him."

Rory nodded. "That wasn't the only reason. I wanted to know if *you* knew that he'd been here, all those years ago."

"Why does it matter?" Evander asked flatly.

"You're uneasy with it, that he was here and didn't tell you. Or"—Rory paused—"are you uneasy with the *why?*"

It was useless. Rory knew. Rory knew, and Rory knew how it made him feel.

Confused.

Lustful.

Flustered.

Exhilarated.

"How did you know you were in love with Gray?" It was difficult to form the words, to ask the question, but he did it.

Rory shot him a look. "You were there, you should already know the answer to that question."

"Yes, of course, I was there. But one minute you were mooning after him like a schoolboy with an embarrassing crush, and then the next, it was entirely different. You looked at each other like . . ." Evander paused, clearing his throat. "You *still* look at each other like that."

"Best thing, and the worst thing, falling in love like that," Rory said contemplatively. His amber eyes shone, like he was remembering those days, which hadn't been so long ago. "At first, it's hard to say if it's the excitement and the terror that makes you want to cling to another person, to *that* person. How did I know I wanted to be with Gray forever and not just because he was conveniently there during the worst point of my life?"

"Yes, *that*," Evander said, in far too deep to feel the sting of humiliation at the fact Rory had discovered his exact worry.

"Because what I really longed for with Gray wasn't excitement, or battles, or clinging to each other when the worst was about to come to pass. What I wanted was this. I wanted peace, with him."

Rory's gaze was knowing, likely because he remembered Evander saying it himself.

All I want is . . . peace. No kingdoms. No wars. No battles. No conquering heroes. Just peace.

When he'd said this, only the day before, he hadn't actually voiced that he wanted it with Marcos, but he'd *thought* it. He'd thought about how much different he would have felt, if he'd given in to Merleen's dogged pursuit, all those months ago.

Peace, Evander thought, would feel very different with the right person next to you.

"Does that help?" Rory asked, raising an eyebrow.

"Yes," Evander said, standing and feeling strangely, utterly resolute. For the first time in what felt like weeks. "Yes, in fact, it does."

Rory grinned. "I thought it might."

Marcos had lived through many battles.

And, as a result, he'd spent many, many nights before a battle.

Sometimes, he could feel the clash, the blood, the destruction coming. Could taste it in the air. Sometimes, he *knew* it was coming, because he had planned it that way. Sometimes he just *felt* it, the impending doom of so many, no matter what he'd do to prevent their deaths.

But he'd never spent the night before a battle with Evander before.

Just the thought of it had his heart beating a little faster.

They might not live to see the next sunset, or the sun rise.

He knew what he wanted to say, the words he'd held in for so long. But the problem with the words was after so long holding them in, Marcos didn't know how to unseal them. If he should.

It would hurt, to confess the truth, even though it was a truth Evander had already guessed, and have him pat him gently on the chest and say, *I know, and it's okay,* but not return the love and devotion he'd felt so long that feeling it felt as natural as breathing.

But it would hurt less *not* to say it, if this was the last chance he would get.

He was very strong, but Deimos was *Death*. Their fate hung on a thousand different decisions, of all kinds and all sizes. They might emerge unscathed, with Deimos destroyed, or Marcos might lose everything. His everlasting life, and his everlasting love.

The door opened before Marcos had quite made up his mind what he *would* say.

Evander didn't knock, merely slipped in, shutting it closed behind him with a click.

"I thought I might find you here," he said with a hint of a smile on his lips.

"In your chambers?"

It had been a bit presumptuous to come to Evander's chambers, where he'd lived as Rhys, but they'd spent the last few nights here, together, and he'd *wanted* to be here, as much as he'd hoped that Evander might want him here.

Still, while Marcos had taken off his chest plate, he'd scrupulously avoided the bed, instead choosing to stand by one of the high arched windows set into the smooth gray stone of the walls.

Evander tugged at the laces of his dark, high-necked tunic. "I *had* hoped you would come here, and I wouldn't have to seek you out," he added.

"Of course I came here," Marcos said, and then hesitated. Evander *knew*, and this was his chance, and yet it was still so difficult to speak of his feelings.

Too many years holding them far too close to his chest.

"Of course you did." His smile had disappeared, and when he finished loosening his tunic, he tugged it off with a very serious expression on his beautiful face. Stepped out of his boots. "Rory had found a drawing of you, in fact when you were Dougal, and asked me if it was you."

"I suppose my expression is rather unchangeable," Marcos allowed.

Evander's fingers slid down his chest, towards his breeches, and Marcos was powerless to watch as he pushed them down.

"*You* are unchangeable," Evander teased, both with his voice, and with his naked body. But he didn't move towards Marcos, just kept staring at him with that inscrutable, opaque expression.

Marcos collected all his courage.

He knew he would need it.

"Actually, in one instance," he said, taking a step closer to where Evander stood, so completely and utterly breathtaking, "I was in fact changeable. But there has only been the one instance." Marcos hesitated. "The most important instance."

Evander tilted his head up, the flawless line of his profile shadowed by the flickering light of the fire in the hearth. "You? Changeable? I find that hard to believe."

"At first," Marcos said, "for many hundreds of years, I had no interest in you. You seemed . . ."

"Petty? Silly?" Evander raised an eyebrow as he made suggestions that were hardly a compliment to his past self. "Entirely preoccupied with selfish matters?"

"No," Marcos said firmly. "Not at all. You weren't spoiled. You cared for all of us, in your own way. Whether you realized it or not. But, inevitably, every time you looked at me, you seemed to see through me, to know me better than I knew myself, and I preferred not to be so exposed. So I avoided you. Until one winter, when I could not, not any longer. And that was when I changed, or rather my *feelings*, they were irrevocably changed."

He reached out, cupping Evander's cheek in one hand. "I could never understand how, or understand why, until I finally accepted that there is no logic and reason in the heart, at least not my heart. Because it is yours, as I am yours, from that winter, for hundreds of years, until now. As long as you wish me to be near you, to be close, to be your friend, and your bed mate, to protect you and the peace you've created, I am yours."

Evander's eyes flickered shut. He pressed more firmly into Marcos' embrace.

Now here is the moment, Marcos thought with terror churning through his veins. *Now he says thank you, or you are kind, or you are steadfast.*

But then Evander's eyes flickered open and he did not look particularly thankful, or particularly kind, or even like he wanted to praise Marcos' loyalty.

He looked . . .

Marcos' breath caught.

"It seems," Evander said, his tone wry, "that I have a secret that *I* did not even realize I possessed, which is that for as long as you want me, or even if you do not want me at all, I believe that I will always love you anyway. Tonight, tomorrow, no matter what befalls us, I will be yours."

Marcos did not hesitate. He reached and pulled him close, pressing Evander's body near to his own. Then Evander's hands were reaching up, tugging his head down into a kiss just as fiery as many they'd shared, but not just full of passion, as they'd first been, but full of love, too.

Marcos could feel the difference, and every fiber of his being rejoiced at the evolution.

He did not know how he'd ever be so lucky to win Evander's love—for ages, he'd never imagined it could even be possible—but in the end, he had done nothing. All he had done was to be himself.

Show himself.

Reveal himself.

"Come," Marcos said roughly, catching Evander's body and lifting it effortlessly, his hands tugging off his own tunic as he set him on the edge of the bed. "I want to love you."

Evander's eyes, as he pulled back, shedding his boots and his breeches, shone brilliantly blue. "You already do, every single day—and for so many days I am not sure I can count them all. I can't . . ." He hesitated.

"I *should* apologize for not seeing it, for not understanding . . . for not realizing sooner . . ."

"No," Marcos said, sliding his body against Evander's, feeling the rush of the skin-to-skin contact. He'd never even dreamt he could have *this*, and to have it, and Evander's love too, it was more than a fantasy come to life, it was a blessing he'd work every day to earn.

"No?" Evander raised an eyebrow.

"No, because I didn't want you to know," Marcos said.

Evander reached up, tracing the lines of his face with the barest touch of his fingertips. "You *are* worthy of this," he said softly. "Of *love*. Of *my* love. No matter what happens tomorrow, if we are both still alive, I intend to show you every day."

With Evander's hands on him, their skin touching in half a dozen places, the knowledge of it rocketing through him like the brightest spark, he felt like he actually might.

But will you tomorrow?

Marcos pushed that voice away, that fear that he might slip into the worst version of himself, the Marcos who would do anything, be anything, slay anything, if only to keep the man he loved and those *he* loved, safe and protected.

It was what you were made for. Deimos' voice echoed in his head.

"I can see the shadow in your eyes." Evander's voice was like a caress.

He could *feel* the shadow, and this time he didn't just absently bat it away, he shoved it.

I am *meant for more than that,* he told himself fiercely, *I am not just meant for blood and mud and war. I can be meant for love, too.*

I am *meant for love. The love of one man.*

"Then," Marcos said lovingly, dipping his head low to brush a kiss along Evander's collarbone, "let's banish it, shall we?"

Evander turned his head, met his mouth eagerly with his own, and it was so easy, so effortless, to sink into the thick lassitude of pleasure he felt whenever they kissed.

Evander was gentle with him at first, only bestowing sweet kisses on him, but then he finally tilted his head, Marcos' fingers tangling in his hair, and *oh*, there was the fire.

It bloomed in his blood, hotter than he had ever thought possible.

"Wait," Evander gasped out as one of Marcos' hands drifted down his body, to where his cock lay hard on his thigh. "Wait, I want . . . I knew . . ."

Marcos sat back, meeting Evander's eyes. "You want?"

Evander reached out for a little vial on the low table next to the bed. "I want you inside me, I want you as close as you can be, before . . ."

"I will make sure nothing happens to you." It was a vow.

But Evander shook his head. "I know, of course I know that, but I want this . . . I want *you*. So badly. I want to feel it tomorrow, and know what I'm fighting for, what I want at the end of the day. Not fighting for kingdoms or territory or endless wars, but peace. With you."

So many over the years had assumed Marcos had no interest in peace; but rather he valued it even more knowing how precious it was. How hard-won.

And it seemed that Evander believed the same.

"This, every day," Marcos said, leaning down and kissing him fiercely, plucking the bottle away from Evander. "Days when we do not even leave this bed."

"Yes," Evander gasped as with oil-damp fingers, Marcos trailed a path down his hip, and then further down still, Evander's legs spreading as he went.

When they snubbed up to his hole, Evander moaned, muffling the sound in Marcos' shoulder.

"You truly want this?" Marcos asked. "I am not small . . . it will not . . ."

Evander's gaze was fierce as they locked eyes. "I want all of you. I *love* you," he said.

Marcos' concern would have been assuaged no matter what, but the desire in Evander's face melted it away completely and he slid a finger inside of Evander, feeling his body contract around it, and then let him in, a little at a time.

He was slow and careful, and by the time a second finger joined the first, Evander's head was thrown back on the bed, groaning in pleasure.

"You are so beautiful like this," Marcos said roughly. Wanting to be inside of him more than he wanted his next breath. His cock was as hard as the steel in his sword, and he could feel the throb of it, with each beat of his heart.

"Please," Evander begged.

"Just . . . one . . . more . . ." Marcos could hear the desperation in his voice. The desire. It was nearly overwhelming him, but he wanted Evander to feel only pleasure as he took him, so he ground his teeth together and a third finger joined the others. He marveled at the way Evander's body opened to his. Like it was just as eager as he was.

Evander reached up, gasping as Marcos' fingers delved deep, and the kiss he gave him was wild and unrestrained, as uninhibited as he had ever seen him, had ever *dreamt* to see him.

The kiss loosened Marcos' control, and he groaned, pulling his fingers free, rubbing them along his cock, hard and twitching, desperate for Evander's body.

"You are mine, and I am yours," Marcos rasped as he began to slide inside. It was so hot and tight, and felt so unbelievably good, he had to squeeze his eyes shut against the sudden need to thrust hard and fast.

But Evander's hand, reaching up, pressing into his chest, kept him in check, his fingertips curling into his skin as he sank in further and further.

And then he was fully seated, and he hesitated, opening his eyes to see Evander's frozen expression. But it wasn't pain. It was more than pleasure.

It was wonder.

"Please," Evander begged again. "Please, oh, *please.*"

Marcos already knew he would give him whatever he wanted, whatever he needed, with every last breath of his body. So it was natural to give him more, short careful thrusts, until Evander's hand slid down, digging into the muscle of his thigh and pulling him in *hard*.

"More," he demanded, "*more.*"

Marcos was helpless to resist, the blood roaring in his ears as he thrust harder and faster, the pleasure lighting up every inch of his body.

His hips stuttered when he saw Evander wrap a hand around his own cock, and felt him tumble off the edge, body spasming around him, stripes of come hitting his chest.

He was lost, driving harder and faster, chasing his own orgasm, until it hit him in a blinding rush.

The pleasure seemed to last forever, until finally it faded, Marcos' racing pulse beginning to fade to normal. He gazed down at his lover, and hoped that he hadn't been too rough at the end.

But then Evander smiled, his eyes a soft glowing blue.

"Why," he said in a soft voice that sounded very unlike Evander, "did we wait so long to do that?"

Marcos carefully pulled out, wiping himself on a corner of the bedding. Reaching up, wiping Evander down, too.

"Because," he said, settling down next to him, pulling him close, "if we had done that, I'd have never let you go, and I don't believe you were ready to be caught, just yet."

"No," Evander said, and then sighed happily. "Tomorrow . . ."

But Marcos didn't let him finish. "Tomorrow is tomorrow," he said. "And tonight is tonight. Let us enjoy this, before tomorrow's destruction."

"I," Evander retorted loftily, "was actually going to say that *tomorrow* Deimos won't even know what hit him, because I will not—not under any circumstances—permit that to be the last time we do that."

Marcos couldn't help the laugh that bubbled out of him.

Evander was quiet a moment. And then, softly, he said, "I have never heard you laugh like that. Or seen you smile, as you did just now."

He felt bared to the quick by the truth in Evander's words.

"I have never been as happy as I am now."

By the truth in his own.

CHAPTER FIFTEEN

The morning dawned clear and cold, a wash of red across the horizon as the sun rose.

Evander watched as Marcos eyed it with a grim expression, his lips in a tight line. "There will be blood today," he said.

"Yes," Gray said vehemently, as he rode up next to him. "The blood of our enemies."

"I would ask if you were always this courageous, but I already know the answer to that. You faced down Sabrina as a twelve-year-old boy, with a knife and a horse, and nothing else, and afterwards, begged to go back and finish her," Evander said lightly as they rode out of the gate, followed by Marthe and her guard, Rory, and a handful of other fighters that Marthe and Marcos had selected personally.

He'd been surprised, at first, that Marcos hadn't wanted to take the entire army. "Why?" he'd asked. "So Deimos can cut them all down without blinking? No, we cannot approach this like a conventional attack. We need to be smarter, *think* smarter. Not necessarily outsmart him, because he thinks he is smarter than anyone else, but perhaps by sticking to our strengths, we can outmaneuver him."

The plan had actually turned out to be fairly simple, simpler than Evander had anticipated, but he hoped that at the very least, it would catch Deimos and his followers off guard.

With Evander in the attack force, Deimos would be anticipating a convoluted battle plan, but instead, Marcos had insisted on keeping it straightforward.

"It's easy to be brave when you're young," Gray said. "Harder when you grow up."

Evander watched as he exchanged glances with Rory. "Which," Rory said wryly, "only makes you sound more impressive."

He knew that Gray hadn't wanted Rory to accompany them—because he'd been very adamantly and vocally opposed to it from the first moment when Rory had declared that he wouldn't be left behind.

But Rory was riding with them today, despite Gray's feelings, and even Evander's argument that he should remain behind, in case things went catastrophically badly, and he was the only one left to rule Fontaine. "What would I rule, then," Rory had asked bitterly, "if everyone is dead and Deimos' poison is spreading across my land and my people? This is our battle, the only one that matters, and I will stand with those who fight for Fontaine."

Rory was right; this was the battle for the future of the surface. If they lost today, it would only be a matter of time before Deimos and his sorcerers spread across the lands, destroying and subverting the humans. Death would rule.

Then we will make sure it does not.

Evander glanced up and found Marcos looking at him intently.

Neither of them had powers of telepathy; in fact, Evander had never heard of any of the Guardians possessing that particular power, but perhaps . . . perhaps the Mother had seen their connection, had *felt* it, and had opened up their minds.

It's you, isn't it? Evander thought, sending the question as hard as he could towards Marcos.

Marcos inclined his head, the corner of his lips curving into a smile. *Yes,* he responded, *perhaps another special gift of the Mother's?*

It was just like the Mother not to *ask* if they wanted to be able to speak to each other in their minds, but merely to gift the power.

Can you read my mind, too? Evander wondered.

Marcos' answer was swift. *No, I think it needs not only purpose to work, but also emotion—I felt it the other day, when Deimos tried to trap me, I could hear your voice in my head. And just now? I saw the expression on your face when you looked at Rory. He will be fine. Acadia and Rowen will be guarding him especially, and he's been training. He's not the useless princeling you once took under your wing.*

No, he was not.

Evander glanced over at Rory and saw the hard resolution on his face, the courage in his eyes, in every line of his figure as they rode towards the caves where Marcos had determined that Deimos and his followers were hiding.

He was no longer a silly prince, he was a *king.*

It was not a long ride to the caves. They lay only an hour or so from Beaulieu, which Evander was convinced was purposeful. There were plenty of villages scattered within an easy ride of the castle, and for Deimos that meant plenty of humans around he could bend to his will. Plenty of humans he could infect with too much power.

He'd been more restrained before, not giving the humans more than they could handle, but now he cared so little for their lives, for their fate, he was turning them into bombs.

The caves, Evander projected towards Marcos as they rode closer, *they will be full. Deimos will meet our small force with a much larger one.*

Marcos' glance was reassuring. *We knew that,* he pointed out, *we always knew he would do whatever he could to defeat us, even if that included conscripting many villagers who couldn't hope to contain the power he gives them.*

Marcos was right, but it made Evander uneasy, all the same.

Trust me, stick to the plan, Marcos thought, his voice a reassuring balm to nerves about the fight to come. *You can do this.*

Evander heard the confidence in his voice, the undeniable love, and raised his chin. He would do it, because the alternative was Death.

Marcos led them through fields, past the burned circle, and then across another field, and suddenly, there were the caves, rising in front of them.

There appeared to be nobody present in them, nothing visible, but Evander could *feel* the darkness residing in them.

"He is here," Marcos said, echoing what Evander also believed. "He may not be expecting us, but he *is* anticipating us, all the same."

Gray nodded, and dismounted. They left the horses tied to a large haystack, with Rory, Acadia, and Rowen. They would join the battle, if necessary, but for now their job was to hang back, to protect the king, and to potentially ride for additional assistance if necessary. "Though," Marcos had said with a rough voice during the council session, "if reinforcements are necessary, we can already call the battle lost."

"Not if we can get Rory away unscathed," Gray had insisted.

Evander didn't know what had ultimately convinced Marcos that Gray's addition to the plan was necessary, but it might have been the gray-blue steel of his gaze.

You taught him well, Evander told himself firmly. *You prepared him for this, as best you could.*

Marcos turned to him as they dismounted. "Are you ready?" he asked, drawing a knife from his boot as Evander pulled the knife Marcos had forged for him from a sheath Gray had found in the armory.

"Yes," Evander said, hearing the certainty in his own voice and letting it bolster his courage, his determination. His part in the plan was not the most vital, but it was still critical that he played it perfectly.

It might mean the safety of the rest of them, vulnerably arrayed in this field.

"You must be quick," Marcos said, as Evander knew.

They had the element of surprise now, but it would not last long. Though the fields and visible cave entrances were empty now, there was no doubt in Evander's mind that Deimos had ways to detect their arrival.

And once they'd arrived, he'd sense their power, just as surely as they had sensed his.

Evander turned to face the caves, but before he could make the final preparations, a hand on his shoulder stopped him.

He turned, and Marcos squeezed his shoulder, over the worked leather armor that Gray had outfitted him with. "Please," he said. *Pleaded.* Evander could not remember at any point in the thousands of years that they'd known each other that the other Guardian had begged for anything. "Please, be careful. Do not be reckless. Not when . . ."

Evander watched as Marcos swallowed hard. "Not when?" he prompted.

"Not when I love you so completely, so utterly," Marcos said quietly, but with purpose.

"I love you, too," Evander said, reaching out and touching him once, on the cheek. He let the certainty, the steadfastness, the brightness of Marcos' love wash over him, steady him. Centering his magic, he reached out for the power in the caves, in the empty spaces he sensed, and then he released all of that gathered force, and the next moment later, he blinked his eyes, refocusing them in the dark.

It took only a second for him to take in his surroundings. That was the only danger with projecting, and why he did it so rarely, even before his banishment, because the risk of being caught off guard and not reacting quickly enough to the new environment was significant.

He was in a cave, with such a low ceiling, Marcos would have been forced to duck. It was dark, only a small, smoldering fire on one side, the smoke making it even harder to see clearly. There were half a dozen men and women in the cave, and as they lifted their arms, gazes haunted by the power that had begun to control them, instead of the other way around, Evander lifted his knife, and let his own power flow.

The fire traveled along the length of the knife like he'd been born to wield it, and maybe, considering the Mother and her knowing gaze, perhaps he had.

The woman there, on the right, who ducked his stream of fire, she was struggling to hold the wind, it was already whipping through her hair, little pieces of her flesh disintegrating into the air as she attempted to hold Gael's power.

"How?" he demanded of her, and she only shook her head, mute terror in her eyes.

Ideally, he would have liberated them, released the power they held, but he could sense how deeply it was buried in them. Deimos had created an army of unstable bombs, in the guise of humans, in the guise of Rory and Gray's subjects, and there was nothing he could do, except permanently free them.

Deimos had finally stopped caring about any collateral damage.

He sent another stream of fire towards her, and this time she could not duck it, as she was too busy frantically trying to hold the tail of the wind, and the fire hit her straight in the chest, and she collapsed to the dirt floor of the cave.

Evander was blessed with a Guardian's quickness again, and it had taken but a moment to eliminate the woman with the wind power, and he turned next to the rest, arraying against him on the other side of the cave.

He sent out another stream of fire, pushing them back further, until one man, young enough to be the shepherd that Anya had spoken of, tried to thrust out with fire of his own. It was unsteady, just as Marcos had described it, and Evander only had a second to be haunted by the fear in the young man's eyes as he lost control of it, screaming as it consumed him, and the woman next to him, who must have had fire as well, because hers leaped to join his.

The other three turned to look at him, dead expressions in their eyes.

"Wind and fire," Evander said out loud, hoping to get through to them.

"Enough to cause a conflagration," one middle-aged man said with a sneer. He shrugged as fire poured out of his hand, and the woman next to him waved wildly, whipping it up.

Evander stared at them, horror coalescing into an ugly ball in his stomach. He'd been afraid of just this, when he'd heard Marcos' plan for him to come into the caves first and hopefully eliminate any of the sorcerers that Deimos had seduced to his cause.

But it was even worse than he could have ever anticipated, and he watched for a second longer as their powers escaped their control, the wind suddenly becoming a gale, and the fire turning bright white at the edges, burning all three of them alive before Evander could do anything to help them.

He had only a moment to reach out for the next cave, and then he was there, opening his eyes.

This time they were prepared for him, and this time he had the chance to lead them out of the caves, running between the craggy rocks, fire streaming from his knife, as he lured them to the open field, where it would be safer and easier to kill them.

Though, Evander though with a horrible dry realization, *it hadn't been particularly difficult to eliminate them where they stood. They are untried, untested, unprepared. Fodder for Deimos' army.*

One woman fell, and Evander almost reached out for her, to steady her, but then he reared back as she shed her skin, writhing along the ground, becoming a massive serpent.

"Hyperion!" Evander called, warning Marcos as he watched the other Guardian brace himself for the fireballs that another of the men was throwing their direction. He batted them away easily with his sword, glowing blue with his protective magic, and then before the serpent could head in Rory's direction, Marcos spun, and raising his sword high over his head, cut the head off the serpent.

"He *would* be here," Marcos answered, his voice grimly resigned.

"I have a few more caves," Evander said, and then he reached out again for the next, and then the next, and then the next.

He did not see Deimos, but he knew he was there; he could sense him in every shadow, in the vile taste on his tongue, from the way the hair on the back of his neck prickled.

He was here, and he was watching.

Evander reached the final cave, having flushed out several dozen of the sorcerers, leading them to Marcos and his relentless sword.

And this one, it was empty.

Or else, Evander *believed* it to be empty, and nearly turned to go back to the field, to help Marcos and Gray and the others kill the sorcerers, when a shadowed figure stepped out of the darkness.

"You are on a fool's errand," Deimos spat.

His face, always pale as milk, had grown gaunt and skeletal, cheekbones seemingly carved into the bone.

"You are not exempt from the rules of this universe," Evander said.

"Neither were you, and yet you circumvent them anyway," Deimos retorted, glancing at the knife in his hand. Evander realized Deimos must be referencing how he'd thwarted his punishment and retrieved his power.

It shouldn't have hurt that Vanya had confessed all to Deimos. But the last bit of hope that he might not turn total traitor died in Evander's heart.

"The Mother informed me how to right a wrong," Evander said, lifting his knife, feeling his power surge.

"The Mother?" Deimos threw his head back and laughed, a grotesque caricature of amusement that grated along every one of Evander's nerves. "That old hag? She's always been too weak, too controlled by her feelings for these . . . these . . . *humans*. Bags of skin and bone and nothing more. Ruled by their emotions, by their instincts. They are not worth the sacrifice you make for them."

Rage billowed alongside the power, strengthening it, buffering it.

"These *bags of skin and bone* are far more honorable than you have ever been in any year of your miserable, eternal life," Evander ground out. "For that alone, I condemn you to death—a state you have become far too familiar with."

Deimos just laughed again.

"You cannot condemn *me*," he said, and pushed back, suddenly, with all his dark power, and it sent Evander flying, hitting the wall with a bone-jarring impact.

"You are no match for me, Guardian or no Guardian," Deimos said, advancing as Evander took a breath, steeling his will against the pain, and lifted himself to his feet.

He flung out one fireball and then another, and Deimos brushed them away like they were nothing, like they were petals falling on a bright summer day.

Gathering his breath, he pushed out with the wall of flame—the one that had sent Vanya scurrying, and it did hold Deimos back, who just smiled, devoid of all humor, at Evander's magic.

He pushed forward, and then forward again, waging his own fire magic against Deimos' pitch-black clouds, and he took an inch, and then another inch.

Just when he thought he might be able to force him back, might be able to at least weaken him with the fire, Evander heard a voice behind him.

Calling him.

Entreating him.

"Evander," Vanya said softly, like he was right in his ear.

Evander shook his head, trying to clear the distraction. Trying not to give in to the desire to turn and see his friend.

Or the Guardian who had *once* been his friend.

You acknowledged it earlier, he reminded himself, *there is no hope for him now. He has betrayed you. He has betrayed the Conclave.*

"Evander," the voice cajoled again.

He might have imagined it was another trick of Deimos' but he knew it was not.

You are prepared for this. You knew it would come to this.

Evander held out a hand, and the wall of fire wavered, glowing blue and white at the edges, Deimos' dark, fathomless eyes glittering with malice.

With his other hand, he released another stream of fire, and as the power flowed through him, like a raging river, he almost imagined how such a feeling could have seduced Deimos into his unspeakable acts.

"You are clever, but not so clever as that," Vanya said, appearing next to Deimos. "I could *almost* make you believe."

"Almost," Evander said grimly. "But not enough. I know your heart, and I do not recognize the black lump that beats in your chest now."

"You cannot defeat us," Deimos pronounced. "You cannot hope, with this small force, even with the great power of Marcos, to banish us."

"No," Evander said, pushing forward with all the power he had, "I mean to *kill* you."

There was surprise in Vanya's eyes then, like he had not imagined that Evander would be willing to go so far.

"Siding with the humans over us, that is the abomination," Deimos pronounced with disgust.

"I am your friend," Vanya said, his face turning from its usual beauty to an ugly, contorted mask. "Join us. Be my friend again."

"No," Evander roared, and flung out the last of his fire. "*Never.*"

Then everything went black.

Marcos swung his sword, a head rolling from a sorcerer who'd become half man, half lion. He'd not been able to complete the change, and it had made him vulnerable.

Hyperion had much to answer for, Marcos thought with disgust.

He had no business interfering here, in Deimos' ugly vendetta, but he was doing it anyway.

Marcos glanced around, taking in the field of battle.

Gray was fighting with Anya against a wind sorcerer quickly losing the hold on her power. Marthe and Diana had a chimera cornered on the other side of the field, Marthe jabbing at it with a long, wickedly sharp poleaxe, as Diana hung back, peppering it with arrows that she fired, one after the other, with deadly accuracy.

Most of the sorcerers had been easy enough to defeat; they, as he and Evander had foretold, defeated themselves with the lack of control they had over their power.

They were distractions from the real fight, the fight that was going to be coming to him shortly.

Marcos took a deep breath, holding his body ready, as he felt Evander's temper rising, flaring, the fire flaming inside of him, and then suddenly, he was screaming.

He ran over to where Evander stood, eyes sightless, with Rory, Acadia, and Rowen, whose task it had been to protect his corporeal form as he sent his spirit to the caves, to flush out the remaining sorcerers.

Suddenly, Evander gasped, and he fell to his knees.

Marcos was beside him in a second, grasping at his shoulders, pulling him close. "Are you alright?" he demanded, feeling everywhere he could touch. Not finding any blood. Not finding any wounds he could identify. In his spirit form, he couldn't be killed. But still, Marcos' heart felt chilled until Evander finally nodded slowly.

"I . . . I do not believe I have any fire left," he said carefully. "I spent the rest of it, trying to get out of the cave. Vanya and Deimos are both in the last one, the farthest one."

Marcos felt relief wash through him, and he helped Evander back to his feet. "We can manage without your fire," he said, even though he knew it was a blow, and *Evander* knew it was a blow, he could sense the truth of it emanating from him.

He heard Gray and Anya jogging up behind him. Clearly they must have finished dispatching their last wind sorcerer.

"This," Evander said carefully, and Marcos watched as he met the eyes of each of them, "is going to be harder than we imagined. Deimos is *very* powerful."

"Then he cannot rage unchecked in these lands." Rory's voice was as harsh as Marcos had ever heard it.

There was a roar behind him, and Marcos turned, slowly. Hyperion and Jae were emerging from the foothills, advancing on Marthe and Diana.

Diana shot an arrow in their direction, and Jae just laughed as he brushed it away with a flick of his fingers.

"I will need to deal with this first," Marcos said, his own voice grim. He pulled a second knife from his belt.

"Do you want me to . . .?" Evander asked but Marcos interrupted him before he could finish the question.

"No," he said. "This is my fight. Deimos will be hanging back, hoping he doesn't need to get his hands particularly dirty. And Vanya? He *never* liked to get his hands dirty. They believe that Hyperion and Jae will finish us. But they will not."

He turned and took off at a slow jog towards where the two Guardians were heading across the field.

Marthe gestured to him as they passed each other, and he gave her a short nod. She and Diana would help Gray and Anya form the second line of defense.

There was no use in sacrificing themselves fighting Hyperion and Jae, when Marcos knew he could handle the two of them.

They are not so easy as you think, he heard Evander think in his head.

I am faster, I am stronger, I am more skilled, and I have power they have never even dreamed of, he told Evander—and himself.

No doubt Evander had confronted Deimos before allowing himself to get drawn into an attack. It was what Marcos had recommended. *You are no match for him, not alone, not in your spirit form*, he'd told him late last night, as they'd lain in bed and discussed today's plan. *Toy with him. He will take the bait.*

And he had, clearly, because Evander had lasted longer than he'd dreamt could be possible.

Leaving him with a clear path to defeating Hyperion and Jae, who would not, unlike Deimos, bother with any silly discussions.

It wasn't their style, and it wasn't Marcos' style either.

Marcos came to stand in front of the pair of them.

Hyperion's long, brown hair partially obscured his face, but he would know the other Guardian's wild, dark eyes anywhere, or the way they narrowed in when they spotted him.

"Marcos," Hyperion said.

For many years they'd sparred together in the gardens and in the armory at the Castle on Top of the World, trading blows and easy-going, harmless jabs at each other. Hyperion had been someone that Marcos had understood, whom he'd believed had understood him, at a time when he hadn't often felt like he belonged with the other Guardians in the Conclave.

But added to the wrinkle of Hyperion knowing how he fought, and how *hard* he could fight, was Jae.

Jae stood next to Hyperion, his stance much more uneasy than his fellow Guardian's. His green eyes and auburn hair were unique among the Conclave, and normally Marcos might have counted Jae in as one of the Guardians least likely to join forces with Deimos. After all, making sure the humans on the surface were well and provided for seemed completely opposite Deimos' goals of death and chaos, but then Marcos wouldn't be surprised if Jae was only here because of Hyperion.

They'd always been close, which had never made much sense to him.

But then, he and Evander didn't make much sense, either.

Hyperion drew his sword. "This isn't your business," he said as he swung around, lifting his sword in a high arc, and then bringing it down, steel clashing against steel, against Marcos' blade.

"It's not yours, either," Marcos claimed. "Why would you join him?"

"He offered us power, immortality, *chaos*," Hyperion crowed.

"Chaos," Jae echoed. "If there is chaos, I can set chaos right. What I want is a *purpose* again."

Marcos thought that defeating Deimos, that evil bastard, was purpose enough, but what did he know?

Hyperion was fast, but Marcos was faster, and as they fought back and forth, he kept waiting for Jae to interfere, but he didn't. Just kept watching and waiting with those bright eyes of his.

Hyperion's fighting style had not changed much in the last thousand years, but Marcos thought his own had evolved, since he'd spent so much time on the surface, learning and teaching the humans.

He worked in a particularly Ardglassian set of parries, heavy and aggressive, big swings of the sword, angling his body so he wouldn't give Hyperion an opening he could use.

Slowly but surely, he began to push Hyperion back, until just when he reached Jae, the other Guardian reached out and unexpectedly sliced out at Marcos with one of his small-handled knives that he always kept to cut a bunch of grapes or to harvest a sheaf of wheat.

Marcos sidestepped, and the knife flashed in the sun as it hit only air.

He fixed Jae with an implacable stare. "You do not want to do this," he said firmly.

Hyperion was probably a lost cause; there was no rationalizing with him. But there was good in Jae. Marcos could feel it still.

"He's with me," Hyperion snarled, and launched another series of heavy-handed attacks. He'd always been too focused on offensive movements, and now Marcos twisted that against him, crouching low and letting him over-commit himself, all while dodging Jae's ineffectual knife slices.

He'd fought two men before. He'd often fought more than two—and because he was faster and quicker to process and analyze his opponents' movements, it had been a challenge, but nothing that he worried might actually overcome him.

But Hyperion and Jae together were proving to be more difficult than he'd anticipated.

Jae was like a bug, constantly hovering around him, lashing out with his knives, always keeping him off-balance and trying to anticipate his next attack, and it divided just enough attention from Hyperion that he was having difficulty neutralizing him.

With Jae joining the fight, he'd pulled back, just enough, refusing to let Marcos bait him into reaching too far, too fast. It made it so much harder to trap him, the way he wanted to.

Hyperion cackled as Marcos smashed into his side, just under his guard, elbowing him hard in the ribs, though he kept his feet.

Annoyingly, Marcos huffed.

He whirled around, trying to outflank Jae, so he could have a few precious seconds alone to finish Hyperion, but he was smart, too, and had watched Marcos fight for thousands of years, and somehow kept one step ahead.

Use them against each other, echoed in his mind, and for a second, Marcos almost froze, and then he realized it was Evander's voice, giving him a suggestion.

And a very good one, too.

He shoved back against Jae, letting the Guardian's knife slice at the side of his armor. He felt the flash of pain, but pushed it away. Instead he focused on spinning out of the way as fast as he could, moving so abruptly that Hyperion couldn't react fast enough, and instead of battering Marcos with his sword on his unprotected side, he caught Jae.

"Ooph," Jae bellowed as the blade sliced through his stomach and blood began to spill and pool on the ground.

Hyperion hesitated, staring at the Guardian in front of him, at his *friend*, and then he howled in pain. Like he'd been the one who'd been hurt. That was all the opening that Marcos needed.

He bashed Hyperion on the head with the heavy steel pommel of his sword, right in the vulnerable part of his skull, and he went down hard.

In an instant, he had his sword pressed against Hyperion's neck and the Guardian dropped his own to the ground.

"And the other knife," Marcos ground out, gesturing with his own.

Hyperion dropped that one too, stark shock in his eyes.

"You will give me your word," Marcos said, "that you will go *only* to the Castle, and have Abram heal Jae, and I will let you go. If you do not, I will kill you both where you stand."

"You could not remove my head," Hyperion blustered.

But he could.

And he would.

Marcos did not want to, but if forced, if he *had* to, to protect Evander and Rory and Gray and the kingdom, he would.

It was the vow he'd taken, ages ago, to protect the humans of the surface with his life and with the lives of the other Guardians.

Hyperion hesitated.

"I could break my word."

"You will not."

Marcos glanced up and saw Evander standing there, and there was an unbelievable fierceness in his expression.

"And do not bother to lie, because I will know if you are lying," Evander added.

"Will you?" Jae gasped out, holding his stomach, blood spilling down his fingers in deep red rivulets.

"Yes," Evander said and he was the Evander of old then, the Evander Marcos had known before his banishment, the impish look in his blue eyes and the resoluteness of his stare.

"Vanya said you got your powers back," Hyperion said cautiously. "He was not lying."

"And neither will you," Evander threatened. "Call Abram, and ask him to transport Jae back to the Castle. Heal him. Stay out of this. We will see you when it is finished."

But still Hyperion hesitated. "How do you know you will be standing after you and *Deimos* . . ."

Evander didn't let him finish the question. "Because I know," he said with finality. "Go back to the Castle, Hyperion. Take Jae. And we will deal with you two later."

"Hyperion . . ." Jae said softly, quietly.

The only way to kill a Guardian, to truly kill them, was to take off their head.

Jae's injury would not be technically life-threatening, but it would be unpleasant. For a long few months his body would knit itself back together.

Marcos knew, because Marcos had dealt with it before.

"Fine," Hyperion said, sounding particularly sulky. "Abram!" he called out, and the Guardian of Healing, who was able to transport patients long distances, the only loophole Evander knew to reach the surface from the Castle quickly, appeared. His eyes were kind and concerned. He reached out for Jae, and in a second, the three of them were gone.

Marcos eyed Evander. "They were not lying?" he asked.

Evander shook his head. "Jae was in considerable pain. He had not even wanted to join Hyperion, but you know Hyperion."

"I do," Marcos said heavily. "We *will* have to deal with them later."

"But first . . ."

"First," an unearthly voice called out, "this annoying interference will *end*."

Marcos looked up and felt his stomach lurch.

Deimos had crossed the field with his unearthly speed, Vanya hovering behind him, and suddenly he had a grip, a *very* firm grip, if the increasingly white skin of Rory's face was to be believed, on the King of Fontaine.

Marcos saw Gray's own expression go ashen.

"Rory!" he called out, desperately.

"How . . ." Marcos began to ask, but Evander just shrugged in response.

"I will kill this pest, right here, right now," Deimos announced, pulling back, until he was at the entrance to the cave, at the highest point of the foothills. "I will put him and the rest of these humans out of their misery."

Marcos exchanged glances with Evander. They had not planned to attack Deimos so directly, but he must have realized that they wouldn't, so he'd forced their hand.

There was terror in Rory's eyes but bravery too. And even with the incredibly hard grip that Deimos had on his throat, he gave a tiny shake of his head.

All the movement he could probably force.

The message was clear enough. Do not save me. Save the kingdom.

But the agony written on Evander's face didn't give Marcos any choice.

He didn't want anyone else to die today, and he especially was not going to let Rory die.

"Let him go," Marcos called out, "let him go, and we will not make you bleed the way we made Jae bleed."

Deimos only laughed, but Marcos couldn't miss how Vanya's face went pale.

"Jae?" Vanya said. "You hurt Jae? One of your own brothers?"

"What does it matter?" Deimos retorted, glancing behind him, seemingly unconcerned, while Vanya looked stricken.

Marcos wasn't particularly surprised—he'd known long before today that Deimos only cared about himself and that the other Guardians were merely fodder in his games—but Vanya . . . he must not have realized how much Deimos was willing to sacrifice.

"It matters because . . ." But Vanya stopped and then clamped his lips together. "It *matters*. He is our *brother*."

But Deimos merely shrugged. "And I have asked you, *repeatedly*, to deal with your *brothers* and return them to the fold, but you have not." The words were dismissive and cruel, and then Deimos completed the trifecta by turning away from him completely.

Marcos had hoped the slight delay in Deimos' threats might give him an idea for an opening on how to attack him, how to save Rory.

Let me do it, Evander's voice echoed in his head. *Some of my fire magic has returned. I can feel it growing again.*

No, Marcos said resolutely. *It's not going to be enough. It wasn't enough before, in the caves. And that was when you were at full strength.*

But we have to try. Evander's thoughts, even in Marcos' head, were despairing.

Deimos advanced, dragging Rory by the throat. He had gone from white to red, and there was panic and a resignation in his eyes.

Marcos knew if they were going to act, they had to act *now.*

But before he could finish formulating a plan—*any* plan—Deimos froze, his face suddenly a stricture of pain.

Something that he had never seen on it before.

Then the arm holding Rory twisted, and then twisted even further, and suddenly he was free, and he was gasping and stumbling away from Deimos, running across the field into Gray's arms.

It was Vanya, Marcos realized. He'd grabbed on to Deimos' back, and was closing his eyes, channeling every bit of power into Deimos, trying to . . . control him?

Marcos had never understood exactly how Vanya's magic worked, how he was able to make people believe in whatever he chose, but he was using it now, and he was using it on *Deimos.*

I didn't think he could use it on one of us, Evander's awed voice proclaimed.

But he was. Holding on and digging in, even though Deimos kept snarling and pushing him, and pulling him, dark smoky power erupting out of him.

Vanya's face paled, and then went even paler, until he was white as the snow that surrounded the Well, as Death tried to conquer him once and for all. But still he held on.

"Quick," Evander said. "He's weakening Deimos, but he can't finish him off. We need to help him."

Marcos still wasn't sure exactly what was happening, and Vanya's about-face was so sudden, he hesitated.

"*Marcos.*" Evander grabbed him by the arm. "You can do this, you can hurt him, you can kill him, but we need to do it *now*, before . . ."

It was clear what Evander was about to say. Marcos could *feel* it. Vanya's eyes were rolling into the back of his head, even as he held on, even as Deimos' power lanced through him, weakening him even further.

"How can we trust him?"

Evander's eyes searched his. He looked desperate. "This is the time," he said. "We trust him because we have to."

Marcos wanted to argue, but he saw Evander's gaze. Saw the plea to trust him, and how could he do anything else, when he loved him the way he did?

"Yes," Marcos finally agreed. "What should we do?"

Evander hesitated and then set his knife down. "Come," he said, and suddenly he was melting away and in his place was a pure white horse—no, a pure white *unicorn*, with a glistening silver horn, and a rippling silvery-white mane.

"Come," Evrard repeated again. "Come ride me. Together, we'll defeat Deimos once and for all."

Marcos didn't hesitate. He leapt onto Evrard's back and he took off in a fierce gallop, winding his way through the fields. Marcos saw his approach, and realized just what he was doing. Reaching up, he steadied himself by gripping Evrard's flanks with his thighs, and he raised his sword, and he watched, in near slow motion as Vanya collapsed, face now totally gray, and Evrard whipped them around, positioning Marcos in exactly the place he needed to be.

He'd been in so many battles, faced so many opponents, and at the time, all of them had seemed vitally important.

But Marcos realized that no strike was ever going to be as important as this one. He lifted his sword, and with every ounce of strength and will he possessed, he smote Deimos. He almost wavered, when the sword struck Deimos' dark magic, but he ignored the sudden nausea and the way every bone in his body seemed suddenly to be made of water, and he pushed through the stroke cleanly.

Deimos' head rolled away from his body, and it was, almost as suddenly as it had begun, over.

Forever.

CHAPTER SIXTEEN

The moment Marcos jumped off his back, Evrard let go of his unicorn form, and without even thinking, took Evander's form.

The next second, he dropped to his knees at Vanya's side, terror lancing through him.

His handsome face was gray, his eyes closed, and when Evander pressed a hand to his chest, it was barely moving.

"Is he . . ."

Evander glanced up, his heart squeezing in his chest at Marcos' question.

"I don't know," Evander said. "All I know . . . he did this for us. To . . ."

"To save us, to save everyone," Marcos finished, his voice heavy. "We never could have defeated Deimos without Vanya holding him with his power. But to push his own power into Deimos, he gave Deimos the chance to push his own back. And his power is Death."

Evander reached down and tugged Vanya's head into his lap. He barely stirred at the movement, his face growing impossibly stiller.

"I think . . ." Evander's voice cracked. "I think we're losing him. We need to do something. *Anything*. If only Abram was here."

"Let me try," Marcos said, dropping down on the other side of Vanya's body. "Abram taught me some things."

He pressed a hand to Vanya's chest and closed his eyes.

Evander didn't need to hear Marcos' thoughts to know that things were bad. Worse even than they'd imagined.

That much was evident when Marcos glanced up at Evander, pain in his eyes.

"I can give him a few minutes, maybe," he admitted gravely. "He's . . . well, he's far gone, Evander. I think Deimos decided that if he was going to hurt him, he was going to drag Vanya with him to Death."

"I don't know why," Evander said, voice low. "I can't figure out *why*. He was . . . he was betraying us. And then he was saving us."

"We were never meant to fight each other," Marcos said, and reached out, tangling his fingers with Evander's, squeezing hard. "He saw that Deimos didn't care that Jae bled. I think he knew that Deimos would let us all fall to further his ambitions. That he'd let *you* fall. Remember what Deimos said, about Vanya refusing to take care of you, even though he'd demanded it? Vanya was protecting you, to the last."

He knew Marcos meant it as a balm, as a path to forgiveness for Vanya's betrayal, but all Evander felt was a harrowing ache spreading through him like wildfire.

Once, they'd been friends and lovers. They'd loved each other.

"It wasn't supposed to be this way." Evander stared down at Vanya's face. "Do whatever you can . . . even if it's not enough."

"I will," Marcos vowed, and Evander knew that he would. That was who he was, and one of the reasons he'd fallen in love with him.

He'd had every reason to be painfully jealous of Vanya, and yet he *would* pull him back from the brink if he could.

Only because it was the right thing to do.

Marcos let go of Evander's fingers, and moved his hand to Vanya's unmoving chest. He pressed down, and Evander could feel the power flowing through him—it tasted like leather and steel, like bravery and courage, every good thing that Marcos had ever done, every sacrifice he'd ever made. He poured it all into Vanya.

For a long moment, Evander held his breath, not sure if it would be enough.

It has to be enough, Marcos thought fiercely. *I will make it enough.*

And then suddenly Vanya gasped, and slowly, his eyes fluttered open.

Evander's hand twitched, grasping at his white linen shift. "Vanya," he cajoled eagerly, "can you hear me? Can you see me?"

"Yes." His voice was weak and so quiet, that if the field of battle hadn't fallen completely, utterly silent, Evander didn't know that he could have heard it.

Evander opened his mouth to praise his actions, to thank him, to tell him *he* was so sorry that he hadn't listened before, even if listening wouldn't have changed his path.

But instead of letting him speak, with difficulty Vanya lifted a hand, pushing a pair of fingers against Evander's lips. "No . . ." he wheezed. "No, let me say this, before it is too late."

"No, we can . . ."

"No," Vanya said more forcefully. "I have only a minute, and I want to . . . I *have* to tell you how sorry I am. I never should have sided with Deimos, never should have betrayed you, and what awaits me is my penance for my actions. I am only glad that I could help, in the end, could save you." He glanced over at Marcos. "And that you will be together, finally."

Pain speared through Evander, and breath clogged in his throat. He didn't know what to say. He'd seen many deaths, but humans were meant to live and then to pass on. Guardians were not. They were supposed to be everlasting, and so Evander had never considered what his last words to his greatest friend might be.

But now he had no choice.

"Please don't . . ." Evander heard the plea in his own voice. "Please don't leave me. Not like this."

Vanya's gaze rested lovingly on his. "I already had, but at least I could do some good in the end." He coughed hard, his chest rattling alarmingly, and Evander felt Marcos push more power through him. But it was like pouring water into a sieve. It didn't matter how much he gave, it wasn't going to be enough. There was too much damage.

"Take the time you have and don't waste it."

"I . . ."

Vanya's gaze hardened. "*Promise me.*"

"I will."

"I might be dying, something I never imagined I'd do," Vanya said wryly between coughs that wracked his whole body, his face growing bluish white. "But . . . but . . . I still want to be remembered not as a traitor but . . ."

"You saved us all, and everyone will know that," Evander vowed.

He glanced over at Marcos. "Don't follow me, giving more power than you can," he warned. "I need you to stay here, stay with Evander. Promise me that."

Evander couldn't miss the pain in Marcos' eyes. For him, and for Evander. He knew just how much this would hurt him. "I promise."

"I . . ." Vanya gasped. "I know you've loved him for thousands of years. Promise me you'll love him for every single one to come."

"I promise. My love will be lasting." Marcos' expression was as grave and serious as he'd ever seen it. Evander knew he meant every word he was saying.

"Good." Vanya shuddered. "Now I . . ."

But Evander never got to know what Vanya was going to say, because his eyes fluttered shut one last time, and then he went utterly still.

For a long time, Evander didn't move a muscle. Barely blinked. Just knelt and stared at the face of his oldest friend, hoping that he would breathe again, that he would laugh and tease again, that he would be there for him once again, but knowing, deep in his heart, that those days had passed forever.

"Come," a voice beckoned him, and for a split second, he knew it must be Marcos, trying to tug him away from the pain of Vanya's death, but it wasn't a man's voice.

It was a woman.

And when he looked up, the Mother was standing there, wreathed in golden light, standing at the feet of one of her creations.

"Come, my child," she said, holding out her hand to him. "There is nothing more you can do for him. He made his decision."

"Can you do nothing for him?" Evander pleaded. "Surely, you are the Mother, and you are the power that created him, surely you can make him live. Surely his sacrifice was enough."

"It was always enough," she said gravely, sadly, "but I cannot give him back the life he gladly traded away. Know, in your heart, that it was enough for him, and it will need to be enough for you. Stop your tears, and rejoice in the chance to make this land new again."

He reached up, and sure enough, his cheeks were wet with tears. Wiping them away, he stood, legs shaky from sitting. The sun was setting over the foothills, and he realized that the day had passed, while he'd knelt at Vanya's body.

"We need to take him to the Castle," Marcos said, and Evander glanced over, realizing he had stood vigil over the two of them for hours, as he'd grieved the loss of his friend.

He was my friend too, though not as good as yours, Marcos reminded him gently. *I grieve for both of you; for him, because in the end, he knew what was right and just, and also for you, because you will miss him so.*

"He should be buried with much honor," the Mother agreed, taking his other hand and squeezing. "But before that, something needs to be done with the betrayer." She glanced over at where Deimos' body lay.

"I know what to do with him," Evander said, and reached for his power, letting it flow through him, fire spreading from his palm and engulfing Deimos' body, and its detached head, purifying the ground.

Purifying the surface, forever.

He poured every bit of hate and anger and frustration and rage into his power, the fire growing as bright and hot as he could make it.

When he finished and the body was gone, the ground underneath it charred black, the Mother nodded in approval.

"Flowers will grow here someday," she said, her eyes glowing with faraway possibilities. "You have sanctified this ground."

"Bluebells," Marcos said lightly. "Those are my favorite."

"Yes," the Mother agreed. "To honor Evander, who never gave up on fighting for what was right, and for Marcos, who loved him for it. But come, let me return you to your rightful place, in the Castle. At the head of the Conclave."

Evander stared at her.

"Yes," she said, "you heard me right. You will lead them. Together. There is much healing to be done, after Deimos' betrayals."

It was not a position that Evander would have ever chosen for himself. But, once he considered it, he could see the advantages. He had long wanted to involve the Conclave in matters on the surface. To bring the Guardians closer to the humans they had sworn to protect and to guide and to love.

Who better to do that than two Guardians who had spent the last thousand years protecting, and guiding, and loving them?

"Yes," Evander said. "There is much to be done." He met Marcos' eyes, and saw not only love and support, but *belief*. And Evander knew he would see it there, in his eyes, forever. "But first, I must say goodbye. If I am to lead . . . I may not be spending much time on the surface."

Understanding dawned on the Mother's face. "Of course, but you are always welcome to have a place here," she said.

"I will," Evander vowed, and turned to Rory and Gray only to find that they had left, leaving only Rowen and Diana behind.

"We were standing guard," Rowen said, ducking her head. "They thought you might want to grieve in peace."

"It is but a short ride to Beaulieu," Marcos pointed out softly. "We can go say goodbye to Rory and Gray, and then come back here, to leave with the Mother."

"In fact," the Mother said, inclining her head, "I would go with you to the Castle. It has been a long time coming for me to meet my Guardians. I will meet you there, in the Castle, and I will bear Vanya with me."

"How will we travel there?" Marcos asked. "We cannot go all the way to the Well and no doubt Abram has his hands busy with Jae."

"Think of me, and you will be taken home," the Mother said. "I promise."

Rowen brought two horses, and in a minute, they were mounting them.

Evander's eyes caught Vanya's body one last time but he resolutely turned away. The Mother was right. Vanya had made his choice, and it had been the right one, no matter how painful it was. He needed to look to the future now, to building a new connection between the surface and the Guardians.

They could no longer live in the shadows.

A short time later, Evander and Marcos rode back through Beaulieu's main gate.

Marthe was standing with a few of the guard, and when they dismounted, she approached.

"Guardians," she said formally, inclining her head out of respect, "my utmost sympathies. We of Fontaine grieve with you today for your loss."

"Thank you, General," Marcos said, mimicking her formal tone, and taking her hand, bowing over it. "And thank you for standing with us today. Without your bravery, I do not know if we would've achieved victory."

Marthe's expression broke into a quick smile. "Now that is questionable," she said lightly, "but I appreciate the sentiment. Are you here to see Their Highnesses?"

"We are, and to say goodbye," Evander said. "There is much to be done in the Conclave, to repair what has been tarnished and corrupted."

"There is no better pair for the task," she said stoutly. "King Emory is in the library, I believe, and I would not be surprised if King Graham was with him."

They met Anya on the central winding staircase, and she confirmed that Gray was with Rory. "I don't think," she said, a serious look in her gray eyes, "that he is wanting him out of his sight. Not after today."

"No, he wouldn't," Evander agreed.

"Shield Maiden of Ardglass," Marcos said, bowing to her, "your bravery on the field today was commendable."

Anya smiled. "You gave us a skill to aspire to, Guardian."

"Protect him," Evander said, before he could stop himself. "Protect *both* of them."

"With my life," she promised solemnly.

When they entered the library, Rory was bent over one of the ancient texts that Evander had seen him consult earlier, and Gray was sitting next to him. Lion's Breath was on the table, and his hand was close enough that when they walked in, his hand automatically strayed to the hilt.

"Oh," Gray said, face breaking into a smile, "it's you."

"For now," Evander said solemnly. He'd never expected, when he'd helped Prince Graham of Ardglass escape in the middle of the night, that he'd end up taking on the role of father to him.

They'd already said goodbye once, and this wasn't a permanent goodbye, not like he'd meant that one to be, but Evander discovered that it hurt nonetheless.

"You are leaving." Rory glanced up, stating rather than questioning.

"We must," Evander said regretfully—truly meaning it. "The Conclave is in chaos and must be led back into the light. I would also strengthen the ties between the surface and the Guardians."

Rory stood, placing a hand on Gray's shoulder. "I think that is an excellent idea," he said. "Don't you?" he asked, looking down at his husband.

"I think if it means that you are not disappearing forever, then it's a good plan." Gray hesitated. His gaze swung to Marcos. "Are there any other Guardians like you?"

"No," Evander said, before Marcos could prevaricate. Because he *would*.

I certainly would not, Marcos told him in amused, mock outrage.

"That will help me rest better at night," Gray said. "As for your friend . . ." Gray's expression turned serious. "I am so sorry for your loss."

"I am, too," Evander said, tilting his head. "But I will make sure he's remembered."

"We will, too," Rory said. "I've been looking through my books for references to him. I would like to create a festival night, an evening of celebration and *belief*, just for him."

For a second, grief slid through Evander with a sickening lurch.

It will take time, Marcos reminded him. *You will heal, in time.*

Marcos smiled. "He would have liked that very much."

"Yes," Evander finally said, finding his voice. "He would have."

"Then, it will be done," Rory said. He turned the book he was examining towards them. "I believe that this is him, is it not?"

It was indeed Vanya. It was not quite his face, but it was his form, and those were his eyes, glowing amber brown, and his traditional white linen shift. Blessing those surrounding him.

"Yes," Evander said softly. "That is him."

"I thought so," Rory said. He reached out and took Evander's hand, squeezing it. "I know you cannot stay, that there are events of much greater importance that need your hand to shape them, but thank you again for bringing us peace."

"I wasn't alone the first time, and not the second time either." Evander took a deep breath, glanced to his right, to where Marcos stood, so solid, so steadfast. "It takes immense courage to stand for something you believe, and immeasurable courage to stand up for something you believe in when you have everything to lose."

"Yes," Gray said, and to Evander's surprise, he skirted around the desk, and pulled him into a tight hug. "I know just how much courage it takes."

You did good, Marcos told him, as Gray let him go.

He turned to Marcos, extending a hand. Marcos shook it seriously. "I assume," Gray said, "that you will make sure he doesn't get into more trouble than he can handle."

"Of course," Marcos said, and then smiled. "But you would be surprised at the amount of trouble he can get into."

"No, I wouldn't," Gray retorted, grinning. "Not remotely."

This is so unfair, Evander told Marcos.

"Please, don't be a stranger," Rory said.

"We won't," Evander promised. And then decided, he might as well try to influence them, one last time.

Who are you kidding, Marcos said, *one last time? You'll be here every few months, giving unasked for advice.*

"Might I add," he continued, ignoring Marcos, "that considering the excitement today, it might be high time to find an heir?"

Gray groaned and Rory just laughed. "You can't help yourself, can you?"

Evander finally had to admit it. "No," he said.

"I suppose it is good, then, that you're going to go lead a whole group of immortal, magical, incredibly powerful beings," Rory teased. "That will at least keep you busy for a while. Might give us a bit more time."

"But," Gray said, glancing down at Rory, "just a bit."

And that, Evander decided, was enough.

He felt satisfied.

Indeed, Marcos said, *a job well done.*

Marcos reached down and took Evander's hand, squeezing it gently. "I believe it's time," he told Evander, "let's go home."

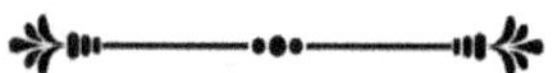

Evander had imagined coming home to the Castle at the Top of the World many times in the last thousand years.

Never had he imagined that he would feel equal amounts of devastating loss and incandescent joy as he took, finally, his chair in the Conclave again. He met Marcos' eyes from across the room, and thought, *I wish it wasn't at this cost.*

Marcos didn't reply, just gazed at him. With love, with longing, with the kind of fierce support he'd always dreamt he might find in a partner.

The Mother stood at the center, a large stone in front of her, Vanya's body resting on it. She placed her hand on the stone, and flowers blossomed wherever she touched.

There was a burn mark scarring Deimos' chair. Evander resolved to keep it there, as a reminder of the danger of believing too fervently in your own power.

Vanya's chair, next to his own, was empty, but the Mother must have already visited it, because flowers covered it, winding through all the arms and legs.

"Much," she said, "has happened. I bear sad news. But all is not lost, because I also bear a new directive."

"A new directive?" Hektor questioned in his gravelly voice. "We knew Deimos was not to be trusted, but to accept back into the fold a Guardian who has been banished?"

Evander told himself not to resent Hektor questioning his authority.

But before he could speak up, the Mother turned her glowing eyes on him. "Banished unfairly, without just cause," she said, "and while he was not the only Guardian who attempted to follow the original directive, he was the solitary Guardian who followed through despite great personal cost. Deimos might have led you before, because I did not know his heart as well as I should have, but now, I know Evander's heart through and through, and it is true."

"I see it," Taavi agreed. "It beats true. And it beats . . ." He glanced over at Marcos. "For one of our own."

"This is a celebration of life, as well as a celebration of death. Vanya sacrificed himself to clear the way for this Conclave to bring some good to the surface. I know some of you were coerced into joining Deimos, and some of you had your powers stolen." First she glanced over at Hyperion. And then she nodded at Gael, who stiffly inclined his head back. "But what we have really come to this Conclave to do is to see about the matter of leadership. Will you follow your brother Marcos? Will you follow Evander? Will you follow them as they lead us? For they both sacrificed their own comfort here to bring justice to the surface." the Mother asked archly.

Marcos raised his hand first. Without even blinking. "I will follow, and I will lead, to the best of my ability," he said.

"I will," Taavi added.

"I will," Abram said, rising.

"I will," Gael proclaimed.

"I will," Osias said.

"I will," Kadir spoke.

"I will," Hektor said, with a hint of resentment in his voice.

"I will," Lyric sang.

Evander looked at where Hyperion sat, glowering. "I am not proud of my actions," he pronounced, "so I will."

"Jae is healing, and cannot be here," the Mother said, "but he has told me that he will." Her gaze swung to Evander. "And you, Guardian of Secrets?"

Evander thought of every time he'd hated his title, and what it represented, and how it had ended up saving them all because he had never given up the fight.

"I will," he said.

The Mother raised her hands, and in chorus, they all spoke together, for the first time in far too long: "We are everlasting."

EPILOGUE

"Where are you taking me?" Evander questioned as Marcos led him through the Castle proper.

"It has been a very long fortnight," Marcos said, reaching out and tangling his fingers with Evander's. "You have been busy playing mediator between far too many of our brothers. You have earned an evening off."

"Perhaps so," Evander conceded, "but I still want to know where you are taking me."

Marcos grinned. "You cannot decipher my secret?"

Evander rolled his eyes. "You wish me to be surprised, and therefore, I must make it clear that I am desperately curious where we are going. This is how it works, correct?"

"Yes," Marcos said with a chuckle, leading him towards the main Conclave chamber and its portal.

Just a few weeks ago, they all had stood in this same chamber, re-dedicating themselves to the Guardians' true purpose, with the Mother overseeing their pledge. It had not been easy afterwards, and Marcos was right—there had been many long days. Hektor was still suspicious. Hyperion was angry—but then Hyperion was perennially angry, so Evander supposed that not much had changed. But Jae was healing, and so were the broken connections in the Conclave. And Evander was discovering that despite his own initial beliefs, Marcos was actually *quite* adept at politics, when he turned his attention to them.

"Imagine, only a month or so ago, I was bored out of my mind," Evander said as they approached the portal.

"Bored *and* lonely," Marcos teased. "And now look at you."

They came to a stop in front of the Well. Evander turned towards Marcos. "I could not have done it without you," he said seriously. "Your support has been invaluable." He hesitated. "Your support *and* your love."

"You will have both, forever," Marcos replied, squeezing Evander's hand with his own.

"Come, then, and show me your surprise," Evander said.

Marcos tugged him forward. One moment, they were standing at the edge of the Well, and the next, they were falling through it, and when Evander opened his eyes again, he was shocked at how familiar this felt.

Once before he'd fallen through the Well, and awoken in this valley.

This valley that was as familiar to him as the Castle. A home that had stood in for the one that he'd lost.

"I wanted you," Marcos said, rising to his knees, staring out at the endless waving grasses surrounding them, "to show me the place you lived, when you were on the surface."

"You never came here, not even in disguise?" Evander couldn't help his surprise.

Marcos shook his head. "It felt like yours, and like I would be trespassing, even to come here as someone else." He hesitated. "And, I hoped, even though I had every faith that it would come to pass, that you might show me yourself, someday."

"Who knew that you were such a romantic at heart?" Evander teased lightly.

"Nobody, except you." Marcos' dark eyes were very serious. Very intent.

Evander leaned forward and pressed their lips together. Sometimes Marcos got lost in all the regrets of the past—he too, could spend far too much time there—but they were good at bringing each other back, now.

Or at least, they were getting better at it.

Evander hardly needed an excuse to want to kiss him, but it was a good reminder for both of them.

They had each other now, and what had occurred years ago mattered much less than that one unassailable fact.

Marcos groaned into his mouth a little, angling his body closer to Evander's, and Evander realized just how long it *had* been since they'd been alone.

Too long.

Yes, indeed, Marcos echoed in his head.

"The first buildings that I labored so hard to build are long gone," Evander said, turning away and looking out into the fields, at the far west, where the sun was beginning to sink below the trees. The sky was a riotous celebration of yellows, golds, and oranges. "But the ones Gray built still stand."

"He would hardly countenance anything else," Marcos observed.

"He did build to last. That is how Gray is, and why I have always believed he will make an excellent king."

Marcos nodded. "But," Evander continued, "you did not bring me here to talk about Gray."

"No, nor Rory, or Fontaine, or even the Ardglassian clans. And definitely not any of the problems still plaguing the Conclave," Marcos said.

"You wanted a night away," Evander guessed.

Marcos nodded solemnly. "The burden lies heavy on your shoulders. I knew it would, but it's good to give yourself a break, every once in a while." His expression brightened. "And," he added, "Rory mentioned a whole field of bluebells, here in this valley, that matched Gray's eyes almost exactly. And I thought, I will stand with you in it, and marvel at your beauty, and marvel at the luck that you are mine."

Evander knew the field he talked of. "Yes," he said simply. "We will." He stood and held out his hand. "Come, my love, and I will show you."

The walk to the field was short, and as they passed the various outbuildings that Gray had spent his childhood and young adulthood building and maintaining, Evander talked of the time they had spent here together. "I did not mean to become his father," he concluded as they finally reached the stream, with its little footbridge. "But I suppose I did."

"You protected him, and kept him company, kept him from becoming too wretched and bitter at his circumstances," Marcos said. "That is a father, whether you meant to be one or not."

Evander nodded.

The bluebells stretched out in every direction.

"This," Evander said, gesturing as they came into the thick of them, "is where I fell."

"When you were banished?" Marcos questioned.

"Yes." Evander gazed out at the flowers' beauty. Remembering how he'd lain here for so long. For months. Not wanting to go on, but knowing, deep down, that he had no other choice. "I wanted to give up."

"But you never did," Marcos said, tugging him closer, until his arms encircled his waist. "I am grateful that you are so stubborn."

"I am the grateful one." Evander gazed up at Marcos' face—it had not always been so beloved to him, but now it was, and he couldn't imagine a time in the future when he felt less love for this man, only more. "If you hadn't been the most stubborn Guardian in the Conclave . . . we would not be here today."

"It would be a loss," Marcos agreed. Leaned down, and touched his forehead to Evander's. "I would be lost without you."

"Then promise me," Evander said softly, "vow to me, that we will be together always."

"Are you . . ." Marcos looked surprised. "Are you committing yourself to me?"

Evander nodded. "Here, in a place where I felt the worst of all my years, I would feel the best."

"I vow," Marcos, said, reaching down and tangling their fingers together, "that I will be only yours."

"And I," Evander repeated, voice none too steady, "will be yours, everlasting."

Don't want to leave Evander, Marcos, Gray and Rory behind?
Make sure to download the bonus scene here.

WANT TO FOLLOW BETH?

MAKE SURE YOU NEVER
MISS A RELEASE?

SCAN THE QR CODE BELOW
OR VISIT HER WEBSITE
FOR A SOCIAL MEDIA LIST,
NEWSLETTER SIGNUP,
AND SO MUCH MORE!

WWW.BETHBOLDEN.COM/ABOUT

www.ingramcontent.com/pod-product-compliance
Lightning Source LLC
Chambersburg PA
CBHW060421310726

48977CB00001B/3